Strange Relations

PHILIP JOSÉ FARMER

Strange Relations

STRANGE RELATIONS

This is a work of fiction. All the characters and events portrayed in this book are
fictional, and any resemblance to real people or incidents is purely coincidental.

A Baen Book

Baen Publishing Enterprises
P.O. Box 1403
Riverdale, NY 10471

ISBN-13: 978-1-61793-375-2

Cover art by Clyde Caldwell

Printed in the United States of America

Contents

The Lovers

1

"I've got to get out," Hal Yarrow could hear someone muttering from a great distance. "There must be a way out."

He woke up with a start, and he realized that he had been the one talking. Moreover, what he had said as he emerged from his dream had no connection at all to it. His half-waking words and the dream were two discrete events.

But what had he meant by those mumbled words? And where was he? Had he actually traveled in time or had he experienced a subjective dream? It had been so vivid that he was slow in returning to this level of the world.

A look at the man sitting beside him cleared his mind. He was in the coach to Sigmen City in the year 550 B.S. (Old Style 3050 A.D., his scholar's mind told him.) He was not, as in the time travel? dream? on a strange planet many light-years from here, many years from now. Nor was he face to face with the glorious Isaac Sigmen, the Forerunner, real be his name.

The man beside him looked sidewise at Hal. He was a lean fellow with high cheekbones, straight black hair, and brown eyes which had a slight Mongoloid fold. He was dressed in the light blue uniform of the engineering class and wore on his left breast an aluminum emblem which indicated he was in the upper echelon. Probably, he was an electronics engineer with a degree from one of the better trade schools.

The man cleared his throat, and he said, in American, "A thousand pardons, *abba*. I know I shouldn't be talking to you without permission. But you did say something to me as you awoke. And, since you're in this cabin, you have temporarily equated yourself. In any event, I've been dying to ask you a question. I'm not called Nosy Sam for nothing."

He laughed nervously and said, "Couldn't help overhearing what you told the stewardess when she challenged your right to sit here. Did I hear you right, or did you actually tell her you was a *goat*?"

Hal smiled and said, "No. Not a goat. I'm a *joat*. From the initial letters of *jack-of-all-trades*. You weren't too mistaken, however. In the professional fields, a *joat* has about as much prestige as a goat."

He sighed and thought of the humiliations endured because he had chosen not to be a narrow specialist. He looked out the window because he did not want to encourage his seatmate to talk, He saw a bright glow far off and up, undoubtedly a military spaceship entering the atmosphere. The few civilian ships made a slower and unobtrusive descent.

From the height of sixty thousand meters, he looked down on the curve of the North American continent. It was a blaze of light with, here and there, some small bands of darkness and an occasional large band. The latter would be a mountain range or body of water on which man had not yet succeeded in building residences or industries. The great city. Megalopolis. Think—only three hundred years ago, the entire continent had a mere two million population. In another fifty years—unless something catastrophic happened, such as war between the Haijac Union and the Israeli Republics—the population of North America would be fourteen, maybe fifteen, billion!

The only area in which living room was deliberately denied was the Hudson Bay Wildlife Preserve. He had left the Preserve only fifteen minutes ago, yet he felt sick because he would not be able to return to it for a long time.

He sighed again. The Hudson Bay Wildlife Preserve. Trees by the thousands, mountains, broad blue lakes, birds, foxes, rabbits, even, the rangers said, bobcats. There were so few, however, that in ten years they would be added to the long list of extinct animals.

Hal could breathe in the Preserve, could feel unconstricted. Free. He also could feel lonely and uneasy at times. But he was just beginning to get over that when his research among the twenty French-speaking Inhabitants of the Preserve was finished.

The man beside him shifted as if he were trying to get up courage to speak again to the professional beside him. After some nervous coughs, he said, "Sigmen help me, I hope I ain't offended you. But I was wondering . . ."

Hal Yarrow felt offended because the man was presuming too much.

Then, he reminded himself of what the Forerunner had said. *All men are brothers, though some are more favored by the father than others.* And it was not this man's fault that the first-class cabin had been filled with people with higher priorities and Hal had been forced to choose between taking a later coach or sitting with the lower echelon.

"It's *shib* with me," said Yarrow. He explained.

The man said, "Ah!" as if he were relieved. "Then, you won't perhaps mind one more question? Don't call me Nosy Sam for nothing, like I said. Ha! Ha!"

"No, I don't mind," said Hal Yarrow. "A *joat*, though a jack-of-all-trades, does not make all sciences his field. He *is* confined to one particular discipline, but he tries to understand as much of all the specialized branches of it as he can. For instance, I am a linguistic *joat*. Instead of restricting myself to one of the many areas of linguistics, I have a good general knowledge of that science. This ability enables me to correlate what is going on in all its fields, to search out things in one specialty which might be of interest to a man in another specialty, and to notify him of this item. Otherwise, the specialist, who doesn't have the time to read the hundreds of journals in his field alone, might be missing something that would aid him.

"All the professional studies have their own *joats* doing this. Actually, I'm very lucky to be in this branch of science. If I were, for example, a medical *joat*, I'd be overwhelmed. I'd have to work with a team of *joats*. Even then, I couldn't be a genuine jack-of-all-trades. I'd have to restrict myself to one area of medical science. So tremendous is the number of publications in each specialty of medicine—or of electronics or physics or just about any science you might want to mention—that no man or team could correlate the entire discipline. Fortunately, my interest has always been in linguistics. I am, in a way, favored. I even have time to do a little research myself and so add to the avalanche of papers.

"I use computers, of course, but even the most complex computer complex is an idiot savant. It takes a human mind—a rather keen one, if I do say so myself—to perceive that certain items have more significance than others and to make a meaningful association between or among them. Then I point these out to the specialists, and they study them. A *joat*, you might say, is a creative correlator.

"However," he added, "that is at the cost of my personal time for sleeping. I must work twelve hours a day or more for the glory and benefit of the Sturch."

His last comment was to ensure that the fellow, if he happened to be an Uzzite or a stool for the Uzzites, could not report that he was cheating the Sturch. Hal did not think it likely that the man was anything other than what he looked, but he did not care to take the chance.

A red light flashed on the wall above the cabin entrance, and a recording told the passengers to fasten their belts. Ten seconds later, the coach began decelerating; a minute later, the vehicle dipped sharply and began dropping at the rate—so Hal had been told—of a thousand meters a minute. Now that they were closer to the ground, Hal could see that Sigmen City (called Montreal until ten years ago when the capital of the Haijac Union had been moved from Rek, Iceland, to this site) was not a single blaze of light. Dark spots, probably parks, could be made out here and there, and the thin black ribbon winding by it was the Prophet (once St. Lawrence) River. The *palis* of Sigmen City rose five hundred meters in the air; each one housed at least a hundred thousand selves, and there were three hundred of this size in the area of the city proper.

In the middle of the metropolis was a square occupied by trees and government buildings, none of which was over fifty stories high. This was the University of Sigmen City, where Hal Yarrow did his work.

Hal, however, lived in the *pali* nearby, and it was toward this that he rode the belt after getting off the coach. Now, he felt strongly something that he had not noticed—consciously—all the days of his waking life. Not until after he had made this research trip to the Hudson Bay Preserve. And that was the crowd, the densely packed, jostling, pushing, and odorous mass of humanity.

They pressed in on him without knowing that he was there except as another body, another man, faceless, only a brief obstacle to their destination.

"Great Sigmen!" he muttered. "I must have been deaf, dumb, and blind! Not to have known! I *hate* them!"

He felt himself turn hot with guilt and shame. He looked into the faces of those around him as if they could see his hate, his guilt, his contrition, on his face. But they did not; they could not. To them, he was only another man, one to be treated with some respect if they encountered him personally because he was a professional. But not here, not on the belt carrying this flood of flesh down the thoroughfare. He was just another pack of blood and bones cemented by tissue and bound in skin. One of them and, therefore, nothing.

Shaken by this sudden revelation, Hal stepped off the belt. He wanted to get away from them, for he felt that he owed them an apology. And, at the same time, he felt like striking them.

A few steps from the belt, and above him, was the plastic lip of Pali No. 30, University Fellowship Residence. Inside this mouth, he felt no better, though he had lost the feeling he should apologize to those on the belt. There was no reason why they should know how he had suddenly been revolted. They had not seen the betraying flush on his face.

And even that was nonsense, he told himself, though he bit his lip as he did so. Those on the belt could not possibly have guessed. Not, that is, unless they, too, felt the same pressing-in and disgust. And, if they did, who were they to point him out?

He was among his own now, men and women clothed in the plastic baggy uniforms of the professional with the plaid design and the winged foot on the left chest. The only difference between male and female was that the women wore floor-length skirts over their trousers, nets over their hair, and some wore the veil. The latter was an article not too uncommon but dying out now, a custom retained by the older women or the more conservative of the young. Once honored, it now marked a woman as old-fashioned. This, despite the fact that the truecaster occasionally praised the veil and lamented its passing.

Hal spoke to several he passed but did not stop to talk. He saw Doctor Olvegssen, his department head, from a distance. He paused to see if Olvegssen wished to speak to him. Even this he did because the doctor was the only man with the authority to make him regret not paying his respects.

But Olvegssen evidently was busy, for he waved at Hal, called out, "Aloha," and walked on. Olvegssen was an old man; he used greetings and phrases popular in his youth.

Yarrow breathed with relief. Though he had thought he was eager to discuss his stay among the French-speaking natives of the Preserve, he now found that he did not want to talk to anybody. Not now. Maybe tomorrow. But not now.

Hal Yarrow waited by the door of the lift while the keeper checked the prospective passengers to determine who had priority. When the doors of the lift shaft opened, the keeper gave Hal's key back to him. He said, "You're first, *abba*."

"Sigmen bless," said Hal. He stepped into the lift and stood against the wall near the door while the others were identified and ranked.

The waiting was not long, for the keeper had been on his job for years and knew almost everybody by sight. Nevertheless, he had to go through the formality. Every once in a while, one of the residents was promoted or demoted. If the keeper had made the mistake of not recognizing the new shift in status, he would have been reported. His years at this post indicated that he knew his job well.

Forty people jammed into the lift, the keeper shook his castanets, and the door closed. The lift shot up swiftly enough to make everybody's knees bend; it continued to accelerate, for this was an express. At the thirtieth floor, the lift stopped automatically, and the doors opened. Nobody stepped out; perceiving this, the optical mechanism of the lift shut the doors, and the lift continued upward.

Three more stops with nobody stepping out. Then, half the crowd left. Hal drew in a deep breath, for if it had seemed crowded on the streets and on the ground floor, it was crushing inside the lift. Ten more stories, a journey in the same silence as that which had preceded it, every man and woman seeming intent on the truecaster's voice coming from the speaker in the ceiling. Then, the doors opened at Hal's floor.

The hallways were fifteen feet wide, room enough at this time of day. Nobody was in sight, and Hal was glad. If he had refused to chat for a few minutes with his neighbors, he would have been regarded as strange. That might have meant talk, and talk meant trouble, an explanation to his floor *gapt* at least. A heart-to-heart talk, a lecture, and Forerunner only knew what else.

He walked a hundred meters. Then, seeing the door to his *puka*, he stopped.

His heart had suddenly begun hammering, and his hands shook. He wanted to turn around and go back down the lift.

That, he told himself, was unreal behavior. He should not be feeling this way.

Besides, Mary would not be home for fifteen minutes at least.

He pushed open the door (no locks on the professional level, of course) and walked in. The walls began glowing and in ten seconds were at full bright. At the same time, the *tridi* sprang into life size on the wall opposite him, and the voices of the actors blared out. He jumped. Saying, "Great Sigmen!" under his breath, he hastened forward and turned off the wall. He knew that Mary had left it on, ready to spring into life when he walked in. He also knew that he had told her so many times how it surprised him that she could not possibly have forgotten. Which meant that she was doing it on purpose, consciously or unconsciously.

He shrugged and told himself that from now on he would not mention the matter. If she thought that he was no longer bothered by it, she might forget to leave it on.

Then, again, she might guess why he had suddenly become silent about her supposed forgetfulness. She might continue with the hope that he would eventually be unnerved, lose his temper, and start shouting at her. And, once more, she would have won a round, for she would refuse to argue back, would infuriate him by her silence and martyred look, and make him even angrier.

Then, of course, she would have to carry out her duty, however painful to her. She would, at the end of the month, go to the block *gapt* and report. And that would mean one more of many black crosses on his Morality Rating, which he would have to erase by some strenuous effort. And these efforts, if he made them—and he was getting tired of making them—would mean time lost from some more—dare he say it even to himself?—worthwhile project.

And if he protested to her that she was keeping him from advancing in his profession, from making more money, from moving into a larger *puka*, then he would have to listen to her sad, reproachful voice asking him if he actually wanted her to commit an *unreal* act. Would he ask her not to tell the truth, to lie by either omission or commission? He surely could not do that, for then both her self and his self would be in grave danger. Never would they see the glorious face of the Forerunner, and never . . . and so on and on—he helpless to answer back.

Yet, she was always asking him why he did not love her. And, when he replied that he did, she continued to say he did not. Then it was his turn to ask her if she thought he was lying. He was not; and if she called him a liar, then he would have to report her to the block *gapt*. Now, sheerly illogical, she would weep and say that she knew he did not love her. If he really did, he could not dream of telling the *gapt* about her.

When he protested that she thought it was *shib* for her to report him, he was answered with more tears. Or would be if he continued to fall into her trap. But he swore again and told himself that he would not.

Hal Yarrow walked through the living room, five-by-three meters, into the only other room—except the unmentionable—the kitchen. In the three- by two-and-a-half-meter room, he swung the stove down from the wall near the ceiling, dialed the proper code on its instrument panel, and walked back into the living room. Here he took off his jacket, crushed it into a ball, and stuffed it under a chair. He knew that Mary might find it and scold him for it, but he did not care. He was, at the moment, too tired to reach up to the ceiling and pull down a hook.

A low pinging sound came from the kitchen. Supper was ready.

Hal decided to leave the correspondence until after he had eaten. He went into the unmentionable to wash his face and hands. Automatically, he murmured the ablution prayer, "May I wash off unreality as easily as water removes this dirt, so Sigmen wills it."

After cleaning himself, he pressed the button by the portrait of Sigmen above the washbasin. For a second, the face of the Forerunner stared at him, the long, lean face with a shock of bright red hair, big projecting ears, straw-colored and very thick eyebrows that met above the huge hooked nose with flaring nostrils, the pale blue eyes, the long orange-red beard, the lips thin as a knife's edge. Then, the face began to dim, to fade out. Another second, and the Forerunner was gone, replaced by a mirror.

Hal was allowed to look into this mirror just long enough to assure himself his face was clean and to comb his hair. There was nothing to keep him from standing before it past the allotted time, but he had never transgressed on himself. Whatever his faults, vanity was not one of them. Or so he had always told himself.

Yet, he lingered perhaps a little too long. And he saw the broad shoulders of a tall man, the face of a man thirty years old. His hair, like the Forerunner's, was red, but darker, almost bronze. His forehead was high and broad, his eyebrows were a dark brown, his widely-spaced eyes were a dark gray, his nose was straight and of normal size, his upper lip was a trifle too long, his lips were full, his chin a shade too prominent.

Hal pressed the button again. The silver of the mirror darkened, broke into streaks of brightness. Then it darkened again and firmed into the portrait of Sigmen. For the flicker of an eyelid, Hal saw his image superimposed on Sigmen's; then, his features faded, were absorbed by the Forerunner, the mirror was gone, and the portrait was there.

Hal left the unmentionable and went to the kitchen. He made sure the door was locked (the kitchen door and unmentionable door were the only ones capable of being locked), for he did not want to be surprised by Mary while eating. He opened the stove door, removed the warm box, placed the box on a table swung down from the wall, and pushed the stove back up to the ceiling. Then, he opened the box and ate his meal. After dropping the plastic container down the recovery-chute opening in the wall, he went back to the unmentionable and washed his hands.

While he was doing so, he heard Mary call his name.

2

Hal hesitated for a moment before answering, though he did not know why or even think of it. Then, he said, "In here, Mary."

Mary said, "Oh! Of course, I knew you'd be there, if you were home. Where else could you be?"

Unsmiling, he walked into the living room. "Must you be so sarcastic, even after I've been gone so long?"

Mary was a tall woman, only half a head shorter than Hal. Her hair was pale blond and drawn tightly back from her forehead to a heavy coil at the nape of her neck. Her eyes were light blue. Her features were regular and petite but were marred by very thin lips. The baggy high-necked shirt and loose floor-length skirt she wore prevented any observer from knowing what kind of figure she had. Hal himself did not know.

Mary said, "I wasn't being sarcastic, Hal. Just realistic. Where else could you be? All you had to do was say, 'Yes.' And you *would* have to be in there"—she pointed at the door to the unmentionable—"when I come home. You seem to spend all your time in there or at your studies. Almost as if you were trying to hide from me."

"A fine homecoming," he said.

"You haven't kissed me," she said.

"Ah, yes," he replied. "That's my duty. I forgot."

"It shouldn't be a duty," she said. "It should be a joy."

"It's hard to enjoy kissing lips that snarl," he said.

To his surprise, Mary, instead of replying angrily, began to weep.

At once, he felt ashamed.

"I'm sorry," he said. "But you'll have to admit you weren't in a very good mood when you came in."

He went to her and tried to put his arms around her, but she turned away from him. Nevertheless, he kissed her on the side of her mouth as she turned her head.

"I don't want you to do that because you feel sorry for me or because it's your duty," she said. "I want you to do it because you love me."

"But I do love you," he said for what seemed like the thousandth time since they had married. Even to himself, he sounded unconvincing. Yet—he told himself—he did love her. He had to.

"You have a very nice way of showing it," she said.

"Let's forget what happened and start all over again," he said. "Here."

And he started to kiss her, but she backed away.

"What in H is the matter with you?" he said.

"You have given me my greeting kiss," she said. "You must not start getting sensual. This is not the time or place."

He threw his hands up in the air.

"Who's getting sensual? I wanted to act as if you had just come in the door. Is it worse to have one more kiss than prescribed than it is to quarrel? The trouble with you, Mary, is that you're absolutely literal-minded. Don't you know that the Forerunner himself didn't demand that his prescriptions be taken literally? He himself said that circumstances sometimes warranted modifications!"

"Yes, and he also said that we must beware of rationalizing ourselves into departing from his law. We must first confer with a *gapt* about the reality of our behavior."

"Oh, of course!" he said. "I'll phone our good guardian angel *pro tempore* and ask him if it's all right if I kiss you again!"

"That's the only safe thing to do," she said.

"Great Sigmen!" he shouted. "I don't know whether to laugh or cry! But I do know that I don't understand you! I never will!"

"Say a prayer to Sigmen," she said. "Ask him to give you reality. Then, we will have no difficulty."

"Say a prayer yourself," he said. "It takes two to make a quarrel. You're just as responsible as I am."

"I'll talk to you later when you're not so angry," she said. "I have to wash and eat."

"Never mind me," he replied. "I'll be busy until bedtime. I have to catch up on my Sturch business before I report to Olvegssen."

"And I'll bet you're happy you have to," she said. "I was looking forward to a nice talk. After all, you haven't said a word of your trip to the Preserve."

He did not reply.

She said, "You needn't bite your lip at me!"

He took a portrait of Sigmen down from the wall and unfolded it on a chair. Then he swung down his projector-magnifier from the wall, inserted the letter in it, and set the controls. After putting on his unscrambling goggles and sticking the phone in his ear, he sat down in the chair. He grinned as he did so. Mary must have seen the grin, and she probably wondered what caused it, but she did not ask. If she had, she would not have been answered. He could not tell her that he got a certain amusement from sitting on the Forerunner's portrait. She would have been shocked or would have pretended to be, he was never sure about her reactions. In any event, she had no sense of humor worth considering, and he did not intend to tell her anything that would downrate his M.R.

Hal pressed the button that activated the projector and then sat back, though not relaxedly. Immediately, the magnification of the film sprang up on the wall opposite him. Mary, not having goggles on, could see nothing except a blank wall. At the same time, he heard the voice recorded on the film. First, as always with an official letter, the face of the Forerunner appeared on the wall. The voice said, "Praise to Isaac Sigmen, in whom reality resides and from whom all truth flows! May he bless us, his followers, and confound his enemies, the disciples of the *unshib* Backrunner!"

There was a pause in the voice and a break in the projection for the viewer to send forth a prayer of his own. Then, a single word—*woggle*—flashed on the wall, and the speaker continued. "Devout believer Hal Yarrow:

"Here is the first of a list of words that have appeared recently in the vocabulary of the American-speaking population of the Union. This word—*woggle*—originated in the Department of Polynesia and spread radially to all the American-speaking peoples of the departments of North America, Australia, Japan, and China. Strangely, it has not yet made an appearance in the Department of South America, which, as you doubtless know, is contiguous to North America."

Hal Yarrow smiled, though there was a time when statements of this type had enraged him. When would the senders of these letters ever realize that he was not only a highly educated man but a broadly educated one, too? In this particular case, even the semiliterates of the lower classes should know where South America was, for the reason that the Forerunner had many times mentioned that continent in his *The Western Talmud* and *The Real World and Time.* It was true, however, that the schoolteachers of the unpros might never have thought to point out the location of South America to their pupils, even if they themselves knew.

"*Woggle,*" continued the speaker, "was first reported on the island of Tahiti. This island lies in the center of the Polynesian Department and is inhabited by people descended from Australians who colonized it after the Apocalyptic War. Tahiti is, at present, used as a military spaceship base.

"*Woggle* apparently spread from there, but its use has been confined mainly to unprofessionals. The exception is the professional space personnel. We feel there is some connection between the appearance of the word and the fact that spacefarers were the first to use it—as far as we know.

"Truecasters have asked permission to use this word on the air, but this has been denied until further study.

"The word itself, as far as can be determined at this date, is used as adjective, noun, and verb. It contains a basically derogatory meaning close to, but not equivalent to, the linguistically acceptable words *fouled-up* and *jinxed.* In addition, it contains the meaning of something strange, otherworldly; in a word, unrealistic.

"You are hereby ordered to investigate the word *woggle*, following Plan No. ST-LIN-476 unless you have received an order with a higher priority number. In either case, you will reply to this letter not later than 12th Fertility, 550 B.S."

Hal ran the letter to the end. Fortunately, the other three words had lower priority. He did not have to accomplish the impossible: investigate all four at once.

But he would have to leave in the morning after reporting to Olvegssen. Which meant not even bothering to unpack his stuff, living for days in the clothes he was wearing, perhaps not having time to have them cleaned.

Not that he did not wish to get away. It was just that he was tired and wished to rest before going on this trip.

What rest? he asked himself after removing the goggles and looking at Mary.

Mary was just getting up from her chair after turning off the *tridi*. She was now bending over to pull a drawer from the wall. He saw that she was getting out their nightclothes. And, as he had for many a night now, he felt sick in his stomach.

Mary turned and saw his face.

"What's the matter?" she said.

"Nothing."

She walked across the room (only a few steps to traverse the length of the chamber, reminding him of how many steps he could take when he was on the Preserve). She handed him a crumpled-up mass of tissue-thin garments and said, "I don't think Olaf had them cleaned. It's not his fault, though. The deionizer isn't working. He left a note saying he called a technician. But you know how long it takes them to fix anything."

"I'll fix it myself, when I get time," he said. He sniffed at the night-clothes. "Great Sigmen! How long has the cleaner been out?"

"Ever since you left," she said.

"How that man does sweat!" Hal said. "He must be in a perpetual state of terror. No wonder! Old Olvegssen scares me, too."

Mary's face became red. "I have prayed and prayed that you wouldn't curse," she said. "When are you going to quit that unreal habit? Don't you know? . . ."

"Yes," he said, interrupting harshly, "I know that every time I take the Forerunner's name in vain, I delay Timestop just that much more. So what?"

Mary stepped back from the loudness of his voice and the curl of his lip.

" 'So what?' " she repeated incredulously. "Hal, you can't mean it?"

"No, of course I don't mean it!" he said, breathing heavily. "Of course I don't! How could I? It's just that I get so mad at your continual reminding me of my faults."

"The Forerunner himself said we must always remind our brother of his unrealities."

"I'm not your brother. I'm your husband," he said. "Though there are plenty of times, such as now, when I wish I weren't."

Mary lost the prim and reproving look, tears filled her eyes, and her lips and chin shook.

"For Sigmen's sake," he said. "Don't cry."

"How can I help it," she sobbed, "when my own husband, my own flesh and blood, united to me by the Real Sturch, heaps abuse on my head? And I have done nothing to deserve it."

"Nothing except turn me in to the *gapt* every chance you get," he said. He turned away from her and pulled the bed down from the wall.

"I suppose the bedclothes will stink of Olaf and his fat wife, too," he said.

He picked up a sheet, smelled it, and said, "Augh!" He tore off the other sheets and threw them on the floor. With them went his nightclothes.

"To H with them! I'm sleeping in my clothes. You call yourself a wife? Why didn't you take our stuff to our neighbor's and get them cleaned there?"

"You know why," she said. "We don't have the money to pay them for the use of their cleaner. If you'd get a higher M.R., then we could afford it."

"How can I get a higher M.R. when you babble to the *gapt* every time I commit a little indiscretion?"

"Why, that's not *my* fault!" she said indignantly. "What kind of Sigmenite would I be if I lied to the good *abba* and told him you deserved a better M.R.? I couldn't live with myself after that, knowing that I had been so grossly unreal and that the Forerunner was watching me. Why, when I'm with the *gapt*, I can feel the invisible eyes of Isaac Sigmen burning into me, reading my every thought. I couldn't! And you should be ashamed because you want me to!"

"H with you!" he said. He walked away and went into the unmentionable.

Inside the tiny room, he shed his clothes and stepped into the shower for the thirty-second fall of water allowed him. Then he stood in front of the blower until he was dried. Afterward, he brushed his teeth vigorously, as if he were trying to scour out the terrible words he had uttered. As usual, he was beginning to feel the shame of what he had said. And with it the fear of what Mary would tell the *gapt*, what he would tell the *gapt*, and what would happen afterward. It was possible that his M.R. would be so devaluated that he would be fined. If that happened, then his budget, strained as it was, would burst. And he would be more in debt than ever, not to mention that he would be passed over when the next promotion time came.

Thinking this, he put his clothes back on and left the little room. Mary brushed by him on her way into the unmentionable. She looked surprised on seeing him dressed, then she stopped and said, "Oh, that's right! You did throw the night-things on the floor! Hal, you can't mean it!"

"Yes, I do," he said. "I'm not sleeping in those sweaty things of Olaf's."

"Please, Hal," she said. "I wish you wouldn't use that word. You know that I can't stand vulgarity."

"I beg your pardon," he said. "Would you rather I used the Icelandic or Hebrew word for it? In either language, the word stands for the same vile human excretion: sweat!"

Mary put her hands to her ears, ran into the unmentionable, and slammed the door behind her.

He threw himself down on the thin mattress and put his arm over his eyes so the light would not get into them. In five minutes, he heard the door open (it was beginning to need oiling but would not get it until their budget and that of the Olaf Marconis could afford to buy the lubricant). And if his M.R. went down, the Marconis might petition to move into another apartment. If they could find one, then another, even more objectionable couple (probably one that had just been elevated from a lower professional class) would move in with them.

Oh, Sigmen! he thought. *Why can't I be content with things as they are? Why can't I accept reality fully? Why must I have so much of the Backrunner in me? Tell me, tell me!*

It was Mary's voice he heard as she settled into bed beside him. "Hal, surely you aren't going to stick to this *unshib*?"

"What *unshib*?" he said, though he knew what she meant.

"Sleeping in your dayclothes."

"Why not?"

"Hal!" she said. "You know very well why not!"

"No, I don't," he replied. He removed his arm from his eyes and stared into total blackness. She had, as prescribed, turned off the light before getting into bed.

Her body, if unclothed, would gleam white in the light of lamp or moon, he thought. *Yet, I have never seen her body, never seen her even half-undressed. Never seen any woman's body except for that picture that man in Berlin showed me. And I, after one half-hungry, half-horrified look, ran as swiftly as I could. I wonder if the Uzzites found him soon after and did to him whatever they do to men who pervert reality so hideously.*

So hideously . . . yet, he could see the picture as if it were before his eyes now in the full light of Berlin. And he could see the man who was trying to sell it to him, a tall, good-looking youth with blond hair and broad shoulders, speaking the Berliner variety of Icelandic.

White flesh gleaming . . .

Mary had been silent for several minutes, but he could hear her breathing. Then, "Hal, haven't you done enough since you came home? Must you make me tell the *gapt* even more?"

"And just what else have I done?" he asked fiercely. Nevertheless, he smiled slightly, for he was determined to make her speak plainly, to come out and ask. Not that she ever would, but he was going to get her to come as close as she was capable.

"That's just it, you haven't done anything," she whispered.

"Now what do you mean?"

"You know."

"No, I don't."

"The night before you left for the Preserve, you said you were too tired. That's no real excuse, but I didn't say anything to the *gapt* about it because you had fulfilled your weekly duty. But you've been gone two weeks, and now—"

"Weekly duty!" he said loudly, resting on one elbow. "Weekly duty! Is that what you think of it?"

"Why, Hal," she said with a surprised note. "What else am I to think?"

Groaning, he lay back down and stared into the dark.

"What's the use?" he said. "Why, why should we? Nine years we've been married; we've had no children; we never will. I've even petitioned for a divorce. So why should we continue to perform like a couple of robots on *tridi*?"

Mary's breath sucked in, and he could imagine the horror on her face.

After a moment which seemed to bulge with her shock, she said, "We must because we must. What else can we do? Surely, you're not suggesting that? . . ."

"No, no," he said quickly, thinking of what would happen if she told their *gapt*. Other things he could get away with, but any hint on her part that her husband was refusing to carry out the specific command of the Forerunner . . . He did not dare to think about that. At least, he now had prestige as a university teacher and a *puka* with some room in it and a chance to advance. But not if . . .

"Of course not," he said. "I know we must try to have children, even if we seem doomed not to."

"The doctors say there's nothing physically wrong with either of us," she said for perhaps the thousandth time in the past five years. "So, one of us must be thinking against reality, denying with his body the true future. And I know that it can't be me. It couldn't be!"

" 'The dark self hides overmuch from the bright self,' " said Hal, quoting *The Western Talmud*. " 'The Backrunner in us trips us, and we know it not.' "

There was nothing that so infuriated Mary, herself always quoting, as to have Hal do the same. But now, instead of beginning a tirade, she cried, "Hal, I'm scared! Do you realize that in another year our time will be up? That we'll go before the Uzzites for another test? And, if we fail, if they find out that one of us is denying the future to our children . . . they made it clear what would happen!"

Artificial insemination by a donor was adultery. Cloning had been forbidden by Sigmen because it was an abomination.

For the first time that evening, Hal felt a sympathy with her. He knew the same terror that was making her body quiver and shake the bed.

But he could not allow her to know it, for then she would break up completely, as she had several times in the past. He would be all night putting the pieces back together and making them stick.

"I don't think there is too much to worry about," he said. "After all, we are highly respected and much needed professionals. They're not about to waste our education and talents by sending us to H. I think that if you don't get pregnant, they'll give us an extension. After all, they do have precedent and authority. The Forerunner himself said that every case should be considered in its context, not judged by an absolute rule. And we—"

"And how often is a case judged by the context?" she said shrilly. "How often? You know as well as I do that the absolute rule is always applied!"

"I don't know any such thing," he replied soothingly. "How naïve can you get? If you go by what the truecasters say, yes. But I've heard some things about the hierarchy. I know that such things as blood relationship, friendship, prestige, and wealth, or usefulness to the Sturch, can make for a relaxation of the rules."

Mary sat upright in bed.

"Are you trying to tell me that the Urielites can be bribed?" she said in a shocked tone.

"I would never ever say that to anybody," he said. "And I will swear by Sigmen's lost hand that I did not mean even to hint at such a vile unreality. No, I am just saying that usefulness to the Sturch sometimes results in leniency or another chance."

"Who do you know to help us?" said Mary, and Hal smiled in the darkness. Mary could be shocked by his outspokenness, but she was practical and would not hesitate to use any means to get them out of their predicament.

There was silence for a few minutes. Mary was breathing hard, like a cornered animal.

Finally, he said, "I don't really know anybody with influence except Olvegssen. And he's been making remarks about my M.R., though he does praise my work."

"See! That M.R.! If you'd only make an effort, Hal . . ."

"If only you weren't so eager to downgrade me," he said bitterly.

"Hal, I can't help it if you go along so easily with unreality! I don't like what I have to do, but it's my duty! You're even making a misstep by reproaching me for what I have to do. Another black mark—"

"Which you will be forced to repeat to the *gapt*. Yes, I know. Let's not go into that again for the ten thousandth time."

"You brought it up," she said righteously.

"That seems to be all we have to talk about."

She gasped, and then she said, "It wasn't always that way."

"No, not for the first year of our marriage. But since then—"

"Whose fault is that?" she cried.

"That's a good question. But I don't think we should go into it. It might be dangerous."

"What do you mean?"

"I don't care to discuss it."

He was himself surprised at what he had said. What did he mean? He did not know; he had spoken, not with his intellect but with his whole being. Had the Backrunner in him made him say that?

"Let's get to sleep," he said. "Tomorrow changes the face of reality."

"Not before—" she said.

"Before what?" he replied wearily.

"Don't play *shib* with me," she said. "This is what started the whole thing. You trying to . . . put off your . . . duty."

"My duty," said Hal. "The *shib* thing to do. Of course."

"Don't talk like that," she said. "I don't want you to do it just because it's your duty. I want you to do it because you love me, as you are enjoined to do. Also, because you *want* to love me."

"I am enjoined to love all of mankind," said Hal. "But I notice that I am expressly forbidden to perform my duty with anyone but my realistically bound wife."

Mary was so shocked that she could not reply, and she turned her back to him. But he, knowing that he was doing it as much to punish her and himself as doing what he should, reached out for her. From then on, having made the formal opening statement, everything was ritualized. This time, unlike some times in the past, everything was executed step by step, the words and actions, as specified by the Forerunner in *The Western Talmud*. Except for one detail: Hal was still wearing his dayclothes. This, he had decided, could be forgiven, for it was the spirit, not the letter, that counted, and what was the difference whether he wore the thick street garments or the bulky nightclothes? Mary, if she had noticed the error, had said nothing about it.

3

Afterward, lying on his back, staring into the darkness, Hal thought as he had many a time before. What was it that cut through his abdomen like a broad, thick steel plate and seemed to sever his torso from his hips? He was excited, in the beginning. He knew he must be because his heart beat fast, he breathed hard. Yet, he could not—really—feel anything. And when the moment came—which the Forerunner called the time of generation of potentiality, the fulfillment and actualization of reality—Hal experienced only a mechanical reaction. His body carried out its prescribed function, but he felt nothing of that ecstasy which the Forerunner had described so vividly. A zone of unfeeling, a nerve-chilling area, a steel plate, cut through him. He felt nothing except the jerkings of his body, as if an electrical needle were stimulating his nerves at the same time it numbed them.

This was wrong, he told himself. Or was it? Could it be that the Forerunner was mistaken? After all, the Forerunner was a man superior to the rest of humanity. Perhaps, he had been gifted enough to experience such exquisite reactions and had not realized that the remainder of mankind did not share his good fortune.

But no, that could not be, if it were true—and perish the thought that it could not be—that the Forerunner could see into every man's mind.

Then, Hal himself was lacking, he alone of all the disciples of the Real Sturch.

Or was he alone? He had never discussed his feelings with anyone. To do so was—if not unthinkable—undoable. It was obscene, unrealistic. He had never been told by his teachers not to discuss the matter; they had not had to tell him, for Hal knew without being told.

Yet, the Forerunner had described what his reactions should be.

Or had he done so directly? When Hal considered that section of *The Western Talmud* which was read only by engaged and married couples, he saw that the Forerunner had not actually depicted a physical state. His language had been poetical (Hal knew what poetical meant, for as a linguist, he had access to various works of literature forbidden to others), metaphorical, even metaphysical. Couched in terms which, analyzed, were seen to have little relation to reality.

Forgive me, Forerunner, thought Hal. *I meant that your words were not a scientific description of the actual electrochemical processes of the human nervous system. Of course, they apply directly on a higher level, for reality has many planes of phenomena.*

Subrealistic, realistic, pseudorealistic, surrealistic, superrealistic, retrorealistic.

No time for theology, he thought, *no wish to make my mind whirl again tonight as on many nights with the unsolvable, unanswerable. The Forerunner knew, but I can't.*

All he knew now was that he was not in phase with the world line; had not been, possibly never would be. He teetered on the brink of unreality every waking moment. And that was not good—the Backrunner would get him, he'd fall into the Forerunner's brother's evil hands . . .

Hal Yarrow woke suddenly as the morning clarion rang through the apartment. For a moment, he was confused, the world of his dream meshing with his waking world.

Then, he rolled out of bed and stood up, looking down at Mary. She, as always, slept on through the first call, loud as it was, because it was not for her. In fifteen minutes, the second blast of bugles over the *tridi* would come, the women's call. By then he must be washed, shaved, dressed, and on his way. Mary would have fifteen minutes to get herself on the road; ten minutes later, the Olaf Marconis would enter from their night's work and prepare to sleep and live in this narrow world until the Yarrows returned.

Hal was even quicker than usual because he still wore his day-clothes. He relieved himself, washed his face and hands, rubbed cream over his face stubble, wiped off the loosened hairs (someday, if he ever rose to the rank of a hierarch, he would wear a beard, like Sigmen), combed his hair, and he was out of the unmentionable.

After stuffing the letters he'd received the previous night into his traveling bag, he started toward the door. Then, impelled by an unexpected and unanalyzable feeling, he turned and went back to the bed and stooped over to kiss Mary. She did not wake up, and he felt regret—for a second—because she had not known what he had done. This act was no duty, no requirement. It had come from the dark depths, where there must also be light. Why had he done it? Last night, he had thought he hated her. Now . . .

She could not help doing what she did any more than he. That, of course, was no excuse. Every self was responsible for its own destiny; if anything good or bad happened to a self, then only one person had caused that happening.

He amended his thought. He and Mary were the generators of their own misery. But not consciously so. Their bright selves did not want their love to be wrecked; it was their dark selves—the deep-down, crouching, horrible Backrunner in them—that was causing this.

Then, as he stood by the doorway, he saw Mary open her eyes and look, somewhat confusedly, at him. And, instead of returning to kiss her again, he hastily stepped into the hallway. He was in a panic, fearing that she might call him back and begin the whole dreary and nerve-racking scene again. Not until later did he realize that he had not had a chance to tell Mary that he would be on his way to Tahiti that very morning. Oh well, he was spared another scene.

By then, the hallway was crowded with men on their way to work. Many, like Hal, were dressed in the loose plaids of the professionals. Others wore the green and scarlet of university teachers.

Hal, of course, spoke to each one.

"Good future to you, Ericssen!"

"Sigmen smile, Yarrow!"

"Did you have a bright dream, Chang?"

"*Shib,* Yarrow! Straight from truth itself."

"Shalom, Kazimuru."

"Sigmen smile, Yarrow!"

Then Hal stood by the lift doors while a keeper, on duty at this level in the morning because of the crowd, arranged the priority of their descent. Once out of the tower, Hal stepped onto a series of belts with increasingly swift speed until he was on the express, the middle belt. Here he stood, pressed in by the bodies of men and women but at ease because they belonged to his class. Ten minutes of travel, and he began to work his way through the crowd from belt to belt. Five minutes later, he stepped off onto the sidewalk and walked into the cavernous entrance of Pali No. 16, University of Sigmen City.

Inside, he had to wait, though not for long, until the keeper had ushered him into the lift. Then, he went straight up on the express to the thirtieth level. Usually, when he got out of the lift, he went directly to his own office to deliver his first lecture of the day, an undergraduate course which went out over *tridi*. Today, Hal headed for the dean's office.

On the way, craving a cigarette and knowing that he could not smoke it in Olvegssen's presence, he stopped to light one and to breathe in the delicious ginseng smoke. He was standing outside the door of an elementary class in linguistics and could hear snatches of Keoni Jerahmeel Rasmussen's lecture.

"*Puka* and *pali* were originally words of the primitive Polynesian inhabitants of the Hawaiian Islands. The English-speaking people who later colonized the islands adopted many terms from the Hawaiian language; *puka*, meaning hole, tunnel, or cave, and *pali*, meaning cliff, were among the most popular.

"When the Hawaiian-Americans repopulated North America after the Apocalyptic War, these two terms were still being used in the original sense. But, about fifty years ago, the two words changed their meanings. *Puka* came to be applied to the small apartments allotted to the lower classes, obviously in a derogatory sense. Later, the term spread to the upper classes. However, if you are a hierarch, you live in an apartment; if you belong to any class below the hierarchy, you live in a *puka*.

"*Pali*, which meant cliff, was applied to the skyscrapers or to any huge building. It, unlike *puka*, also retains its original meaning."

Hal finished his cigarette, dropped it in an ashtray, and walked on down the hall to the dean's office. There he found Doctor Bob Kafziel Olvegssen sitting behind his desk.

Olvegssen, the senior, spoke first, of course. He had a slight Icelandic accent.

"Aloha, Yarrow. And what are you doing here?"

"Shalom, *abba*. I beg your pardon for appearing before you without an invitation. But I had to arrange several matters before I left."

Olvegssen, a gray-haired middle-aged man of seventy, frowned. "Left?"

Hal took the letter from his suitcase and handed it to Olvegssen.

"You may process it yourself later, of course. But I can save you valuable time by telling you it's another order to make a linguistic investigation."

"You just got back from one!" said Olvegssen. "How can they expect me to run this college efficiently and to the glory of the Sturch if they continually drag my staff away on wild word chases?"

"You're surely not criticizing the Urielites?" said Hal, not without a touch of malice. He did not like his superior, try though he had to overcome this unrealistic thinking on his part.

"Harumph! Of course not! I am incapable of doing so, and I resent your imputation that I might be!"

"Your pardon, *abba*," said Hal. "I would not dream of hinting at such a thing."

"When must you leave?" said Olvegssen.

"On the first coach. Which, I believe, takes off in an hour."

"And you will return?"

"Only Sigmen knows. When my investigation and the report are finished."

"Report to me at once when you return."

"I beg your pardon again, but I can't do that. My M.R. will be long overdue by then, and I am compelled to clear that out of the way before I do anything else. That may take hours."

Olvegssen scowled and said, "Yes, your M.R. You didn't do so well on your last, Yarrow. I trust your next shows some improvement. Otherwise . . ."

Suddenly, Hal felt hot all through his body, and his legs quivered. "Yes, *abba*?"

His own voice sounded weak and distant.

Olvegssen made a steeple of his hands and looked at Yarrow over the tip.

"Much as I would regret it, I would be forced to take action. I can't have a man with a low M.R. on my staff. I'm afraid that I . . ."

There was a long silence. Hal felt the sweat trickling down from his armpits and the beads forming on his forehead and upper lip. He knew that Olvegssen was purposely hanging him in suspense, and he did not want to ask him anything. He did not want to give the smug gray-haired *gimel* the satisfaction of hearing him speak. But he did not dare seem to be uninterested. And, if he did not say anything, he knew that Olvegssen would only smile and dismiss him.

"What, *abba*?" said Hal, striving to keep a choking sound from his voice.

"I'm very much afraid that I could not even allow myself the leniency of merely demoting you to secondary school teaching. I would like to be merciful. But mercy in your case might only be enforcing unreality. And I could not endure the possibility of that. No . . ."

Hal swore at himself because he could not control his trembling. "Yes, *abba*?"

"I am very much afraid that I would have to ask the Uzzites to look into your case."

"No!" said Hal loudly.

"Yes," said Olvegssen, still speaking behind the steeple of his hands. "It would pain me to do that, but it would be *unshib* not to. Only by seeking their help could I dream correctly."

He broke the steeple of his hands, swung around in his chair so his profile was to Hal, and said, "However, there is no reason that I should have to take such steps, is there? After all, you and you alone are responsible for whatever happens to you. Therefore, you've nobody to blame but yourself."

"So the Forerunner has revealed," said Hal. "I will see that you are not pained, *abba*. I will make certain that my *gapt* has no reason to give me a low M.R."

"Very good," said Olvegssen as if he did not believe it. "I will not hold you up by examining your letter, for I should have a duplicate in today's mail. Aloha, my son, and good dreaming."

"See real, *abba*," said Hal, and he turned and left. In a daze of terror, he scarcely knew what he was doing. Automatically, he traveled to the port and there went through the process of obtaining priority for his trip. His mind still refused to function clearly when he got onto the coach.

Half an hour later, he got off at the port of LA and went to the ticket office to confirm his seat on the coach to Tahiti.

As he stood in the ticket line, he felt a tap on his shoulder.

He jumped, and then he turned to apologize to the person behind.

He felt his heart hammer as if it would batter through his chest.

The man was a squat broad-shouldered potbellied fellow in a loose, jet black uniform. He wore a tall, conical, shiny black hat with a narrow rim, and on his chest was the silvery figure of the angel Uzza.

The officer leaned forward to examine the Hebrew numbers on the lower rim of the winged foot Hal wore on his chest. Then he looked at a paper in his hand.

"You're Hal Yarrow, *shib*," said the Uzzite. "Come with me."

Afterward, Hal thought that one of the strangest aspects of the business was his lack of terror. Not that he had not been scared. It was just that the fear was pushed far down into a corner of his mind while the greater part devoted itself to considering the situation and how to get out of it. The vagueness and confusion that had filled him during his interview with Olvegssen and that had lasted long afterward now seemed to dissolve. He was left cold and quick-thinking; the world was clear and hard.

Perhaps, it was because the threat given by Olvegssen was distant and uncertain, whereas being taken into custody by the Uzzites was immediate and certainly dangerous.

He was taken to a small car on a strip by the ticket building. Here he was ordered into the seat. The Uzzite with him also got in, and he set the controls for his destination. The car rose vertically to about five hundred meters and then shot, sirens screaming, toward its destination. Hal, though not in a humorous mood, could not help reflecting that cops had not changed in the last thousand years. Even though no emergency warranted, the guardians of the law must make noise.

Within two minutes, the car had entered a port of a building at the twentieth level. Here the Uzzite, who had spoken not a word to Hal since the initial conversation, gestured to him to get out. Hal had not said anything either because he knew that it would be useless.

The two walked up a ramp and then through many corridors filled with hurrying people. Hal tried to keep the route straight just in case he was able to escape. He knew that flight was ridiculous, that he could not possibly get away. Also, he had no reason as yet to think that he would be in a situation where running was the only way out.

Or so he hoped.

Finally, the Uzzite stopped before an office door which bore no legend. He jerked his thumb at it, and Hal walked in ahead of him. He found himself in an anteroom; a female secretary sat behind a desk.

"Angel Patterson reporting," said the Uzzite. "I have Hal Yarrow,

Professional LIN-56327."

The secretary relayed the information through a speaker, and a voice came from the wall telling the two to enter.

The secretary pressed a button, and the door swung open.

Hal, still in the lead, walked in.

He was in a room large by his standards, larger even than his classroom or his whole *puka* in Sigmen City. At its far end was a huge desk whose top curved like a crescent or a pair of sharp horns. Behind it sat a man, and the sight of the man shattered Hal's calm composure. He had expected a *gapt* of high rank, a man dressed in black and wearing a conical hat.

But this man was not an Uzzite. He was clad in flowing purple robes with a cowl over his head, and on his chest was a large golden Hebrew *L*, the *lamedh*. And he had a beard.

He was among the highest of the high, a Urielite. Hal had seen his kind only a dozen times in his life and only once before in the flesh.

He thought, Great Sigmen, what have I done? I'm doomed, doomed!

The Urielite was a very tall man, almost half a head higher than Hal. His face was long, his cheekbones protruding, his nose large, narrow, and curved, his lips thin, and his eyes pale blue with a slight internal epicanthic fold.

Behind Hal, the Uzzite said in a very low voice, "Halt, Yarrow! Stand at attention! Do everything the Sandalphon Macneff says, without hesitation and with no false moves."

Hal, who would not have thought of disobeying, nodded his head.

Macneff looked at Yarrow for at least a minute, meanwhile stroking his bushy brown beard.

Then, after making Hal sweat and quiver inwardly, Macneff finally spoke. His voice was surprisingly deep for such a thin-necked man.

"Yarrow, how would you like to leave this life?"

4

Afterward, Hal had time to thank Sigmen that he had not followed his impulse.

Instead of becoming paralyzed with terror, he had considered whirling swiftly and attacking the Uzzite. The officer, though he wore no visible arms, undoubtedly had a gun in a holster under his robes. If Hal could knock him out and get the weapon, he might be able to take Macneff as a hostage. With him as a shield, Hal could flee.

Where?

He had no idea. To Israel or the Malay Federation? Both were a long way off, though distance meant little if he could steal or commandeer a ship. Even if he succeeded in doing that, he had no chance of getting past the antimissile stations. Unless he could fool the guards, and he did not know enough of military usage or codes to do that.

Meanwhile, thinking of the possibilities, he felt the impulse die. It would be more intelligent to wait until he found out what he was accused of. Perhaps, he could prove that he was innocent.

Macneff's thin lips curved slightly in a smile that Hal was to know well. He said, "That is good, Yarrow."

Hal did not know if he had been given an implication to speak, but he took a chance of not offending the Urielite.

"What is good, Sandalphon?"

"That you turned red instead of pale. I am a reader of selves, Yarrow. I can see into a man within a few seconds after meeting him. And I saw that you were not ready to faint with terror, as many would have done if they had just heard my first words to you. No, you became flushed with the hot blood of aggressiveness. You were ready to deny, to argue, to fight against anything I might say.

"Now, some might say that that would not be a favorable reaction, that your attitude showed wrong thinking, a leaning toward unreality.

"But I say, *What is reality?* That was the question propounded by the Forerunner's evil brother in the great debate. The answer is the same, that only the real man can tell.

"I am real; otherwise, I would not be a Sandalphon. *Shib?*"

Hal, trying to keep from breathing noisily, nodded. He was thinking that Macneff must not be able to read as clearly as he thought he could, for he had said nothing about knowing Hal's first intention to resort to violence.

Or did Macneff know but was wise enough to forgive?

"When I asked you how you would like to leave this life," said Macneff, "I was not suggesting that you were a candidate for H."

He frowned, and he said, "Though your M.R. suggests that if you keep on your present level, you may soon be. However, I am certain that if you volunteer for what I propose, you will soon straighten out. You would then be in close contact with many *shib* men; you could not escape their influence. 'Reality breeds reality.' So said Sigmen.

"However, I may be rushing things. First, you must swear on this book"—he picked up a copy of *The Western Talmud*—"that nothing that we say in this office will be divulged to any person under any circumstances. You will die or undergo any torture before you betray the Sturch."

Hal put his left hand on the book (Sigmen used his left hand because of the early loss of his right), and he swore by the Forerunner and all the levels of reality that his lips would be locked forever. Otherwise, he cut himself off forever from any hope of the glory of seeing the Forerunner face to face and of some day having his own universe to rule.

Even as he swore, he began to feel guilty because he had thought of striking an Uzzite and using force on a Sandalphon. How could he have given in to his dark self so suddenly? Macneff was the living representative of Sigmen while Sigmen was voyaging through time and space to prepare the future for his disciples. To refuse to obey Macneff in any degree was to strike the Forerunner in the face, and that was a thing so terrible he could not bear to think of it.

Macneff put the book back on the desk, and he said, "First, I must tell you that your getting that order to investigate the word *woggle* in Tahiti was a mistake. Probably because certain departments of the Uzzites were not working as closely together as they should. The reason for the mistake is even now being researched, and effective measures will be taken to make sure similar errors do not occur in the future."

The Uzzite behind Hal sighed heavily, and Hal knew that he was not the only man in the room capable of feeling fear.

"One of the hierarchy noticed, while going over his reports, that you had applied for permission to travel to Tahiti. Knowing how high a security rating the island has, he investigated. As a result, we were able to intercept you. And I, after examining your record, concluded that you might be just the one we needed to fill a certain position on the ship."

By now, Macneff had walked from behind his desk and was pacing back and forth, his hands clasped behind him, his body stooped forward. Hal could see how pale yellow Macneff's skin was, much the same color as the elephant tusk Hal had once seen in the Museum of

Extinct Animals. The purple of the cowl over his head brought out the sallowness.

"You will be asked to volunteer," said Macneff, "because we want none but the most dedicated men aboard. However, I hope you do join us, because I would feel uneasy about leaving on Earth any civilian who knew the existence and destination of the *Gabriel.* Not that I doubt your loyalty, but the Israeli spies are very clever, and they might trick you into revealing what you know. Or kidnap you and use drugs to make you talk. They are devoted followers of the Backrunner, those Israeli."

Hal wondered why the use of drugs by the Israeli was so unrealistic and by the Haijac Union so *shib*, but he forgot about that when he heard Macneff's next words.

"A hundred years ago, the first interstellar spaceship of the Union left Earth for Alpha Centaurus. About the same time, an Israeli ship left. Both returned in twenty years and reported they had found no habitable planets, A second Haijac expedition came back ten years after that and a second Israeli vessel twelve years after it. None found a star with any planets human beings could colonize."

"I never knew that," murmured Hal Yarrow.

"Both governments have kept the secret well from their people, though not from each other," said Macneff. "The Israeli, as far as we know, have sent no more interstellar craft out since the second one. The expense and time involved are astronomical. However, we sent a third vessel out, a much smaller and faster one than the first two. We have learned much about interstellar drives since a hundred years ago; that is all I can tell you about them.

"But the third ship came back several years ago and reported—"

"That it had found a planet on which human beings could live and which was already inhabited by sentient beings!" said Hal, forgetting in his enthusiasm that he had not been asked to speak.

Macneff stopped pacing to stare at Hal with his pale blue eyes.

"How did you know?" he said sharply.

"Forgive me, Sandalphon," said Hal. "But it was inevitable! Did not the Forerunner predict in his *Time and the World Line* that such a planet would be found? I believe it was on page five seventy-three!"

Macneff smiled and said, "I am glad that your scriptural lessons have left such an impression."

How could they not? Hal thought. Besides, they were not the only impressions. Pornsen, my *gapt*, whipped me because I had not learned my lessons well enough. He was a good impresser, that Pornsen. Was? Is! As I grew older and was promoted, so was he, always where I was. He was my *gapt* in the creche. He was the dormitory *gapt* when I went to college and thought I was getting away from him. He is now my block *gapt*. He is the one responsible for my getting such low M.R.s.

Swiftly came the revulsion, the protest. No, not he, for I, and I alone, am responsible for whatever happens to me. If I get a low M.R., I do so because I want it that way, or my dark self does. If I die, I die because I willed it so. So, forgive me, Sigmen, for the contrary-to-reality thoughts!

"Please pardon me again, Sandalphon," said Hal. "But did the expedition find any records of the Forerunner having been on this planet? Perhaps, even, though this is too much to wish, find the Forerunner himself?"

"No," said Macneff. "Though that does not mean that there may not be such records there. The expedition was under orders to make a swift survey of conditions and then to return to Earth. I can't tell you now the distance in light-years or what star this was, though you can see it with the naked eye at night in this hemisphere. If you volunteer, you will be told where you're going after the ship leaves. And it leaves very soon."

"You need a linguist?" said Hal.

"The ship is huge," said Macneff, "but the number of military men and specialists we are taking limits the linguists to one. We have considered several of your professionals because they were *lamedhians* and above suspicion. Unfortunately . . ."

Hal waited. Macneff paced some more, frowning. Then, he said, "Unfortunately, only one *lamedhian joat* exists, and he is too old for this expedition. Therefore—"

"A thousand pardons," said Hal. "But I have just thought of one thing. I am married."

"No problem at all," said Macneff. "There will be no women aboard the *Gabriel*. And, if a man is married, he will automatically be given a divorce."

Hal gasped, and he said, "A divorce?"

Macneff raised his hands apologetically and said, "You are horrified, of course. But, from our reading of *The Western Talmud*, we Urielites believe that the Forerunner, knowing this situation would arise, made reference to and provision for divorce. It's inevitable in this case, for the couple will be separated for, at the least, eighty objective years. Naturally, he couched the provision in obscure language. In his great and glorious wisdom, he knew that our enemies the Israelites must not be able to read therein what we planned."

"I volunteer," said Hal. "Tell me more, Sandalphon."

Six months later, Hal Yarrow stood in the observation dome of the *Gabriel* and watched the ball of Earth dwindle above him. It was night on this hemisphere, but the light blazed from the megalopolises of Australia, Japan, China, Southeast Asia, India, Siberia. Hal, the linguist, saw the glittering disks and necklaces in terms of the languages spoken therein. Australia, the Philippine Islands, Japan, and northern China were inhabited by those members of the Haijac Union that spoke American.

Southern China, all of southeast Asia, southern India, and Ceylon, these states of the Malay Federation spoke Bazaar.

Siberia spoke Icelandic.

Hal's mind turned the globe swiftly for him, and he visualized Africa, which used Swahili south of the Sahara Sea. All around the Mediterranean Sea, Asia Minor, northern India, and Tibet, Hebrew was the native tongue. In southern Europe, between the Israeli Republics and the Icelandic-speaking peoples of northern Europe, was a thin but long stretch of territory called March. This was no man's land, disputed by the Haijac Union and the Israeli Republics, a potential source of war for the last two hundred years. Neither nation would give up their claim on it, yet neither wished to make any move that might lead to a second Apocalyptic War. So, for all practical purposes, it was an independent nation and by now had its own government (unrecognized outside its own borders). Its citizens spoke all of the world's surviving tongues, plus a new one called Lingo, a pidgin whose vocabulary was derived from the other six and whose syntax was so simple it could be contained on half a sheet of paper.

Hal saw in his mind the rest of Earth: Iceland, Greenland, the Caribbean Islands, and the eastern half of South America. Here the peoples spoke the tongue of Iceland because that island had gotten the jump on the Hawaiian-Americans who were busy resettling North America and the western half of South America after the Apocalyptic War.

Then there was North America, where American was the native speech of all except the twenty descendants of French-Canadians living on the Hudson Bay Preserve.

Hal knew that when that side of Earth rotated into the night zone, Sigmen City would blaze out into space. And, somewhere in that enormous light, was his apartment. But Mary would soon no longer be living there, for she would be notified in a few days that her husband had died in an accident. She would weep in private, he was sure, for she loved him in her frigid way, though in public she would be dry-eyed. Her friends and professional associates would sympathize with her, not because she had lost a beloved husband, but because she had been married to a man who thought unrealistically. If Hal Yarrow had been killed in a crash, he must have wanted it that way. There was no such thing as an "accident." Somehow, all the other passengers (also supposed to have died in this web of elaborate frauds to cover up the disappearance of the personnel of the *Gabriel*) had simultaneously "agreed" to die. And, therefore, being in disgrace, they would not be cremated and their ashes flung to the winds in public ceremony. No, the fish could eat their bodies for all the Sturch cared.

Hal felt sorry for Mary; he had a time keeping the tears from welling to his own eyes as he stood in the crowd in the observation dome.

Yet, he told himself, this was the best way. He and Mary would no longer have to tear and rend at each other; their mutual torture would be over. Mary was free to marry again, not knowing that the Sturch had secretly given her a divorce, thinking that death had dissolved her marriage. She would have a year in which to make up her mind, to choose a mate from a list selected by her *gapt*. Perhaps, the psychological barriers that had prevented her from conceiving Hal's child would no longer be present. Perhaps. Hal doubted if this happy event would occur. Mary was as frozen below the navel as he. No matter who the candidate for marriage selected by the *gapt* . . .

The *gapt*. Pornsen. He would no longer have to see that fat face, hear that whining voice . . .

"Hal Yarrow!" said the whining voice.

Slowly, icy yet burning, Hal turned.

There was the squat, loose-jowled, thick-lipped, vulture-nosed, narrow-eyed man smiling at him. Under the narrow-brimmed conical azure hat, gray-flecked black hair hung down to a high-ruffed black collar. The azure jacket fit snugly over a large paunch—Pornsen had endured many a lecture from his superiors because of his overeating—and a broad blue belt held a metal clasp for the handle of his whip. The thick legs were enclosed in tight azure pants with a black stripe running vertically along the outer and inner sides and with azure knee-high boots. The feet, however, were so tiny they looked ridiculous. On the toes of each boot was a seven-sided mirror.

There were some dirty stories about the origin of the mirrors circulating among lower-class elements. Hal had once overheard one, and he still blushed whenever he recalled it.

"My beloved ward, my perennial gadfly," Pornsen whined. "I'd no idea that you would be on this glorious voyage. But I might've known! We seem to be bound by love. Sigmen himself must have foreseen it. Love to you, my ward."

"Sigmen love you, too," Hal said, and he coughed. "How wonderful to see your cherished self. I had thought we'd never see each other again."

5

The *Gabriel* pointed toward her destination and, under one-gee acceleration, began to build toward her ultimate velocity, 33.1 percent of the speed of light. Meanwhile, all the personnel except those few needed to carry out the performance of the ship went into the suspensor. Here they would lie in suspended animation for many years. Some time later, after a check had been made of all automatic equipment, the crew would join the others. They would sleep while the *Gabriel's* drive would increase the acceleration to a point which the unfrozen bodies of the personnel could not have endured. Upon reaching the desired speed, the automatic equipment would cut off the drive, and the silent but not empty vessel would hurl toward the star which was its journey's end.

Many years later, the photon-counting apparatus in the nose of the ship would determine that the star was close enough to actuate deceleration. Again, a force too strong for unfrozen bodies to endure would be applied. Then, after slowing the vessel considerably, the drive would adjust to a one-gee deceleration. And the crew would be automatically brought out of their suspended animation. These members would then unthaw the rest of the personnel. And, in the half-year left before reaching their destination, the men would carry out whatever preparations were needed.

Hal Yarrow was among the last to go into the suspensor and among the first to come out. He had to study the recordings of the language of the chief nation of Ozagen, Siddo. And, from the first, he faced a

difficult task. The expedition that had discovered Ozagen had succeeded in correlating five thousand Siddo words with an equal number
of American words. The description of the Siddo syntax was very
restricted. And, as Hal found out, obviously mistaken in many cases.

This discovery caused Hal anxiety. His duty was to write a school
text and to teach the entire personnel of the *Gabriel* how to speak
Ozagen. Yet, if he used all of the little means at his disposal, he would
be instructing his students wrongly. Moreover, getting even this across
would be difficult.

For one thing, the organs of speech of the Ozagen natives differed
somewhat from Earthmen's; the sounds made by these organs were,
therefore, dissimilar. It was true that they could be approximated, but
would the Ozagenians understand these approximations?

Another obstacle was the grammatical construction of Siddo.
Consider the tense system. Instead of inflecting a verb or using an
unattached particle to indicate the past or future, Siddo used an entirely
different word. Thus, the masculine animate infinitive
dabhumaksanigalu'ahai, meaning *to live*, was, in the perfect tense,
ksu'u'peli'afo, and, in the future, *mai'teipa*. The same use of an entirely
different word applied for all the other tenses. Plus the fact that Siddo
not only had the normal (to Earthmen) three genders of masculine,
feminine, and neuter, but the two extra of inanimate and spiritual.
Fortunately, gender was inflected, though the expression of it would
be difficult for anybody not born in Siddo. The system of indicating
gender varied according to tense.

Other parts of speech—nouns, pronouns, adjectives-adverbs, and
conjunctions—operated under the same system as the verbs. To con-
fuse the use of the tongue, different social classes quite often used
different words to express the same meaning.

The writing of Siddo could only be compared to that of ancient
Japanese. There was no alphabet; instead, ideograms, lines whose
length, shape, and relative angle to each other were meaningful, were
used. Signs accompanying each ideogram indicated the correct inflection of gender.

In the privacy of his study cubicle, Hal swore mildly by the lost
right hand of Sigmen.

The captain of the first expedition had picked out the continent in
the Ozagenian antipodes as his base for research. This happened to be
occupied by natives who spoke the most difficult language (for Earthmen) to master. If he had chosen the other continent in the northern

hemisphere, he could have had (rather, his linguist could have had) forty different tongues to choose from, some of them comparatively easy in their syntax and with short words. That is, they were if Hal could believe the random sample of them that the linguist had taken.

Siddo, the land mass in the southern hemisphere, was about the size, though not the shape, of Africa and was separated from the other by ten thousand miles of ocean. If the wog geologists were correct, it had once been part of a Gondwanaland, but then it had drifted away. Evolution had then taken a somewhat different path from that on the other continent. Whereas the other continent had been dominated by insects and their distant cousins, the endoskeletal pseudoarthropods, this land mass had been very hospitable to mammals. Though, Sigmen knew, there was an abundance of insect life on it.

The sentient species on Abaka'a'tu, the northern land mass, had been, until five hundred years ago, the wogglebug. On Siddo it had been a remarkably human-looking animal. There *Homo ozagen* had developed a culture at a stage analogous to that of ancient Egypt or Babylon. And then almost all the humans, civilized or savage, had perished.

This had happened only a thousand years before the first wogglebug Columbus had landed on their great continent. At the time of the discovery and for two centuries after, the wogs had presumed that the indigenes were extinct. But, as the wog colonists began penetrating the jungles and mountains of the ulterior, they encountered a few small groups of humanoids. These had retreated into the wilderness, where they could hide as successfully as the African pygmies had hidden before the great rain forests were cut down. It was estimated that there might be a thousand, maybe two thousand, scattered over an area of 100,000 square kilometers.

A few specimens, all males, had been captured by the wogs. Before releasing them, the wogs had learned their languages. They'd also tried to find out why the humanoids had so suddenly and mysteriously disappeared. Their informants had explanations, but these were contradictory and of obvious mythical origin. They just did not know the truth, though it might be concealed in their myths. Some explained the catastrophe as a plague sent by the Great Goddess or All-Mother. Others said she had sent a horde of demons to wipe out her worshippers because they had sinned against her laws. One story had it that she had shaken loose the stars so that they fell on all but a few of the people.

In any event, Yarrow did not have all the data he needed for his study. The linguist on the first expedition had had only eight months to gather his data, and a good part of that had been spent teaching several wogs American before he could really get started. The ship had stayed ten months on Ozagen, but for the first two months the crew had remained aboard while robots collected atmospheric and biota specimens, which were analyzed to make sure that the Terrans could venture forth without being poisoned or stricken by disease.

Despite all precautions, two had died of insect bites, one had been killed by a peculiar form of predator, and then half of the personnel had been stricken with a very debilitating but not fatal disease. This was caused by a bacterium which was innocuous to the natives but which had mutated in the bodies of its non-Ozagen hosts.

Fearing that other diseases might occur, and being under orders to make only a survey, not a thorough exploration, the captain had ordered a return to home. The personnel had been quarantined for a long time on a satellite station before they were allowed to touch Earth again. The linguist had died a few days after the landing.

While the second ship was being built, a vaccine for the disease was prepared. And other collected bacteria and viruses were tested on animals and then on human beings who had been sent to H. This had resulted in a number of vaccines, some of which had made the crew of the *Gabriel* sick.

For some reason known only to the hierarchy, the captain of the first ship had been disgraced. Hal thought that this could be because he had failed to get samples of the blood of the natives. From what little Hal had learned, and this was only through some rumors, the wogs had just refused to allow their blood to be taken. Perhaps, this was because the suspicious behavior of the Haijacs had infected the wogs. When the Terrestrial scientists had then asked for corpses to dissect—for purely scientific reasons, of course—the wogs had again refused. All of their dead, they claimed, were cremated and their ashes strewn on the fields. It was true that they were often dissected by their own doctors before cremation, but it was part of their religion that this be done ritually. And a wog physician-priest had to perform it.

The captain had considered abducting some wogs just before the takeoff. But he'd felt that it wouldn't be wise to antagonize them at this time. He knew that a second expedition in a much larger vessel would be sent to Ozagen after he'd made his report. If its biologists couldn't talk the wogs into supplying blood samples, then force would be used.

While the *Gabriel* was being built, a top-echelon linguist had read the notes and listened to the recordings of his predecessor. But he'd spent too much time in trying to make comparisons with various aspects of Siddo to those of Terran languages, dead or alive. Where he should have been setting up a system by which the crew could learn Siddo in the quickest manner, he'd indulged his scholarly inclinations. Maybe this was the reason he wasn't going on the ship. Hal didn't know. He'd been given no explanation of why he was a last-minute substitute.

So Hal swore and bent to his work. He listened to the sounds of Siddo and studied their waveforms on the oscilloscope. He labored at reproducing them with his un-Ozagenian tongue, lips, teeth, palate, and larynx. He worked on a Siddo-American dictionary, an essential which his predecessor had somewhat neglected.

Unfortunately, before he or any of his crew mates could become fully conversant in Siddo, its native speakers would be dead.

Hal worked six months, long after all but the skeleton crew had gone into the suspensor. What annoyed him most about the project was the presence of Pornsen. The *gapt* would have gone into deep freeze, but he had to stay awake to watch Hal, to correct any unreal behavior on his part. The only redeeming feature was that Hal did not have to talk to Pornsen unless he felt like it, because he could use the urgency of his work as an excuse. But he tired of it after a while and of the loneliness. Pornsen was the most available human being to talk to, so Hal talked to him.

Hal Yarrow was also among the first to come out of the suspensor. This, he was told, was forty years later. Intellectually, he accepted the statement. But he never really believed it. There was no change in the physical appearance of himself or his shipmates. And the only change outside the ship was in the increased brightness of the star that was their destination.

Eventually, the star became the brightest object in the universe. Then, the planets circling it became visible. Ozagen, the fourth from the star, loomed. Approximately the size of Earth, it looked—from a distance—exactly like Earth. The *Gabriel* slipped into orbit after feeding data into the computer. For fourteen days, the vessel whirled around the planet while observations were made from the *Gabriel* itself and from gigs which descended into the atmosphere and even made several landings.

Finally, Macneff told the captain to take the *Gabriel* down.

Slowly, using immense quantities of fuel because of her vast mass, the *Gabriel* eased into the atmosphere and toward Siddo, the capital city, on the central-eastern coast. It settled gently as snowfall toward an open stretch in a park in the heart of the city. Park? The entire city was a park; the trees were so plentiful that from the air Siddo looked as if only a few people lived in it, not the estimated quarter of a million. There were many buildings, some ten stories high, but they were so widely separated they did not make an aggregate impression. The streets were wide, but they were overgrown by a grass so tough it could withstand any amount of wear. Only on the busy harbor front did Siddo resemble anything like an Earth city. Here the buildings were clustered close together, and the water was packed with sail ships and paddle-wheeled steamboats.

Down came the *Gabriel* while the crowd that had gathered below it ran to the borders of the meadow. Its colossal gray bulk settled upon the grass and at once began imperceptibly sinking into the soil. The Sandalphon, Macneff, ordered the main port opened. And, followed close behind by Hal Yarrow, who was to assist him if he stumbled in his speech to the welcoming delegation, Macneff stepped out into the open air of the first habitable planet discovered by Earthmen.

Like Columbus, thought Hal. *Will the story be the same?*

Afterward, the Terrans discovered that the mighty vessel lay at right angles across and above two underground steam-railroad tunnels. There was, however, no danger of their collapsing. The holes went through solid rock with six meters of another stratum of rock and twenty meters of dirt above it. Moreover, the ship was so long that most of its weight pressed on the area outside the tunnels. After determining this, the captain decided that the *Gabriel* should stay where it was.

From sunrise to sunset, its personnel ventured among the natives, learning all they could of their language, customs, history, biology, and other things, data which the first expedition had failed to get.

To make sure that the wogs didn't think the Terrans were suspiciously eager to get blood samples, Hal didn't bring up the matter for six weeks. In the meantime he spent much time—with Pornsen usually present—with a native named Fobo. He was one of the two who had learned American and a little Icelandic during the first expedition. Though he didn't know any more of the former language than Hal knew of Siddo, he did know enough to speed up Hal's mastery of

Siddo. Sometimes, they talked quite fluently, on a simple level, by mixing up the two tongues.

One of the things about which the Earthmen were covertly curious was the Ozagen technology. Logically, there was nothing to fear from them. As far as could be determined, the wogs had progressed no further than Earth's early-twentieth-century (A.D.) science. But the human beings had to make sure that what met the eye was all that was there. What if the wogs were hiding weapons of devastating power, waiting to catch the visitors unawares?

Missiles and atomic warheads were not to be feared. Obviously, Ozagen was not, as yet, capable of making these. But the wogs did seem to be very advanced in biological science. And this was to be dreaded as much as thermonuclear weapons. Moreover, even if disease was not used to attack the Earthmen, disease remained a deadly threat. What might be a nuisance to an Ozagenian with millennia of acquired immunity could be a swift death to a Terrestrial.

So—slow and cautious was the order. Find out everything possible. Gather data, correlate, interpret. Before beginning Project Ozagenocide, make sure that retaliation is impossible. *Make sure.*

Thus it was that four months after the appearance of the *Gabriel* above Siddo, two presumably friendly (to wogs) Terrans set out on a trip with two presumably friendly (to Terrans) wogglebugs. They were going to investigate the ruins of a city built two thousand years ago by now nearly extinct humanoids. They were inspired by a dream that had been dreamed on the planet Earth years before and light-years distant.

They rode in a vehicle fantastic to the human beings.

6

The motor hiccoughed, and the car jerked. The Ozagenian sitting on the right side of the rear seat leaned over and shouted something.

Hal Yarrow turned his head and yelled, "What?" He repeated in Siddo, "'*Abhudai'akhu?*" Fobo, sitting directly behind Hal, stuck his mouth against the Earthman's ear. He translated for Zugu, though his American sounded weird with its underlying trill and resonant approximations.

"Zugu says and emphasizes that you should pump that little rod to your right. It gives the . . . carburetor . . . more alcohol."

The antennae on Fobo's skullcap tickled Hal's ears. Hal spoke a word-sentence consisting of thirty syllables. This meant, roughly, "I thank you." It consisted initially of the verb used in the present masculine animate singular first person form. Attached to the verb was a syllable indicating freedom from obligation on the part of either the speaker or hearer, the inflected first person pronoun, another syllable indicating that the speaker acknowledged the hearer as most knowledgeable of the two, the third person masculine animate singular pronoun, and two syllables which, in their order of sequence, classified the whole present situation as semihumorous. Reversed in sequence, the classifier would indicate that the situation was serious.

"What did you say?" shouted Fobo, and Hal shrugged. He suddenly realized that he had forgotten a palatal click, the lack of which either changed the meaning of the phrase or else made it completely meaningless. In either case, he did not have the time or the will to repeat.

Instead, he worked the throttle as Fobo had directed. To do so, he had to lean across the *gapt*, sitting at his right.

"A thousand pardons!" Hal bellowed. Pornsen did not look at Yarrow. His hands, lying on his lap, were locked together. The knuckles were white. Like his ward, he was having his first experience with an internal combustion motor. Unlike Hal, he was scared by the loud noise, the fumes, the bumps and bangs, and the idea of riding in a manually controlled ground vehicle.

Hal grinned. He loved this quaint car, which reminded him of the pictures in the history books of Earth's automobiles during the second decade of the twentieth century. It thrilled him to be able to twist the stiff-acting wheel and feel the heavy body of the vehicle obey his muscles. The banging of the four cylinders and the reek of burning alcohol excited him. As for the rough riding, that was fun. It was romantic, like putting out to sea in a sailboat—something else he hoped to do before he left Ozagen.

Also, though he would not admit it to himself, anything that scared Pornsen pleased him.

His pleasure ended. The cylinders popped, then sputtered. The car bucked and jerked and rolled to a stop. The two wogglebugs hopped over the side of the car (no doors) and raised the hood. Hal followed.

Pornsen remained on the seat. He pulled a package of Merciful Seraphim (if angels smoked, they'd prefer Merciful Seraphim) out of his uniform pocket and lit one. His hands shook.

Hal noted it was the fourth he'd seen Pornsen smoking since morning prayers. If Pornsen wasn't careful, he'd be going over the quota allowed even first-class *gapts*. That meant that the next time Hal got into trouble, he could ask the *gapt* for help by reminding him . . . No! That was too shameful a thought to keep in his head. Definitely unreal, belonging only in a pseudofuture. He loved the *gapt* as the *gapt* loved him, and he should not be planning such an un-Sigmenlike path of behavior.

Yet, he thought, judging from the difficulties he'd been in so far, he could use some help from Pornsen.

Hal shook his head to clear himself of such thoughts and bent over the motor to watch Zugu work on it. Zugu seemed to know what he was doing. He should, since he was the inventor and builder of the only—as far as the Terrans knew—Ozagenian vehicle driven by an internal combustion motor.

Zugu used a wrench to unscrew a long narrow pipe from a round glass case. Hal remembered that this was a gravity feed system. The fuel ran from the tank into the glass case, which was a sediment chamber. From there it ran into the feed pipe, which in turn passed the fuel on to the carburetor.

Pornsen called harshly, "Beloved son, are we going to be stuck here all day?"

Though he wore the mask and goggles which the Ozagenians had given him as windbreaker, his tight lips were enough expression. It was evident that unless events unproved, the *gapt* would turn in a report unfavorable to his ward.

The *gapt* had wanted to wait the two days that would be needed until he could requisition a gig. The trip to the ruins could then have been made in fifteen minutes, a soundless and comfortable ride through the air. Hal had argued that driving would give more valuable espionage in this heavily forested country than surveying from the air. That his superiors had agreed was another thing that had exasperated Pornsen. Where his ward went, he had to go.

So, he had sulked all day while the young Terran, coached by Zugu, wheeled the jalopy down the forest roads. The only time Pornsen spoke was to remind Hal of the sacredness of the human self and to tell him to slow down.

Hal would reply, "Forgive me, cherished guardian," and would ease his foot off the accelerator. But, after a while, he would slowly press down. Once again, they would roar and leap down the rough dirt road.

Zugu unscrewed both ends of the pipe, stuck one end in his V-shaped mouth, and blew. Nothing, however, came out of the other end. Zugu shut his big blue eyes and puffed his cheeks out again. Nothing happened, except that his lightly tinged green face turned a dark olive. Then, he rapped the copper tubing against the hood and blew once more. Same result.

Fobo reached into a large leather pouch slung from a belt around his big belly. His finger and thumb came out, holding between them a tiny blue insect. Gently, he pushed the creature into one end of the pipe. After five seconds, a small red insect in a hurry dropped out of the other end. Behind it, hungrily crossing its mandibles, came the blue insect. Fobo deftly snared his pet and replaced it in the pouch. Zugu squashed the red bug beneath his sandal.

"Behold!" said Fobo. "An eater of alcohol! It lives in the fuel tank and imbibes freely and unmolested. It extracts the carbohydrates therein. A swimmer upon the golden seas of alcohol. What a life! But now and then it becomes too adventurous, travels into the sediment chamber, eats and devours the filter, and passes into the feedpipe. *See!* Zugu is even now replacing the filter. In a moment, we will be on our way down the road."

Fobo's breath had a strange and sickening odor. Hal wondered if the wog had been drinking liquor. He had never smelled it on anybody's breath before, so he had no experience to go on. But even the thought of it made Hal nervous. If the *gapt* knew a bottle was being passed back and forth in the rear seat, he would not allow Hal out of his sight for a minute.

The wogs climbed into the back of the car. "Let's go and depart!" said Fobo.

"Just a minute," said Pornsen in a low voice to Hal. "I think it's better that Zugu drive this thing."

"If you ask the wog to drive, he'll know you lack confidence in me, your fellow Terran," said Hal. "You wouldn't want him to think it was your belief that a wog is superior to a human being, would you?"

Pornsen coughed as if he had trouble swallowing Hal's remarks, then sputtered, "Of-of-of course not! Sigmen forbid! It was just that I had your welfare in mind. I thought you might be tired after the strain of piloting this primitive and dangerous contraption all day."

"Thank you for your love for me," said Hal. He grinned and added, "It is comforting to know you are always at my side, ready to direct me away from the peril of pseudofutures."

Pornsen said, "I have sworn by *The Western Talmud* to guide you through this life."

Chastened by the mention of the sacred book, Hal started the car. At first, he drove slowly enough to suit the *gapt*. But, inside five minutes, his foot became heavy, and the trees began whizzing by. He glanced at Pornsen. The *gapt's* rigid back and set teeth showed that he was again thinking of the report he would make to the chief Uzzite back in the spaceship. He looked furious enough to demand the 'Meter for his ward.

Hal Yarrow breathed deeply of the wind battering his face mask. To H with Pornsen! To H with the 'Meter! The blood lurched in his veins. The air of this planet was not the stuffy air of Earth. His lungs sucked it in like a happy bellows. At that moment, he felt as if he could have snapped his fingers under the nose of the Archurielite himself.

"Look out!" screamed Pornsen.

Hal, out of the corners of his eyes, glimpsed the large antelope-like beast that leaped from the forest onto the road just ahead of the right side of the car. At the same time, he twisted the wheel to swing the vehicle away from it. The vehicle skidded on the dirt. Its rear swung around. And Hal was not grounded enough in the elements of driving to know that he should turn the wheels in the direction of the skid to straighten the car out.

His lack of knowledge was not fatal, except to the beast, for its bulk struck the vehicle's right side. Its long horns caught in Pornsen's jacket and ripped open the sleeve on his right arm.

The car, its skid checked by the big bulk of the antelope, straightened out. But it was going in a straight line that angled off the road and led it up a sloping ridge of earth. Reaching the end of the ridge, it leaped out into the air and landed with an all-at-once bang of four tires blowing.

Even that impact did not halt it. A big bush loomed before Hal. He jerked on the wheel. Too late.

His chest pushed hard against the wheel as if it were trying to telescope the steering shaft against the dashboard. Fobo slammed into Hal's back, increasing the weight on his chest. Both cried out, and the wog fell away.

Then, except for a hissing, there was silence. A pillar of steam from the broken radiator shot through the branches that held Hal's face in a rough, barky embrace.

Hal Yarrow stared through steamshapes into big brown eyes. He shook his head. Eyes? And arms like branches? Or branches like arms? He thought he was in the grip of a brown-eyed nymph. Or were they called dryads? He couldn't ask anybody. They weren't supposed to know about such creatures. *Nymph* and *dryad* had been deleted from all books including Hack's edition of the *Revised and Real Milton*. Only because Hal was a linguist had he had the chance to read an unexpurgated *Paradise Lost* and thus learn of classical Greek mythology.

Thoughts flashed off and on like lights on a spaceship's control board. Nymphs sometimes turned into trees to escape their pursuers. Was this one of the fabled forest women staring at him with large and beautiful eyes through the longest lashes he'd ever seen?

He shut his eyes and wondered if a head injury was responsible for the vision and, if so, if it would be permanent. Hallucinations like that were worth keeping. He didn't care if they conformed to reality or not.

He opened his eyes. The hallucination was gone.

He thought, *It was that antelope looking at me. It got away after all. It ran around the bush and looked back. Antelope eyes. And my dark self formed the head around the eyes, the long black hair, the slender white neck, the swelling breasts . . . No! Unreal! It was my diseased mind, stunned by the shock, momentarily opened to that which has been festering, seething all that time on the ship without ever seeing a woman, even on the tapes . . .*

He forgot about the eyes. He was choking. A heavy nauseating odor hung over the car. The crash must have frightened the wogs very much. Otherwise, they would not have involuntarily relaxed the sphincter muscles which controlled the neck of the "madbag." This organ, a bladder located near the small of the back, had been used by the presentient ancestors of the Ozagenians as a powerful defensive weapon, much like that of the bombardier beetle. Now an almost vestigial organ, the madbag served as a means of relieving extreme nervous tension. Its function was effective, but its use presented problems. The wog psychiatrists, for instance, either had to keep their windows wide open during therapy or else wear gas masks.

Keoki Amiel Pornsen, assisted by Zugu, crawled out from under the bush into which he had been thrown. His big paunch, the azure color of his uniform, and the white nylon angel's wings sewn on the back of his jacket made him resemble a fat blue bug. He stood up and removed his windmask, showing a bloodless face. His shaking fingers fumbled over the crossed hourglass and sword, symbol of the Haijac Union. Finally, they found the flap for which he was searching. He pulled the magnetic lips of the pocket loose and took out a pack of Merciful Seraphim. Once the cigarette was in his lips, he had a shaky time holding his lighter to it.

Hal held the glowing coil of his own lighter to the tip of Pornsen's cigarette. His hand was steady.

Thirty-one years of discipline shoved back the grin he felt deep inside his face.

Pornsen accepted the light. A second later, a tremor around his lips revealed that he knew he had lost much of his advantage over Yarrow. He realized he couldn't allow a man to do him a service—even one as slight as this—and then crack the whip on him.

Nevertheless, he began formally, "Hal Shamshiel Yarrow . . ."

"*Shib, abba,* I hear and obey," replied Hal as formally.

"Just how do you explain this accident?" Hal was surprised. Pornsen's voice was much milder than he had expected. He did not relax, however, for he suspected that Pornsen meant to take him off guard and lash out at him when he was not mentally braced for an attack.

"I—or, rather, the Backrunner in me—departed from reality. I— my dark self—willfully precipitated a pseudofuture."

"Oh, really?" said Pornsen, quietly but with a note of sarcasm. "You say your dark self, the Backrunner in you, did that? That is what you have said ever since you were able to talk. Why must you always blame someone else? You know—you should, for I have been forced to whip you many times—that you and you alone are responsible. When you were taught that it was your dark self that caused departures from reality, you were also taught that the Backrunner could cause nothing unless you—your real self, Hal Yarrow—fully cooperated."

"That is as *shib* as the Forerunner's left hand," said Hal. "But, my beloved *gapt,* you forgot one thing in that little lecture of yours."

Now, his voice had a sarcasm to match that in Pornsen's.

Pornsen, shrilly, said, "What do you mean?"

"I mean," said Hal triumphantly, "that you were in the accident, too! Therefore, you caused it just as much as I did!"

Pornsen goggled at him. He said, whining, "But—but, you were driving the car!"

"Makes no difference according to what you have always told me!" said Hal. He was grinning smugly. "You agreed to be in the collision. If you had not, we would have missed the beast."

Pornsen stopped to puff on the cigarette. His hand shook. Yarrow watched the hand that hung free by Pornsen's side, its fingers twisting the seven leather lashes of the whip handle stuck in his belt.

Pornsen said, "You have always shown signs of a regrettable pride and independence. That smacks of behavior that does not conform to the structure of the universe as revealed to mankind by the Forerunner, real be his name.

"I have [puff]—may the Forerunner forgive them!—sent two dozen men and women to H. I did not like to do that, for I loved them with all my heart and self. I wept when I reported them to the holy hierarchy, for I am a tender-hearted man. [Puff!] But it was my duty as a Guardian Angel *Pro Tempore* to watch out for the loathsome diseases of self that may spread and infect the followers of Sigmen. Unreality must not be tolerated. The self is too weak and precious to be subjected to temptation.

"I have been your *gapt* since you were born. [Puff!] You always were a disobedient child. But you could be loved into submissiveness and contrition; you felt my love often. [Puff!]"

Yarrow felt his back tingle. He watched the *gapt's* hand tighten around the handle of the "lover" projecting from the belt.

"However, not until you were eighteen did you really depart from the true future and show your weakness for pseudofutures. That was when you decided to become a *joat* instead of a specialist. I warned you that as a *joat* you'd get only so far in our society. But you persisted. And since we do have need of *joats*, and since I was overruled by my superiors, I allowed you to become one.

"That was [puff] *unshib* enough. But when I picked out the woman most suitable to be your wife—as was my duty and right—for who but your loving *gapt* knows the type of woman best suited for you?—I saw just how proud and unreal you were. You argued and protested and tried to go over my head and held out for a year before you consented to marry her. In that year of unreal behavior, you cost the Sturch one self . . ."

Hal's face paled, revealing seven thin red marks that rayed out from the left corner of his lips and across his cheek to his ear.

"I cost the Sturch nothing!" Hal growled. "Mary and I were married nine years, but we had no children. Tests showed that neither of

us was physically sterile. Therefore, one or both was not thinking fertile. I petitioned for a divorce, even though I knew I might end up in
H. Why didn't you insist on our divorce, as your duty required, instead
of pigeonholing my petition?"

Pornsen blew out smoke nonchalantly enough, but he dropped
one shoulder lower than the other as if something had caved inside
him. Yarrow, seeing this, knew that he had his *gapt* on the defensive.

Pornsen said, "When I first realized you were on the *Gabriel*, I
was sure that you were not on it because of a desire to serve the Sturch.
I [puff] thought at the time that you signed up for one reason. And
now I am *shib, shib* to the bone, that your reason was your wicked
desire to get away from your wife. And, since barrenness, adultery,
and interstellar travel are the only legal grounds for divorce, and adultery means going to H, you [puff] took the only way out. You became
legally dead by becoming a crewman of the *Gabriel*. You—"

"Don't talk about anything legal to me!" shouted Hal. He shook
with rage and, at the same time, hated himself because he could not
hide his emotion.

"You know you were not carrying out the proper functions of a
gapt when you sidetracked my request! I had to sign up—"

"Ah, I thought so!" said Pornsen. He smiled and puffed out smoke
and said, "I turned it down because I thought it would be unreal. You
see, I had a dream, a very vivid dream, in which I saw Mary bearing
your child at the end of two years. It was not a false dream but one
that had the unmistakable signs of a revelation sent by the Forerunner. I knew after that dream that your desire for a divorce was a desire
for a pseudofuture. I knew that the true future was in my hands and
that only by guiding your conduct could I bring it about. I recorded
this dream the day after I had it, which was only a week after I reviewed
your petition, and—"

"You proved that you were betrayed by a dream sent by the Backrunner and did not see a revelation sent by the Forerunner!" shouted
Hal again. "Pornsen, I am going to report this! Out of your own mouth
you have convicted yourself!"

Pornsen turned pale; his mouth hung open so the cigarette dropped
to the ground; his jowls quivered with fright. "Wha—what do you
mean?"

"How could she have my child at the end of two years when I am
not on Earth to father it? So, what you *say* you dreamed can't possibly
become a real future! Therefore, you allowed yourself to be deceived

by the Backrunner. And you know what that means! That you are a candidate for H!"

The *gapt* stiffened. His lower left shoulder drew level with the other. His right hand shot to the handle of the whip, closed around the *crux ansata* on its end, and he pulled it from his belt. It cracked in the air, a few inches from Hal's face.

"See this?" shrieked Pornsen. "Seven lashes! One for each of the Seven Deadly Unrealities! You've felt them before; you'll feel them again!"

Harshly, Hal said, "Shut up!"

Again, Pornsen's jaw dropped. Whining, he said, "How, how dare you? I, your beloved *gapt*, am—"

"I told you to shut up!" said Hal, less loudly but just as bitingly. "I'm sick of your whine. I've been sick of it for years, my whole life."

Even as he spoke, he watched Fobo walking toward them. Behind Fobo, the antelope lay dead on the road.

The animal is dead, Hal thought. *I thought it had managed to get away. Those eyes staring through the bush at me. Antelope eyes? But if it is dead, whose eyes did I see?*

Pornsen's voice recalled Hal to the present.

"I think, my son, that we spoke in anger, not in premeditated evil. Let us forgive one another, and we'll say nothing to the Uzzites when we get back to the ship."

"*Shib* with me if it's with you," said Hal.

Hal was surprised to see tears welling in Pornsen's eyes. And he was even more surprised, almost shocked, when Pornsen made an attempt to put his arm around Hal's shoulder.

"Ah, my boy, if you only knew how much I loved you, how much it has hurt me when I've had to punish you."

"I find that rather hard to believe," said Hal, and he walked away from Pornsen and toward Fobo.

Fobo, too, had large tears in his unhumanly large and round eyes. But they were from another cause. He was weeping because of sympathy for the beast and shock from the accident. However, with every step toward Hal, his expression became less grieved, and tears dried. He was making a circular sign over himself with his right index finger.

It was, Hal knew, a religious sign which the wogs used in many different situations. Now, Fobo seemed to be using it to relieve his tension. Suddenly, he smiled the ghastly V-in-V smile of a wogglebug. And he was in good spirits. Though supersensitive, his nervous system was hit and run. Charge and discharge came easily.

Fobo stopped before them and said, "A clash of personalities, gentlemen? A disagreement, an argument, a dispute?"

"No," replied Hal. "We were just a little shaken up. Tell me, how far will we have to walk to get to the humanoid ruins? Your car's wrecked. Tell Zugu I'm sorry."

"Do not bother your skulls . . . heads. Zugu was ready to build a new and better vehicle. As for the walk, it will be pleasant and stimulating. It is only a . . . kilometer? Or thereabouts."

Hal threw his mask and goggles into the car, where the Ozagenians had put theirs. He picked up his suitcase from the floor in the compartment back of the rear seat. He left the *gapt's* on the floor. Not without a slight pang of guilt, however, for he knew that as Pornsen's ward, he should have offered to carry it.

"To H with him," he muttered.

He said to Fobo, "Aren't you afraid the driving clothes will be stolen?"

"Pardon?" said Fobo, eager to learn a new word. "Stolen means what?"

"To take an article of property from someone by stealth, without their permission, and keep it for yourself. It is a crime, punishable by law."

"A crime?"

Hal gave up and began walking swiftly up the road. Behind him the *gapt*, angry because he had been rejected and because his ward was breaking etiquette by forcing him to carry his own case, shouted, "Don't presume too far, you—you *joat*!"

Hal didn't turn back but plunged on ahead. The angry retort he had been phrasing beneath his breath fizzed away. Out of the corner of his eye, he had glimpsed white skin in the green foliage.

It was only a flash, gone as quickly as it had come. And he could not be sure that it was not a bird's white wing opening. Yes, he could be. There were no birds on Ozagen.

7

"*Soo Yarrow. Soo Yarrow. Wuhjvayfvoo, soo Yarrow.*"

Hal woke up. For a moment, he had trouble placing himself. Then, as he became wider awake, he recalled that he was sleeping in one of the marble rooms of the ruins. The moonlight, brighter than Earth's, poured in through the doorway. It shone on a small shape clinging upside down to the arch of the doorway. It glittered briefly on a flying insect that passed below the shape. Something long and thin flickered down and caught the flier and pulled it into a suddenly gaping mouth.

The lizard loaned by the ruins custodians was doing a fine job of keeping out pests.

Hal turned his head to look at the open window a foot above him. The bugcatcher there was also busily tonguing the area clean of mosquitoes.

The voice had seemed to come from beyond that moonwashed and narrow rectangle. He strained his ears as if he could force the silence to yield the voice again. But there was only more silence. Then, he jumped and whirled around as a snuffling and rattling came from behind him. A thing the size of a raccoon stood in the doorway. It was one of the quasi-insects, the so-called lungbugs, that prowled the forest at night. It represented a development of arthropod not found on Earth. Unlike its Terran cousins, it did not depend solely on tracheae or breathing tubes for oxygen. A pair of distensible sacs, like a frog's, swelled out and fell in behind its mouth. It was these that had made the snuffling sound.

Though the lungbug was shaped like the sinister praying mantis, Hal didn't worry. Fobo had told him it was not dangerous to a man.

A shrill sound like that of an alarm clock suddenly filled the room. Pornsen sat up on the cot against the wall. Seeing the insect, he yelled. It scurried off. The noise, which had come from the mechanism on Pornsen's wrist, stopped.

Pornsen lay back. He groaned, "That makes the sixth time those *sib* bugs have woke me up."

"Turn off the wristbox," said Hal.

"So you can sneak out of the room and spill your seed on the ground," replied Pornsen.

"You have no right to accuse me of such unreal conduct," said Hal. He spoke mechanically, without deep anger. He was thinking of the voice.

"The Forerunner himself said no one was beyond reproach," muttered Pornsen. He sighed and mumbled as he fell asleep, "Wonder if the rumor is true . . . Forerunner himself may be on this planet . . . watching us . . . he predicted . . . aah . . ."

Hal sat on his cot and watched Pornsen until he began snoring. Hal's own lids felt heavy. Surely, he must have dreamed of that soft, low voice speaking in a tongue neither Terran nor Ozagenian. He must have, because it had been human, and he and the *gapt* were the only specimens of *Homo sapiens* for two hundred miles in any direction.

It had been a woman's voice. Forerunner! To hear a woman again! Not Mary. He never wanted to hear her voice again or even hear *of* her. She was the only woman he had ever—dare he say it to himself?— *had.* That had been a sorry, disgusting, and humiliating ordeal. But it had not taken from him the wish—he was glad that the Forerunner was not there to read his mind—to meet another woman who might give him that ecstasy of which he knew nothing except from spilling his seed—Forerunner help him!—and which was, he was sure, only a paleness and a hollowness compared to that which waited . . .

"*Soo Yarrow. Wuhfvayfvoo. Sa mfa, zh'net Tastinak. R'gateh wa f'net.*"

Slowly, Hal rose from the cot. His neck was cased in ice. The whisper *was* coming from the window. He looked at it. The outline of a woman's head tilted into the solid box of moonlight that was window. The solid box became a cascade. Moonwash flowed over white shoulders. The white of a finger crossed the black of a mouth.

"*Poo wamoo tu baw choo. E'ooteh. Seelahs. Fvooneh. Fvit, seelfvoopleh.*"

Numbed, but obeying as if shot full of hypno-lipno, he began walking toward the doorway. He was not so shocked, however, that he did not look at Pornsen to make sure he was still sleeping.

For a second, his reflexes almost overcame him and forced him to wake up the *gapt*. But he withdrew the hand reaching for Pornsen. He must take a chance. The urgency and fear in the woman's voice told him that she was desperate and needed him. And it was evident that she did not want him to arouse Pornsen.

What would Pornsen say, do, if he knew there was a woman outside this very room?

Woman? How could a woman be here?

Her words had clicked something familiar. He had had the strange and fleeting notion that he should know the language. But he did not.

He stopped. What was he thinking of? If Pornsen woke and looked over at the cot to make sure his ward was still in it . . . He went back to the cot and shoved his suitcase under the sheet which the custodian had provided for him. He rolled up his jacket and packed it next to the case. One end of it stuck out of the sheet and lay on the pillow. Perhaps, if Pornsen was very sleepy, he might mistake the dark lump on the pillow and the bulk under the sheet for Hal.

Softly, on bare feet, he walked again toward the doorway. An object about eight decimeters high stood on guard in it. A statuette of the archangel Gabriel, pale, wings half-extended, a sword in its right hand held above its head.

If any object with a mass larger than a mouse's came within two feet of the field radiating from the statuette, it would cause a signal to be transmitted to the small case mounted on the silver bracelet around Pornsen's wrist. The case would shrill—as it had at the appearance of the lungbug—and up would come Pornsen from the bottom of his sleep.

The statuette's purpose was not only to insure against trespassers. It was also there to make certain that Hal would not leave the room without his *gapt's* knowledge. As the ruins had no working plumbing, Hal's only excuse to step outside would be to relieve himself. The *gapt* would go along to see that he did not try to do something else.

Hal picked up a fly swatter. It had a three-foot-long handle made of some flexible wood. Its mass would not be enough to touch off the field. Hand trembling, he very gently pushed the statuette to one side with the end of the handle. He had to be careful not to upset it, for tilting triggered its alarm. Fortunately, the stone floor was one of those which had had the debris, piled on by centuries, cleaned out. The stone beneath was smooth, polished by generations of feet.

Once outside, Hal reached back in and slid the object back to its former spot. Then, with his heart pounding under the double strain of tampering with the statuette and of meeting a strange woman, he walked around the corner.

The woman had moved from the window into the shadow of a statue of a kneeling goddess about forty yards away. He began walking toward her, then he saw why she was hiding. Fobo was strolling toward him. Hal walked faster. He wanted to intercept the wog before he noticed the girl and also before Fobo was so close that their voices might waken Pornsen.

"Shalom, aloha, good dreaming, Sigmen love you," said Fobo. "You seem nervous. Is it that incident of the forenoon?"

"No. I am just restless. And I wanted to admire these ruins by moonlight."

"Grand, beautiful, weird, and a little sad," said Fobo. "I think of these people, of the many generations that lived here, how they were born, played, laughed, wept, suffered, gave birth, and died. And all, all, every one dead and turned to dust. Ah, Hal, it brings tears to my eyes and a premonition of my own doom."

Fobo pulled a handkerchief from the pouch on his belt and blew his nose.

Hal looked at Fobo. How human—in some respects—was this monster, this native of Ozagen. Ozagen. A strange name with a story. What was the story? That the discoverer of this planet, upon first seeing the natives, had exclaimed, "Oz again!"

It was only natural. The aborigines resembled Frank Baum's Professor Wogglebug. Their bodies were rather round, and their limbs were skinny in proportion. Their mouths were shaped like two broad and shallow V's, one set inside the other. The lips were thick and lobular. Actually, a wogglebug had four lips, each leg of the two V's being separated by a deep seam at the connection. Once, far back on the evolutionary path, those lips had been modified arms. Now they were rudimentary limbs, so disguised as true labial parts and so functional that no one could have guessed their origin. When the wide V-in-V mouths opened in a laugh, they startled the Terrans. They had no teeth but serrated ridges of jawbone. A fold of skin hung from the roof of the mouth. Once the epipharynx, it was now a vestigial upper tongue. It was this organ which gave the underlying trill to so many Ozagen sounds and gave the human beings so much trouble reproducing them.

Their skins were as lightly pigmented as Hal's, and he was a redhead. But where his was pink, theirs was a very faint green. Copper, not iron, carried oxygen in their blood cells. Or so they said. So far they had refused to allow the Haijac to take blood samples. But they had promised that they might give permission within the next four or five weeks. Their reluctance, so they had stated, was caused by certain religious taboos. If, however, they could be assured that the Earthmen would not be drinking the blood, they might let them have it.

Macneff thought they were lying, but he had no good reasons for this. It was impossible for the Ozagenians to know just why their blood was wanted.

That their blood cells used copper instead of iron should have made the Ozagenians considerably less strong and less enduring in physical exertion than the Terrans. Their corpuscles would not transport oxygen as efficiently. But Nature had made certain compensations. Fobo had two hearts, which beat faster than Hal's and drove blood through arteries and veins larger than Hal's.

Nevertheless, the fastest sprinter or marathon runner of this planet would be left behind by his Terrestrial counterpart.

Hal had borrowed a book on evolution. But, since he could read very little of it, he had so far had to content himself with looking at the many illustrations. The wog, however, had explained what they represented.

Hal had refused to believe Fobo.

"You say that mammalian life originated from a primeval sea worm! That has to be wrong! We know that the first land lifeform was an amphibian. Its fins developed into legs; it lost its ability to get oxygen from sea water. It evolved into a reptile, then a primitive mammal, then an insectivorous creature, then a presimian, then a simian, and eventually into the sapient bipedal stage, and then into modern man!"

"Is that so?" Fobo had said calmly. "I don't doubt that things went just as you said. On Earth. But here evolution took a different course. Here there were three ancestral *se"ba'takufu*, that is, *motherworms*. One had hemoglobin-bearing blood cells; one, copper-bearing; one, vanadium-bearing. The first had a natural advantage over the other two, but for some reason it dominated this continent but not the other. We have some evidence that the first also split early into two lines, both of which were notochords but one of which wasn't mammalian.

"Anyway, all the motherworms did have fins, and these evolved into limbs. And—"

"But," Hal had said, "evolution can't work that way! Your scientists have made a serious, a grievous, error. After all, your paleontology is just beginning; it's only about a hundred years old."

"Ah!" Fobo had said. "You're too terrocentric. Hidebound. You have an anemic imagination. Your thought arteries are hardened. Consider the possibility that there might be billions of habitable planets in this universe and that on each evolution may have taken slightly, or even vastly, different paths. The Great Goddess is an experimenter. She'd get bored reproducing the same thing over and over. Wouldn't you?"

Hal was sure that the wogs were mistaken. Unfortunately, they weren't going to live long enough to be illuminated by the superior and much older science of the Haijac.

Now Fobo had removed his skullcap with its two imitation antennae, the symbols of the Grasshopper clan. But, even though this removal lessened his resemblance to Professor Wogglebug, his bald forepate and the stiff blond corkscrew fuzz on his backpate reasserted it. And the bridgeless, comically long nose shooting straight out from his face doubly strengthened it. Concealed in its cartilaginous length were two antennae, his organs of smell.

The Terran who first saw the Ozagenians would have been justified in his remark, if he had made it. But it was doubtful if he had. In the first place, the local tongue used the word *Ozagen* for Mother Earth. In the second place, even if the man on the first expedition had thought this, he would not have uttered it. The Oz books were forbidden in the Haijac Union; he could not have read the term unless he had taken a chance on buying it from a booklegger. It was possible he had. In fact, that was the only explanation. Otherwise, how could the spaceman who told Hal the story have come by the word? The originator of the story may not have cared if the authorities found out he was reading condemned books. Spacemen were famous, or infamous, for their disregard of danger and lax conduct in following the precepts of the Sturch when not on Earth.

Hal became aware that Fobo was talking to him.

". . . this *joat* that Monsieur Pornsen called you when he was so angry and furious. What does that mean?"

"It means," he said, "a person who is not a specialist in any of the sciences but who knows much about all of them. Actually, I am a liaison officer between various scientists and government officials. It is my business to summarize and integrate current scientific reports and then present them to the hierarchy."

He glanced at the statue.

The woman was not in sight.

"Science," he continued, "has become so specialized that intelligible communication even among scientists in the same field is very difficult. Each scientist has a deep vertical knowledge of his own little area but not much horizontal knowledge. The more he knows about his own subject, the less aware he is of what others in allied subjects are doing. He just does not have the time to read even a fraction of the overwhelming mass of articles. It is so bad that of two doctors who specialize in nose dysfunctions, one will treat the left nostril and the other will treat the right."

Fobo threw up his hands in horror.

"But science would come to a standstill! Surely you exaggerate!"

"About doctors, yes," said Hal, managing to grin a little. "But I do not exaggerate much. And it is true that science is not advancing in geometric progression as it once did. There is a lack of time for the scientist and too little communication. He cannot be aided in his own research by a discovery in another field because he just will not hear of it."

Hal saw a head stick out from the base of the statue and then withdraw. He began to sweat.

Fobo questioned Hal about the religion of the Forerunner. Hal was as taciturn as possible and completely ignored some questions, though he felt embarrassed by doing so. The wog was nothing if not logical, and logic was a light that Hal had never turned upon what he had been taught by the Urielites.

Finally, he said, "All I can say to you is that it is absolutely true that most men can travel subjectively in time but that the Forerunner, his evil disciple, the Backrunner, and the Backrunner's wife are the only people who can travel objectively in time. I know it is true because the Forerunner predicted what would happen in the future, and his every prediction was fulfilled. And—"

"Every prediction?"

"Well, all but one. But that turned out to be an unreal forecast, a pseudofuture somehow inserted by the Backrunner into *The Western Talmud*."

"How do you know those predictions which haven't been fulfilled aren't also false insertions?"

"Well . . . we don't. The only way to tell is to wait until the time for them to happen arrives. Then . . ."

Fobo smiled and said, "Then you know that that particular prediction was written and inserted by the Backrunner."

"Of course. But the Urielites have been working for some years now on a method which they say will prove, by internal evidence, whether the future events are real futures or false. When we left Earth, we expected to hear at any time that an infallible method had been discovered. Now, of course, we won't know until we return to Earth."

"I feel that this conversation is making you nervous," said Fobo. "Perhaps, we can pursue it some other time. Tell me, what do you think of the ruins?"

"Very interesting. Of course, I take an almost personal interest in this vanished people because they were mammals, so much like us Terrans. What I cannot imagine is how they could almost die out. If they were like us, and they seem to have been, they would have thrived."

"They were a very decadent, quarrelsome, greedy, bloody, pernicious breed," Fobo said. "Though, no doubt, there were many fine people among them. I doubt that they all killed each other off, except for a few dozen or so. I doubt also that a plague killed almost all their kind. Maybe someday we'll find out. Right now, I'm tired, so I'm going to bed."

"I'm restless. If you don't mind, I'll poke around. These ruins are so beautiful in this bright moonlight."

"Reminds me of a poem by our great bard Shamero. If I could remember it and could translate it effectively enough into American, I'd recite it to you."

Fobo's V-in-V lips yawned.

"I shall go to bed, retire, wrap the arms of Morpheus around me. However, first, do you have any weapons, firearms, with which to defend yourself against the things that prowl the night?"

"I am allowed to carry a knife in my bootsheath," said Hal.

Fobo reached under his cloak and brought out a pistol. He handed it to Hal and said, "Here! I hope you won't have to use it, but you never know. We live in a savage, predatory world, my friend. Especially out here in the country."

Hal looked curiously at the weapon, similar to those he had seen in Siddo. It was crude compared to the small automatics in the *Gabriel*, but it had all the aura and fascination of an alien weapon. Plus the fact that it resembled very much the early steel pistols of Earth. Its hexagonal barrel was not quite three decimeters long; the caliber looked to be about ten millimeters. A revolving chamber contained five brass cartridges; these were loaded with black gunpowder, lead bullets, and percussion caps containing, he guessed, fulminate of mercury. Strangely, the pistol had no trigger; a strong spring pulled the hammer down against the cartridge when the finger released the hammer.

Hal would have liked to see the mechanism that turned the revolving cartridge chamber when the hammer was pulled back. But he did not want to keep Fobo around any longer than he could help.

Nevertheless, he could not refrain from asking him why the Siddo did not use a trigger. Fobo was surprised at the question. When he had heard Hal's explanation, he blinked his large round eyes (a weird and at first unnerving sight because the lower eyelid made the motion), and he said, "I have never thought of it! It does seem to be more efficient and less tiring on the handler of the gun, does it not?"

"Obvious to me," said Hal. "But then, I am an Earthman and think like one. I have noticed the not unsurprising fact that you Ozagens do not always think as we do."

He handed the gun back to Fobo, and he said, "I am sorry I can't take it. But I am forbidden to carry firearms."

Fobo looked puzzled, but evidently he did not think it politic to inquire why not. Or else he was too tired.

He said, "Very well. Shalom, aloha, good dreaming, Sigmen visit you."

"Shalom to you, too," said Hal. He watched the broad back of the wog disappear into the shadows, and he felt a strange warmth for the creature. Despite his utterly alien and unhuman appearance, Fobo appealed to Hal.

Hal turned and walked toward the statue of the Great Mother. When he got to the shadows at its base, he saw the woman slipping into the darkness cast by a three-story heap of rubble. He followed her to the rubble only to see her several stone-throws ahead, leaning against a monolith. Beyond was the lake, silvery and black in the moonlight.

Hal walked toward her and was about five meters from her when she spoke in a low and throaty voice.

"*Baw sfa, soo Yarrow.*"

"*Baw sfa,*" he echoed, knowing that it must be a greeting in her language.

"*Baw sfa,*" she repeated, and then, obviously translating the phrase for his benefit, she said, in Siddo, "'*Abhu'umaigeitsi'i.*"

Which meant, very roughly, "Good evening."

He gasped.

8

Of course! Now he knew why the words had sounded vaguely familiar and the rhythm of her speech reminded him so strongly of a not too unrecent experience. Something about it stirred up a memory of his research in the tiny community of the last of the French speakers in the Hudson Bay Preserve.

Baw sfa. Baw sfa was *bon soir.*

Even though her speech was, linguistically speaking, a very decayed form, it could not disguise its ancestry. *Baw sfa.* And those other words he had heard through the window. *Wuhfvayfvoo.* That would be *levez-vous*, French for "get up."

Soo Yarrow. Could that be, must be, *Monsieur* Yarrow? The initial *m* dropped, the French *eu* evolved to something resembling the American *u* sound? Must be. And there were other changes to this degenerate French. Development of aspiration. The abandonment of nasalization. Vowel shift. Replacement of *k* before a vowel by a glottal stop. Change of *d* to *t; l* to *w; f* shifted to a sound between v and f; *w* changed to *f.* What else? There must also be a transmutation in the meanings of some words, and new words replacing old ones.

Yet, despite its unfamiliarity, it was subtly Gallic.

"*Baw sfa,*" he repeated.

And he thought, How inadequate that greeting! Here were two human beings meeting forty-odd light-years from Earth, a man who had not seen a woman for one subjective year, a woman obviously hiding and in great fear, perhaps the only woman left on this planet. And he could only say, "Good evening."

He stepped closer. And he flushed with the heat of embarrassment. Almost, he turned and ran. Her white skin was relieved only by two black narrow strips of cloth, one across her breasts, the other diapered around the hips. It was a sight such as he had never seen in his life except in a forbidden photograph.

The embarrassment was forgotten almost at once as he saw that she was wearing lipstick. He gasped and felt a shock of fear. Her lips were as scarlet as those of the monstrously evil wife of the Backrunner.

He forced himself to quit shaking. He must think rationally. This woman could not be Anna Changer, come from the far distant past to this planet to seduce him, to turn him against the real religion. She would not speak this degraded French if she were Anna Changer. Nor would she appear to as insignificant a person as Hal. She would have come to the chief Urielite, Macneff.

His mind gave the problem of the lipstick a quick flip and considered its other side. Cosmetics had gone out with the coming of the Forerunner. No woman dared . . . well, that wasn't true . . . it was just in the Haijac Union that cosmetics were not used. Israeli, Malay, and Bantu women wore rouge. But then everybody knew what kind of women they were.

Another step, and he was close enough to determine that the scarlet was natural, not paint. He felt an immense relief. She could not be the wife of the Backrunner. She could not even be Earthborn. She had to be an Ozagen humanoid. The murals on the walls of the ruins depicted red-lipped women, and Fobo had told him that these had been born with the flaming labile pigment.

The answer to one question bore another. Why was she speaking a Terran language, or, rather, a descendant of one? This tongue, he was sure, did not exist on Earth.

The next moment, he forgot his questions. She was clinging to him, and he had his arms around her, clumsily trying to comfort her. She was weeping and pouring out words, one so fast after the other that even though he knew they came from the French he could only make out a word here and there.

Hal asked her to slow down and to go over what she had said. She paused, her head cocked slightly to the left, then brushed back her hair. It was a gesture he was to find characteristic of her when she was thinking.

She began to repeat very slowly. But, as she continued, she speeded up, her full lips working like two bright red creatures independent of her, packed with their own life and purpose.

Fascinated, Hal watched them.

Ashamed, he looked away from them, tried to look into her wide dark eyes, could not meet them, and looked to one side of her head.

She told her story disconnectedly and with much repetition and backtracking. Many of her words he could not understand but had to supply the meaning from the context. But he could understand that her name was Jeannette Rastignac. That she came from a plateau in the central mountains of this continent. That she and her three sisters were, as far as she knew, the only survivors of her kind. That she had been captured by an exploring party of wogs who'd intended to take her to Siddo. That she had escaped and had been hiding in the ruins and in the surrounding forest. That she was frightened because of the terrible things that prowled the forest at night. That she lived on wild fruit and berries or on food stolen from wog farmhouses. That she had seen Hal when his vehicle hit the antelope. Yes, it had been her eyes he had thought were those of the antelope.

"How did you know my name?" Hal said.

"I followed you and listened to you talk. I could not understand you. But, after a while, I heard you respond to the name of Hal Yarrow. Learning your name was nothing at all. What puzzled me was that you and that other man looked like my father, must be human beings. Yet, because you did not speak my father's language, you could not have come from his planet.

"Then, I thought, of course! My father had once told me that his people had come to *Wuhbopfey* from another planet. So, it was a matter of logic. You must be from there, the original world of human beings."

"I don't understand at all," said Hal. "Your father's ancestors came to this planet, Ozagen? But . . . but there is no record of that! Fobo told me—"

"No, no, you do not understand, yes! My father, Jean-Jacques Rastignac, was born on another planet. He came to this one from that. His ancestors came to that other planet which revolves around a star far from here from an even more distant star."

"Oh, then they must have been colonists from Earth. But there is no record of that. At least, none that I have ever seen. They must have been French. But if that is true, they left Earth and went to that other system over two hundred years ago. And they could not have been Canadian French, for there were too few of them left after the Apocalyptic War. They must have been European French. But the last speaker of French in Europe died two and a half centuries ago. So—"

"It is confusing, *nespfa*? All I know is what my father told me. He said he and some others from *Wuhbopfey* found Ozagen during an exploration. They landed on this continent, his comrades were killed, he found my mother—"

"Your mother? Worse and worse," Hal said, groaning.

"She was an indigene. Her people have always been here. They built this city. They—"

"And your father was an Earthman? And you were born of his union with an Ozagen humanoid? Impossible! The chromosomes of your father and of your mother could not possibly have matched!"

"I do not care about these chromosomes!" said Jeannette in a quavering voice. "You see me before you, do you not? I exist, do I not? My father lay with my mother, and here I am. Deny me if you can."

"I did not mean . . . I mean . . . it seemed . . ." He stopped and looked at her, not knowing what to say.

Suddenly, she began sobbing. She tightened her arms around him, and his hands pressed down on her shoulders. They were soft and smooth, and her breasts pressed against his ribs.

"Save me," she said brokenly. "I cannot stand this any more. You must take me with you. You must save me."

Yarrow thought swiftly. He had to get back to the room in the ruins before Pornsen woke up. And he couldn't see her tomorrow, because a gig from the ship was picking up the two Haijacs in the morning. Whatever he was going to do would have to be unfolded to her in the next few minutes.

Suddenly, he had a plan; it germinated from another idea, one he had long carried around buried in his brain. Its seeds had been in him even before the ship had left Earth. But he hadn't had the courage to carry it out. Now, this girl had appeared, and she was what he needed to spark his guts, make him step onto a path that could not be retraced.

"Jeannette," he said fiercely, "listen to me! You'll have to wait here every night. No matter what things haunt the dark, you'll have to be here. I can't tell you just when I'll be able to get a gig and fly here. Sometime in the next three weeks, I think. If I'm not here by then, keep waiting. *Keep waiting!* I'll be here! And when I am, we'll be safe. Safe for a while, at least. Can you do that? Can you hide here? And wait?"

She nodded her head and said, "*Fi.*"

9

Two weeks later, Yarrow flew from the spaceship *Gabriel* to the ruins. His needle-shaped gig gleamed in the big moon as it floated over the white marble building and settled to a stop. The city lay silent and bleached, great stone cubes and hexagons and cylinders and pyramids and statues like toys left scattered by a giant child who has gone to bed to sleep forever.

Hal stepped out, glanced to his left and right, and then strode to an enormous arch. His flashlight probed its darkness; his voice echoed from the faraway roof and walls.

"*Jeannette! Sah mfa. Fo tami,* Hal Yarrow. *Jeannette! Ou eh tu?* It's me. Your friend. Where are you?"

He walked down the fifty-meter-broad staircase that led to the crypts of the kings. The beam bounced up and down the steps and suddenly splashed against the black and white figure of the girl.

"Hal!" she cried, looking up at him. "Thank the Great Stone Mother! I've waited every night! But I knew you'd come!"

Tears trembled on the long lashes; her scarlet mouth was trembling as if she were doing her best to keep from sobbing. He wanted to take her in his arms and comfort her, but it was a terrible thing even to look at an unclothed woman. To embrace her would be unthinkable. Nevertheless, that was what he was thinking.

The next minute, as if divining the cause of his paralysis, she moved to him and put her head on his chest. Her own shoulders hunched forward as she tried to burrow into him. He found his arms going around her. His muscles tightened, and blood lunged down into his loins.

He released her and looked away. "We'll talk later. We've no time to lose. Come."

Silently, she followed him until they came to the gig. Then, she hesitated by the door. He gestured impatiently for her to climb in and sit down beside him.

"You will think I'm a coward," she said. "But I have never been in a flying machine. To leave this earth . . ."

Surprised, he could only stare at her.

It was hard for him to understand the attitude of a person totally unaccustomed to air travel.

"Get in!" he barked.

Obediently enough, she got in and sat down in the copilot's seat. She could not keep from trembling, however, or looking with huge brown eyes at the instruments before and around her.

Hal glanced at his watchphone.

"Ten minutes to get to my apartment in the city. One minute to drop you off there. A half-minute to return to the ship. Fifteen minutes to report on my espionage among the wogs. Thirty seconds to return to the apartment. Not quite half an hour in all. Not bad."

He laughed. "I would have been here two days ago, but I had to wait until all the gigs that were on automatic were in use. Then, I pretended that I was in a hurry, that I had forgotten some notes, and that I had to go back to my apartment to pick them up. So, I borrowed one of the manually controlled gigs used for exploration outside the city. I never could have gotten permission from the O.D. for that if he had not been overwhelmed by this."

Hal touched a large golden badge on his left chest. It bore a Hebrew L.

"That means I'm one of the Chosen. I've passed the 'Meter."

Jeannette, who had seemingly forgotten her terror, had been looking at Hal's face in the glow from the panel light.

She gave a little cry. "Hal Yarrow! What have they done to you?" Her fingers touched his face.

A deep purple ringed his eyes; his cheeks were sunken, and in one a muscle twitched; a rash spread over his forehead; the seven whipmarks stood out against a pale skin.

"Anybody would say I was crazy to do it," he said. "I stuck my head in the lion's mouth. And he didn't bite my head off. Instead, I bit his tongue."

"What do you mean?"

"Listen. Didn't you think it was strange that Pornsen wasn't with me tonight, breathing his sanctimonious breath down my neck? No? Well, you don't know us. There was only one way I could get permission to move out of my quarters in the ship and get an apartment in Siddo. That is, without having a *gapt* living with me to watch my every move. And without having to leave you out here in the forest. And I couldn't do *that*."

She ran her finger down the line from his nose to the corner of his lip. Ordinarily he would have shrunk from the touch because he hated close contact with anybody. Now, he didn't move back.

"Hal," she said softly. "*Maw sheh.*"

He felt a glow. My *dear*. Well, why not?

To stave off the headiness her touch gave, he said, "There was only one thing to do. Volunteer for the 'Meter."

"*Wuh Met? 'Es'ase'asah?*"

"It's the only thing that can free you from the constant shadow of a *gapt*. Once you've passed it, you're pure, above suspicion—theoretically, at least.

"My petition caught the hierarchy off guard. They never expected any of the scientists—let alone me—to volunteer. Urielites and Uzzites have to take it if they hope to advance to the hierarchy—"

"Urielites? Uzzites?"

"To put it in ancient terminology, priests and cops. The Forerunner adopted those terms—the names of angels—for religious-governmental use—from the Talmud. See?"

"No."

"I'll explain that later. Anyway, only the most zealous ask to face the 'Meter. It's true that many people do, but only because they are compelled to. The Urielites were gloomy about my chances, but they were forced by law to let me try. Besides, they were bored, and they wanted to be entertained—in their grim fashion."

He scowled at the memory. "A day later, I was told to report to the psych lab at twenty-three hundred S.T.—Ship's Time, that is. I went into my cabin—Pornsen was out—opened my labcase, and took out a bottle labeled 'Prophetsfood.' It is supposed to contain a powder whose base is peyote. That's a drug that was once used by American Indian medicine men."

"*Kfe?*"

"Just listen. You'll get the main points. Prophets-food is taken by everybody during Purification Period. That's two days of locking yourself in a cell, fasting, praying, being flagellated by electric whips, and seeing visions induced by hunger and Prophetsfood. Also subjective time-traveling."

"*Kfe?*"

"Don't keep saying 'What?' I haven't got time to explain dunnology. It took me ten years of hard study to understand it and its mathematics. Even then, there were a lot of questions I had. But I didn't ask them. I might be thought to be doubting.

"Anyway, my bottle did not hold Prophetsfood. Instead, it contained a substitute I'd secretly prepared just before the ship left Earth. That powder was the reason why I dared face the 'Meter. And why I was not as terrified as I should have been . . . though I was scared enough. Believe me."

"I do believe you. You were brave. You overcame your fear."

He felt his face reddening. It was the first time in his life he had ever been complimented.

"A month before the expedition took off for Ozagen, I had noticed, in one of the many scientific journals that I must review, an announcement that a certain drug had been synthesized. Its efficacy was in destroying the virus of the so-called Martian rash. What interested me was a footnote. It was in small print and in Hebrew, which showed that the biochemist must have realized its importance."

"*Pookfe?*"

"Why? Well, I imagine it was in Hebrew in order to keep any laymen from understanding it. If a secret like that became generally known . . .

"The note commented briefly that it had been found that a man suffering from the rash was temporarily immune to the effects of hypno-lipno. And that the Urielites should take care during any sessions with the 'Meter that their subject was healthy."

"I have trouble understanding you," she said.

"I'll go slower. Hypno-lipno is the most widely used so-called truth-drug. I saw at once the implications in the note. The beginning of the article described how the Martian rash was narcotically induced for experimental purposes. The drug used was not named, but it did not take me long to look it and its processing up in other journals. I thought if the true rash would make a man immune to hypno-lipno, why wouldn't the artificial?

"No sooner said than done. I prepared a batch, inserted a tape of questions about my personal life in a psychotester, injected the rash drug, injected the truth-drug, and swore that I would lie to the tester about my life. And I *could* lie, even though shot full of hypno-lipno!"

"You're so clever to think of that," she murmured.

She squeezed his biceps. He hardened them. It was a vain thing to do, but he wanted her to think he was strong.

"Nonsense!" he said. "A blind man would have seen what to do. In fact, I wouldn't be surprised if the Uzzites had arrested the chemist and put out orders for some other truth-drug to be used. If they did, they were too late. Our ship left before any such news reached us.

"Anyway, the first day with the 'Meter was nothing to worry about. I took a twelve-hour written and oral test in serialism. That's Dunne's theories of time and Sigmen's amplifications on it. I've been taking that same test for years. Easy but tiring.

"The next day I rose early, bathed, and ate what was supposed to be Prophetsfood. Breakfastless, I went into the Purification Cell. Alone, I lay two days on a cot. From time to time I took a drink of water or a shot of the false drug. Now and then, I pressed the button that sent the mechanical scourge lashing against me. The more flagellations, you know, the higher your credit.

"I didn't see any visions. I did break out with the rash. That didn't worry me. If anybody got suspicious, I could explain that I had an allergy to Prophetsfood. Some people do."

He looked below. Moon-frosted forest and an occasional square or hexagonal light from a farmhouse. Ahead was the high range of hills that shielded Siddo.

"So," he continued, unconsciously talking faster as the hills loomed closer, "at the end of my purification I rose, dressed, and ate the ceremonial dinner of locusts and honey."

"Ugh!"

"Locusts aren't so bad if you've been eating them since childhood."

"Locusts are delicious," she said. "I've eaten them many times. It's the combination with honey that sickens me."

He shrugged and said, "I'm going to turn out the cabin lights. Get down on the floor. And put on that cloak and nightmask. You can pass for a wog."

Obediently she slid off the seat. Before he flicked the lights off, he glanced down. She was leaning over while picking up the cloak, and he could not help getting a full glimpse of her superb breasts. Her nipples were as scarlet as her lips. Though he jerked his head away, he kept the image in his head. He felt deeply aroused. The shame, he knew even then, would come later.

He continued uncomfortably: "Then the hierarch came in. Macneff the Sandalphon. After him, the theologians and the dunnological specialists: the psychoneural parallelists, the interventionists, the substratumists, the chronentropists, the pseudotemporalists, the cosmobserverists.

"They sat me down in a chair that was the focus of a modulating magnetic-detector field. They injected hypno-lipno into my arm. They turned out the lights. They said prayers for me, and they chanted chapters from *The Western Talmud* and the *Revised Scriptures.* Then a spotlight was directed upon the Elohimeter—"

"*'Es'ase'asah?*"

"*Elohim* is Hebrew for 'God.' A meter is, well, those." He pointed at the instrument panel. "The Elohimeter is round and enormous, and its needle, as long as my arm, is straight up and down. The circumference of the dial's face is marked with Hebraic letters that are supposed to mean something to those giving the test.

"Most people are ignorant of what the needle indicates. But I'm a *joat.* I've access to the books that describe the test."

"Then you knew the answers, *nespfa?*"

"*Fi.* Though that means nothing, because hypno-lipno brings out the truth, the reality . . . unless, of course, you are suffering from Martian rash, natural or artificial."

His sudden laugh was a mirthless bark.

"Under the drug, Jeannette, all the dirty and foul things you've done and thought, all the hates you've had for your superiors, all the doubts about the realness of the Forerunner's doctrines—these rise up from your lower-level minds like soap released at the bottom of a dirty bathtub. Up it comes, slick and irresistibly buoyant and covered with layers of scum.

"But I sat there, and I watched the needle. It's just like watching the face of God, Jeannette—you can't understand that, can you?—and I lied. Oh, I didn't overplay it. I didn't pretend to be incredibly pure and faithful. I confessed to minor unrealities. Then the needle would flicker and go back around the circumference a few square letters. But, on the big issues, I answered as if my life depended on them. Which it did.

"And I told them my dreams—my subjective time-traveling."

"*Soopji'tiw?*"

"*Fi.* Everybody travels in time subjectively. But the Forerunner is the only man, except for his first disciple and his wife and a few of the scriptural prophets, who has traveled objectively.

"Anyway, my dreams were beauties—architecturally speaking. Just what they liked to hear. My last, and crowning, creation—or lie—was one in which the Forerunner himself appeared on Ozagen and spoke to the Sandalphon, Macneff. That event is supposed to take place a year from now."

"Oh, Hal," she breathed. "Why did you tell them that?"

"Because now, *maw sheh,* the expedition will not leave Ozagen until that year is up. They couldn't go without giving up the chance of seeing Sigmen in the flesh as he voyages up and down the stream of time. Not without making a liar of him. And of me. So, you see, that colossal lie will make sure that we have at least a year together."

"And then?"

"We'll think of something else then."

Her throaty voice murmured in the darkness by the seat, "And you would do all that for me . . ."

Hal did not reply. He was too busy keeping the gig close to the rooftop level. Clumps of buildings, widely separated by woods, flashed by. So fast was he going that he almost overshot Fobo's castlelike house. Three stories high, medieval in appearance with its crenellated towers and gargoyle heads of stone beasts and insects leering out from many niches, it was no closer than a hundred yards to any other building. Wogs built cities with plenty of elbow room.

Jeannette put on the long-snouted nightmask; the gig's door swung open; they ran across the sidewalk and into the building. After they dashed through the lobby and up the steps to the second floor, they had to stop while Hal fumbled for the key. He had had a wog smith make the lock and a wog carpenter install it. He hadn't trusted the carpenter's mate from the ship because there was too much chance of duplicate keys being made.

He finally found the key but had trouble inserting it. He was breathing hard by the time he succeeded in opening the door. He almost pushed Jeannette through. She had taken her mask off.

"Wait, Hal," she said, leaning her weight against his. "Haven't you forgotten something?"

"Oh, Forerunner! What could it be? Something serious?"

"No. I only thought," and she smiled and then lowered her lids, "that it was the Terran custom for men to carry their brides across the threshold. That is what my father told me."

His jaw dropped. Bride! She was certainly taking a lot for granted!

He couldn't take time to argue. Without a word, he swept her up in his arms and carried her into the apartment. There he put her down and said, "Back as soon as possible. If anybody knocks or tries to get in, hide in that special chamber I had the wog carpenter build for you inside our closet. Don't make a sound or come out until you're sure it's me."

She suddenly put her arms around him and kissed him.

"*Maw sheh, maw gwah, maw fooh.*"

Things were going too fast. He didn't say a word or even return her kiss. Vaguely he felt that her words, applied to him, were somewhat ridiculous. If he translated her degenerate French correctly, she had called him her dear, her big strong man.

Turning, he closed the door but not so quickly that he did not see the hall light shine on a white face haloed blackly by a hood. A red mouth stained the whiteness.

He shook. He had a feeling that Jeannette was not going to be the frigid mate so much admired, officially, by the Sturch.

10

Hal was an hour late returning home from the *Gabriel* because the Sandalphon asked for more details about the prophecy he had made concerning Sigmen. Then, Hal had to dictate his report on the day's espionage. Afterward, he ordered a sailor to pilot his gig back to the apartment. While he was walking toward the launching rack, he met Pornsen.

"Shalom, *abba*," Hal said.

He smiled and rubbed his knuckles against the raised *lamedh* on the shield.

The *gapt's* left shoulder, always low, sagged even more, as if it were a flag dipping in surrender. If there were any whip cuts to be given, they would be struck by Yarrow.

Hal puffed out his chest and started to walk on, but Pornsen said, "Just a minute, son. Are you going back to the city?"

"*Shib.*"

"*Shib.* I'll ride back with you. I have an apartment in the same building. On the third floor, right opposite Fobo's."

Hal opened his mouth to protest, then closed it. It was Pornsen's turn to smile. He turned and led the way. Hal followed with tight lips. Had the *gapt* trailed him and seen his meeting with Jeannette? No. If he had, he would have had Hal arrested at once.

The *gapt* had one distinguishing feature: a small mind. He knew his presence would annoy Hal and that living in the same building with him would poison Hal's joy at being free from surveillance.

Under his breath Hal quoted an old proverb: "A *gapt's* teeth never let loose."

The sailor was waiting by the gig. They all got in and dropped silently into the night.

At the apartment building, Hal strode into the doorway ahead of Pornsen. He felt a slight glow of satisfaction at thus breaking etiquette and expressing his contempt for the man.

Before opening his door, he paused. The guardian angel passed silently behind him. Hal, struck with a devilish thought, called out, "*Abba.*"

Pornsen turned.

"What?"

"Would you care to inspect my rooms and see if I'm hiding a woman in there?"

The little man purpled. He closed his eyes and swayed, dizzy with sheer fury. When he opened them, he shouted, "Yarrow! If ever I saw an unreal personality, you're it! I don't care how you stand with the hierarchy! I think you're—you're—just not simply *shib*! You've changed. You used to be so humble, so obedient. Now, you're arrogant."

Hal said, evenly at first, his voice rising as he continued, "It wasn't so long ago that you described me as unruly from the day I was born. Suddenly, it seems that I am an example of splendid behavior, one the Sturch may point to with—pardon the cliché—pride. I suggest that I have always behaved as well as could be expected. I suggest that you were and are a picayunish, malicious, nasty, bird-brained pimple on the ass of the Sturch and that you ought to be squeezed until you pop!"

Hal stopped shouting because he was breathing so hard. His heart was hammering; his ears, roaring; his sight, getting dim.

Pornsen backed away, his hands held out before him.

"Hal Yarrow! Hal Yarrow! Control yourself! Forerunner, how you must hate me! And all these years I thought you loved me, that I was your beloved *gapt* and you were my beloved ward. But you hated me. Why?"

The roaring faded away. Hal's vision cleared.

"Are you serious?"

"Of course! I never dreamed, dreamed! Anything that I ever did to you was for you; when I punished you, my heart broke. But I drove myself to it by reminding myself that it was for your good."

Hal laughed and laughed while Pornsen ran down the hall and disappeared into his apartment with a single white-faced look.

Weakly, shaking, Hal leaned against the doorway. This was the most unexpected thing of all. He had been absolutely certain that Pornsen loathed him as a contrary and unnatural monster and that he took a bitter delight in humiliating and whipping him.

Hal shook his head. Surely, the *gapt* was scared and was trying to justify himself.

He unlocked the door and entered. Around and around in his head flew the thought that the courage to speak out against Pornsen had come from Jeannette. Without her, he was nothing, a resentful but scared rabbit. A few hours with her had enabled him to overcome many years of rigid discipline.

He clicked on the front room lights. Looking beyond into the dining room, he could see the closed kitchen door. The rattling of pots came through it. He sniffed deeply.

Steak!

The pleasure was replaced by a frown. He'd told her to hide until he returned. What if he had been a wog or an Uzzite?

When the door swung open, the hinges squeaked. Jeannette's back was to him. At the first protest of unoiled iron, she whirled. The spatula in her hand dropped; the other hand flew to her open mouth.

The angry words on his lips died. If she were to be scolded now, she would probably break out in embarrassing tears.

"*Maw choo!* You startled me!"

He grunted and went by her to lift the lids on the pots.

"You see," she said, her voice trembling as if she divined his anger and were defending herself. "I have lived such a life, being afraid of getting caught, that anything sudden scares me. I am always ready to run."

"How those wogs fooled me!" Hal said sourly. "I thought they were so kind and gentle."

She glanced at him out of the side of her large eyes. Her color had come back; her red lips smiled.

"Oh, they weren't so bad. They really were kind. They gave me everything I wanted, except my freedom. They were afraid I'd make my way back to my sisters."

"What did they care?"

"Oh, they thought there might be some males of my race left in

the jungle and that I might give them children. They are terribly frightened of my race becoming numerous and strong again and making
war on them. They do not like war."

"They are strange beings," he said. "But we cannot expect to understand those who do not know the reality of the Forerunner. Moreover,
they are closer to the insect than to man."

"Being a man does not necessarily mean being better," Jeannette
said with a tinge of asperity.

"All God's creatures have their proper place in the universe," he
replied. "But man's place is everywhere and everywhen. He can occupy
any position in space and can travel in any direction in time. And if he
must dispossess a creature to gain that place or time, he is doing only
what is right."

"Quoting the Forerunner?"

"Of course."

"Perhaps, he is right. Perhaps. But what is man? Man is a sentient
being. A wog is a sentient being. Therefore, the wog is a man. *Nespfa?*"

"*Shib* or *sib*, let's not argue. Why don't we eat?"

"I wasn't arguing."

She smiled and said, "I will set the table. You will see if I can cook
or not. There'll be no argument about that."

After the dishes were placed on the table, the two sat down. Hal
joined his hands together, put them on the table, bowed his head, and
prayed.

"Isaac Sigmen, runner before man, real be your name, we thank
you for having made certain this blessed present, which once was the
uncertain future. We thank you for this food, which you have actualized from potentiality. We hope and know that you will slay the
Backrunner, forestall his wicked attempts to unshake the past and so
alter the present. Make this universe solid and real, and omit the flu-
idity of time. These selves gathered at this table thank you. So be it."

He unfolded his hands and looked at Jeannette. She was staring at
him.

Obeying an impulse, he said, "You may pray if you wish."

"Won't you regard my prayer as unreal?"

He hesitated before saying, "Yes. I do not know why I asked you. I
certainly would not ask an Israeli or Bantu to pray. I wouldn't eat at
the same table with one. But you . . . you are special . . . maybe because
unclassified. I . . . I do not know."

"Thank you," she said.

She described a triangle in the air with the middle finger of her right hand. Looking upward, she said, "Great Mother, we thank you."

Hal repressed showing the strange feeling it gave him to hear an unbeliever. He slid open the drawer beneath the table and took out two objects. One he handed to Jeannette. The other he put on his head.

It was a cap with a wide brim from which hung a long veil. It entirely covered his face.

"Put it on," he said to Jeannette.

"Why?"

"So we can't see each other eat, of course," he said impatiently. "There is enough space between the veil and your face for you to manipulate your fork and spoon."

"But why?"

"I told you. So we can't see each other eat."

"Would the sight of me eating make you sick?" she said with a rising inflection.

"Naturally."

"Naturally? Why naturally?"

"Why, eating is so . . . uh . . . I don't know . . . animalistic."

"And have your people always done this? Or did they begin when they found out they were animals?"

"Before the coming of the Forerunner, they ate naked and unashamed. But they were in a state of ignorance."

"Do the Israeli and Bantu hide their faces when they eat?"

"No."

Jeannette rose from the table.

"I cannot eat with this thing over my face. I would feel ashamed."

"But . . . I have to wear my eating cap," he said with a shaky voice. "I couldn't keep my food down."

She spoke a phrase in a language he did not know. But the unfamiliarity did not conceal the bewilderment and hurt.

"I'm sorry," he said. "But that's the way it is. That's the way it should be."

Slowly, she sat down again. She put the cap on.

"Very well, Hal. But I think we must talk about this later. This makes me feel as if I am isolated from you. There is no closeness, no sharing in the good things that life has given us."

"Please don't make any noise while you're eating," he said. "And if you must speak, swallow all your food first. I've turned my face when a wog was eating before me, but I couldn't close my ears."

"I'll try not to make you sick," she said. "Just one question. How do you keep your children quiet when they're eating?"

"They never eat with adults. Rather, the only adults at their tables are *gapts*. And these soon teach them the proper behavior."

"Oh."

The meal passed in silence except for the unavoidable sound of cutlery on plate. When Hal finished, he took off his cap.

"Ah, Jeannette, you are a rare cook. The food is so good I almost felt sinful that I should be enjoying it so much. The soup was the best I ever tasted. The bread was delicious. The salad was superb. The steak was perfect."

Jeannette had removed her cap first. Her meal was scarcely touched. Nevertheless, she smiled.

"My aunts trained me well. Among my people, the female is taught at an early age all that will please a man. All."

He laughed nervously and, to cover his uneasiness, lit a cigarette.

Jeannette asked if she might try a cigarette, too.

"Since I am burning, I may as well smoke," she said, and she giggled.

Hal wasn't sure of what she meant, but he laughed to show her that he wasn't angry with her about the eating caps.

Jeannette lit her own cigarette, drew in, coughed, and rushed to the sink for a glass of water. She came back with her eyes streaming, but she at once picked up the cigarette and tried again. In a short time, she was inhaling like a veteran.

"You have amazing imitative powers," Hal said. "I've watched you copying my movements, heard you mimic my speech. Do you know that you pronounce American as well as I do?"

"Show or tell me something once, and you seldom have to do it again. I'm not claiming a superior intelligence, however. As you said, I have an instinct for imitation. Not that I'm not capable of an original thought now and then."

She began chattering lightly and amusingly about her life with her father, sisters, and aunts. Her good spirits seemed genuine; apparently, she was not talking just to conceal the depression caused by the incident at mealtime. She had a trick of raising her eyebrows as she laughed. They were fascinating, almost bracket-shaped. A thin line of black hair rose from the bridge of her nose, turned at right angles, curved slightly while going over the eye sockets, and then made a little hook at the ends.

He asked her if the shape of her eyebrows was a trait of her mother's people. She laughed and replied that she inherited it from her father, the Earthman.

Her laughter was low and musical. It did not get on his nerves, as his ex-wife's had. Lulled by it, he felt pleasant. And every time he thought of how this situation might end and his spirits sagged, he was pulled back into a better mood by something amusing she said. She seemed to be able to anticipate exactly what he needed to blunt any gloominess or sharpen any gaiety.

After an hour, Hal rose to go into the kitchen. On his way past Jeannette, he impulsively ran his fingers through her thick, wavy black hair.

She raised her face and closed her eyes, as if she expected him to kiss her. But, somehow, he could not. He wanted to but just couldn't bring himself to make the first move.

"The dishes will have to be washed," he said. "It would never do for an unexpected visitor to see a table set for two. And another thing we'll have to watch. Keep the cigarettes hidden and the rooms aired out frequently. Now that I've been 'Metered, I'm supposed to have renounced such minor unrealities as smoking."

If Jeannette was disappointed, she did not show it. She at once busied herself in cleaning up. He smoked and speculated about the chances of getting ginseng tobacco. She so enjoyed the cigarettes that he could not stand the idea of her missing out on them. One of the crewmen with whom he had good relations did not smoke but sold his ration to his mates. Maybe a wog could act as middleman, buy from the sailor, and pass it on to Hal. Fobo might do it, but the whole transaction would have to be handled carefully. Maybe it wasn't worth the risk . . .

Hal sighed. Having Jeannette was wonderful, but she was beginning to complicate his life. Here he was, contemplating a criminal action as if it were the most natural thing in the world.

She was standing before him, hands on her hips, eyes shining.

"Now, Hal, *maw namoo*, if we only had something to drink, it would make a perfect evening."

He got to his feet. "Sorry. I forgot you wouldn't know how to make coffee."

"No. No. It is the liquor I am thinking of. Alcohol, not coffee."

"Alcohol? Great Sigmen, girl, we don't *drink*! That'd be the most disgust—"

He stopped. She was hurt. He mastered himself. After all, she couldn't help it. She came from a different culture. She wasn't even, strictly speaking, all human.

"I'm sorry," he said. "It's a religious matter. Forbidden."

Tears filled her eyes. Her shoulders began to shake. She put her face into her hands and began to sob. "You don't understand. I have to have it. I have to."

"But why?"

She spoke from behind her fingers. "Because during my imprisonment, I had little to do but entertain myself. My captors gave me liquor; it helped to pass the time and make me forget how utterly homesick I was. Before I knew it, I was an—an alcoholic."

Hal clenched his fists and growled, "Those sons of . . . bugs!"

"So you see, I have to have a drink. It would make me feel better, just for the time being. And later, maybe later, I can try to overcome it. I know I can, if you'll help me."

He gestured emptily. "But—but where can I get you some?" His stomach revolted at the idea of trafficking in alcohol. But, if she needed it, he'd try his best to get it.

Swiftly, she said, "Perhaps Fobo could give you some."

"But Fobo was one of your captors! Won't he suspect something if I come asking for alcohol?"

"He'll think it's for you."

"All right," he said, somewhat sullenly, and at the same time guiltily because he was sullen. "But I hate for anybody to think *I* drink. Even if he is just a wog."

She came up to him and seemed to flow against him. Her lips pressed softly. Her body tried to pass through his. He held her for a minute and then took his mouth away.

"Do I have to leave you?" he whispered. "Couldn't you pass up the liquor? Just for tonight? Tomorrow, I'll get you some."

Her voice broke. "Oh, *maw namoo*, I wish I could. How I wish I could. But I can't. I just can't. Believe me."

"I believe you."

He released her and walked into the front room, where he took a hood, cloak, and nightmask out of the closet. His head was bent; his shoulders sagged. Everything would be spoiled. He would not be able to get near her, not with her breath stinking of alcohol. And she'd probably wonder why he was cold, and he wouldn't have the nerve to tell her how revolting she was, because that would hurt her feelings. To make it worse, she'd be hurt anyway if he offered no explanation.

Before he left, she kissed him again on his now frozen lips.

"Hurry! I'll be waiting."

"Yeah."

11

Hal Yarrow knocked lightly on the door of Fobo's apartment. The door did not open at once. No wonder. There was so much noise inside. Hal beat on the door, though reluctantly, for he did not want to attract Pornsen's attention. The *gapt* lived across the hall from Fobo and might open his door to see what was going on. Tonight was not a good time for Pornsen to see him visiting the empathist. Even though Hal had every right to enter a wog's home without being accompanied by a *gapt*, he felt uneasy because of Jeannette. He would not put it past the *gapt* to enter his, Hal's, *puka* while he was gone for a bit of unofficial spying. And, if Pornsen did, he would have Hal. All would be up.

But Hal comforted himself with the thought that Pornsen was not a very brave man. If he took the liberty of entering Hal's place, he would also take the chance of being discovered. And Hal, as a *lamedhian*, could bring so much pressure to bear that Pornsen might not only be disgraced and demoted, he might even be a candidate for H.

Loudly, impatiently, Hal rapped on the door again. This time it swung open. Abasa, Fobo's wife, was smiling at him.

"Hal Yarrow!" she said in Siddo. "Welcome! Why didn't you come in without knocking?"

Hal was shocked. "I couldn't do that!"

"Why not?"

"We just don't do that."

Abasa shrugged her shoulders, but she was too polite to comment. Still smiling, she said, "Well, come on in. I won't bite!"

Hal stepped in and shut the door behind him, though not without a backward glance at Pornsen's door. It was closed.

Inside, the screams of twelve wog children at play bounced off the walls of a room as large as a basketball court. Abasa led Hal across the uncarpeted floor to the opposite end, where a hallway began. They passed by one corner where three wog females, evidently Abasa's visitors, sat at a table. They were occupied in sewing, drinking from tall glasses before them, and chattering. Hal could not understand the few words he could hear; wog females, when talking among themselves, used a vocabulary restricted to their sex. This custom, however, so Hal understood, was swiftly dying out under the impact of increasing urbanization. Abasa's female children were not even learning woman-talk.

Abasa led Hal down to the end of the hall, opened a door, and said, "Fobo, dear! Hal Yarrow, the No-nose, is here!"

Hal, hearing himself so described, smiled. The first time he had met this phrase, he had felt offended. But he had learned that the wogs did not mean it to be insulting.

Fobo came to the door. He was dressed only in a scarlet kilt. Hal could not help thinking for the hundredth time how strange the Ozagen's torso was, with its nippleless chest and the curious construction of shoulder blades attached to the ventral spine. (Would it be called a forebone as opposed to the Earthman's backbone?)

"You are welcome indeed, Hal," said Fobo in Siddo. He switched to American, "Shalom. What happy occasion brings you here? Sit down. I'd offer you a drink, but I'm fresh out."

Hal did not think his dismay showed on his face, but Fobo must have discerned it.

"Anything wrong?"

Hal decided not to waste time. "Yes. Where can I get a quart of liquor?"

"You need some? *Shib. I* will go out with you. The nearest tavern is a low-class hangout; it will give you a chance to see at close range an aspect of Siddo society you doubtless know little about."

The wog went into the closet and returned with an armful of clothes. He put a broad leather belt around his fat stomach and to it fastened a sheath containing a short rapier. Then, he stuck a pistol in the belt. Over his shoulders he fastened a long, kelly green cloak with many black ruffles. On his head he put a dark green skullcap with two artificial antennae. This head covering was the symbol for the Grasshopper clan. Once, it would have been important for a wog of that clan to have always worn it outside his house. Now, the clan system had degenerated to the point where it represented a minor social function, though its political use was still great.

"I need a drink, an alcoholic beverage," Fobo said. "You see, as a professional empathist, I encounter many nerve-racking cases. I give therapy to so many neurotics and psychotics. I must put myself in their shoes, feel their emotions as they feel them. Then I wrench myself out of their shoes and take an objective look at their problems. Through the use of this"—he tapped his head—"and this"—he tapped his nose—"I become them, then become myself, and so, sometimes, enable them to cure themselves."

Hal knew that when Fobo indicated his nose, he meant that the two extremely sensitive antennae inside the projectilelike proboscis could detect the type and flux of his patients' emotions. The odor from a wog's sweat told even more than the expression of his face.

Fobo led Hal down the hall to the big room. He told Abasa where he was going and affectionately rubbed noses with her.

Then, Fobo handed Hal a mask shaped like a wog's face, and he put his own on. Hal did not ask what it was for. He knew that it was the custom for all Siddo to wear nightmasks. They did serve a utilitarian purpose, for they kept the many biting insects off. Fobo explained their social function.

"We upper-class Siddo keep them on inside when we go—what's the American word?"

"Slumming?" said Hal. "When an upper-class person goes to a lower-class place for amusement?"

"Slumming," said Fobo. "Ordinarily, I do not keep the mask on when I go into a low-class resort, for I go there to have fun with people, not to laugh at them. But, tonight, inasmuch as you are a—I blush to say it, a No-nose—I think it would be more relaxing if you kept the mask on."

When they had walked out of the building, Hal said, "Why the gun and sword?"

"Oh, there isn't too much danger in this—neck of the woods?—but it's best to be careful. Remember what I told you at the ruins? The insects of my planet have developed and specialized far beyond those of your world, according to what you have told me. You know of the parasites and mimics that infest ant colonies? The beetles that look like ants and freeload off the ants because of that resemblance? The pygmy ants and other creatures that live in the walls of the colonies and prey on the eggs and young?

"We have things analogous to those, but they prey off us. Things that hide in sewers or basements or hollow trees or holes in the ground and creep around the city at night. That is why we do not allow our children out after dark. Our streets are well lighted and patrolled, but they are often separated by wooded stretches."

They walked through a park over a path lit with tall lamps that burned gas. Siddo was still in the transition between electricity and the older forms of energy; it was not unusual to find one area illuminated by light bulbs, the next by gaslights. Coming out of the park and onto a broad street, Hal saw other evidences of Ozagen's culture, the old and the brand new side by side. Buggies drawn by hoofed animals belonging to the same subphylum as Fobo and steam-driven wheeled vehicles. The animals and cars passed over a thoroughfare covered with tough short-bladed grass that resisted all efforts to wear it out.

And the buildings were so widely separated that it was difficult to think of oneself as being in a metropolis. Too bad, thought Hal. The wogs had more than enough Lebensraum now. But their expanding population made it inevitable that the wide spaces would be filled with houses and buildings; someday, Ozagen would be as crowded as Earth.

Then, he corrected himself. Crowded, yes, but not with wogglebugs. If the *Gabriel* carried out her planned function, human beings from the Haijac Union would replace the natives.

He felt a pang at this and also had the thought—unrealistic, of course—that such an event would be hideously wrong. What right did beings from another planet have to come here and callously murder all the inhabitants?

It was right, because the Forerunner had said so. *Or was it?*

Fobo said, "Ah, there it is."

He pointed to a building ahead of them. It was three stories high, shaped something like a ziggurat, and had arches running from the upper stories to the ground. These arches had steps on them on which the residents of the upper stories walked. Like many of the older Siddo buildings, it had no internal stairways; the residents went directly from the outside into their apartments.

However, though old, the tavern on the first story had a big electric sign blazing above the front door.

"Duroku's Happy Vale," said Fobo, translating the ideograms.

The bar was in the basement. Hal, after stopping to shudder at the blast of liquor fumes that came up the steps, followed the wog. He paused in the entrance.

Strong odors of alcohol mingled with loud bars of a strange music and even louder talk. Wogs crowded the hexagonal-topped tables and leaned across big pewter steins to shout in each other's face. Somebody waved his hands uncoordinatedly and sent a stein crashing. A waitress hurried up with a towel to mop up the mess. When she bent over, she was slapped resoundingly on the rump by a jovial, green-faced, and very fat wogglebug. His tablemates howled with laughter, their broad V-in-V lips wide open. The waitress laughed, too, and said something to the fat one that must have been witty, for those at the neighboring tables guffawed.

On a platform at one end of the room a five-piece band slammed out fast and weird notes. Hal saw three instruments that looked Terranlike: a harp, a trumpet, and a drum. A fourth musician, however, was not producing any music himself, but he was now and then prodding with a long stick a rat-sized locustoid creature in a cage. When so urged, the insect rubbed its hind wings over its back legs and gave four loud chirps followed by a long, nerve-scratching screech.

The fifth player was pumping away at a bellows connected to a bag and three short and narrow pipes. A thin squealing came out.

Fobo shouted, "Don't think that noise is typical of our music. It's cheap, popular stuff. I'll take you to a symphony concert one of these days, and you'll hear what great music is like."

The wog led the man to one of the curtained-off booths scattered along the walls. They sat down. A waitress came to them. Sweat ran off her forehead and down her tubular nose.

"Keep your mask on until we've gotten our drinks," said Fobo. "Then we can close the curtains."

The waitress said something in Wog.

Fobo repeated in American for Hal's benefit. "Beer, wine, or beetlejuice. Myself, I wouldn't touch the first two. They're for women and children."

Hal didn't want to lose face. He said, with a bravado he didn't feel, "The latter, of course."

Fobo held up two fingers. The waitress returned quickly with two big steins. The wog leaned his nose into the fumes and breathed deeply. He closed his eyes in ecstasy, lifted the stein, and drank a long time. When he put the container down, he belched loudly and then smacked his lips.

"Tastes as good coming up as going down!" he bellowed.

Hal felt queasy. He had been whipped too many times as a child for his uninhibited eructations.

"But Hal," said Fobo, "you are not drinking!"

Yarrow said weakly, "*Damif'ino,*" Siddo for, "I hope this doesn't hurt," and he drank.

Fire ran down his throat like lava down a volcano's slope. And, like a volcano, Hal erupted. He coughed and wheezed; liquor spurted out of his mouth; his eyes shut and squeezed out big tears.

"Very good, isn't it?" said Fobo calmly.

"Yes, very good," croaked Yarrow from a throat that seemed to be permanently scarred. Though he had spat most of the stuff out, some of it must have dropped straight through his intestines and into his legs, for he felt a hot tide down there swinging back and forth as if pulled by some invisible moon circling around and around in his head, a big moon that bulged and brushed against the inside of his skull.

"Have another."

The second drink he managed better—outwardly, at least, for he did not cough or sputter. But inwardly he was not so unconcerned. His belly writhed, and he was sure he would disgrace himself. After a few deep breaths, he thought he would keep the liquor down. Then, he belched. The lava got as far as his throat before he managed to stop it.

"Pardon me," he said, blushing.

"Why?" said Fobo.

Hal thought that was one of the funniest retorts he had ever heard. He laughed loudly and sipped at the stein. If he could empty it swiftly and then buy a quart for Jeannette, he could get back before the night was completely wasted.

When the liquor had receded halfway down the stein, Hal heard Fobo, dimly and far-off as if he were at the end of a long tunnel, ask him if he cared to see where the alcohol was made.

"*Shib,*" Hal said.

He rose but had to put a hand on the table to steady himself. The wog told him to put his mask back on.

"Earthmen are still objects of curiosity. We don't want to waste all evening answering questions. Or drinking drinks that'll be forced on us."

They threaded through the noisy crowd to a back room. There Fobo gestured and said, "Behold! The *kesarubu!*"

Hal looked. If he had not had some of his inhibitions washed away in the liquorish flood, he might have been overwhelmingly repulsed. As it was, he was curious.

The thing sitting on a chair by the table might, at first glance, have been taken for a wogglebug. It had the blond fuzz, the bald pate, the nose, and the V-shaped mouth. It also had the round body and enormous paunch of some of the Ozagens.

But a second look in the bright light from the unshaded bulb overhead showed a creature whose body was sheathed in a hard and light green tinted chitin. And, though it wore a long cloak, the legs and arms were naked. They were not smooth-skinned but were ringed, segmented with the edges of armor-sections, like stovepipes.

Fobo spoke to it. Yarrow understood some of the words; the others, he was able to fill in.

"Ducko, this is Mr. Yarrow. Say hello to Mr. Yarrow, Ducko."

The big blue eyes looked at Hal. There was nothing about them to distinguish them from a wog's, yet they seemed inhuman, thoroughly arthropodal.

"Hello, Mr. Yarrow," Ducko said in a parrot's voice.

"Tell Mr. Yarrow what a fine night it is."

"It's a fine night, Mr. Yarrow."

"Tell him Ducko is happy to see him."

"Ducko is happy to see you."

"And serve him."

"And serve you."

"Show Mr. Yarrow how you make beetlejuice."

A wog standing by the table glanced at his wrist-watch. He spoke in rapid Ozagen. Fobo translated.

"He says Ducko ate a half hour ago. He should be ready to serve. These creatures eat a big meal every half hour and then they—watch!"

Duroku set on the table a huge earthenware bowl. Ducko leaned over it until a half-inch-long tube projecting from his chest was poised above the edge of the bowl. The projection, thought Hal, was probably a modified tracheal opening. From the tube a clear liquid shot into the bowl until it was filled to the brim. Duroku grabbed the bowl and carried it off. An Ozagen came from the kitchen with a plate of what Hal later found out was highly sugared spaghetti. He set it down, and Ducko began eating from it with a big spoon.

Hal's brain was by then not working very fast, but he began to see what was going on. Frantically, he looked around for a place to vomit. Fobo shoved a drink under his nose. For lack of anything better to do, he swallowed some. Whole hog or none. Surprisingly, the fiery stuff settled his stomach. Or else burned away the rising tide.

"Exactly," replied Fobo to Hal's strangled question. "These creatures are a superb example of parasitical mimicry. Though quasi-insectal, they look much like us. They live among us and earn their room and board by furnishing us with a cheap and smooth alcoholic drink. You noticed its enormous belly, *shib*? It is there that they so rapidly manufacture the alcohol and so easily upchuck it. Simple and natural, yes? Duroku has two others working for him, but it is their night off, and doubtless they are in some neighborhood tavern, getting drunk. A sailor's holiday—"

Hal burst out, "Can't we buy a quart and get out? I feel sick. It must be the closeness of the air. Or something."

"Something, probably," Fobo murmured.

He sent a waitress after two quarts. While they were waiting for her, they saw a short wog in a mask and blue cloak enter. The newcomer stood in the doorway, black boots widespread and the long tubular projection of the mask pointing this way and that like a sub's periscope peering for prey.

Hal gasped and said, "Pornsen! I can see his uniform under the cloak!"

"*Shib*," replied Fobo. "That drooping shoulder and the black boots also give him away. Who does he think he's fooling?"

Hal looked wildly around. "I've got to get out of here!"

The waitress returned with the bottles. Fobo paid her and gave one to Hal, who automatically put it in the inside pocket of his cloak.

The *gapt* saw them through the doorway, but he must not have recognized them. Yarrow wore his mask, while the empathist probably looked to Pornsen like any other wog. Methodical as always, Pornsen evidently was determined to make a thorough search. He brought up his sloping shoulder in a sudden gesture and began parting the curtains of the booths along the walls. Whenever he saw a wog with his or her mask still on, he lifted the grotesque covering and looked behind.

Fobo chuckled, and he said, in American, "He won't keep that up long. What does he think we Siddo are? A bunch of mouses?"

What he had been waiting for happened. A burly wog suddenly stood up as Pornsen reached for his mask and instead lifted the *gapt's*. Surprised at seeing the non-Ozagenian features, the wog stared for a second. Then, he gave a screech, yelled something, and punched the Earthman in the nose.

At once, there was bedlam. Pornsen staggered back into a table, knocking it and its steins over, and fell to the floor. Two wogs jumped him. Another hit a fourth. The fourth struck back. Duroku, carrying a short club, ran up and began thumping his fighting customers on the backs and legs. Somebody threw beetlejuice in his face.

And, at that moment, Fobo threw the switch that plunged the tavern into darkness.

Hal stood bewildered. A hand seized his. "Follow me!" The hand tugged. Hal turned and allowed himself to be led, stumbling, toward what he thought was the back door.

Any number of others must have had the same idea. Hal was knocked down and trampled upon. Fobo's hand was torn from his. Yarrow cried out for the wog, but any possible answer was drowned out in a chorus of *Beat it! Get off my back, you dumb son-of-a-bug! Great Larva, we're piled up in the doorway!*

Sharp reports added to the noise. A foul stench choked Hal as the wogs, under nervous stress, released the gas in their madbags. Gasping, Hal fought his way through the door. A few seconds later, his mad scrambling over twisting bodies earned him his freedom. He lurched down an alleyway. Once on the street, he ran as fast as he could. He didn't know where he was going. His one thought was to put as much distance as possible between himself and Pornsen.

Arc lights on top of tall, slender iron poles flashed by. He ran with his shoulder almost scraping the buildings. He wanted to stay in the shadows thrown by the many balconies jutting out from above. After a minute, he slowed down at a narrow passageway. A glance showed him it wasn't a blind alley. He darted down it until he came to a large square can, one that by its odor must have been used for garbage. Squatting behind it, he tried to lessen his gaspings. Presently, his lungs regained their balance; he no longer had to sob for air. He could listen without having his heart thudding in his ears.

He heard no pursuer. After a while, he decided it was safe to rise. He felt the bottle in his cloak pocket. Miraculously, it had not been broken. Jeanette would get her liquor. What a story he would have to tell her! After all he had gone through for her, he would surely get a just reward . . .

He shivered with goose pimples at the thought and began to walk briskly down the alley. He had no idea where he was, but he carried a map of the city in his pocket. It had been printed in the ship and bore street names in Ozagen with American and Icelandic translations beneath. All he had to do was read the street signs under one of the many lamps, orient himself with the map, and return home. As for Pornsen, the fellow had no real evidence against him and would not be able to accuse him until he got some. Hal's golden *lamedh* made him above suspicion. Pornsen . . .

12

Pornsen! No sooner had he muttered the name than the flesh appeared. There was a click of hard boot heels behind him. He turned. A short, cloaked figure was coming down the alley. A lamp's glow outlined the droop of a shoulder and shone on black leather boots. His mask was off.

"Yarrow!" shrilled the *gapt*, triumphantly. "No use running! I saw you in that tavern. You won't be able to save yourself now!"

He click-clacked up to his ward's tall rigid form. "Drinking! I know you were drinking!"

"Yeah?" Hal croaked. "What else?"

"Isn't that enough?" screamed the *gapt*. "Or are you hiding something in your apartment? Maybe you are! Maybe you've got the place filled with bottles. Come on! Let's get back to your apartment. We'll go over it and see what we see. I wouldn't be surprised to find all sorts of evidence of your unreal thinking."

Hal hunched his shoulders and clenched his fists, but he said nothing. When he was told by the *gapt* to precede him back to Fobo's building, he walked without a sign of resistance. Like conqueror and conquered, they marched from the alley into the street. Yarrow, however, spoiled the picture by reeling a little and having to put his hand to the wall to steady himself.

Pornsen sneered. "You drunken *joat*! You make me sick to my stomach!"

Hal pointed ahead. "I'm not the only one who's sick. Look at that fellow."

He was not really interested, but he had a wild hope that anything he said or did, however trivial, might put off the final and fatal moment when they would return to his apartment. He was pointing at a large and evidently intoxicated wogglebug hanging onto a lamppost to keep from falling on his needle-shaped nose. He might have been a nineteenth- or twentieth-century drunk, complete to top hat, cloak, and lamppost. Now and then, the creature groaned as if he were deeply disturbed.

"Perhaps we'd better stop to see if he's hurt," said Hal.

He had to say something, anything to delay Pornsen. Before his captor could protest, he went up to the wog. He put his hand on the free arm—the other was wrapped around the post—and spoke in Siddo.

"Can we help you?"

The big wog looked as if he, too, had been in a brawl. His cloak, besides being ripped down the back, was spotted with dried green blood. He kept his face away from Hal, so that the Earthman had a hard time understanding his muttering.

Pornsen jerked at his arm. "Come on, Yarrow. He'll get by all right. What's one sick bug more or less?"

"*Shib*," agreed Hal tonelessly. He let his hand drop and started to walk on. Pornsen, behind, took one step and then bumped into Hal as Hal stopped.

"What are you stopping for, Yarrow?" The *gapt's* voice was suddenly apprehensive.

And then the voice was screaming in agony.

Hal whirled—to see in grim actuality what had flashed across his mind and caused him to stop in his tracks. When he had put his hand on the wog's arm, he had felt, not warm skin, but hard and cool chitin. For a few seconds, the meaning of that had not cleared the brain's switchboard. Then it had come through, and he had remembered the talk he and Fobo had had on the way to the tavern, and why Fobo wore a sword. Too late, he had wheeled to warn Pornsen.

Now the *gapt* was holding both hands to his eyes and shrieking. The big thing that had been leaning against the lamppost was advancing toward Hal. Its body seemed to grow huger with every step. A sac across its chest swelled until it looked like a palpitating gray balloon and a wheezing sound accompanied its deflation. The hideous insectal face, with two vestigial arms waving on each side of its mouth and the funnel-shaped proboscis below the mouth, was pointed at him. It was that proboscis which Hal had mistakenly thought was a wog's nose. In reality, the thing must have breathed through tracheae and two slits below the enormous eyes. Normally, its breath must saw loudly through the slits, but it must have suppressed the sound in order not to warn its victims.

Hal yelled with fright. At the same time he grabbed his cloak and threw it up before his face. His mask might have saved him, but he did not care to take the chance.

Something burned the back of his hand. He yelped with pain but leaped forward. Before the thing could breathe in air to bloat the sac again and expel the acid through the funnel, Hal rammed his head against its paunch.

The thing said, "Oof!" and fell backward where it lay on its back and thrashed its legs and arms like a giant poisonous bug—which it was. Then, as it recovered from the shock and rolled over and tried to get back on its feet, Hal kicked hard. His leather toe drove with a crunching sound through the thin chitin.

The toe withdrew; blood, dark in the lamplight, oozed out; Hal kicked again in the open place. The thing screamed and tried to crawl away on all fours. The Terran leaped upon it with both feet and drove it sprawling to the cement. He pressed his heel against its thin neck and shoved with all the strength of his leg. The neck cracked, and the thing lay still. Its lower jaw dropped open and exposed two rows of tiny needle teeth. The mouth's rudimentary arms wigwagged feebly for a while and then drooped.

Hal's chest heaved in agony. He couldn't get enough *air*. His guts quivered and threatened to force their way through his throat. Then they did, and Hal bent over, retching.

All at once, he was sober. By that time Pornsen had quit screaming. He was lying huddled on his side in the gutter. Hal turned him over and shuddered at what he saw. The eyes were partly burned out, and the lips were gray with large blisters. The tongue, sticking from the mouth, was swollen and lumpy. Evidently, Pornsen had swallowed some of the venom.

Hal straightened up and walked away. A wog patrol would find the *gapt's* body and turn it over to the Earthmen. Let the hierarchy figure out what had happened. Pornsen was dead, and now that he was, Yarrow admitted to himself what he had never allowed himself to admit before this time. He had hated Pornsen. And he was glad that he was dead. If Pornsen had suffered horribly, so what? His pains were brief, but the pain and grief he had caused Hal had lasted for almost thirty years.

A sound behind him made him whirl around.

"Fobo?"

There was a moan, followed by pain-garbled words.

"Pornsen? You can't be . . . you're . . . dead."

But Pornsen was alive. He was standing up, swaying.

He held his hands out before him to feel his way and took a few weak, exploratory steps.

For a moment, Hal was so panicked he thought of running away. But he forced himself to remain rooted and to think rationally.

If the wogs did find Pornsen, they'd turn him over to the doctors of the *Gabriel.* And the doctors would give Pornsen new eyes from the meat bank and would inject regeneratives into him. In two weeks, Pornsen's tongue would grow out again. And he'd talk. Forerunner, how he'd talk!

Two weeks? *Now!* There was nothing to prevent Pornsen from writing.

Pornsen groaned with physical pain; Hal, with mental.

There was only one thing to do.

He went up to Pornsen and seized his hand. The *gapt* flinched and said something unintelligible.

"It's Hal," said Yarrow.

Pornsen reached out his free hand and pulled a notebook and pen from his pocket. Hal released the other hand. Pornsen wrote on the paper and then handed the notebook to Hal.

The moonlight was bright enough to read by. The handwriting was a scrawl, but, even blind, Pornsen could write legibly.

> Take me to the *Gabriel*, son. I swear by the Fore-
> runner I won't say a word about the liquor to anybody.
> I'll be eternally grateful. But don't leave me here in my
> pain at the mercy of monsters. I love you.

Hal patted Pornsen on the shoulder and said, "Take my hand. I'll lead you."

At the same time, he heard a noise from down the street. A group of noisy wogs was heading his way.

He pulled Pornsen into the nearby park, guiding the stumbling man around the trees and bushes. After they'd walked a hundred yards, they came to an especially thick grouping of trees. Hal halted. Unfamiliar sounds were coming from the center of the grove—clicking and wheezing sounds.

He peered around a tree and saw the origin of the noise. The bright moonlight fell on the corpse of a wog, or, rather, on what was left of it. The upper part was stripped of flesh. Around it and on it were many silvery-white insects. These resembled ants but were at least a foot high. The clicking came from their mandibles working on the corpse. The wheezing came from the air sacs on their heads breathing in and out.

Hal had thought he was hidden, but they must have detected him. Suddenly, they had disappeared into the shadows of the trees on the side of the grove opposite him.

He hesitated, then decided that they were scavengers and would give a healthy person no trouble. Probably, the wog was a drunk who had passed out and been killed by the ants.

He led Pornsen to the corpse and examined it because this was his first chance to inspect the bone structure of the indigenes. The spinal column of the wog was located in the anterior of the torso. It rose from unhumanly shaped hips in a curve that was the mirror image of the curve of a man's spine. However, two sacs of the intestinal tract lay on each side of the spine, forward of the hips. They made a stomach with a hollow in its center. The stomach of a live wog concealed the depression, for the skin stretched tightly over it.

Such an internal construction was to be expected in a being that had developed from the ancestors similar to those of the insects. Hundreds of millions of years ago, the ancestors of the wogs had been unspecialized, wormlike prearthropods. But evolution had intended to make a sentient being from the worm. And, realizing the limitations of true arthropods, evolution had split the wogs' Nth-great-grandfather from the phylum of Arthropoda. When the Crustacea, arachnida, and insecta had formed exoskeletons and many legs, Grandfather Wog the Nth had not gone along with them. He had refused to harden his delicate cuticle skin into chitin. Instead, he had erected a skeleton inside the flesh. But his central nervous system was still ventral, and the feat of shifting spinal nerves and spine from front to back was beyond him. So, he had formed the spine where it had to be. And the rest of his skeleton had to go along. The inner parts of a wog were unmistakably different from a mammal's. But if the form was different, the function was similar.

Hal would have liked to investigate further, but he had work to do.

Work which he hated.

Pornsen wrote something in the notebook and handed it to Hal.

> Son, I am in terrible pain. Please don't hesitate about
> taking me to the ship. I will not betray you. Have I
> ever broken a promise to you? I love you.

Hal thought, *The only promise you ever made to me was to whip me.*

He looked at the shadows between the trees. The pale bodies of the ants were like a forest of mushrooms. Waiting until he left.

Pornsen mumbled something and sat down on the grass. His head drooped.

"Why do I have to do this?" murmured Hal.

He thought, *I don't have to. Jeannette and I could throw ourselves on the mercy of the wogs. Fobo would be the one to go to. The wogs could hide us. But would they do it? If I could be sure. But I can't. They might surrender us to the Uzzites.*

"No use putting it off," he murmured.

He groaned, and he said, "Why must I do this? Why couldn't he have died back there?"

He drew a long knife from a sheath in his boot.

At that moment, Pornsen raised his head and looked upward with scarred eyes. His hand groped for Hal. A ghastly caricature of a smile formed on his burned lips.

Hal raised his knife until its point was about six inches from Pornsen's throat.

"Jeannette, I am doing this for you!" Hal said loudly.

But the knifepoint did not move, and, after a few seconds, it dropped.

"I can't do it," Hal said. "Can't."

Yet, he must do something, something which would either keep Pornsen from informing on him or would remove him and Jeannette from the scene of danger.

Moreover, he had to see that Pornsen was given medical care. The suffering of the man was making him sick, making him writhe with empathy. If he could have killed Pornsen, he would have put an end to that suffering. But he could not do it.

Pornsen, mumbling with burned lips, took a few steps forward, his hands held out at chest level and rotating as he felt for Hal. Hal stepped to one side. He was thinking furiously. There was only one course of action. That was to get Jeannette and make a run for it. His first thought to get a wog to take Pornsen to the ship was discarded. Pornsen would have to be in agony for a while. Hal needed every second of time he could get, and to try to ease the *gapt's* pain quickly would be treachery to Jeannette—not to mention himself.

Pornsen had been walking slowly forward, exploring the air with his hands, shuffling his feet across the grass so he wouldn't stumble over an obstacle. Presently, his foot came into contact with the bones of the native. He halted, and he stooped to feel. When he closed his hands around the ribs and pelvis, he froze. For several seconds, he kept his stance, then he began feeling the length of the skeleton. His fingers touched the skull, moved around it, tested the fragments of flesh clinging to it.

Abruptly, seemingly terrified, perhaps realizing that whatever had stripped the wog of flesh might be close and that he was helpless, he straightened up and ran headlong. A choking scream came from him as he sped across the glade. The high-pitched ululation ended abruptly. He had rammed into a tree trunk and fallen on his back.

Before he could rise, he was overwhelmed by a wheezing and clicking horde of mushroom-white bodies.

Hal did not think of the fact that he was not behaving rationally. Instead, giving a cry, he ran toward the ants. Halfway across the glade, Hal saw them disappear into the shadows, but not so far that he could not discern their massed whiteness.

Reaching Pornsen, Hal sank down to one knee and examined him.

In those few moments, the man's clothing had been torn to shreds and his flesh bitten in many places.

His eyes stared straight upward; his jugular vein had been severed.

Hal, moaning, rose and walked swiftly from the grove. Behind him was a rustling and wheezing as the ants surged forward from the protection of the trees. Hal did not look back.

And, when he stepped under the light of the street-lamp, the pressure inside him found vent. Tears ran down his cheeks. His shoulders shook with sobs. He staggered like a drunk. His intestines felt as if they were being pulled apart.

He did not know if it was grief or if it was hate at last finding expression because the cause of his hate could no longer retaliate against him. Perhaps, it was both grief and hate. Whatever it was, it was working out of his body like a poison; his body was expelling it. At the same time, it was boiling him alive.

Yet, it was coming out. Though he felt he was dying, by the time he had walked to his home, he was rid of the poison. Fatigue leadened his arms and legs, and he could scarcely find the energy to walk up the flight of steps to the front door of the building.

At the same time, his heart felt light. It was strong, pumping unimpeded as if a hand around it had released its clutch.

13

A tall ghost in a light blue shroud was waiting for the Terran in the false dawn. It was Fobo, the empathist, standing in the hexagonal-shaped arch that led into his building. He threw back the hood and exposed a face that was scratched on one cheek and blackened around the right eye.

He chuckled and said, "Some son-of-a-bug pulled my mask off and plowed me good. But it was fun. It helps if you blow off steam now and then. How did you come out? I was afraid you might have been picked up by the police. Normally, that wouldn't worry me, but I know your colleagues at the ship would frown upon such activities."

Hal smiled wanly.

"Frown misses it by a mile."

He wondered how Fobo knew what the hierarch's reactions would be. How much did these wogs know about the Terrestrials? Were they onto the Haijac game and waiting to pounce? If so, with what? Their technology, as far as could be determined, was far behind Earth's. True, they seemed to know more of psychic functions than the Terrans did, but that was understandable. The Sturch had long ago decreed that the proper psychology had been perfected and that further research was unnecessary. The result had been a standstill in the psychical sciences.

He shrugged mentally. He was too tired to think of such things. All he wanted was to go to bed.

"I'll tell you later what happened."

Fobo replied, "I can guess. Your hand. You'd better let me fix that burn. Nightlifer venom is nasty."

Like a little child, Hal followed him to the wog's apartment and let him put a cooling salve on it.

"*Shib* as *shib*," Fobo said. "Go to bed. Tomorrow you can tell me all about it."

Hal thanked him and walked down to his floor. His hand fumbled with the key. Finally, after using Sigmen's name in vain, he inserted the key. When he had shut and locked the door, he called Jeannette. She must have been hiding in the closet-within-a-closet in the bedroom, for he heard two doors bang. In a moment she was running to him. She threw her arms around him.

"Oh, *maw num, maw num!* What has happened? I was so worried. I thought I would scream when the night went by, and you didn't return."

Though he was sorry he had caused her pain, he could not help a prickling of pleasure because she cared enough about him to worry. Mary, perhaps, might have been sympathetic, but she would have felt duty-bound to repress it and to lecture him on his unreal thinking and the resulting injury to himself.

"There was a brawl."

He had decided not to say anything about the *gapt* or the nightlifer. Later, when the strain had passed, he'd talk.

She untied his cloak and hood and took off his mask. She hung them up in the front room closet, and he sank into a chair and closed his eyes.

A moment later, they were opened by the sound of liquid pouring into a glass. She was standing in front of him and filling a large glass from the quart. The odor of beetlejuice began to turn his stomach, and the picture of a beautiful girl about to drink the nauseating stuff spun it all the way around.

She looked at him. The delicate brackets of her brows rose.

"*Kyetil?*"

"Nothing's the matter!" he groaned. "I'm all right."

She put down the glass, picked up his hand, and led him into the bedroom. There she gently sat him down, pressed on his shoulders until he lay down, and then took off his shoes. He didn't resist. After she unbuttoned his shirt, she stroked his hair.

"You're sure you're all right?"

"*Shib*. I could lick the world with one hand tied behind my back."

"Good."

The bed creaked as she got up and walked out of the room. He began to drift into sleep, but her return awakened him. Again, he opened his eyes. She was standing with a glass in her hand.

She said, "Would you like a sip now, Hal?"

"Great Sigmen, don't you understand?" Fury roused him and he sat up.

"Why do you think I got sick? I can't stand the stuff! I can't stand to see you drink it. It makes me sick. You make me sick. What's the matter with you? Are you stupid?"

Jeannette's eyes widened. Blood drained from her face and left the pigment of her lips a crimson moon in a white lake. Her hand shook so that the liquor spilled.

"Why—why—" she gasped—"I thought you said you felt fine. I thought you were all right. I thought you wanted to go to bed with me."

Yarrow groaned. He shut his eyes and lay back down. Sarcasm was lost on her. She insisted on taking everything literally. She would have to be reeducated. If he weren't so exhausted, he would have been shocked by her open proposal—so much like that of the Scarlet Woman in *The Western Talmud* when she had tried to seduce the Forerunner.

But he was past being shocked. Moreover, a voice on the edge of his conscience said that she had merely put into hard and unrecallable words what he had planned in his heart all this time. But when they were spoken!

A crash of glass shattered his thoughts. He jerked upright. She was standing there, face twisted, lovely red mouth quivering, and tears flowing. Her hand was empty. A large wet patch against the wall, still dripping, showed what had become of the glass.

"I thought you loved me!" she shouted.

Unable to think of anything to say, he stared. She spun and walked away. He heard her go into the front room and begin to sob loudly. Unable to endure the sound, he jumped out of bed and walked swiftly after her. These rooms were supposed to be soundproof, but one never knew. What if she were overheard?

Anyway, she was twisting something inside him, and he had to straighten it out.

When he entered the front room, he saw she was looking downcast. For a while, he stood silent, wanting to say something but utterly unable to because he had never been forced to solve such a problem before. Haijac women didn't cry often, and if they did, they wept alone in privacy.

He sat down by her and put his hand on her soft shoulder.

"Jeannette."

She turned quickly and laid her dark hair against his chest. She said, between sobs, "I thought maybe you didn't love me. And I couldn't stand it. Not after all I've been through!"

"Well, Jeannette, I didn't—I mean—I wasn't . . ."

He paused. He had had no intention of saying he loved her. He'd never told any woman he loved her, not even Mary. Nor had any woman ever told him. And here was this woman on a faraway planet, only half-human at that, taking it for granted that he was hers, body and self.

He began speaking in a soft voice. Words came easily because he was quoting Moral Lecture AT-16:

" ' . . . all beings with their hearts in the right place are brothers . . . Man and woman are brother and sister . . . Love is everywhere . . . but love . . . should be on a higher plane . . . Man and woman should rightly loathe the beastly act as something the Great Mind, the Cosmic Observer, has not yet eliminated in man's evolutionary development . . . The time will come when children will be produced through thought alone. Meanwhile, we must recognize sex as necessary for only one reason: children . . . ' "

Slap! His head rang, and points of fire whirled off into the blackness before his eyes.

It was a moment before he could realize that Jeannette had leaped to her feet and slammed him hard with the palm of her hand. He saw her standing above him with her eyes slitted and her red mouth open and drawn back in a snarl.

Then, she whirled and ran into the bedroom. He got up and followed her. She was lying on the bed, sobbing.

"Jeannette, you don't understand!"

"*Fva tuh fe fu!*"

When he understood that, he blushed. Then he became furious. He grabbed her by the shoulder and turned her over so that she faced him.

Suddenly he was saying, "But I do love you, Jeannette. I *do.*"

He sounded strange, even to himself. The concept of love, as she meant it, was alien to him—rusty, perhaps, if it could be put that way. It would need much polishing. But it would, he knew, be polished. Here in his arms was one whose very nature and instinct and education were pointed toward love.

He had thought he had drained himself of grief earlier that night;

but now, as he forgot his resolve not to tell her what had happened, and as he recounted, step by step, the long and terrible night, tears ran down his face. Thirty years made a deep well; it took a long time to pump out all the weeping.

Jeannette, too, cried, and said that she was sorry that she had gotten angry at him. She promised never again to do so. He said it was all right. They kissed again and again until, like two babies who have wept themselves and loved themselves out of frustration and fury, they passed gently into sleep.

14

At 0900 Ship's Time, Yarrow walked into the *Gabriel*, the scent of morning dew on the grass in his nostrils. As he had a little time before the conference, he looked up Turnboy, the historian *joat*. Casually, he asked Turnboy if he knew anything of a space flight emigration from France after the Apocalyptic War. Turnboy was delighted to show off his knowledge. Yes, the remnants of the Gallic nation had gathered in the Loire country after the Apocalyptic War and had formed the nucleus of what might have become a new France.

But the swiftly growing colonies sent from Iceland to the northern part of France, and from Israel to the southern part, had surrounded the Loire. New France found itself squeezed economically and religiously. Sigmen's disciples invaded the territory in waves of missionaries. High tariffs strangled the little state's trade. Finally, a group of Frenchmen, seeing the inevitable absorption or conquest of their state, religion, and tongue, had left in six rather primitive spaceships to find another Gaul rotating about some far-off star. It was highly improbable that they had succeeded.

Hal thanked Turnboy and walked to the conference room. He spoke to many. Half of them, like him, had a Mongolian tinge to their features. They were the English-speaking descendants of Hawaiian and Australian survivors of the same war which had decimated France. Their many-times great-grandfathers had repopulated Australia, the Americas, Japan, and China.

Almost half of the crew spoke Icelandic. Their ancestors had sailed from the grim island to spread across northern Europe, Siberia, and Manchuria.

About a sixteenth of the crew knew Georgian as their native tongue. Their foreparents had moved down from the Caucasus Mountains and resettled depopulated southern Russia, Bulgaria, northern Iran, and Afghanistan.

The conference was a memorable one. First, Hal was moved from twentieth place to the Archurielite's left to sixth from his right. The *lamedh* on his chest made the difference. Second, there was little difficulty about Pornsen's death. The *gapt* was considered a casualty of the undeclared war. Everyone was warned, again, about the nightlifers and other things that sometimes prowled Siddo after dusk. It was not, however, suggested that the Haijacs quit their moonlit espionage.

Macneff ordered Hal, as the dead *gapt's* spiritual son, to arrange for the funeral the following day. Then he pulled down a huge map from a long roller on the wall. This was the representation of Earth that would be given to the wogs.

It was a good example of the Haijacs' subtlety and Chinese box-within-a-box thinking. The two hemispheres of Earth were depicted on the map with colored political boundaries. It was correct as far as the Bantu and Malay states were concerned. But the positions of the Israeli and Haijac nations had been reversed. The legend beneath the map indicated that green was the color of the Forerunner states and yellow the Hebrew states. The green portion, however, was a ring around the Mediterranean, and a broad band covering Arabia, the southern half of Asia Minor, and northern India.

In other words, if, by an inconceivable chance, the Ozagen succeeded in capturing the *Gabriel* and built ships with it as a model, and used the navigational data aboard to find Sol, they would still attack the wrong country. Undoubtedly, they would not bother to contact personally the people of Earth, for they would want to use the element of surprise. Thus, the Israeli would never get a chance to explain before the bombs went off. And the Haijac Union, warned, would hurl its space fleet against the invaders.

"However," said Macneff, "I do not think that the pseudofuture I have just suggested could ever become reality. Not unless the Back-runner is more powerful than I believe. Of course, you could take the attitude that this course might be best. What better shape could the future take than to wipe out our Israeli enemies through means of these nonhumans?

"But, as you all know, our ship is well guarded against attack by open assault or stealth. Our radar, lasers, audiodetection equipment, and starlight scopes are operating at all times. Our weapons are ready. The wogs are inferior in technology; they have nothing to bring against us that we could not easily crush.

"Nevertheless, if the Backrunner were to inspire them to superhuman cunning, and they did get into the ship, they would fail. If the wogs should reach a certain point in the ship, one of two officers always on duty on the bridge will press a button. This will wipe out all navigational data in the memory banks; the wogs will never be able to locate Sol.

"And if the wogs—Sigmen forbid—should reach the bridge, then the officer on duty there will press another button."

Macneff paused and looked at those around the conference table. Most of them were pale, for they knew what he was going to say.

"An H-bomb will utterly destroy this ship. It will also annihilate the city of Siddo. And we will be honored forever in the eyes of the Forerunner and the Sturch.

"Naturally, we would all prefer that this not happen. And I wish I could warn Siddo so that they would not dare to attack. However, to do so would spoil our present good relations with them and might result in our having to launch Project Ozagenocide before we are ready,"

After the conference, Hal gave orders for the funeral arrangements. Other duties kept him till dark, when he returned home.

When Hal locked the door behind him, he heard the shower running. He hung his coat up in the closet; the water stopped splashing. As he went toward his bedroom door, Jeannette stepped out from the bathroom. She was drying her hair with a big towel, and she was naked.

She said, "*Baw yoo,* Hal," and walked into the bedroom, unselfconsciously. Feebly, Hal replied. He turned and went back into the front room. He felt foolish because of his timorousness and, at the same time, vaguely wicked, unreal, because of the pounding of his heart, his heavy breathing, the hot and fluid fingers that wrapped themselves, half-pain, half-delight, around his loins.

She came out dressed in a pale green robe which he had bought for her and which she had recut and re-sewn to fit her figure. Her heavy black hair was piled on her head in a Psyche knot. She kissed him and asked if he wanted to come into the kitchen while she cooked. He said that would be fine.

She began making a sort of spaghetti. He asked her to tell him about her life. Once started, she was not hard to keep going.

"... and so my father's people found a planet like Earth and settled there. It was a beautiful planet; that is why they called it *Wuhbopfey*, the beautiful land.

"According to my father, there are about thirty million living there on one continent. My father was not content to live the life his grand-fathers had lived—tilling the soil or running a shop and raising many children. He and some other young men like him took the only space-ship left of the original six that had come there, and they sailed off to the stars. They came to Ozagen. And crashed. No wonder. The ship was so old."

"Is the wreck still around?"

"*Fi*. Close to where my sisters and aunts and cousins live."

"Your mother is dead?"

She hesitated, then nodded. "Yes. She died giving birth to me. And my sisters. My father died later. Or rather, we think he did. He went on a hunting party and never came back."

Hal frowned, and he said, "You told me that your mother and aunts were the last of the native human beings on Ozagen. That isn't so. Fobo told me that there are at least a thousand small isolated groups in the backlands. And you said once before that Rastignac was the only Earthman to get out alive from the wreck. He was your mother's husband, naturally . . . and incredible as it sounds, their union—one of a terrestrial and an extraterrestrial—was fertile! That alone would rock my colleagues on their heels. It's completely contrary to accepted science that their body chemistry and chromosomes should match! But—what I'm getting at is that your mother's sisters had children, too. If the last human male of your group died years before Rastignac crashed, who was their father?"

"My father, Jean-Jacques Rastignac. He was the husband of my mother and my three aunts. They all said that he was a superb lover, very experienced, very virile."

Hal said, "Oh."

Until she had the spaghetti and salad ready, he watched her in silence. By then he had regained some of his moral perspective. After all, the Frenchman was not too much worse than he himself was. Maybe not as bad. He chuckled. How easy it was to condemn some-body else for giving way to temptation until you yourself faced the same situation. He wondered what Pornsen would have done if Jean-nette had contacted him.

". . . and so, after we'd been going down that jungle river," she was saying, "they quit watching me so closely. We'd taken two months to get from my home, near where they'd captured me, so they thought I'd never dare to try to get home alone. There are too many deadly things in the jungle. They make the nightlifer look like a minor nuisance."

She shuddered.

"When we got to a village which was on the very edge of their civilization, they let me wander around in the enclosure. By then I'd learned some of their language and they some of mine. But our conversation was on a very simple level. One of their party, a scientist named 'Asa"atsi, put me through all sorts of examinations and tests, physical and mental. There was a machine at the village hospital which took photographs of my insides. My skeleton, my organs. *Maw tyuh!* My everything.

"They said it was most interesting. Imagine that! I am exposed as no woman has ever been exposed, and to them I am just most interesting. Indeed!"

"Well." Hal laughed. "You can't expect them to take the viewpoint of a male mammal toward a female mammal . . . that is . . ."

She looked archly at him. "And am I a mammal?"

"Obviously, unmistakably, indisputably, and enthusiastically."

"For that, you get a kiss."

She leaned over him and placed her mouth over his. He stiffened, reacting as he had when his ex-wife had offered to kiss him. But she must have anticipated this, for she said, "You are a man, not a pillar of stone. And I am a woman who loves you. Kiss me back; don't just take my kisses."

"Oh, not so hard," she murmured. "Kiss me. Don't try to ram your lips through mine. Go soft, melt, merge your lips with mine. See."

She vibrated the tip of her tongue against his. Then she stood back, smiling, her eyes half-closed, her red lips wet. He was shaking and breathing hard.

"Do your people think the tongue is only to talk with? Do they think that what I did is wicked, unreal?"

"I don't know. Nobody ever discussed that."

"You liked it, I know. Yet this is the same mouth with which I eat. The one I must hide behind a veil when I sit across the table from you."

"Don't put the cap on," he blurted. "I have been thinking about that. There is no rational reason why we should be veiled when we eat. The only reason is that I have been taught it is disgusting. Pavlov's dog salivated when it heard the bell; I get sick when I see food go into a naked mouth."

"Let's eat. Then we will drink and we will talk of us. And later do whatever we feel like doing."

He was learning fast. He didn't even blush.

15

After the meal she diluted a pitcher of beetle-juice with water, poured in a purplish liquid which made the drink smell like grapes, and dropped sprigs of an orange plant on the surface. Placed into a glass of ice cubes, it was cool and even tasted like grapes. It did not gag him at all.

"Why did you pick me instead of Pornsen?"

She sat on his lap, one arm around his neck, the other on the table, drink in hand.

"Oh, you were so good-looking, and he was so ugly. Besides, I could *feel* that you could be trusted. I knew I had to be careful. My father had told me about Earthmen. He said they couldn't be trusted."

"How true. But you must have an intuition for doing the right thing, Jeannette. If you had antennae, I'd say you could detect nervous emanations. Here, let's see!" He went to run his fingers through her hair, but she ducked her head and laughed.

He laughed with her and dropped his hand to her shoulder, rubbing the smooth skin. "I was probably the only person on the ship who wouldn't have betrayed you. But I'm in a quandary now. You see, your presence here raises the Backrunner. It puts me in grave danger— but a danger I wouldn't miss for anything else in the world.

"However, what you tell me of the X-ray machines worries me. So far, we've seen none. Are the wogs hiding them? If so, why? We know that they have electricity, and that they're theoretically capable of inventing X-ray machines. Perhaps, they're hiding them only because they're indications of an even more developed technology.

"But that doesn't seem reasonable. And, after all, we don't know too much of Siddo culture. We've not been here long enough; we don't have enough men to do extensive investigation.

"Maybe I'm being too suspicious. That's more than likely. Nevertheless, Macneff should be informed. But I can't tell him how I found out; I wouldn't even dare make up a lie about my source of information.

"I'm on the horns of a dilemma."

"A dilemma? A beast I never heard of before."

He hugged her and said, "I hope you never do."

"Listen," she said, looking eagerly at him with her beautiful brown eyes, "why bother to tell Macneff? If the Siddo should attack the Haijac—or, as you say their enemies call them so aptly, Highjackers—and conquer them, why not? Couldn't we make our way to my homeland and live there?"

Hal was shocked. "Those are my people, my countrymen! They—we—are Sigmenites. I couldn't betray them!"

"You are doing just that now by keeping me here," she said gravely.

"I know that," said Hal slowly. "But it's not a gross betrayal, not a real betrayal at all. How am I hurting them by having you?"

"I don't worry at all about what you may be doing to them. I do worry about what you may be doing to yourself."

"To myself? I am doing the best thing I ever did!"

She laughed delightedly and gave him a light kiss on the lips.

But he frowned, and he said, "Jeannette, it's serious. Sooner or later, and probably sooner, we have to do something definite. By that, I mean find a hiding place deep underground. Later, after it's all over, we can come out. And we'll have at least eighty years to ourselves, which will be more than enough. Because it will take that long for the *Gabriel* to return to Earth and for the colonizing ships to come back. We'll be like Adam and Eve, just us two and the beasts."

"What do you mean?" she said, her eyes widening.

"This. Our specialists are working night and day on samples of blood the wogs gave us. They hope to make an artificial semivirus that will attach itself to the copper in the wog's blood cells and change the cells' electrophoretic properties."

"*'Ama?*"

"I'll try to explain even if I have to use a mixture of American, French, and Siddo to get it across.

"A form of this artificial semivirus is what killed most of Earth's people during the Apocalyptic War. I won't go into the historical details; it's enough to say that the virus was disseminated secretly from outside the Earth's atmosphere by the ships of Martian colonists. The descendants of Earthmen on Mars, who considered themselves true Martians, were led by Sigfried Russ, as evil a man as ever lived. Or so say the history books."

"I do not know what you are talking about," she said.

Her face was grave, her eyes fixed upon his face.

"You can pick up the gist of it. The four Martian ships, pretending to be merchant vessels orbiting before entry, dropped billions of these viruses. Invisible knots of protein molecules that drifted through the atmosphere, spreading throughout the world, covering it in a very tenuous mist. These molecules, once they penetrated a human being's skin, locked onto the hemoglobin in the red blood cells and gave them a positive charge. This charge caused one end of a globin molecule to bind with the end of the other. And the molecule would go into a kind of crystallization. This would twist the doughnut-shaped cells into scimitars and thus cause an artificial sickle-cell anemia.

"The lab-created anemia was much swifter and more certain than the natural anemia, because every blood cell in the body would be affected, not just a small percentage. Every cell would soon break down. No oxygen would be carried through the human organism; the body died.

"The body did die, Jeannette—the body of humanity. Almost an entire planet of human beings perished from lack of oxygen."

"I think I understand most of what you have told me," said Jeannette. "But everybody, they did not die?"

"No. And at the beginning, the governments of Earth found out what was going on. They launched missiles toward Mars; and the missiles, designed to cause earthquakes, destroyed most of the Martian underground colonies.

"On Earth, perhaps a million survived on each continent. With the exception of certain areas where almost the entire population was untouched. Why? We don't really know. But something, perhaps favorable wind currents, bent the fall of virus away until the virus had fallen to the ground. After a certain time outside of a human body, the virus died.

"Anyway, the islands of Hawaii and Iceland were left with organized governments and a full population. Israel, too, was left untouched, as if the hand of God had covered it during the deadly fall. And southern Australia and the Caucasus Mountains were spared.

"These groups spread out afterward, resettling the world, absorbing the survivors in the areas which they took over. In the jungles of Africa and the Malayan peninsula, enough were left alive to venture out. These reestablished themselves in their native lands before colonies from the islands and Australia could take over.

"And what happened to Earth is destined to happen here on this planet. When the order is given, missiles will leave the *Gabriel*, missiles laden with the same deadly cargo. Only, the viruses will be fitted for the blood cells of the Ozagen. And the missiles will circle and circle and drop their invisible rain of death. And . . . everywhere . . . the skulls—"

"Hush!" Jeannette put her finger on his quivering lips. "I don't know what you mean by proteins and molecules and those—those electrofrenetic charges! They're way above my head. But I do know that the longer you've been talking, the more scared you've been getting. Your voice was getting higher, and your eyes were growing wider.

"Somebody has frightened you in the past. No! Don't interrupt! They've scared you, and you've been man enough to hide most of your fear. But they've done such a horribly efficient job that you haven't been able to get over it.

"Well—" and she put her soft lips to his ear and whispered—"I'm going to wipe that fear out. I'm going to lead you out of that valley of fright. No! Don't protest! I know it hurts your ego to think that a woman could know you're afraid. But I don't think any the less of you. I admire you all the more because you've conquered so much of it. I know what courage it took to face the 'Meter. I know you did it because of me. I'm proud that you did. I love you for it. And I know what courage it takes to keep me here, when at any time a slip would send you to certain disgrace and death. I know what it all means. It's my nature and instinct and business and love to know.

"Now! Drink with me. We're not outside these walls where we have to worry ourselves about such things and be scared. We're in here. Away from everything except ourselves. Drink. And love me. I'll love you, Hal, and we'll not see the world outside nor need to. For the time being. Forget in my arms."

They kissed and ran their hands over each other and said the things lovers have always said.

Between kisses, Jeannette poured more of the purplish liquor, and they drank this. Hal had no trouble swallowing it. He decided that it wasn't the idea of drinking alcohol so much as it was the odor that sickened him. When his nose was deceived, his stomach was also. And every drink made it easier for the next one.

He downed three tall glasses and then rose and lifted Jeannette in his arms and carried her into the bedroom. She was kissing the side of his neck, and it seemed to him that an electric charge was passing from her lips to his skin and on up to his brain and on down through his beating chest and warming stomach and swelling genital and on down through the soles of his feet, which, strangely, had become ice. Certainly, holding her did not make him want to withdraw as when he had carried out his duty toward Mary and the Starch.

Yet, even in his ecstasy of anticipation, there was a stronghold of retreat. It was small, but it was there, dark in the middle of the fire. He could not completely forget himself, and he doubted, wondering if he would fail as he had sometimes when he had crawled into bed in the dark and reached out for Mary.

There was also a black seed of panic, dropped by the doubt. If he failed, he would kill himself. He would be done forever.

Yet, he told himself, it could not possibly happen, must not. Not when he had his arms around her and her lips were on his.

He put her on the bed and then turned off the ceiling light. But she turned on the lamp over the bed.

"Why are you doing *that*?" he said, standing at the foot of the bed, feeling the rise of panic and the fall of his passion. At the same time he wondered how she could so swiftly, unseen by him, have unclothed herself.

She smiled and said, "Remember what you told me the other day? That beautiful passage: *God said, Let there be light.*"

"We do not need it."

"I do. I must see you at every moment. The dark would take away half of the pleasure. I want to see you in love."

She reached upward to adjust the angle of the bed-lamp, her breasts rising with the movement and sending an almost intolerable pang through him.

"There. Now I can see your face. Especially, at the moment when I will know best that you love me."

She extended a foot and touched his knee with her toe. Skin upon skin . . . it drew him forward as if it were the finger of an angel gently directing him toward destiny. He knelt upon the bed, and she drew back her leg with her toe still placed upon his leg as if it had grown roots into his flesh and could not be dislodged. "Hal, Hal," she murmured. "What have they done to you? What have they done to all your men? I know from what you have told me that they are like you. What have they done? Made you hate instead of love, though they call hate love. Made you half-men so you will turn your drive into yourself and then outward against the enemy. So you will become fierce warriors because you are such timid lovers."

"That's not true," he said. "Not true."

"I can see you. It is true."

She removed her foot and placed it beside his knee and said, "Come closer," and when he had moved closer, still on his knees, she reached up and pulled him down against her breasts.

"Place your mouth here. Become a baby again. And I will raise you so you forget your hate and know only love. And become a man."

"Jeannette, Jeannette," he said hoarsely. He put out his hand to pull the cord of the bedlamp and said, "Not the light."

But she put her hand on his and said, "Yes, the light."

Then she took her hand away and said, "All right, Hal. Turn it off. For a little while. If you must go back into the darkness, go far back. Far back. And then be reborn . . . for a little while. Then, the light."

"No! Let it stay on!" he snarled. "I am not in my mother's womb. I do not want to go back there; I do not need to. And I will take you as an army takes a city."

"Don't be a soldier, Hal. Be a lover. You must love me, not rape me. You can't take me, because I will surround you."

Her hand closed gently on him, and she arched her back slightly, and suddenly he was surrounded. A shock ran through him, comparable to that he had felt when she kissed his neck, but comparable only in kind and not in intensity.

He started to bury his face against her shoulder, but she put both hands on his chest and with surprising strength, half-raised him.

"No. I must see your face. Especially at *the time* I must, for I want to see you lose yourself in me."

And she kept her eyes wide open throughout as if she were trying to impress forever upon every cell of her body her lover's face.

Hal was not disconcerted, for he would not have paid attention to the Archurielite himself knocking on the door. But he noticed, though he did not think of it, that the pupils of her eyes had contracted to a pencil point.

16

The alcoholics in the Haijac Union were sent to H. Therefore, no psychological or narcotic therapies had been worked out for addicts. Hal, frustrated by this fact in his desire to wipe out Jeannette's weakness, went for medicine to the very people who had given her the disease. But he pretended that the cure was for himself.

Fobo said, "There is widespread drinking on Ozagen, but it is light. Our few alcoholics are empathized into normality with the help of medicine, of course. Why don't you let me empathize you?"

"Sorry. My government forbids that." He had given Fobo the same excuse for not inviting the wog into his apartment.

"You have the most forbidding government," said Fobo and went into one of his long, howling laughs.

When he recovered, he said, "You're forbidden to touch liquor, too, but that doesn't hold you back. Well, there's no accounting for inconsistency. Seriously, though, I have just the thing for you. It's called Easyglow. We put it into the daily ration of liquor, slowly increasing the Easyglow and diminishing the alcohol. In two or three weeks, the patient is drinking from a fluid ninety-six percent Easyglow. The taste is much the same; the drinker seldom suspects. Continued treatment eases the patient from his dependence on the alcohol. There is only one drawback."

He paused and said, "The drinker is now addicted to Easyglow!"

He whooped and slapped his thigh and shook his head until his long cartilaginous nose vibrated, and laughed until the tears came.

When he managed to quit laughing and had dried his tears with a starfish-shaped handkerchief, he said, "Really, the peculiar effect of Easyglow is that it opens the patient for discharge of the strains that have driven him to drink. He may then be empathized and at the same time weaned from the stimulant. Since I have no opportunity to slip the stuff to you secretly, I'm taking the chance that you are seriously interested in curing yourself. When you're ready for therapy, tell me."

Hal took the bottle to his apartment. Every day, its contents went quietly and carefully into the beetlejuice he got for Jeannette. He hoped that he was psychologist enough to cure her once the Easyglow took effect.

Although he didn't know it, he was himself being "cured" by Fobo. His almost daily talks with the empathist instilled doubts about the religion and science of the Haijacs. Fobo read the biographies of Isaac Sigmen and the *Works:* the *Pre-Torah, The Western Talmud,* the *Revised Scriptures,* the *Foundations of Serialism, Time and Theology, The Self and the World Line.* Calmly sitting at his table with a glass of juice in his hand, the wog challenged the mathematics of the dunnologists. Hal proved; Fobo disproved. He pointed out that the mathematics was based mainly on false-to-fact assumptions; that Dunne's and Sigmen's reasoning was buttressed by too many false analogies, metaphors, and strained interpretations. Remove the buttresses, and the structure fell.

"Moreover and to continue," Fobo said, "allow and permit me to point out one more in a score of contradictions embodied in your theology. You Sigmenites believe that every person is responsible for any event happening to him, that no one else but the self may be blamed. If you, Hal Yarrow, stumbled on a toy left by some careless child—happy, happy infant with no responsibilities!—and skinned your elbow, you did so because you really wanted to hurt yourself. If you are seriously hurt in an 'accident,' it was no accident; it was you agreeing to actualize a potentiality. Contrarily, you could have agreed with your self not to be involved, and so actualized a different future.

"If you commit a crime, you wish to do so. If you get caught, it is not because you were stupid in the commission of the crime or because the Uzzites were more clever or because circumstances worked out to make you fall into the hands of—what is your vernacular for them, the uzz? No, it was because you wished to be caught; you, somehow, controlled the circumstances.

"If you die, it is because you wanted to die, not because someone pointed a gun at you and pulled the trigger. You died because you willed to intercept the bullet; you agreed with the killer that you could be killed.

"Of course, this philosophy, this belief, is very *shib* for the Sturch, for it relieves them of any blame if they have to chastise or execute or unjustly tax you or in any way take uncivil liberties with you. Obviously, if you did not wish to be chastised or executed or taxed or dealt with in an unfair way, you would not permit it.

"Of course, if you do disagree with the Sturch or try to defy it, you do so because you are trying to realize a pseudofuture, one condemned by the Sturch. You, the individual, can't win.

"Yet, hear and listen to this: You also believe that you yourself have perfect free will to determine the future. But the future has been determined because Sigmen has gone ahead in time and arranged it. Sigmen's brother, Jude Changer, may temporarily disarrange the future and the past, but Sigmen will eventually restore the desired equilibrium.

"Let me ask and question you, how can you yourself determine the future when the future has been determined and forecast by Sigmen? One state or the other may be correct, but not both."

"Well," Hal said, his face hot, his chest feeling as if a heavy weight were on it, his hands shaking, "I have thought of that very question."

"Did you ask anyone?"

"No," Hal said, feeling trapped. "We were allowed to ask questions, of course, of our teachers. But that question was not on the list."

"You mean to tell me that your questions were written out for you and you were confined to those?"

"Well, why not?" Hal said angrily. "Those questions were for our benefit. The Sturch knew from long experience what questions students ask, so it listed them for the less bright."

"Less bright is right," said Fobo. "And I suppose that any questions not on the list were considered too dangerous, too conducive to unrealistic thinking?" Hal nodded miserably.

Fobo went on in his relentless dissection. Worse, far worse than anything he had said were his next words, for they were a personal attack on the sacrosanct self of Sigmen himself.

He said that the Forerunner's biographies and theological writings revealed him to an objective reader as a sexually frigid and woman-hating man with a Messiah complex and paranoid and schizophrenic tendencies which burst through his icy shell from time to time in religious-scientific frenzies and fantasies.

"Other men," Fobo said, "must have stamped their personalities and ideas upon their times. But Sigmen had an advantage over those great leaders who came before him. Because of Earth's rejuvenation serums, he lived long enough, not only to set up his kind of society, but also to consolidate it and weed out its weaknesses. He didn't die until the cement of his social form had hardened."

"But the Forerunner didn't die," Yarrow protested. "He left in time. He is still with us, traveling down the fields of presentation, skipping here and there, now to the past, now to the future. Always, wherever he is needed to turn pseudotime into real time, he is there."

"Ah, yes," Fobo smiled. "That was the reason you went to the ruins, was it not? To check up on a mural which hinted that the Ozagen humans had once been visited by a man from another star? You thought it might have been the Forerunner, didn't you?"

"I still think so," said Hal. "But my report showed that though the man resembled Sigmen somewhat, the evidence was too inconclusive. The Forerunner may or may not have visited this planet a thousand years ago."

"Be that as it may, I maintain your theses are meaningless. You claim that his prophecies came true. I say, first, that they were ambiguously stated. Second, if they have been realized it is because your powerful state-church—which you economically term the Sturch—has made strenuous efforts to fulfill them.

"Furthermore, this pyramidal society of yours—this guardian-angel administration—where every twenty-five families have a *gapt* to supervise their most intimate and minute details, and every twenty-five family-*gapts* have a block-*gapt* at their head, and every fifty block-*gapts* are directed by a supervisor-*gapt*, and so on—this society is based on fear and ignorance and suppression."

Hal, shaken, angered, shocked, would get up to leave. Fobo would call him back and ask him to disprove what he'd said. Hal would let loose a flood of wrath. Sometimes, when he had finished, he would be asked to sit down and continue the discussion. Sometimes, Fobo would lose his temper; they would shout and scream insults. Twice, they fought with fists; Hal got a bloody nose, and Fobo a black eye. Then the wog, weeping, would embrace Hal and ask for his forgiveness, and they would sit down and drink some more until their nerves were calmed.

Hal knew that he should not listen to Fobo, should not allow himself to be in a situation where he could hear such unrealism. But he could not stay away. And, though he hated Fobo for what he said, he derived a strange satisfaction and fascination from the relationship. He could not cut himself off from this being whose tongue cut and flayed him far more painfully than Pornsen's whip ever had.

He told Jeannette of these incidents. She encouraged him to tell them over and over again until he had talked away the stress and strain of grief and hate and doubt. Afterward, there was always love such as he had never thought possible. For the first time, he knew that man and woman could become one flesh. His wife and he had remained outside the circle of each other, but Jeannette knew the geometry that would take him in and the chemistry that would mix his substance with hers.

Always, too, there was the light and the drink. But they did not bother him. Unknown to her, she was now drinking a liquor almost entirely Easyglow. And he had gotten used to the light above their bed. It was one of her quirks. Fear of the dark wasn't behind it, because it was only while making love that she required that the lamp be left on. He didn't understand it. Perhaps she wanted to impress his image on her memory, always to have it if she ever lost bun. If so, let her keep the light.

By its glow he explored her body with an interest that was part sexual and part anthropological. He was delighted and astonished at the many small differences between her and Terran women. There was a small appendage of skin on the roof of her mouth that might have been the rudiment of some organ whose function had been long ago cast aside by evolution. She had twenty-eight teeth; the wisdom teeth were missing. That might or might not have been a characteristic of her mother's people.

He suspected that she had either an extra set of pectoral muscles or else an extraordinarily well developed normal set. Her large and cone-shaped breasts did not sag. They were high and firm and pointed slightly upward: the ideal of feminine beauty so often portrayed through the ages by male sculptors and painters and so seldom existing in nature.

She was not only a pleasure to look at; she was pleasing to be with. At least once a week she would greet him with a new garment. She loved to sew; out of the materials he gave her she fashioned blouses, skirts, and even gowns. Along with the change in dress went new hairdos. She was ever new and ever beautiful, and she made him realize for the first time that a woman could be beautiful. Or perhaps she made him realize that a human being could be beautiful. And a thing of beauty was a joy, if not forever, then for a long time.

His enjoyment of her, and hers of him, was hastened and strengthened by her linguistic fluency. She seemed to have switched from her French to American almost overnight. Within a week she was speaking, within her limited but quickly increasing vocabulary, faster and more expressively than he.

However, his delight in her company made him neglect his duties.

His progress in learning to read Siddo slowed down.

One day, Fobo asked him how he was doing with the books he'd loaned him. Hal confessed that they were too difficult for him—so far. Fobo then gave him a book on evolution which was used in the wog elementary schools.

"Try these. They're two volumes, but they're rather slim in text. The many pictures will enable you to grasp the text more quickly. It's an abridgement for the youngsters by a famous educator, We'enai."

Jeannette had much more time to study than Hal, since she had little to do in the apartment while he was gone during the day. She tackled the new books, and so Hal fell into the lazy habit of allowing her to translate for him. She would first read the Siddo aloud and then translate into American. Or, if her vocabulary failed her, into French.

One evening, she started out energetically enough. But she was sipping beetlejuice between paragraphs, and after a while she began to lose interest in the translating.

She went through the first chapter, which described the formation of the planet and the beginnings of life. In the second chapter, she yawned quite openly and looked at Hal, but he closed his eyes and pretended not to notice. So she read of the rise of the wogs from a prearthropod that had changed its mind and decided to become a chordate. We'enai made some heavy jests about the contrariness of the wogglebugs since that fateful day, and then took up, in the third chapter, the story of mammalian evolution on the other large continent of Ozagen which climaxed in man.

She quoted, " 'But man, like us, had its mimical parasites. One was a different species of the so-called tavern beetle. It, instead of resembling a wog, looked like a man. Like its counterpart, it could fool no intelligent person, but its gift of alcohol made it very acceptable to man. It, too, accompanied its host from primitive times, became an integral part of his civilization, and, finally, according to one theory, a large cause of man's downfall.

" 'Humanity's disappearance from the face of Ozagen is due not only to the tavern beetle, if it was at all. That creature can be controlled. Like most things, it can be abused or its purpose distorted so that it becomes a menace.

" 'This is what man did with it.

" 'He had, it must be noted, an ally to help him in the misuse of the insect. This was another parasite, one of a somewhat different kind; one that was, indeed, our cousin, in a manner speaking.

"'One thing, however, distinguishes it from us, and from man, and from any other animal on this planet with the exception of some very low species. That is, that from the very first fossil evidence we have of it, it was wholly—'"

Jeannette put the book down. "I don't know the next word. Hal, do I have to read this? It's so boring."

"No. Forget it. Read me one of those comics that you and the *Gabriel*'s sailors like so much."

She smiled, a beautiful sight, and she began reading Volume 1037, Book 56, *The Adventures of Leif Magnus, Beloved Disciple of the Forerunner, When He Met the Horror from Arcturus.*

He listened to her efforts to translate the American into the vernacular wog until he grew tired of the banalities of the comic and pulled her down to him.

Always, there was the light left on above them.

Yet, they had their misunderstandings, their disagreements, their conflicts.

Jeannette was neither puppet nor slave. When she did not like something Hal did or said, she was often quick to say so. And, if he replied sarcastically or violently, he was likely to find himself attacked verbally.

Not too long after he had hidden Jeannette in his *puka*, he returned after a long day at the ship with a heavy growth of stubble on his face.

Jeannette, after kissing him, made a face and said, "That hurts; it is like a file. I'll get your cream and rub off your whiskers myself."

"No, don't do that," he said.

"Why not?" she said as she walked toward the unmentionable. "I love to do things for you. And I especially love to make you look nice."

She returned with the can of depilatory in her hand.

"Now, you sit down, and I will do all your work for you. You can think of how much I love you while I'm removing those so-scratchy wires on your face."

"You don't understand, Jeannette. I can't shave. I am a *lamedhian* now, and *lamedhians* must wear beards."

She stopped walking toward him and said, "You *must*? You mean that it is the law, that you will be a criminal if you don't?"

"No, not exactly," he said. "The Forerunner himself never said a word about it, nor has any law been passed making it compulsory. But—it is the custom. And it is a sign of honor, for only a man worthy to wear a *lamedh* is allowed to grow a beard."

"What would happen if a *non-lamedhian* grew one?"

"I don't know," he said, annoyance apparent in his voice. "It has never happened. It's—just one of those things you take for granted. Something only an outsider would think about."

"But a beard is so ugly," she said. "And it scratches my face. I would as soon kiss a pile of bedsprings."

"Then," he said angrily, "you'll either have to learn to kiss bedsprings or learn to get along without kisses. Because I *have* to have a beard!"

"Listen to me," she said, going up close to him. "You don't *have* to! What is the use of being a *lamedhian* if you don't have any more freedom than before, if you must do what is expected of you? Why can't you just ignore the custom?"

Hal began to feel both fury and panic. Panic because he might alienate her so far she would leave and because he knew that if he gave in to her he would be regarded suspiciously by the other *lamedhians* on the *Gabriel*.

As a result, he accused her of being a stupid fool. She replied with equal heat and harshness. They quarreled; the night was half over before she made the first movement toward a reconciliation. Then, it was dawn before they were through proving they loved each other.

In the morning, he shaved. Nothing happened at the *Gabriel* for three days, nobody made any remarks, and he put down to guilt and imagination the strange looks he saw—or thought he saw. Finally, he began to think that either nobody had noticed or else they were so busy with their duties that they did not think it worthwhile to comment. He even began wondering if there were other annoyances connected with being a *lamedhian* which he could do away with.

Then, the morning of the fourth day, he was called to the office of Macneff.

He found the Sandalphon sitting behind his desk and fingering his own beard. Macneff stared with his pale blue eyes at Hal for some time before replying to Hal's greeting.

"Perhaps, Yarrow," he said, "you have been too concerned with your researches among the wogs to think about other things. It is true we live in an abnormal environment here, and we are all concentrating on the day we start the project."

He rose and began pacing back and forth before Hal.

"You surely must know that as a *lamedhian*, you not only have privileges, you have responsibilities?"

"*Shib, abba.*"

Macneff suddenly wheeled on Hal and pointed a long bony finger at him.

"Then, why aren't you growing a beard?" he said loudly. And he glared.

Hal felt himself grow cold, as he had so often when he was a child and his *gapt*, Pornsen, had made this same maneuver toward him. And he felt the same mental confusion.

"Why, I—I—"

"We must strive not only to attain the *lamedh*, we must strive to continue to be worthy of it. Purity and purity alone will make us succeed, unending effort to be pure!"

"Your pardon, *abba*," said Hal, his voice quivering. "But I am making a never-ending effort to be pure."

He dared to look the Sandalphon in the eyes when he said that, though where he got the courage he did not know. To lie so outrageously, he who was living in unreality, to lie in the presence of the great and pure Sandalphon!

"However," Hal continued, "I did not know that shaving would have anything to do with my purity. There is nothing in *The Western Talmud* or any of the Forerunner's books about the reality or unreality of a beard."

"Are you telling me what is in the scriptures?" shouted Macneff.

"No, of course not. But, what I said is true, isn't it?"

Macneff resumed his pacing, and he said, "We must be pure, must be pure. And even the slightest hint of pseudofuture, the smallest departure from reality, may dirty us. Yes, Sigmen never said anything about this. But it has long been recognized that only the pure are worthy to emulate the Forerunner by having a beard. Therefore, to be pure, we must look pure."

"I agree with you wholeheartedly," said Hal.

He was beginning to find courage in himself, a firmness. It had suddenly occurred to him that he felt so shaken because he was reacting to Macneff as he had to Pornsen. But Pornsen was dead, defeated, his ashes thrown to the wind. And it had been Hal himself who had scattered them at the ceremony.

"Under ordinary circumstances, I would let my whiskers grow," he said. "But I am living among the wogs now so I may do more effective espionage, besides conducting my researches. And I have found out that the wogs regard a beard as an abomination; they have no beards themselves, you know. They do not understand why we let ours grow if we have means to remove them. And they feel uneasy and disgusted when in the presence of a bearded man. I can't gain their confidence if I have one.

"However, I plan to grow one the moment the project is begun."

"Hmm!" said Macneff, fingering the hairs on his face. "You may have something there. After all, these are unusual circumstances. But why didn't you tell me?"

"You are so busy, from morning to bedtime, that I did not want to bother you," said Hal. He was wondering if Macneff would take the time and trouble to investigate the truth of his statement. For the wogs had never said one word to Hal about beards. He had been inspired to make his excuse when he remembered having read about the initial reactions of the American Indians to the facial growth of white men.

Macneff, after a few more words on the importance of keeping pure, dismissed Hal.

And Hal, shaking from the reaction of the lecture, went home. There, he had a few drinks to calm himself, then a few more to uninhibit himself for the supper with Jeannette. He had discovered that if he drank enough, he could overcome the disgust he felt on seeing food go into her naked mouth.

17

One day, Yarrow, returning from the market with a large box, said, "You've really been putting away the groceries lately. You're not eating for two? Or maybe three?"

She paled. "*Maw choo!* Do you know what you're saying?"

He put the box on a table and grabbed her shoulders.

"*Shib.* I do. Jeannette, I've been thinking about that very thing for a long time, but I haven't said anything. I didn't want to worry you. Tell me, are you?"

She looked him straight in the eye, but her body was shaking. "Oh, no. It is impossible!"

"Why should it be?"

"*Fi.* But I know—don't ask me how—that it cannot be. But you must never say things like that. Not even joking. I can't stand it."

He pulled her close and said over her shoulder, "Is it because you can't? Because you know you'll never bear my children?"

Her thick, faintly perfumed hair nodded.

"I know. Don't ask me how I know."

He held her at arm's length again.

"Listen, Jeannette. I'll tell you what's been troubling you. You and I are of different species. Your mother and father were, too. Yet they had children. However, you may know that the ass and the mare have young, too, but the mule is sterile. The lion and the tigress may breed, but the liger or tigon can't. Isn't that right? You're afraid you're a mule!"

She put her head on his chest; tears fell on his shirt.

He said, "Let's be real about this, honey. Maybe you are. So what? Forerunner knows that our situation is bad enough without a baby to complicate it. We'll be lucky if you are . . . uh . . . well, we have each other, haven't we? That's all I want. You."

He couldn't keep from being reflective as he dried her tears and kissed her and helped her put the food in the refrigerator.

The quantities of groceries and milk she had been consuming were more than a normal amount, especially the milk. There had been no telltale change in her superb figure. She could not eat that much without some kind of effect. A month passed. He watched her closely. She ate enormously. Nothing happened.

Yarrow put it down to his ignorance of her alien metabolism.

Another month. Hal was just leaving the ship's library when Turnboy, the historian *joat*, stopped him.

"The rumor is that the techs have finally made the globin-locking molecule," the historian said. "I think that this time the grapevine's right. A conference is called for fifteen hundred."

"*Shib.*"

Hal kept his despair out of his voice.

When the meeting broke up at 1650, it left him with sagging shoulders. The virus was already in production. In a week, a large enough supply would be made to fill the disseminators of six prowler torpedoes. The plan was to release them to wipe out the city of Siddo. The prowlers would fly in spirals whose range would expand until a large territory was covered. Eventually, as the prowlers returned for reloading and then went out again, the entire planet of wogs would be slain.

When he got home, he found Jeannette lying in bed, her hair a black corona on the pillow. She smiled weakly.

He forgot his mood in a thrill of concern.

"What's the matter, Jeannette?"

He laid his hand on her forehead. The skin was dry, hot, and rough.

"I don't know. I haven't been feeling really well for two weeks, but I didn't complain. I thought I'd get over it. Today, I felt so bad I just had to go back to bed after breakfast."

"We'll get you well."

He sounded confident. Inside himself, he was lost. If she had contracted a serious disease, she could get no doctor, no medicine.

For the next few days she continued to lie in bed. Her temperature fluctuated from 99.5 in the morning to 100.2 at night. Hal attended her as ably as he could. He put wet towels and ice bags on her head and gave her aspirin. She had stopped eating so much food; all she wanted was liquid. She was always asking for milk. Even the beetlejuice and the cigarettes were turned down.

Her illness was bad enough, but her silences stung Yarrow into a frenzy. As long as he had known her, she had chattered lightly, merrily, amusingly. She could be quiet, but it was with an interested wordlessness. Now she let him talk; and when he quit, she did not fill his silence with questions or comments.

In an effort to arouse her, he told her of his plan to steal a gig and take her back to her jungle home. A light came into her dulled eyes; the brown looked shiny for the first time. She even sat up while he put a map of the continent on her lap. She indicated the general area where she had lived, and then she described the mountain range that rose from the jungle and the tableland on its top where her aunts and sisters lived in the ruins of an ancient metropolis.

Hal sat down at the little hexagon-shaped tabletop by the bed and worked out the coordinates from the maps. Now and then, he glanced up. She was lying on her side, her white and delicate shoulder rising from her nightgown, her eyes large in the shadows around them.

"All I have to do is steal a little key," he said. "You see, the meter gauge on a gig is set at zero before every flight from the field. The boat will run fifty kilometers on manual. But, once the tape passes fifty, the gig automatically stops and sends out a location signal. That's to keep anybody from running away. However, the autos can be unlocked and the signal turned off. A little key will do it. I can get it. Don't worry."

"You must love me very much."

"You're *shib* as *shib* I do!"

He rose and kissed her. Her mouth, once so soft and dewy, felt dry and hard. It was almost as if the skin were turning to horn.

He returned to his calculations. An hour later, a sigh from her made him look up. Her eyes were closed and her lips were slightly open. Sweat ran down her face.

He hoped her fever had broken. No. The mercury had risen to 100.3.

She said something.

He bent down.

"What?"

She was muttering in an unknown language, the speech of her mother's people. Delirious.

Hal swore. He had to act. No matter what the consequences. He ran into the bathroom, shook from a bottle a ten-grain rockabye tablet, returned, and propped Jeannette up. With difficulty he managed to get her to wash the pill down with a glass of water.

After he locked her bedroom door, he put on a hood and cloak and walked fast to the nearest wog pharmacy. There he purchased three 20-gauge needles, three syringes, and some anti-coagulant. Back in his apartment, he tried to insert the needle in her arm vein. The point refused to go in until the fourth attempt when, in a fit of exasperation, he pressed hard.

During none of the jabbings did she open her eyes or jerk her arm.

When the first fluid crept into the glass tube, he gasped with relief. Though he hadn't known it, he had been biting his lip and holding his breath. Suddenly, he knew that he had for the last month been pushing a horrible suspicion back to the outlands of his mind. Now, he realized the thought had been ridiculous.

The blood was red.

He tried to arouse her in order to get a specimen of urine. She twisted her mouth over strange syllables, then lapsed back into sleep or a coma—he didn't know which. In an anguish of despair, he slapped her face, again and again, hoping he could bring her to. He swore once more, for he realized all at once that he should have gotten the specimen before giving her the rockabye. How stupid could he get! He wasn't thinking straight; he was too excited over her condition and what he had to do at the ship.

He made some very strong coffee and managed to get part of it down her. The rest dribbled down her chin and soaked her gown.

Either the caffeine or his desperate tone awoke her, for she opened her eyes long enough to look at him while he explained what he wanted her to do and where he was going afterward. After he had gotten the urine into a previously boiled jar, he wrapped the syringes and jar in a handkerchief and dropped them into the cloak pocket.

He had wristphoned the *Gabriel* for a gig. A horn beeped outside. He took another look at Jeannette, locked the bedroom door, and ran down the stairs. The gig hovered above the curb. He entered, sat down, and punched the GO button. The boat rose to a thousand feet and then flashed at an 11-degree angle toward the park where the ship squatted.

The medical section was empty, except for one orderly. The fellow dropped his comic and jumped to his feet.

"Take it easy," said Hal. "I just want to use the Labtech. And I don't want to be bothered with making out triplicate forms. This is a little personal matter, see?"

Hal had taken off his cloak, so the orderly could see the bright golden *lamedh*.

"*Shib*," the orderly grunted.

Hal gave him two cigarettes.

"Geez, thanks." The orderly lit a cigarette, sat down, and picked up *The Forerunner and Delilah in the Wicked City of Gaza.*

Yarrow went around the corner of the Labtech, where the orderly couldn't see him, and set the proper dials. After he inserted his specimens, he sat down. Within a few seconds, he jumped up and began pacing back and forth. Meanwhile, the huge cube of the Labtech purred like a contented cat as it digested its strange food. A half-hour later, it rumbled once and then flashed a green light: ANALYSIS COMPLETE.

Hal pressed a button. Like a tongue out of a metal mouth, a long tape slid out. He read the code. Urine was normal. No infection there. Also normal were the pH and the blood count.

He hadn't been sure the "eye" would recognize the cells in her blood. However, the chances had been strong that her red cells would be Terranlike. Why not? Evolution, even on planets separated by light-years, follows parallel paths; the biconcave disk is the most efficient form for carrying the maximum of oxygen.

Or at least he'd thought so until he'd seen the corpuscles of an Ozagenian.

The machine chattered. More tape. Unknown hormone! Similar

in molecular structure to the parathyroid hormone primarily concerned in the control of calcium metabolism.

What did that mean? Could the mysterious substance loosed in her bloodstream be the cause of her trouble?

More clicks. The calcium content of the blood was 40 milligram percent.

Strange. Such an abnormally high percentage should mean that the renal threshold was passed and that an excess of calcium should be "spilling" into the urine. Where was it going?

The Labtech flashed a red light: FINISHED.

He took a hematology textbook down from the shelf and opened it to the Ca section. When he quit reading, he straightened his shoulders. New hope? Perhaps. Her case sounded as if she had a form of hypercalcemia, which was manifested by any number of diseases ranging from rickets and steomalacia to chronic hypertrophic arthritis. Whatever she had, she was suffering from a malfunction of the parathyroid glands.

The next move was to the Pharm machine. He punched three buttons, dialed a number, waited for two minutes, and then lifted a little door at waist level. A tray slid out. On it was a cellophane sheath containing a hypodermic needle and a tube holding 30 cubic centimeters of a pale blue fluid. It was Jesper's serum, a "one-shot" readjustor of the parathyroid.

Hal put on his cloak, stuck the package in the inside pocket, and strode out. The orderly didn't even look up.

The next step was the weapons room. There he gave the storekeeper an order—made out in triplicate—for one 1 mm. automatic and a clip of one hundred explosive cartridges. The keeper only glanced over the forged signatures—he, too, was awed by the *lamedh*—and unlocked the door. Hal took the gun, which he could easily hide in the palm of his hand, and stuck it in his pants pocket.

At the key room, two corridors away, he repeated the crime. Or rather, he tried to.

Moto, the officer on duty, looked at the papers, hesitated, and said, "I'm sorry. My orders are to check on any requests with the Chief Uzzite. That won't be possible for about an hour, though. He's in conference with the Archurielite."

Hal picked up his papers.

"Never mind. My business'll hold. Be back in the morning."

On the way home, he planned what he would do. After injecting

Jesper's serum into Jeannette, he would move her into the gig. The floor beneath the gig's control panel would have to be ripped up, two wires would be unhooked, and one connected to another lead. That would remove the fifty-mile limit. Unfortunately, it would also set off an alarm back in the *Gabriel.*

He hoped that he could take off straight up, level off, and dive behind the range of hills to the west of Siddo. The hills would deflect the radar. The autopilot could be set long enough for him to demolish the box that would be sending out the signal by which the *Gabriel* might track him down.

After that, with the gig hedgehopping, he could hope to be free until daybreak. Then, he'd submerge in the nearest lake or river deep enough until nightfall. During the darkness, he could rise and speed toward the tropics. If his radar showed any signs of pursuit, he could plunge again into a body of water. Fortunately, there was no sonar equipment on the *Gabriel.*

He left the long needle-shaped gig parked by the curb. His feet pounded the stairs. The key missed the hole the first two tries. He slammed the door without bothering to lock it again.

"Jeannette!"

Suddenly, he was afraid that she might have gotten up while delirious and somehow opened the doors and wandered out.

A low moan answered him. He unlocked the bedroom door and shoved it open. She was lying with her eyes wide.

"Jeannette. Do you feel better?"

"No. Worse. Much worse."

"Don't worry, baby. I've got just the medicine that'll put new life in you. In a couple of hours you'll be sitting up and yelling for steaks. And you won't even want to touch that milk. You'll be drinking your Easyglow by the gallon. And then—"

He faltered as he saw her face. It was a stony mask of distress, like the grotesque and twisted wooden masks of the Greek tragedians.

"Oh, no . . . *no!*" she moaned. "What did you say? Easyglow?" Her voice rose. "Is *that* what you've been giving me?"

"*Shib*, Jeannette. Take it easy. You liked it. What's the difference? The point is that we're going—"

"Oh, Hal, Hal! What have you done?"

Her pitiful face tore at him. Tears were falling; if ever a stone could weep, it was weeping now.

He turned and ran into the kitchen where he took out the sheath, removed the contents, and inserted the needle in the tube. He went back into the bedroom. She said nothing as he thrust the point into her vein. For a moment, he was afraid the needle would break. The skin was almost brittle.

"This stuff cures Earthpeople in a jiffy," he said, with what he hoped was a cheery bedside manner.

"Oh, Hal, come here. It's—it's too late now." He withdrew the needle, rubbed alcohol on the break, and put a pad on it. Then he dropped to his knees by the bed and kissed her. Her lips were leathery.

"Hal, do you love me?"

"Won't you ever believe me? How many times must I tell you?"

"No matter what you'll find out about me?"

"I know all about you."

"No, you don't. You can't. Oh, Great Mother, if only I'd told you! Maybe you'd have loved me just as much, anyway. Maybe—"

"Jeannette! What's the matter?"

Her lids had closed. Her body shook in a spasm. When the violent trembling passed, she whispered with stiff lips. He bent his head to hear her.

"What did you say? Jeannette! Speak!"

He shook her. The fever must have died, for her shoulder was cold. And hard.

The words came low and slurring.

"Take me to my aunts and sisters. They'll know what to do. Not for me . . . but for the—"

"What do you mean?"

"Hal, will you always love—"

"Yes, yes. You know that! We've got more important things to do than talk about that."

If she heard him, she gave no sign. Her head was tilted far back with her exquisite nose pointed at the ceiling. Her lids and mouth were closed, and her hands were by her side, palms up. The breasts were motionless. Whatever breath she might have was too feeble to stir them.

18

Hal pounded on Fobo's door until it opened.

The empathist's wife said, "Hal, you startled me!"

"Where's Fobo?"

"He's at a college board meeting."

"I've got to see him at once."

Abasa yelled after him, "If it's important, go ahead! Those meetings bore him, anyway!"

By the time Yarrow had taken the steps three at a time and beelined across the nearby campus, his lungs were on fire. He didn't slacken his pace; he hurtled up the steps of the administration building and burst into the board room.

When he tried to speak, he had to stop and suck in deep breaths.

Fobo jumped out of his chair.

"What's up?"

"You—you've—got to come. Matter—life—death!"

"Excuse me, gentlemen," Fobo said.

The ten wogs nodded their heads and resumed the conference. The empathist put on his cloak and skullcap with its artificial antennae and led Hal out.

"Now, what is it?"

"Listen. I've got to trust you. I know you can't promise me anything. But I think you won't turn me in to my people. You're a real person, Fobo."

"Get to the point, my friend."

"Listen. You wogs are as advanced as we in endocrinology, even if you lag way behind in other sciences. And you've got an advantage. You have made some medical examinations and tests on her. You should know something about her anatomy and physiology and metabolism. You—"

"Jeannette? Oh, Jeannette Rastignac! The *lalitha*!"

"Yes. I've been hiding her in my apartment."

"I know."

"You know? But how? I mean—"

The wog put his hand on Hal's shoulder.

"There's something you should know. I meant to tell you tonight after I got home. This morning a man named Art Hunah Pukui rented an apartment in a building across the street. He claimed he wanted to live among us so he could learn our language and our mores more swiftly.

"But he's spent most of his time in this building carrying around a case which I imagine contains various devices to enable him to hear from a distance the sounds in your apartment. However, the landlord kept an eye on him, so he wasn't able to plant any of his devices."

"Pukui is an Uzzite."

"If you say so. Right now he's in his apartment watching this building through a powerful telescope."

"And he could be listening to us right now, too," Hal said. "His instruments are extremely sensitive. Still, the walls are heavily sound-proofed. Anyway, forget about him!"

Fobo followed him into his rooms. The wog felt Jeannette's forehead and tried to lift her lid to look at her eye. It would not bend.

"Hmm! Calcification of the outer skin layer is far advanced."

With one hand he threw the sheet from her figure and with the other he grabbed her gown by the neckline and ripped the thin cloth down the middle. The two parts fell to either side. She lay nude, as silent and pale and beautiful as a sculptor's masterpiece.

Her lover gave a little cry at what seemed like a violation. But he said nothing because he realized that Fobo's move was medical. In any case, the wog would not have been sexually interested.

Puzzled, he watched. Fobo had tapped his fingertips against her flat belly and then put his ear against it. When he stood up, he shook his head.

"I won't deceive you, Hal. Though we'll do the best we can, we may not be good enough. She'll have to go to a surgeon. If we can cut her eggs out before they hatch, that, plus the serum you gave her, may reverse the effect and pull her out."

"Eggs?"

"I'll tell you later. Wrap her up. I'll run upstairs and phone Dr. Kuto."

Yarrow folded a blanket around her. Then he rolled her over. She was as stiff as a show-window dummy. He covered her face. The stony look was too much for him.

His wristphone shrilled. Automatically, he reached to flick the stud and just in time drew his hand back. It shrilled loudly, insistently. After a few seconds of agony, he decided that if he didn't answer, he would stir up their suspicion far faster.

"Yarrow!"

"*Shib?*"

"Report to the Archurielite. You will be given fifteen minutes."

"*Shib.*"

Fobo came back in and said, "What're you going to do?"

Hal squared his mouth and said, "You take her by the shoulders, and I'll carry her feet. Rigid as she is, we won't need a stretcher."

As they carried her down the steps, he said, "Can you hide us after the operation, Fobo? We won't be able to use the gig now."

"Don't worry," the wog said enigmatically over his shoulder. "The Earthmen are going to be too busy to run after you."

It took sixty seconds to get her into the gig, hop to the hospital, and get her out.

Hal said, "Let's put her on the ground a minute. I've got to set the gig on auto and send her back to the *Gabriel*. That way, at least, they won't know where I am."

"No. Leave it here. You may be able to use it afterward."

"After what?"

"Later. Ah, there's Kuto."

In the waiting room, Hal paced back and forth and puffed Merciful Seraphim out in chains of smoke. Fobo sat on a chair and rubbed his bald pate and the thick golden corkscrew fuzz on the back of his head.

"All of this might have been avoided," he said unhappily. "If I had known the *lalitha* was living with you, I might have guessed why you wanted the Easyglow. Though not necessarily so. Anyway, I didn't find out until two days ago that she was in your apartment. And I was too busy with Project Earthman to think much about her."

"Project Earthman?" said Hal. "What's that?"

Fobo's V-in-V lips parted in a smile to reveal the sharp serrated ridges of bone.

"I can't tell you now because your colleagues on the *Gabriel* might, just possibly, learn about it from you before it takes effect. However, I think I can safely tell you that we know about your plan for spreading the deadly globin-locking molecule through our atmosphere."

"There was a time when I would have been horrified to learn that," Hal said. "But now it doesn't matter."

"You don't want to know how we found out about it?"

"I suppose so," Hal said dully.

"When you asked us for samples of blood, you aroused our suspicion."

He tapped the end of his absurdly long nose.

"We can't read your thoughts, of course. But concealed in this flesh are two antennae. They are very sensitive; evolution has not dulled our sense of smell as it has among you Terrans. They allow us to detect, through odor, very slight changes in the metabolism of others. When we were asked by one of your emissaries to donate blood for their scientific research, we smelled a—shall I call it *furtive*?—emanation. We finally did give you the blood. But it was that of a barnyard creature which uses copper in its blood cells. We wogs use magnesium as the oxygen-carrying element in our blood cells."

"Our virus is useless!"

"Yes. Of course, in time, when you'd learned to read our writing and got hold of our textbooks, you'd have discovered the truth. But before that happened it would be too late, I trust, hope, and pray, for the truth to be of any importance or consequence.

"Meanwhile, we've determined just what you were up to. I'm sorry to say that we had to use force to do it, but since our survival was at stake and you Earthmen were the aggressor, the means justified the ends. A week ago we finally found an opportunity to catch a biochemist and his *gapt* while they were visiting a laboratory in the college. We injected a drug and hypnotized them. It was difficult getting the truth out of them but only because of the language barrier. However, I've learned a certain amount of American.

"We were horrified. But not really surprised. In fact, because we suspected something was afoot that we wouldn't like, and from the very first contact, we were ready to take action. So, from the first day your ship landed, we've been busy. The vessel, as you know, is directly—"

"Why didn't you hypnotize me?" Hal said. "You could have done it easily and a long time ago."

"Because we doubted that you'd be privy to anything that had to do with our blood. Anyway, we needed someone who had the necessary technical knowledge. However, we've been watching you, though not so successfully, since you managed to sneak in the *lalitha* past us."

"How did you find out about Jeannette?" Hal said. "And may I see her?"

"I am sorry; I must say no to your second question," said Fobo.

"As for the first, it was not until two days ago that we managed to develop a listening device sensitive enough to justify installing it in your rooms. As you know, we are far behind you in some departments."

"I searched the *puka* every day for a long time," said Hal. "Then, when I learned of the stage of development of your electronics, I quit."

"Meanwhile, our scientists have been busy," said Fobo. "The visit of you Earthmen has stimulated us to research in several fields."

A nurse entered and said, "Phone, Doctor."

Fobo left.

Yarrow paced back and forth and smoked another cigarette. Within a minute, Fobo returned.

He said, "We're going to have company. One of my colleagues, who is watching the ship, tells me Macneff and two Uzzites left in a gig. They should be arriving at the hospital any second now."

Yarrow stopped in midstride. His jaw dropped. "Here? How'd they find out?"

"I imagine they have means about which they failed to inform you. Don't be afraid."

Hal stood motionless. The cigarette, unnoticed, burned until it seared his fingers. He dropped it and crushed it beneath his sole.

Boot heels clicked in the corridor.

Three men entered. One was a tall and gaunt ghost—Macneff, the Archurielite. The others were short and broad-shouldered and clad in black. Their meaty hands, though empty, were hooked, ready to dart into their pockets. Their heavy-lidded eyes stabbed at Fobo and then at Hal.

Macneff strode up to the *joat*. His pale blue eyes glared; his lipless mouth was drawn back in a skull's smile.

"You unspeakable degenerate!" he shouted.

His arm flashed, and the whip, jerked out of his belt, cracked. Thin red marks appeared on Yarrow's white face and began oozing blood.

"You will be taken back to Earth in chains and there exhibited as an example of the worst pervert, traitor, and—and—!"

He drooled, unable to find words.

"You—who have passed the Elohimeter, who are supposed to be so pure—you have lusted after and lain with an insect!"

"What!"

"Yes. With a thing that, is even lower than a beast of the field! What even Moses did not think of when he forbade union between man and beast, what even the Forerunner could not have guessed when he reaffirmed the law and set the utmost penalty for it—you have done! You, Hal Yarrow, the pure, the *lamedh*-wearer!"

Fobo rose and said in a deep voice, "Might I suggest and stress that you are not quite right in your zoological classification? It is not the class of *Insecta* but the class of the *Chordata pseudarthropoda*, or words to that effect."

Hal said, "What?" He could not think.

The wog growled, "Shut up. Let me talk."

He swung to face Macneff. "You know about her?"

"You are *shib* that I know her! Yarrow thought he was getting away with something. But, no matter how clever these unrealists are, they're always tripped up. In this case, it was his asking Turnboy about those Frenchmen that fled Earth. Turnboy, who is very zealous in his attitude toward the Sturch, reported the conversation. It lay among my papers for quite a while. When I came across it, I turned it over to the psychologists. They told me that the *joat's* question was a deviation from the pattern expected of him; a thing totally irrelevant unless it was connected to something we didn't know about him,

"Moreover, his refusal to grow a beard was enough to make us suspicious. A man was put on his trail. He saw Yarrow buying twice the groceries he should have. Also, when you wogs learned the tobacco habit from us and began making cigarettes too, he bought them from you. The conclusion was obvious. He had a female in his apartment.

"We didn't think it'd be a wog female, for she wouldn't have to stay hidden. Therefore, she must be human. But we couldn't imagine how she got here on Ozagen. It was impossible for him to have stowed her away on the *Gabriel.* She must either have come here in a different ship or be descended from people who had.

"It was Yarrow's talk with Turnboy that furnished the clue. Obviously, the French had landed here and she was a descendant. We didn't know how the *joat* had found her. It wasn't important. We'll find out, anyhow."

"You're due to find out some other things, too," Fobo said calmly. "How did you discover she wasn't human?"

Yarrow muttered, "I've got to sit down."

19

He swayed to the wall and sank into a chair. One of the Uzzites started to move toward him. Macneff waved the man back and said, "Turnboy got a wog to read to him a book on the history of man on Ozagen. He came across so many references to the *lalitha* that the suspicion was bound to rise that the girl might be one.

"Last week one of the wog physicians, while talking to Turnboy, mentioned that he had once examined a *lalitha*. Later, he said, she had run away. It wasn't hard for us to guess where she was hiding!"

"My boy," said Fobo, turning to Hal, "didn't you read We'enai's book?"

Hal shook his head. "We started it, but Jeannette mislaid it."

"And doubtless saw to it that you had other things to think of . . . they are good at diverting a man's mind. Why not? That is their purpose in life.

"Hal, I'll explain. The *lalitha* are the highest example of mimetic parasitism known. Also, they are unique among sentient beings. Unique in that all are female.

"If you'd read on in We'enai, you'd have found that fossil evidence shows that about the time that Ozagenian man was still an insectivorous marmoset-like creature, he had in his family group not only his own females but the females of another phylum. These animals looked and probably stank enough like the females of prehomo marmoset to be able to live and mate with them. They seemed mammalian, but dissection would have indicated their pseudoarthropodal ancestry.

"It's reasonable to suppose that these precursors of the *lalitha* were man's parasites long before the marmosetoid stage. They may have met him when he first crawled out of the sea. Originally bisexual, they became female. And they adapted their shape, through an unknown evolutionary process, to that of the reptile's and primitive mammal's. And so on.

"What we do know is that the *lalitha* was Nature's most amazing experiment in parasitism and parallel evolution. As man metamorphosed into higher forms, so the *lalitha* kept pace with him. All female, mind you, depending upon the male of another phylum for the continuance of the species.

"It is astonishing the way they became integrated into the prehuman societies, the pithecanthropoid and neanderthaloid steps. Only when *Homo sapiens* developed did their troubles begin. Some families and tribes accepted them; others killed them. So they resorted to artifice and disguised themselves as human women. A thing not hard to do—unless they became pregnant.

"In which case, they died."

Hal groaned and put his hands over his face.

"Painful but real, as our acquaintance Macneff would say," said Fobo. "Of course—such a condition required a secret sorority. In those societies where the *lalitha* was forced to camouflage, she would, once pregnant, have to leave. And perish in some hidden place among her kind, who would then take care of the nymphs"—here Hal shuddered—"until they were able to go into human cultures. Or else be introduced as foundlings or changelings.

"You'll find quite a tribal lore about them—fables and myths make them central or peripheral characters quite frequently. They were regarded as witches, demons, or worse.

"With the introduction of alcohol in primitive times, a change for the better came to the *lalitha*. Alcohol made them sterile. At the same time, barring accident, disease, or murder, it made them *immortal*."

Hal took his hands off his face. "You—you mean Jeannette would have lived—forever? That I cost her—that?"

"She could have lived many thousands of years. We know that some did. What's more, they did not suffer physical deterioration but always remained at the physiological age of twenty-five. Let me explain all this. In due order. Some of what I'm going to tell you will distress you. But it must be said.

"The long lives of the *lalitha* resulted in their being worshipped as goddesses. Sometimes, they lived so long they survived the downfall of mighty nations that had been small tribes when the *lalitha* first joined their groups. The *lalitha*, of course, became the repositories of wisdom, wealth, and power. Religions were established in which the *lalitha* was the immortal goddess, and the ephemeral kings and priests were her lovers.

"Some cultures outlawed the *lalitha*. But these either directed the nations they ruled into conquering the people that rejected them or else infiltrated and eventually ruled as powers behind the throne. Being always very beautiful, they became the wives and mistresses of the most influential men. They competed with the human female and beat them at their own game, hands down. In the *lalitha*, Nature wrought the complete female.

"And so they gained mastery over their lovers. But not over themselves. Though they belonged to a secret society in the beginning, they soon enough split up. They began to identify themselves with the nations they ruled and to use their countries against the others. Moreover, their long lives resulted in younger *lalitha* becoming impatient. Result: assassinations, struggles for power, and so on.

"Also, their influence was technologically too stabilizing. They tried to keep the *status quo* in every aspect of culture, and as a result the human cultures had a tendency to eliminate all new and progressive ideas and the men that espoused them."

Fobo paused, then said, "You must realize that most of this is speculative. It's based largely on what the very few human natives we've captured in the jungle have told us. However, we recently discovered some pictographs in a long-buried temple that gave us additional information. So we think our reconstruction of the history of the *lalitha* is valid.

"Oh, by the way, Jeannette didn't have to run away from us. After we'd learned all we could from her, we'd have returned her to her family. We told her we would, but she didn't believe us."

A wog nurse came out of the operating room and said something to the empathist in a low voice.

Macneff walked by her and obviously tried to eavesdrop. But as the nurse was speaking in Ozagenian, which he did not understand, he continued pacing back and forth. Hal wondered why he, Hal, had not been dragged away at once, why the priest had waited to hear Fobo out. Then, a flash of insight told Hal that Macneff wanted him to hear all about Jeannette and realize the enormity of his deeds.

The nurse went back into the operating room. The Archurielite said loudly, "Is the beast of the fields dead yet?"

Hal shook as if he had been struck when he heard the word *dead*. But Fobo ignored the priest.

He spoke to Hal. "Your larv—that is, your children, have been removed. They are in an incubator. They are . . ." he hesitated—"eating well. They will live."

Hal knew from his tone that it was no use asking about the mother. Big tears rolled from Fobo's round blue eyes.

"You won't understand what has happened, Hal, unless you comprehend the *lalitha's* unique method of reproduction. Three things the *lalitha* needs to reproduce. One thing must precede the other two. That primary event is to be infected at the age of puberty by another adult *lalitha*. This infection is needed to transmit genes."

"Genes?" said Hal. Even in his shock, he could feel interest and amazement at what Fobo was telling him.

"Yes. Since *lalitha* receive no genes from the human males, they must exchange hereditary material between each other. Yet—they must use man as a means.

"Allow and permit me to elucidate. An adult *lalitha* has three so-called banks of genes. Two are duplicates of each other's chromosomal stuff.

"The third, I will explain in a moment.

"A *lalitha's* uterus contains ova, the genes of which are duplicated in the bodies of microscopic wrigglers formed in the giant salivary glands in a *lalitha's* mouth. These wrigglers—salivary ova—are continually released by the adult.

"The adult *lalitha* pass genes by means of these invisible creatures; they infect each other as if the carriers of heredity were diseases. They cannot escape it; a kiss, a sneeze, a touch, will do it.

"Preadolescent *lalitha*, however, seem to have a natural immunity against being infected by these wrigglers.

"The adult *lalitha*, once infected, then builds up antibodies against reception of salivary ova from a second *lalitha*.

"Meanwhile, the first wrigglers she is exposed to have made their way through the bloodstream, the intestinal tract, the skin, boring, floating, until they arrive at the uterus of the host.

"There, the salivary ovum unites with the uterine ovum. Fusion of the two produces a zygote. At this point, fertilization is suspended. True, all genetic data needed to produce a new *lalitha* is provided. All except the genes for the specific features of the face of the baby. This data will be given by the male human lover of the *lalitha*. Not, however, until the conjunction of two more events.

"These two must occur simultaneously. One is excitation by orgasm. The other is stimulation of the photokinetic nerves. One cannot take place without the other. Neither can the last two come about unless the first happens. Apparently, fusion of the two ova causes a chemical change in the *lalitha* which then makes her capable of orgasm and fully develops the photokinetic nerves."

Fobo paused and cocked his head as if he were listening for something outside. Hal, who knew from familiarity with the wogs what their facial expressions meant, felt that Fobo was waiting for something important to happen. Very important. And, whatever it was, it involved the Earthmen.

Suddenly, he thrilled to the knowledge that he was on the wogs' side! He was no longer an Earthman, or, at least, not a Haijac.

"Are you sufficiently confused?" said Fobo.

"Sufficiently," replied Hal. "For instance, I have never heard of the photokinetic nerves."

"The photokinetic nerves are the exclusive property of the *lalitha*. They run from the retina of the eye, along with the optic nerves, to the brain. But the photokinetic nerves descend the spinal column and leave its base to enter the uterus. The uterus is not that of the human female. Do not even compare them. You might say that the *lalitha* uterus is the darkroom of the womb. Where the photograph of the father's face is biologically developed. And, in a manner of speaking, attached to the daughters' faces.

"This is done by means of photogenes. These are in the third bank of which I spoke. You see, during intercourse, at the moment of orgasm, an electrochemical change, or series of changes, takes place in that nerve. By the light that the *lalitha* requires during intercourse if she is to experience orgasm, the face of the male is photographed. An arc-reflex makes it impossible for her to close her eyes at that time. Moreover, if she throws her arm over her eyes, she at once loses the orgasm.

"You must have noticed during your intercourse with her, for I'm sure she insisted you keep your eyes open, that her pupils contracted to a pinpoint. That contraction was an involuntary reflex which would narrow her field of vision to your face. Why? So the photokinetic nerves could receive data from only your face. Thus, the information about the specific color of your hair could be passed on to the bank of photogenes. We don't know the exact manner in which the photokinetic nerves transmit this data. But they do it.

"Your hair is auburn. Somehow, this information becomes known to the bank. The bank then rejects the other genes controlling other colors of hair. The 'auburn' gene is duplicated and attached to the zygote's genetic makeup. And so with the other genes that fix the other features of the face-to-be. The shape of the nose—modified to be feminine—is selected by choosing the correct combination of genes in the bank. This is duplicated, and the duplicates are then incorpo-rated into the zygote—"

"You hear that?" shouted Macneff in an exultant voice. "You have begat larvae! Monsters of an unholy unreal union! Insect children! And they will have your face as witness of this revolting carnality—"

"Of course, I am no connoisseur of human features," Fobo inter-rupted. "But the young man's strike me as vigorous and handsome. In a human way, you understand."

He turned to Hal. "Now you see why Jeannette desired light. And why she pretended alcoholism. As long as she had enough liquor before copulation, the photokinetic nerve—very susceptible to alcohol—would be anesthetized. Thus, orgasm but no pregnancy. No death from the life within her. But when you diluted the beetlejuice with Easy-glow . . . unknowing, of course—"

Macneff burst into a high-pitched laughter. "What irony! Truly it has been said that the wages of unrealism are death!"

20

Fobo spoke loudly. "Go ahead, Hal. Cry, if you like. You'll feel better. You can't, eh? I wish you could.

"Very well, I continue. The *lalitha*, no matter how human she looks, cannot escape her arthropod heritage. The nymphs that develop from the larvae can easily pass for babies, but it would pain you to see the larvae themselves. Though they are not any uglier than a five months' human embryo. Not to me, anyway.

"It is a sad thing that the *lalitha* mother must die. Hundreds of millions of years ago, when a primitive pseudoarthropod was ready to hatch the eggs in her womb, a hormone was released in her body. It calcified the skin and turned her into a womb-tomb. She became a shell. Her larvae ate the organs and the bones, which were softened by the draining away of their calcium. When the young had fulfilled the function of the larva, which is to eat and grow, they rested and became nymphs. Then they broke the shell in its weak place in the belly.

"That weak point is the navel. It alone does not calcify with the epidermis but remains soft. By the time the nymphs are ready to come out, the soft flesh of the navel has decayed. Its dissolution lets loose a chemical which decalcifies an area that takes in most of the abdomen. The nymphs, though weak as human babies and much smaller, are activated by instinct to kick out the thin and brittle covering.

"You must understand, Hal, that the navel itself is both functional and mimetic. Since the larvae are not connected to the mother by an umbilical cord, they would have no navel. But they grow an excrescence that resembles one.

"The breasts of the adult also have two functions. Like the human female's, they are both sexual and reproductive. They never produce milk, of course, but they are glands. At the time the larvae are ready to hatch from the eggs, the breasts act as two powerful pumps of the hormone which carries out the hardening of the skin.

"Nothing wasted, you see—Nature's economy. The things that enable her to survive in human society also carry out the death process."

"I can understand the need for photogenes in the humanoid stage of evolution," Hal said. "But when the *lalitha* were in the animal stage of evolution, why should they need to reproduce the characteristics of the father's face? There isn't much difference between the face of a male animal and a female animal of the same species."

"I do not know," said Fobo. "Perhaps, the prehuman *lalitha* did not utilize the photokinetic nerves. Perhaps, those nerves are an evolutionary adaptation of an existing structure which had a different function. Or a vestigial function. There is some evidence that photokinesis was the means by which the *lalitha* changed her body to conform with the change in the human body as it passed up the evolutionary ladder. It seems reasonable to suppose that the *lalitha* needed such a biological device. If the photokinetic nerves were not involved, some other organ may have been. It is unfortunate that by the time we were advanced enough to scientifically study the *lalitha*, we had no specimens available. Finding Jeannette was pure luck. We did discover in her several organs whose functions remain a mystery to us. We need many of her kind for fruitful research."

"One more question," said Hal. "What if a *lalitha* had more than one lover? Whose features would her baby have?"

"If a *lalitha* were raped by a gang, she would not have an orgasm because the negative emotions of fear and disgust would bar it. If she had more than one lover—and she weren't drinking alcohol—she would reproduce young whose features would be those of the first lover. By the time she lay with her second lover—even if it were immediately afterward—the complete fertilization would have already been initiated."

Sorrowfully, Fobo shook his head.

"It is a sad thing, but it has not changed in all these epochs. The mothers must give their lives for their young. Yet Nature, as a sort of recompense, has given them a gift. On the analogy of reptiles, which, it is said, do not stop growing larger as long as they are alive, the *lalitha* will not die if they remain unpregnant. And so—"

Hal leaped to his feet and shouted, "Stop it!"

"I'm sorry," Fobo said softly. "I'm just trying to make you see why Jeannette felt that she couldn't tell you what she truly was. She must have loved you, Hal. She possessed the three factors that make love: a genuine passion, a deep affection, and the feeling of being one flesh with you, male and female so inseparable it would be hard to tell where one began and the other ended. I know she did, believe me, for we empathists can put ourselves into somebody else's nervous system and think and feel as they do.

"Yet, Jeannette must have had a bitter leaven in her love. The belief that if you knew she was of an utterly alien branch of the animal kingdom, separated by millions of years of evolution, barred by her ancestry and anatomy from the true completion of marriage—children—you would turn from her with horror. That belief must have shot with darkness even her brightest moments—"

"*No!* I would have loved her anyway! It might have been a shock. But I'd have gotten over it. Why, she was human; she was more human than any woman I've known!"

Macneff sounded as if he were going to retch. When he had recovered himself, he howled, "You abysmal thing! How can you stand yourself now that you know what utterly filthy monster you have lain with! Why don't you try to tear out your eyes, which have seen that vile filth! Why don't you bite off your lips, which have kissed that insect mouth! Why don't you cut off your hands, which have pawed with loathsome lust that mockery of a body! Why don't you tear out by the roots those organs of carnal—"

Fobo spoke through the storm of wrath. "Macneff! Macneff!"

The gaunt head swiveled toward the empathist. His eyes stared, and his lips had drawn back into what seemed to be an impossibly large smile; a smile of absolute fury.

"What? What?" he muttered, like a man waking from sleep.

"Macneff, I know your type well. Are you sure you weren't planning on taking the *lalitha* alive and using her for your own sensual purposes? Doesn't most of your fury and disgust result from being balked in your desires? After all, you've not had a woman for a year, and . . ."

The Sandalphon's jaw fell. Red flooded his face and became purple. The violent color faded, and a corpse-like white replaced it.

He screeched like an owl.

"*Enough!* Uzzites, take this—this thing that calls itself a man to the gig!"

The two men in black circled to come at the *joat* from front and back. Their approach was based on training, not caution. Years of taking prisoners had taught them to expect no resistance. The arrested always stood cowed and numb before the representatives of the Sturch. Now, despite the unusual circumstances and the knowledge that Hal carried a gun, they saw nothing different in him,

He stood with bowed head and hunched shoulders and dangling arms, the typical arrestee.

That was one second; the next, he was a tiger striking.

The agent in front of him reeled back, blood flowing from his mouth and spilling on his black jacket. When he bumped into the wall, he paused to spit out teeth.

By then, Yarrow had whirled and rammed a fist into the big soft belly of the man behind him.

"*Whoof!*" went the Uzzite.

He folded. As he did so, Hal brought his knee up against the unguarded chin. There was a crack of bone breaking, and the agent fell to the floor.

"Watch him!" Macneff yelled. "He's got a gun!"

The Uzzite by the wall shoved his hand under his jacket, feeling for the weapon in his armpit holster. Simultaneously, a heavy bronze bookend, thrown by Fobo, struck his temple. He crumpled.

Macneff screamed, "You are resisting, Yarrow! You are resisting!"

Hal bellowed, "You're damn *shib* I am!"

Head down, he plunged at the Sandalphon.

Macneff slashed with his whip at his attacker. The seven lashes wrapped themselves around Hal's face, but he rammed into the purple-clad form and knocked it down on the floor.

Macneff got to his knees; Hal, also on his knees, seized Macneff by the throat and squeezed.

Macneff's face turned blue, and he grabbed Hal's wrists and tried to tear them away. But Hal squeezed harder.

"You . . . can't do . . . this!" said Macneff, wheezing. "Can't . . . impossi—"

"I can! I can!" screamed Hal. "I've always wanted to do this, Pornsen! I mean . . . Macneff!"

At that moment, the floors shook, the windows rattled. Almost immediately, a tremendous *boom*! blew in the windows. Glass flew; Hal was hurled to the floor.

Outside, the night became day. Then, night again.

Hal rose to his feet. Macneff lay on the floor, his hands feeling his neck.

"What was that?" Hal said to Fobo.

Fobo went to the broken window and looked out. He was bleeding from a cut on his neck, but he did not seem to notice it.

"It's what I've been waiting for," Fobo said.

He turned to face Hal.

"From the moment the *Gabriel* landed, we've been digging under it, and—"

"Our sound-detection equipment—"

"—caught the noise of the underground trains directly below the ship. But we dug only when the trains were moving through so the digging would be covered up. Normally, a tram would go through the tunnels every ten minutes. But we routed them through every two minutes or so and made sure that they were long freight trains.

"Only a few days ago we completed filling the hole under the *Gabriel* with gunpowder. Believe me, we all breathed easier after it was done, for we'd feared we might be heard despite our precautions or that our shorings might break under the great weight of the ship. Or that, for some reason, the captain might decide to move the ship."

"Then you blew it up?" Hal said dazedly.

Things were going too fast for him.

"I doubt that. Even with the tons of explosives we set off, they could not damage too much a vessel built as solidly as the *Gabriel*. As a matter of fact, we did not wish to damage it, for we want to study it.

"But our calculations showed that the shock waves going through the metal plates of the ship would kill every man in the ship."

Hal went to the window and looked out. Against the moon-bright sky was a pillar of smoke; soon, the entire city would be covered with it.

"You had better get your men aboard at once," Hal said. "If the explosion only knocked out the officers on the bridge, and they regain consciousness before you reach them, they will press a button that will trigger an H-bomb.

"This will blow every thing up for miles around. Its explosion will make your powder charge seem a baby's breath. Far worse, it will release a deadly radioactivity that will kill millions more—if the winds go inland."

Fobo turned pale, though he tried to smile.

"I imagine our soldiers are on board by now. But I'll phone them just to make sure."

He returned after a minute. Now, he did not have to make an effort to smile.

"Everyone on board the *Gabriel* died instantly, including the personnel on the bridge. I've told the captain of the boarding party not to tamper with any mechanisms or controls."

"You've thought of everything, haven't you?" Hal said.

Fobo shrugged, and he said, "We are fairly peaceful. But, unlike you Terrans, we are really 'realists.' If we have to take action against vermin, we do our best to exterminate them. On this insect-ridden planet we have had a long history of battling killers."

He looked at Macneff, who was on all fours, eyes glazed, shaking his head like a wounded bear.

Fobo said, "I do not include you in the vermin, Hal. You are free to go where you want, do what you want."

Hal sat down in a chair. He said, in a grief-husked voice, "I think that all my life I've wanted just that. Freedom to go where I wanted, do what I wanted. But, now, what is there left for me? I have no one—"

"There is much for you, Hal," said Fobo. Tears ran down his nose and collected at the end.

"You have your daughters to care for, to love. In a short time, they will be through with their feeding in the incubator—they survived the premature removal quite well—and will be beautiful babies. They will be yours as much as any human infants could be.

"After all, they look like you—in a modified feminine way, of course. Your genes are theirs. What's the difference whether genes act by cellular or photonic means?

"Nor will you be without women. You forget that she has aunts and sisters. All young and beautiful. I'm sure that we can locate them."

Hal buried his face in his hands, and he said, "Thanks, Fobo, but that's not for me."

"Not now," Fobo said softly. "But your grief will soften; you will think life worth living again."

Someone came into the room. Hal looked up to see a nurse.

"Doctor Fobo, we are bringing the body out. Does the man care for one last look?"

Hal shook his head. Fobo walked over to him and put his hand on his shoulder.

"You look faint," he said. "Nurse, do you have some smelling salts?"

Hal said, "No, I won't need them."

Two nurses wheeled a carrier out. A white sheet was draped over the shell. Black hair cascaded from beneath the sheet and fell over the pillow.

Hal did not rise. He sat in the chair, and he moaned, "Jeannette! Jeannette! If you had only loved me enough to tell me . . ."

Flesh

For Bette,

Courageous and Loving Wife

PRELUDE

The crowd in front of the White House talked, shouted, and laughed. Women shrilled; men boomed. The high-pitched cut of children's voices was missing. They were home and being cared for by their older but prepubescent brothers and sisters or cousins. It was not fitting that children should see what would happen tonight. They would not understand the rites, one of the most holy in honor of the Great White Mother.

It also would not be safe for the children to be present. Centuries before the present date (2860 Old Style), when the rites were first held, children had been allowed to attend. Many had been killed, literally ripped apart, during the frenzies.

Tonight was dangerous enough for the adults. Always, a number of women were badly mauled or killed. Always, a number of men were overpowered by long-nailed, sharp-toothed women who ripped off by the roots that which made men men and who ran screaming down the streets with the trophies held high in the air or clenched between their teeth before placing them on the altar of the Great White Mother in the Temple of Dark Earth.

The following week, on Friday Sabbath, the white-robed Speakers for the Mother, priests and priestesses, would reprimand the survivors for carrying their zeal just a little too far. However, harsh words were the worst that those preached to could expect, and not always these were hurled at them. A man or woman truly possessed by the Goddess, and who was not then, could not be blamed. Besides, what else did the Speakers expect? Did not this happen every night a Sun-hero or Stag-king was born? Oh, well, the Speakers felt that it was necessary to quiet the worshipers down so that they could resume a normal life. Listen, pray, and forget. And look forward to the next ceremony.

Besides, the victims had nothing to complain about. They would be buried in a shrine, prayers said over them, and deer sacrificed over them. The ghosts of the slain would drink the blood and be thrice-glorified and sustained.

The bloody sun slid down past the horizon; night rushed in with cool dark whispering wings. The crowd became quieter while the representatives of the great frats lined up on Pennsylvania Avenue. There was a violent argument between the chief of the Moose frat and the chief of the Elks. Each claimed that his frat should lead the parade. Were they not both antlered men? Was not the Sunhero antler-bearing this year?

John Barleycorn, green from head to foot in his ritual costume, scarlet in face, staggering, tried to settle the dispute. As usual, he was too far gone by nightfall to speak clearly or to care much whether or not he spoke at all. His few discernible words only succeeded in making both chiefs angry. They were likely to be easily angered since both were more than a little drunk. They even went so far as to grip their knife handles, though it would have taken far greater provocation for them to unsheathe the knives at this time.

A detachment of the White House Honor Guard left their posts to straighten matters out. The tall girls marched from the porch, their high conical helmets shining in the torchlight, long hair hanging down their backs, their white robes gleaming. They carried their bows in one hand and an arrow in the other. Unlike the rest of the virgins in the city of Washington, they exposed only one breast, the left. The robe concealed the other—or, rather, the lack of the other. Traditionally, a White House archer gladly allowed her breast to be removed so it would not interfere with her handling of the bow. The lack was no disadvantage in getting a husband when she retired. Tonight, after the Sunhero planted the seed of divinity in them, they could have their choice of men to marry. A man whose wife had been a one-breasted Honor Guard was a proud man.

The captain of the Honor Guard sternly asked about the disturbance. After hearing both chiefs out, she said, "This is the first time matters have ever been so badly arranged. Perhaps we need a new John Barleycorn!"

She pointed the arrow in her hand at the chief of the Elk frat.

"You will take the lead in the parade. And you and your brothers will have the honor of bringing out the Sunhero."

The chief of the Moose frat was either a brave man or a foolish man. He protested. "I was out drinking with the Barleycorn last night, and he told me the Moose would have the honor! I demand to know why the Elks have been chosen instead of us!"

The captain stared coldly at him, and then fitted the nock of her arrow to the string of her bow. But she was too well trained in politics to shoot one of the powerful Moose frat.

"The Barleycorn must have been possessed with spirits other than those the Goddess gives him," she said. "It has been planned for some time that the Elks would escort the Sunhero to the Capitol. Is not the Sunhero a stag? Isn't he Stagg? You know that a male Elk is a stag, but a male Moose is a bull!"

"That is true," said the chief Moose, pale from the moment the arrow had been fitted. "I should not have listened to John Barleycorn. But it normally would have been the turn of the Moose. Last year it was the Lions, and the year before it was the Lambs. We should have been next."

"And so you would have been—except for that."

She pointed behind him down Pennsylvania Avenue.

He turned to look. The street ran straight for six blocks from the White House and then ended suddenly in a towering baseball stadium. Rising even over it was the shining needle shape of a craft that had not been seen for seven hundred and sixty years. Not until a month ago, when it had come thundering and flaming out of the late November skies and settled in the center of the ball park.

"You are right," said the chief Moose. "Never before has the Sunhero descended to us from the skies, sent by the Great White Mother Herself. And, certainly, She made it clear what frat he honors by being its brother when She named him Stagg."

He marched away at the head of his men and just in time.

There was a scream from the Capitol, now only six blocks away from the White House. The scream silenced the crowd; it paralyzed them and made the men turn pale. The women in the crowd became wide-eyed, eager, and expectant. Several fell on the ground, writhing and moaning. There came another scream, and now it could be seen that the terrible sound was from the throats of many young girls running down the steps of Congress.

They were priestesses, newly graduated from the divinity college of Vassar. They wore tall conical narrow-brimmed black hats, their hair was unbound and hung to their hips, their breasts were as bare as those of any other virgins; but those would have to serve for five years more before they put on the matronly bras. Not for them tonight the seed of the Sunhero; their participation was confined to initiating the ceremonies. They wore flaring bell-shaped white skirts with many petticoats beneath; some of these were belted with live and hissing rattlesnakes, the rest carried the deadly snakes around their shoulders. In their hands they held ten-foot whips made of snake hide.

Drums began beating; a bugle blared out above the drums; cymbals clanged; syrinxes shrilled.

Screaming, wild-eyed, the young priestesses ran down Pennsylvania Avenue, clearing a way before them with their whips. Suddenly they were at the gate surrounding the yard of the White House. There was a brief mock struggle as the Honor Guard pretended to resist the invasion. Some of it was not so harmless, since the archers and the priestesses had well-deserved reputations as vicious little bitches. There was a hair-pulling and scratching and breast-twisting, but the older priestesses applied their whips to the bare backs of the overenthusiastic. Howling, the girls sprang apart and quickly came to a sense of the business at hand.

These pulled out little golden sickles from their belts and brandished them in the air in a threatening but at the same time obviously ritualistic air. Suddenly, as if he had dramatically staged his entrance— and he had—John Barleycorn appeared in the main doorway of the White House. In one hand he carried a half-empty bottle of whiskey. There was no doubt where its contents had gone. He swayed back and forth and fumbled the cord at his neck before he managed to find the whistle at its end. Then he stuck the whistle in his mouth and blew shrilly.

Immediately, a howl rose from the street where the Elks were assembled.

A number of them burst past the Guard and onto the porch. These men wore little deerskin caps with toy antlers protruding from the sides, deerskin capes, and belts from which hung the tails of deer. Their breechclouts were balloons in phallic shapes. They did not run or walk but pranced on the ends of their toes, like ballet dancers, simulating the gait of a deer. They threatened the priestesses; the priestesses shrieked as if frightened and scattered to one side so the Elks could pass into the White House.

Here, inside the great reception room, John Barleycorn blew his whistle once again and lined them up according to their rank in the frat. Then he began walking unsteadily up the broad curving staircase that led to the second floor.

He disgraced himself by losing his balance and falling backwards into the arms of the chief Elk.

The chief caught the Barleycorn and shoved him to one side. In ordinary circumstances he would not have dared to deal so strongly with the Speaker of the House, but knowing that the fellow was in disgrace made him bold. The Barleycorn staggered to one side of the staircase. He fell backwards over the railing and fell on his head on the marble floor of the reception room. There he lay, his neck at an odd angle. A young priestess rushed forward, felt his pulse, looked at the glazing eyes, then drew out her golden sickle.

At that moment, a whip cracked across her bare shoulders and breasts and left a line from which blood oozed.

"What do you think you are doing?" screamed an older priestess.

The young priestess crouched low, head averted, but she did not dare to hold out her hands to protect herself from the whip.

"I was exercising my right," she whimpered. "Great John Barleycorn is dead. I am an incarnation of the Great White Mother; I was going to reap the crop."

"And I would not stop you," said the older priestess. "It would be your right to castrate him—except for one thing. He died by accident, not during the Planting Rites. You know that."

"Columbia forgive me," whimpered the priestess. "I could not help myself. It is tonight's doing; the coming to manhood of the son, the crowning of the Horned King, the defloration of the mascots."

The stern face of the older priestess splintered into a smile. "I am sure that Columbia will forgive you. There is something in the air that takes us all out of our senses. It is the divine presence of the Great White Mother in Her aspect as Virginia, Bride of the Sunhero and the Great Stag. I feel it too, and—"

At that moment there was a bellow from the second story. Both women looked up. Down the steps poured the mob of Elks, and on their shoulders and hands they bore the Sunhero.

The Sunhero was a naked man magnificently built in every respect. Though he was sitting on the shoulders of two Elks, he obviously was very tall. His face, with its prominent supraorbital ridges, long hooked nose, and massive chin, could have been that of a good-looking heavyweight champion. But at this moment anything that might have evoked such terms as "handsome" or "ugly" was gone from his face. It bore a look that could only be described as "possessed." That was exactly the term anybody in the city of Washington of the nation of Deecee would have used. His long red-gold hair hung to his shoulders. Out of the curly masses, just above the forehead and the hairline, sprouted a pair of antlers.

These were not the artificial antlers that the Elk frat wore. They were living organs.

They stood twelve inches above his head and measured sixteen inches from the outer tip of one to the outer tip of the other. They were covered with a pale shiny skin, shot through with blue blood vessels. At the base of each a great artery pulsed with the throb of the Sunhero's heart. It was obvious that they had been grafted onto the man's head very recently. There was dried blood at the base of the antlers.

The face of the man with the antlers would have been distinguished instantly in a crowd of citizens. The faces of the Elks and of the priest-esses were individual, but all had a look that belonged to their era and could be called cervine. Triangular, with large dark eyes and long eye-lashes, high cheekbones, small but full-fleshed mouths and tapering chins, they were cast in the mold of their times. But a sensitive onlooker would have known that this man on the shoulders of the cervines, this man with the face emptied of intellect, belonged to an earlier era. Just as a student of the portraits of humanity can say by looking at this face, "He belongs to the Ancient world," or "This man was born dur-ing the Renaissance," or "This man lived when the Industrial Age was just getting its stride," so the student could have said, "This man was born when the Earth swarmed with humanity. He looks vaguely insectal. Yet there is a difference. He also bears the look of the original of those times—the man who managed to be an individual among the insects."

Now the crowd carried him down the broad steps and out onto the great porch of the White House.

At his appearance a tremendous shout rose from the mob in the street. Drums thundered; bugles blared like Gabriel's trumpet; syr-inxes shrilled. The priestesses on the porch waved sickles at the men dressed like elks, but they did not cut—except by accident. The Elks on the outside of the mob shoved at the priestesses so they staggered back and fell on their backs. There they lay, their legs up in the air, screaming and writhing.

The antlered man was rushed down the sidewalk, out through the iron gates and onto the middle of Pennsylvania Avenue. Here he was seated on the back of a wild-eyed black stag. The stag tried to buck and rear; but the men held on to his antlers and the long hair of his flanks and prevented him from racing headlong down the street. The man on the beast's back grabbed its antlers to keep from being thrown. His own back arched. The muscles on his arms knotted as he forced the mighty neck back. The stag bellowed, and the whites of his eyes shone in the torchlight. Suddenly, just as it seemed his neck must break under the force of the man's arms, he relaxed and stood trembling. Saliva drooled from his mouth, and his eyes were still wide, but they were frightened. His rider was master.

The Elks formed in ranks of twelve behind the stag and rider. Behind them was a band of musicians, also of the Elk frat. Behind them were the Moose and their musicians. Next was a group of Lions wearing panther skulls as helmets and panther skins as cloaks, the long tails dragging on the cement. They held on to the ropes of a balloon that rose twelve feet over them. This had a long sausage-shape and a swelling round nose. Beneath it hung two round gondolas in each of which sat pregnant women, throwing flowers and rice on the crowd lining the street. Behind them were the representatives of the Rooster frat carrying their totem, a tall pole surmounted by the carved head of an enormous rooster with a tall red comb and a long straight beak knobbed at the end.

Behind them, the leader of the other frats of the nation: the Elephants, the Mules, the Jackrabbits, the Trouts, the Billy Goats, and many others. Behind them, the representatives of the great sisterhoods: the Wild Does, the Queen Bees, the Wood Cats, the Lionesses, the Shrikes.

The Sunhero paid no attention to those behind him. He was staring down the street. Both sides were lined with crowds, but evidently they had not assembled by accident. They were organized into definite ranks. The group closest to the streets was composed of girls from fourteen to eighteen. They wore the high-necked, long-sleeved blouses which opened at the front to exhibit their breasts. Their legs were concealed by white bell-shaped skirts with many petticoats beneath, and their red-nailed feet wore white sandals. Their long hair was unbound and fell to their waists. Each carried a bouquet of white roses in her right hand. They were wide-eyed and eager; they screamed, over and over, "Sunhero! Horned King! Mighty Stag! Great Son and Lover!"

Behind them stood matrons who seemed, from the advice they shouted at them, to be their mothers. Those wore high-necked, long-sleeved blouses too, but their breasts were covered. Their skirts lacked the petticoats to give them the bell shape; they fell straight to the ground except in the front, where they wore, beneath the skirt, bustles to give them a pregnant appearance. Their hair was coiled up into buns and Psyche knots, and in each were stuck the stems of red roses, one for each child they had borne.

Behind the matrons stood the fathers, each clad in the garment of his particular frat and holding in one hand the totem of his frat. In the other he held a bottle from which he drank frequently and occasionally passed forward to his wife.

All were shouting and screaming, straining forward as if they would crowd onto the street. This was not in the plan, since the way had to be left open for the passage of the parade. The Honor Guards and the Vassar graduates rushed out in front of the stag and its rider. The Guard jabbed with arrows at those who crossed a white line on the curb, and the priestesses struck out with their whips. The virgins in the front ranks did not whimper or shrink at the blood drawn from them, but instead yelled as if they liked the sight of their own blood.

There was a hush. The drums and bugles and Panpipes ceased for a moment.

Maidens appeared from the White House, carrying on their shoulders and hands a chair in which lolled the body of John Barleycorn. These maidens were dressed in the garb of their sisterhood, long stiff cloths dyed green to look like corn leaves and on their heads tall yellow crowns like ears of corn. They belonged to the Corn sisterhood. They were carrying out the single male member. He was dead. But apparently the crowd did not realize it, since they laughed at the sight of the body. It was not the first time he had passed out in public, and nobody except the Corn Maidens knew the difference. They took their appointed place in the procession just behind the Guard and priestesses and just ahead of the Sunhero.

The drums began again; the bugles blared; the syrinxes shrilled; the men roared; the women screamed.

The stag lurched forward with its rider.

The man on its back had to be restrained from climbing down and joining the teen-aged girls who lined the street. They were shouting suggestions that would have made a sailor blush, and he was shouting back at them in kind. His face, which had been emptied of intellect as he came down the steps, was now demoniac. He struggled to leave the beast. When the Elks pushed him back, he hit at them with his fists. They reeled back, their noses broken and bloody, and fell on the street where the marchers trampled them. Others took their places and gripped the Sunhero with many hands.

"Hold on, Great Stag!" they shouted. "Wait until we get to the domes! There we will release you, and you may do what you want! There the High Priestess Virginia waits in the aspect of the Great White Mother as maiden! And there wait also the most beautiful mascots of Washington, tender maidens filled with the divine presence of Columbia and of America, her daughter! Waiting to be filled with the divine seed of the Son!"

The man with the antlers did not seem to hear them or to understand them—part of which might be explained by the fact that his speech, though American, was a variant of theirs. The other part was explained by the thing that possessed him. It made him deaf to anything but the roar of blood in him.

Though the paraders made an attempt to pace slowly toward their destination, six blocks away, they could not help increasing speed as they came closer. Perhaps the insults and threats of the young girls to tear them apart if they didn't hurry had something to do with it. The whips and arrows drew more blood. The girls nevertheless pressed in, and once a girl made a fantastically high jump into the air and knocked over a priestess. She scrambled up and leaped again onto the shoulders of an Elk, but she lost her footing and fell headlong into the group. There she was treated savagely; the men ripped off her clothes, pinched and gripped her everywhere until they drew blood. One man intended to anticipate the Sunhero, but this blasphemy was prevented by others. They knocked him over the head, and then kicked the girl back into line.

"Wait your turn, honey!" they shouted. They laughed, and one yelled, "If the Great Stag isn't enough, the little stags will accommodate you later, baby!"

By the time this incident had passed, the procession was halted at the foot of the steps to the Capitol Building. Here there was some momentary confusion, as the Guards and priestesses tried to shove the girls back. The Elks pulled the Sunhero off the stag and began to lead him up the steps.

"Hold on just a minute, Great Stag!" they said. "Hold on until you get to the top of the steps. And we will let you go!"

Raving, the Sunhero glared at them, but he allowed them to hang on to him. He looked at the statue of the Great White Mother on the top of the steps by the entrance to the building. Carved marble, it was fifty feet high with enormous breasts. She was suckling her baby Son. One of her feet was crushing the life out of a bearded dragon.

The crowd broke into a mighty roar, "Virginia! Virginia!"

The high priestess of Washington had appeared from the shadows of the columns of the immense porch that ran around the Capitol.

The light from the torches gleamed whitely on her long skirt and bare shoulders and breasts. It turned dark her honey-colored hair, which fell to her calves. It turned dark the mouth which in the daylight was red as a wound. It turned dark the eyes which in the sun were a deep blue.

The Sunhero bellowed like a stag who scents a female during rutting season. He shouted, "Virginia! You'll not put me off any longer! Nothing can stop me now!"

The dark mouth opened, and the teeth flashed white in the torchlight. A long slim white arm beckoned to him. He tore loose from the many hands holding him and ran up the steps. He was only faintly aware that the drums and bugles and pipes behind him had risen to a crescendo and that the screaming was the high-pitched lust of a mob of young girls. He was only dimly aware of these . . . and not at all aware that his bodyguard was fighting for its life, trying to keep from being trampled underfoot or torn apart by the long sharp nails of the virgins. Nor did he see that mingled with the fallen bodies of the men were the white skirts and blouses of the girls, cast aside.

Only one thing made him pause for even a second. That was the sudden appearance of a girl in an iron cage, set at the base of the statue of the Great Mother. She was a young woman, too, but clad differently than the others. She wore a long-billed cap like a baseball player's, a loose shirt with some indistinguishable marking on it, loose calf-length pants, thick stockings, and thick-soled shoes.

Above the cage was a large sign with thick-limbed letters in Dee-cee spelling.

MAESST
GAKAETI REA KESILAE

Translated:

MASCOT
CAPTURED IN A RAID ON CASEYLAND

The girl gave him one horrified look, then covered her eyes and turned her back on him.

His puzzled look disappeared, and he ran toward the high priestess. She was facing him with her two arms spread out, as if bestowing a benediction upon him. But the arc of her back bending backwards and the outthrust of her hips made plain that his long waiting was over. She would not resist.

He growled so deeply that it seemed to come from the root of his spine, and he seized her robe and pulled.

Behind him the many throats rose to an insane screeching, and, surrounded by flesh, he disappeared from the view of the fathers and mothers assembled at the foot of the steps.

I

Around and around the Earth the starship sped.

Where air ends and space begins, it skimmed from north pole to south pole and around and around.

Finally, Captain Peter Stagg turned away from the viewplate.

"Earth has changed very much since we were here eight hundred years ago. How do you interpret what you've seen?"

Dr. Calthorp scratched his long white beard and then turned a dial on the panel below the viewplate. The fields and rivers and forests below expanded and shot out of sight. Now the magnifier showed a city on both sides of a river, presumably the Potomac. The city was roughly ten miles square, and could be seen in the same detail as if the men on the ship were five hundred feet above it.

"How do I interpret what I see?" said Calthorp. "Your guess would be as good as mine. As Earth's oldest anthropologist, I should be able to make a fair analysis of the data presented—perhaps even explain how some of these things came to be. But I can't. I'm not even sure

that is Washington, If it is, it's been rebuilt without much planning. I
don't know; you don't either. So why don't we go down and see?"

"We've little choice," said Peter Stagg. "We're almost out of fuel."

Suddenly, he smacked his palm with his huge fist.

"Once we land, then what? I didn't see a single building anywhere
on Earth that looked as if it might house a reactor. Or anything like
the machines we knew. Where's the technology? It's back to the horse
and buggy—except that they don't have any horses. The horse seems
to be extinct, but they've got a substitute. Some sort of hornless deer."

"To be exact, deer have antlers, not horns," Calthorp said. "I'd say
the latter-day Americans have bred deer or elk or both, not only to
take the place of the horse but of cattle. If you've noticed, there's a
great variety among the cervines. Big ones for draft and pack and meat
animals, some bred with the lines of race horses. Millions of them."
He hesitated. "But I'm worried. Even the seeming non-existence of
radioactive fuel doesn't bother me as much . . ."

"As what?"

"As what kind of reception we'll get when we land. Much of Earth
has become a desert. Erosion, the razor of God, has slashed its face.
Look at what used to be the good old U.S.A. A chain of volcanoes
belching fire and dust along the Pacific coast! As a matter of fact, the
Pacific coast all around—both Americas, upper Asia, Australia, the
Pacific islands—is alive with active volcanoes. All that carbon dioxide
and dust released into the atmosphere has had a radical effect on the
terrestrial climate. The icecaps of the arctic and antarctic are melting.
The oceans have risen at least six feet and will rise more. Palm trees
grow in Pennsylvania. The once-reclaimed deserts of the American
Southwest look as if they'd been blasted by the hot breath of the Sun.
The Midwest is a dust bowl. And . . ."

"What has this got to do with the reception we might get?" said
Peter Stagg.

"Just this. The central Atlantic seaboard seems to be on the road
to recovery. That is why I'm recommending we land there. But the
technological and social setup there is apparently that of a peasant
state. You've seen how the coast is busy as a hive of bees. Gangs planting trees, digging irrigation ditches, buildings dams, roads. Almost
every activity out of which we've been able to make sense is directed
at rebuilding the soil.

"And the ceremonies we've seen through the plate were obviously
fertility rites. The absence of an advanced technology might indicate

several things. One, science as we knew it has been lost. Two, a revulsion against science and its practitioners exists—because science is blamed, fairly or not, for the holocaust that has scourged Earth."

"So?"

"So these people probably have forgotten that Earth once sent out a starship to explore interstellar space and locate virgin planets. They may look upon us as devils or monsters—especially if we represent the science they may have been taught to loathe as the spirit of evil. I'm not just conjecturing on the basis of pure imagination, you know. The images on their temple walls and the statues, and some of the pageants we've witnessed, clearly show a hatred of the past. If we come to them out of the past, we might be rejected. Rather fatally for us."

Stagg began pacing back and forth.

"Eight hundred years since we left the Earth," he muttered. "Was it worth it? Our generation, our friends, enemies, our wives, sweethearts, children, their children and their children's children . . . shoveled under and become grass. And that grass turned to dust. The dust that blows around the planet is the dust of the ten billion who lived when we lived. And the dust of God knows how many more tens of billions. There was a girl I didn't marry because I wanted this great adventure more . . ."

"You're alive," said Calthorp. "And eight hundred and thirty-two years old, Earth-time."

"But only thirty-two years old in physiological time," Stagg said. "How can we explain to those simple people that as our ship crept toward the stars, we slept, frozen like fish in ice? Do they know anything about the techniques of suspended animation? I doubt it. So how will they comprehend that we only stayed out of suspended animation long enough to search for Terrestrial-type planets? That we discovered ten such, one of which is wide open for colonization?"

"We could go around Earth twice while you make a speech," said Calthorp. "Why don't you get down off your soapbox and take us to Earth so we can find out what's facing us? And so you might find a woman to replace the one you left behind?"

"Women!" shouted Stagg, no longer looking dreamy.

"What?" said Calthorp, startled by his captain's sudden violence.

"Women! Eight hundred years without seeing a single, solitary, lone, forlorn woman! I've taken one thousand ninety-five S.P. pills—enough to make a capon out of a bull elephant! But they're losing their effect! I've built up a resistance! Pills or not, I want a woman. I could make love to my own toothless and blind great-grandmother. I feel like Walt Whitman when he boasted he jetted the stuff of future republics. I've a dozen republics in me!"

"Glad to see you've quit acting the nostalgic poet and are now yourself," said Calthorp, "But quit pawing the ground. You'll get your fill of women soon enough. From what I've seen in the plate, women seem to have the upper hand, and you know you can't stand a domineering female."

Gorilla-fashion, Stagg pounded his big hard chest.

"Any woman comes up against me will run into a hard time!"

Then he laughed and said, "Actually, I'm scared. It's been so long since I've talked to a woman, I won't know how to act."

"Just remember that women don't change. Old Stone Age or Atomic Age, the colonel's lady and Judy O'Grady are still the same."

Stagg laughed again and affectionately slapped Calthorp's thin back. Then he gave orders to make planetfall. But during the descent, he said, "Do you think there's a chance we might get a decent reception?"

Calthorp shrugged.

"They might hang us. Or they might make us kings."

As it happened, two weeks after he made a triumphal entry into Washington, Stagg was crowned.

II

"Peter, you look every inch a king," Calthorp said. "Hail to Peter the Sixth!"

Calthorp, despite his ironic tone, meant what he said.

Stagg was six feet six inches tall, weighed two hundred and thirty-five pounds, and had a forty-eight inch chest, thirty-two inch waistline, and thirty-six inch hips. His red-gold hair was long and wavy. His face was handsome as an eagle's was handsome. Just now he looked like an eagle in his cage, for he was pacing back and forth, hands behind his back like folded wings, his head bent forward, his dark blue eyes fierce and intent. Now and then he scowled at Calthorp.

The anthropologist was slumped in a huge, gold-plated chair, a long jeweled cigar-holder dangling from his lips. He, like Stagg, had permanently lost his facial hair. One day after landing, they had been showered, shampooed, and massaged. The servants had shaved them by simply applying a cream to their faces and then wiping the cream off with a towel. Both men thought this was a delightfully easy way to shave until they discovered that the cream had deprived them forever of their right to grow whiskers if they felt like it.

Calthorp cherished his beard, but he had not objected to being shaved because the natives made it clear that they regarded beards as an abomination and a stench in the nostrils of the Great White Mother. Now he lamented its disappearance. He had not only lost his patriarchal appearance, he had exposed his weak chin.

Suddenly, Stagg halted his pacing to stand before the mirror that covered one wall of the tremendous room. He looked hard at his image and at the crown on his head. It was gold, with fourteen points, each tipped by a large diamond. He looked at the inflated green velvet collar around his neck, at his bare chest, on which was painted a flaming sun. He regarded distastefully the broad jaguarskin belt around his waist, the scarlet kilt, the enormous black phallic symbol stitched to the front of the kilt, the shiny, white leather, knee-length boots. He looked at the King of Deecee in all his splendor, and he snarled. He jerked off the crown and savagely threw it across the room. It struck the far wall and rolled back across the room to his feet.

"So I've been crowned ruler of Deecee!" he shouted. "King of the Daughters of Columbia. Or, as they say in their degenerate American, *Ken-a dot uh K'lumpaha.*

"What kind of a monarch am I? I am not allowed to exercise any of the powers and privileges a king should have. I have been ruler of this woman-ridden land for two weeks, and I've had all sorts of parties in my honor. I've had my praises sung, literally, everywhere I go with my one-breasted Guard of Honor. I am initiated into the totem frat of the Elks—and, let me repeat, they were the weirdest rites I've ever heard of. And I was chosen Big Elk Of The Year . . ."

"Naturally, with a name like Stagg, you'd belong to the Elks," Calthorp said. "It's a good thing they didn't find out your middle name was Leo. They'd have had a hell of a time deciding whether you belonged to the Elks or the Lions. Only . . ."

He frowned. Stagg kept on raving.

"They tell me I am Father of My Country. If I am, why don't I get a chance to be one? They won't allow a woman to be alone with me!

When I complain about it, that lovely bitch, the Chief Priestess, tells me I am not allowed to discriminate in favor of any one woman. I am the father, lover and son, of every woman in Deecee!"

Calthorp was looking gloomier and gloomier. He rose from his chair and walked to the huge French windows on the second story of the White House. The natives thought the royal mansion was named so in honor of the Great White Mother. Calthorp knew better, but he was too intelligent to argue. He motioned to Stagg to come by him and look out.

Stagg did so, but he sniffed loudly and made a face.

Calthorp pointed out the window to the street. Several men were lifting a large barrel onto the back of the wagon.

"Honeydippers was the ancient name for them," said Calthorp. "Every day they come by and collect their stuff for the fields. This is a world where every little grunt is for the glory of the nation and the enrichment of the soil."

"You'd think we'd be used to it by now," Stagg said. "But the odor seems to get stronger every day."

"Well, it's not a new odor around Washington. Though in the old days there was less of the human and more of the bull."

Stagg grinned and said, "Who ever thought America, land of the two-bathroom house, would go back to the little house with the crescent on the door? Except the little houses don't have doors. It's not because they don't know anything about plumbing. We have running water in our apartments."

"Everything that comes out of the earth must go back to the earth. They don't sin against Nature by piping millions of tons of phosphates and other chemicals, which the soil needs, into the ocean. They're not like we were, blind stupid fools killing our earth in the name of sanitation."

"This lecture wasn't why you called me to the window," Stagg said.

"Yes, it was. I wanted to explain the roots of this culture. Or try to. I'm handicapped because I've spent most of my time learning the language."

"It's English. But farther from our brand than ours was from Anglo-Saxon."

"It's degenerated, in the linguistical sense, far faster than was predicted. Probably because of the isolation of small groups after the Desolation. And also because the mass of the people are illiterate. Literacy is almost the exclusive property of the religious ministers and the *diradah*."

"*Diradah?*"

"The aristocrats. I think the word originally was deer-riders. Only the privileged are allowed to ride deer. *Diradah.* Analogous to the Spanish *caballero* or French *cavalier.* Both originally meant *horseman.* I've several things to show you, but let's look at that mural again."

They walked to the far end of the long room and stopped before an enormous and brightly colored mural.

"This painting," Calthorp said, "depicts the great basic myth of Deecee. As you can see"—he pointed at the figure of the Great White Mother towering over the tiny plains and mountains and even tinier people—"she is very angry. She is helping her son, the Sun, to blast the creatures of Earth. She is rolling back the blue shield she once flung around Earth to protect it from the fierce arrows of her son.

"Man, in his blindness, greed, and arrogance, has fouled the Goddess-given earth. His ant-heap cities have emptied their filth into the rivers and seas and turned them into vast sewers. He has poisoned the air with deadly fumes. These fumes, I suppose, were not only the products of industry but of radioactivity. But the Deecee, of course, know nothing of atomic bombs.

"Then Columbia, unable any longer to endure man's poisoning of Earth and his turning away from her worship, ripped away her protective shield around Earth—and allowed the Sun to hurl the full force of his darts upon all living creatures."

"I see all those people and animals falling down all over Earth," Stagg said. "On the streets, in the fields, on the seas, in the air. The grasses shrivel, and the trees wither. Only the humans and animals lucky enough to have been sheltered from the Sun's arrows survived."

"Not so lucky," Calthorp said. "They didn't die from sunburn, but they had to eat. The animals came forth at night and ate the carrion and each other. Man, after devouring all the canned goods, ate the animals. And then man ate man.

"Fortunately, the deadly rays lasted only a short time, perhaps less than a week. Then the Goddess relented and replaced her protective shield."

"But what *was* the Desolation?"

"I can only surmise. Do you remember that just before we left Earth the government had commissioned a research company to develop a system for broadcasting power over the entire planet? A shaft was to be sunk into the earth deep enough to tap the heat radiating from the core. The heat was to be converted into electricity and transmitted around the world, using the ionosphere as a medium of conduction.

"Theoretically, every electrical system on the planet could tap this power. That meant, for instance, that the city of Manhattan could draw down from the ionosphere all the power it needed to light and heat all buildings, run all TV sets, and, after electric motors were installed, power all vehicles.

"I believe that the idea was realized about twenty-five years after we left Earth. I also believe that the warnings of some scientists, notably Cardon, were justified. Cardon predicted that the first full-scale broadcast would strip away a part of the ozone layer."

"My God!" Stagg said. "If enough ozone in the atmosphere was destroyed . . . !"

"The shorter waves of the ultraviolet spectrum, no longer absorbed by the ozone, would fall upon every living creature exposed to the sunlight. Animals—including man—died of sunburn. Plants, I imagine, were sturdier. Even so, the effect on them must have been devastating enough to account for the great deserts we saw all over Earth.

"And as if that wasn't enough, Nature—or the Goddess, if you prefer—struck man just as he was shakily getting to his feet. The ozone imbalance must have lasted a very short time. Then natural processes restored the normal amount. But about twenty-five years later, just as man was beginning to form small isolated societies here and there—the population must have dropped from ten billion to a million in a year's time—extinct volcano ranges all over Earth began erupting.

"I don't know. Maybe man's probings into the Earth caused this second cataclysm—twenty-five years delayed because Earth works slowly, but surely.

"Most of Japan sank. Krakatoa disappeared. Hawaii blew up. Sicily cracked in two. Manhattan sank under the sea a few meters and then rose again. The Pacific was ringed by belching volcanoes. The Mediterranean was a lesser inferno. Tidal waves roared far inland, stopping only at the feet of the mountains. The mountains shook, and those who had escaped the tidal waves were buried under avalanches.

"Result: man reduced to the Stone Age, the atmosphere filled with the dust and carbon dioxide that make for the magnificent sunsets and subtropical climate in New York, melting icecaps . . ."

"No wonder there was so little continuity between our society and that of the survivors of the Desolation," Stagg said. "Even so, you'd think they would have rediscovered gunpowder."

"Why?"

"Why? Because making black gunpowder is so simple and so obvious!"

"Sure," Calthorp said. "So simple and so obvious it only took mankind a mere half a million years to learn that mixing charcoal, sulfur, and potassium nitrate in the proper proportions resulted in an explosive mixture. That's all.

"Now, you take a double cataclysm like the Desolation. Almost all books perished. There was a period of over a hundred years in which the extremely few survivors were so busy scratching out a living they didn't have time to teach their youngsters the three R's. The result? Abysmal ignorance, an almost complete loss of history. To these people, the world was created anew in 2100 A.D. or 1 A.D., their time. A.D. After the Desolation. Their myths say it is so.

"I'll give you an example. Cotton-raising. When we left Earth, cotton was no longer raised, because plastics had replaced fiber clothing. Did you know that the cotton plant was rediscovered only two hundred years ago? Corn and tobacco never vanished. But until three centuries ago, people wore animal skins or nothing. Mostly nothing."

Calthorp led Stagg from the mural back to the open French windows. "I digress, though we've little else to do. Look out there, Pete. You see a Washington, or Wazhtin as it's now called, like none we knew. Washington has been leveled twice since we left, and the present city was built two hundred years ago over the site of the dead cities. An attempt was made to model it after the previous metropolis. But a different *Zeitgeist* possessed the builders. They built it as their beliefs and myths dictated."

He pointed to the Capitol. In some respects, it resembled the one they remembered. But it had two domes instead of one, and on top of each dome was a red tower.

"Modeled after the breasts of the Great White Mother," Calthorp said. He pointed at the Washington Monument, now located about a hundred yards to the left of the Capitol. It was three hundred feet high, a tower of steel and concrete, painted like a barber pole with red, white, and blue stripes and topped with a round red structure.

"No need to tell you what that is supposed to represent. The myth is that it belonged to the Father of His Country. Washington himself is supposed to be buried under it. I heard that story last night, told in all devoutness by John Barleycorn himself."

Stagg stepped through the open French windows onto the porch outside his second-story apartment. The porch ran completely around the second story, but Calthorp walked no farther than around the corner. Stagg, who had delayed following him, found him leaning on the porch railing. This was composed of small marble caryatids which supported broad trays on their heads. Calthorp pointed over the tops of the thick orchard in the White House yard.

"See that white building with the enormous statue of a woman on top? She is Columbia, the Great White Mother, watching over and protecting her people. To us she is just a figure in a heathen religion. But to her people—our descendants—she is a vivid and vital force that directs this nation toward its destiny. And does so through ruthless means. Anybody who stands in her way is crushed—one way or another."

"I saw the Temple when we first came into Washington," Stagg said. "We passed it on the way to the White House. Remember how Sarvant almost died of shame when he saw the sculptured figures on the walls?"

"What did you think of them?"

Stagg turned red, and he growled, "I thought I was hardened, but those statues! Disgusting, obscene, absolutely pornographic! And decorating a place dedicated to worship."

Calthorp shook his head. "Not at all. You have been to two of their services. They were conducted with great dignity and great beauty. The state religion is a fertility cult, and those figures are representations of various myths. They tell stories whose obvious moral is that man has once almost destroyed the earth because of his terrible pride. He and his science and arrogance upset the balance of Nature. But now that it is restored, it is up to man to retain his humility, to work hand in hand with Nature—whom they believe to be a living goddess, whose daughters mate with heroes. If you noticed, the goddesses and heroes depicted on the walls emphasized through their postures the importance of the worship of Nature and fertility."

"Yes? From some of the positions they were in, I'd say they certainly weren't going to fertilize anything."

Calthorp smiled. "Columbia is also the goddess of erotic love."

"I have the feeling," Stagg said, "that you're trying to tell me something. But you're taking a very indirect route. I also have a feeling that I won't like what you're trying to tell me,"

At that moment they heard the clanging of a gong in the room they'd just left. They hurried back to see what was going on.

They were greeted by a blast of trumpets and roll of drums. In marched a band of musician-priests from the nearby Georgetown University. These were fat well-fed fellows who had castrated themselves in honor of the Goddess—and, incidentally, to get a lifelong position of prestige and security. Like women, they were dressed in high-necked, long-sleeved blouses and ankle-length skirts.

Behind them walked the man known as John Barleycorn. Stagg didn't know his real name; "John Barleycorn" was evidently a title. Nor did Stagg know Barleycorn's exact position in the government of Deecee. He lived in the White House, on the third floor, and seemed to have much to do with the administration of the country. His function was probably similar to that of the Prime Minister of ancient Great Britain.

The Sunheroes, like the monarch of that country, were more figureheads, binders of loyalty and tradition, than actual rulers. Or so it seemed to Stagg, who had been forced to guess at the meaning of most of the phenomena that flashed and buzzed with him during his imprisonment.

John Barleycorn was a very tall and very thin man of about thirty-five. His long hair was dyed a bright green, and he wore green spectacles. His long ski-slope nose and his face were covered with broken red veins. He wore a tall green plug hat. Around his neck hung a string of ears of corn. His torso was bare. His kilt was green, and the sporran hanging from his belt was made of stiff cloth shaped like the leaves of corn. His sandals were yellow.

In his right hand he carried his emblem of office, a large bottle of white lightning.

"Hail, man and myth!" he said to Stagg. "Greetings to the Sunhero! Greetings to the ramping, snorting stag of the Elk totem! Greetings to the Father of His Country and the Child and Lover of the Great White Mother!"

He took a long swig from the bottle, smacked his lips, and passed it to Stagg.

"I need that," said the captain, and swallowed a mouthful. A minute later, after choking, gasping, and weeping great tears, he returned the bottle.

Barleycorn was elated. "You gave a splendid performance, Noble Elk! You must have been visited by the special potency of Columbia

Herself to be so stricken by the white lightning. Indeed, you are divine! Now take me, I am only a poor mortal, and when I first drank white lightning, I was affected. Still, I must confess that when I first assumed office as a lad I was able to feel the holy presence of the Goddess in the bottle and to be affected as much as yourself. But a man may become hardened even to divinity, may She pardon my saying so. Have I ever told you the story of how Columbia first liquified a lightning bolt and then bottled it? And how She gave it to the first man, none other than Washington himself? And how disgracefully he behaved and thereby incurred the wrath of the Goddess?

"I have? Well, to business, then. I am preceding the Chief Priestess herself to give you a message. To whit and to-whooooo! Tomorrow is the birthday of the Son of the Great White Mother. And you, the child of Columbia, will be born tomorrow. And then what has been will be."

He took another drink, bowed to Stagg, almost fell on his face, recovered, and staggered out of the room.

Stagg called him back. "Just a minute! I want to know what has happened to my crew!"

Barleycorn blinked. "I told you that they were in a building on the campus of Georgetown University."

"I want to know where they are now—at this moment!"

"They are being treated very well. Anything they want they may have, except their freedom. And they will get that day after tomorrow."

"Why then?"

"Because you, too, will be released. Of course, you won't be able to see them then. You'll be on the Great Route."

"What is that?"

"It will be revealed."

Barleycorn turned to leave, but Stagg said, "Tell me, why is that girl being kept in a cage? You know, the one with the sign that says: 'Mascot, Captured in a Raid on Caseyland.'"

"That, too, will be revealed, Sunhero. Meanwhile, I suggest that it is unbecoming in a man of your importance to lower himself by asking questions. The Great White Mother will explain everything in due time."

After Barleycorn had left, Stagg said to Calthorp, "What nonsense is he trying to cover up?"

The little man frowned. "Wish I knew. After all, my chances for an examination into the social mechanisms of this culture have been rather limited. It's just that there is . . ."

"There's what?" Stagg said anxiously. Calthorp was looking very gloomy.

"Tomorrow is the winter solstice. Midwinter—when the sun is weakest in the northern hemisphere and has reached its most southerly station. On the calendar we knew, it was December twenty-first or twenty-second. As near as I can remember, that was a very important date in prehistoric and even historic times. All sorts of ceremonies connected with it, such as . . . ahhh!"

It was more a wail than an exclamation of sudden remembrance.

Stagg became even more alarmed. He was about to ask him what was wrong, but he was interrupted by another blast from the band. The musicians and the attendants faced the door and fell on their knees.

They cried in unison, "Chief Priestess, living flesh of Virginia, daughter of Columbia! Holy maiden! Beautiful one! Virginia, soon to lose to the raging stag—heedless, savage, tearing male—your sanctified and tender fold! Blessed and doomed Virginia!"

A tall girl of eighteen walked haughtily into the apartment. She was beautiful, though she had a high-bridged nose and a very white face. Her full lips were red as blood. Her blue eyes were piercing and unflinching as a cat's. Her curling honey-colored hair fell to her hips. She was Virginia, graduate of Vassar College for Oracular Priestesses and incarnate daughter of Columbia.

"Hello, mortals," she said in a high clear voice.

She looked at Stagg.

"Hello, immortal."

"Hello, Virginia," he answered. He felt the blood spurting through his flesh and the ache building up in his chest and loins. Every time he met her, he experienced this almost irrepressible desire for her. He knew that if he were left alone with her, he would take her, no matter what the consequences.

Virginia gave no sign that she was aware of her effect upon him. She regarded him with the cool unfaltering stare of a lioness.

Virginia, like all mascots, was clothed in a high-necked and ankle-length garment, but her garment was covered with large pearls. A large triangular opening in the dress exposed her large but upthrusting breasts. The areola of each was rouged and circled by two rings of blue and white paint.

"Tomorrow, immortal, you will become both Child and Lover of the Mother. Therefore, it is necessary that you prepare yourself."

"Just what do I have to do to prepare myself?" Stagg said. "And why should I?"

He looked at her and ached through his whole body.

She motioned with one hand. Instantly John Barleycorn, who must have been waiting around the corner, appeared. He now carried two bottles, the white lightning and some dark liquor. A priest-eunuch offered him a cup. He filled it with the dark stuff, and handed it to the priestess.

"Only you, Father of Your Country, may drink this," she said, giving the cup to Stagg. "This is the best. Made from the waters of the sticks."

Stagg took the cup. He looked at it dubiously, but he tried to be nonchalant. "Real mountain hooch, hey? Well, here goes. Never let anybody say that Peter Stagg couldn't outdrink the best of them. Aaourrwhoosh!"

The trumpets blew, the drums beat, the attendants clapped their hands and whooped.

It was then that he heard Calthorp protesting. "Captain, you misunderstood! She didn't say sticks. She said *Styx*. Waters of the S-T-Y-X! Get it?"

Stagg had gotten it, but there was nothing he could do about it. The room whirled around and around, and darkness rushed in like a great black bat.

Amid the trumpets and the cheering, he fell headlong toward the floor.

III

"What a hangover!" Stagg groaned.

"I'm afraid they do," said a voice that Stagg faintly recognized as Calthorp's.

Stagg sat up and then yelled from the pain and the shock. He rolled out of bed, fell to his knees from weakness, struggled to his feet, and staggered to the three full-length mirrors set at angles to each other. He was naked. His testicles were painted blue; his penis, red; his buttocks, white. He did not think about that. He could think about nothing except the two things he saw sticking at a 45-degree angle from his forehead for a foot and then branching out into many points.

"Horns! What're they doing there? Who put them there? By God, if I get my hands on the practical joker . . ." and he tried to pull the things from his head. He yelled with pain and let his hands drop to his side while he stared into the mirror. There was a stain of blood at the base of one of the horns.

"Not horns." Calthorp said. "Antlers. I like to be specific. Antlers— and not the hard, dead, horny kind, either. They're fairly soft, warm and velvety, as a matter of fact. If you will put your thumb there, you can feel an artery pulsing, just under the surface. Whether they will later become the hard dead antlers of the mature—pardon the pun— stag, I don't know."

The captain was scared and looking for something at which to get angry.

"All right, Calthorp!" he roared. "Are you in on this monkey business? Because if you are, I'll tear you limb from limb!"

"You not only look like a beast, you're beginning to act like one," Calthorp murmured.

Stagg could have struck the little anthropologist for his ill-timed humor. Then he saw that Calthorp was pale and his hands were shaking. His attitude was a cover-up for his very real fright.

"All right," Stagg said, calming down somewhat. "What happened?"

Voice trembling, Calthorp told him that the priests had carried his unconscious body toward his bedroom. But a mob of priestesses had rushed in and seized him. For a terrible moment Calthorp had feared that Stagg would be torn apart by the two factions. However, the fight was a mock one, a ritual; the priestesses were supposed to win the body.

Stagg had been carried into the bedroom. Calthorp tried to follow, but he was literally thrown out.

"I soon got the point. They didn't want a man in the room—except you. Even the surgeons were women. I tell you, when I saw them enter your room carrying saws and drills and bandages and all sorts of paraphernalia, I about went out of my mind. Especially when I saw that the surgeons were drunk. In fact, all the women were drunk. What a wild bunch! But John Barleycorn made me leave. He told me that at this time the women were likely to tear apart—literally—any man they encountered. He hinted that some of the musicians had not voluntarily qualified for candidacy as priests; they had just not been spry enough to get out of the way of the ladies on the evening of the winter solstice.

"Barleycorn asked me if I were an Elk. Only the totem brothers of the Great Stagg were comparatively safe during this time. I replied that I wasn't an Elk, but I was a member of Lions Club—though my dues hadn't been paid for a long time. He said I would have been safe last year, when the Sunhero was a Lion. But I was in great danger now. And he insisted on my leaving the White House until the Son—by which he meant you—was born. So I did. I came back at dawn and found everyone gone, except you. I stayed by your bedside until you woke up."

He shook his head and clucked with sympathy.

"Do you know," Stagg said, "some things are coming back to me. It's vague and mixed up, but I can remember coming to after taking that drink. I was weak and helpless as a baby. There was a great noise around me. Women screaming as if they were in the pain of childbirth . . ."

"You were the baby," Calthorp said.

"Yes. How did you know?"

"Things are beginning to shape a not unfamiliar pattern."

"Don't leave me in the dark when you see the light!" Stagg pleaded. "Anyway, I was only half-conscious most of the time. I tried to resist when they put me on a table and then placed a little white lamb on top of me. I didn't have the slightest idea of what they intended—until they cut its throat. I was drenched in the blood from head to foot.

"Then it was taken away, and I was being forced through a narrow triangular opening. The opening must have had a skeleton of metal, but it was surrounded by some pinkish spongy stuff. Two priestesses had me by the shoulders and were pulling me through the opening. The others were caterwauling like banshees. Dopey as I was, my blood was chilled. You never heard such God-awful shrieks in your life!"

"Yes, I did," Calthorp said. "All Washington heard them. The entire adult population was standing right outside the White House gates."

"I was stuck in the opening, and the priestesses were pulling violently at me. My shoulders were jammed. Suddenly, I felt water squirting on my back; somebody must have turned a hose on me. I remember thinking that they must have some sort of pump in the house, for the water had terrific pressure behind it.

"Then, I had slipped through the opening—but I didn't fall to the floor. Two priestesses grabbed my legs. I was lifted into the air and held upside down. And I was spanked, spanked hard. I was so surprised I yelled."

"Which was what they wanted you to do."

"Then I was placed on another table. My nose and mouth and eyes were cleaned out. It's funny, but up to then I hadn't noticed that I had a thick mucus-like stuff in my mouth and up my nostrils. I must have had some trouble breathing, but I wasn't aware of it. Then . . . then . . ."

"Then?"

Stagg turned red.

"Then they carried me to this enormously fat priestess, lying propped up on pillows on my bed. I'd never seen her before."

"Maybe she came down from Manhattan," Calthorp said. "Barleycorn told me the Chief Priestess there is enormously fat."

"Enormous is the word for her," Stagg continued. "That woman was the biggest I've ever seen. I'll bet that if she'd stood up, she'd have been as tall as I am. And she must have weighed over three hundred and fifty pounds. She was powdered all over her body—it must have taken a barrel of powder to cover her. She was huge and round and white. A human Queen Bee, born to do nothing but lay millions of eggs and . . ."

"And what?" Calthorp asked after Stagg had been silent for at least a minute.

"They placed me so my head was on one of her breasts. It's the hugest in the world, I'll swear it. It seemed like the curve of Earth itself. Then she took my head and turned it. I tried to fight, but I was so weak, I could not resist. I could do nothing.

"Suddenly, I did feel like a little baby. I wasn't a full grown man; I was Peter Stagg, just born. It must have been the effect of that drug. It's a hypnotic agent, I'll swear it. Anyway, I was . . . I was . . ."

"Hungry?" Calthorp said quietly.

Stagg nodded his head.

Then, in an obvious desire to get away from the subject, he put his hand on one of the antlers and said, "Hmmm. The horns are rooted solidly."

"Antlers," Calthorp said. "But you may as well continue misusing the term. I notice the Deecee use the inexact word too. Well, even if they don't distinguish between antlers and horns in common speech, their scientists are wonderful biologists. Maybe not so hot in physics and electronics, but superb artists in flesh. By the way, those antlers are more than symbolical and ornamental. They function. A thousand to one that they contain glands that are pumping all sorts of hormones into your bloodstream."

Stagg winced. "What makes you think that?"

"For one thing, Barleycorn dropped a few hints that they would. For another, there's your phenomenally rapid recovery from a major operation. After all, it was necessary to cut two holes in your skull, plant the antlers, tie off blood vessels, connect the bloodstream of the antlers with your bloodstream, and who knows what else?"

Stagg growled and said, "Somebody's going to be sorry for this. That Virginia is behind this! I'll rip her apart the next time I see her. I'm tired of being kicked around."

Calthorp had been anxiously watching him. He said, "You feel all right now?"

Stagg flared his nostrils and thumped his chest. "I didn't. But now I feel like I could lick the world. Only thing is, I'm hungry as a bear that's just come out of hibernation. How long have I been out?"

"About thirty hours. As you can see, it's getting dark outside." Calthorp put his hand on Stagg's forehead. "You have a fever. No wonder. Your body is roaring like a furnace, building new cells right and left, pumping hormones like mad into your blood. You need fuel for the furnace."

Stagg crashed his fist on a table top. "I need drink, too! I'm burning up!"

He rammed his fist into the gong repeatedly, until the notes rang throughout the palace. As if they'd been waiting for the signal, servants exploded through the door. They carried trays with many dishes and goblets.

Stagg, all politeness forgotten, tore a tray from the hands of a servant and began stuffing the meat, potatoes, gravy, corn, tomatoes, bread, and butter into his rapidly working jaws, only stopping to wash them down with tremendous draughts of beer. The food and beer slopped on his bare chest and legs but, though he'd always been a fastidious eater, he paid no attention.

Once, after a huge belch that almost knocked over a servant, he roared, "I can outbeat, outdrink . . ." Another giant belch interrupted him, and he fell again to eating like a hog in a trough.

Sickened not only at the sight but at its implications, Calthorp turned away. Evidently the hormones were washing away his captain's inhibitions and exposing the purely animal part of the human being. What would come next?

Finally, his belly sticking out like a bull gorilla's, Stagg rose. He thumped his chest and howled, "I feel great, great! Hey, Calthorp, you ought to get yourself a pair of horns! Oh, that's right, I forgot, you got a pair. That's why you left Earth the first time, wasn't it? Haw, haw!"

The little anthropologist, his face flaming and twisted, screeched and ran at Stagg. Stagg laughed and picked him up by his shirt and held him out at arm's length while Calthorp cursed and swung futilely with his short arms. Suddenly, Calthorp felt the room go by him with a rush. He slammed hard into something behind him. There was a loud clang, and he knew dimly, even as he sat half-unconscious on the floor, that he had been thrown into the gong.

He became aware that a huge hand had gripped him painfully around his wrist, hauling him to his feet. Frightened that Stagg was going to finish him off, he clenched his fist to strike a brave but futile blow. Then he dropped his fist.

Tears were running out of Stagg's eyes.

"Great God, what's the matter with me? I must be completely out of my head ever to do anything like that to you, my best friend! What's *wrong*? How could I do that?"

He sobbed and pulled Calthorp close to his great body and squeezed him affectionately. Calthorp shrieked with pain as his ribs threatened to give way. Stagg, looking hurt, released him.

"Okay, you're forgiven," Calthorp said, retreating cautiously. By now he realized that Stagg was not responsible for what he did. He had become a child in some ways. But a child is not absolutely selfish and may often be tenderhearted. Stagg was genuinely sorry and ashamed.

Calthorp went to the French windows and looked out.

"The street is alive with people and blazing with torches," he said. "They must be having another shindig tonight."

Even to himself, he sounded false. He knew well enough that the Deecee were assembled for a ceremony which would have his captain as its guest of honor.

"Skin-dig, you mean," Stagg said. "These people stop at nothing when they hold a party. Inhibitions are discarded like last year's snakeskin. And they don't care who gets hurt."

Then he made a statement that surprised Calthorp.

"I hope they get the party started soon. The sooner the better."

"For God's sake, why?" Calthorp said. "Haven't you seen enough to scare the living soul right out of your body?"

"I don't know. But there's something in me that wasn't there before. I can feel an eagerness and a power, a real power I've never known before. I feel . . . I feel . . . like a god! A god! I'm bursting with the power of all the world! I want to explode! You can't know how I feel! No mere man could!"

Outside, the priestesses screamed as they raced down the street.

The two men stopped talking to listen. They stood like stone statues while they listened to the mock-fight between the priestesses and the Honor Guards. Then, the battle as the Elks beat off the priestesses.

Then, the rush of feet in the hall outside their apartment, the crash as the Elks hit the doors with their bodies so violently they tore them from their hinges.

Stagg was lifted on their shoulders and carried out.

Just for a second, Stagg seemed to be his normal self. He turned and yelled, "Help me, Doc! Help me!"

Calthorp could do nothing except weep.

IV

There were eight of them: Churchill, Sarvant, Lin, Yastzhembski, Al-Masyuni, Steinberg, Gbwe-hun, and Chandra.

These, together with the absent Stagg and Calthorp, were the ten survivors of the original thirty that had left Earth eight hundred years ago. They were congregated in the large recreation room of the building in which they had been kept prisoners for six weeks. They were listening to Tom Tobacco.

Tom Tobacco was not his birth-name. What that was, none of them knew. They had asked, but Tom Tobacco had replied that he was not to mention it or hear it spoken. As of the day he had become Tom Tobacco, he was no longer a man but a *dim*. Apparently *dim* was the word for demigod.

"If affairs had gone normally," he was saying, "it would not be me talking to you but John Barleycorn. But the Great White Mother saw fit to end his life before Planting Rites. An election was held, and I, as chief of the great Tobacco frat, took his place as ruler of Deecee. And so I will be until I am too old and feeble—and then what will be will be."

In the short time that the starship personnel had been in Washington, they had learned the phonology, morphology, syntax, and basic vocabulary of standard Deecee speech. The machines in the laboratory of the *Terra* enabled them to speak Deecee with fluency although they could not utter the phonemes exactly as a native would, and probably never would. The structure of English had changed much; there were some sounds that had never been in English or even in its Germanic parent speech; there were many words that had come into being from unknown sources; a combination of stress and tone played an important part in meaning.

Moreover, the lack of knowledge of Deecee culture impeded understanding. To add to the trouble, Tom Tobacco himself could not speak standard Deecee with much ease. He had been born and raised in Norfolk, Virginia, the southernmost city of the nation of Deecee. Nafek, or Norfolkese, differed as much from Wazhdin, of Washingtonese, as Spanish from French, or Swedish from Icelandic.

Tom Tobacco, like his predecessor John Barleycorn, was a tall, thin man. He wore a brown plug hat, a breastplate made of stiff brown cloth in the shape of tobacco leaves, a brown cloak, a greenish kilt from which hung a two-foot-long cigar, and brown calf-length boots. His long hair was brown, his purely decorative spectacles were brown-tinted, and a big brown cigar was stuck in his tobacco-stained teeth. While he talked, he pulled cigars from a pocket in his kilt and passed them around the group. Everybody except Sarvant accepted them and found them excellent.

Tom Tobacco blew out a thick cloud of green smoke and said, "You will be released as soon as I leave. Which will be soon. I am a busy man. I have many decisions to make, many papers to sign, many functions to attend. My time is not my own; it belongs to the Great White Mother."

Churchill puffed on his cigar to allow himself time to think before speaking. The others were all talking at the same time, but when Churchill spoke they were silent. He was the first mate of the *Terra*, and now that Stagg was gone he was not only the official leader but, by force of his personality, the real one.

He was a short stocky man with a thick neck, thick arms, and thick legs. His face was babyish but at the same time strong. He had thick curly red hair and a reddish complexion with a light sprinkling of freckles. His eyes were round and clear blue as a baby's; his nose was short and round. Yet, if he had at first glance all a baby's helplessness, he also had a baby's ability to command those around him. His voice, completely at variance with his appearance, boomed out richly.

"You may be a busy man, Mr. Tobacco, but you are not so busy you can't at least tell us what is going on. We've been prisoners. We've not been allowed to communicate with our captain or with Dr. Calthorp. We have reason to suspect they may have met with foul play. Yet, when we ask about them, we're told that *what will be will be.* Very fine! Very comforting!

"Now, Mr. Tobacco, I demand that we get answers to our questions. And don't think that just because you've guards stationed outside the door, we couldn't tear you apart right now. We want answers, and we want them now!"

"Have a cigar and cool off," said Tom Tobacco. "Certainly, you're mystified and infuriated. But don't talk of rights. You are not citizens of Deecee, and you are in a very precarious situation.

"However, I will give you some answers; that's why I came here. First, you will be released. Second, you will be given a month to fit into the life of Deecee. Third, if, at the end of the month, you show no promise of becoming a good citizen, you will be killed. Not exiled, but killed. If we escorted you across the borders to another country, we would be increasing the population of our enemy states. And we've no intention of doing that."

"Well, at least we know where we stand," Churchill said. "That is, in a vague way. Do we get access to the *Terra*? The results of ten years of unique study are in that ship."

"No, you do not. However, your personal property will be returned to you."

"Thanks," Churchill said. "Do you realize that except for a few books, we *had* no personal property? What will we do for money while we're looking for jobs? Jobs we may not be able to get in this rather primitive society."

"I really can't say," replied Tom Tobacco. "After all, we've allowed you to keep your lives. There were those who didn't want to give you even that."

He stuck two fingers in his mouth and whistled. A man with a small bag in his hand appeared.

"I must go now, gentlemen. Official business. However, in order that you may not break the laws of this blessed nation through ignorance, and also to remove any temptation to steal, this man will enlighten you about our laws and loan you enough coin to buy food for a week. You will repay it after you have jobs—if you have jobs. Columbia bless you."

An hour later, the eight men stood in front of the building out of which they had just been escorted.

Far from being elated, they felt a trifle dazed and more than a little helpless.

Churchill looked at them, and, though he felt as they did, he said, "For God's sake, buck up! What's the matter with you? We've been through worse than this. Remember when we were on Wolf 69 III, crossing that big Jurassic-type swamp on a raft? And the balloon-creature upset us and we lost our weapons in the water and had to make our way back to the ship unarmed? We were far worse off then, and we didn't look nearly so woebegone. What's happened? Aren't you the men you used to be?"

"I'm afraid not," Steinberg said. "It's not that we've lost our courage. It's just that we expected too much. When we were landing on a newly discovered planet, we expected the unexpected and the disastrous. We even looked forward to it. But here, well, we anticipated too much—plus the fact that we are helpless. We're unarmed, and if we run into a bad situation, we can't just shoot our way out and make our way back to the ship."

"So you're going to stand around and hope everything's turned out all right?" Churchill said. "For God's sake! You men were the cream of the crop of Earth, chosen out of tens of thousands of candidates because of your I.Q., your education, your ingenuity, your physical hardihood. And now you're marooned among a people who haven't the knowledge you have in your little finger! You men should be gods—and you're mice!"

"Knock it off," Lin said. "We're still suffering from shock. We don't know what to do, and that's what is scaring us."

"Well, I'm not going to stand around until some kind soul comes along and takes me in hand," Churchill said. "I am going to act—now!"

"And just what are you going to do?" Yastzhembski asked.

"I'm going to walk around Washington until I see something that calls for action. If you men want to come with me, you can. But if you want to go your own ways, that's all right, too. I'll be your leader, but I won't be your shepherd."

"You don't understand," Yastzhembski said. "Six of us don't even belong on this continent. I would like to return to Holy Siberia. Gbwehun wants to go back to Dahomey. Chandra, to India. Al-Masyuni, to Mecca. Lin, to Shanghai. But that seems impossible. Steinberg could conceivably get back to Brazil, yet, if he did, he'd find nothing but desert and jungle and howling savages. So . . ."

"So you have to stay here and do as Tobacco suggested—fit in. Well, that's what I'm going to do. Anybody coming along?"

Churchill didn't wait for more argument. He began walking down the street and did not look back once. When he had turned a corner, however, he stopped to watch a bunch of naked little girls and boys playing ball in the street.

After perhaps five minutes, he sighed. Apparently no one was following him.

He was wrong. Just as he turned to go on, he heard someone calling to him. "Hold on a minute, Churchill."

It was Sarvant.

"Where are the others?" Churchill said.

"The Asiatics have decided to try to get back to their homelands. When I left they were still arguing about whether they should steal a boat and cross the Atlantic, or steal deer and ride up to the Bering Strait, where they'll cross on boat to Siberia."

"I'll give them credit for the greatest guts in the world—or the most stupid brains. Do they really think they can make it? Or that they'll find any better conditions there than here?"

"They don't know what they'll find, but they're desperate."

"I'd like to go back and wish them good luck," Churchill said. "But I'd just end up trying to argue them out of the idea. They are brave men. I knew it when I called them mice, but I was just trying to arouse them. Maybe I succeeded too well."

"I gave them my blessing, even if most of them are agnostics," Sarvant said. "But I fear their bones will bleach on this continent."

"What about you? Are you going to try for Arizona?"

"From what I saw of Arizona while we were still circling Earth, I'd say there's not only no organized government there, there are almost no people. I would try for Utah, but it doesn't look much better. Even the Salt Lake is dried up. There's nothing to go back to. It doesn't matter. There is a lifetime of work here."

"Work? You don't mean preaching?"

Churchill looked incredulously at Sarvant as if seeing his true character for the first time.

Nephi Sarvant was a short, dark, and bony man of about forty. His chin jutted out so far it gave the impression of curving upwards at its end. His mouth was so thin-lipped it was only a thread. His nose, like his chin, was overdeveloped. It hooked downwards as if trying to meet the chin. His crewmates said that in profile he looked like a human nutcracker.

His large brown eyes were very expressive and just now seemed to glow with inner light. They had glowed often during the star-trip when he had extolled the merits of his church as the only true one left on Earth. He belonged to a sect known as the Last Slanders, the strictly orthodox core of a church that had undergone the suburbanization most churches had experienced. Once thought a peculiar people, the members of this sect now could be distinguished from other Christians only by the fact that they still attended their church. But the spiritual fires had died out.

Not so the group to which the Sarvant belonged. The Last Slanders had refused to adopt the so-called vices of their neighbors. They had collected in a body at the city of Fourth of July, Arizona, and from there had sent out missionaries to an indifferent or amused world.

Sarvant had been chosen to be a crew member of the *Terra* because he was the foremost authority in his field of geology. He had been accepted only after he had promised not to proselytize. He had never explicitly made an attempt to convert. But he had offered to others the Book of his church, asking only that they read. And he had argued with the others about the authenticity of the Book.

"Of course I mean to preach!" he said. "This country is as wide open to the Gospel as it was when Columbus landed. I'll tell you, Rud, that when I saw the desolation of the Southwest I was filled with despair. It seemed that my church had vanished from the face of the Earth. And if that were true, then my church was false, for it was supposed to be eternal. But I prayed, and at once the truth came to me. That is—I still exist! And through me the church can grow again— grow as it never did, for these pagan minds, once convinced of the Truth, will become as the First Disciples. The Book will spread like a flame. You see, we Last Slanders could make little headway among Christians because they thought they already had the true church. But the true church meant little more to them than a social club. It wasn't a way of truth and life, the only way. It . . ."

"I get your point," Churchill said. "The only thing I have to say is, don't implicate me. Things are going to be tough enough. Well, let's go."

"Go where?"

"Someplace where we can trade these monkeys suits in for native clothes."

They were on a street called Conch. It ran north and south, so Churchill felt that if they followed it south it would bring them eventually to the port area. Here, unless things changed very much, there would be more than one shop where they could trade their clothes and perhaps make a little profit in the bargain. In this neighborhood, Conch Street was a mixture of well-to-do residences and large government buildings. The residences were set far back on well-tended yards and were of brick or cement. Single-storied, they presented a broad front, and most of them had two wings at right angles to the front buildings. They were painted in many colors and various designs. Every one had a large totem pole in front of it. These were, for the most part, of carved stone, since wood was reserved for shipbuilding, wagons, weapons, and stove fuel.

The government buildings were set close to the street and were of brick or marble. They had curving walls and were surrounded by roofless porches with tall pillars. On top of each dome roof was a statue.

Churchill and Sarvant walked on the asphalt pavement—there was no sidewalk—for ten blocks. Occasionally, they had to step close to the buildings to avoid being run over by men furiously riding deer or driving carriages. The riders were richly dressed and obviously expected the pedestrians to jump out of the way or get trampled. The carriage drivers seemed to be couriers of one type or another.

Abruptly, the street became shabby.

The buildings presented a solid front except for alleys here and there. They were evidently government buildings that had been sold to private agents and had become little shops or tenements. Naked children played in front of them.

These were not nearly as clean as those they had just passed.

Churchill found the shop he was looking for. With Sarvant at his heels, he entered. The inside of the shop was a small room crowded with clothes of every kind. The store window and the cement floor were dirty; the odor of dog excrement filled the shop. Two dogs of indeterminate breed tried to put their paws on the two men.

The owner was a short big-paunched double-chinned bald man

with two enormous earrings of brass. He looked much like any shop-keeper of his breed of any century, except that he had the cervine stamp of the times on his features.

"We want to sell our clothes," Churchill said.

"Are they worth anything?" said the owner.

"As clothes, not much," Churchill replied. "As curios, they may be worth a great deal. We are men from the starship."

The owner's little eyes widened. "Ah, brothers to the Sunhero!"

Churchill didn't know all the implications of the exclamation. He knew only that Tom Tobacco had casually mentioned that Captain Stagg had become a Sunhero.

"I'm sure that you could sell each article of our clothing for quite a sum. These clothes have been to the stars, to places so distant that if you were to walk there without stopping to eat or rest it would take you halfway through eternity. The light of alien suns and the air of exotic worlds are caught in the fibers of these suits. And the shoes still bear the traces of earth where monsters bigger than this building have walked like earthquakes."

The shopkeeper was unimpressed. "But has the Sunhero touched these garments?"

"Many times. Once, he wore this jacket."

"Ahhh!"

The owner must have realized that he was betraying his eager-ness. He lower his eyelids and stiffened his face.

"This is all very well, but I am a poor man. The sailors who come to this shop do not have much money. By the time they get past the taverns, they are ready to sell their own clothes."

"Probably true. But I'm sure you have contacts who can sell these to wealthier patrons."

The owner took some coins from the pocket on his kilt.

"I'll give you four columbias for the lot."

Churchill motioned to Sarvant and started to walk out. Before he reached the door, he found the owner blocking his way.

"Perhaps I could offer you five columbias."

Churchill pointed to a kilt and sandals. "How much are those worth? Or I should say, how much are you charging for them?"

"Three fish."

Churchill considered. A Columbia was roughly equal to a five-dollar bill of his time. A fish was equal to a quarter.

"You know as well as I do that you'll be making a thousand-percent-profit off us. I want twenty columbias for these."

The owner threw his hands up in the air in a gesture of despair.

"Come off it," Churchill said. "I'd go from house to house on Millionaire's Row and peddle these. But I haven't the time. Do you want to give us twenty or not? Last offer."

"You're snatching the bread from the mouths of my poor children . . . but I'll take your offer."

Ten minutes later, the two starmen stepped out of the shop. They wore sandals and kilts and round hats with floppy brims. Their broad leather belts held sheaths with long steel knives, and their pockets contained eight columbias each. They held bags in their hands, and in these bags were rainproof ponchos.

"Next stop, the docks," Churchill said. "I used to sail yachts for the rich during the summers when I was working my way through college."

"I know you can sail," Sarvant said. "Have you forgotten that you commanded that sailing-ship we stole when we escaped from prison on the planet Vixa?"

"I forgot," Churchill said. "I want to size up the chances for getting a job. Afterwards, we'll start sniffing around. Maybe we can find out what's happened to Stagg and Calthorp."

"Rud," Sarvant said, "there must be more to this than just getting a job. Why boats particularly? I know you well enough to know you're operating on more than one level."

"O.K. I know you're no blabbermouth. If I can find a suitable ship, we'll get hold of Yastzhembski's boys and take off for Asia, via Europe."

"I'm very glad to hear that," Sarvant said. "I thought you'd just walked out on them, washed your hands of them. But how will you find them?"

"Are you kidding?" Churchill said, laughing. "All I have to do is ask at the nearest temple."

"Temple?"

"Sure. It's evident that the government'll be keeping an eye on us. In fact, it's had a tail on us ever since we left our prison."

"Where is he?"

"Don't look around now. I'll point him out to you later. Just keep walking."

Abruptly, Churchill stopped. His way was barred by a circle of men kneeling on the road. There was nothing to keep Churchill from walking around them. But he stopped to look over the shoulders.

"What are they doing?" Sarvant asked.

"Playing the twenty-ninth century version of craps."

"It's against my principles even to watch gambling. I sincerely hope you're not planning on joining them."

"Yes, I think that's exactly what I'm planning on doing."

"Don't, Rud," Sarvant said, putting his hand on Churchill's arm. "Nothing good can come of this."

"Chaplain, I'm not a member of your parish. They probably abide by the rules. That's all I want." Churchill took three columbias out of his pocket and spoke loudly. "Can I get into this shoot?"

"Sure," a huge dark man with a patch over one eye said. "You can play as long as your money lasts. You just get off the ship?"

"Not so long ago," Churchill said. He sank to his knees and laid a Columbia on the ground. "My turn for the bones, eh? Come on, babies, Poppa needs a pocketful of rye."

Thirty minutes later a grinning Churchill walked toward Sarvant with a handful of silver coins. "The wages of sin," he said.

He lost his grin when he heard a loud shout behind him. Turning, he saw the dice players walking toward him. The big one-eyed man was yelling at him.

"Wait a minute, buddy, we got a couple of questions!"

"Oh, oh," Churchill said out of the side of his mouth. "Get ready to run. These guys are poor losers."

"You didn't cheat, did you?" Sarvant said nervously.

"Of course not! You ought to know me better than that. Besides, I wouldn't take a chance in that rough bunch."

"Listen, buddy," the one-eyed man said. "You talk kinda funny. Where you come from? Albany?"

"Manitowoc, Wisconsin," Churchill said.

"Never heard of that place. What is it, some small burg up north?"

"North by west. Why do you want to know?"

"We don't like strangers that can't even talk Deecee straight. Strangers got queer tricks, especially when they are shooting craps. Only a week ago we caught a tar from Norfolk who was using magic to control the dice. We knocked his teeth out and threw him off the dock with a weight around his neck. Never saw him again."

"If you thought I was cheating, you should have said something while we were playing."

The one-eyed sailor ignored Churchill's remark and said, "I don't notice no frat mark on you. What frat you belong to?"

"Lambda Chi Alpha," Churchill said. He put his hand on his knife-blade.

"What kind of lingo is that? You mean the Lamb frat?"

Churchill could see that he and Sarvant would be considered lambs for the slaughter unless they could prove they were under the protection of some powerful frat. He didn't mind telling a lie in a situation like this if it got him out of it. But a resentment that had been building up for the past six weeks broke into a sudden fury.

"I belong to the human race!" he shouted. "And that's more than you can say for yourself!"

The one-eyed sailor turned red. He growled, "By the breasts of Columbia, I'll cut your heart out! No stinking foreigner can talk that way to me!"

"Come on, you thieves!" Churchill snarled. He pulled his knife from its sheath and at the same time shouted at Sarvant, "Run like hell!"

The one-eyed sailor had also pulled his knife and came at Churchill with the blade. Churchill threw the handful of silver coins in the man's eyes and at the same time stepped forward. The palm of his left hand struck outwards against the wrist of the other man's knife-hand. The knife fell, and Churchill sank his blade into the bulging paunch of the sailor.

He withdrew the knife and stepped back, crouching, to face the others. But they knew dirty fighting as well as any sailor. One of them picked up a loose brick from a pile of rubble and threw it at Churchill's head. The world grew dim, and he was vaguely aware that blood was streaming over his eyes from a cut on his forehead. By the time he regained his senses, he found his knife taken away and his arms gripped by two strong sailors.

A third, a short skinny fellow with a broken-toothed snarl, stepped up and shoved his blade straight at Churchill's belly.

V

Peter Stagg awoke. He was flat on his back, lying on something soft, with the branches of a large oak tree above him. Through the branches he could see a bright, cloudless sky. There were birds on the branches, a sparrow, a catbird—and a huge jay which sat on its rear and dangled bare and human legs.

The legs were brown and slim and nicely curved. The rest of the body was disguised in the costume of a giant jaybird. Shortly after Stagg opened his eyes, the jay took off its mask and revealed the pretty face of a dark, big-eyed girl. She reached behind her and pulled a bugle that had been hanging from a cord from over her shoulder. Before Stagg could stop her, she blew a long wavering call.

Immediately, a hubbub arose from somewhere behind him.

Stagg sat up and turned around to face the source of the noise. It came from a mob of people standing on the other side of the road. The road was a broad cement highway running past farm fields. Stagg was sitting a few feet from its edge on a thick pile of blankets which someone had thoughtfully placed beneath him.

He had no idea of when or how he had gotten to this spot. Or where it was. He remembered only too vividly events up to shortly before dawn; after that, all was blank. The height of the sun indicated that the time was about eleven in the morning.

The jay-girl lowered herself from the branch, hung for a moment, then dropped the five feet to the ground. She picked herself up and said, "Good morning, Noble Stag. How do you feel?"

Stagg groaned and said, "I'm stiff and sore in every muscle. And I've an awful headache."

"You'll be all right after you have breakfast. And may I say that you were magnificent last night? I've never seen a Sunhero who could come up to you. Well, I must go now. Your friend, Calthorp, said that when you woke you'd want to be alone with him for a while."

"Calthorp!" Stagg said. He groaned again. "He's the last man I want to see." But the girl had run off across the road and joined the group of people.

Calthorp's white head appeared from behind a tree. He approached with a large covered tray in his hands. He was smiling, but it was obvious he was desperately trying to cover up his concern.

"How do you feel?" he shouted.

Stagg told him. "Where are we?"

"I'd say we're on what used to be U.S. 1 but is now called Mary's Pike. We're about ten miles out of the present limits of Washington. Two miles down the road is a little farming town called Fair Grace. Its normal population is two thousand, but just now it's about fifteen thousand. The farmers and the farmers' daughters from miles around have gathered here. Everyone in Fair Grace is eagerly awaiting you. But you are not at their beck and call. You are the Sunhero, so you may rest and take your ease. That is, until sundown. Then you must perform as you did last night."

Stagg looked down and for the first time became aware that he was still nude.

"You saw me last night?" He looked up pleadingly at the old man.

It was Calthorp's turn to stare at the ground. He said, "Ringside seat—for a while, anyway. I sneaked around the edge of the crowd and went into a building. There I watched the orgy from a balcony."

"Don't you have any decency?" Stagg said angrily. "It's bad enough that I couldn't help myself. It's worse that you'd witness my humiliation."

"Some humiliation! Yes, I saw you. I'm an anthropologist. This was the first time I'd ever had a chance to see a fertility rite at close range. Also, as your friend, I was worried about you. But I needn't have; you took care of yourself. Others, too."

Stagg glared. "Are you making fun of me?"

"God forbid! No. I wasn't expressing humor, just amazement. Perhaps envy. Of course, it's the antlers that gave you the drive and the ability. Wonder if they'd give me just a little shot of the stuff those antlers produce."

Calthorp placed the tray in front of Stagg and removed the cloth over it. "Here's a breakfast such as you never had."

Stagg turned his head to one side. "Take it away. I'm sick. Sick to my stomach and sick to my soul with what I did last night."

"You seemed to be enjoying yourself." Stagg growled with sheer fury, and Calthorp put out a reassuring hand. "No, I meant no offense. It's just that I saw you, and I can't get over it. Come on, lad, eat. Look what we have for you! Fresh baked bread. Fresh butter. And jam. Honey.

Eggs, bacon, ham, trout, venison—and a pitcher of cool ale. And you can have second helpings on anything you want."

"I told you, I'm sick! I couldn't eat a thing." Stagg sat silent for a few minutes, staring across the road at the brightly colored tents and the people clustered around them. Calthorp sat down by him and lit up a large green cigar.

Suddenly, Stagg picked up the pitcher and drank deeply of the ale. He put the pitcher down, wiped the foam off his lips with the back of his hand, belched, and picked up a fork and knife.

He began eating as if this were the first meal in his life—or the last.

"I have to eat," he apologized between bites. "I'm weak as a new-born kitten. Look how my hand's shaking."

"You'll have to eat enough for a hundred men," Calthorp said. "After all, you did the work of a hundred—two hundred!"

Stagg reached up with one hand and felt his antlers. "Still there. Hey! They're not standing up straight and stiff like they did last night. They're limp! Maybe they are going to shrink up and dry away,"

Calthorp shook his head. "No. When you get your strength back, and your blood pressure rises, they'll become erect again. They're not true antlers. Those of deer consist of bony outgrowth with no covering of keratin. Yours seem to have a bony base, but the upper part is mainly cartilage surrounded by skin and blood vessels.

"It's no wonder they're deflated. And it's a wonder that you didn't rupture a blood vessel. Or something."

"Whatever it is the horns pump into me," Stagg said, "it must be gone. Except for being weak and sore, I feel normal. If only I could get rid of these horns! Doc, could you cut them off?"

Sadly, Calthorp shook his head.

Stagg turned pale. "Then I have to go through that *again*?"

"I'm afraid so, my boy."

"Tonight, at Fair Grace? And the next night at another town? And so on until . . . when?"

"Peter, I'm sorry, I have no way of knowing how long."

Calthorp cried out with pain as a huge hand bent his wrist bones towards each other.

Stagg loosened his grip. "Sorry, Doc. I got excited."

"Well, now," Calthorp said, rubbing his wrist tenderly, "there's one possibility. It seems to me that, if all this business started at the winter solstice, it should end at the summer solstice. That is, about June 21 or 22.

You are the symbol of the sun. In fact, these people probably regard you as being literally the sun himself—especially since you came down in a flaming iron steed out of the sky."

Stagg put his head in his hands. Tears welled out from between his fingers, and his naked shoulders shook. Calthorp patted his golden head, while tears ran from his own eyes. He knew how terribly grieved his captain must be, if he could weep through the armors of his inhibitions.

Finally, Stagg rose and began walking across the fields toward a nearby creek. "Have to take a bath," he muttered. "I'm filthy. If I have to be a Sunhero, I'm going to be a clean one."

"Here they come," Calthorp said, pointing to the crowd of people who had been waiting about fifty yards away. "Your devout worshipers and bodyguards."

Stagg grimaced. "Just now I loathe myself. But last night I enjoyed what I was doing. I had no inhibitions. I was living the secret dream of every man—unlimited opportunity and inexhaustible ability. I was a *god*!"

He stopped and seized Calthorp's wrist again.

"Go back to the ship! Get a gun, if you have to sneak it past the guards. Come back and shoot me in the head—so I won't have to go through this again!"

"I'm sorry. In the first place, I wouldn't know where to get the gun. Tom Tobacco told me that all weapons have been taken from the ship and locked in a secret room. In the second place, I can't kill you. While there's life, there's hope. We'll get out of this mess."

"Tell me how," Stagg said.

He didn't have time to continue the conversation. The mob had come across the field and surrounded them. Continuity of talk was difficult to maintain when bugles and drums were roaring in your ears, Panpipes shrilling, men and women chattering away at the tops of their voices, and a group of beautiful girls was insisting on bathing you and afterward toweling you down and perfuming you. In a short time the pressure of the crowd forced the two apart.

Stagg began to feel better.

Under the skillful hands of the girls, his soreness was massaged away, and, as the sun climbed toward the zenith, Stagg's strength rose. By two o'clock he was brimming over with vitality. He wanted to be up and doing.

Unfortunately, this was siesta hour. The crowd dispersed to seek shade under which to lie down.

A few faithful stood around Stagg. From their sleepy expression Stagg decided that they, too, would like to lie down. They couldn't; they were his guards, lean hard men armed with spears and knives. A few yards away stood several bowmen. These carried strange arrows. The shafts were tipped with long needles instead of the broad, sharp steel heads. Undoubtedly, the tips were smeared with a drug that would temporarily paralyze any Sunheroes who might dare to run away.

Stagg thought that it was foolish of them to post a guard. Now that he felt better, he didn't care one bit about escaping. Indeed, he wondered why he could have contemplated such a stupid move.

Why should he want to run and take a chance of being killed— when there was so much living to be done?

He walked back across the field, his guards trailing along at a respectful distance. There were about forty tents pitched on a meadow and three times that many people stretched out sleeping. Stagg was not at the moment interested in them.

He wanted to talk to the girl in the cage.

Ever since he had been moved into the White House, he had wondered who she was and why she was kept prisoner. His questions had invariably been answered with the infuriating *What will be will be.* He remembered seeing her as he approached Virginia, the Chief Priestess. The memory brought back a pang of the shame he had felt a little while ago, but it quickly faded.

The wheeled cage was under the shadow of a plane tree, the deer that drew it browsing nearby. There were no guards within earshot.

The girl was sitting on a built-in cucking stool at one end of the cage. Near her stood a peasant smoking a cigar while he waited for her to finish. When she was through, he would remove the chamber pot from the recess underneath the stool and carry it off to his fields to enrich the soil.

She wore the long-billed jockey cap, gray shirt, and calf-length pants that all mascots wore, though the pants were now down around her ankles. Her head was bowed, but Stagg did not think it was because she was ashamed to be performing this need in public view. He had seen too much of the casual, animal-natural—to him—attitude of these people. They could feel shame and inhibition about many things but public excretion was not one of them.

A hammock was pulled tight against the ceiling. A broom stood in the corner and in the opposite corner a cabinet was bolted to the floor. Probably it contained toilet articles, since a rack on the side of the cabinet contained a washbasin and towels.

He looked again at the sign rising from the top of her cage like a shark's fin. "Mascot, captured in a raid on Caseyland." What did it mean?

He understood that "mascot" was the word the Deecees used for human virgins. The term "virgin" was reserved for maiden goddesses. But there was much he did not understand.

"Hello," he said.

The girl started as if she had been dozing. She raised her head to look at him. She had large dark eyes and petite features. Her skin was white, and it went even whiter when she saw him, and she turned her head away.

"Hello, I said. Can't you speak? I won't hurt you."

"I don't want to talk to you, you beast," she replied in a shaky voice. "Go away."

He had taken a step toward the cage, but now he stopped.

Of course, she had had to witness last night. Even if she kept her head turned and eyes shut, she couldn't have stopped up her ears. And curiosity would have forced her to open her eyes. At least for brief periods.

"I couldn't help what happened," he said. "It's these that did it, not me." He touched the antlers. "They do something to me. I'm not myself."

"Go away," she said. "I won't talk to you. You're a pagan devil."

"Is it because I'm not clothed?" he said. "I'll put a kilt on."

"Go away!"

One of the guards walked up to him. "Great Stag, do you want this girl? You may have her, eventually, but not now. Not until the end of the journey. Then the Great White Mother will give her to you."

"I just want to talk to her."

The guard smiled. "A little fire applied to her cute little ass might get her to talking. Unfortunately we're not allowed to torture her— yet."

Stagg turned away. "I'll find some way to make her talk. But later. Just now, I want some more cold ale."

"At once, sire."

The guard, not caring that he was waking most of the camp, blew shrilly on his whistle. A girl ran from around the corner of a tent.

"Cold ale!" the guard cried.

The girl ran toward the tent and quickly returned with a tray on which stood a copper pitcher, its sides beaded with sweat.

Stagg took the pitcher without thanking the girl and held it to his mouth. He did not lower it until it was empty.

"That was good," he said loudly. "But ale bloats you. Do you have any lightning on ice?"

"Of course, sire."

She returned from the tent with a silver pitcher full of chunks of ice and another pitcher brimming with clear whiskey. She poured the lightning into the pitcher of ice and then handed it to Stagg.

He drank half of the pitcher before he set it back on the tray.

The guard became alarmed. "Great Stag, if you continue at this rate, we'll have to carry you into Fair Grace!"

"A Sunhero can drink as many as ten men," said the girl, "and he will still tumble a hundred mascots in one night."

Stagg laughed like a trumpet blaring. "Of course, mortal, don't you know that? Besides, what's the use of being the Great Stag if I can't do exactly what I want to do?"

"Forgive me, sire," the guard said. "It's just that I know how anxious the people of Fair Grace are to greet you. Last year, you know, when the Sunhero was a Lion, he took the other road out of Washington. The people of Fair Grace could not attend the ceremonies. So they would feel very bad if you did not show up."

"Don't be a fool," the girl said. "You shouldn't talk this way to the Sunhero. What if he got mad and decided to kill you? That's happened, you know."

The guard blanched. "With your permission, sire, I'll join my friends."

"Do that!" Stagg said, laughing.

The guard trotted away to a group standing about fifty yards off.

"I'm hungry again," Stagg said. "Get me some food. Lots of meat."

"Yes, sire."

Stagg began to prowl around the camp. When he came across a gray-haired fat man snoring away in a hammock stretched between two tripods, he turned the hammock over and dumped the fat man on the ground. Roaring with laughter, he strode around the camp and began shouting in the ear of every sleeper he came across. They sat up, their eyes wide and their hearts beating with shock. He laughed and moved on and seized the leg of a girl and began tickling her on the sole of her foot. She shrieked with laughter and wept and begged him to let her go. A young man, her fiancé, stood by but made no move to free her. His fists were clenched, but it would have been blasphemy to interfere with the Sunhero.

Stagg looked up and saw him. He frowned, released the girl, and rose to his feet. At that moment the girl whom he'd sent for food came with a tray. There were two pitchers of ale on it. Stagg took one and calmly poured it over the head of the young man. Both girls laughed, and that seemed to be a signal to the whole camp. Everybody howled.

The girl with the tray took the other pitcher of ale and poured it over the fat man who had been dumped out of the hammock. The cold liquid brought him sputtering to his feet. He ran into his tent and came out with a small keg of beer. Holding it upside down, he drenched the girl with its contents.

A beer-throwing party exploded across the camp. There wasn't a person on the meadow who wasn't dripping with ale and beer and whiskey, except for the girl in the cage. Even the Sunhero was showered. He laughed when he felt the cool liquid and ran for more to throw back. But on the way he got a new idea. He began pushing the tents over so they would imprison the occupants. Howls of anguish rose from the interiors of the collapsed tents. The others began imitating Stagg's actions, and shortly there was hardly a tent standing on the meadow.

Stagg seized the girl who had served him and the girl whose foot he'd tickled. "You two must be mascots," he said. "Otherwise you'd not be half-naked. How did I happen to miss you last night?"

"We weren't beautiful enough for the first night."

"The judges must be blind," Stagg roared. "Why, you're two of the most beautiful and desirable girls I've ever seen!"

"We thank you. It's not just beauty that enables you to be chosen as the bride of the Sunhero, sire, though I hesitate to say it for fear of what might happen if a priestess overheard me. But it's true that if your father happens to have wealth and connections, you stand a much better chance of being picked."

"Then why were you two chosen to be in my entourage?"

"We were second-place winners in the Miss America contests, sire. Being in your entourage isn't as great an honor as having one's debut in Washington. But it is still a great honor. And we are hoping that tonight at Fair Grace . . ."

Both were looking at him with wide eyes. Their lips and nipples were swelling, they were breathing heavily.

"Why wait until tonight?" he bellowed.

"It's not customary to do anything until the rites begin, sire. Anyway, most Sunheroes don't recover from the previous night until evening . . ."

Stagg downed another drink. He drew the empty pitcher as high in the air as he could and laughed.

"I'm a Sunhero like you've never had! I'm the genuine Stagg!"

He picked up the two girls by their waists, one in each arm, and carried them into the tent.

VI

Churchill reared back and tried to kick more teeth out of the snaggle-toothed sailor's mouth. The blow from the brick had taken more than he realized out of him. He could barely lift his legs.

"Yer would, wouldjer?" Snaggletooth squeaked.

He had jumped back at Churchill's threatening move. Now he stepped forward confidently and shoved the knife toward Churchill's solar plexus.

There was a screech, and a little man jumped forward and thrust his arm in the path of the blade. The point went through the open palm and came out redly on the other side.

It was Sarvant, who had taken this clumsy but effective means of keeping his friend from death.

The knife was stopped for only a moment. Another sailor pushed Sarvant so hard he fell backwards, the knife still protruding from his hand. The sailor drew back to plunge his blade into the original target.

A whistle sounded shrilly almost in his ear. He stopped. The whistler reached out a long shepherd's staff and crooked the end around Snaggletooth's scrawny neck.

The whistler was dressed in light blue, and he had light blue eyes to match. They were as cold as eyes could get.

"These men are protected by Columbia Herself," he said. "You men will disperse at once, unless you want to be strung up by the neck inside ten minutes. And you will not attempt to take revenge on these two later on. Do you understand?"

The sailors had turned pale under their deeply tanned skins. They nodded, gulped, and then ran.

"I owe you my life," Churchill said, shakily.

"You owe the Great White Mother," the man in blue said. "And She will collect as it pleases her. I am merely Her servant. For the next four weeks, you are under Her protection. I hope you will prove yourself worthy of Her consideration."

He looked at Sarvant's dripping hand. "I think you owe this man your life, too. Though he was only the tool of Columbia, he served Her well. Come with me. We will fix up that hand."

They followed him down the street, Sarvant moaning with the pain, Churchill supporting him.

"That's the man who was tailing us," Churchill said. "Lucky for us. And—thanks for what you did."

Sarvant's face lost its look of pain and became ecstatic.

"I was glad to do it for you, Rud. It's something I'd do again, even knowing how it would hurt. It made me feel justified."

Churchill didn't know how to reply to that statement, so he said nothing.

Both men were silent until they walked out of the dock area and came to a temple set far back of the street. Their guide led them into the cool interior. He spoke to a priestess in long white robes, who, in turn, led them to a small room. Churchill was asked to wait while Sarvant was taken away.

He didn't object. He was certain they had no evil intentions against Sarvant—at the present.

He paced back and forth for an hour by a huge sandglass on a table. The chamber was quiet and dark and cool.

He was just in the act of turning the big sandglass over when Sarvant reappeared.

"How's the hand?"

Sarvant held it up for Churchill to see. There was no bandage on it. The hole had been glued together, and a transparent film of some substance covered the wound.

"They tell me I can use it at this very moment for hard work," Sarvant said wonderingly. "Rud, these people may be backwards in many respects, but when it comes to biology, they bow to no one. The priestess told me this thin stuff is a pseudoflesh that will grow and make the wound as if it had never been. They gave me a blood transfusion, and then made me eat some food that seemed to charge me with energy at once. But it wasn't for nothing," he concluded wryly. "They said they'd send me the bill."

"The impression I get is that this culture just doesn't tolerate freeloaders," Churchill said. "We'd better get a job of some kind, and fast."

They left the temple and resumed their interrupted journey toward the docks. This time they passed without incident to the Potomac River.

The docks extended along the banks for at least two kilometers. There were ships tied up alongside the wharves and many anchored in the river itself. "Looks like a picture of an early nineteenth-century port," Churchill said. "Sailing ships of every size and type. I didn't expect to find any steamships, though it's unreasonable to suppose that these people don't know how to build one."

"The coal and oil supplies were exhausted long before we left Earth," Sarvant said. "They could burn wood, but the impression I have is that, while there's no scarcity of trees, they aren't chopped down except for the utmost necessity. And it's evident they either have forgotten the techniques of making nuclear fuel, or else are suppressing the knowledge."

"Wind power may be slow," Churchill said. "But it's free for the taking, and it'll get you there in time. Man, here comes a beautiful ship!"

He gestured at a single-masted yacht with white keel and scarlet sail. It was tacking to come into a slip just below the wharf on which they were standing.

Churchill, motioning to Sarvant, walked down the long steps running down the bank. He liked to talk to sailors, and the people on this yacht looked as if they were the type he had worked for during his college summers.

The man at the wheel was a gray-haired, heavily built man of about fifty-five. The other two looked like his son and daughter. The son was tall, well-built, handsome, a blond of about twenty; his sister was a short girl with a well-developed bust, slim waist, long legs, extremely beautiful face, and long honey-blond hair. She could have been anywhere from sixteen to eighteen years old. She wore loose bell-bottomed trousers and a short blue jacket. Her feet were bare.

She stood in the prow of the boat, and, seeing the two men waiting on the slip, she flashed white teeth and called, "Catch this rope, sailor!"

Churchill caught it and pulled the yacht alongside the slip. The girl leaped down onto the boards and smiled. "Thanks, sailor!"

The blond youth reached into the pocket of his kilt and tossed Churchill a coin. "For your trouble, my man."

Churchill turned the coin over. It was a Columbia. If these people could tip so generously for such a small service, they must be worth making acquaintance.

He flipped the coin back at the youth, who, though surprised, deftly caught it with one hand.

"I thank you," Churchill said, "but I am no man's servant."

The eyes of the girl widened, and Churchill saw that they were a dark blue-gray.

"We meant no offense," she said. She had a rich throaty voice.

"No offense taken," Churchill said.

"I can tell by your accent you're not a Deecee," she said. "Would it offend you if I asked what your native city is?"

"Not at all. I was born in Manitowoc, a city that no longer exists. My name is Rudyard Churchill, and my companions is Nephi Sarvant. He was born in Mesa, Arizona. We are eight hundred years old and remarkably well preserved for our advanced age."

The girl sucked in her breath. "Oh, the brothers of the Sunhero!"

"Shipmates of Captain Stagg, yes." Churchill was pleased that he was making such a strong impression.

The father held out his hand, and by that gesture Churchill knew he and Sarvant were accepted as equals, at least for the time being.

"I am Res Whitrow. This is my son, Bob, and my daughter, Robin."

"You have a beautiful ship," Churchill said, knowing that was the best way to stimulate a flow of talk.

Res Whitrow at once began explaining the virtues of his craft, and his children added their enthusiastic comments. After a while, there was a brief pause in the conversation, and Robin said, breathlessly, "Oh, you must have seen so many things, so many wonderful things, if it's true that you have been out to the stars. I wish I could hear of them!"

"Yes," Whitrow said, "I'm eager to hear of them too. Why don't you two become my guests for the evening? That is, unless you've an engagement for tonight?"

"We would be honored," Churchill said. "But I'm afraid we're not dressed to sit at your table."

"Don't worry about that," Whitrow said, heartily. "I shall see that you are dressed as a brother of the Sunhero should be!"

"Perhaps you can tell me what has happened to Stagg?"

"You mean you don't know? Ah well, I suppose not. We can talk about that tonight. Evidently there are some things you do not know about the Earth you left behind such a fantastically long time ago. Can it be true? Eight hundred years! Columbia preserve us!"

Robin had taken off her jacket and stood stripped to the waist. She had a magnificent bust but seemed no more self-conscious about it than she would have been about any other attribute of hers. That is, she knew she was worth looking at, but she wasn't going to let the knowledge interfere with her grace of movement or impose any coquettishness upon her.

Sarvant seemed quite affected, since he would not allow his gaze to rest upon her except for very brief intervals. That was strange, thought Churchill. Sarvant, despite his condemnation of the dress of Deecee virgins, had not seemed to be bothered when they were walking through the streets. Perhaps it was because he could look at the other girls impersonally, as savage natives of a foreign country, until acquaintanceship made a personal relationship.

They walked up the steps to the top of the bank, where a carriage waited. It was drawn by a team of two large reddish deer, and had, besides a driver, two armed men who stood on a little platform at its rear.

Whitrow and his son sat down and invited Sarvant to a place beside them. Robin placed herself without hesitation beside Churchill and very close to him. One breast was against his arm. He felt heat radiate from it up his arm to his face and he cursed himself for showing how she affected him.

They drove at a fast clip through the streets, the driver taking it for granted that the pedestrians would get out of his way or suffer the consequences. In fifteen minutes, they had passed the government buildings and were in a district reserved for the wealthy and the powerful. They turned into a long gravel-strewn driveway and then stopped before a large white house.

Churchill jumped down and held out his hand to help Robin down. She smiled and said, "Thank you," but he was examining the huge totem pole in the yard. It bore stylized heads of several animals, the most numerous of which was the cat.

Whitrow recognized what Churchill was doing. He said, "I am a

Lion. My wife and daughters belong to the Wood Cat sorority."

"I was just wondering," Churchill answered. "I know that the totem is a powerful factor in your society. But the idea is strange to me."

"I noticed you were wearing nothing to identify you with a frat," Whitrow said. "I think that perhaps I can do something to get you into mine. It is better to belong to one. In fact, I know of no one, besides you two, who doesn't belong."

They were interrupted by five youngsters who burst out of the front door and threw themselves affectionately upon their father. Whitrow introduced the naked boys and girls and then, as they reached the porch, he introduced his wife, a fat middle-aged woman who had probably once been very beautiful.

They went into a small anteroom, then stepped into a room that ran the length of the house. This was a combination living room, recreation room, and dining hall.

Whitrow charged his son Bob to see that his guests were washed. The two went into the interior of the house, where they took a shower and then put on the fine clothes that Bob insisted were theirs to keep.

Afterwards, they went back to the main room, where they were handed two glasses of wine by Robin. Churchill intercepted Sarvant's refusal to drink.

"I know it's against your principles," he whispered, "but turning it down might offend them. At least take a little sip."

"If I give in on a little thing, I'll give in later to the big things," said Sarvant.

"All right, be a stubborn fool," Churchill whispered savagely. "But you can't get drunk on one glass, you know."

"I'll touch the glass to my lips," said Sarvant. "That's as far as I'll go."

Churchill was angry but not so angry he couldn't appreciate the exquisite bouquet of the wine. By the time he was down to the bottom of the glass, he was called to the table. Here Whitrow directed them to sit on his right, the place of honor. He seated Churchill next to him.

Robin sat across the table from him. He was happy; it was a joy just to look at her.

Angela sat at the other end of the table. Whitrow said prayers, carved the meat, and passed it to his guests and family. Angela talked a lot, but she did not interrupt her husband. The children, though they giggled and whispered among themselves, were careful not to annoy their father. Even the twenty or so house-cats that prowled around the room were well behaved.

The table was certainly no indication of a land where food was rationed. Besides all the customary fruits and vegetables, there were venison and goat steaks, chicken and turkey, ham, fried grasshoppers and ants. Servants kept the glasses full of wine or beer.

"I certainly intend to hear of your journey to the stars," Whitrow boomed. "But let us talk of that later. During the meal, we will have small talk. I will tell you of us, so that you may feel you know us and will be at ease."

Whitrow shoved large gobs of food into his mouth, and while he chewed, he talked. He was born on a small farm in southern Virginia, he said, not too far from Norfolk. His father was an honorable man, since he raised pigs, and as everybody except possibly the starmen knew, a pig raiser was a highly respected man in Deecee.

Whitrow did not cotton to pigs, however. He had a liking for boats, so, as soon as his schooling was over, he left the farm and went to Norfolk. The schooling apparently was equivalent to the eighth grade of Churchill's time. Whitrow implied that education was not compulsory and that it had cost his father a respectable sum to send him. Most people were illiterate.

Whitrow shipped out on a fishing vessel as an apprentice seaman. After a few years, he saved enough money to go back to school in Norfolk, where nautical navigation was taught. From the anecdotes told about his stay there, Churchill knew that the compass and the sextant were still used.

Whitrow, though a seaman, had not been initiated into any of the sailor's frats. Even at that early age he was looking far ahead. He knew that the most powerful frat in Washington was the Lions. It was not an easy frat for a relatively poor youth to get into, but he had a stroke of luck.

"Columbia Herself took me under Her wing," he said. He knocked on the table top three times. "I do not boast, Columbia, I merely let men know of Your goodness!

"Yes, I was only a common seaman, despite being a graduate of the Norfolk College of Mathematics. I needed the patronage of a wealthy man to get an appointment as officer-in-training. And I got my patron. It was while I was on the merchant brigantine *Petrel*, bound for Miami in Florida. The Floridians had just lost a big naval battle and had to sue for peace. We were the first Deecee ship with a cargo to Florida in ten years, so we expected to make quite a haul. The Floridians would welcome our goods, even if they might not like our faces. On the way, however, we were attacked by Karelian pirates."

Churchill thought at first that the Karelians were Carolinians, but some of the details Whitrow gave about them changed Churchill's mind. He got the impression that they were from overseas. If that were true, then America was not as isolated as he had thought.

The Karelian ships rammed the brigantine, and the pirates boarded. It was during the fighting that followed that Whitrow saved a wealthy passenger from being cut in two by a Karelian broadsword. The Karelians were beaten off, though with great loss. All the officers were killed, and Whitrow took command. Instead of turning back, he sailed the ship on to Miami and sold the cargo at profit.

From that time on, he rose rapidly.

He was given a ship of his own. As a captain he had many chances to advance his own fortunes. Moreover, the man whose life he had saved knew what was going on in the business world of Washington and Manhattan, and he steered financial opportunities toward Whitrow.

"I was often a guest at his house," said Whitrow, "and there I met Angela. After I married her, I became her father's partner. And so now you see me, owner of fifteen great merchant ships and many farms and proud father of these healthy and handsome children, may Columbia continue to make us prosper."

"A toast to that," Churchill said, and he drank another wine, his tenth. He had made an effort to be temperate to keep his wits ready. But Whitrow had insisted that every time he drank, his guests drank. Sarvant had refused. Whitrow said nothing, but he no longer talked to Sarvant except when Sarvant directly spoke to him.

The table had become very noisy by now. The children drank beer and wine, even the youngest, a boy of six. They no longer giggled but laughed loudly, especially when Whitrow told jokes that would have delighted Rabelais. The servants, standing behind the chairs, laughed until tears ran from their eyes and they had to hold their aching sides.

These people had few visible inhibitions. They chewed noisily and did not mind talking when their mouths were full. When their father belched loudly, the children tried to outdo him.

At first, seeing the lovely Robin eating like a hog had sickened Churchill. It made him aware of the gulf between them, a gulf that meant more than just years. After his fifth wine, he seemed to lose his revulsion. He told himself that their attitude toward food was really healthier than that of his time. Besides, table manners were not intrinsically good or bad. The custom of the land determined what was or was not acceptable.

Sarvant did not seem to think so. As the meal progressed he became more silent and at the end he would not raise his eyes from his plate.

Whitrow became more boisterous. When his wife passed him on her way to direct a servant in the kitchen, he gave her a hard but affectionate slap on her broad rear. He laughed and said that that reminded him of the night Robin was conceived, and then he proceeded to go into the details of that night.

Suddenly, in the middle of the story, Sarvant stood up and walked out of the house. He left a complete silence behind him.

Finally, Whitrow said, "Is your friend sick?"

"In a way," Churchill said. "He comes from a place where talking of sex is taboo."

Whitrow was amazed. "But . . . how could that be? What a curious custom!"

"I imagine you have your own taboos," Churchill said, "and they would be just as curious to him. If you'll excuse me, I'll go ask him what he intends to do; but I'll be right back."

"Tell him to come back. I would like to get another look at a man who thinks so crookedly."

Churchill found Sarvant in a very peculiar situation. He was halfway up the totem pole, clinging tightly to the head of one of the animals to keep from falling.

Churchill looked once at the moonlit scene and leaped back into the house. "There's a lioness outside! She's treed Sarvant!"

"Oh, that'd be Alice," Whitrow said. "We let her out after dark to discourage burglars. I'll let Robin take care of her. She and her mother can handle big cats much better than I. Robin, will you take Alice back to her den?"

"I'd rather take her with me," Robin said. She looked at her father. "Would you mind if Mr. Churchill took me to the concert now? He can talk to you later. I'm sure he'll accept your invitation to be our guest for an indefinite period."

Something seemed to pass between father and daughter. Whitrow grinned and said, "Of course. Mr. Churchill, would you be my house guest? You are welcome to stay until you care to leave."

"I am honored," Churchill said. "Does that invitation include Sarvant?"

"If he wishes to accept. But I am not so sure he'll be at ease with us."

Churchill opened the door and allowed Robin to precede him. She walked out without hesitation and took the lioness by the collar. Churchill called up, "Come on down, Sarvant. It's not yet time to throw a Christian to the lions."

Reluctantly, Sarvant climbed down. "I should have stood my ground. But it took me by surprise. It was the last thing I would have expected."

"Nobody's blaming you for getting out of reach," Churchill said. "I'd have done the same thing. A mountain lion is nothing to treat with contempt."

"Wait a minute," Robin said. "I have to get a leash for Alice."

She stroked the lioness' head and chucked her under the chin. The big cat purred like distant thunder and then, at her mistress' command, followed her around the side of the house.

"All right, Sarvant," Churchill said. "Why did you take off like the proverbial bird? Didn't you know you could have gravely offended your hosts? Luckily, Whitrow didn't get mad at me. You could have queered the best stroke of luck we've had so far."

Sarvant looked angry. "Surely you didn't expect me to sit there and tolerate such bestial behavior? And his obscene descriptions of his cohabitations with his wife?"

"I gather there's nothing wrong with that in this time and place," Churchill said. "These people are, well, just earthy. They enjoy a good tumble in bed, and they enjoy rehashing it in conversation."

"Good God, you're not defending them?"

"Sarvant, I don't understand you. You encountered hundreds of customs more disgusting, actually repulsive, when we were on Vixa. Yet I never saw you flinch."

"That was different. The Vixans weren't human."

"They were humanoid. You can't judge these people by our standards."

"Do you mean to tell me you enjoyed his anecdotes about his sexual behavior?"

"I did get kind of queasy when he was talking about conceiving Robin. But I think that was because Robin was there. Certainly she wasn't suffering—she was laughing her beautiful head off."

"These people are degenerate! They need scourging!"

"I thought you were the minister of the Prince of Peace."

"What?" Sarvant said. He was silent for a moment, then he spoke in a quieter voice. "You're right. I hated when I should have been loving. But, after all, I'm only human. However, even a pagan like yourself is right to rebuke me when I talk of scourging."

"Whitrow invited you to come back in."

Sarvant shook his head. "No, I just haven't the stomach for it. God only knows what would happen if I spent the night there. I wouldn't be surprised if he offered me his wife."

Churchill laughed and said, "I don't think so. Whitrow's no Eskimo. And don't think that just because they're loose in talk they may not have a far stricter sexual code, in some ways, than we had in our time. What *are* you going to do?"

"I'm going to find some sort of motel and spend the night there. What are *you* going to do?"

"Just now I think Robin intends to take me out on the town. Later, I'm to spend the night here. I don't want to throw away this opportunity. Whitrow could be the wedge to get us into a nice position in Deecee. Washington hasn't changed in some respects; it still pays to know somebody with pull."

Sarvant held out his hand. His nutcracker face was serious.

"God be with you," he said, and walked away into the darkness of the street.

Robin came back around the corner of the house. She was holding the leash in one hand and in the other she held a large leather bag. Evidently she'd spent time in doing more than snapping the leash on the lioness' collar. Even though the moon furnished the only light, Churchill could see that she had changed her clothes and had put on fresh make-up. She had also exchanged her sandals for high-heeled shoes.

"Where did your friend go?" she said.

"Somewhere to spend the night."

"Good! I didn't like him very much. And I was afraid that I would have to be rude and not invite him to come along with us."

"I can't imagine you being rude—and don't waste too much sympathy on him. I think he likes to suffer. Where are we going?"

"I was thinking of going to the concert in the park. But that would mean sitting still too long. We could go to the amusement park. Did you have such things in your time?"

"Yes. It might be interesting to see if they've changed much. But I don't care where I go. Just as long as I'm with you."

"I thought you liked me," she said, smiling.

"What man wouldn't? But I must admit I'm surprised that you seem to like me so much. I'm not much to look at, just a red-haired wrestler with a face like a baby's."

"I like babies," she replied, laughing. "But you needn't act surprised. I'll bet you've laid a hundred girls."

Churchill winced. He wasn't as insensitive to the direct speech of Deecee as Sarvant had thought.

He was wise enough not to boast. He said, "I can truthfully swear you're the first woman I've touched in eight hundred years."

"Great Columbia, it's a wonder you don't explode all over the place!"

She laughed merrily, but Churchill blushed. He was glad that they were not in a bright light.

"I've an idea," she said. "Why don't we go sailing tonight? There's a full moon, and the Potomac will be beautiful. And we can get away from this heat. There'll be a breeze."

"Fine, but it's a long walk."

"Virginia preserve us! You didn't think we'd walk? Our carriage is in back, waiting."

She reached into the pocket of her bell-shaped skirt and pulled out a small whistle. Immediately following the shrill sound came the beat of hoofs and the crunch of gravel under wheels. Churchill assisted her aboard. The lioness leaped after them and lay down on the floor at their feet. The driver shouted, "Giddyap!" and the carriage sped down the moonlit street. Churchill wondered why she wanted to bring along the lioness, since two armed servants rode the platform on the rear of the carriage. He decided that having Alice along was being doubly fortified. She would be worth ten men in a fight.

The three got down off the carriage. Robin ordered the servants to wait until she came back from the sail. On the way down the long steps to the ship, Churchill said, "Won't they get bored, just waiting for us?"

"I don't think so. They've got a bottle of white lightning and dice."

Alice leaped aboard the yacht first and settled down in the small cabin where she probably hoped the water wouldn't touch her. Churchill untied the craft, gave her a shove, and jumped on. Then he and Robin were busy unfurling the sails and doing everything necessary.

They had a delightful sail. The full moon gave them all the light they needed or wanted, and the breeze was just strong enough to send them at a good clip when they headed downwind. The city was a black monster with a thousand blazing fitful eyes, the torches of the people in the streets. Churchill, seated with the rudder bar in his hand and Robin by his side, told her how Washington looked in his day.

"It was many towers crowded together and connected in the air with many bridges and underground with many tunnels. The towers soared into the air for a mile, and they plunged into the ground a mile deep. There was no night, because the lights were so bright."

"And now it is all gone, melted and covered with dirt," Robin said.

She shivered as if she thought of all that splendor of stone and steel and the millions of people now gone had made her cold. Churchill put his arm around her and, as she did not resist, he kissed her.

He thought that now would be the time to furl the sails and throw out the anchor. He wondered if the lioness would get upset, but decided that Robin must know how she would act under such circumstances. Perhaps he and Robin could go down into the small cabin, though he preferred to stay above decks. It was possible that she would not object if she were locked in the cabin.

But it was not to be. When he told her bluntly why he wanted to haul down the sails, he was informed that this could not be. Not now, anyway.

Robin spoke in a soft voice and smiled at him. She even said she was sorry.

"You have no idea what you do to me, Rud," she said. "I think I am in love with you. But I am not sure if it is you I love, or if it is the brother of the Sunhero I love. You are more than a man to me, you are a demigod in many ways. You were born eight hundred years ago and you have traveled to places that are so far away my head spins to think of it. To me, there is a light around you that shines even in the daytime. But I am a good girl. I cannot allow myself—though Columbia knows I want to—to do this with you. Not until I'm sure . . . But I know you must feel. Why don't you go to the Temple of Gotew tomorrow?"

Churchill did not know what she was talking about. He was only concerned about having offended her so much she wouldn't see him again. It wasn't lust alone that drew him toward her. He was sure of that. He loved this beautiful girl; he would have wanted her if he had just had a dozen women.

"Let's go back," she said. "I'm afraid this has killed your good spirits.

It's my fault. I shouldn't have kissed you. But I wanted to kiss you."

"Then you're not mad at me?"

"Why should I be?"

"No reason. But I'm happy again."

After they'd tied the craft to the slip, and were just beginning to walk back up the steps, he stopped her.

"Robin, how long do you think it'll be before you're sure?"

"I am going to the temple tomorrow. I'll be able to tell you when I get back."

"You're going to pray for guidance? Or something like that?"

"I'll pray. But I'm not going primarily for that. I want to have a priestess make a test on me."

"And after this test, you'll know whether or not you want to marry me?"

"Goodness no!" she said. "I'll have to know you much better than I do before I'd think of marrying you. No, I have to have this test made so I'll know whether or not I should go to bed with you."

"What test?"

"If you don't know, then you'll not be worried about it. But I'll be sure tomorrow."

"Sure of what?" he said angrily.

"Then I'll know if it's all right for me to quit acting like a virgin."

Her face became ecstatic.

"I'll know if I'm carrying the Sunhero's child!"

VII

It rained the morning that Stagg was to lead the parade into Baltimore. Stagg and Calthorp were in a large open-walled tent and drinking hot white lightning to keep warm. Stagg was motionless as a model while submitting to the usual morning repainting of his genitals and buttocks, necessary because he wore the paint off at nights. He was silent and paying no attention to the giggles and compliments of the three girls whose only work was this daily redecorating of the Sunhero. Calthorp, who generally talked like a maniac to keep Stagg's sprits up, was also glum.

Finally, Stagg said, "Do you know, Doc, it's been ten days since we left Fair Grace. Ten days and ten towns. By now you and I should have worked out a plan for escape. In fact, if we were the men we used to be, we'd have been over the hills and far away. But the only time I get to thinking is in the mornings, and I'm too exhausted and wretched to do anything constructive. And by noon I just don't give a damn. I *like* the way I am!"

"And I've not been much help to you, have I?" Calthorp said. "I get as drunk as you do, and I'm too sick in the morning to do anything but take a hair of the dog that bit me."

"What the hell's happened?" Stagg said. "Do you realize that I don't even know where I'm going, or what's going to happen to me when I get there? I don't even know, really, what a Sunhero is!"

"It's mostly my fault," Calthorp said. He sighed and sipped some more of his drink. "I just can't seem to get organized."

Stagg looked at one of his guards, who was standing in the entrance of a nearby tent. "Do you suppose that if I threatened to wring his neck, he'd tell me everything I want to know?"

"You could try it."

Stagg rose from his chair. "Hand me that cloak, will you? I don't think they'll object if I wear this while it's raining."

He was referring to an incident of the previous day when he had put on a kilt before going over to talk to the girl in the cage. The attendants had looked shocked, then summoned the guards. These surrounded Stagg. Before he could find out what they intended, a man behind him had torn off his kilt and run off with it into the woods.

He did not reappear all day, apparently dreading Stagg's wrath, but the lesson had been taught. The Sunhero was supposed to display his naked glory to the worshiping people.

Now Stagg slipped the cloak on and strode on bare feet across the wet grass. The guards stepped out from their tents and followed him, but they did not come close.

Stagg halted before the cage. The girl sitting inside looked up, then turned her face away.

"You don't need to be ashamed to look at me," he said. "I'm covered."

There was silence. Then he said, "For God's sakes, speak to me! I'm a prisoner too, you know! I'm in as much of a cage as you."

The girl clutched the bars and pressed her face against them. "You said, 'For God's sake!' What does that mean? That you're a Caseylander too? You can't be. You don't talk like my countrymen. But then you don't talk like a Deecee, either—or like anyone I ever heard before. Tell me, are you a believer in Columbia?"

"If you'll stop talking for a minute, I'll explain," Stagg said. "Thank God, you're talking, though."

"There you go again," she said. "You couldn't possibly be a worshiper of the foul Bitch-Goddess. But if you're not, why are you a Horned King?"

"I was hoping you could tell me that. If you can't, you can tell me some other things I'd like to know."

He held out the bottle to her. "Would you like a drink?"

"I'd like one, yes. But I won't accept one from an enemy. And I'm not sure you're not one."

Stagg understood her with difficulty. She used enough words similar to those of Deecee for him to grasp the main idea of her sentences. But her pronunciation of some of the vowels was different, and the tonal pattern was not that of Deecee.

"Can you speak Deecee?" he said. "I can't keep up with you in Caseylander."

"I speak Deecee fairly well," she replied. "What is your native tongue?"

"Twenty-first-century American."

She gasped, and her big eyes became even wider.

"But how could that be?"

"I was born in the twenty-first century. January 30, 2030 A.D. . . . let's see that would be . . ."

"You don't need to tell me," she replied in his native speech. "That would be . . . uh . . . well, 1 A.D. is 2100 A.D. So, Deecee style, you were born 70 B.D. Before the Desolation. But what does that matter? We Caseylanders use the Old Style."

Stagg finally quit goggling at her and said, "You spoke twenty-first-century American! Something like it, anyway!"

"Yes. Usually only priests can, but my father is a wealthy man. He sent me to Boston University, and I learned Church American there."

"You mean it's a liturgical language?"

"Yes. Latin was lost during the Desolation."

"I think I need a drink," Stagg said. "You first?"

She smiled and said, "I don't understand much of what you've said, but I'll take the drink."

Stagg slipped the bottle through the bars. "At least I know your name. It's Mary I-Am-Bound-for-Paradise Little Casey. But that's all I ever got out of my guards."

Mary handed back the bottle. "That was wonderful. It's been a long dry spell. You said guard? Why do you need a guard? I thought all Sunheroes were volunteers."

Stagg launched into his story. He didn't have time to go into the details, even though he could tell by Mary's expression that she comprehended only half of what he told her. And occasionally he had to shift back into Deecee because it was evident that Mary might have studied Church American at college but she hadn't mastered it.

"So you see," he concluded, "that I am a victim of these horns. I am not responsible for what I do."

Mary turned red. "I don't want to talk about it. It makes me sick to my soul."

"Me too," Stagg said. "In the mornings, that is. Later . . ."

"Can't you run away?"

"Sure. And I'd run back even faster."

"Oh, these evil Deecee! They must have bewitched you, it could only be a devil in your loins that could possess you so! If only we could escape to Caseyland, a priest could exorcise it."

Stagg looked around him. "They're beginning to break camp. We'll be on the march in a minute. Then, Baltimore. Listen! I've told you about myself. But I still know nothing about you, where you come from, how you happened to be a prisoner. And there are things you could tell me about myself, what this Sunhero stuff is about."

"But I can't understand why Cal . . ."

She put her hand over her mouth.

"Cal! You mean Calthorp! What's he got to do with this? Don't tell me he's been talking to you? He told me he didn't know a thing!"

"He's been talking to me. I thought that he must have told you so."

"He didn't say a thing to me! In fact, he said he didn't know any more than I did about what's going on! Why, that . . ."

Speechless, he turned and ran away from the cage.

Halfway across the field, he regained his voice and began bellowing the name of the little anthropologist.

The people in his path scattered; they thought that the Great Stag had gone amok again. Calthorp stepped out of the tent. Seeing Stagg running toward him, he scuttled across the road. He did not allow himself to be stopped by the stone fence in his path but put one hand on it and vaulted over. Once on the other side, he ran as fast as his spindly legs would carry him across a field and around a farmhouse.

Stagg screamed after him, "If I catch you, Calthorp, I'll break every bone in your body! How could you do this to me?"

He stood for a moment, panting with rage. Then he turned away, muttering to himself. "Why? Why?"

At that moment, the rain ceased. A few minutes later, the clouds cleared, and the midnoon sun shone fiercely.

Stagg tore off his cloak and threw it on the ground. "To hell with Calthorp! I don't need him and never did! The traitor! Who cares!"

He called to Sylvia, an attendant, to bring him food and drink. He ate and drank as he always did in the afternoon, and when he had finished, he glared wildly about him. The antlers, which had been flopping limply with every movement of his head, now rose stiff and hard.

"How many kilometers to Baltimore?" he roared.

"Two and a half, sire. Shall I call your carriage?"

"To hell with the carriage! I can't be slowed down by wheels! I am going to run to Baltimore! I am going to take the city by surprise! I'll be on them before they know it! They'll think the Grandfather of all Staggs hit them! I'll ravage among them, lay them all low! It'll not just be the mascots who'll get it this time! I'll not just take what's handed to me! No Miss Americas only for me! Tonight, the whole city!"

Sylvia was horrified. "But, sire, things just . . . just aren't done that way! Since time immemorial . . ."

"I am the Sunhero, am I not? The Horned King? I will do as I want to do!"

He seized a bottle from the tray she was holding and began to run off down the road.

At first he stayed on the cement. But even though the soles of his feet were by now as hard as iron, he found the pavement too rough, so he ran on the soft grass by the side of the road.

"It's better this way," he said to himself. "The closer I get to Mother Earth, the better for me and the better I like it. It may be superstitious nonsense that a man is refreshed by direct contact with the earth. But I'm inclined to believe the Deecee. I can *feel* the strength surging up from the heart of Mother Earth, surging up like an electric current and recharging my body. And I can feel the strength coming with such power, such overflowing power, that my body isn't big enough to contain it. And the excess spurts from the crown of my head and flames upward toward the sky. I can feel it."

He stopped running for a moment to uncap the bottle and take a drink. He noticed that the guards were running toward him, but they were at least two hundred yards behind. They just did not have his speed and strength. Besides his native muscle, he had the additional power given him by the antlers. He was, he thought, probably the fastest and strongest human being that had ever existed.

He took another drink. The guards were getting closer but they were winded, their pace slowing. They held their bows and arrows nocked, but he didn't think they would shoot as long as he stayed on the road to Baltimore. He had no intention of straying from it. He just wanted to run along on the curving breast of Earth and feel her strength surge through him and feel the ecstasy of his thoughts.

He ran faster, now and then giving great bounds into the air and uttering strange cries. They were sheer delight, exuberance, and nameless longings and their fulfillment. They were spoken in the language of the first men on Earth, the broken chaotic feeling-toward-speech the upright apes must have formed with clumsy tongues when they were trying to name the things around them. Stagg was not trying to name things. He was trying to name feelings. And he was having as little success as his ancestors a hundred thousand years before.

But he was, like them, gaining joy from the effort. And he was gaining a consciousness of something never before experienced, something new to his kind and perhaps to every creature in the world.

He ran toward a man, woman, and child who had been walking on the road. They stopped when they saw him, and then, recognizing him for what he was, fell on their knees.

Stagg did not stop but raced past them. "I may seem to be alone!" he cried at them. "But I am not! Earth comes along with me, your Mother and mine! She is my Bride and goes with me wherever I go. I cannot get away from Her. Even when I traveled through space to places so distant it takes light-years to get there, She was with me. And the proof is that I am back and now have carried out my eight-hundred-years-old promise to marry Her!"

By the time he had finished speaking, he was far past them. He did not care if they heard or not. All he wanted was to talk, talk, talk. Shout, shout, shout. Burst his lungs if he must, but scream out the truth.

Suddenly, he stopped. A large red stag grazing in a meadow beyond a fence had caught his eye. It was the only male of a herd of hind, and, like those deer bred for milk and meat, the stag had a distinctly bovine quality. Its body was thick, its legs short, its neck powerful, its eyes stupid but lustful. It was probably a thoroughbred male, highly prized as a stud.

Stagg leaped over the fence, though it was five feet high and composed of hard stone that would not have yielded if he had tripped. He landed on his feet and then ran toward the stag. The stag bellowed and stood his ground. The hinds ran off toward a corner of the field and there turned to see what was going to happen. They barked like dogs in their alarm, setting up such a clamor that the owner came running from a nearby barn.

Stagg ran up to the big male. The beast waited until the man was about twenty yards away. Then it lowered its antlers, bugled a challenge, and charged.

Stagg laughed with joy and ran very close. Timing his steps exactly, he leaped into the air just as the great branched horns swept the air where he had been. He drew up his knees so the horns would miss him, and then extended his legs so his feet landed beyond the base of the antlers and on the back of the neck. A second later, the stag reared his head, hoping to catch the man with his horns and throw him high in the air. The stag succeeded only in acting as a springboard for the man and propelling him along the line of his back. The man landed on the stag's broad rump.

There, instead of jumping down to the ground, he somersaulted backwards, intending to come down on the stag's neck. However, his feet slipped, and he rolled off the beast and fell on the ground on his side.

The stag wheeled and trumpeted another challenge and lowered his antlers and charged again. But Stagg was on his feet. As the beast lunged, Stagg jumped to one side, caught one of the big ears in his hand, and swung himself onto its back.

During the next five minutes, the amazed farmer watched the naked man ride the bucking, rearing, wheeling, snorting, bugling stag and stay on its back despite all its furious maneuvers. Suddenly, the stag stopped. Its eyes were bulging, saliva dripping from its open mouth, through which wheezed a tired breath, its sides pumping agonizedly for more air.

"Open the gate!" shouted Stagg to the farmer. "I'm going to ride this beast into Baltimore in style, like a Horned King should!"

The farmer silently swung open the gate to the field. He was not going to object if the Sunhero appropriated his prize stag. He would not have objected if the Sunhero had wanted his house, his wife, his daughter, his own life.

Stagg rode the beast onto the road toward Baltimore. Far ahead, he saw a carriage racing toward the city. Even at the distance he could perceive that it was Sylvia, going ahead to warn the people of Baltimore that the Horned King was arriving ahead of schedule—and doubtless to relay the Horned King's boast that he would ravish the entire city.

Stagg would have liked to race after her and arrive on her heels. But the deer was still breathing heavily, so he allowed it to walk until it could regain its breath.

Half a kilometer from Baltimore, Stagg kicked the beast in the ribs with his bare heels and shouted in its ears. It began trotting, then, under its rider's continued urgings, to gallop. It raced between two low hills, and suddenly was on the main street of Baltimore. This led straight for twelve blocks to the central square, where a large crowd was hastily being assembled. Even as Stagg crossed the city limits, a band struck up *Columbia, Gem of the Ocean,* and a group of priestesses began to march toward the Sunhero.

Behind them, the mascots who had been lucky enough to be chosen as the Sunhero's brides ranged themselves in a solid body. They looked very beautiful in their white bellshaped skirts and white lace veils, and their breasts were edged in white frilly lace. Each carried a bouquet of white roses.

Stagg allowed the big deer to slow to a trot so it could reserve its strength for the final spurt. He bowed and waved his hand at the men and women who lined the street and cheered frantically. He called to the teen-aged girls who stood by their parents, the girls who had failed to get first place in the Miss America contest.

"Don't cry! I won't neglect you tonight!"

Then the blare of bugles, thunder of drums, shrilling of syrinxes swelled and filled the street. The priestesses marched toward him. They were clad in gowns of light blue, the color reserved for the goddess Mary, patron deity of Maryland. Mary, according to the myth, was the granddaughter of Columbia and the daughter of Virginia. It was she who had formed a fondness for the natives of this region and had taken them under her protection.

The priestesses, fifty strong, marched toward Stagg. They sang and threw marigolds before them and occasionally gave long shuddering screams.

Stagg waited until he was about fifty meters from them. He kicked the animal in the ribs and beat on its head with his fists. It bugled and reared, and then began galloping straight toward the group of priestesses. These stopped singing to stand in astonished silence. Suddenly, perceiving that the Sunhero did not intend to pull up his mount, that it was not slackening speed but was increasing it, they screamed and tried to scatter to one side. Here they found that the number of the crowd formed an impenetrable body. And then they turned and tried to outrun the galloping stag, they knocked each other down, tripped over each other, got in each other's way.

Only one priestess did not stampede. She was the Chief Priestess, a woman of fifty who had kept her virginity in honor of her patron goddess. Now she remained, as if bolted by her courage to the ground. She held out one hand as she would have held it out to bless him if he had arrived in normal fashion. She tossed her bouquet of marigolds at him, and with the other hand, which held a golden sickle, she described a religious symbol.

The marigolds landed in front of the hoofs of the stag, were trampled, and then the Chief Priestess was knocked down to the ground and her head split open by a flying hoof.

The impact of the priestess' body scarcely checked the onslaught of the stag, which weighed at least a ton. It rammed head-on into the solidly packed mob of struggling, writhing women.

The animal stopped as if it had run into a stone wall, but Stagg continued.

He rose over the lowered neck and antlers and floated through the air. For a moment, he seemed to be suspended. Beneath was the group of blue-clad priestesses, splitting into two from the crash of the great body, flying in all directions, some of them soaring away on their backs, others upside down, several describing cartwheels. There was a severed head spinning by him, a head that had been caught under the chin by the tip of the antler and ripped off.

He was past the blue ruin and descending upon a field of white veils and red mouths behind the veils, of white flaring bell-shaped skirts and bare virginal breasts.

Then he had fallen into the trap of lace and flesh and disappeared from view.

VIII

Peter Stagg did not awake until the evening of the following day. Yet he was the first of his group to rise, except for one. That was Dr. Calthorp, who sat by his captain's bedside.

"How long have you been here?" Stagg said.

"In Baltimore? I followed right on your heels. I saw you charge that deer into the priestesses—and everything that went on afterwards."

Stagg sat up and moaned. "I feel as if every muscle in my body has been strained."

"Every muscle has been. You didn't go to sleep until about ten in the morning. But you ought to feel more than muscle-ache. Doesn't your back hurt much?"

"A little. Feels like a slight burn in my lower back."

"Is that all?" Calthorp's white brows rose high. "Well, all I can say is that the antlers must be doing more than pouring out philoprogenitive hormones into your bloodstream. They must also be conducive to cell-repair."

"What does all that mean?"

"Why, last night a man stabbed you in the back with a knife. Yet it didn't slow you down much, and the wound seems to be almost healed. Of course, the knife didn't go in more than an inch. You've got some pretty solid muscles."

"I have a vague memory of that," Stagg said. He winced. "And what happened to the man afterwards?"

"The women tore him apart."

"But why did he stab me?"

"It seems he was mentally unbalanced. He resented your intense interest in his wife, and he stuck a knife into you. Of course, he was committing a horrible blasphemy. The women used tooth and nail to punish him."

"Why do you say he was mentally unbalanced?"

"Because he was—at least, from this culture's viewpoint. Nobody in his right mind would object to his wife cohabiting with a Sunhero. In fact, it was a great honor, because Sunheroes usually devote their time to nobody but virgins. However, last night you made an exception . . . of the whole city. Or tried to, anyway."

Stagg sighed and said, "Last night was the worst ever. Weren't there more than the usual number mangled?"

"You can hardly blame the Baltimoreans for that. You started things off on a grand scale when you trampled those priestesses. By the way, whatever inspired that move?"

"I don't know. It just seemed a good idea at the time. But I think it might have been my unconscious directing me to get revenge on the people responsible for these."

He touched his antlers. Then he fixed a stare on Calthorp.

"You Judas! Why have you been holding out on me?"

"Who told you? That girl?"

"Yes. That doesn't matter. Come on, Doc, spill it. If it hurts, spill it, anyway. I won't harm you. My antlers are an index of whether I'm in my right mind or not. You can see how floppy they are."

"I began to suspect the true pattern of events as soon as I started understanding the language," Calthorp said. "I wasn't sure, however, until they grafted those antlers on you. But I didn't want to tell you until I could figure out some way of escape. I thought you might try to make a break and would get shot down. I soon began seeing that even if you ran away in the morning, you'd be back by evening—if not sooner. That biological mechanism on your forehead gives you more than an almost inexhaustible ability to scatter your seed; it also gives you an irresistible compulsion to do so. Takes you over completely—possesses you. You're the biggest case of satyriasis known to history."

"I know how it affects me," Stagg said, impatiently. "I want to know just what kind of a role I am playing? Toward what goal? And why is all this Sunhero routine necessary?"

"Wouldn't you like a drink first?"

"No! I'm not going to drown my sorrow in liquor. I'm going to accomplish something today. I would like a big cold drink of water. And I'm dying to take a bath, get all this sweat and crud off me. But that can wait. Your story, please. And make it damn quick!"

"I haven't time now to go into the myth and history of Deecee," Calthorp said. "We can do that tomorrow. But I can elucidate fairly well what position of dubious honor you hold.

"Briefly, you combine several religious roles, that of the Sunhero and that of the Stag-King. The Sunhero is a man who is chosen every year to enact the passage of the Sun around the Earth in symbolic form. Yes, I know the Earth goes around the Sun, and so do the priest-esses of Deecee, and so does the unlettered mass, But for all practical purposes, the Sun circles the Earth, and that is how even the scientist thinks of it when he is not thinking scientifically.

"So, the Sunhero is chosen, and he is symbolically born during a ceremony which takes place around December 21. Why then? Because that is the date of the winter solstice. When the Sun is weakest and has reached the most southerly station.

"That is why you went through the birth scene.

"And that is why you are taking the northern route now. You are destined to travel as the Sun travels after the winter solstice, north-ward. And like the Sun, you will get stronger and stronger. You have noticed how the antlers' effect has been getting more powerful; proof of that is the crazy stunt you pulled when you subdued that stag and rode down the priestesses."

"And what happens when I reach the most northerly station?" Stagg said. His voice was quiet and well controlled, but the skin under the deep brown tan had turned pale.

"That will be the city we used to know as Albany, New York. It is now the northernmost limit of the country of Deecee, And it is also where Alba, the Sow-Goddess, lives. Alba is Columbia in her aspect of the Goddess of Death. The pig is sacred to her because, like Death, it is omnivorous. Alba is also the White Moon Goddess, another sym-bol of death."

Calthorp stopped. He looked as if he could not bear to continue the conversation; his eyes were moist.

"Go on," Stagg said. "I can take it."

Calthorp took a deep breath and said, "The north, according to Deecee myth, is the place where the Moon Goddess imprisons the Sunhero. A circuitous way of saying that he . . ."

"Dies," Stagg finished for him.

Calthorp gulped. "Yes. The Sunhero is scheduled to complete the Great Route at the time of the summer solstice—about June 22."

"What about the Great Stag aspect, the Horned King?"

"The Deecee are nothing if not economical. They combine the role of Sunhero with that of the Stag-King. He is a symbol of man. He is born as a weak and helpless infant, he grows to become a lusty, virile male, lover, and father. But he, too, completes the Great Route and must, willy-nilly, face Death. By the time he meets her, he is blind, bald, weak, sexless. And . . . he fights for his last breath, but . . . Alba relentlessly chokes it out of him."

"Don't use symbolic language, Doc," Stagg said. "Give me the facts, in plain English."

"There will be one tremendous ceremony at Albany, the final. There you will take, not the tender young virgins, but the white-haired sag-breasted old priestesses of the Sow-Goddess. And your natural distaste for the old women will be overcome by keeping you restrained in a cage until you are at such a point of lust that you will take any woman, even a hundred-year-old great-grandmother. Afterwards . . ."

"Afterwards?"

"Afterwards, you will be blinded, scalped, castrated, and then hung. There will be a week of national mourning for you. Then you will be buried in the position of a foetus beneath a dolmen, an archway of great slabs of stone. And prayers will be said to you and stags will be sacrificed over your tomb."

"That's quite a consolation," Stagg said. "Tell me, Doc, why was I picked for this role? Isn't it true that the Sunheroes are usually volunteers?"

"Men strive for the honor, just as the virgins strive to become the Bride of the Stag. The man who is chosen is the strongest, most handsome, most virile youth in the nation. It was your misfortune to be not only that, but the captain of men who had actually ascended to the heavens on a fiery steed and then returned. They've a myth about a Sunhero who did that. I think that the government of Deecee decided that if they got rid of you they'd disorganize all of the crew. And so diminish any danger of us bringing back the old and abominated science.

"I see Mary Casey waving at you. I think she wants to speak to you."

IX

Peter Stagg said, "Why do you look to one side when you talk to me?"

"Because," May Casey said, "it's hard for me to keep you two separated."

"What two?"

"The Peter I know in the morning, and the Peter I know at night. I'm sorry, but I can't help it. I shut my eyes at night and try to think of something else, but I can't shut my ears. And even though I know you can't help what you do, I loathe you. I'm sorry. I just can't help it."

"Then why did you call me over to talk to me?"

"Because I know that I am not acting charitably. Because I know that you would like to get out of your cage of flesh as much as I want to get out of this cage of iron. Because I hope we can think of some way to escape."

"Calthorp and I have worked out several plans for getting away, but we don't know how to keep me from running back. As soon as the horns began affecting me, I'd come running back to the women."

"Can't you use your will power?"

"A saint wouldn't be able to resist the horns."

"Then it's hopeless," she said dully.

"Not entirely. I don't intend to go all the way to Albany, you know. Somewhere between Manhattan and Albany, I'm taking off for the wilderness. Better to die trying than going like an ox to the slaughterhouse.

"Let's change the subject. Tell me about yourself and your people. One thing that's handicapping me is my ignorance. I just don't know enough to figure a way out."

Mary Casey said, "I'll be glad to. I need somebody to talk to, even if it's . . . I'm sorry."

During the next hour, while Stagg stood outside her cage and she kept her eyes on the floor, she told him of herself and Caseyland. He broke in now and then with questions, because she had a tendency to take knowledge of fundamental matters for granted.

Caseyland occupied the area once known as New England. It was not as thickly populated as Deecee or as rich. Its people were engaged in rebuilding the soil, but they depended largely on the raising of pigs and deer and on the sea for their food. Even though at war with the Deecee to the southwest, the Karelians to the north, and the Iroquois to the northwest, they traded with their enemies. They had a peculiar institution known as Treaty War. This limited, by mutual agreement, the number of warriors to be sent across the borders on raids in a year's time, and also regulated the rules of warfare. The Deecee and the Iroquois abided by the rules, but every once in a while the Karelians broke them.

"How can either side expect to win?" Stagg said in amazement.

"Neither side does. I think that the Treaty War was adopted by our ancestors for one reason. To allow an outlet for the energies of belligerent men while keeping the majority of the population busy in rebuilding the earth. I think that when the population of any country gets too large, you will see wholesale warfare without any rules at all. But in the meantime, no nation feels powerful enough to start a treatyless war. The Karelians break the treaties because they are a people who live by a wartime economy."

She continued with a brief résumé of her nation's origins. There were two myths concerning the reason why Caseyland had been so named. One proposed that, after the Desolation, an organization known as the Knights of Columbus had succeeded in founding a city-state near Boston. This, like the original small city of Rome, had expanded to absorb its neighbors. The city-state was called K.C., and over a period of time the initials had somehow been converted into the name of an eponymous and mythical ancestor, Casey.

The other story was that there actually was a Casey family which had founded a town, named after him. And they had originated the present clan system whereby everybody in their country was named Casey.

There was a third version, not widely accepted, that the truth was a combination of the first two myths. A man named Casey had been the leader of the Knights of Columbus.

"Perhaps none of those myths are true," Stagg said, said.

Mary did not seem pleased at this suggestion, but she was essentially fair-minded. She said that it was possible.

"What about the claim of the Deecee?" he said. "They say you worship a father-god named Columbus and you got the name from their goddess Columbia. You masculinized both the goddess and her name. Isn't it true that your god has two names, Jehovah and/or Columbus?"

"That is not so!" she said angrily. "The Deecee have confused the name of our god with that of St. Columbus. It is true that we pray quite often to St. Columbus for intercession with Jehovah. But we do not worship him."

"And who was St. Columbus?"

"Why, everybody knows that he came from the east, from over the ocean, and landed in Caseyland. It was he who converted the citizens of the father-city of Casey to the true religion and founded the

Knights of Columbus. If it weren't for St. Columbus, we would all be heathens."

Stagg was beginning to get restless, but he managed to ask her one more question before he left.

"I know that *mascot* is the word used for *virgin*. Do you have any idea how mascot came to be used in its present sense?"

"It has always been used so," she replied, looking directly at him for the first time. "A mascot brings good luck with her, you know. Perhaps you've observed how the Deecee touch the hair of a pubescent mascot when they get a chance. That is because the good luck sometimes rubs off on the toucher. And, of course, a raiding party of men always take along a mascot for good luck. I was with a war expedition against Poughkeepsie when I was captured. That sign lies when it says I was captured on a raid by the Deecee into Caseyland. It was the other way around. But, of course, you can't expect the truth from people who worship the Mother of Lies."

Stagg decided that the Caseylanders were as mixed up and mistaken as the Deecee. It would be useless to argue or try to entangle myth from history.

The great arteries at the base of his antlers were beginning to pulse strongly, and the antlers themselves were stiffening.

"I have to go now," he said. "See you tomorrow."

He turned and walked swiftly away. It was only by an effort of will that he kept from running.

So the days and the nights passed. Mornings filled with weakness and discussion of plans to escape. Afternoons of eating, drinking, and wild and sometimes savage horseplay. Nights . . . the nights were visions of screaming white flesh, of being one great pulse that throbbed in unison with the buried heart of earth itself, of transformation from an individual man into a force of nature. Mindless ecstasy, body obeying the will of a Principle. He was an agent who had no choice but to obey that which possessed him.

The Great Route led from Washington to Columbia Pike, once U.S. Route 1, through Baltimore, where it switched to what had once been U.S. Route 40 but was now known as Mary's Way. It turned from Mary's Way outside of Wimlin (Wilmington, Delaware) to follow the former New Jersey Turnpike. This road was also named after one of Columbia's daughters, Njuhzhi.

Stagg stayed a week in Kaept (Camden) and noticed the large number of soldiers in the city. He was told that this was because

Philadelphia, across the Dway (Delaware) River, was the capital city of the hostile nation of Pants-Elf (eastern Pennsylvania).

The soldiers accompanied Stagg out of Camden on the former U.S. Route 30 until he was deep enough inland to be safe. There they left him, and he and his entourage continued to the town of Berlin.

After the pageant and the orgies that followed, Stagg continued on ex-U.S. 30 to Talant (Atlantic City).

Atlantic City kept Stagg for two weeks. It was a metropolis of thirty thousand, whose population quintupled when the country people poured in to attend the Sunhero rites. From there Stagg followed the former Garden State Parkway until he turned off at what had been State Highway 72. It led to 70 and 70 led to ex-U.S. Route 206. Stagg took this road to Trint (Trenton), where he was again met by a large bodyguard.

When he left Trenton, he was once more on Columbia Pike, the ex-U.S. Route 1. After making the usual progress through the relatively large cities of Elizabeth, Newark, and Jersey City, he took a ferry to Manhattan Island. He made his most extended stay in the Greater New York area, because Manhattan held fifty thousand people and the surrounding cities were almost as large.

Moreover, this was the beginning of the Great Series.

Stagg not only had to throw the first baseball of the season, he had to attend every game. For the first time, he became aware of how much the game had changed. Now it was conducted in such a fashion that it was an unusual match in which both teams did not suffer numerous injuries and several fatalities.

The first part of the Great Series was taken up by games between the champions of the various state leagues. The final game for national championship was between the Manhattan Big Ones and the Washington Sentahs. The Big Ones won, but they lost so many men they were forced to use half of the Sentahs for their reserves in the international games that followed.

The international half of the Great Series was between the national champions of Deecee, Pants-Elf, Caseyland, the Iroquois League, the Karelian pirates, Florida, and Buffalo. The last-mentioned nation occupied a territory stretching out from the city of Buffalo to include a part of the coastal sections of Lake Ontario and Lake Erie.

The final game of the Great Series was a bloody struggle between the Deecee team and the Caseylanders. The Caseylanders wore red leggings as part of their uniform, but by the end of the game the players were red from head to foot. Feelings were very bitter, not only among the players but among the rooters. The Caseylanders had a section of the stadium reserved for them and enclosed from the other sections by a tall fence of barbed wire. Moreover, the Manhattan Police Force had men stationed nearby to protect them if feelings ran too high.

Unfortunately, the umpire—a Karelian who was supposed to be neutral because he hated both sides equally—made a decision disastrous in its effects.

It was the ninth inning, and the score was 7-7. The Big Ones were batting. One man was on third base and, though he had a gash in his neck, he was strong enough to run for home if he got a chance. Two men were out—literally. One, covered by a sheet, lay where he had been struck down between second and third. The other was sitting in the dugout and groaning, while a doctor glued up the cuts on his scalp.

The man at bat was the greatest hitter of Deecee, and he faced the greatest pitcher of Caseyland. He wore a uniform that had not changed much since the nineteenth century, and his cheek was swelled with a big quid of tobacco. He swung his bat back and forth. The sunlight glittered on its metal sides, for the upper half of the bat was covered with thin vertical strips of brass. He waited for the umpire to call *Play Ball!* and when he heard the cry, he did not step up to the plate at once.

Instead, he turned and waited until the mascot had run from the dugout to him.

She was a beautiful petite brunette who wore a baseball player's uniform. The only departure from ancient tradition was the triangular opening in her shirt which exposed her small but firm breasts.

Big Bill Appletree, the batter, rubbed his knuckles against the black hair of the mascot, kissed her on the forehead, and then gave her fanny a playful slap as she ran back to the dugout. He stepped into the box, a square drawn with chalk on the ground, and assumed the ancient stance of the batter ready for the pitcher.

Lanky John Up-The-Hill-And-Over-The-River-Jordan Mighty Casey spat tobacco, then began to wind up. He held in his right hand a ball of regulation size. Four half-inch steel spikes projected from the ball, one from each pole of the sphere and two from the equator. John Casey had to hold the ball so he wouldn't cut his fingers when he hurled it. This handicapped him somewhat from the view of an ancient pitcher. But he stood six meters closer to the batter, thus more than making up for the awkwardness of hurling the ball.

He waited until the Caseylander mascot had come to him to have her head knuckled. Then he wound up and let fly.

The spike-bearing ball whizzed by an inch from Big Bill Appletree's face. Appletree blinked, but he did not flinch.

A roar went up from the crowd at this show of courage.

"Ball one!" cried the umpire.

The Caseyland rooters booed. From where they sat, it looked as if the ball, though coming close to Appletree's face, had been exactly in line with the chalk mark of the box. Therefore, the throw should have been a strike.

Appletree struck at the next one and missed.

"Strike one!"

At the third pitch, Appletree swung and connected. The ball, however, soared to the left. It was obviously a foul.

"Strike two!"

The next pitch came sizzling in, directed at Appletree's belly. He sucked it in and jumped back, just far enough to keep from being hit but not so far he stepped outside the box, which would constitute a strike.

The next pitch, Appletree swung and missed. The ball did not. Appletree fell to the ground, the spike of the ball sticking in his side.

The crowd screamed, and then became comparatively silent as the ump began counting.

Appletree had ten seconds to get up and bat or else have a strike called on him.

The Deecee mascot, a tall beautiful girl with exceptionally long legs and rich red hair that fell past her buttocks, round and hard as apples, ran out to him. She brought her knees up high in the prancing gait affected by mascots on such occasions. When she got to Appletree, she dropped to her knees and bent her head over him and threw her hair forward so he could stroke it. The strength of a virgin, of a mascot dedicated to the Great White Mother in her aspect as Unfekk, was supposed to flow from her to him. Apparently this was not enough. He said something to her, and she rose, unbuttoned a flap over her pubes, and then bent down to him again. The crowd roared, because this meant that Appletree was so badly hurt he needed a double dose of spiritual-physical power.

At the count of eight, Appletree rose to his feet. The crowd cheered. Even the Caseylander rooters gave him an ovation—all honored a man with guts.

Appletree pulled the spike from his side, took a bandage from the mascot, and placed it over the wound. The bandage clung without being taped, as its pseudo-flesh at once put out a number of little claw-tipped tendrils that anchored it.

He nodded to the ump that he was ready.

"Play ball!"

Now it was Appletree's turn to pitch. He was allowed one try to knock the pitcher down. If he did so, he could walk to first.

He wound up and hurled the ball. John Casey stood within the narrow square used for this occasion. If he stepped outside it, he would be in disgrace—the showers for him—and Appletree could walk all the way to second.

He stood his ground, but his knees were bent so he could sway his body either way.

The ball was a technical miss, though the edge of one of the rotating spikes did cut his right hip.

Then he picked up the ball and wound up.

The Deecee rooters prayed silently, their fingers crossed or their hands stroking the hair on the heads of any nearby mascots. The Casey-landers screamed themselves hoarse. The Pants-Elf, Iroquois, Floridians, and Buffaloes yelled insults at whichever team they hated most.

The Deecee man on third base edged out, ready to run for home if he got a chance. Casey eyed him but made no threatening move.

He threw one straight over the plate, preferring to make Apple-tree hit for a long one rather than dodge and perhaps get another ball called. Four balls, and Appletree could walk to first.

The big Deecee batter hit the ball square. But, as often happened, one of the spikes was also hit. The ball rose high over the path from home plate to first and then dropped toward a point halfway between home and first.

Appletree threw the bat at the pitcher, as was his right, and sprinted for first. Halfway to first, the ball hit him on the head. The first base-man, running to catch it, also rammed into him. Appletree hit the ground hard but bounced up like a rubber ball, ran several steps, and took a belly skid toward first.

However, the first baseman, while still on the ground, had picked up the ball and made a pass with it at Appletree. Immediately after, he jumped up and threw to home. The ball smacked into the huge and thick mitt of the catcher just before the man who had been on third slid into the plate.

The ump called the Deecee player out, and there was no argument there. But the first baseman walked up to the ump and submitted, in a loud voice, that he had touched Appletree as he ran away. Therefore, Appletree was also out.

Appletree denied that he had been touched.

The first baseman said that he could prove it. He had nicked the Deecee on the side of the right ankle with a spike on the ball.

The ump made Appletree take off his stocking.

"You've a fresh wound there, still bleeding," he said. "You're out!"

"I am not!" roared Appletree, spraying tobacco juice into the ump's face. "I'm bleeding from two cuts on my thigh, too, and that was done last inning! That father-god worshiper is a liar!"

"How would he know to tell me to look at your right ankle unless he had nicked you?" roared the ump back at Appletree. "I'm the ump, and I say you're out!"

He spelled it out in Deecee phonetics. "A-U-T! Out!"

The decision did not go over well with the Deecee rooters. They booed and screamed the traditional, "*Kill the ump!*"

The Karelian turned pale, but he stood his ground. Unfortunately, his courage and integrity did him no good, as the mob spilled out of the stadium and hung him by the neck from a girder. The mob also began beating up the Caseylander team. These might have died under the savage blows, but the Manhattan police surrounded them and beat back the frenzied rooters with the flat of their swords. They also managed to cut down the Karelian before the noose had finished its work.

Meanwhile, the Caseylander rooters had attempted to come to the rescue of their team. Although they never reached the players, they did tangle with the Deecee fans.

Stagg watched the melee for a while. At first he thought of leaping into the mass of furiously struggling bodies and striking blows right and left with his great fists. His bloodlust was aroused. He rose to make the leap into the mob below, but at that moment a group of women, also aroused by the fight, but in a different sense, descended on him.

X

Churchill did not sleep well that night. He could not rid himself of the ecstatic expression on Robin's face when she had said she hoped she would bear the Sunhero's child.

First, he cursed himself for not having guessed that she would have been among the one hundred virgins selected to make their debut during the rites. She was too beautiful, and her father was too prominent, for her to have been rejected.

Then he excused himself on the grounds that he really knew little of Deecee's culture. His own attitudes were too much those of his own time. He had treated her as if she were a girl of the early twenty-first century.

He cursed himself for having fallen in love with Robin. He was reacting more like a youth of twenty than a man of thirty-two—no, a man of eight hundred and thirty-two. A man who had traveled thousands of millions of miles and had made interstellar space his domain. Fallen for a girl of eighteen, who knew only a tiny section of Earth and a tiny section of time!

But Churchill was practical. A fact was a fact. And it was a fact that he wanted Robin Whitrow for his wife—or had, up to that moment last night when she had stunned him with her announcement.

For a while he hated Peter Stagg. He had always had a slight resentment against his captain, because Stagg was so tall and handsome and held a position which Churchill knew he was just as capable of holding. He liked and respected Stagg, but, being honest, he had admitted to himself that he was jealous.

It was almost unendurable to think that Stagg, as usual, had beaten him. Stagg was always first.

Almost unendurable.

As the night crept on, and Churchill rose from bed to smoke a cigar and pace back and forth, he forced himself to be frank with himself.

It was neither Stagg's fault nor Robin's that this had happened. And Robin certainly was not in love with Stagg. Stagg, poor devil, was doomed to a short but ecstatic life.

The immediate fact for Churchill to deal with was that he wanted to marry a woman who was going to bear another man's child. That neither she nor the father could be blamed was beside the point. What mattered was whether he wanted to marry Robin and to raise the child as his own.

Eventually, by lying still in bed and relaxing himself through yogoid techniques, he managed to go to sleep.

He woke about an hour after dawn and left his bedroom. A servant informed him that Whitrow had gone to his offices downtown and that Robin and her mother had left for the temple. The women should be back in two hours, if not sooner.

Churchill asked after Sarvant, but he had not as yet appeared.

Churchill ate breakfast with some of the children. They asked him to tell them a story about his trip to the stars. He described the incident on Wolf when the crew, while crossing a swamp on a raft in their escape from the Lupines, had been attacked by a balloon-octopus. This was an enormous creature that floated through the air by means of a gas-filled sac and seized its prey with long dangling tendrils. The tendrils could deliver an electric shock that paralyzed or killed its victims, after which the balloon-octopus tore the corpse apart with sharp claws on the ends of its eight muscular tentacles.

The children were wide-eyed and silent while he told the tale, and at the end they looked at him as if he were a demigod. He was in a bitter mood by the time he'd finished breakfast, especially when he remembered that it was Stagg who had saved his life by chopping off a tentacle that had seized him.

When he rose from the table, the children begged him for other stories. Only by promising to relate others when he returned that day was he able to free himself.

He gave orders to the servants that they should tell Sarvant to wait for him and tell Robin that he was going in search of his crew-mates. The servants insisted on his taking a carriage and team. He did not like to be any more in debt to Whitrow than he was but decided that refusing the offer would probably insult him. He drove away at a fast clip down Conch Avenue, heading toward the stadium in which the *Terra* stood.

Churchill had some difficulty in finding the proper authorities. Washington had not changed in some respects. A little money here and there got him the correct information, and presently he was in the office of the man in charge of the *Terra*.

"I would also like to know where the crew is," he said.

The official excused himself. He was gone for fifteen minutes, during which time he must have been checking on the whereabouts of the *Terra*'s ex-personnel. Returning, he told Churchill that all but one were at the House of Lost Souls. This, he explained, was a rooming and eating house for foreigners and traveling men who could not find a hostelry run for their particular frats.

"If you were the Sunhero and in a city, you could stay at the Elks' Hall," the official said. "But until you are initiated into a frat, you must find whatever public or private lodging you can. It is not always easy."

Churchill thanked him and walked out. Following the official's directions, he drove to the House of Lost Souls.

Here he found all the men he had left. Like him, they were dressed in native costume. Like him, they had sold their clothing.

They exchanged news of what had happened since the day before. Churchill asked where Sarvant was.

"We haven't heard a word about him," Gbwe-hun said. "And we still don't know what we're going to do."

"If you're willing to be patient," Churchill said, "you might be able to sail back to home."

He outlined for them what he knew about the maritime industry of Deecee and the chances they might have for seizing a ship. He concluded, "If I get a ship, I'll see that you have a berth on it. First, you have to be capable of filling a seaman's position. That means you're going to have to be initiated into one of the nautical frats, and then you will have to ship out for training. The whole plan will take time. If you can't stand the idea, you can always try it overland."

They discussed their chances and, after two hours, decided to follow Churchill.

He rose from the table. "All right. You make this your headquarters until further notice. You know where to contact me. So long and good luck."

Churchill allowed the deer pulling the carriage to set their own preferred slow pace. He dreaded what he might find when he returned to the Whitrow home, and he still did not know what he would do.

Eventually, the carriage pulled up before the house. The servants drove the team off. Churchill forced himself to enter the house. He found Robin and her mother sitting at the table, chattering away like a pair of happy magpies.

Robin jumped up from her chair and ran to him. Her eyes were shining, and she was smiling ecstatically.

"Oh, Rud, it has happened! I am carrying the Sunhero's child—and the priestess said it will be a boy!"

Churchill tried to smile, but he could not do it. Even when Robin had thrown her arms around him and kissed him and then had danced merrily around the room, Churchill could not smile.

"Have a cold beer," Robin's mother said. "You look as if you'd had some bad news. I hope not. Today should be a day of rejoicing. I am the daughter of a Sunhero, and my daughter is the child of a Sunhero, and my grandchild will be the son of a Sunhero. This house has been triply blessed by Columbia. We should reward her with the gratitude of laughter."

Churchill sat down and drank deep of the cold dark beer in the huge stone mug. He wiped the foam from his lips and said, "You must forgive me. I have been listening to the troubles of my men. However, that is no concern of yours. What I would like to know is, what will Robin do now?"

Angela Whitrow looked shrewdly at him as if she guessed what was going on inside him.

"Why, she will accept some lucky young man as her husband. She may have trouble making up her mind, since at least ten men are very serious about her."

"Does she favor anyone in particular?" Churchill asked in what he hoped was a nonchalant manner.

"She hasn't told me so," Robin's mother said. "But if I were you, Mr. Churchill, I'd ask her here and now—before the others get here."

Churchill was startled, but he kept a stiff face.

"How did you know I had that in mind?"

"You're a man, aren't you? And I know that Robin favors you. I think you'd make her the best of husbands."

"Thank you," he murmured. He sat for a moment, drumming his fingers on the table top. Then he rose and walked to where Robin was petting one of her cats, and seized her by the shoulders.

"Robin, will you marry me?"

"Oh yes!" she said, and she went into his arms.

That was that.

Once Churchill had made up his mind, he proceeded on the assumption that he had no grounds for resenting Stagg's child or Robin's conceiving it. After all, he told himself, if Robin had been married to

Stagg and borne his child, and then Stagg had died, he, Churchill, would have had nothing to resent. And the situation in effect amounted to the same. For one night, Robin had been married to his former captain.

And though Stagg wasn't dead yet, he soon would be.

The upsetting factor had been his reacting with a set of values to a situation in which they did not apply. Churchill would have liked his bride to be a virgin. She wasn't, and that was that.

Nevertheless, he had more than one moment of feeling that, somehow, he had been betrayed.

There wasn't much time to think. Whitrow was called home from his office. He wept and embraced his daughter and son-in-law-to-be and then got drunk, Meanwhile, Churchill was taken away by the female servants and given a hair-trimming and a bath. Afterwards, he was massaged and oiled and perfumed. When he came out of the bathhouse, he found Angela Whitrow busy with some friends arranging a party to be held that night.

Shortly after supper, the guests began pouring in. By this time, both Whitrow and his daughter's fiancé were deep in their cups. The guests did not mind. In fact, they seemed to expect such a condition, and they tried to catch up with the two.

There was much laughter, much talking, much boasting. Only one ugly incident happened. One of the men who had been courting Robin made an allusion to Churchill's foreign pronunciation and then challenged Churchill to a duel. It was to be knives at the foot of the totem pole, the two to be tied by their waists to the pole, and the winner to take Robin.

Churchill punched the young man on the jaw, and his friends, laughing and whooping, carried off the unconscious body to its carriage.

About midnight Robin left her friends and took Churchill by the hand.

"Let's go to bed," she whispered.

"*Where? Now?*"

"To my room, silly. And now, of course."

"But, Robin, we've not been married. Or was I so drunk I didn't notice?"

"No, the marriage will take place in the temple next weekend. But what does that have to do with our going to bed?"

"Nothing," he said, shrugging his shoulders. "Other times, other mores. Lead on, Macduff."

She giggled and said, "What are you muttering about?"

"What would you do if I backed out before we got married?"

"You're joking, of course?"

"Of course. But you must realize, Robin darling, that I don't know much about Deecee customs. I'm just curious."

"Why, I'd do nothing. But it would be a deadly insult to my father and brother. They'd have to kill you."

"I just wanted to know."

The following week was a very busy one. In addition to the normal preparations for the wedding ceremony, Churchill had to decide what frat he was going to join. It was unthinkable that Robin would marry a man without a totem.

"I would suggest," Whitrow said, "my own totem, the Lion. But it would be better for you to be in a frat directly concerned with your work and one which is blessed by the tutelary spirit of the animal with which you will be dealing."

"You mean one of the fish frats or the porpoise frat?"

"What? No, I do not! I mean the Pig totem. It would not be wise to be breeding hogs and at the same time have as your totem the Lion, a beast which preys on pigs."

"But," Churchill protested, "what do *I* have to do with pigs?"

It was Whitrow's turn to be surprised. "Then you've not discussed it with Robin? No wonder. She's had so little time to talk. Although you two have been alone every night from midnight until morning. But then I suppose you're too busy tumbling each other. Oh, to be young again! Well, my boy, the situation is this. I inherited some farms from my father, who was also no slouch when it came to making money. I need you to run these farms for me for several reasons.

"One, I don't trust the present manager. I think he's cheating me. Prove to me that he is, and I'll have him hung.

"Two, the Karelians have been making raids on my farms, stealing the best of my stock and the good-looking women. They haven't burned the houses and barns down or left the help to starve, since they don't want to kill the golden goose. You will stop the raids.

"Three, I understand that you're a geneticist. Therefore, you should be able to improve my stock.

"Four, when I return to the bosom of the Great White Mother, you will inherit some of the farms. The merchant fleet goes to my sons."

Churchill rose. "I'll have to talk to Robin about this."

"Do that son. But you'll find she agrees with me."

Whitrow was right. Robin did not want her husband to be a sea-captain. She couldn't stand being separated from him so frequently.

Churchill protested that she could go with him on his voyages.

Robin replied that that wasn't so. The wives of seamen could not accompany them. They got in the way, they were extra expense, and, worst of all, they brought bad luck to the ship. Even when the ships carried paying women passengers, the ship had to be given an especially strong blessing by a priest in order to avert ill-fortune.

Churchill retaliated with the argument that, if she loved him, she'd put up with his long absences.

Robin retorted that if he really loved her, he wouldn't want to leave her for any length of time. Besides, what about the children? It was well known that children raised in a family where the father was weak or was often absent had a tendency to grow up psychically twisted. Children needed a strong father who was always available for love or discipline.

Churchill took ten minutes to reflect.

If he went back on his promise to marry her, he would have to fight Whitrow and his son. Somebody would be killed, and he had a conviction that eventually it would be he. Even if he could stand his ground against her father and brother and killed them, he'd have to fight the next of kin, who were very numerous.

Of course, he could force Robin to reject him. But he did not want to lose her.

Finally, he said, "All right, darling. I'll be a pig-raiser. I only ask one thing. I want to take one last sea voyage before settling down. Can we take a ship to Norfolk and then travel overland to the farms?"

Robin wiped away her tears, smiled, and kissed him, and said she would indeed be a hardhearted bitch if she denied him that.

Churchill left to tell his crewmates that they must buy passage on the ship that he and Robin would be taking. He'd arrange it so they had money enough for the tickets. After the ship was out of sight of land, they must seize it. They would then sail across the Atlantic and points east. It was too bad they hadn't had a chance to learn seamanship. They must learn as they sailed.

"Won't your wife be angry?" Yastzhembski said.

"More than that," Churchill said. "But if she really loves me, she'll go with me. If she doesn't, we'll put her and the crew ashore before we set out."

As it turned out, the crew of the *Terra* never got a chance to seize the vessel. The second day of their voyage, they were attacked by Karelian pirates.

XI

When Stagg entered the campus of Vassar, he heard the same song, or variation thereof, he always heard when being presented the keys to the city, or, in this case, an honorary doctorate. Now, however, there was no large crowd to sing the welcome. A choir of freshmen, novitiates, greeted him. The older women, the priestesses and professors, arrayed in scarlet or blue, stood in a half-moon behind the white-clad choir, massed to form a delta. While the novitiates sang, the others nodded in approval at the quality of the performance or pounded the butts of their caducei on the ground in joy at sight of Stagg.

The Pants-Elf war party took the Vassar College for Oracular Priestesses completely by surprise. Somehow, the raiders had gotten the information that the Sunhero was to attend a private ceremony at midnight on the campus of Vassar. They knew that the people of Poughkeepsie had been warned to stay away. The only male on the college grounds was Stagg, and the priestesses numbered perhaps a hundred.

The war party burst out of the darkness and into the torchlight. The women were too busy chanting and observing Stagg and a young novitiate to notice the raiders. Not until the Pants-Elf gave a concerted scream and began cutting off the heads of those on the outside circle did the priestesses know they were attacked.

Stagg had no memory of what happened immediately after that. He raised his head just in time to see a man jump at him and swing the flat of a broadsword at his head.

He woke to find himself hanging like a slain deer from a pole carried on the shoulders of two men. His arms and legs were numb, the circulation cut off by rawhide strips binding them to the pole. His head felt as if it would burst; it ached not only from the blow but from the excess of blood which had drained into it because of its down-hanging position.

The moon was up and full. By its bright light he could see the bare legs and chest of the man behind him. Twisting his head, he could make out the gleam of moon on deeply tanned skins of men and on the white robes of a priestess.

Abruptly, he was lowered heavily on the hard ground.

"Old Horney is awake," a deep male voice said.

"Can't we cut the big bastard loose so he can walk?" another voice said. "I'm worn out carrying his useless hulk. That pole's cut an inch-deep groove in my shoulder."

"Okay," a third voice said, one that obviously belonged to a leader. "Cut him loose. But tie his hands behind his back, and tie a noose around his neck. If he tries to make a getaway, we can choke him. And be careful. He looks strong as a bull moose!"

"Oh, so strong, so superbly built!" a fourth voice said, higher-pitched than the others. "What a lover-boy!"

"You trying to make me jealous?" one of the men said. "Because if you are, dove, you're doing a good job. But don't push me. I'll cut out your liver and feed it to your mother."

"Don't you dare to say anything about my mother, you hairy thing!" the high-pitched voice said. "I'm beginning not to like you very much!"

"In the name of Columbia, our Blessed Mother! Cut out that lovers' quarreling. I'm sick of it. We're on a war party, not lounging around a totem hall. Go ahead, cut him loose. But watch him."

"I couldn't possibly watch him," the high-pitched voice said breathlessly.

"You trying to put his horns on my forehead?" said the man who had threatened to cut his friend's liver out. "Try it, and I'll gouge your face so another man will never look at you again."

"For the last time I said shut up!" the leader said, gratingly. "Next time, I slit the throat of the first man who provides the reason. Understood? Okay! Let's get going. We've a hell of a long way to go before we get out of enemy territory, and it won't be long before they have the bloodhounds on our trail."

Stagg was able to follow the conversation fairly well. The language was akin to Deecee, probably closer than German was to Dutch. He had heard it spoken before, in Camden. A group of Pants-Elf prisoners, taken on a raid, had had their throats cut during a ceremony in his honor. Some of them had been very brave men, jibing obscenely at Stagg until the knife severed their windpipes.

Just now Stagg wished that every man in the Pants-Elf had had his throat cut. His legs and arms were beginning to hurt terribly. He wanted to cry out, but he knew that the Pants-Elf would probably knock him out again to keep him quiet. He also did not want to give them the satisfaction of knowing they had hurt him.

The raiders tied his hands behind his back, placed a noose around his neck and promised to put a knife into his back if he made any suspicious moves. Then they shoved him ahead.

At first, Stagg was not capable of trotting. After a while, as the blood reached its normal circulation and the pains went away, he was able to keep up with the others. It was a good thing, he thought. Every time he stumbled, he felt the noose tighten around his neck and his breath choked off.

They were going downhill in sparsely wooded territory. The raiders numbered about forty, strung out in a double file. They carried broadswords, assegais, clubs, bows and arrows. They wore no armor at all, probably to increase their mobility. They did not wear their hair long, like the men of Deecee, but cut it very short and close to the scalp. Their faces presented an odd appearance, since they all had broad dark mustaches. These were the first men with hair on their faces that he had seen since landing on Earth.

They left the wooded area and approached the bank of the Hudson River. He got a closer and brighter view of the Pants-Elf and saw that the mustaches had been painted or tattooed on.

Moreover, each of them had tattooed across his bare chest, in large letters, the word *Mother.*

There were seven prisoners: himself, five priestesses, and—his heart skipped a beat—Mary Casey. They, too, had their hands tied behind their backs. Stagg tried to edge over to Mary Casey to whisper to her, but the rope around his neck pulled him back.

The party halted. Some of the men began clearing away a pile of brush. In a short time they exposed a number of large canoes piled in a hollow in the ground. These were carried to the river's edge.

The prisoners were forced to step into the canoes, one prisoner to a canoe, and the fleet paddled toward the other shore.

When the other shore was reached, the canoes were pushed out into the river for the current to carry away. The party set out at a trot through the woods. Occasionally, one of the prisoners stumbled and fell on her knees or face. The Pants-Elf kicked them and threatened to slit their throats on the spot if they didn't quit behaving like awkward cows.

Once, Mary Casey fell. A man kicked her in the ribs, and she writhed in agony. Stagg growled with fury and said, "If I ever get loose, Pants-Elf, I'll tear your arms off and wrap them around your neck!"

The man laughed and said, "Do that, dearie. It'd be a *pleasure* to be manhandled by the likes of *you*."

"For mother's sake, clam up!" the leader snarled. "Is this a war party or a courting?"

There was little said the rest of the night. They trotted a while and then walked a while. By dawn they had covered many miles, though not so many as the crow flies. The path wound through many hills.

Just after the eastern horizon began to pale, the leader called a halt. "We'll hole up and sleep until noon. Then, if the neighborhood looks deserted enough, we'll push on. We can make better time in the daylight, even if there is more chance of being seen."

They found a semicave formed by the overhang of a cliff. Here each man spread his single blanket on the hard earth and stretched out on it. In a few minutes all were asleep, except the four guards posted to keep an eye on the prisoner and any approaching Deecee.

Stagg was the other exception. He called softly to one of the guards. "Hey, I can't sleep! I'm hungry!"

"You'll eat when the rest of us do," said the guard. "That is, if you get anything to eat."

"You don't understand," Stagg said. "I don't have the normal requirements for food. If I don't eat every four hours, and twice as much as everybody else, my body starts to eat itself. It's these horns that do it. They affect my body so I have to eat like a bull moose to keep alive."

"I'll get you some hay," the guard said, and he snickered.

Somebody behind Stagg whispered, "Don't worry, honey. I'll get you something to eat. I couldn't let a monstrously handsome man like you starve to death. That would be a waste!"

There was a stirring behind him as somebody opened a knapsack. The guards looked curiously and then began grinning.

"Looks like you made a hit with Abner," said one. "But his buddy, Luke, isn't going to like it one bit when he wakes up."

Another said, "Good thing it's not Abner who's hungry. Then he could eat you. Haw, haw!"

The owner of the whisper walked into Stagg's view. It was the little man who had openly admired Stagg the previous night. He held a half loaf of bread, two huge slices of ham, and a canteen.

"Here, sit up, baby. Mother will feed big Horneycums."

The guards laughed, though not loudly. Stagg turned red, but he was too hungry to refuse food. He could feel the fire raging within him, flesh devouring flesh.

The little man was a youth about twenty, short and very slim-hipped. Unlike the other Pants-Elf, his hair had not been cut close to the scalp. It was wheat-brown and very curly. His face would have been called "cute" by a woman, though the painted mustache gave him a bizarre appearance. His large brown eyes were fringed by very long dark lashes. His teeth were so white they looked false, and his tongue was very red, probably because of some gum-like substance he was chewing.

Stagg hated to owe a debt to a being like Abner, but his mouth seemed to open automatically and gulp the food.

"There," Abner said, fondling Stagg's antlers and then running his long, slim fingers through Stagg's hair. "Does Horneycums feel better now? What about a big kiss to show big Horneycums' thanks?"

"Horneycums will kick hell out of you if you come any closer," Stagg said.

Abner's big eyes became even larger. He stepped back, his lower lip swelling with resentment.

"Is that any way to treat a buddy after he's kept you from starving to death?" he asked in a very hurt tone.

"Admittedly not," Stagg said. "But I just wanted you to know that if you try what I think you have in mind, you'll get killed."

Abner smiled and fluttered his long lashes. "Oh, you'll get over that absurd prejudice, baby. Besides, I've heard that you horned men are oversexed and once you're aroused you stop for nothing. What're you going to do if there are no women available?"

His lip curled in a sneer when he spoke of women. "Women" was a free translation of the word he used, a word that in Stagg's time had been used in a very derogatory, anatomical sense. Later, Stagg found that the Pants-Elf males always used that word among themselves, though in the presence of their females, they referred to them as "angels."

"Let the future take care of itself," Stagg said, and he closed his eyes and went to sleep.

It seemed to him only a minute later when he was awakened, but the sun was at its zenith. He blinked and sat up and looked around for Mary Casey. She had her hands untied, and was eating, while a man with a sword stood guard beside her.

The leader's name was Raf. He was a big man with broad shoulders and slim waistline and a strikingly handsome but cold face and blond hair. His blue eyes were very pale and very cold.

"That Mary Casey tells me you aren't a Deecee," he said. "She says you came down from the skies in a fiery metal ship, and that you left Earth over eight hundred years ago to explore the stars. Is she a liar?"

Stagg outlined his story, watching Raf closely while he told it. He was hoping that Raf would decide not to give him the usual treatment a Pants-Elf gave a Deecee who was in his power.

"Say, you're quite a dish," Raf enthusiastically said, though his pale blue eyes were as icy as before. "And those horns are *crazy*. They give you a real masculine look. I hear that when you Horned Kings are in heat, you've the staying power of fifty bucks."

"That is a well-known fact," Stagg replied smoothly. "What I'd like to know is, what's going to happen to us?"

"We'll decide that after we get out of Deecee territory and get across the Delaware River. We've two days' hard marching ahead of us, though we'll be fairly safe once we get over the Shawangunk Mountains. Beyond the Shawangunk is a no-man's land, where the only people we'll meet are raiding parties, friendly or hostile."

"What about untying me?" Stagg said. "I can't go back to Deecee, and I'd just as soon throw in my lot with you."

"You kidding?" Raf said. "I'd just as soon let loose a mad elk! I'm a damn good man, baby, but I wouldn't want to tangle with you—that is—not in combat. No, you'll stay tied up."

The party set out at a fast pace. Two scouts ran ahead to make sure they didn't fall into ambush. When they came to the Shawangunk Mountains, they approached the pass cautiously, hiding until the scouts gave the go-ahead signal. At midnight the party bedded down behind a high rocky ridge.

Stagg tried to talk to Mary Casey to raise her morale. She was beginning to look very fatigued. Every time she started to lag, she was struck and cursed. Abner was especially hard on her; he seemed to hate her.

The evening of the third day, they forded the Delaware River at a shallow place. They slept, rose at dawn, and pushed on. By eight o'clock in the morning, the raiders made a triumphal entry into the small frontier town of High Queen.

High Queen had a population of about fifty, huddled in cubical stone buildings surrounded by a twenty-five foot high stone and cement wall. Each building was windowless on the street side, and its entranceways were set deep within the walls. The windows were on the inside walls, facing the court.

The houses had no front yards, since they were set flush with the street. However, they were separated by vacant weed-grown lots on which goats grazed, chickens pecked, and dirty, naked children played.

The crowd that greeted the raiders was composed mainly of men; the few women present soon left at the orders of their husbands. The women were veiled and wore robes that concealed the body from shoulder to ground. Evidently women held an inferior position in Pants-Elf, despite the fact that the only idol in the town was a granite statue of the Great White Mother.

Later, Stagg found out that the Pants-Elf worshiped Columbia, but that the Deecee regarded them as belonging to a heretical sect. In the theology of the Pants-Elf, every woman was a living incarnation of Columbia and therefore a sacred vessel of motherhood. But the men of Pants-Elf knew also that the flesh was weak. They made sure that their women had no chance to dirty their purity.

They were to be good servants and good mothers, but that was all; therefore, they were to be sealed from view as much as possible and also sealed from temptation. The males had sexual intercourse with their wives only to have children, and as little other type of intercourse, social and familial, as possible. They were polygamous—on the theory that polygamy was an *excellent* institution for repopulating a sparsely settled country.

The women, shut off from men and confined to each other's company, often became Lesbians. They were even encouraged by the males to become so; but they went to bed with the men at least three times a week. This was enjoined on husband and wife as a sacred duty, distasteful as it might be to either or both. The result was almost perpetual pregnancy.

This was a state which the man desired. According to his heretical sect, a pregnant woman was ritually unclean. She was not to be touched, except by other unclean women or priests.

The prisoners were shut within one of the larger stone buildings. Women came to bring them food, but first Stagg was forced to put on kilts so he wouldn't shock the women. The raiders and townsmen then celebrated by getting very drunk.

At about nine at night, they burst into the cell and took Stagg, Mary Casey and the priestesses to the town square. Here stood the statue of Columbia, and around her were a circle of woodpiles. From the center of each pile rose a stake.

A priestess was bound to each stake.

Stagg and Mary were not tied to a stake, but they were forced to stand and watch.

"It is necessary to purify these evil witches through fire," Raf said. "That is why we brought along those young women. We felt sorry for them. You see, those we killed with the sword are forever lost, doomed souls that will wander through eternity. But these will be purified through fire. They will go to the land of happy souls.

"It is too bad," he added, "that High Queen doesn't have any sacred bears, because then we'd feed the wretches to the bears. Bears are just as much instruments of salvation as fire, you know.

"You needn't worry about anything happening to you here. We wouldn't waste you on this hick town. You're to go to Pheelee, where the government will take the responsibility for you."

"Pheelee? Philadelphia, the City of Brotherly Love?" Stagg said with the last attempt at humor he made that night.

The fires were touched off, and the purifying ritual begun.

Stagg watched for a moment, then closed his eyes. Fortunately, he couldn't hear the women screaming, because they were gagged. The priestesses who were burned had the habit of calling down curses upon the Pants-Elf; the gags were to prevent this.

The stench of burning flesh could not be shut out. Stagg and Mary both became sick—and then had to endure the amused laughter of their captors.

Finally, the fires went out and the two prisoners were marched back to the cell. Mary was held while two men stripped her, locked an iron chastity belt around her and then put a kilt on over it.

Stagg protested; the men looked at him in amazement.

"What?" Raf said. "Leave her open to temptation? Allow the pure vessel of Columbia to be defiled? You must be mad! Inasmuch as she will be left alone with you, and you're a Horned King, the result would be inevitable. And—knowing your endurance—probably fatal for her. You should thank us for this. You know what you would do!"

"Unless you feed me more than you have," Stagg said, "I could not do anything. I'm weak from starvation."

Stagg did not want to eat, in one sense. His meager diet had considerably diminished the action of the antlers. He still suffered from a drive that was embarrassingly evident and had been the object of numerous amused and admiring comments from his captors; but it was almost nothing compared to the satyriasis that had possessed him in Deecee.

Now he was afraid that, if he ate, he would attack Mary Casey—chastity belt or no chastity belt. But he was also afraid that if he didn't eat he'd be dead by morning.

Perhaps, he thought, he could eat enough to feed his body and antlers but not enough so the compulsion would become uncontrollable.

"Why don't you put me in another room if you're so sure I'll attack her?" he said.

Raf looked amazed. But he overdid it, and Stagg knew that Raf had been maneuvering him into making just such a suggestion.

"Of course! I'm so tired, I'm stupid," Raf said. "We'll lock you up in another room."

The other room was located in the same building, across the inner court. From his window Stagg could see the window of Mary's room. Although she had no light of her own, the moon cast beams into the court. They glimmered palely upon her face, pressed against the iron bars.

Stagg waited for twenty minutes; then the expected sound came, a key inserted into the lock of the iron door.

The door swung open with the creak of unoiled hinges. Abner entered with a huge tray. He set it down on the table and told the guard he'd call him when he wanted him. The guard opened his mouth to object, but, seeing Abner's glare, he withdrew. He was a local and therefore awed by this Philadelphia raider.

"See, Horneycums?" said Abner. "Look at all the nice food for you! Don't you think you owe me something for this?"

"I certainly do," Stagg said. He would have gone along with almost anything for the sake of a meal. "You've got more than enough. But in case I want more later, could you get it easily?"

"You bet. The kitchen is just down the hall. The woman has gone back to her quarters, but I'd be delighted to do a woman's work for *you*. How about a kiss to show your gratitude?"

"I couldn't put anything into it until I eat," Stagg replied, forcing himself to smile at Abner. "Then we'll see."

"Don't be coy, Horneycums," Abner said. "And please, pretty please, hurry up and eat. We don't have too much time. I think that big bitch Raf is planning to come here tonight. And I'm nervous, too, about my buddy, Luke. If he knew I was here alone with you . . . !"

"I can't eat with my hands tied behind my back."

"I don't know," Abner said, hesitatingly. "You're so big and strong. You could tear me apart with your bare hands—such *huge* hands, too."

"I'd be stupid to do that," Stagg said. "Then I'd have nobody to sneak me food. I'd starve."

"That's right. Besides, you wouldn't hurt little old me, would you? I'm so small and helpless. And you do like me, just a little, don't you? You didn't mean what you said on the trail, did you?"

"Of course not," Stagg said, munching on cold ham, bread and butter, and pickles. "I just said that so your buddy Luke wouldn't get any ideas about us."

"You're not only devastatingly handsome, you're clever, too," Abner said. He was panting slightly. "Do you feel strong enough, now?"

Stagg was about to say that he had to eat everything in sight before he would get his strength back, but thought better of the remark. He did not have to say anything, because there was a commotion just outside the door. He put his ear against the iron to hear.

"It's your buddy, Luke. He's telling the guard he knows you're in here with me, and he's demanding that he be let in."

Abner turned pale. "Oh, Mother! He'll kill me and you, too! He's such a jealous bitch!"

"Call him in. I'll take care of him. I won't kill him; just rough him up a bit. Let him know how things are between you and me."

Abner squealed with delight. "That would be *divine*!"

He squeezed Stagg's arm, and rolled his eyes upward with ecstasy. "Mother, what *biceps*! So big and *hard*!"

Stagg beat on the door with his fist and called to the guard. "Abner says it's all right to let him in!"

"Yes," Abner said behind him. "It's perfectly all right. Let Luke in."

He kissed Stagg on the back of the neck. "I can just see the expression on his face when you tell him about us. I've been getting pretty tired of his jealous moods, anyway."

The door squeaked open. Luke rushed in, sword in hand. The guard slammed the door shut behind Luke, and the three were locked in.

Stagg wasted no time. He chopped down with the edge of his palm against Luke's neck. Luke fell, and the sword clanged as it hit the stone floor.

Abner gave a little shriek. Then he opened his mouth for a scream as he saw Stagg bound at him. Before he could give vent to it, he, too, fell on the floor.

His head lay at a grotesque angle. Stagg had hit him so hard with his fist that he'd broken his neck.

Stagg dragged the bodies to one side so they wouldn't be visible from the doorway. He took Luke's sword and with one hard swing cut off Luke's head.

Then he rapped on the door and called in what he hoped was a passable imitation of Abner's voice, "Guard! Come in here and make Luke quit abusing the prisoner!"

The key was turned, and the guard stepped inside. He had his sword in hand, but Stagg struck from behind the door. The head of the guard rolled a foot from his body, the open neck gushing a stream of blood.

Stagg put the guard's knife in his belt and stepped out into the hall, which was narrow and dimly lit by a torch at the far end. He took a chance that the kitchen was at the far end and walked down to it. The door opened onto a large room well stocked with food. He found a cloth sack and filled it with food and several bottles of wine. Then he went back into the hall.

At the same time, Raf opened the door to the hall and stepped inside.

His manner was furtive, and it was probably his nervousness that made him not notice the guard was gone. He was unarmed except for a knife in a scabbard at his belt.

Stagg ran down the hall toward him. Raf looked up and saw the horned man bearing down on him, a lifted bloody sword in one hand, the other holding a large sack slung over his shoulder.

Raf turned and tried to get out of the door. The blade cut all the way through his neck.

Stagg stepped over the corpse, still spouting blood, and went out into the court. There he found two men sleeping on the pavement. Like most of the men in High Queen that night, they had passed out. Stagg did not care to take a chance on their barring his way later, and besides he wanted to kill every Pants-Elf he came across. He gave two quick strokes across their necks and went on.

He crossed the court and entered another hall, exactly like the one he had left. There was a guard posted outside the door of Mary's room, a bottle tilted to his lips.

He did not see Stagg until Stagg was almost on him. For a second, he was too paralyzed with astonishment to make a move. It was all the time Stagg needed. He threw the sword, point foremost.

The point stuck the guard exactly in the "O" of the *Mother* tattooed on his bare chest. The guard staggered backward with the impact, his hand clutching the blade. Strangely, his other hand did not drop the bottle.

The point had not gone in deeply, but Stagg dropped his sack, leaped after the sword, seized it and pushed hard on the hilt. The blade went all the way through the breastbone and deep into the organ beneath.

Mary Casey almost fainted when the door opened and the horned and bloody man stepped inside. Then she gasped. "Peter Stagg! How . . . ?"

"Later!" he said. "No time to talk!"

Together they ran from the shadow of one building to another until they reached the wall and high gate through which they had entered the town. There were two guards posted at the foot of the gate, and two men in small towers above it.

Fortunately, all four were sleeping off their drunk. Stagg had no trouble in plunging his knife into the throats of the two men on the ground. Then he walked softly up the steps leading to the towers and treated the two there the same way. He did not have any trouble in withdrawing the huge bolt of oak that held the two gates together.

They went back by the path on which they had come. They trotted a hundred steps, walked a hundred, trotted a hundred, walked a hundred.

They came to the Delaware and crossed on the same shallow ford. Mary asked for rest, but Stagg said they'd have to push on.

"When the town wakes up and finds all those headless corpses, they'll be hot on our trail. They won't stop till they find us, unless we can reach Deecee territory before they do. And then we'll have to watch out for the Deecee, too. We're going to try to get to Caseyland."

The time came when they had to slow down to a walk; Mary couldn't keep up the pace. By nine in the morning, she sat down.

"I can't go another step unless I get some sleep first."

They found a hollow about a hundred meters from the path. Here Mary fell asleep at once. Stagg ate and drank first and then he lay down to sleep also. He would have liked to stay on guard, but he knew that he had to have rest to continue in a few hours. He needed his strength because he might have to carry Mary.

He woke before Mary did, and he ate again.

When she opened her eyes a few minutes later, she saw Stagg bending over her.

"What are you doing?"

He said, "Shut up. I'm trying to get your chastity belt off."

XII

The face of Nephi Sarvant was an index to his character. It looked in profile like a nutcracker or the curved jaws of a pair of pliers. He was faithful to his face; once he fastened down upon something, he would not let go.

Having left Whitrow's house, he swore that he would never set foot in a place where such iniquity thrived. He swore also to dedicate his life, if need be, to bringing the Truth to the idolatrous heathen.

He walked the five kilometers to the House of Lost Souls and spent a night of uneasy sleep there. Shortly after dawn, he left the house. Though it was so early, the street was alive with wagons piled with freight, sailors, merchantmen, children, women marketing. He looked into several restaurants, found them too dirty, and decided to make his breakfast on fruit from a street stand. He talked with the fruit-merchant about his chances for getting a job and was told that there was an opening for a janitor at the temple of the goddess Gotew. The merchant knew this because his brother-in-law had been fired from the job the previous evening.

"It doesn't pay much but you get your board and room. And there are other compensations, provided you are a man who has fathered many children," the merchant said. He winked at Sarvant. "My brother-in-law was fired because he neglected his sweeping and scrubbing for the other advantages."

Sarvant didn't ask what he meant. He got directions for getting to the temple and left.

This job, if he secured it, would be an excellent post for observation of the Deecee religion. And it would afford a first-rate battleground for proselytizing. Oh, it would be dangerous, but what missionary worthy of his faith ever considered that a drawback?

The directions were complicated; Sarvant lost his way. He found himself far into a wealthy residential district, with no one to ask directions from except a few people who rode by in carriages or on deerback. These did not look as if they would stop to talk to a pedestrian, a man of the lower classes.

He decided to go back to the dock area and start over. He had not gone a block before he saw a woman who had just left a large house. She was dressed strangely, covered from head to foot with a hooded robe. At first, he thought she must be a servant; he knew now that an aristocrat never walked when she could ride. On approaching her, he saw that the robe was of too fine a material to belong to one of the lower class.

He followed her for several blocks before he took a chance of offending her by speaking to her. Finally, he called to her, "Lady, may I humbly ask a question?"

She turned and looked haughtily at him. She was a tall woman of about twenty-two with a face that would have been beautiful if it had been less sharp. Her large eyes were a deep blue, and her hair, where it was not hidden by the hood, was rich yellow.

Sarvant repeated his question, and she nodded her head. He then asked her directions to the Temple of Gotew.

She looked angry and said, "Are you making fun of me?"

"No, no," Sarvant said. "Why would I do that? I don't understand."

"Perhaps you don't, she said. "You sound like a foreigner. Certainly, you've no reason to deliberately insult me. My people would kill you—even if I am not worthy of the insult."

"Believe me, I had no such intention. If I have offended, I apologize."

She smiled slightly and said, "Accepted, stranger. And now, tell me, why do you want to go to the Temple of Gotew? Do you have a wife who is as wretched and cursed as I am?"

"She has been long dead," Sarvant said. "And I do not know what you mean by saying you are wretched and cursed. No, I am looking for a job as janitor in the temple. You see, I am one of those who came down to Earth . . ." and he launched into his story, though he told it in the briefest outline.

She said, "Then you may talk to me as an equal, I suppose, though it is hard to think of a *diradah* sweeping floors. A true *diradah* would starve to death first. And I see you're not wearing a totem symbol. If you belonged to one of the great totems, you could find a job worthy of you. Or do you lack a sponsor?"

"Totems are superstitious idolatry!" he said. "I would never join one."

Her eyebrows rose. "You *are* a queer one! I don't know how to classify you. As a brother of the Sunhero, you are a *diradah*. But you certainly don't look or act like one. My advice to you is to behave like one so we may know how to behave toward you."

"I thank you," he said. "But I must be what I am. Now, could you please tell me how to get to the temple."

"Just follow me," she said, and she began walking.

Perplexed, he trailed her by a few steps. He would have liked to have clarified some of the statements she made, but there was something about her attitude that discouraged questions.

The Temple of Gotew was on the borderline between the dock area and a wealthy residential district. It was an imposing building of prestressed concrete, shaped like an enormous half-open oyster shell and painted in scarlet and white stripes. Broad steps of granite slabs ran up to the lower lip of the shell, and the interior was cool and dimly lit. The upper part of the shell was supported by a few slim pillars of stone carved in the likeness of the goddess Gotew, a stately figure with a sad and brooding face and an open hollow where her stomach should have been.

In the hollow sat a large stone reproduction of a hen surrounded by eggs.

At the base of each caryatid of the goddess sat women. Every one wore a robe similar to that of the woman he had followed. Some robes were shabby; some, rich. Wealthy and poor sat together.

The woman walked without hesitation to a group that sat on the cement floor deep within the gloom. There were about twelve around the caryatid, and they must have been expecting the tall thin blonde, since they had a space reserved for her.

Sarvant found a white-faced priest who was standing at the rear by a row of large stone booths. He inquired about the janitor's job. To his surprise, he found he was talking to the chief official of the temple; he had expected a priestess in charge.

Bishop Andi was curious about Sarvant's accent and asked him the same sort of questions others had. Sarvant replied truthfully, but he sighed relief when the bishop failed to ask him if he was a worshiper of Columbia. The bishop turned Sarvant over to a lesser priest, who told him what his duties would be, how much he'd be paid, where he would eat and sleep and when. He concluded by asking, "Are you the father of many children?"

"Seven," replied Sarvant, neglecting to add that they had been dead for eight centuries. It was possible that the priest himself was one of Sarvant's descendants; indeed, it was conceivable that everyone under the roof could claim him as their grandfather thirty-odd generations removed.

"Seven? Excellent!" the priest said. "In that case, you will have the same privileges as any other man of proven fertility. You will have to undergo a medical examination, however, because we take no man's word for such a grave responsibility. I warn you, do not abuse the privilege. Your predecessor was discharged for neglecting his push broom."

Sarvant began sweeping in the rear of the temple. He had just reached the pillar where the blonde was sitting when he noticed a man talking to a woman by the blonde's side. He could not hear what they were saying, but presently the woman arose and opened her robe. She was wearing nothing under the robe.

The man apparently liked what he saw since he nodded his head. The woman took his hand and led him to one of the booths at the rear. They entered, and the woman closed a curtain over the front of the booth.

Sarvant was speechless. It was minutes before he was able to begin pushing the broom again. By then he saw that the same actions were being repeated everywhere in the temple.

His first impulse was to drop the broom, run out of the temple, and never come back. But he told himself that wherever he went in Deecee he would find evil. He might as well stay here and see if he could do anything in the service of the Truth.

Then he was forced to witness something that almost made him vomit. A big sailor approached the thin blonde and began talking to her. She rose and opened her robe, and in a moment the two had gone into a booth.

Sarvant shook with rage. He had been shocked enough that the others would do this, but that she, *she* . . . !

He made himself stand still and think.

Why should her actions offend him more than the actions of the others? Because—admit it—he had felt attracted to her. Very much attracted. He had felt about her as he had not felt about a woman since the day he had met his wife.

He picked up his brush, walked to the office of the underling priest, and demanded to be told what was going on.

The priest was astonished. "Are you so new to our religion that you did not know Gotew is the patroness of sterile women?"

"No, I did not," Sarvant replied, his voice shaking. "What does that have to do with this . . ." He stopped, because Deecee had no words, as far as he knew, for prostitution or whoring. Then he said, "Why do these women offer themselves to strangers, what does the worship of Gotew have to do with this?"

"Why, everything of course! These are unlucky women, cursed with a sterile womb. They came to us after a year's endeavor to conceive by their husbands, and we gave them a thorough physical examination. Some women have troubles we can diagnose and rectify, but not these. There is nothing we could do for them.

"So, when science fails, faith must be called upon. These unfortunate women come here every day—except on holy days, when there is a ceremony to attend elsewhere—and they pray that Gotew will send them a man whose seed will quicken their dead wombs. If, after a year's time, they are not blessed with a child, they usually enter an order where they may dedicate their life to serving their goddess and their people."

"What about Arva Linkon?" Sarvant said, naming the blonde. "It's unthinkable that a woman with her beauty and aristocratic family should lie with any man who comes along."

"Tut, tut, my dear fellow! Not *any* man. Perhaps you didn't observe that those males who come here went into a side room first. My good brothers examine them there to make sure they are brimming with healthy sperm. Also, any man who is diseased or in any way unfit to be a father is rejected. As for ugliness or handsomeness of the male, we pay no attention to that; here the desideratum is the seed and the womb. Personalities and personal taste do not enter. By the way, why don't you take the examination too? No reason to selfishly restrict your offspring to one woman. You owe as much a debt to Gotew as to any other aspect of the Great White Mother."

"I have to get back to my sweeping," muttered Sarvant, and he left hastily.

He did manage to finish the main floor, but it was only by an extreme effort of will. He could not keep from looking at Arva Linkon from time to time. She left at noon and did not return the rest of the day.

He did not sleep well that night. He dreamed of Arva entering the booth with those men—ten in all; he had counted them. And though he knew he should love the sinners and loathe the sin, he loathed every one of the ten sinners.

When morning came, he swore that he would not hate the men who came to her today. But even as he swore he knew he could not keep his vow.

That day he counted seven men. By the time the seventh strolled out, he had to retreat to his quarters to keep from running after the man and closing his hands around his throat.

The third night, he prayed for guidance.

Should he leave the temple, look elsewhere for work? If he stayed, he would be indirectly approving of and directly maintaining this abomination. Moreover, he might have the terrible sin of murder on his conscience, the blood of a man on his hands. He did not want that. Yes, he wanted it! But he must not want it, he must not!

And if he left, he would not have done a thing to wipe out the evil; he would have fled like a coward. Moreover, he would not have made Arva realize that she was slapping God in the face by carrying on this loathsome travesty of a religious rite. He wanted to get her out of the temple more than he had wanted anything in his life—even more than he had wanted to be on the *Terra* so he could carry the Word to the ignorant heathen of the other planets.

He had not made a single convert during those eight hundred years. But he had tried. He had done his best; he could not help it if their ears were deaf to the Word, their eyes blind to the light of the Truth.

The next day, he waited until Arva began to walk out of the temple at noon. Then he leaned his brush against the wall and followed her out into the sunshine and the buzz and crash of Deecee street life.

"Lady Arva!" he called. "I must speak with you!"

She stopped. Her face was shadowed by the overhanging hood, but it seemed to him that she looked as if she were deeply ashamed and were suffering. Or did she look that way because he wanted her to?

"May I walk home with you?" he asked.

She was startled, "Why?"

"Because I will go crazy if I do not."

"I do not know," she said. "It is true that you are a brother of the Sunhero, so that there should be no loss of dignity in having you walk by my side. On the other hand, you have no totem, and you do the work of the lowest of menials."

"And who are you, of all people, to talk to me about being lowly!" he snarled. "You, who take on all comers?"

Her eyes widened. "What have I done wrong? How dare you talk to a Linkon in that manner?"

"You are a . . . a whore!" he shouted, using the English word even though he knew she would not understand.

"What's that?" she said.

"Prostitute! A woman who sells herself for money!"

"I never heard of anything like that," she said. "What kind of country do you come from, that a vessel of the Holy Mother would so dishonor herself?"

He tried to calm down. He spoke in a low but quivering voice.

"Arva Linkon, I just want to talk to you. I have something to say that will be the most important thing you have ever heard in your life. Indeed, the only important thing."

"I don't know. I think you are a little crazed."

"I swear that I would not dream of doing you harm!"

"Swear on the sacred name of Columbia?"

"No, I cannot do that. But I will swear by my God that I will not lay a hand on you."

"God! You worship the god of the Caseylanders?"

"No, not theirs! Mine! The true God!"

"Now I know you are crazy! Otherwise, you would not be talking of this god in this country, and especially not to me. I won't listen to the foul blasphemy that would pour from your wicked mouth."

She walked away.

Sarvant took a step after her. Then, realizing that now was not the time to talk to her, and that he was not conducting himself as he would have wished, he turned away. His fists were clenched, and he was grinding his teeth together. He walked like a blind man, several times bumping into people. They swore at him, but he paid no attention.

He went back to the temple and picked up his broom.

Again, he did not sleep well at night. He planned a hundred times how he would talk softly and wisely to Arva. He would show her the errors of her belief in a manner she could not refute. Eventually, she would be his first convert.

Side by side, they would begin the work that would sweep the country clean, as the Primitive Christians had swept ancient Rome.

The following day, however, Arva did not come into the temple. He despaired. Perhaps she would never come back.

Then he realized that that was one of the things he had wanted her to do. Perhaps he was making more progress than he had thought.

But how would he get to see her again?

The morning of the next day, Arva, still clad in the hooded robe of the sterile woman, walked into the temple. She averted her eyes and was silent when he greeted her. After praying at the foot of the caryatid at which she customarily sat, she went to the rear of the temple and began talking earnestly to the bishop.

Sarvant was seized with a fear that she was denouncing him. Was it reasonable to expect that she would keep silent? After all, in her eyes, he was committing blasphemy by even being in this—to her—holy place.

Arva resumed her place at the foot of the caryatid. The bishop beckoned to Sarvant.

He put his broom down and walked to him, his legs weak with anxiety. Was this mission to stop here and now, before he had planted one seed of faith that would grow after he was gone? And if he failed now, then the Word was lost forever, since he was the last of his sect.

"My son," said the bishop, "up to now the knowledge that you are not as yet a believer has been confined to the hierarchy. You must remember that you were granted a great privilege because you are a brother to the Sunhero. If you had been anybody else, you would have been hanged long ago. But you were given a month to see the error of your ways and to testify to the truth. Your month is not up yet; but I must warn you that you will have to keep your mouth shut about your false belief. Otherwise, the time will be shortened. I am disturbed, since I had hoped that your application to work here meant that you were about to announce your desire to sacrifice to the Mother of Us All."

"Then Arva told you?"

"Bless her for a truly devout woman, she certainly did! Now, do I have your promise that you will not repeat the incident of the day before?"

"You have it," Sarvant said. The bishop had not asked him to quit proselytizing. He had just asked him not to repeat the incident. From now on he would be cunning as the dove, wise as the serpent.

Five minutes later, he had forgotten his resolution.

He saw a tall and handsome man, an aristocrat by his bearing and his expensive clothes, approach Arva. She smiled at him, rose, and led him to the booth.

It was the smile that did it.

Never before had she smiled at the men who came to her. Her face had been as expressionless as if cut from marble. Now, seeing the smile, Sarvant felt something well up in him. It spread from his loins, roared through his chest, raced through his throat, cutting off his wind. It filled his skull until it exploded; he could see only blackness before him and could hear nothing.

He did not know how long he had been in that condition, but when he partially regained his senses, he was standing in the office of the priest-physician.

"Bend over, and I'll massage your prostate and get a specimen," the priest was saying.

Automatically, Sarvant obeyed. While the priest was examining the slide through a microscope, Sarvant stood like a block of ice. Inside, he was fire. He was filled with a fierce joy he had never known; he knew what he was going to do, but he did not care. At that moment he would have defied any being or Being who tried to stop him.

A few minutes afterward, he strode from the office, Unhesitatingly, he walked up to Arva, who had just returned from the booth and was about to sit down.

"I want you to come with me!" he said in a loud clear voice.

"Where?" she said, and then, seeing the expression on his face, she understood.

"What did you say about me the other day?" she asked scornfully.

"That was not today."

He seized her hand and began to pull her toward the booth. She did not resist, but when they were in the booth and he had closed the curtain, she said, "Now I know! You have decided to sacrifice to the Goddess!"

She threw off her robe and smiled ecstatically. But she was looking upwards, not at him.

"Great Goddess, I thank You for having allowed me to become the instrument to convert this man to the true faith!"

"No!" said Sarvant hoarsely. "Don't say that! I do not believe in your idol. It is just—God help me!—I want you! I cannot stand seeing you go into this booth with every man that asks you. Arva, I love you!"

For a moment, she stared at him with horror. Then she stopped and picked up her robe and held it in front of her. "Do you think that I would allow you to defile me by touching me? A pagan! And under this holy roof!"

She turned to walk out. He leaped at her, spun her around. She opened her mouth to scream, and he stuffed the hem of the robe into her mouth. He wrapped the rest of the robe around her head and shoved her backwards so she fell upon the bed and he on top of her.

She writhed and twisted to get from his grip, but he held her with fingers that cut deep into her flesh. Then she tried to hold her knees together. He gave a great flop like a giant fish, coming down hard with his hips; it broke the lock of her legs.

She tried to go backwards, like a snake attempting to crawl on its back, but her head was stopped by the wall behind her. Suddenly, she stopped struggling.

Sarvant moaned and gripped her back with his hands, pressing his face against the robe over her face. He wanted to feel his lips upon hers, but the cloth was doubled where he had shoved it into her mouth; he could feel nothing through the thickness.

There was a spark of sanity, the thought that he had always hated violence and especially rape, and yet he was forcing himself upon this woman he loved. And worse, far worse, she had willingly given herself to at least a hundred men in the last ten days, men who did not care at all about her but merely wanted to spew out their lust upon her. Yet she was resisting him like a virgin martyr of ancient Rome at the mercy of a pagan emperor! It did not make sense; nothing did.

He screamed with the sudden release of eight hundred years.

He did not know that he was screaming. He was absolutely unaware of his surroundings. When the bishop and priest rushed in, and Arva, weeping and sobbing, told her story, he did not comprehend what was happening. Not until the temple was crowded with furious men from the street, and someone appeared with a rope, did he understand what was happening.

Then it was too late.

Too late to try to tell them what had impelled him. Too late even if they could have known what he was talking about. Too late even if they had not knocked him down and beaten him until his teeth were knocked out and his lips too puffed to do anything but mumble.

The bishop tried to intervene, but the mob pushed him to one side and carried Sarvant out into the street. There they dragged him by the legs, his head bumping on the cement, until they came to a square where a gallows stood. This was in the shape of a hideous old goddess, Alba, the Throttler of Men's Breath. Her iron hands, painted a dead-white, reached out as if clutching for every man that passed.

The rope was thrown over one of her hands and its end tied around the wrist. Men brought a table out from a house and set it beneath the dangling rope. They lifted Sarvant upon it and tied his hands behind his back. Two men held him while a third put a noose around his neck.

There was a moment of silence when the cries of outraged men ceased, and they quit trying to get their hands upon him and tear his blasphemer's flesh.

Sarvant looked about him. He could not see clearly, since his eyes were puffed up, and blood was running over them from gashes in his scalp. He mumbled something.

"What did you say?" one of the men holding him asked.

Sarvant could not repeat it. He was thinking that he had always wanted to be a martyr. It was a terrible sin, that desire; the sin of pride. But he had desired martyrdom. And he had always pictured himself coming to the end with dignity and with the courage given him by the knowledge that his disciples would carry on and would eventually triumph.

This was not to be. He was to hang like a criminal of the worst sort. Not for preaching the Word, but for rape.

He had not a single convert. He would die unmourned, die practically nameless. His body would be thrown to the hogs. Not that his body mattered; it was the thought that his name and his deed would die, too, that made him want to scream out to the heavens. Somebody, even if just one soul, should carry on.

He thought, No new religion succeeds unless the old religion first becomes weak. And these people believe without a shadow of a doubt to relieve the blinding intensity of conviction. They believe with a strength that the people of my time certainly did not have.

He mumbled again. By now he was standing alone on the table, swaying back and forth but determined that he would not show any fear.

"Too soon," he said in a language his hearers could not have understood even if he had spoken clearly. "I came back to Earth too soon. I should have waited another eight hundred years, when men might have begun to lose faith and to scoff in secret. Too soon!"

Then the table was dragged out from under him.

XIII

Two tall-masted schooners, sailing out of the dawn mists, were on the Deecee brigantine before the lookout had time to cry a warning. The sailors aboard *The Divine Dolphin*, however, had no doubt about the identity of the attackers. The simultaneous shout, "The Karelians!" arose; then all was confusion.

One of the pirate vessels ran up alongside *The Divine Dolphin*. Grappling hooks from the Karelian ship secured the two ships tightly. In an incredibly swift time, the pirates were aboard.

They were tall men who wore nothing but brightly colored shorts and broad leather belts bristling with weapons. They were tattooed from head to foot, and they brandished cutlasses and big clubs with spiked knobs. They shouted ferociously in their native Finnish, and they swung cutlass and club as if berserk, sometimes felling their own men in their fury.

The Deecee were caught by surprise but they fought bravely. They did not think of surrender; that meant being sold into slavery and worked to death.

The crew of the *Terra* were among the defenders. Though they knew nothing of swordplay, they slashed away as best they could. Even Robin seized a sword and fought by Churchill's side.

The second schooner closed in on the other side. The Karelians from her swarmed aboard and attacked the Deecee before they could turn around to face them. Gbwe-hun, the Dahomeyan, was the first casualty among the starmen. He had killed a pirate with a lucky stroke and wounded another before a cutlass wielder from behind cut off the Dahomey's sword arm and then lopped off his head. Yastzhembski went down next, bleeding from a gash across his forehead.

Suddenly, Robin and Churchill were struggling in the folds of a net thrown over them from a yardarm. They were beaten unconscious with fists.

Churchill awoke to find his hands tied behind him. Robin was on the deck beside him, also tied. The clang of blade on blade had ceased, and even the shrieks of the wounded were still. The badly wounded

Deecee had been thrown overboard, and the badly wounded Karelians refused to cry out.

The pirate captain, a Kirsti Ainundila, stood in front of the captives. He was a tall dark man with a patch over one eye and a scar running across his left cheek. He spoke in a heavily accented Deecee.

"I have been through the ship's log," he said, "and I know who you are. So there is no use lying to me. Now! You two"—he pointed to Churchill and Robin—"are worth a huge ransom. I think that this Whitrow will pay much to get his daughter and son-in-law back unharmed. As for the rest, they will fetch a fair price on the block when we get back to Aino."

Aino, Churchill knew, was a Karelian-held city on the coast of what had once been North Carolina.

Kirsti ordered all the prisoners taken below and chained to the bulkhead. Yastzhembski was among them, since he had been judged fit to recover from his wound.

After they had been chained and the pirates had left, Lin spoke up.

"I see now that it was foolish to think we could go back to our homelands. Not because we've been captured, but because we no longer have homelands. We'd be no better off there than here. We'd find our descendants as alien and hostile as Churchill has found his.

"Now, I've been thinking for some time of a thing that we forgot because of our desire to get back to Earth. That is, what happened to the Earthmen who colonized Mars?"

"I don't know," Churchill said, "but it does seem to me that if the Martians weren't wiped out for some reason or other, they would have sent spaceships to Earth long before this. After all, they were self-supporting. They had their own ships."

"Apparently something prevented them," Chandra said. "But I think I know what Lin is getting at. There are radioactive minerals on Mars. The means for making ore should still be there even if the people no longer are."

"Let me get this straight," Churchill said. "You are proposing that we take the *Terra* there? We *do* have enough fuel to get us to Mars, but there's not enough to get us back. Are you suggesting we use the equipment in the Martian domes to make more fuel? And then leave for the stars once more?"

"We found one planet where the aborigines are not advanced enough, technologically, to fight us," Lin said. "I mean the second planet of Vega. It had four large continents, each about the size of Australia, each separated by a large body of water. One of the land-masses is inhabited by humanoids who are, technologically speaking, at the level of the ancient Greeks. Two are inhabited by Neolithics. The fourth is uninhabited. If we can get to Vega, we can colonize the fourth continent."

They were all silent for a while.

Churchill could see that Lin's proposal had its points; the biggest objection was that they had no means of carrying it out. First, they must get free. Then they must seize the *Terra*—and it was so heavily guarded that the starmen, who had discussed it after being released from their Washington prison, had discarded the idea.

"Even if we can seize the ship," he said, "and that's a big *if*, we must get to Mars. That's the biggest gamble of all. What if conditions there are such that we can't get fuel?"

"Then we hole in and start making equipment," Al-Masyuni said.

"Yes, but assuming that Mars gives us what we want, and we do reach Vega, we have to have women. Otherwise the race dies out. That means I have to take Robin, willy-nilly. And it also means that we have to abduct Deecee women."

"Once they come out of deep-freeze on Vega, there's not much they can do about it," Steinberg said.

"Violence, abduction, rape," Churchill said. "What a way to start a brave new world!"

"Is there any other way?" Wang said.

"Don't forget the Sabine women," Steinberg said.

Churchill did not reply to that but brought up another objection. "We are so few that in a short time our descendants would be highly inbred. We don't want to found a race of idiots."

"We kidnap children as well as women and take them along in deep-freeze."

Churchill frowned. There seemed to be no way to get away from violence. But then it had always been so throughout man's history.

"Even if we take infants who are too small to talk and therefore will not remember earth, we still have to take along enough women to raise them. And that brings up another problem. Polygamy. I don't know about the other women, but I do know that Robin will strongly object."

Yastzhembski said, "Explain to her it's only temporary. Anyway, you could be the exception, the monogamous one, if you wish. Let us have all the fun. I suggest we raid a Pants-Elf village. I've been told that the Pants-Elf women are accustomed to polygamy, and from what I heard, they'd welcome having husbands who'd pay attention to them. They sure as hell can't like the so-called men they got now."

"All right," Churchill said. "Agreed. But there's one thing that really bothers me."

"What's that?"

"How do we get out of this immediate mess?"

There was a gloomy silence.

Yastzhembski said, "Do you think Whitrow would put up the money to ransom all of us?"

"No. It's going to strain his purse to get Robin and me out of this tight-fisted pirate's hands."

"Well," Steinberg said, "at least you've a way out. What of us?"

Churchill stood up and began banging his manacles against each other and shouting loudly for the captain.

"Why are you doing that?" Robin said. She had not understood more than a few words of the conversation so far because it had been conducted in twenty-first-century American.

"I'm going to try to talk the captain into some sort of a deal," he replied in Deecee. "I think I've a way out. But it depends on how glibly I can talk and how receptive he is."

A sailor stuck his head through the hatch and asked what the hell was going on.

"Tell your captain I've a way for him to make a thousand times more money than he expects," Churchill said. "And enough glory to make him a hero."

The head disappeared. Within five minutes, two sailors came down into the hold and unlocked Churchill.

"See you," for he said to the others as he left. "But don't wait up for me."

He did not know how true his joking words would be.

The day passed, and he did not return. Robin was close to hysteria. She speculated that the captain had gotten angry at her husband and had killed him. The others tried to calm her down with the reasonable argument that a good businessman like the Karelian would not destroy such a heavy investment. Nevertheless, despite their reassurances, they were worried. Churchill might have inadvertently insulted the captain and therefore forced him to murder Churchill to save his face. Or he might have been slain trying to escape.

Some of them dozed off. Robin stayed awake to murmur prayers to Columbia.

Finally, close to dawn, the hatch opened. Churchill came down the ladder, accompanied by two sailors. He staggered and almost fell down, and once he hiccupped loudly. After he had been chained, the others could understand his behavior. His breath stank of beer, and he slurred his words.

"Been drinking like a camel about to go on a caravan," he said. "All day, all night. I outtalked Kirsti, but I think he outdrank me. Found out a lot about these Finns. They were spared more than other people during the Desolation, and afterwards they exploded all over Europe, just like the ancient Vikings. They mingled with what was left of the Scandinavians, Germans, and the Baltic peoples. They now hold northwest Russia, the eastern part of England, most of northern France, the coastal regions of Spain and North Africa, Sicily, south Africa, Iceland, Greenland, Nova Scotia, Labrador, and North Carolina. God knows what else, because they have sent expeditions to India and China . . ."

"Very interesting, but some other time," Steinborg said. "How did you come out with the captain? Make a deal?"

"He's a pretty shrewd fellow and awfully suspicious. I had a hell of a time convincing him."

"What happened?" Robin said.

Churchill told her, in Deecee, not to worry, that they'd all be out soon. Then he switched back to the language of his birth.

"Have you ever tried to explain antigravity generators and antimatter propulsion to a man who doesn't even know there are such things as molecules or electrons? Among other things, many other things, I had to give a lecture in basic atomic theory, and . . ."

His voice trailed off, and his head dropped. He was asleep.

Exasperated, Robin shook him until he struggled up from his befuddlement.

"Oh, it's you, Robin," he mumbled. "Robin, you won't like this little scheme I've cooked up. You'll hate me . . ."

He went back to sleep. This time all her efforts to arouse him were in vain.

XIV

"I wish I *could* get the belt off," Mary Casey said. "It's very cumbersome and irritating. It chafes my skin so I can hardly walk. And it's not very sanitary, either. It has two small outlets, but I have to pour water down it to clean myself."

"I know that," Stagg said impatiently. "That's not what's bothering me."

Mary looked at him and said, "Oh, no!"

His antlers had lost their floppiness and were standing stiff and erect.

"Peter," she said, trying to keep her voice calm, "please don't. You mustn't. You'll kill me."

"No, I won't," he answered, almost sobbing—but whether from his desire or from agony at not being able to control himself, she could not tell.

"I'll be as gentle as possible. I promise it won't be too much for you."

"Once is too much!" she said. "We've not been married by a priest. It would be a sin."

"No sin if you don't do it willingly," he said hoarsely. "And you've no choice. Believe me, you've no choice!"

"I won't do it," she said. "I won't! I won't!"

She continued protesting, but he paid no attention. He was too busy concentrating on getting the belt open. It presented a problem that only a key or a file could solve; since neither was available, it looked as if he would have to be frustrated.

But he was under the stress of a thing that did not acknowledge rationality.

The belt was composed of three parts. The two parts that went around the waist were made of steel. It was hinged at the back so it could be put on open and then snapped shut with a lock in front. The third part was made of many small links and was fastened to the belt by a second lock. Its chain mail effect allowed a certain amount of flexibility. Like the band around the waist, it was padded with thick cloth on the inside to prevent chafing and cutting. However, the whole contrivance was necessarily tight. Otherwise, the wearer could have slipped out of it or have been pulled out, with force and a little lost skin. This belt was a very snug fit, so tight that Mary complained about breathing.

Stagg managed to work his hands inside the front of the belt, though Mary protested that he was hurting her very much. He did not answer but began trying to work the two ends of the belt back and forth with the intention of twisting them loose from the lock.

"Oh, God!" Mary cried. "Don't, don't! You're crushing my insides! You'll kill me! Don't, don't!"

Suddenly, he released her. For a moment he seemed to have regained control. He was breathing hard.

"I'm sorry, Mary," he said. "I don't know what to do. Maybe I should run away as fast as I can until this thing in me turns me around and sets me to looking for you again."

"We might never find each other again," she said. She looked sad and then spoke softly. "I would miss you, Peter. I like you very much when you're not under the influence of the antlers. But there's no use pretending. Even if you got over this today, you might do the same tomorrow."

"I'd better go now while I still have a grip on myself. What a dilemma! Leaving you here to die because, if I stay, you might die!"

"You can't do anything else," she said.

"There's just one thing," he said slowly and hesitatingly. "That belt doesn't absolutely mean that I can't get what I want. There's more than one way . . ."

She turned white and screamed, "No, no!"

He turned away and ran as fast as he could down the path.

Then it occurred to him that she would be coming along the same trail. He left the path and went into the forest. It was not much of a forest, since this country was still a wasteland in the slow process of recovering from the Desolation. Its earth had not been seeded and water diverted through it, as much as the Deecee land had been. The trees were relatively scarce; most of the growth was weeds and under-brush and not too much of those. Nevertheless, where there was water at any time of the year, the forest was thicker. He had not run far before he came across a small creek. He lay down in it, hoping that the shock of the water would cool off the fire in his loins, but the water was warm.

He rose and crossed the creek and began running again. He rounded a tree and ran headlong into a bear.

Since he and Mary had left High Queen he had been watching for just such an animal.

He knew they were comparatively numerous in this area, because of the Pants-Elf custom of tying up their prisoners and rebellious women and leaving them for the sacred bears to eat.

The bear was a huge black male. He may or may not have been hungry. Perhaps he might have been as frightened by Stagg's sudden appearance as Stagg was by his. If he'd had a chance, he might have retreated. Stagg was on him so swiftly he must have thought he was being attacked—and being attacked meant attacking back.

He reared back on his hind legs, as was his habit in seizing his helpless human prey. He swung his immense right paw at Stagg's head. If it had connected it would have scattered the man's skull like a jigsaw puzzle dumped on a floor.

It did not land, though it came close enough for the claws to tear across Stagg's scalp. He was knocked to the ground, partly by the force of the blow and partly because his own forward impetus unbalanced him.

The bear dropped to all fours and went after Stagg. Stagg rolled to his feet. He drew his sword and screamed at the bear. The beast, unshaken by the noise, reared up again. Stagg swung his sword, and its edge sliced into the outstretched paw.

Though the bear roared with pain, it advanced. Stagg swung again. This time the paw flicked out with such stunning force against the blade that it knocked it from Stagg's grip and sent it flying into the weeds.

Stagg leaped after it, bent down to pick it up—and was buried under the enormous weight of the bear. His head was shoved flat into the earth, and his body felt as if it were being pressed flat by a giant iron.

There was a moment when even the bear was confused, for it had overextended its lunge and the man was covered only by its hindquarters. It quickly rolled over and away and then reversed itself. Stagg jumped up and tried to run away. Before he could take two steps, the bear had reared up and folded its front legs around him.

Stagg knew that it was not true that the bear hugs its victim to death, but in that moment he thought that he had met a bear who did not know his natural history. However, the bear was trying to hold

Stagg while it raked Stagg's chest open.

He did not succeed because Stagg broke loose from the embrace. He did not have time to be amazed at his Herculean feat of pushing the extremely powerful legs of the bear apart. If he had, he would have known that the superhuman strength given him by the antlers was responsible.

He jumped away and whirled around to face the animal. Fast as he was, he was too close for flight. Inside fifty meters, a bear could outrun even an Olympic champion.

The bear was on him. Stagg did the only thing he could think of. He hit the animal as hard as he could with his fist on its black snout.

The impact would have broken a man's jaw. The bear said, "Oof!" and stopped in its tracks. Blood ran from its nostrils, and its eyes crossed.

Stagg did not stay to admire his fistwork. He ran past the stunned beast and tried to pick up his sword. His right hand would not close round the hilt. It hung numbly, paralyzed by the blow he had given the bear.

He reached down with his left hand, picked up the sword, and turned. He was just in time. The bear had recovered enough to make another lunge, though this time it had lost some of its original speed.

Carefully, Stagg raised the sword and then, just as the bear closed in, he swung the edge downward across the thick short neck.

The last thing he saw was the blade sinking deep into the black fur and the spray of crimson that followed.

He woke some time later to find himself in deep pain, the bear lying dead by his side and Mary weeping over him.

Then the pain became overbearing, and he fainted.

When he regained consciousness, his head was on Mary's lap and water from a canteen was running into his open mouth. His head still hurt abominably. Reaching upward to find out why, he discovered bandages around his head.

The right-hand branch of his antlers was missing.

Mary said, "The bear must have torn it off. I heard the fight from a distance. I could hear the bear roaring and you screaming. I came as fast as I could, though I was scared."

"If you hadn't," he said, "I'd have died."

"I think so," she said matter-of-factly. "You were bleeding terribly from the hole left in the bony base of the torn-off antler. I ripped up part of my kilt and managed to stop the flow with it."

Suddenly, great hot tears fell on his face.

"Now it's over," he said, "you can cry all you want. But I'm glad you're so brave. I couldn't have blamed you if you'd run away from here."

"I couldn't have done that," she sobbed. "I—I think I love you. Of course, I wouldn't have left anyone to die like this. Besides I was scared to be alone."

"I heard what you said the first time," he replied. "I can't see how you could love a monster like me. But if it'll make you feel better, and not worse, I love you, too—even if it didn't look like it a while ago."

He touched the broken-off part of the base of the antlers and winced. "Do you think this will cut my . . . my compulsion in half?"

"I don't know. I wish it would. Only . . . I thought that if the antlers were removed, you'd die from the shock."

"I did too. Maybe the priestesses lied. Or may be the whole set has to be removed before a fatal shock occurs. After all, the bony base is still intact, and one of the antlers is still operating. I don't know."

"You quit thinking about it," she said. "Do you think you could eat? I've cooked some bear steak."

"Is that what I smell?" he said, sniffing. He looked at the carcass. "How long was I out?"

"You were unconscious all day and night and part of the morning," she said. "And don't worry about the smoke from the fire. I know how to make a small smokeless fire."

"I think I'll be all right then," he said. "The horns have great regenerative powers. I wouldn't be surprised if it grew back."

"I will pray that it won't," she said. She went to the fire and removed two slices of bear steak from a wooden spit. In a moment, he was eating a loaf of bread and the steaks.

"I must be getting better," he said. "All of a sudden I'm hungry enough to eat a bear."

Two days later he could look back on what he had said and laugh, because he *had* eaten the bear. There was nothing left except skin, bones, and entrails; even the brains had been cooked and devoured.

By then he felt ready to move again. The bandage had been removed from the wound just above the bony base of the antlers, and a cleanly healing scar was disclosed.

"At least, it's not going to grow out again," he said. He looked at Mary. "Well, here we are again. Just where we started when I ran away from you. I'm beginning to feel the urge again."

"Does that mean we have to separate again?" From her tone, it was impossible to tell if she wanted him to leave or not.

"I've been doing a lot of thinking while I was convalescing," he said. "One thing that I thought of was that when the Pants-Elf were taking us to High Queen, I felt a definite diminution of the drive. I think it happened because I was underfed. I'm going to propose that we stay together, but I go on a starvation diet. I'll eat just enough to keep me going, but not enough to stimulate this . . . this desire. It'll be hard, but I can do it."

"That's wonderful," she said. She hesitated, then blushed and said, "We're going to have to do one thing, though. I must get rid of this belt. No, not for the reason you might be thinking. It's driving me out of my mind. It cuts and chafes, and it presses me so tightly around the middle I can scarcely breathe."

"As soon as we get into Deecee territory and find a farmhouse," he said, "I'll steal a file. We'll get rid of that devil's device."

"All right. Just so you don't misunderstand my motives," she said. He picked up the sack, and they started off.

They proceeded as swiftly as they could, considering the handicap the belt gave Mary. They were very cautious, sensitive to any strange noise. There was not only a chance of running into the inevitable party from High Queen searching for them but a chance of encountering hostile Deecee.

They crossed the Shawangunk Mountains. Then, as they came into a glade through which the path ran, they saw the men who had come out of High Queen to avenge the deaths of their friends.

They must have been so intent on running down the two escapees that they had been utterly surprised by the ambushing Deecee. Now they hung from the trunks of trees where they had been tied before their throats were cut, or their bones lay at the foot of the trees. What the bears had not eaten, the foxes had; and what the foxes had overlooked, the crows were now picking.

"We'll have to be more cautious than ever," Stagg said. "I doubt if the Deecee have given up looking for us yet."

He did not speak with his accustomed vigor. He was pounds lighter, and his eyes were ringed with black. His horn flopped with every motion of his head. When he sat down to eat, he finished his short rations and then looked longingly at Mary's portion. Sometimes, he left the campsite and lay down where he could not see her until she was through eating.

The worst of it was, he could not forget food even when he slept. He dreamed of tables bending beneath the weight of a hundred savory dishes and huge stone mugs filled with cold dark beer. And when he was not distressed by these visions, he dreamed again of the maidens he had met during the Great Route. Though his drive was considerably lessened by lack of food, it was still stronger than most men's. There were times when, after Mary had fallen asleep, he had to go into the woods to relieve the terrible tension. He felt deeply ashamed afterwards, but it was preferable to taking Mary by force.

He did not dare kiss Mary. She seemed to understand this, since she made no attempt to kiss him. Nor did she again refer to having told him she loved him. Perhaps, he thought, she did not love him. She had been overcome with emotion because he had not been killed; the words might just have been an expression of relief.

After coming across the bones of the Pants-Elf, they left the trail and cut straight across the woodlands. Their speed was reduced, but they felt safer.

They reached the banks of the Hudson. That night, Stagg broke into a barn and found a file. He had to kill the watch dog, which he did by strangling it before it managed to bark more than twice. They returned to the woods where Stagg took four hours to cut through the belt with the file. The steel was hard, and he had to be careful not to hurt Mary. Then he gave her some ointment he had found in the barn, and she went into the brush to rub it on the chafed and infected places. Stagg shrugged at his shoulders at this incongruous modesty. They had seen each other unclothed many times. But, of course, she had not been able to control the situation then.

When she came back, they walked along the bank until they found a boat tied to a wooden dock. They untied it and rowed across. Stagg shoved the boat out into the current, and they began walking eastward. For two nights they walked, hiding and sleeping during the days. Stagg stole some more food from a farmhouse just outside the town of Poughkeepsie. When he returned to Mary in the woods, he sat down and devoured three times what he was supposed to eat. Mary was alarmed, but he told her that he had to because he could feel his cells turning cannibal.

After he had eaten half of the food and also drank a whole bottle of wine, he sat quietly for a while. Then he said to Mary, "I'm sorry, but I just can't stand it any more. I have to go back to the farmhouse."

"Why?" she said alarmedly.

"Because the men there are gone, probably into town. And there are three women there, two of them good-looking girls. Mary, can you understand?"

XV

"No!" she said, "I can't. Even if I could, do you think you should endanger us by returning there? Those women will tell their men when they return, and the priestesses at Vassar will be notified. And we'll have them on our track. We'd be sure to get caught if they knew we were in this neighborhood."

"I know you're right," he said. "But I can't stand it. I ate too much. It's either those two women or you."

Mary rose to her feet. She looked as if she were going to attempt something she disliked but must do.

"If you'll turn around a moment," she said, her voice quivering, "I think I can solve your problem."

Ecstatically, he said, "Mary, would you really? You don't know what this means to me!"

He turned away, and, despite his almost unbearably keen anticipation, he had to smile. How like her to be so modest about unclothing just before she bedded with him.

He heard her stir behind him. "Can I turn around now?"

"Not yet," she said. "I'm not ready."

He heard her approach him and he said, impatiently, "Is it all right to turn around now?"

"Not yet," she said, standing behind him.

"I can't stand waiting much longer . . ."

Something hit him hard on the back of the head. He blacked out.

When he awoke, he was on his side, his arms bound behind him and his legs tied together at the ankles. She had cut into two the thin rope he had put into the bag before escaping from the Pants-Elf. Near him was a large rock which he supposed she had used to knock him out.

Seeing his eyes open, she said, "I'm terribly sorry, Peter. I had to do that. If you'd put the Deecee on our trail, we might not have escaped."

"There are two bottles of whiskey in the sack," he said. "Prop me up against a tree trunk and put a bottle to my lips. I want to drink the whole quart. One, because I need something to kill this pain in my head. Two, because unless I drink myself unconscious, I'll go crazy from frustration. Three, I want to forget what a black-hearted bitch you are!"

She did not reply but did obey him, holding the bottle to his mouth and withdrawing it from time to time when he quit gulping.

"I'm sorry, Peter."

"To hell with you! Why did I have to get stuck with somebody like you? Why couldn't I have run off with a real woman? Keep feeding me the whiskey."

In two hours, he had drunk two-thirds of the fifth. He sat quietly for a few seconds, his eyes staring straight ahead. Then he groaned and fell asleep.

The next morning, he woke to find himself untied. He did not complain of his hangover or say anything to her. He merely watched her while she placed his rations before him. After breakfast, during which he drank much water, they began walking east in silence.

Toward midmorning, Mary spoke. "No farms in the last two hours. And the forest is thinning out and the land getting rockier. We're in the wastelands between Deecee and Caseyland. We must be more careful than ever, because we're likely to run into war parties of either nation."

"What's wrong with meeting your people?" Stagg said. "They're the boys we want, aren't they?"

"They might shoot first and identify us later," Mary said, nervously.

"Okay," he answered harshly. "So we'll holler out at them from a distance. Tell me, Mary, are you certain I'll not be treated as a Deecee captive? After all, this horn might prejudice them."

"Not after I tell them how you saved my life. And that you can't help being a Sunhero. Of course . . ."

"Of course what?"

"You'll have to submit to an operation. I don't know if my people have medical skill enough to remove your horn without killing you, but you'll have to take that chance. Otherwise, you'll be locked up. And you know that would drive you crazy. You can't be allowed to run loose in this condition. And, naturally, I wouldn't think of marrying you while you still have that horn. Oh yes, you must first be baptized in our belief. I wouldn't marry a heathen. I couldn't if I wanted to; we kill heathens."

Stagg didn't know whether to roar with anger, bellow with laughter, or weep with sadness. As a result, he expressed no emotion. Instead, he spoke levelly, "I don't remember asking you to marry me."

"Oh, but you don't have to," she replied. "It is enough that we spent one night together without chaperones. In my country, that means that a man and a woman must get married. In fact, that is often one way to announce your engagement."

"But you've done nothing to justify a forced marriage," he said. "You're still a virgin. At least, as far as I know."

"I most certainly am! But it makes no difference. It is taken for granted that a man and a woman who spend the night together must succumb to the flesh, however strong the will. That is, unless they are saints. And if they're saints, they don't allow such situations to happen."

"Then why in blue skies and rocketing nonsense have you been so determined to be a good girl?" he said loudly. "If you're going to have the name, you might as well have the game."

"Because I wasn't brought up that way. Because," she added somewhat smugly, "it doesn't matter what people think. It is what the Mother sees that counts."

"Sometimes you're so sanctimonious I could wring your pretty little neck! Here I've been suffering agonies of frustration such as you'll never know, and all the time you could have eased my pain without any moral blemish on your part—and had a time such as few women ever get!"

"There's no need to get angry," she said. "After all, it wasn't as if it had occurred at home, where we could be killed before we could be married. And then I would have sinned. Besides, you're not in the normal category. You have that horn. That puts you in a special case. I'm sure it'll take a learned priest to straighten out all the complexities."

Stagg shook with rage. He said, "We haven't reached Caseyland yet!"

Noon came. Stagg ate much more than his normal allowance. Mary said nothing about it, but she kept eyeing him. Every time he came near, she flinched. They repacked the bag and resumed walking. Stagg obviously was beginning to feel the benefit of food. The fleshy upper part of the antler began to swell and to stand stiff. His eyes sparkled, and he gave little leaps into the air, grunting with suppressed joy.

Mary began to lag behind. He was so affected by the approaching rush of desire that he did not notice. When she was about twenty yards behind him, she ran off into the bushes. He walked another twenty yards before he turned around and saw that she was gone. Then he roared and darted after her into the woods, losing all sense of caution and shouting her name.

He found her trail in a bed of crushed weeds, followed it to a small, almost dry creek bed, crossed the creek, and entered a grove of oaks. There he lost the trail. Emerging on the other side, he faced a broad meadow.

He also faced a dozen or more swords, behind every uplifted point of which was the grim face of a Caseylander.

Beyond them he saw a girl of about twenty.

This girl wore a costume such as Mary had worn when he first saw her in the cage. She was a mascot. The men were dressed in the red-soxed uniform of a Caseylander champion baseball team. There was one incongruous item among their clothes. Instead of long-billed caps, they wore feather-plumed hats, like an admiral's headgear.

Beyond them stood deer, nineteen for the first team and substitutes, one for the mascot, four to carry food and equipment.

The leader of the Caseys, titled "Mighty" as all the Casey captains were, was a tall rangy man with a long lean face, one cheek of which was swelled with a quid of tobacco. He grinned savagely at Stagg. "So, Old Horney! You expected to find soft curved young flesh? And instead you find the hard biting edge of a sword. Disappointed, monster? Don't be. We'll give you the embrace of a woman—only her arms are thin and bony and her breasts are flabby and wrinkled, and her breath stinks of the open grave."

"Don't be so damned melodramatic, Mighty," growled one of the men. "Let's hang him and get it over with. We've a game to play in Poughkeepsie."

Stagg understood then what they were doing there. It was no war party but a ball club that had been invited to compete in Deecee. As such, they would have a safe-conduct pass guaranteeing them against being ambushed.

Furthermore, the guarantee involved the promise not to hurt any Deecee they might encounter in the wasteland.

"Let's not talk of hanging," he said to Mighty. "According to the rules, you're not to harm a Deecee unless he attacks you."

"That's true," Mighty said. "But it just so happens that we've heard of you through our spies. You're not a native of Deecee; therefore our promise doesn't hold for you."

"Then why hang me?" Stagg said. "If I'm not a Deecee, I'm also not your enemy. Tell me, didn't you see a woman running ahead of me? Her name's Mary Casey. She'll tell you I should be treated as a friend!"

"A likely story," said the man who had urged hanging Stagg. "You're one of those devil-possessed horned men! That's enough for us."

"Shut up, Lonzo!" Mighty said. "I'm captain here."

He spoke to Stagg. "I wish now I'd had you cut down before you could open your mouth. Then you'd be no problem. But I would like to hear about this Mary Casey." Suddenly he said, "What's her middle name?"

"I-Am-Bound-For-Paradise."

"Yes, that's my cousin's name. But I guess your knowing it doesn't prove anything. She was hauled along with you in the Great Route. We have a good spy system, and we know you and she disappeared after the fairy-boys made a raid on Vassar. But the witches substituted another Horned King and then sent secret war parties out looking for you."

"Mary is somewhere nearby in these woods," Stagg said. "Find her, and she'll verify that I was helping her escape to your country."

"And what were you doing separated?" Mighty said, suspiciously. "Why were you running?"

Stagg was silent. Mighty said, "I thought so. One look at you would tell anybody why you were chasing her. I'll tell you what, Horned King. I'm going to give you a break. Ordinarily, I'd roast you over a low fire first, then rip out your eyes and stuff them down your throat. But we've the game to make and no time to waste, so I'm going to give you a quick death. Tie his hands, boys, and string him up!"

A rope was thrown over the branch of an oak and noose put around his neck. Two men seized his arms, while a third prepared to tie them. He did not resist, though he could easily have tossed the two aside.

He said, "Wait! I challenge you to a game according to the rules of One against Five, and I call God to witness that I have challenged you!"

"What?" Mighty said, incredulously. "Columbus' sake, man, we're late now! Besides, why should we accept the challenge? We don't know if you're our equal. We're all *diradah*, you know, and a challenge from a *shet hed* is not acceptable. In fact, come to think of it, it's unthinkable."

"I am not a *shet hed*," Stagg said, also using the term for a peasant. "Have you ever heard of a Sunhero being chosen from any but the ranks of the aristocrats?"

"That's right," Mighty said. He scratched his head. "Well, it can't be helped. Let him loose, boys. Maybe the game won't take long."

There was not even a flicker of thought in his mind to ignore Stagg's challenge and hang him. He had a code of honor, and he would not think of breaking it. Especially since Stagg had called on the name of his deity.

The Caseys who were to play on the first five removed their plumed admiral's hats and put on long-billed caps. They took their equipment from the bags on the sides of their deer and began laying out a diamond on the nearby meadow. From a leather bag they poured out a heavy white powder to mark the lanes from plate to plate and from each plate to the pitcher's box. They drew a narrow square around each plate, since in the rules of One against Five, Stagg might have to bat from any one of the bases during the course of the game. They drew a somewhat larger box for the pitcher.

"Is it okay if our mascot is the ump?" Mighty asked. "She will swear before the Father, Mother, and the Son that she will not favor us over you. If she isn't fair, lightning will strike her down. Worse, she'll become sterile."

"There's not much choice," Stagg said, hefting the brass-bound bat they'd given him. "I'm ready when you are."

His desire for women was gone now, sublimated in an eagerness to spill the blood of these men.

The mascot, wearing a barred iron mask and a heavily padded uniform, waddled up to her place behind the catcher.

"Batter up!"

Stagg waited for the Mighty's pitch. The Mighty stood only thirty-nine meters away from him, holding the hard leather ball with the four sharp steel spikes. He eyed Stagg, then wound up and let fly.

The ball sped like a cannon shot straight toward Stagg's head. It came so fast and so true that it was doubtful if a man of normal reflexes could have avoided it. Stagg, however, bent his knees. The ball skimmed an inch over his head.

"Ball one!" the mascot cried in a high, clear voice.

The catcher made no effort to catch the ball. In this game his duty was to chase after the ball and return it to the pitcher. Of course, he also guarded home plate and would try to catch the ball in his immense padded glove if Stagg ever tried to slide into home.

Mighty Casey wound up again and aimed this time for Stagg's midriff.

Stagg swung. The bat connected with a dull sound that contrasted strangely with the sharp crack he had automatically expected

The ball bounced off to Stagg's left and rolled out of the diamond, crossing the foul line.

"Strike one!"

The catcher returned the ball. Mighty Casey feinted winding up, then threw it suddenly in one smooth motion.

Stagg was almost caught. He had no time to swing, just barely enough time to stick the bat out. The ball struck the side and clung for a second, one of its spikes embedded in the brass.

Stagg ran for first, clinging to his bat as the rules said he could do if the ball stuck to it. Mighty Casey ran after him, hoping the ball would fall off on the way. Otherwise, if Stagg reached first and had possession of the ball, he became the pitcher and Mighty Casey became the batter.

Halfway toward first, the ball fell off.

Stagg ran like the deer he resembled, launched himself head foremost and slid on the grass into the plate. The bat, which he held out before him in his extended arm, hit the first baseman in the shinbone, knocking him off his feet.

Something struck Stagg in the shoulder. He groaned with pain as he felt the spike sticking in the flesh. But he leaped up, reached behind him, and pulled the spike out, heedless of the warm gush down his shoulder.

Now, according to the rules, if he survived the impact of the ball and had strength enough, he could throw it at either the pitcher or the first baseman.

The first baseman had tried to run away, but he had been so badly hurt by Stagg's bat that he could not even walk. He had removed his own bat from the sheath hanging over his back and stood ready to knock down the ball if Stagg would throw it at him.

Stagg threw, and the first, his face contorted with the pain of this leg, swatted at the ball.

There was a thump. The first swayed back and forth, then slumped, the spike buried in his throat.

Stagg had the choice of staying safe on first or trying to steal second. He chose to run, and again had to slide in face first. The second baseman, unlike the first, stood to one side. So great was Stagg's momentum that he slid past the plate. At once he twisted around and rolled back to touch second base.

There was a smack as the ball caught in the second's enormous thickly padded glove.

Stagg was—theoretically—safe on second. But he did not relax because of the look of fury on the second's face. He jumped up, his bat ready to hit the fellow over the head if he forgot the rules long enough to try to hit Stagg with the ball.

The second, seeing the bat poised, let the ball drop to the ground. Blood dripped from his fingers where he had cut himself on the spikes in his eagerness to get the ball loose from the glove.

Time out was called, while the first baseman had some brief rites said over him as he was being covered with a blanket.

Stagg asked for more food and water because he was beginning to feel faint from hunger. He had a right to demand such if the other side called time out.

He ate. Just as he finished, the mascot called, "Play ball!"

Now Stagg, standing within the narrow box marked around second base, was at bat again. Mighty wound up and let loose. Stagg knocked the ball to his left just inside the foul line. He began running, but this time the fellow who had replaced the dead first baseman was on the ball as soon as it landed and stuck in the ground. Stagg broke his run for a split second, not knowing whether to run on for third or return to second.

The first tossed the ball in an underhand motion to Mighty, who, by now, was crouched close to the lane between second and third, almost in Stagg's path. Stagg's back would be unprotected if he continued. He spun around; his bare feet slipped on the grass, and he fell on his back.

For one terrible second, he thought he was done for. Mighty was very close and had drawn back to throw at his prostrate target.

But Stagg had clung to his bat. Desperately, he raised it before him. The ball hit it glancingly, knocking the bat out of his hand and itself rebounding to a spot a few feet away.

Stagg roared with triumph, leaped to his feet, picked up the bat, and stood there, swinging the bat warningly. Unless he was actually hit by the ball while between bases, he could not pick it up and hurl it back at his opponents. Nor could he leave the white-marked lane to threaten anyone who tried to pick it up. However, if the ball was lying on the ground close enough for him to bat anybody who tried to pick it up, he could do so.

The ump's feminine voice shrilled over the field as she began counting to ten. Stagg's opposition had ten seconds in which to decide whether to try for the ball or allow him to stroll safe to third.

"Ten!" called the mascot, and Mighty turned away from the swinging bat.

Mighty threw again. Stagg swung and missed. Mighty smiled and threw at Stagg's head. Stagg swung and missed the ball, but the ball also missed him.

Mighty grinned wolfishly because, if Stagg struck out, Stagg would have to throw aside his bat and stand unmoving while Mighty tried to hit him between the eyes with the ball.

However, if Stagg managed to get to home plate, then he became the pitcher. He would still be at a disadvantage because he had no teammates to help; on the other hand, his greater speed and strength made him a one-man team.

There was a hush with only the murmurs of the prayers from the Caseys to be heard. Then Mighty hurled.

Straight for Stagg's belly the ball flew, giving him the choice of trying to bunt it down or else lean to one side and still keep his feet in the narrow box. If he stepped or fell outside, he had a strike against him.

Stagg chose to lean.

The ball shot by his shrinking flesh. So close was it that a whirling spike point ripped out a tiny gobbet. Blood trickled down his stomach.

"Ball one!"

Mighty hurled for the belly again. To Stagg the ball seemed to swell enormously, pregnant with doom, a planet toward which he was falling.

He swung hard, the bat coming around in a swift arc, parallel to the ground. Its tip connected with the ball, and a shock ran down the bat. It broke in two, and the ball soared back to Mighty.

The pitcher was caught off guard. He could not believe that the heavy ball could fly so far. Then, as Stagg raced for home, Mighty ran forward and caught the ball in his glove. At the same time, the other players, breaking out of their paralytic astonishment, closed in for the kill.

Two men stood between Stagg and home, one on each side of the white lines of the path. Both begged for Mighty to throw them the ball. But he chose the honor of tackling Stagg himself.

Desperately, Stagg struck the ball down with the stub end of his bat, the wooden part which had separated from the brassbound half. The ball did not rebound but stuck in the ground at his feet.

A Casey dived for it.

Stagg caved in the hat and the skull beneath it.

The others stopped running.

The mascot had thrown her hands over her mask, shielding the sight of the dead man from her eyes. But in a moment she put her hands down and looked beseechingly at Mighty. Mighty hesitated for a moment, as if he were going to give the signal to rush at Stagg and dispose of him, to hell with the rules.

Then he took a deep breath and called out, "Okay, Katie, start the count. We are *diradah*. We do not cheat."

"One!" quavered the mascot.

The other players looked at Mighty. He grinned and said, "Okay, Everybody line up behind me. I'll try first. I wouldn't ask you boys to do anything that's my duty."

One of the men said, "We could let him walk home."

"What?" cried Mighty. "And have every henpecked, skirt-wearing, idol-worshiping man in Deecee laughing at us? No! If we must die— and we have to die some time—we'll die like men!"

"Five!" the mascot called, sounding as if her heart were breaking.

"We haven't a chance!" a Casey groaned. "He's twice as fast as any of us. It'll be a lamb to the slaughter."

"I'm no lamb!" Mighty roared. "I'm a Casey! I'm not afraid to die! I'll go to heaven, while this fellow'll roast in hell!"

"Seven!"

"Come on!" Stagg bellowed, swinging the broken half of the bat. "Step up, gentlemen, and try your luck!"

"Eight!"

Mighty crouched for the leap, his lips working in a silent prayer.

"Nine!"

"STOP IT!"

XVI

Mary Casey ran from the woods, her hands held out in protest. She threw her arms around Mighty and began kissing him, weeping all the while.

"Oh, cousin, cousin, I thought I'd never see you again!"

"Thank the Mother you're safe," he said. "So what this horned man said was true, heh?" He held her away from him and looked carefully at her. "Or did he harm you?"

"No, no! He didn't touch me. He was a true *diradah* all the time," she said. "And he's not a worshiper of Columbia. He swears by God and the Son. I've heard him many times! And you know no Deecee would do that."

"I wish I'd known that," Mighty said. "We'd not have two good men dead for nothing."

He turned to Stagg. "If what she says is true, friend, there's no reason to continue the game. Of course, if you insist, we will."

Stagg threw the stump of the bat to the ground and said, "My original purpose was to go to Caseyland and live there the rest of my life."

"We've no time to talk!" Mary said. "We have to get out of here! Fast! I climbed a tree to get a better look around, and I saw a pack of hellhounds and a group of men and women on deer following them. And the death-hogs!"

The Caseys turned pale.

"Death-hogs!" Mighty said. "Alba is riding! But what's she doing here?"

Mary pointed at Stagg. "They must know he's in this area, and they must have picked up his scent. They were coming too fast just to be casting around."

"We're in a hell of a dilemma," Mighty said. "She won't bother us, I think, because we've a safe-conduct pass. But you never know about Alba. She's above such things as treaties."

"Yes," Mary said, "but even if they don't harm you, what about Peter—and me? I'm not included in the safe-conduct."

"I could give you two a couple of extra deer. You could run for the Housatonic River; once across it, you'd be safe. There's a fort there. But Alba still might catch you."

He twisted his face into a mask of intense concentration. Then he said, "Only one honorable thing to do. We can't allow two God-believers to fall into the foul hands of Alba. Especially when one of them is my cousin!

"All right, men!" he shouted. "What do you say? Shall we give up the safe-conduct and fight for these two? Or be chickens before the hawk and hide in the forest?"

"We live like Caseys and we die like Caseys!" the team roared.

"Okay, we fight," Mighty said. "But first we make a run for it. We'll make them work for their blood."

At that moment, they heard the baying of the hounds.

"On your mounts! Let's go!"

Mary and Stagg untied the packs from the deer given them, climbed on the bare backs of the beasts, and gripped the reins.

"You women ride first," Stagg said. "We'll drop behind a little."

Mary looked despairingly at Stagg. "If he stays behind, I stay behind with him."

"No time to argue," Mighty said. "We'll ride together."

They began galloping down the rough and winding trail. Behind them, the baying increased as the hounds caught the scent of many men and deer. The fugitives had scarcely left the meadow before the first of the hounds burst out of the woods. Stagg, looking back, saw a large dog built like a cross between a greyhound and a wolf. Its body was snow-white, and its wolflike ears were auburn. Behind it came a pack of twenty more like it.

Then he was too busy guiding his deer over the rough trail to risk many more backward glances. He did not have to urge the frightened beast to run at top speed.

Half a kilometer sped beneath the flying hoofs, and then Stagg took another quick look behind him. Now he saw about twenty deer and riders. At their head, riding a white stag with scarlet-painted antlers, was an old woman who wore only a tall black conical hat and a live snake around her neck. Her long white hair trailed out behind her, and her flat hanging breasts bounced with every motion of the beast under her.

She was enough to frighten any man. Alongside of the riders, running swiftly as the deer, was a herd of pigs. These were tall, long-legged, rangy swine, built for speed. They were black, their tusks long and painted with scarlet, and they squealed hideously as they ran.

Stagg had just turned his head when he heard crash and then a deer screaming with pain in front of him.

He looked ahead. There were two deer on the ground, and beside them their riders. The worst had happened. The deer of the mascot had stepped into a hole and gone down.

Mary, just behind her, had not been able to pull to one side quickly enough.

Stagg reined in his deer and leaped down.

"Are you all right?" he cried.

"A little shaken up," Mary said. "But I think Katie's deer has broken its leg. And mine has bolted into the woods."

"Get on the back of my deer," he said. "One of the others can carry Katie."

Mighty rose from Katie's side and came to Stagg. He said, "She can't move her legs. I think her back is broken."

Katie must have known what he was saying. She called, "Somebody kill me! I won't commit the sin of doing it myself! But if you kill me, I'm sure it would be forgiven. Even the Mother wouldn't want me to fall into Alba's hands!"

"Nobody's going to kill you, Katie," Mighty said. "Not while one of us is alive to defend you."

He barked orders, and the rest of the Caseys dismounted.

"Form into two lines. The dogs will hit us first; use your swords on them. Then grab your spears because either the hogs or the cavalry will charge next."

His men had just enough time to form in front of the two women when the hellhounds reached them. These dogs were no hangers-back but vicious beasts trained to kill. Snarling, they leaped into the air at the throats of the defenders.

There was confusion for a moment as the dogs bowled over many of the men. But in two minutes, despite all the snarling, shouting, yelping, screaming, it was over. Four dogs, badly wounded, limped to the woods to die. The rest were dead, their heads half severed or their legs cut off.

One Casey was on his back, eyes staring, throat ripped out. Five had been bitten deeply in several places but could still wield their swords.

"Here come the others!" Mighty shouted. "Reform ranks and stand ready to cast spears!"

The Deecee had reined in. The white-haired hag rode out a little in front of them, shouting in a high thin voice.

"Men of Caseyland! We do not want *you*! Give us our Horned King, and all of you, even that girl who was our prisoner, may go back to your country in safety. If you don't, I will release my death-hogs on you—and all will die!"

"Go screw yourself!" Mighty roared. "I'm sure you're the only one you could find to do it, you withered stinking old she-goat!"

Alba shrieked with rage. She turned to her priests and priestesses and signaled with her hand.

They unsnapped the leashes on the big tuskers.

"Use your spears as if you were on a pig-sticking!" Mighty shouted. "You've hunted wild hogs since you were old enough to hold a spear! Don't let them panic you!"

To Stagg he said, "Use your sword. I saw you fight the dogs. You're quicker and stronger than we—quick enough to wield a sword even on a tusker . . . okay, men, steady! Here they come!"

Mighty rammed his spear into the neck of a huge boar. The boar slumped to the ground; an enormous sow just behind it charged for Mighty. Stagg leaped over the carcass of the dead boar and brought his broadsword down with such force it cut through the sow's spinal cord just back of the neck.

Then he repeated the feat on another sow that had knocked a man down and was ripping his legs open with her teeth.

He heard a scream from Mary and saw that she was holding onto the end of her spear, the head of which was stuck in the side of a boar. The boar was not hurt badly, he was just angry and was trying to get at Mary. She clung to the end of the spear while she went around and around in a circle with the wheeling boar in its center.

Stagg shouted and leaped through the air. He landed with his feet on the back of the hog, and its legs crumpled under the impact. Stagg rolled off onto the ground. The boar regained its hoofs with lightning speed and swiveled toward Stagg. He thrust the point of his sword out; it drove into the open mouth of the tusker and down its throat.

He rose to his feet, assuring himself with a glance that Mary, though frightened, was not hurt. Then he saw that a hog had reached Katie. The Casey who had been protecting her was also on the ground, screaming because his legs had been ripped open and his ribs were sticking out of his flesh.

Stagg was too late to help Katie. By the time he had chopped off one of the hog's hind legs and slashed its jugular vein, Katie was dead.

He took a quick survey of the situation.

It was bad. The sixteen Caseys left alive after the onslaught of the dogs had been reduced to ten by the swine. Of the ten, only five were still on their feet.

Stagg helped the Caseys dispatch three more hogs. The remainder of the original twenty beasts, four wounded ones, ran squealing for the woods.

Mighty panted, "Alba will charge now, and we'll be done for. But I want to say, Stagg, that this is a fight they'll sing of for a long time to come in the halls of Caseyland!"

"They're not going to get Mary!" Stagg screamed. His eyes were wild, his face emptied of human expression. He was possessed—but it was blood he wanted, not women.

He turned toward Alba's group. They were being marshaled into files of five, their long spears glittering in the sunlight.

"Alba!" he roared, and he ran toward her.

She did not see him at first, but when her retainers warned her, she wheeled the white stag to face him.

"I'll kill you, you bloody old bitch!" he shouted. He swung his sword in great circles above his head. "I'll kill you all!"

And then a strange thing happened.

The priests and priestesses had been conditioned from childhood to regard the Sunhero as a demigod. Now they were in an abnormal and upsetting situation. They were being led by the Death-Goddess, who was invincible. But they were also being asked to battle a man whom their religion told them was also invincible. Every myth about the Sunhero stressed his inevitable triumph over his enemies. One of the myths even told of his victory over Death.

Moreover, they had witnessed his killings of the hellhounds and the death-hogs, animals sacred to Alba, and seen his superhuman swiftness and terrible sword-play. So, when the incarnation of the Death-Goddess ordered them to level spears and charge the Horned King, they hesitated.

Their pause lasted only a few seconds, but that time was long enough for Stagg to be upon Alba.

He slashed at her spear and cut through the wood of the shaft so that the steel head fell on the ground. At the same time, the deer on which Alba sat reared up.

She fell off backwards.

Alba landed on her feet like a cat. For a moment she had a chance to run among her retainers, since her deer was between her and Stagg.

He slashed at it, and the beast fled.

For a second, he stared into her pale blue eyes. He saw a tall, bent-backed old woman, old, old. She looked as if she were two hundred, so lined and seamed and wrinkled was her face. Long thin white hairs sprouted from her chin, and hairs formed a white film like milk on her upper lip. Her eyes seemed to have seen generations of men come and pass, and their stoniness said that she would see more. She was Death Herself!

Stagg felt cold, as if he were facing the inevitable Destroyer.

The rattlesnake, writhing and hissing around her neck, added the extra note of fatality.

Then he shook himself, reminding himself that she was, after all, only human. He charged.

He never reached her.

Her face contorted with pain, she clutched at her chest, and she fell, stricken dead with a heart attack.

There was panic among her followers, a panic of which Stagg took advantage. Running into their midst, he struck left and right. He was berserk, unmindful of the gashes from their spear heads or sabers.

He slashed riders and mounts alike. The deer reared up and threw men and women onto the ground, and Stagg cut them down before they could get to their feet.

For a while, it looked as if he would defeat the whole band. He had killed and wounded at least six on deer-back and upset four more and struck them down. Then a rider who had kept cool urged her beast forward. She rode directly toward Stagg. He looked up just in time to see her bearing down on him.

He saw the lovely face of Virginia, the one-time chief virgin of Washington, the woman with the long honey-colored hair and nose like a delicate hawk's and lips as red as blood and breasts that tilted upwards. Her bosom was covered now, for she was full in the belly with his child. She had only four months to go before delivering the baby—and yet she was riding deer-back.

Stagg had raised his sword to cut at her.

Then, recognizing her—and realizing that she carried his child, he froze.

That was enough time for her. Her beautiful face cold and expressionless, she slashed out with her weapon, a keen-edged light saber. The edge whistled through the air, thwacked into his antler. And that was the end for Peter Stagg.

XVII

The plan called for months of careful preparation.

First, spies, disguised as Deecee of various classes, drifted into Washington. They investigated any sources that might be able to inform them about the equipment left on the *Terra*. They also used their many means to find out what had happened to the Sunhero. During their inquiries, they discovered that Doctor Calthorp was back in Washington.

It was not long before he was contacted, and, a few days later, he slipped out by boat down the Potomac to Chesapeake Bay and on out into the ocean. Here a Karelian ketch picked him up and took him to the port of Aino.

He had a happy reunion with Churchill and the others, marred only by news of the deaths of Sarvant and Gbwe-hun and the doubts about Stagg's whereabouts.

Churchill explained the deal he had made with the Karelians. Calthorp chuckled and said that it might work. If it didn't, they would at least have tried. He himself was the most profitable source of information on the conditions of the *Terra*. He knew exactly what they would find in it and what they needed to get elsewhere.

Finally, they were ready.

They left Aino with Captain Kirsti Ainundila and three Karelians to each one of the crew of the *Terra*. The Karelians carried knives which they would use at the first suspicious action of the starmen.

They sailed in a swift brigantine that preceded the vast fleets to follow. This fleet was composed of vessels manned by Karelians from the colonies south of Deecee and the colonies of what had once been called Nova Scotia and Labrador.

The brigantine sailed boldly into Chesapeake Bay and let the small party of invaders out on a sailboat at the mouth of the Potomac. Disguised as a fishing vessel of Deecee, the sailboat tied up at night on a dock near Washington.

At midnight, the party rushed the building where the arms from the *Terra* were stored.

The few guards went down silently, their throats cut. The armory was broken into, and the starmen took the rapid-fire rifles and passed out the rest to the Karelians. These had never handled such weapons before, but they had worked in Aino with mock-ups made by Churchill.

Churchill also armed the starmen with self-propelled grenades.

They walked without hindrance to the great baseball stadium, now a shrine sacred to the Sunhero. Inside it, the *Terra* still reared her needle nose toward the stars she had left.

The group was challenged by the sentries; a fight took place—slaughter, rather. Thirty archers were killed by the automatic rifles, and forty more badly wounded. The invaders, unscratched, blasted open the gate to the stadium.

The starship was designed so that one man could operate it. Churchill sat in the pilot's seat, Kirsti and two Karelians standing beside him, knives in their hands.

"You will see what this ship can do," Churchill said. "It can destroy Washington simply by letting its bulk down on the buildings. Your fleet will have no trouble sacking the city. And we can fly to Camden and Baltimore and New York and do the same there. If we had not been taken in by the Deecee at first, we'd never have been captured. But we let them sweet-talk us into coming out of the ship after they made Stagg their king."

He tested the controls, checked the indicators, found everything working. He closed the main port and then looked at the clock on the instrument board.

"It's time to go into action," he said, loudly.

Every starman held his breath, at this prearranged code.

Churchill punched a button. Sixty seconds later, the Karelians keeled over. Churchill pressed another button, and air from outside swept out the gas.

It was a trick they had used to get away from the avianthropes of the planet Vixa when they had been in a similar situation.

"Do we put them in deep-freeze?" Steinberg said.

"For the time being," Churchill replied. "Later, we'll put them on the ground. If we took them to Vega II, they might murder us."

He took hold of the wheel, pulled back on a lever, and the *Terra* rose from the ground, her antigravs lifting the fifty-thousand ton bulk easily.

"Due to atmospheric resistance," Churchill said, "it'll take us fifteen minutes to get to Aino. We'll pick up your wives there and mine—and then it's Poughkeepsie ho!"

The wives he was referring to were the Karelian women Yastzhembski and Al-Masyuni had married during their stay in Aino.

"They're not expecting this. What'll they do once we get them aboard?"

"Give them the gas and put them in deep-freeze," Churchill said. "It's a dirty trick, but we can't waste time arguing with them."

"I hate to think of what they'll say when they thaw out on Vega."

"Not much they can do about it," Churchill said. But he frowned, thinking of Robin's sharp tongue.

However, for now at least, there was no trouble. Robin and the two women came aboard, and the starship took off. The Karelians still on the ground discovered the abduction too late and hurled harmless invectives at them which they did not hear. Again, the gas was released. The women were put in the tanks.

On the way to Poughkeepsie, Churchill said to Calthorp, "According to what the spies said, Stagg was seen in a little village on the east bank of the Hudson a few days ago. That means he escaped from the Pants-Elf. Where he now is, I don't know."

"He must be trying for Caseyland," Calthorp said. "But he'll just be jumping from fire to pan. What I don't understand is how he's had will power enough to keep from going back on the Great Route. That man is possessed by something to which no man can say no."

"We'll land outside Poughkeepsie," Churchill said. "Near Vassar. There's a large clearinghouse for orphans, operated by the priestesses. The orphans are kept there until families are found who'll adopt them. We'll pick the infants up and deep-freeze them. And we'll kidnap a priestess and use a hypnotic on her to make her reveal what she knows about Stagg's whereabouts."

That night, they hovered above the clearinghouse. There was a slight wind, so the starship moved upwind a little and then released the anaesthetic.

It took an hour to install sixty sleeping infants in the deep-freeze. Then they revived the head of the clearinghouse, a priestess of about fifty years of age.

They did not bother trying to get her to talk voluntarily. They injected the drug. Within a few minutes, they learned that Alba and her hunting party had left Poughkeepsie the night before on Stagg's trail.

They carried her back into the house and put her in bed.

"When morning comes," Churchill said, "we'll cruise over the vicinity where they should be. We could use black light, but our chances of finding somebody who'll be hiding under cover of trees are very remote."

The starship rose shortly after dawn from the little valley in which it had been hiding. It sped at a height of thirty meters above ground, heading due east. When it reached the Housatonic River, Churchill turned it back to the west. He calculated that Stagg could not have reached the river yet and so must be somewhere in the wasteland.

Returning, they were delayed a dozen times, because they saw people in the woods and descended to investigate. Once a man and a woman disappeared into a cave and the starmen went after them to interrogate them. They had trouble getting them out of the winding tunnels of what turned out to be an abandoned mine. By the time they had questioned them, and found out the two knew nothing of Stagg's location, they had lost several hours.

Reaching the Hudson again, the starship went due north a few miles and then began her eastward hunting.

"If Stagg sees the *Terra*, he'll come out of hiding," Calthorp said.

"We'll go up a few more meters and turn on the full power of the magnifier," Churchill said. "We have to find him!"

They were above five kilometers from the Housatonic River when they saw a number of deer riders racing pellmell down a trail. They dropped down but, seeing a lone figure on foot leading a deer about a kilometer behind the others, they decided to interrogate the straggler.

She was Virginia, the ex-chief maiden-priestess of Washington. Heavy with child, unable to endure the hard riding any longer, she had gotten off her mount. She tried to escape into the woods, but the ship sent a cloud of gas around her, and she crumpled. Revived a short time later by an injection of antidote, she proved willing enough to talk.

"Yes, I know where the so-called Sunhero is," she said viciously. "He is lying on the path about two and a half kilometers from here. But you need be in no hurry. He'll wait for you. He is dead."

"Dead!" Churchill gasped. He thought, *So close to success. Half an hour sooner, and we could have saved him!*

"Yes, dead!" Virginia spat. "I killed him. I cut off his remaining antler, and he bled to death. And I am glad! He was not a true Sun-hero. He was a traitor and a blasphemer, and he killed Alba."

She looked pleadingly at Churchill and said, "Give me a knife so I can kill myself. I was proud once, because I was to bear the child of the Horned King. But I want no brat of a false god! And I do not want the shame of bearing it."

"You mean that if we let you go, you'll kill yourself and the unborn child?"

"I swear by the sacred name of Columbia that I will!"

Churchill nodded to Calthorp, who pressed the syringe against her arm and pushed in on the button which sent a blast of anaesthetic into her flesh. She slumped, and the two men carried her to the deep-freeze tank.

"We certainly can't allow her to kill Stagg's child," Calthorp said. "If he is dead, his son will live."

"I wouldn't worry about his not having descendants, if I were you," Churchill said. He did not elaborate on the statement, but he thought of Robin, frozen in the tank. In about fifty years, she would give birth to Stagg's boy.

Oh well, there was nothing he could do to change the situation, so he quit thinking about it. The immediate concern was Stagg.

He raised the ship and shot it straight east. Below, the trail was a thin brown curving line bordered by green. It went around a small mountain, a hill and then another hill; and there was the scene of the battle.

Bodies of dogs and deer and pigs. And a few human forms. Where were the many reported killed?

The ship touched ground, settling on the path and crushing many trees on either side. The men, armed with rifles, stepped out of the main port and surveyed the scene. Steinberg stayed behind in the pilot's seat.

"I think," Churchill said, "that the dead Caseys have been taken off the trail into the woods. They're probably being buried. You'll notice that all the corpses here wear Deecee clothes."

"Maybe they're burying Stagg," Calthorp said.

"I hope not," Churchill replied. He was sad because his captain, who had led him successfully through so many dangers, was gone. Yet he knew that there was a reason why he could not find it in him to mourn very much. If Stagg were alive, what complications would exist once they arrived on Vega? Stagg would not be able to help taking more than a mild interest in Robin's child. Every time Churchill loved or punished the boy, Stagg would be wanting to interfere. And he, Churchill, would be wondering if Robin still regarded Stagg as more than human.

What if she wanted to keep her religion alive?

The men separated, looking for the burial party. Presently, a whistle sounded. It could not be heard by the Caseys, because it was pitched too high. The starmen wore in one ear a device which lowered the frequency to an audible noise, yet did not block normal sound.

They came swiftly, stealthily, and assembled behind Al-Masyuni, who had blown the whistle. There, inside a ring of trees, they saw the worst: a girl and four men, smoothing out the mound of what was obviously a common grave.

Churchill stepped out from the trees and said, "Do not be alarmed. We are friends of Stagg."

The Caseys were startled, but, hearing Churchill repeat his assurance, they relaxed somewhat. However, they did keep their hands upon their weapons.

Churchill advanced a few steps, stopped and explained who he was and why he had come here.

The girl's eyes were red-rimmed and her face tear-streaked. Upon hearing Churchill ask about Stagg, she burst into weeping again.

"He is dead!" she sobbed. "If only you had come sooner!"

"How long has he been dead?"

One of the Caseys eyed the sun. "About half an hour. He bled much for a long time and did not give up without a fight."

"Okay, Steinborg," Churchill said into his walkie-talkie. "Bring the ship up and send out a couple of walking shovels. We have to dig Stagg out of this ground fast. Calthorp, do you think there's a chance?"

"That we can resurrect him? A good chance. That he'll escape brain damage? No chance at all. But we can build up the damaged tissue and then see what happens."

They did not tell the Caseys their real reason for wanting to exhume Stagg. By now they knew a little of Mary's love for him, and they did not want to rouse false hopes. They told her they wished to take the captain back to the stars, where he would have wished to be buried.

The other corpses were left in the grave; they were badly mangled and had been dead too long.

Inside the ship, Calthorp, directing the delicate robo-surgeon, cut the bony base of the antlers out of Stagg's skull and removed the top of his skull.

His chest was laid open, electrodes implanted in the heart and the brain. A blood pump was attached to his circulatory system. Then the body was lifted by the machine and placed in a lazarus tank.

The tank was filled with biogel, a thin fluid which nourished the cells swarming in it. There were two kinds of cells. One would eat away the damaged or decomposed cells of the corpse. The other was a multitude descended from cells from Stagg's own body. These would seek out and attach themselves to the mother organs and replace those which had been scourged from his body.

Stagg's heart began pumping under the electrical stimulus. His body temperature began to rise. Gradually, the grayish color of skin was replaced by a healthy pink.

Five hours passed, while the biogel did its work. Calthorp studied for the hundredth time the indications on the meters and the waves on the oscilloscopes.

Finally he said, "No use keeping him in there any more."

He twisted a dial on the instrument panel of the robo-surgeon, and Stagg was slowly lifted from the tank.

He was deposited on a table, where he was washed off, the needles withdrawn from heart and brain, his chest sewed up, a metal skull cap fitted on, the scalp rolled back over the cap and the skin sewn up.

From there the men took over. They carried Stagg to a bed and put him in it. He slept like a new-born baby.

Churchill went outside, where the Caseys waited. They had refused to enter the ship, because they were too filled with superstitious fear and awe.

The men were talking in low tones. Mary Casey sat slumped against a tree trunk, her face a Greek mask of tragedy.

Hearing Churchill approach, she raised her head and said, emotionlessly, "May we go now? I'd like to be with my people."

"Mary," Churchill said, "you may go wherever you wish. But first I must tell you why I asked you to wait all these hours."

Mary listened to his plans for going to Mars, picking up or making fuel there and then going on to Vega II to settle. She lost some of her grief-stricken look at first, but after a while she seemed to fall back into her apathy.

"I am glad for you that you have something to look forward to," she said. "Although, somehow it sounds blasphemous. However, it does not really concern me. Why are you telling me this?"

"Mary, when we left Earth in 2050 A.D., it was common practice to bring men back from the dead. It was not black magic or witchcraft, but application of knowledge that did it . . ."

She leaped to her feet and seized his hands.

"Do you mean that you have brought Peter back to life?"

"Yes," he said. "He is sleeping now. Only . . ."

"Only what?"

"When a man has been dead as long as he was, he suffers a certain inevitable amount of brain damage. Usually this can be repaired. But sometimes the man is an idiot."

She lost her smile. "Then we won't know until morning. Why didn't you wait until then to tell me?"

"Because you would have gone on home unless I told you this. There's something else. Every man aboard the *Terra* knew what might happen if he died and was resurrected. All of us, except Sarvant, agreed that if he came out of the lazarus tank an idiot, he was to be killed again. No man wants to live without his mind."

"To kill him would be a terrible sin!" she said. "It would be murder!"

"I will not waste time arguing with you," he said. "I just want you to know what might happen. However, if it's any help to you, I can tell you that when we were on the planet Vixa, Al-Masyuni was killed. A poisonous plant which shot little darts by means of air pressure got him twice. He died at once, and then the plant opened up and about twenty centipede-like insects raced out. They were enormous for insects, two feet long and armed with great pincers. They apparently intended to drag Al-Masyuni's body into the plant, where everybody—including the plant—would share in the feast.

"We stayed out of range of the darts and blasted the insects with rifle fire and the plant with grenades. Then we took Al-Masyuni's body to the ship and resurrected him, after we'd gotten rid of the alkaloid in his system. He suffered no physical or mental effects from his death at all. But Stagg's case is somewhat different."

"May I see him in the morning?" she said.

"For better or for worse."

The night went slowly. Neither the starmen nor Mary slept, though the Caseys sprawled in the woods and snored lustily. Some of the crew asked Churchill why they did not proceed with their plans while waiting for Stagg to waken. They could gas a village or two, put more babies and women in deep-freeze, and be on their way to Mars.

"Because of that girl," Churchill said. "Stagg might want to take her with us."

"Why don't we just put her in the tank, too," Yastzhembski said. "After all, it's rather delicate hairsplitting, isn't it? Being sensitive about her feelings and yet kidnaping dozens of babies and women?"

"We don't know them. And we're doing the babies, and the Pants-Elf women a favor by getting them out of this savage world. But we do know her, and we know that she and Stagg were going to get married. We'll wait and see what Stagg has to say about it."

Morning came at last. The men ate breakfast and did various chores until Calthorp summoned them.

"Time," he said. He filled a hypodermic syringe, plunged it into Stagg's huge biceps, swabbed the invisible break, and then stood back.

Churchill had gone to Mary Casey and told her that Stagg would awaken very soon. It was a measure of her love for Stagg that she had the courage to enter the ship. She did not look around her as she was led through the corridors filled with what to her must have been weird and evil-looking devices. She looked straight ahead, at Churchill's broad back.

Then she was at Stagg's side, weeping.

Stagg mumbled something. His eyelids fluttered, became still again. His deep breathing resumed.

Calthorp said loudly, "Wake up, Pete!"

He lightly slapped his captain's cheek.

Stagg's eyes opened. He looked around at them, at Calthorp, Churchill, Steinberg, Al-Masyuni, Lin, Yastzhembski, Chandra, and looked puzzled. When he saw Mary Casey, he was startled.

"What the hell happened?" he said, trying to roar but succeeding only in croaking. "Did I black out? Are we on Earth? We must be! Otherwise, that woman wouldn't be on board. Unless you Don Juans had her stowed away all this time."

It was Churchill who first grasped what had happened to Stagg.

"Captain," he said, "what's the last thing you remember?"

"Remember? Why, you know what I ordered just before I blacked out! Land on Earth, of course!"

Mary Casey became hysterical. Churchill and Calthorp took her out of the room and Calthorp gave her a sedative. She fell asleep in two minutes. Then Calthorp and the first mate went into the control room.

"It's too early to tell for certain," Calthorp said, "but I don't think he's suffered any loss of I.Q. He's no idiot; but that part of his brain which contained the memory of the last five and a half months was destroyed. It's been repaired, so it's as good as ever, but the memory content is gone. To him, we've just returned from Vixa, and we're preparing to descend to Earth."

"I thought so," Churchill said. "Now, what are we going to do with Mary Casey?"

"Tell her the situation and allow her to decide for herself. She may want to try to make him fall in love with her."

"We'll have to tell her about Virginia. And Robin. She may not like the idea."

"No time like the present," Calthorp said. "I'll have to give her a shot to bring her out of her sleep. Then I'll tell her. She can make up her mind now. We've no time to dillydally."

He left.

Churchill sat thinking in the pilot's seat. He wondered what the future held. Certainly events wouldn't be boring. He would have troubles enough of his own, but he would not be in Stagg's shoes for anything. To have fathered hundreds of children in the wildest and most extended orgy a man could dream of, yet be innocent of any knowledge of it! To go to Vega II and there be presented with two babies by different women, and perhaps a third if Mary Casey came along. To be told what had happened—and yet be absolutely unable to visualize it, perhaps not to believe it even when a dozen witnesses swore it was true! To have incidents of which he had no remembrance at all hurled at him during the inevitable marital quarrels.

No, thought Churchill, he would not care to be Stagg. He was content to be Churchill, though that was going to be bad enough when Robin awakened.

He looked up. Calthorp had returned.

"What's the verdict?" Churchill said.

"I don't know whether to laugh or cry," Calthorp said. "Mary is coming with us."

POSTLUDE

Thunder, lightning, and rain.

A small tavern in a neutral area on the border of Deecee and Casey-land. Three women sitting at a table in a private room in the rear of the tavern. Their heavy hooded robes hanging from pegs on the walls. All three wearing tall black conical hats.

One, Virginia, the younger sister of the woman on the *Terra*. Now, like her older sister when Stagg came to Washington, maiden priest-ess of the holy city. Tall, beautiful, hair like honey, eyes so deep blue, nose curved like a delicate hawk's, lips like a wound, exposed breasts full and upthrusting.

One, the abbess of a great sisterhood of Caseyland. Thirty-five years old, graying hair, heavy-breasted, protruding stomach, and, under the robe, broken veins on the legs, tokens of childbirth, though she is sworn to chastity. In public, she prays to Columbus the Father, and the Son, and the Mother. In private, she prays to Columbia, the God-dess, the Great White Mother.

One, Alba, white-haired, toothless, withered hag, successor to the Alba slain by Stagg.

They drink from tall glasses filled with red wine. *Or is it wine?*

Virginia, the maiden, asks if they have lost. The starmen have escaped them and taken with them the Sunhero and her dear sister, heavy with his child.

The gray-haired matron replies that they never lose. Did she think that her sister would allow the thought of the Goddess to die in her child's mind? Never!

But Stagg, the maiden protests, has also taken with him a devout maiden of Caseyland, a worshiper of the Father.

Alba, the old hag, cackles and says, Even if he takes the religion of the Caseys as his, young and beautiful but ignorant girl, do you not know that the Goddess has already won in Caseyland? The people pay thin-blooded homage to the Father and the Son on their Sabbath, but it is to the Mother they pray most fervently. It is Her statues that fill the land, She who fills their thoughts. What does it matter whether the Goddess is called Columbia or some other name? If She cannot enter the front door, She enters the back.

But Stagg has escaped us, the maiden protests.

No, the matron replies, he did not escape us or the Great Route. He was born in the south and went north, and he met Alba and was killed. It does not matter that he slew a human being called Alba, since Alba lives today in this old flesh that sits with us. And he was killed, and buried, and he rose again, as it was told. And he is like a new-born baby, for I have heard that he has no memory of the life he spent on the Great Route.

Pay attention to what Alba says about the Goddess always winning even when She loses! It will not matter if he rejects Virginia and chooses Mary. He is ours. Mother Earth goes with him to the stars.

They talk of other things and make their plans. Then, though the thunder and lightning rage, and the rain falls, they leave the tavern. Now their faces are shadowed by hoods so no man will know who they are. They pause for a moment before the parting of the ways, one south, one north, one to remain halfway between them.

The maiden says, When shall we three meet again?

The matron replies, When man is born and dies and is born.

The hag replies, When the battle is lost and won.

Strange Relations

. . . Mother

Chapter 1

"Look, mother. The clock is running backwards."

Eddie Fetts pointed to the hands on the pilot room dial.

Dr. Paula Fetts said, "The crash must have reversed it."

"How could it do that?"

"I can't tell you. I don't know everything, son."

"Oh!"

"Well, don't look at me so disappointedly. I'm a pathologist, not an electronician."

"Don't be so cross, mother. I can't stand it. Not now."

He walked out of the pilot room. Anxiously, she followed him. The burial of the crew and her fellow scientists had been very trying for him. Spilled blood had always made him dizzy and sick; he could scarcely control his hands enough to help her sack the scattered bones and entrails.

He had wanted to put the corpses in the nuclear furnace, but she had forbidden that. The Geigers amidships were ticking loudly, warning that there was invisible death in the stern.

The meteor that struck the moment the ship came out of Translation into normal space had probably wrecked the engine-room. So she had understood from the incoherent high-pitched phrases of a colleague before he fled to the pilot room. She had hurried to find Eddie. She feared his cabin door would still be locked, as he had been making a tape of the aria "Heavy Hangs the Albatross" from Gianelli's *Ancient Mariner*.

Fortunately, the emergency system had automatically thrown out the locking circuits. Entering, she had called out his name in fear he'd been hurt. He was lying half-unconscious on the floor, but it was not the accident that had thrown him there. The reason lay in the corner, released from his lax hand; a quart free-fall thermos, rubber-nippled. From Eddie's open mouth charged a breath of rye that not even Nodor pills had been able to conceal.

Sharply she had commanded him to get up and on to the bed. Her voice, the first he had ever heard, pierced through the phalanx of Old Red Star. He struggled up, and she, though smaller, had thrown every ounce of her weight into getting him up and on to the bed.

There she had lain down with him and strapped them both in. She understood that the lifeboat had been wrecked also, and it was up to the captain to bring the yacht down safely to the surface of this charted but unexplored planet, Baudelaire. Everybody else had gone to sit behind the captain, strapped in crashchairs, unable to help except with their silent backing.

Moral support had not been enough. The ship had come in on a shallow slant. Too fast. The wounded motors had not been able to hold her up. The prow had taken the brunt of the punishment. So had those seated in the nose.

Dr. Fetts had held her son's head on her bosom and prayed out loud to her God. Eddie had snored and muttered. Then there was a sound like the clashing of the gates of doom—a tremendous bong as if the ship were a clapper in a gargantuan bell tolling the most frightening message human ears may hear—a blinding blast of light—and darkness and silence.

A few moments later Eddie began crying out in a childish voice, "Don't leave me to die, mother! Come back! Come back!"

Mother was unconscious by his side, but he did not know that. He wept for a while, then he lapsed back into his rye-fogged stupor—if he had ever been out of it—and slept. Again, darkness and silence.

It was the second day since the crash, if "day" could describe that twilight state on Baudelaire. Dr. Fetts followed her son wherever he went. She knew he was very sensitive and easily upset. All his life she had known it and had tried to get between him and anything that would cause trouble. She had succeeded, she thought, fairly well until three months ago when Eddie had eloped.

The girl was Polina Fameux, the ash-blonde, long-legged actress whose tridi image, taped, had been shipped to frontier stars where a small acting talent meant little and a large and shapely bosom much. Since Eddie was a well-known Metro tenor, the marriage made a big splash whose ripples ran around the civilized Galaxy.

Dr. Fetts had felt very bad about the elopement, but she had, she hoped, hidden her grief very well beneath a smiling mask. She didn't regret having to give him up; after all, he was a full-grown man, no longer her little boy. But, really, aside from the seasons at the Met and his tours, he had not been parted from her since he was eight.

That was when she went on a honeymoon with her second husband. And then she and Eddie had not been separated long, for Eddie had got very sick, and she'd had to hurry back and take care of him, as he had insisted she was the only one who could make him well.

Moreover, you couldn't count his days at the opera as a total loss, for he vised her every noon and they had a long talk—no matter how high the vise bills ran.

The ripples caused by her son's marriage were scarcely a week old before they were followed by even bigger ones. They bore the news of the separation of Eddie and his wife. A fortnight later, Polina applied for divorce on grounds of incompatibility. Eddie was handed the papers in his mother's apartment. He had come back to her the day he and Polina had agreed they "couldn't make a go of it," or, as he phrased it to his mother, "couldn't get together."

Dr. Fetts was, of course, very curious about the reason for their parting, but, as she explained to her friends, she "respected" his silence. What she didn't say was that she had told herself the time would come when he would tell her all.

Eddie's "nervous breakdown" started shortly afterwards. He had been very irritable, moody, and depressed, but he got worse the day a so-called friend told Eddie that whenever Polina heard his name mentioned, she laughed loud and long. The friend added that Polina had promised to tell someday the true story of their brief merger.

That night his mother had to call in a doctor.

In the days that followed, she thought of giving up her position as research pathologist at De Kruif and taking all her time to help him "get back on his feet." It was a sign of the struggle going on in her mind that she had not been able to decide within a week's time. Ordinarily given to swift consideration and resolution of a problem, she could not agree to surrender her beloved quest into tissue regeneration.

Just as she was on the verge of doing what was for her the incredible and the shameful, tossing a coin, she had been vised by her superior. He told her she had been chosen to go with a group of biologists on a research cruise to ten preselected planetary systems.

Joyfully, she had thrown away the papers that would turn Eddie over to a sanatorium. And, since he was quite famous, she had used her influence to get the government to allow him to go along. Ostensibly, he was to make a survey of the development of opera on planets colonized by Terrans. That the yacht was not visiting any colonized globes seemed to have been missed by the bureaus concerned. But it was not the first time in the history of a government that its left hand knew not what its right was doing.

Actually, he was to be "rebuilt" by his mother, who thought herself much more capable of curing him than any of the prevalent A, F, J, R, S, K, or H therapies. True, some of her friends reported amazing results with some of the symbol-chasing techniques. On the other hand, two of her close companions had tried them all and had got no benefits from any of them. She was his mother; she could do more for him than any of those "alphabatties;" he was flesh of her flesh, blood of her blood. Besides, he wasn't so sick. He just got awfully blue sometimes and made theatrical but insincere threats of suicide or else just sat and stared into space. But she could handle him.

Chapter 2

So now it was that she followed him from the backward-running clock to his room. And saw him step inside, look for a second, and then turn to her with a twisted face. "Neddie is ruined, mother. Absolutely ruined." She glanced at the piano. It had torn loose from the wallracks at the moment of impact and smashed itself against the opposite wall. To Eddie it wasn't just a piano; it was Neddie. He had a pet name for everything he contacted for more than a brief time. It was as if he hopped from one appellation to the next, like an ancient sailor who felt lost unless he was close to title familiar and designated points of the shoreline. Otherwise, Eddie seemed to be drifting helplessly in a chaotic ocean, one that was anonymous and amorphous.

Or, analogy more typical of him, he was like the night-clubber who feels submerged, drowning, unless he hops from table to table, going from one well-known group of faces to the next, avoiding the featureless and unnamed dummies at the strangers' tables.

He did not cry over Neddie. She wished he would. He had been so apathetic during the voyage. Nothing, not even the unparalleled splendour of the naked stars nor the inexpressible alienness of strange planets had seemed to lift him very long. If he would only weep or laugh loudly or display some sign that he was reacting violently to what was happening. She would even have welcomed his striking her in anger or calling her "bad" names.

But no, not even during the gathering of the mangled corpses, when he looked for a while as if he were going to vomit, would he give way to his body's demand for expression. She understood that if he were to throw up, he would be much better for it, would have got rid of much of the psychic disturbance along with the physical.

He would not. He had kept on raking flesh and bones into the large plastic bags and kept a fixed look of resentment and sullenness.

She hoped now that the loss of his piano would bring tears and shaking shoulders. Then she could take him in her arms and give him sympathy. He would be her little boy again, afraid of the dark, afraid of the dog killed by a car, seeking her arms for the sure safety, the sure love.

"Never mind, baby," she said. "When we're rescued, we'll get you a new one."

"When—!"

He lifted his eyebrows and sat down on the bed's edge. "What do we do now?"

She became very brisk and efficient.

"The ultrad automatically started working the moment the meteor struck. If it's survived the crash, it's still sending SOS's. If not, then there's nothing we can do about it. Neither of us knows how to repair it.

"However, it's possible that in the last five years since this planet was located, other expeditions may have landed here. Not from Earth but from some of the colonies. Or from non-human globes. Who knows? It's worth taking a chance. Let's see."

A single glance was enough to wreck their hopes. The ultrad had been twisted and broken until it was no longer recognizable as the machine that sent swifter-than-light waves through the no-ether.

Dr. Fetts said with false cheeriness, "Well, that's that! So what? It makes things too easy. Let's go into the storeroom and see what we can see."

Eddie shrugged and followed her. There she insisted that each take a panrad. If they had to separate for any reason, they could always communicate and also, using the DF's—the built-in direction finders—locate each other. Having used them before, they knew the instruments' capabilities and how essential they were on scouting or camping trips.

The panrads were lightweight cylinders about two feet high and eight inches in diameter. Crampacked, they held the mechanisms of two dozen different utilities. Their batteries lasted a year without recharging, they were practically indestructible and worked under almost any conditions.

Keeping away from the inside of the ship that had the huge hole in it, they took the panrads outside. The long wave bands were searched by Eddie while his mother moved the dial that ranged up and down the shortwaves. Neither really expected to hear anything, but to search was better than doing nothing.

Finding the modulated wave-frequencies empty of any significant noises, he switched to the continuous waves. He was startled by a dot-dashing.

"Hey, mom! Something in the 100 kilocycles! Unmodulated!"

"Naturally, son," she said with some exasperation in the midst of her elation. "What would you expect from a radio-telegraphic signal?"

She found the band on her own cylinder. He looked blankly at her. "I know nothing about radio, but that's not Morse."

"What? You must be mistaken!"

"I—I don't think so."

"Is it or isn't it? Good God, son, can't you be certain of anything!"

She turned the amplifier up. As both of them had learned Galacto-Morse through sleeplearn techniques, she checked him at once.

"You're right. What do you make of it?"

His quick ear sorted out the pulses.

"No simple dot and dash. Four different time-lengths."

He listened some more.

They've got a certain rhythm, all right. I can make out definite groupings. Ah! That's the sixth time I've caught that particular one. And there's another. And another."

Dr. Fetts shook her ash-blonde head. She could make out nothing but a series of zzt-zzt-zzt's.

Eddie glanced at the DF needle.

"Coming from NE by E. Should we try to locate?"

"Naturally," she replied. "But we'd better eat first. We don't know how far away it is, or what we'll find there. While I fix a hot meal, you get our field trip stuff ready."

"O.K.," he said with more enthusiasm than he had shown for a long time.

When he came back he ate everything in the large dish his mother had prepared on the unwrecked galley stove.

"You always did make the best stew," he said.

"Thank you. I'm glad you're eating again, son. I am surprised. I thought you'd be sick about all this."

He waved vaguely but energetically.

"The challenge of the unknown. I have a sort of feeling this is going to turn out much better than we thought. Much better."

She came close and sniffed his breath. It was clean, innocent even of stew. That meant he'd taken Nodor, which probably meant he'd been sampling some hidden rye. Otherwise, how explain his reckless disregard of the possible dangers? It wasn't like him.

She said nothing, for she knew that if he tried to hide a bottle in his clothes or field sack while they were tracking down the radio signals, she would soon find it. And take it away. He wouldn't even protest, merely let her lift it from his limp hand while his lips swelled with resentment.

Chapter 3

They set out. Both wore knapsacks and carried the panrads. He carried a gun over his shoulder, and she had snapped on to her sack her small black bag of medical and lab supplies.

High noon of late autumn was topped by a weak red sun that barely managed to make itself seen through the eternal double layer of clouds. Its companion, an even smaller blob of lilac, was setting on the northwestern horizon. They walked in a sort of bright twilight, the best that Baudelaire ever achieved. Yet, despite the lack of light, the air was warm. It was a phenomenon common to certain planets behind the Horsehead—one being investigated but as yet unexplained.

The country was hilly, with many deep ravines. Here and there were prominences high enough and steep-sided enough to be called embryo mountains. Considering the roughness of the land, however, there was a surprising amount of vegetation. Pale green, red and yellow bushes, vines, and little trees clung to every bit of ground, horizontal or vertical. All had comparatively broad leaves that turned with the sun to catch the light.

From time to time, as the two Terrans strode noisily through the forest, small multicoloured insect-like and mammal-like creatures scuttled from hiding place to hiding place. Eddie decided to carry his gun in the crook of his arm. Then, after they were forced to scramble up and down ravines and hills and fight their way through thickets that became unexpectedly tangled, he put it back over his shoulder, where it hung from a strap.

Despite their exertions, they did not tire quickly. They weighed about twenty pounds less than they would have on Earth, and, though the air was thinner, it was richer in oxygen.

Dr. Fetts kept up with Eddie. Thirty years the senior of the twenty-three-year-old, she passed even at close inspection for his older sister. Longevity pills took care of that. However, he treated her with all the courtesy and chivalry that one gave one's mother and helped her up the steep inclines, even though the climbs did not appreciably cause her deep chest to demand more air.

They paused once by a creek bank to get their bearings.

"The signals have stopped," he said.

"Obviously," she replied.

At that moment the radar-detector built into the panrad began to ping. Both of them automatically looked upwards.

"There's no ship in the air."

"It can't be coming from either of those hills," she pointed out. "There's nothing but a boulder on top of each one. Tremendous rocks."

"Nevertheless, it's coming from there, I think. Oh! Oh! Did you see what I saw? Looked like a tall stalk of some kind being pulled down behind that big rock."

She peered through the dim light. "I think you were imagining things, son. I saw nothing."

Then, even as the pinging kept up, the zzting started again. After a burst of noise, both stopped.

"Let's go up and see what we shall see," she said.

"Something screwy," he commented. She did not answer.

They forded the creek and began the ascent. Half-way up, they stopped to sniff in puzzlement at a gust of some heavy odour coming downwind.

"Smells like a cageful of monkeys," he said.

"In heat," she added. If his were the keener ears, hers was the sharper nose.

They went on up. The RD began sounding its tiny hysterical gonging. Nonplussed, Eddied stopped. The DF indicated the radar pulses were not coming from the top of the hill they were climbing, as formerly, but from the other hill across the valley. Abruptly, the panrad fell silent.

"What do we do now?"

"Finish what we started. This hill. Then we go to the other one."

He shrugged and then hastened after her tall slim body in its long-legged coveralls. She was hot on the scent, literally, and nothing could stop her. Just before she reached the bungalow-sized boulder topping the hill, he caught up with her. She had stopped to gaze intently at the DF needle, which swung wildly before it stopped at neutral. The monkey-cage odour was very strong.

"Do you suppose it could be some sort of radio-generating mineral?" she asked, disappointedly.

"No. Those groupings were semantic. And that smell . . ."

"Then what—"

He didn't know whether to feel pleased or not that she had so obviously and suddenly thrust the burden of responsibility and action on him. Both pride and a curious shrinking affected him. But he did feel exhilarated. Almost, he thought, he felt as if he were on the verge of discovering what he had been looking for for a long time. What the object of his search had been, he could not say. But he was excited and not very much afraid.

He unslung his weapon, a two-barrelled combination shotgun and rifle. The panrad was still quiet.

"Maybe the boulder is camouflage for a spy outfit," he said. He sounded silly, even to himself.

Behind him, his mother gasped and screamed. He whirled and raised his gun, but there was nothing to shoot. She was pointing at the hilltop across the valley, shaking, and saying something incoherent.

He could make out a long slim antenna seemingly projecting from the monstrous boulder crouched there. At the same time, two thoughts struggled for the first place in his mind: one, that it was more than a coincidence that both hills had almost identical stone structures on their brows, and two, that the antenna must have been recently stuck out, for he was sure he had not seen it the last time he looked.

He never got to tell her his conclusions, for something thin and flexible and irresistible seized him from behind. Lifted into the air, he was borne backwards. He dropped the gun and tried to grab the bands or tentacles around him and tear them off with his bare hands. No use.

He caught one last glimpse of his mother running off down the hillside. Then a curtain snapped down, and he was in total darkness.

Chapter 4

Eddie sensed himself, still suspended, twirled around. He could not know for sure, of course, but he thought he was facing in exactly the opposite direction. Simultaneously, the tentacles binding his legs and arms were released. Only his waist was still gripped. It was pressed so tightly that he cried out with pain.

Then, boot-toes bumping on some resilient substances, he was carried forward. Halted, facing he knew not what horrible monster, he was suddenly assailed—not by a sharp beak or tooth or knife or some other cutting or mangling instrument—but by a dense cloud of that same monkey perfume.

In other circumstances, he might have vomited. Now his stomach was not given the time to consider whether it should clean house or not. The tentacle lifted him higher and thrust him against something soft and yielding—something fleshlike and womanly—almost breast-like in texture and smoothness and warmth and in its hint of gentle curving.

He put his hands and feet out to brace himself, for he thought for a moment he was going to sink in and be covered up—enfolded—ingested. The idea of a gargantuan amoeba-thing hiding within a hollow rock—or a rock-like shell—made him writhe and yell and shove at the protoplasmic substance.

But nothing of the kind happened. He was not plunged into a smothering and slimy jelly that would strip him of his skin and then his flesh and then dissolve his bones. He was merely shoved repeatedly against the soft swelling. Each time, he pushed or kicked or struck at it. After a dozen of these seemingly purposeless acts, he was held away, as if whatever was doing it was puzzled by his behaviour.

He had quit screaming. The only sounds were his harsh breathing and the zzzts and pings from the panrad. Even as he became aware of them, the zzzts changed tempo and settled into a recognizable pattern of bursts—three units that crackled out again and again.

"Who are you? Who are you?"

Of course, it could just as easily have been, "What are you?" or "What the hell!" or "Nor smoz ka pop?"

Or nothing—semantically speaking.

But he didn't think the latter. And when he was gently lowered to the floor, and the tentacle went off to only-God-knew-where in the dark, he was sure that the creature was communicating—or trying to—with him.

It was this thought that kept him from screaming and running around in the lightless and fetid chamber, brainlessly seeking an outlet. He mastered his panic and snapped open a little shutter in the panrad's side and thrust in his right-hand index finger. There he poised it above the key and in a moment, when the thing paused in transmitting, he sent back, as best he could, the pulses he had received. It was not necessary for him to turn on the light and spin the dial that would put him on the 1,000 kc. band. The instrument would automatically key that frequency in with the one he had just received.

The oddest part of the whole procedure was that his whole body was trembling almost uncontrollably—one part excepted. That was his index finger, his one unit that seemed to him to have a definite function in this otherwise meaningless situation. It was the section of him that was helping him to survive—the only part that knew how—at that moment. Even his brain seemed to have no connection with his finger. That digit was himself, and the rest just happened to be linked to it.

When he paused, the transmitter began again. This time the units were unrecognizable. There was a certain rhythm to them, but he could not know what they meant. Meanwhile, the RD was pinging. Something somewhere in the dark hole had a beam held tightly on him.

He pressed a button on the panrad's top, and the built-in flashlight illuminated the area just in front of him. He saw a wall of reddish-grey rubbery substance. On the wall was a roughly circular, light grey swelling about four feet in diameter. Around it, giving it a medusa appearance, were coiled twelve very long, very thin tentacles.

Though he was afraid that if he turned his back to them the tentacles would seize him once more, his curiosity forced him to wheel about and examine his surroundings with the bright beam. He was in an egg-shaped chamber about thirty feet long, twelve wide, and eight to ten high in the middle. It was formed of reddish-grey material, smooth except for irregular intervals of blue or red pipes. Veins and arteries?

A door-sized portion of the wall had a vertical slit running down it. Tentacles fringed it. He guessed it was a sort of iris and that it had opened to drag him inside. Starfish-shaped groupings of tentacles were scattered on the walls or hung from the ceiling. On the wall opposite the iris was a long and flexible stalk with a cartilaginous ruff around its free end. When Eddie moved, it moved, its blind point following him as a radar antenna tracks the thing it is locating. That was what it was. And unless he was wrong, the stalk was also a C.W. transmitter-receiver.

He shot the light around. When it reached the end farthest from him, he gasped. Ten creatures were huddled together facing him! About the size of half-grown pigs, they looked like nothing so much as unshelled snails; they were eyeless, and the stalk growing from the forehead of each was a tiny duplicate of that on the wall. They didn't look dangerous. Their open mouths were little and toothless, and their rate of locomotion must be slow, for they moved like snails, on a large pedestal of flesh—a foot-muscle.

Nevertheless, if he were to fall asleep they could overcome him by force of numbers, and those mouths might drip an acid to digest him, or they might carry a concealed poisonous sting.

His speculations were interrupted violently. He was seized, lifted, and passed on to another group of tentacles. He was carried beyond the antenna-stalk and towards the snail-beings. Just before he reached them, he was halted, facing the wall. An iris, hitherto invisible, opened. His light shone into it, but he could see nothing but convolutions of flesh.

His panrad gave off a new pattern of dit-dot-deet-dats. The iris widened until it was large enough to admit his body, if he were shoved in head first. Or feet first. It didn't matter. The convolutions straightened out and became a tunnel. Or a throat. From thousands of little pits emerged thousands of tiny, razor-sharp teeth. They flashed out and sank back in, and before they had disappeared thousands of other wicked little spears darted out and past the receding fangs.

Meat-grinder.

Beyond the murderous array, at the end of the throat, was a huge pouch of water. Steam came from it, and with it an odour like that of his mother's stew. Dark bits, presumably meat, and pieces of vegetables floated on the seething surface.

Then the iris closed, and he was turned around to face the slugs. Gently, but unmistakably, a tentacle spanked his buttocks. And the panrad zzzted a warning.

Eddie was not stupid. He knew now that the ten creatures were not dangerous unless he molested them. In which case he had just seen where he would go if he did not behave.

Again he was lifted and carried along the wall until he was shoved against the light grey spot. The monkey-cage odour, which had died out, became strong again. Eddie identified its source with a very small hole which appeared in the wall.

When he did not respond—he had no idea yet how he was supposed to act—the tentacles dropped him so unexpectedly that he fell on his back. Unhurt by the yielding flesh, he rose.

What was the next step? Exploration of his resources. Itemization: the panrad. A sleeping-bag, which he wouldn't need as long as the present too-warm temperature kept up. A bottle of Old Red Star capsules. A free-fall thermos with attached nipple. A box of A-2-Z rations. A Foldstove. Cartridges for his double-barrel, now lying outside the creature's boulderish shell. A roll of toilet paper. Toothbrush. Paste. Soap. Towel. Pills: Nodor, hormone, vitamin, longevity, reflex, and sleeping. And a thread-thin wire, a hundred feet long when uncoiled, that held prisoner in its molecular structure a hundred symphonies, eighty operas, a thousand different types of musical pieces, and two thousand great books ranging from Sophocles and Dostoyevsky to the latest bestseller. It could be played inside the panrad.

He inserted it, pushed, a button, and spoke "Eddie Fetts's recording of Puccini's *Che gelida manina*, please."

And while he listened approvingly to his own magnificent voice, he zipped open a can he had found in the bottom of the sack. His mother had put into it the stew left over from their last meal in the ship.

Not knowing what was happening, yet for some reason sure he was for the present safe, he munched meat and vegetables with a contented jaw. Transition from abhorrence to appetite sometimes came easily for Eddie.

He cleaned out the can and finished with some crackers and a chocolate bar. Rationing was out. As long as the food lasted, he would eat well. Then, if nothing turned up, he would . . . But then, he reassured himself as he licked his fingers, his mother, who was free, would find some way to get him out of his trouble.

She always had.

Chapter 5

The panrad, silent for a while, began signalling. Eddie spotlighted the antenna and saw it was pointing at the snailbeings, which he had, in accordance with his custom, dubbed familiarly. Sluggos he called them.

The Sluggos crept towards the wall and stopped close to it. Their mouths, placed on the tops of their heads, gaped like so many hungry young birds. The iris opened, and two lips formed into a spout. Out of it streamed steaming-hot water and chunks of meat and vegetables. Stew! Stew that fell exactly into each waiting mouth.

That was how Eddie learned the second phrase of Mother Polyphema's language. The first message had been, "What are you?" This was, "Come and get it!"

He experimented. He tapped out a repetition of what he'd last heard. As one, the Sluggos—except the one then being fed—turned to him and crept a few feet before halting, puzzled.

Inasmuch as Eddie was broadcasting, the Sluggos must have had some sort of built-in DF. Otherwise they wouldn't have been able to distinguish between his pulses and their Mother's.

Immediately after, a tentacle smote Eddie across the shoulders and knocked him down. The panrad zzzted its third intelligible message: "Don't ever do that!"

And then a fourth, to which the ten young obeyed by wheeling and resuming their former positions.

"This way, children."

Yes, they were the offspring, living, eating, sleeping, playing, and learning to communicate in the womb of their Mother—the Mother. They were the mobile brood of this vast immobile entity that had scooped up Eddie as a frog scoops up a fly. This Mother. She who had once been just such a Sluggo until she had grown hog-size and had been pushed out of her Mother's womb. And who, rolled into a tight ball, had free-wheeled down her natal hill, straightened out at the bottom, inched her way up the next hill, rolled down, and so on. Until she found the empty shell of an adult who had died. Or, if she wanted to be a first class citizen in her society and not a prestigeless *occupée*, she found the bare top of a tall hill—any eminence that commanded a big sweep of territory—and there squatted.

And there she put out many thread-thin tendrils into the soil and into the cracks in the rocks, tendrils that drew sustenance from the fat of her body and grew and extended downwards and ramified into other tendrils. Deep underground the rootlets worked, the instinctive chemistry; searched for and found the water, the calcium, the iron, the copper, the nitrogen, the carbons, fondled earthworms and grubs and larvae, teasing them for the secrets of their fats and proteins; broke down the wanted substance into shadowy colloidal particles; sucked them up the thready pipes of the tendrils and back to the pale and slimming body crouched on a flat space atop a ridge, a hill, a peak.

There, using the blueprints stored in the molecules of the cerebellum, her body took the building blocks of elements and fashioned them into a very thin shell of the most available materials, a shield large enough so she could expand to fit it while her natural enemies—the keen and hungry predators that prowled twilighted Baudelaire—nosed and clawed it in vain.

Then, her evergrowing bulk cramped, she would resorb the hard covering. And if no sharp tooth found her during that process of a few days, she would cast another and a larger. And so on through a dozen or more.

Until she had become the monstrous and much reformed body of an adult and virgin female. Outside would be the stuff that so much resembled a boulder, that was, actually, rock; either granite, diorite, marble, basalt, or maybe just plain limestone. Or sometimes iron, glass, or cellulose.

Within was the centrally located brain, probably as large as a man's. Surrounding it, the tons of organs: the nervous system, the mighty heart, or hearts, the four stomachs, the microwave and longwave generators, the kidneys, bowels, tracheae, scent and taste organs, the perfume factory which made odours to attract animals and birds close enough to be seized, and the huge womb. And the antennae—the small one inside for teaching and scanning the young, and a long and powerful stalk on the outside, projecting from the shelltop, retractable if danger came.

The next step was from virgin to Mother, lower-case to upper-case as designated in her pulse-language by a longer pause before a word. Not until she was deflowered could she take a high place in her society. Immodest, unblushing, she herself made the advances, the proposals, and the surrender.

After which, she ate her mate.

The clock in the panrad told Eddie he was in his thirtieth day of imprisonment when he found out that little bit of information. He was shocked, not because it offended his ethics, but because he himself had been intended to be the mate. And the dinner.

His finger tapped, Tell me, Mother, what you mean."

He had not wondered before how a species that lacked males could reproduce. Now he found that, to the Mothers, all creatures except themselves were male. Mothers were immobile and female. Mobiles were male. Eddie had been mobile. He was, therefore, a male.

He had approached this particular Mother during the mating season, that is, midway through raising a litter of young. She had scanned him as he came along the creek-banks at the valley bottom. When he was at the foot of the hill, she had detected his odour. It was new to her. The closest she could come to it in her memory banks was that of a beast similar to him. From her description, he guessed it to be an ape. So she had released from her repertoire its rut stench. When he seemingly fell into the trap, she had caught him.

He was supposed to attack the conception-spot, that light grey swelling on the wall. After he had ripped and torn it enough to begin the mysterious workings of pregnancy, he would have been popped into her stomach-iris.

Fortunately, he had lacked the sharp beak, the fang, the claw. And she had received her own signals back from the panrad.

Eddie did not understand why it was necessary to use a mobile for mating. A Mother was intelligent enough to pick up a sharp stone and mangle the spot herself.

He was given to understand that conception would not start unless it was accompanied by a certain titillation of the nerves—a frenzy and its satisfaction. Why this emotional state was needed, Mother did not know.

Eddie tried to explain about such things as genes and chromosomes and why they had to be present in highly-developed species.

Mother did not understand.

Eddie wondered if the number of slashes and rips in the spot corresponded to the number of young. Or if there were a large number of potentialities in the heredity-ribbons spread out under the conception-skin. And if the haphazard irritation and consequent stimulation of the genes paralleled the chance combining of genes in human male-female mating. Thus resulting in offspring with traits that were combinations of their parents.

Or did the inevitable devouring of the mobile after the act indicate more than an emotional and nutritional reflex? Did it hint that the mobile caught up scattered gene-nodes, like hard seeds, along with the torn skin, in its claws and tusks, that these genes survived the boiling in the stew-stomach, and were later passed out in the faeces? Where animals and birds picked them up in beak, tooth, or foot, and then, seized by other Mothers in this oblique rape, transmitted the heredity-carrying agents to the conception-spots while attacking them, the nodules being scraped off and implanted in the skin and blood of the swelling even as others were harvested? Later, the mobiles were eaten, digested, and ejected in the obscure but ingenious and never-ending cycle? Thus ensuring the continual, if haphazard, recombining of genes, chances of variations in offspring, opportunities for muta-tions, and so on?

Mother pulsed that she was nonplussed.

Eddie gave up. He'd never know. After all, did it matter?

He decided not, and rose from his prone position to request water. She pursed up her iris and spouted a tepid quartful into his thermos. He dropped in a pill, swished it around till it dissolved, and drank a reasonable facsimile of Old Red Star. He preferred the harsh and pow-erful rye, though he could have afforded the smoothest. Quick results were what he wanted. Taste didn't matter, as he disliked all liquor tastes. Thus he drank what the Skid Row bums drank and shuddered even as they did, renaming it Old Rotten Tar and cursing the fate that had brought them so low they had to gag such stuff down.

The rye glowed in his belly and spread quickly through his limbs and up to his head, chilled only by the increasing scarcity of the cap-sules. When he ran out—then what? It was at times like this that he most missed his mother.

Thinking about her brought a few large tears. He snuffled and drank some more and when the biggest of the Sluggos nudged him for a back-scratching, he gave it instead a shot of Old Red Star. A slug for Sluggo. Idly, he wondered what effect a taste for rye would have on the future of the race when these virgins became Mothers.

At that moment he was shaken by what seemed a lifesaving idea.

These creatures could suck up the required elements from the earth and with them duplicate quite complex molecular structures. Provided, of course, they had a sample of the desired substance to brood over in some cryptic organ.

Well, what easier to do than give her one of the cherished capsules? One could become any number. Those, plus the abundance of water pumped up through hollow underground tendrils from the nearby creek, would give enough to make a master-distiller green!

He smacked his lips and was about to key her his request when what she was transmitting penetrated his mind.

Rather cattily, she remarked that her neighbour across the valley was putting on airs because she, too, held prisoner a communicating mobile.

Chapter 6

The Mothers had a society as hierarchical as table-protocol in Washington or peck-order in a barnyard. Prestige was what counted, and prestige was determined by the broadcasting power, the height of the eminence on which the Mother sat, which governed the extent of her radar-territory, and the abundance and novelty and wittiness of her gossip. The creature that had snapped Eddie up was a queen. She had precedence over thirty-odd of her kind; they all had to let her broadcast first, and none dared start pulsing until she quit. Then, the next in order began, and so on down the line. Any of them could be interrupted at any time by Number One, and if any of the lower echelon had something interesting to transmit, she could break in on the one then speaking and get permission from the queen to tell her tale.

Eddie knew this, but he could not listen in directly to the hilltop-gabble. The thick pseudo-granite shell barred him from that and made him dependent upon her womb-stalk for relayed information.

Now and then Mother opened the door and allowed her young to crawl out. There they practiced beaming and broadcasting at the Sluggos of the Mother across the valley. Occasionally that Mother deigned herself to pulse the young, and Eddie's keeper reciprocated to her offspring.

Turnabout.

The first time the children had inched through the exit-iris, Eddie had tried, Ulysses-like, to pass himself off as one of them and crawl out in the midst of the flock. Eyeless, but no Polyphemus, Mother had picked him out with her tentacles and hauled him back in.

It was following that incident that he had named her Polyphema.

He knew she had increased her own already powerful prestige tremendously by possession of that unique thing—a transmitting mobile. So much had her importance grown that the Mothers on the fringes of her area passed on the news to others. Before he had learned her language, the entire continent was hooked-up. Polyphema had become a veritable gossip columnist; tens of thousands of hill crouchers listened in eagerly to her accounts of her dealings with the walking paradox: a semantic male.

That had been fine. Then, very recently, the Mother across the valley had captured a similar creature. And in one bound she had become Number Two in the area and would, at the slightest weakness on Polyphema's part, wrest the top position away.

Eddie became wildly excited at the news. He had often daydreamed about his mother and wondered what she was doing. Curiously enough, he ended many of his fantasies with lip-mutterings, reproaching her almost audibly for having left him and for making no try to rescue him. When he became aware of his attitude, he was ashamed. Nevertheless, the sense of desertion coloured his thoughts.

Now that he knew she was alive and had been caught, probably while trying to get him out, he rose from the lethargy that had lately been making him doze the clock around. He asked Polyphema if she would open the entrance so he could talk directly with the other captive. She said yes. Eager to listen in on a conversation between two mobiles, she was very co-operative. There would be a mountain of gossip in what they would have to say. The only thing that dented her joy was that the other Mother would also have access.

Then, remembering she was still Number One and would broadcast the details first, she trembled so with pride and ecstasy that Eddie felt the floor shaking.

Iris open, he walked through it and looked across the valley. The hillsides were still green, red, and yellow, as the plants on Baudelaire did not lose their leaves during the winter. But a few white patches showed that winter had begun. Eddie shivered from the bite of cold air on his naked skin. Long ago he had taken off his clothes. The womb-warmth had made garments too uncomfortable; moreover, Eddie, being human, had had to get rid of waste products. And Polyphema, being a Mother, had had periodically to flush out the dirt with warm water from one of her stomachs. Every time the tracheae-vents exploded streams that swept the undesirable elements out through her door-iris, Eddie had become soaked. When he abandoned dress, his clothes had gone floating out. Only by sitting on his pack did he keep it from a like fate.

Afterwards, he and the Sluggos had been dried off by warm air pumped through the same vents and originating from the mighty battery of lungs. Eddie was comfortable enough—he'd always liked showers—but the loss of his garments had been one more thing that kept him from escaping. He would soon freeze to death outside unless he found the yacht quickly. And he wasn't sure he remembered the path back.

So now, when he stepped outside, he retreated a pace or two and let the warm air from Polyphema flow like a cloak from his shoulders. Then he peered across the half-mile that separated him from his mother, but he could not see her. The twilight state and the dark of the unit interior of her captor hid her.

He tapped in Morse, "Switch to the talkie, same frequency." Paula Fetts did so. She began asking him frantically if he were all right.

He replied he was fine.

"Have you missed me terribly, son?"

"Oh, very much."

Even as he said this he wondered vaguely why his voice sounded so hollow. Despair at never again being able to see her, probably.

"I've almost gone crazy, Eddie. When you were caught I ran away as fast as I could. I had no idea what horrible monster it was that was attacking us. And then, half-way down the hill, I fell and broke my leg . . . "

"Oh, no, mother!"

"Yes. But I managed to crawl back to the ship. And there, after I'd set it myself, I gave myself B.K. shots. Only, my system didn't react like it's supposed to. There are people that way, you know, and the healing took twice as long.

"But when I was able to walk, I got a gun and a box of dynamite. I was going to blow up what I thought was a kind of rock-fortress, an outpost for some kind of extee. I'd no idea of the true nature of these beasts. First, though, I decided to reconnoitre. I was going to spy on the boulder from across the valley. But I was trapped by this thing.

"Listen, son. Before I'm cut off, let me tell you not to give up hope.

I'll be out of here before long and over to rescue you."

"How?"

"If you remember, my lab kit holds a number of carcinogens for field work. Well, you know that sometimes a Mother's conception-spot when it is torn up during mating, instead of begetting young, goes into cancer—the opposite of pregnancy. I've injected a carcinogen into the spot and a beautiful carcinoma has developed. She'll be dead in a few days."

"Mom! You'll be buried in that rotting mass!"

"No. This creature has told me that when one of her species dies, a reflex opens the labia. That's to permit their young—if any—to escape. Listen, I'll—"

A tentacle coiled about him and pulled him back through the iris, which shut.

When he switched back to C.W., he heard, "Why didn't you communicate? What were you doing? Tell me! Tell me!"

Eddie told her. There was a silence that could only be interpreted as astonishment. After Mother had recovered her wits, she said, "From now on, you will talk to the other male through me."

Obviously she envied and hated his ability to change wavebands, and, perhaps, had a struggle to accept the idea.

"Please," he persisted, not knowing how dangerous were the waters he was wading in, "please let me talk to my mother di—"

For the first time, he heard her stutter.

"Wha-wha-what? Your Mo-Mo-Mother?"

"Yes. Of course."

The floor heaved violently beneath his feet. He cried out and braced himself to keep from falling and then flashed on the light. The walls were pulsating like shaken jelly, and the vascular columns had turned from red and blue to grey. The entrance-iris sagged open, like a lax mouth, and the air cooled. He could feel the drop in temperature in her flesh with the soles of his feet.

It was some time before he caught on.

Polyphema was in a state of shock.

What might have happened had she stayed in it, he never knew. She might have died and thus forced him out into the winter before his mother could escape. If so, and he couldn't find the ship, he would die. Huddled in the warmest corner of the egg-shaped chamber, Eddie contemplated that idea and shivered to a degree for which the outside air couldn't account.

Chapter 7

However, Polyphema had her own method of recovery. It consisted of spewing out the contents of her stew-stomach, which had doubtless become filled with the poisons draining out of her system from the blow. Her ejection of the stuff was the physical manifestation of the psychical catharsis. So furious was the flood that her foster son was almost swept out in the hot tide, but she, reacting instinctively, had coiled tentacles about him and the Sluggos. Then she followed the first upchucking by emptying her other three waterpouches, the second hot and the third lukewarm and the fourth, just filled, cold.

Eddie yelped as the icy water doused him.

Polyphema's irises closed again. The floor and walls gradually quit quaking; the temperature rose; and her veins and arteries regained their red and blue. She was well again. Or so she seemed.

But when, after waiting twenty-four hours he cautiously approached the subject, he found she not only would not talk about it, she refused to acknowledge the existence of the other mobile.

Eddie, giving up hope of conversation, thought for quite a while. The only conclusion he could come to, and he was sure he'd grasped enough of her psychology to make it valid, was that the concept of a mobile female was utterly unacceptable.

Her world was split into two: mobile and her kind, the immobile. Mobile meant food and mating. Mobile meant—male. The Mothers were—female.

How the mobiles reproduced had probably never entered the hill-crouchers' minds. Their science and philosophy were on the instinctive body-level. Whether they had some notion of spontaneous generation or amoeba-like fission being responsible for the continued population of mobiles, or they'd just taken for granted they "growed," like Topsy, Eddie never found out. To them, they were female and the rest of the protoplasmic cosmos was male.

That was that. Any other idea was more than foul and obscene and blasphemous. It was—unthinkable.

Polyphema had received a deep trauma from his words. And though she seemed to have recovered, somewhere in those tons of unimaginably complicated flesh, a bruise was buried. Like a hidden flower, dark purple, it bloomed, and the shadow it cast was one that cut off a certain memory, a certain tract, from the light of consciousness. That bruise-stained shadow covered that time and event which the Mother, for reasons unfathomable to the human being, found necessary to mark KEEP OFF.

Thus, though Eddie did not word it, he understood in the cells of his body, he felt and knew, as if his bones were prophesying and his brain did not hear, what came to pass.

Sixty-six hours later by the panrad clock, Polyphema's entrance-lips opened. Her tentacles darted out. They came back in, carrying his helpless and struggling mother.

Eddie, roused out of a doze, horrified, paralysed, saw her toss her lab kit at him and heard an inarticulate cry from her. And saw her plunged, headforemost, into the stomach-iris.

Polyphema had taken the one sure way of burying the evidence.

Eddie lay face down, nose mashed against the warm and faintly throbbing flesh of the floor. Now and then his hands clutched spasmodically as if he were reaching for something that someone kept putting just within his reach and then moving away.

How long he was there he didn't know, for he never again looked at the clock.

Finally, in the darkness, he sat up and giggled inanely, "Mother always did make good stew."

That set him off. He leaned back on his hands and threw his head back and howled like a wolf under a full moon.

Polyphema, of course, was dead-deaf, but she could radar his posture, and her keen nostrils deduced from his body-scent that he was in terrible fear and anguish.

A tentacle glided out and gently enfolded him.

"What is the matter?" zzted the panrad.

He stuck his finger in the keyhole.

"I have lost my mother!"

"?"

"She's gone away, and she'll never come back."

"I don't understand. *Here I am.*"

Eddie quit weeping and cocked his head as if he were listening to some inner voice. He snuffled a few times and wiped away the tears, slowly disengaged the tentacle, patted it, walked over to his pack in a corner, and took out the bottle of Old Red Star capsules. One he popped into the thermos; the other he gave to her with the request she duplicate it, if possible. Then he stretched out on his side, propped on one elbow like a Roman in his sensualities, sucked the rye through the nipple, and listened to a medley of Beethoven, Moussorgsky, Verdi, Strauss, Porter, Feinstein, and Waxworth.

So the time—if there were such a thing there—flowed around Eddie. When he was tired of music or plays or books, he listened in on the area hookup. Hungry, he rose and walked—or often just crawled—to the stew-iris. Cans of rations lay in his pack; he had planned to eat those until he was sure that—what was it he was forbidden to eat? Poison? Something had been devoured by Polyphema and the Sluggos. But sometime during the music-rye orgy, he had forgotten. He now ate quite hungrily and with thought for nothing but the satisfaction of his wants.

Sometimes the door-iris opened, and Billy Greengrocer hopped in. Billy looked like a cross between a cricket and a kangaroo. He was the size of a collie, and he bore in a marsupialian pouch vegetables and fruit and nuts. These he extracted with shiny green, chitinous claws and gave to Mother in return for meals of stew. Happy symbiote, he chirruped merrily while his many-faceted eyes, revolving independently of each other, looked one at the Sluggos and the other at Eddie.

Eddie, on impulse, abandoned the 100 kc. band and roved the frequencies until he found that both Polyphema and Billy were emitting a 108 wave. That, apparently, was their natural signal.

When Billy had his groceries to deliver, he broadcast. Polyphema, in turn, when she needed them, sent back to him. There was nothing intelligent on Billy's part; it was just his instinct to transmit. And the Mother was, aside from the "semantic" frequency, limited to that one band. But it worked out fine.

Chapter 8

Everything was fine. What more could a man want? Free food, unlimited liquor, soft bed, air-conditioning, shower-baths, music, intellectual works (on the tape), interesting conversation (much of it was about him), privacy, and security.

If he had not already named her, he would have called her Mother Gratis.

Nor were creature comforts all. She had given him the answers to all his questions, all . . .

Except one.

That was never expressed vocally by him. Indeed, he would have been incapable of doing so. He was probably unaware that he had such a question.

But Polyphema voiced it one day when she asked him to do her a favour.

Eddie reacted as if outraged.

"One does not—! One does not—!"

He choked, and then he thought, how ridiculous. She is not—

And looked puzzled, and said, "But she is."

He rose and opened the lab kit. While he was looking for a scalpel, he came across the carcinogens. He threw them through the half-opened labia far out and down the hillside.

Then he turned and, scalpel in hand, leaped at the light grey swelling on the wall. And stopped, staring at it, while the instrument fell from his hand. And picked it up and stabbed feebly and did not even scratch the skin. And again let it drop.

"What is it? What is it?" crackled the panrad hanging from his wrist.

Suddenly, a heavy cloud of human odour—mansweat—was puffed in his face from a nearby vent

"????"

And he stood, bent in a half-crouch, seemingly paralysed. Until tentacles seized him in fury and dragged him towards the stomach-iris, yawning man-sized.

Eddie screamed and writhed and plunged his finger in the panrad and tapped, "All right! All right!"

And once back before the spot, he lunged with a sudden and wild joy; he slashed savagely; he yelled. "Take that! And that, P . . ." and the rest was lost in a mindless shout.

He did not stop cutting, and he might have gone on and on until he had quite excised the spot had not Polyphema interfered by dragging him towards her stomach-iris again. For ten seconds he hung there, helpless and sobbing with a mixture of fear and glory.

Polyphema's reflexes had almost overcome her brain. Fortunately, a cold spark of reason lit up a corner of the vast, dark, and hot chapel of her frenzy.

The convolutions leading to the steaming, meat-laden pouch closed and the foldings of flesh rearranged themselves. Eddie was suddenly hosed with warm water from what he called the "sanitation" stomach. The iris closed. He was put down. The scalpel was put back in the bag.

For a long time Mother seemed to be shaken by the thought of what she might have done to Eddie. She did not trust herself to transmit until her nerves were settled. When they were, she did not refer to his narrow escape. Nor did he.

He was happy. He felt as if a spring, tight-coiled against his bowels since he and his wife had parted, was now, for some reason, released. The dull vague pain of loss and discontent, the slight fever and cramp in his entrails, the apathy that sometimes afflicted him, were gone. He felt fine.

Meanwhile, something akin to deep affection had been lighted, like a tiny candle under the draughty and over-towering roof of a cathedral. Mother's shell housed more than Eddie; it now curved over an emotion new to her kind. This was evident by the next event that filled him with terror.

For the wounds in the spot healed and the swelling increased into a large bag. Then the bag burst and ten mouse-sized Sluggos struck the floor. The impact had the same effect as a doctor spanking a newborn baby's bottom; they drew in their first breath with shock and pain; their uncontrolled and feeble pulses filled the ether with shapeless SOS's.

When Eddie was not talking with Polyphema or listening in or drinking or sleeping or eating or bathing or running off the tape, he played with the Sluggos. He was, in a sense, their father. Indeed, as they grew to hog-size, it was hard for their female parent to distinguish him from her young. As he seldom walked any more, and was often to be found on hands and knees in their midst, she could not scan him too well. Moreover, something in the heavywet air or in the diet had caused every hair on his body to drop off. He grew very fat. Generally speaking, he was one with the pale, soft, round, and bald offspring. A family likeness.

There was one difference. When the time came for the virgins to be expelled, Eddie crept to one end, whimpering, and stayed there until he was sure Mother was not going to thrust him out into the cold, hard, and hungry world.

That final crisis over, he came back to the centre of the floor. The panic in his breast had died out, but his nerves were still quivering. He filled his thermos and then listened for a while to his own tenor singing the "Sea Things' aria from his favourite opera, Gianelli's *Ancient Mariner*. Suddenly, he burst out and accompanied himself, finding himself thrilled as never before by the concluding words.

> And from my neck so free
> The Albatross fell off, and sank
> Like lead into the sea.

Afterwards, voice silent but heart singing, he switched off the wire and cut in on Polyphema's broadcast.

Mother was having trouble. She could not precisely describe to the continent-wide hook-up this new and almost inexpressible emotion she felt about the mobile. It was a concept her language was not prepared for. Nor was she helped any by the gallons of Old Star in her bloodstream.

Eddie sucked at the plastic nipple and nodded sympathetically and drowsily at her search for words. Presently the thermos rolled out of his hand.

He slept on his side, curled in a ball, knees on his chest and arms crossed, neck bent forward. Like the pilot room chronometer whose hands reversed after the crash, the clock of his body was ticking backwards, ticking backwards . . .

In the darkness, in the moistness, safe and warm, well fed, much loved.

. . . Daughter

Cq! Cq!

This is Mother Hardhead pulsing.

Keep quiet all you virgins and Mothers, while I communicate. Listen, listen, all you who are hooked into this broadcast. Listen, and I will tell you how I left my Mother, how my two sisters and I grew our shells, how I dealt with the olfway, and why I have become the Mother with the most prestige, the strongest shell, the most powerful broadcaster and beamer, and the pulser of a new language.

First, before I tell my story, I will reveal to all you who do not know it that my father was a mobile.

Do not be nervequivered. This is a so-story. It is not a not-so-story.

Father was a mobile.

Mother pulsed, "Get out!"

Then, to show she meant business, she opened her exit-iris.

That sobered us up and made us realize how serious she was. Before, when she snapped open her iris, she did it so we could practice pulsing at the other young crouched in the doorways to their Mothers' wombs, or else send a respectful message to the Mothers themselves, or even a quick one to Grandmother, far away on a mountainside. Not that she received, I think, because we young were too weak to transmit that far. Anyway, Grandmother never acknowledged receipt.

At times, when Mother was annoyed because we would all

broadcast at once instead of asking her permission to speak one at a time or because we would crawl up the sides of her womb and then drop off the ceiling on to the floor with a thud, she would pulse at us to get out and build our own shells. She meant it, she said.

Then, according to our mood, we would either settle down or else get more boisterous. Mother would reach out with her tentacles and hold us down and spank us. If that did no good, she would threaten us with the olfway. That did the trick. That is, until she used him too many times. After a while, we got so we didn't believe there was an olfway. Mother, we thought, was creating a not-so-story. We should have known better, however, for Mother loathed not-so-stories.

Another thing that quivered her nerves was our conversation with Father in Orsemay. Although he had taught her his language, he refused to teach her Orsemay. When he wanted to send messages to us that he knew she wouldn't approve, he would pulse at us in our private language. That was another thing, I think, that finally made Mother so angry she cast us out despite Father's pleadings that we be allowed to remain four more seasons.

You must understand that we virgins had remained in the womb far longer than we should have. The cause for our overstay was Father.

He was the mobile.

Yes, I know what you're going to reply. All fathers, you will repeat, are mobiles.

But he was Father. He was the *pulsing* mobile.

Yes, he could too. He could pulse with the best of us. Or maybe he *himself* couldn't. Not directly. We pulse with organs in our body. But Father, if I understand him correctly, used a creature of some kind which was separate from his body. Or maybe it was an organ that wasn't attached to him.

Anyway, he had no internal organs or pulse-stalks growing from him to pulse with. He used this creature, this r-a-d-i-o, as he called it. And it worked just fine.

When he conversed with Mother, he did so in Mother-pulse or in his own language, mobilepulse. With us he used Orsemay. That's like mobilepulse, only a little different. Mother never did figure out the difference.

When I finish my story, dearie, I'll teach you Orsemay. I've been beamed that you've enough prestige to join our Highest Hill sorority and thus learn our secret of communication.

Mother declared Father had two means of pulsing. Besides his radio, which he used to communicate with us, he could pulse in another and totally different manner. He didn't use dotdeetditdashes, either. His pulses needed air to carry them, and he sent them with the same organ he ate with. Boils one's stomach to think of it, doesn't it?

Father was caught while passing by my Mother. She didn't know what mating-lust perfume to send downwind towards him so he would be lured within reach of her tentacles. She had never smelled a mobile like him before. But he did have an odour that was similar to that of another kind of mobile, so she wafted that towards him. It seemed to work, because he came close enough for her to seize him with her extra-uterine tentacles and pop him into her shell.

Later, after I was born, Father radioed me—in Orsemay, of course, so Mother wouldn't understand—that he had smelled the perfume and that it, among other things, had attracted him. But the odour had been that of a hairy tree-climbing mobile, and he had wondered what such creatures were doing on a bare hilltop. When he learned to converse with Mother, he was so surprised that she had identified him with that mobile.

Ah, well, he pulsed, it is not the first time a female has made a monkey of a man.

He also informed me that he had thought Mother was just an enormous boulder on top of the hill. Not until a section of the supposed rock opened out was he aware of anything out of the ordinary or that the boulder was her shell and held her body within. Mother, he radioed, is something like a dinosaur-sized snail, or jellyfish, equipped with organs that generate radar and radio waves and with an egg-shaped chamber big as the living room of a bungalow, a womb in which she bears and raises her young.

I didn't understand more than half of these terms, of course. Nor was Father able to explain them satisfactorily.

He did make me promise not to pulse Mother that he had thought she was just a big lump of mineral. Why, I don't know.

Father puzzled Mother. Though he fought her when she dragged him in, he had no claws or teeth sharp enough to tear her conception-spot. Mother tried to provoke him further, but he refused to react. When she realized that he was a pulse-sending mobile and released him to study him, he wandered around the womb. After a while he understood that Mother was beaming from her womb pulse-stalk. He learned how to talk with her by using his detachable organ which he termed a panrad. Eventually, he taught her his language, mobilepulse. When Mother learned that and informed other Mothers about it, her prestige became the highest in all the area. No Mother had ever thought of a new language. The idea stunned them.

Father said he was the only communicating mobile on this world. His s-p-a-c-e-s-h-i-p had crashed, and he would now remain forever with Mother.

Father learned the dinnerpulses when Mother summoned her young to eat. He radioed the proper message. Mother's nerves were quivered by the idea that he was semantic, but she opened her stew-iris and let him eat. Then Father held up fruit or other objects and let Mother beam at him with her wombstalk what the proper dotditdeet-dashes were for each. Then he would repeat on his panrad the name of the object to verify it.

Mother's sense of smell helped her, of course. Sometimes it is hard to tell the difference between an apple and a peach just by pulsing it. Odors aid you.

She caught on fast. Father told her she was very intelligent—for a female. That quivered her nerves. She wouldn't pulse with him for several mealperiods after that.

One thing that Mother especially liked about Father was that when conception-time came, she could direct him what to do. She didn't have to depend on luring a non-semantic mobile into her shell with perfumes and then hold it to her conception-spot while it scratched and bit the spot to fight its way from the grip of her tentacles. Father had no claws, but he carried a detachable claw. He named it a s-c-a-l-p-e-l.

When I asked him why he had so many detachable organs, he replied that he was a man of parts.

Father was always talking nonsense.

But he had trouble understanding Mother, too.

Her reproductive processes amazed him.

"By G-o-d," he beamed, "who'd believe it? That a healing process in a wound would result in conception? Just the opposite of cancer."

When we were adolescents and about ready to be shoved out of Mother's shell, we received Mother asking Father to mangle her spot again. Father replied no. He wanted to wait another four seasons. He had said farewell to two broods of his young, and he wanted to keep us around longer so he could give us a real education and enjoy us instead of starting to raise another group of virgins.

This refusal quivered Mother's nerves and upset her stew-stomach so that our food was sour for several meals. But she didn't act against him. He gave her too much prestige. All the Mothers were dropping Motherpulse and learning mobile from Mother as fast as she could teach it.

I asked, "What's prestige?"

"When you send, the others have to receive. And they don't dare pulse back until you're through and you give your permission."

"Oh, I'd like prestige!"

Father interrupted, "Little Hardhead, if you want to get ahead, you tune in to me. I'll tell you a few things even your Mother can't. After all, I'm a mobile, and I've been around."

And he would outline what I had to expect once I left him and Mother and how, if I used my brain, I could survive and eventually get more prestige than even Grandmother had.

Why he called me Hardhead, I don't know. I was still a virgin and had not, of course, grown a shell. I was as soft-bodied as any of my sisters. But he told me he was f-o-n-d of me because I was so hardheaded. I accepted the statement without trying to grasp it.

Anyway, we got eight extra seasons in Mother because Father wanted it that way. We might have got some more, but when winter came again, Mother insisted Father mangle her spot. He replied he wasn't ready. He was just beginning to get acquainted with his children—he called us Sluggos—and, after we left, he'd have nobody but Mother to talk to until the next brood grew up.

Moreover, she was starting to repeat herself, and he didn't think she appreciated him like she should. Her stew was too often soured or else so overboiled that the meat was shredded into a neargoo.

That was enough for Mother.

"Get out!" she pulsed.

"Fine! And don't think you're throwing me out in the cold, either!" zzted back Father. "Yours is not the only shell in this world."

That made Mother's nerves quiver until her whole body shook. She put up her big outside stalk and beamed her sisters and aunts. The Mother across the valley confessed that, during one of the times Father had basked in the warmth of the s-u-n while lying just outside Mother's opened iris, she had asked him to come live with her.

Mother changed her mind. She realized that, with him gone, her prestige would die and that of the hussy across the valley would grow.

"Seems as if I'm here for the duration," radioed Father.

Then, "Whoever would think your Mother'd be j-e-a-l-o-u-s?'

Life with Father was full of those incomprehensible semantic groups. Too often he would not, or could not, explain.

For a long time Father brooded in one spot. He wouldn't answer us or Mother.

Finally, she became overquivered. We had grown so big and boisterous and sassy that she was one continual shudder. And she must have thought that as long as we were around to communicate with him, she had no chance to get him to rip up her spot.

So, out we went.

Before we passed forever from her shell, she warned, "Beware the olfway."

My sisters ignored her, but I was impressed. Father had described the beast and its terrible ways. Indeed, he used to dwell so much on it that we had dropped the old term for it and used Father's. It began when he reprimanded her for threatening us too often with the beast when we misbehaved.

"Don't 'cry wolf.'"

He then beamed me the story of the origin of that puzzling phrase. He did it in Orsemay, of course, because Mother would lash him with her tentacles if she thought he was pulsing something that was not-so. The very idea of not-so strained her brain until she couldn't think straight.

I wasn't sure myself what not-so was, but I enjoyed his stories. And I, like the other virgins and Mother herself, began terming the killer "the olfway."

Anyway, after I'd beamed, "Good sending, Mother," I felt Father's strange stiff mobile-tentacles around me and something wet and warm falling from him on to me. He pulsed, "Good l-u-c-k, Hardhead. Send me a message via hook-up sometimes. And be sure to remember what I told you about dealing with the olfway."

I pulsed that I would. I left with the most indescribable feeling inside me. It was a nervequivering that was both good and bad, if you can imagine such a thing, dearie.

But I soon forgot it in the adventure of rolling down a hill, climbing slowly up the next one on my single foot, rolling down the other side, and so on. After about ten warm-periods, all my sisters but two had left me. They found hilltops on which to build their shells. But my two faithful sisters had listened to my ideas about how we should not be content with anything less than the highest hilltops.

"Once you've grown a shell, you stay where you are."

So they agreed to follow me.

But I led them a long, long way, and they would complain that they were tired and sore and getting afraid of running into some meat-eating mobile. They even wanted to move into the empty shells of Mothers who had been eaten by the olfway or died when cancer, instead of young, developed in the conception spots.

"Come on," I urged. "There's no prestige in moving into empties. Do you want to take bottom place in every community-pulsing just because you're too lazy to build your own covers?"

"But we'll resorb the empties and then grow our own later on."

"Yes? How many Mothers have declared that? And how many have done it? Come on, Sluggos."

We kept getting into higher country. Finally, I scanned the set-up I was searching for. It was a flat-topped mountain with many hills around it. I crept up it. When I was on top, I test-beamed. Its summit was higher than any of the eminences for as far as I could reach. And I guessed that when I became adult, and had much more power, I would be able to cover a tremendous area. Meanwhile, other virgins would sooner or later be moving in and occupying the lesser hills.

As Father would have expressed it, I was on top of the world.

It happened that my little mountain was rich. The search-tendrils I grew and then sunk into the soil found many varieties of minerals. I could build from them a huge shell. The bigger the shell, the larger the Mother. The larger the Mother, the more powerful the pulse.

Moreover, I detected many large flying mobiles. Eagles, Father termed them. They would make good mates. They had sharp beaks and tearing talons.

Below, in a valley, was a stream. I grew a hollow tendril under the soil and down the mountainside until it entered the water. Then I began pumping it up to fill my stomachs.

The valley soil was good. I did what no other of our kind had ever done, what Father had taught me. My far-groping tendrils picked up seeds dropped by trees, flowers, and birds and planted them. I spread an underground net of tendrils around an apple tree. But I didn't plan on passing the tree's fallen fruit from tendril-frond to frond and so on up the slope and into my iris. I had a different destination in mind for them.

Meanwhile, my sisters had topped two hills much lower than mine. When I found out what they were doing, my nerves quivered. Both had built shells! One was glass; the other, cellulose!

"What do you think you're doing? Aren't you afraid of the olfway?"

"Pulse away, old grouch. Nothing's the matter with us. We're just ready for winter and mating-heat, that's all. We'll be Mothers, then, and you'll still be growing your big old shell. Where'll your prestige be? The others won't even pulse with you 'cause you'll still be a virgin and a half-shelled one at that!"

"Brittlehead! Woodenhead!"

"Yah! Yah! Hardhead!"

They were right—in a way. I was still soft and naked and helpless, an evergrowing mass of quivering flesh, a ready prey to any meat-eating mobile that found me. I was a fool and a gambler. Nevertheless, I took my leisure and sunk my tendrils and located ore and sucked up iron particles in suspension and built an inner shell larger, I think, than Grandmother's. Then I laid a thick sheath of copper over that so the iron wouldn't rust. Over that I grew a layer of bone made out of calcium I'd extracted from limestone rocks. Nor did I bother, as my sisters had done, to resorb my virgin's stalk and grow an adult one. That could come later.

Just as fall was dying, I finished my shells. Body-changing and growing began. I ate from my crops, and I had much meat, too, because I'd put up little cellulose latticework shells in the valley and raised many mobiles from the young that my far-groping tendrils had plucked from their nests.

I planned my structure with an end in mind. I grew my stomach much broader and deeper than usual. It was not that I was overly hungry. It was for a purpose, which I shall transmit to you later, dearie.

My stew-stomach was also much closer to the top of my shell than it is in most of us. In fact, I intentionally shifted my brain from the top to one side and raised the stomach in its place. Father had informed me I should take advantage of my ability to partially direct the location of my adult organs. It took me time, but I did it just before winter came.

Cold weather arrived.

And the olfway.

He came as he always does, his long nose with its retractable antennae sniffing out the minute encrustations of pure minerals that we virgins leave on our trails. The olfway follows his nose to wherever it will take him. This time it led him to my sister who had built her shell of glass. I had suspected she would be the first to be contacted by an olfway. In fact, that was one of the reasons I had chosen a hilltop further up the line. The olfway always takes the nearest shell.

When sister Glasshead detected the terrible mobile, she sent out wild pulse after pulse.

"What will I do? Do? *Do?*"

"Sit tight, sister, and hope."

Such advice was like feeding on cold stew, but it was the best, and the only, that I could give. I did not remind her that she should have followed my example, built a triple shell, and not been so eager to have a good time by gossiping with others.

The olfway prowled about, tried to dig underneath her base, which was on solid rock, and failed. He did manage to knock off a chunk of glass as a sample. Ordinarily, he would then have swallowed the sample and gone off to pupate. That would have given my sister a season of rest before he returned to attack. In the meanwhile, she might have built another coating of some other material and frustrated the monster for another season.

It just so happened that that particular olfway had, unfortunately for sister, made his last meal on a Mother whose covering had also been of glass. He retained his special organs for dealing with such mixtures of silicates. One of them was a huge and hard ball of some material on the end of his very long tail. Another was an acid for weakening the glass. After he had dripped that over a certain area, he battered her shell with the ball. Not long before the first snowfall he broke through her shield and got to her flesh.

Her wildly alternating beams and broadcasts of panic and terror still bounce around in my nerves when I think of them. Yet I must admit my reaction was tinged with contempt. I do not think she had even taken the trouble to put boron oxide in her glass. If she had, she might . . .

What's that? How dare you interrupt? . . . Oh, very well, I accept your humble apologies. Don't let it happen again, dearie. As for what you wanted to know, I'll describe later the substances that Father termed silicates and boron oxides and such. After my story is done.

To continue: the killer, after finishing Glasshead off, followed his nose along her trail back down the hill to the junction. There he had his choice of my other sister's trail or of mine. He decided on hers.

Again he went through his pattern of trying to dig under her, crawling over her, biting off her pulse-stalks, and then chewing a sample of shell.

Snow fell. He crept off, sluggishly scooped a hole, and crawled in for the winter.

Sister Woodenhead grew another stalk. She exulted, "He found my shell too thick! He'll never get me!"

Ah, sister, if only you had received from Father and not spent so much time playing with the other Sluggos. Then you would have remembered what he taught. You would have known that an olfway, like us, is different from most creatures. The majority of beings have functions that depend upon their structures. But the olfway, that nasty creature, has a structure that depends upon his functions.

I did not quiver her nerves by telling her that, now that he had secreted a sample of her cellulose-shell in his body, he was pupating around it. Father had informed me that some arthropods follow a life-stage that goes from egg to larva to pupa to adult. When a caterpillar pupates in its cocoon, for instance, practically its whole body dissolves, its tissues disintegrate. Then something reforms the pulpy whole into a structurally new creature with new functions, the butterfly.

The butterfly, however, never repupates. The olfway does. He parts company with his fellow arthropods in this peculiar ability. Thus, when he tackles a Mother, he chews off a tiny bit of the shell and goes to sleep with it. During a whole season, crouched in his den, he dreams around the sample—or his body does. His tissues melt and then coalesce. Only his nervous system remains intact, thus preserving the memory of his identity and what he has to do when he emerges from his hole.

So it happened. The olfway came out of his hole, nested on top of sister Woodenhead's dome, and inserted a modified ovipositor into the hole left by biting off her stalk. I could more or less follow his plan of attack, because the winds quite often blew my way, and I could sniff the chemicals he was dripping.

He pulped the cellulose with a solution of something or other, soaked it in some caustic stuff, and then poured on an evil-smelling fluid that boiled and bubbled. After that had ceased its violent action, he washed some more caustic on the enlarging depression and finished by blowing out the viscous solution through a tube. He repeated the process many times.

Though my sister, I suppose, desperately grew more cellulose, she was not fast enough. Relentlessly, the olfway widened the hole. When it was large enough, he slipped inside.

End of sister . . .

The whole affair of the olfway was lengthy. I was busy, and I gained time by something I had made even before I erected my dome. This was the false trail of encrustations that I had laid, one of the very things my sisters had mocked. They did not understand what I was doing when I then back-tracked, a process which took me several days, and concealed with dirt my real track. But if they had lived, they would have comprehended. For the olfway turned off the genuine trail to my summit and followed the false.

Naturally, it led him to the edge of the cliff. Before he could check his swift pace, he fell off.

Somehow, he escaped serious injury and scrambled back up to the spurious path. Reversing, he found and dug up the cover over the actual tracks.

That counterfeit path was a good trick, one my Father taught me. Too bad it hadn't worked, for the monster came straight up the mountain, heading for me, his antennae ploughing up the loose dirt and branches which covered my encrustations.

However, I wasn't through. I had collected a number of large rocks and cemented them into one large boulder. The boulder itself was poised on the edge of the summit. Around its middle I had deposited a ring of iron, grooved to fit a rail of the same mineral. This rail led from the boulder to a point half-way down the slope. Thus, when the mobile reached that ridge of iron and followed it up the slope, I removed with my tentacles the little rocks that kept the boulder from toppling over the edge of the summit.

My weapon rolled down its track with terrific speed. I'm sure it would have crushed the olfway if he had not felt the rail vibrating with his nose. He sprawled aside. The boulder rushed by, just missing him.

Though disappointed, I did get another idea to deal with future olfways. If I deposited two rails half-way down the slope, one on each side of the main line, and sent three boulders down at the same time, the monster could leap aside from the centre, either way, and still get it on the nose!

He must have been frightened, for I didn't pip him for five warm-periods after that. Then he came back up the rail, not, as I had expected, up the opposite if much steeper side of the mountain. He was stupid, all right.

I want to pause here and explain that the boulder was my idea, not Father's. Yet I must add that it was Father, not Mother, who started me thinking original thoughts. I know it quivers all your nerves to think that a mere mobile, good for nothing but food and mating, could not only be semantic but could have a higher degree of semanticism.

I don't insist he had a higher quality. I think it was different, and that I got some of that difference from him.

To continue, there was nothing I could do while the olfway prowled about and sampled my shell. Nothing except hope. And hope, as I found out, isn't enough. The mobile bit off a piece of my shell's outer bone covering. I thought he'd be satisfied, and that, when he returned after pupating, he'd find the second sheath of copper. That would delay him until another season. Then he'd find the iron and have to retire again. By then he would be so frustrated he'd give up and go searching for easier prey.

I didn't know that an olfway never gives up and is very thorough. He spent days digging around my base and uncovered a place where I'd been careless in sheathing. All three elements of the shell could be detected. I knew the weak spot existed, but I hadn't thought he'd go that deep.

Away went the killer to pupate. When summer came, he crawled out of his hole. Before attacking me, however, he ate up my crops, upset my cage-shells and devoured the mobiles therein, dug up my tendrils and ate them, and broke off my waterpipe.

But when he picked up all the apples off my tree and consumed them, my nerves tingled. The summer before, I had transported, via my network of underground tendrils, an amount of a certain poisonous mineral to the tree. In so doing I killed the tendrils that did the work, but I succeeded in feeding to the roots minute amounts of the stuff—selenium, Father termed it. I grew more tendrils and carried more poison to the tree. Eventually, the plant was full of the potion, yet I had fed it so slowly that it had built up a kind of immunity. A kind of, I say, because it was actually a rather sickly tree.

I must admit I got the idea from one of Father's not-so-stories, tapped out in Orsemay so Mother wouldn't be vexed. It was about a mobile—a female, Father claimed, though I find the concept of a female mobile too nervequivering to dwell on—a mobile who was put into a long sleep by a poisoned apple.

The olfway seemed not to have heard of the story. All he did was retch. After he had recovered, he crawled up and perched on top of my dome. He broke off my big pulse-stalk and inserted his ovipositor in the hole and began dripping acid.

I was frightened. There is nothing more panic-striking, than being deprived of pulsing and not knowing at all what is going on in the world outside your shell. But, at the same time, his actions were what I had expected. So I tried to suppress my nervequiverings. After all, I knew the olfway would work on that spot. It was for that very reason that I had shifted my brain to one side and jacked up my oversize stomach closer to the top of my dome.

My sisters had scoffed because I'd taken so much trouble with my organs. They'd been satisfied with the normal procedure of growing into Mother-size. While I was still waiting for the water pumped up from the stream to fill my sac, my sisters had long before heated theirs and were eating nice warm stew. Meanwhile, I was consuming much fruit and uncooked meat, which sometimes made me sick. However, the rejected stuff was good for the crops, so I didn't suffer a complete loss.

As you know, once the stomach is full of water and well walled up, our body heat warms the fluid. As there is no leakage of heat except when we iris meat and vegetables in or out, the water comes to the boiling point.

Well, to pulse on with the story, when the mobile had scaled away the bone and copper and iron with his acids and made a hole large enough for his body, he dropped in for dinner.

I suppose he anticipated the usual helpless Mother or virgin, nerves numbed and waiting to be eaten.

If he did, his own nerves must have quivered. There was an iris on the upper part of my stomach, and it had been grown with the dimensions of a certain carnivorous mobile in mind.

But there was a period when I thought I hadn't fashioned the opening large enough. I had him half through, but I couldn't get his hindquarters past the lips. He was wedged in tight and clawing my flesh away in great gobbets. I was in such pain I shook my body back and forth and, I believe, actually rocked my shell on its base. Yet, despite my jerking nerves, I strained and struggled and gulped hard, oh, so hard. And finally, just when I was on the verge of vomiting him back up the hole through which he had come, which would have been the end of me, I gave a tremendous convulsive gulp and popped him in.

My iris closed. Nor, much as he bit and poured out searing acids, would I open it again. I was determined that I was going to keep this meat in my stew, the biggest piece any Mother had ever had.

Oh, he fought. But not for long. The boiling water pushed into his open mouth and drenched his breathing-sacs. He couldn't take a sample of that hot fluid and then crawl off to pupate around it.

He was through—and he was delicious.

Yes, I know that I am to be congratulated and that this information for dealing with the monster must be broadcast to everyone of us everywhere. But don't forget to pulse that a mobile was partly responsible for the victory over our ancient enemy. It may quiver your nerves to admit it, but he was.

Where did I get the idea of putting my stew-sac just below the hole the olfway always makes in the top of our shells? Well, it was like so many I had. I came from one of Father's not-so-stories, told in Orsemay. I'll pulse it sometime when I'm not so busy. After you, dearie, have learned our secret language.

I'll start your lessons now. First . . .

What's that? You're quivering with curiosity? Oh, very well, I'll give you some idea of the not-so-story, then I'll continue my lessons with this neophyte.

It's about eethay olfway and eethay eethray ittlelay igspay.

. . . Father

Chapter 1

The first mate of the *Gull* looked up from the navigation desk and pointed to the magnified figures cast upon the information screen by the spoolmike.

"If this is correct, sir, we're a hundred thousand kilometres from the second planet. There are ten planets in this system. Luckily, one is inhabitable. The second one."

He paused. Captain Tu looked curiously at him, for the man was very pale and had ironically accented the *luckily.* "Sir, the second planet must be Abatos." The captain's swarthy skin whitened to match the mate's. His mouth opened as if to form an oath, then clamped shut. At the same time his right hand made an abortive gesture towards his forehead, as if he had meant to touch it. His hand dropped.

"Very well, Mister Givens. We shall make an attempt to land. That is all we can do. Stand by for further orders." He turned away so none could see his face. "Abatos, Abatos," he murmured. He licked his dry lips and locked his hands behind his back.

Two short buzzes sounded. Midshipman Nkrumah passed his hand over an activating plate and said, "Bridge," to a plate that sprang into life and colour on the wall. A steward's face appeared.

"Sir, please inform the captain that Bishop André and Father Carmody are waiting for him in cabin 7."

Captain Tu glanced at the bridge clock and tugged at the silver crucifix that hung from his right ear. Givens, Nkrumah, and Merkalov watched him intently, though they looked to one side when their eyes met his. He smiled grimly when he saw their expressions, unlocked his hands, and straightened his back. It was as if he knew his men were depending on him to preserve a calm that would radiate confidence in his ability to get them to safety. So, for a half minute, he posed monolithic in his sky-blue uniform that had not changed since the Twenty-First Century. Though it was well known that he felt a little ridiculous when he wore it planetside, when he was on his ship he walked as a man clad in armour. If coats and trousers were archaic and seen only at costume balls or in historical stereos or on officers of interstellar vessels, they did give a sense of apartness and of glamour and helped enforce discipline. The captain must have felt as if he needed every bit of confidence and respect he could muster. Thus, the conscious striking of the pose; here was the thoughtful and unnervous skipper who was so sure of himself that he could take time to attend to social demands.

"Tell the bishop I'll be in to see him at once," he ordered the midshipman.

He strode from the bridge, passed through several corridors, and entered the small lounge. There he paused in the doorway to look the passengers over. All except the two priests were there. None of them as yet was aware that the *Gull* was not merely going through one of the many transitions from normal space to perpendicular space. The two young lovers, Kate Lejeune and Pete Masters, were sitting in one corner on a sofa, holding hands and whispering softly and every now and then giving each other looks that ached with suppressed passion. At the other end of the room Mrs. Recka sat at a table playing double solitaire with the ship's doctor, Chandra Blake. She was a tall voluptuous blonde whose beauty was spoiled by an incipient double chin and dark halfmoons under her eyes. The half-empty bottle of bourbon on the table told of the origin of her dissipated appearance; those who knew something of her personal history also knew that it was responsible for her being on the *Gull*. Separated from her husband on Wildenwooly, she was going home to her parents on the faraway world of Diveboard on the Galaxy's rim. She'd been given the choice of him or the bottle and had preferred the simpler and more transportable item. As she was remarking to the doctor when the captain entered, bourbon never criticized you or called you a drunken slut.

Chandra Blake, a short dark man with prominent cheekbones and large brown eyes, sat with a fixed smile. He was very embarrassed at her loud conversation but was too polite to leave her.

Captain Tu touched his cap as he passed the four and smiled at their greetings, ignoring Mrs. Recka's invitation to sit at her table. Then he went down a long hall and pressed a button by the door of cabin 7.

It swung open and he strode in, a tall stiff gaunt man who looked as if he were made of some dark inflexible metal. He stopped abruptly and performed the seeming miracle of bending forward. He did so to kiss the bishop's extended hand, with a lack of grace and a reluctance that took all the meaning out of the act. When he straightened up, he almost gave the impression of sighing with relief. It was obvious that the captain liked to unbend to no man.

He opened his mouth as if to give them at once the unhappy news, but Father John Carmody pressed a drink into his hand.

"A toast, captain, to a quick trip to Ygdrasil," said Father John in a low gravelly voice. "We enjoy being aboard, but we've reason for haste in getting to our destination."

"I will drink to your health and His Excellency's," said Tu in a harsh clipped voice. "As for the quick trip, I'm afraid we'll need a little prayer. Maybe more than a little."

Father Carmody raised extraordinarily thick and tufted eyebrows but said nothing. This act of silence told much about his inner reactions, for he was a man who must forever be talking. He was short and fat, about forty, with heavy jowls, a thick shock of blue-black slightly wavy hair, bright blue and somewhat bulging eyes, a drooping left eyelid, a wide thick mouth, and a long sharp rocket-shaped nose. He quivered and shook and bounced with energy; he must always be on the move lest he explode; must be turning his hand to this and that, poking his nose here and there, must be laughing and chattering; must give the impression of vibrating inside like a great tuning fork.

Bishop André, standing beside him, was so tall and still and massive that he looked like an oak turned into a man, with Carmody the squirrel that raced around at his feet. His superb shoulders, arching chest, lean belly, and calves bursting with muscle told of great strength rigidly controlled and kept at a prizefighter's peak. His features did justice to the physique; he had a large high-cheekboned head topped by a mane of lion-yellow hair. His eyes were a glowing golden-green, his nose straight and classical in profile though too narrow and pinched when seen from the front; his mouth full and red and deeply indented at the corners. The bishop, like Father John, was the darling of the ladies of the diocese of Wildenwooly, but for a different reason. Father John was fun to be around. He made them giggle and laugh and made even their most serious problems seems not insurmountable. But Bishop André made them weak-kneed when he looked into their eyes. He was the kind of priest who caused them regret that he was not available for marrying. The worst part of that was that His Excellency knew the effect he had and hated it. At times he had been downright curt and was always just a little standoffish. But no woman could long remain offended at him. Indeed, as was well known, the bishop owed some of his meteoric rise to the efforts of the ladies behind the scenes. Not that he wasn't more than capable; it was just that he'd attained his rank faster than might have been expected.

Father John poured out a drink from a wine bottle, then filled two glasses with lemonade.

"I shall drink of the wine," he said. "You, Captain, will be forced to gag down this non-alcoholic beverage because you are on duty. His Excellency, however, refuses the cup that cheers, except as a sacrament, for reasons of principle. As for me, I take a little wine for my stomach's sake."

He patted his large round paunch. "Since my belly constitutes so much of me, anything I take for it I also take for my entire being. Thus, not only my entrails benefit, but my whole body glows with good health and joy and calls for more tonic. Unfortunately, the bishop sets me such an unendurably good example, I must restrain myself to this single cup. This, in spite of the fact that I am suffering from a toothache and could dull the pain with an extra glass or two."

Smiling, he looked over the rim of his glass at Tu, who was grinning in spite of his tension, and at the bishop, whose set features and dignified bearing made him look like a lion deep in thought.

"Ah, forgive me, Your Excellency," said the padre. "I cannot help feeling that you are most immoderate in your temperance, but I should not have intimated as much. Actually, your asceticism is a model for all of us to admire, even if we haven't the strength of character to imitate it."

"You are forgiven, John," said the Bishop gravely. "But I'd prefer that you confine your raillery—for I cannot help thinking that that is what it is—to times when no one else is around. It is not good for you to speak in such a manner before others, who might think you hold your bishop in some measure of contempt."

"Now, God forgive me, I meant no such thing!" cried Carmody. "As a matter of fact, my levity is directed at myself, because I enjoy too much the too-good things of this life, and instead of putting on wisdom and holiness, add another inch to my waistline."

Captain Tu shifted uneasily, then suppressed his telltale movements. Obviously, this mention of God outside of church walls embarrassed him. Also, there just was no time to be chattering about trivial things.

"Let's drink to our good healths," he said. He gulped his ale. Then, setting the glass on the table with an air of finality as if he would never get a chance to drink again, he said, "The news I have is bad. Our translator engine cut out about an hour ago and left us stranded in normal space. The chief says he can't find a thing wrong with it, yet it won't work. He has no idea of how to start it again. He's a thoroughly competent man, and when he admits defeat, the problem is unsolvable."

There was silence for a minute. Then Father John said, "How close are we to an inhabitable planet?"

"About a hundred thousand kilometres," replied Tu, tugging at the silver crucifix hanging from his ear. Abruptly realizing that he was betraying his anxiety, he let his hand fall to his side.

The padre shrugged his shoulders. "We're not in free fall, so there's nothing wrong with our interplanetary drive. Why can't we set down on this planet?"

"We're going to try to. But I'm not confident of our success. The planet is Abatos."

Carmody whistled and stroked the side of his long nose. André's bronzed face paled.

The little priest set down his glass and made a moue of concern.

"That is bad." He looked at the bishop. "May I tell the captain why we're so concerned about getting to Ygdrasil in a hurry?"

André nodded, his eyes downcast as if he were thinking of something that concerned the other two not at all.

"His Excellency," said Carmody, "left Wildenwooly for Ygdrasil because he thought he was suffering from hermit fever."

The captain flinched but did not step back from his position close to the bishop. Carmody smiled and said, "You needn't worry about catching it. He doesn't have it. Some of his symptoms matched those of hermit fever, but an examination failed to disclose any microbes. Not only that, His Excellency didn't develop a *typical* antisocial behaviour. But the doctors decided he should go to Ygdrasil, where they have better facilities than those on Wildenwooly, which is still rather primitive, you know. Also, there's a Doctor Ruedenbach there, a specialist in epileptoid diseases. It was thought best to see him, as His Excellency's condition was not improving."

Tu held out his palms in a gesture of helplessness.

"Believe me, Your Excellency, this news saddens me and makes me regret even more this accident. But there is nothing. . . ."

André came out of his reverie. For the first time he smiled, a slow, warm, and handsome smile. "What are my troubles compared to yours? You have the responsibility of this vessel and its expensive cargo. And, far more important, the welfare of twenty-five souls."

He began pacing back and forth, speaking in his vibrant voice.

"We've all heard of Abatos. We know what it may mean if the translator doesn't begin working again. Or if we meet the same fate as those other ships that tried to land on it. We're about eight light years from Ygdrasil and six from Wildenwooly, which means we can't get to either place in normal drive. We either get the translator started or else land. Or remain in space until we die."

"And even if we are allowed to make planetfall," said Tu, "we may spend the rest of our lives on Abatos."

A moment later, he left the cabin. He was halted by Carmody, who had slipped out after him.

"When are you going to tell the other passengers?"

Tu looked at his watch.

"In two hours. By then we'll know whether or not Abatos will let us pass. I can't put off telling them any longer, because they'll know something's up. We should have been falling to Ygdrasil by now."

The bishop is praying for us all now," said Carmody. "I shall concentrate my own request on an inspiration for the engineer. He's going to need it.

"There's nothing wrong with that translator," said Tu flatly, "except that it won't work."

Carmody looked shrewdly at him from under his thatched eyebrows and stroked the side of his nose.

"You think it's not an accident that the engine cut out?"

"I've been in many tough spots before," replied Tu, "and I've been scared. Yes, scared. I wouldn't tell any man except you—or maybe some other priest—but I have been frightened. Oh, I know it's a weakness, maybe even a sin . . ."

Here Carmody raised his eyebrows in amazement and perhaps a little awe of such an attitude

". . . but I just couldn't seem to help it, though I swore that I'd never again feel that way, and I never allowed anyone to see it. My wife always said that if I'd allow myself now and then to show a little weakness, not much, just a little . . . Well, perhaps that may have been why she left me, I don't know, and it doesn't really matter any more, except . . ."

Suddenly realizing that he was wandering, the captain stopped, visibly braced himself, squared his shoulders, and said, "Anyway, Father, this set-up scares me worse than I've ever been scared. Why, I couldn't exactly tell you. But I've a feeling that something caused that cut-out and for a purpose we won't like when we find out. All I have to base my reasoning on is what happened to those other three ships. You know, everybody's read about them, how the *Hoyle* landed and was never heard of again, how the *Priam* investigated its disappearance and couldn't get any closer than fifty kilometres because her normal space drive failed, and how the cruiser *Tokyo* tried to bull its way in with its drive dead and only escaped because it had enough velocity to take it past the fifty kilo limit. Even so, it almost burned up when it was going through the stratosphere."

"What I cant understand," said Carmody, "is how such an agent could affect us while we're in translation. Theoretically, we don't even exist in normal space then."

Tu tugged at the crucifix. "Yes, I know. But we're *here*. Whatever did this has a power unknown to man. Otherwise it wouldn't be able to pinpoint us in translation so close to Its home planet."

Carmody smiled cheerfully. "What's there to worry about? If it can haul us in like fish in a net, it must want us to land. So we don't have to fret about planetfall."

Suddenly he grimaced with pain. "This rotten molar of mine," he explained. "I was going to have it pulled and a bud put in when I got to Ygdrasil. And I'd sworn to quit eating so much of the chocolate of which I'm perilously overfond and which has already cost me the loss of several teeth. And now I must pay for my sins, for I was in such a hurry I forgot to bring along any painkiller, except for the wine. Or was that a Freudian slip?"

"Doctor Blake will have pain pills."

Carmody laughed. "So he does! Another convenient oversight! I'd hoped to confine myself to the natural medicine of the grape, and ignore the tasteless and enervating laboratory-born nostrums. But I have too many people looking out for my welfare. Well, such is the price of popularity."

He slapped Tu on the shoulder. "There's adventure awaiting us, Bill, Let's get going."

The captain did not seem to resent the familiarity. Evidently, he'd known Carmody for a long time.

"I wish I had your courage, Father."

"Courage!" snorted the priest. "I'm shaking in my hair shirt. But we must take what God sends us, and if we can like it, all the better."

Tu allowed himself to smile. "I like you because you can say something like that without sounding false or unctuous or—uh—priestly. I know you mean it."

"You're blessed well right I do," answered Carmody, then shifted from cheeriness to a more grave tone. "Seriously, though, Bill, I do hope we can get going soon. The bishop is in a bad way. He looks healthy, but he's liable at any moment to have an attack. If he does, I'll be pretty busy with him for a while. I can't tell you much more about him because he wouldn't want me to. Like you, he hates to confess to any weakness; he'll probably reprimand me when I go back to the cabin for having mentioned the matter to you. That's one reason why he has said nothing to Doctor Blake. When he has one of his . . . spells, he doesn't like anyone but me to take care of him. And he resents that little bit of dependency."

"It's pretty bad, then? Hard to believe. He's such a healthy-looking man; you wouldn't want to tangle with him in a scrap. He's a *good* man, too. Righteous as they make them. I remember one sermon he gave us at St. Pius' on Lazy Fair. Gave us hell and scared me into living a clean life for all of three weeks. The saints themselves must have thought they'd have to move over for me, and then . . ."

Seeing the look in Carmody's eyes, Tu stopped, glanced at his watch, and said, "Well, I've a few minutes to spare and I've not been doing as well as I might, though I suppose we all could say that, eh, Father? Could we step into your cabin? There's no telling what might happen in the next few hours and I'd like to be prepared."

"Certainly. Follow me, my son."

Chapter 2

Two hours later, Captain Tu had told crew and passengers the truth over the bridge-viser. When his voice died and his grim gaunt face faded off the screen in the lounge, he left behind him silence and stricken looks. All except Carmody sat in their chairs as if the captain's voice had been an arrow pinning them to the cushions. Carmody stood in the centre of the lounge, a soberly clad little figure in the midst of their bright clothes. He wore no rings on his ears, his legs were painted a decent black, his puffkilts were only moderately slashed, and his quilted dickie and suspenders were severe, innocent of golden spangles or jewels. Like all members of the Jairusite Order, he wore his Roman collar only when on planetside in memory of the founder and his peculiar but justified reason for doing so.

He shrewdly watched the passengers. Rocking back and and forth on his heels, his forefinger tracing the length of his nose, he seemed to be interested in the announcement only from the viewpoint of how it was affecting them. There was no sign that he was concerned about himself.

Mrs. Recka was still sitting before her cards, her head bent to study them. But her hand went out more often to the bottle, and once she upset it with a noise that made Blake and the two young lovers jump. Without bothering to get up from her chair, she allowed the fifth to spill on the floor while she rang for the steward. Perhaps the significance of the captain's words had not penetrated the haze in her brain. Or perhaps she just did not care.

Pete Masters and Kate Lejeune had not moved or spoken a word. They huddled closer, if that were possible, and squeezed hands even more tightly—pale-faced, their heads nodded like two white balloons shaken by an internal wind, Kate's red painted mouth, vivid against her bloodless skin, banging open like a gash in the sphere and by some miracle keeping the air inside her so her head did not collapse.

Carmody looked at them with pity, for he knew their story far better than they realized. Kate was the daughter of a rich "pelterpiper" on Wildenwooly. Pete was the son of a penniless "tinwoodman," one of those armoured lumberjacks who venture deep into the planet's peculiarly dangerous forests in search of wishing-wood trees. After his father had been dragged into an underwater cavern by a snoligoster, Pete had gone to work for Old Man Lejeune. That he had courage was quickly proved for it took guts to pipe the luxuriously furred but savage-tempered agropelters out of their hollow trees and conduct them into the hands of the skinners. That he was also foolhardy was almost as swiftly demonstrated for he had fallen as passionately in love with Kate as she had with him.

When he had summoned up enough bravery to ask her father for her hand—Old Man Lejeune was as vicious and quickly angered as an agropelter itself and not to be charmed by any blowing on a pipe—he had been thrown out bodily with several bruises and contusions, a slight brain concussion, and a promise that if he got within speaking distance of her again he would lose both life and limb. Then had followed the old and inevitable story. After getting out of the hospital Pete had sent Kate messages through her widowed aunt. The aunt disliked her brother and was moreover such an intense devotee of the stereo romance-serials that she would have done almost anything to smooth the path of true love.

Thus it was that a copter had suddenly dropped on to the port outside Breakneck just before the *Gull* was to take off. After identifying themselves and purchasing tickets—which was all they had to do to get passage for there were no visas or passports for human beings who wanted transportation between planets of the Commonwealth—they had entered cabin 9 next to the bishop's, and there stayed until just before the translator had broken down.

Kate's aunt had been too proud of her part as Cupid to keep her mouth shut. She'd told a half dozen friends in Breakneck after getting their solemn promises not to tell anyone. Result: Father Carmody had all the facts and some of the lies about the Masters-Lejeune affair. When the couple had slipped aboard he'd known at once what had happened and indeed was waiting for the outraged father to follow them with a band of tough skinners to take care of Pete. But the ship had flashed away, and now there was little chance they'd be met at Ygdrasil port with an order for the couple's detention. They'd be lucky if they ever arrived there.

Carmody walked to a spot before them and halted. "Don't be frightened, kids," he said. "The captain's private opinion is that we won't have any trouble landing on Abatos."

Pete Masters was a red-haired hawk-nosed youth with hollow cheeks and a too large chin. His frame was large but he'd not yet filled out with a man's muscles nor got over the slouch of the adolescent who grows too fast. He covered the delicate long-fingered hand of Kate with his big bony hand and said, glaring up at the priest, "And I suppose he'll turn us over to the authorities as soon as we land?"

Carmody blinked at the brassiness of Pete's voice and leaned slightly forward as if he were walking against the wind of it.

"Hardly," he said softly. "If there's an authority on Abatos, we haven't met him yet. But we may, we may."

He paused and looked at Kate. She was pretty and petite. Her long wheaten hair was caught up in the back with a silver circlet; her large violet eyes turned up to meet his with a mixture of guilelessness and pleading.

"Actually," said the padre, "your father can't do a thing—legally—to stop you two unless you commit a crime. Let me see, you're nineteen, aren't you, Pete? And you, Kate, are only seventeen, right? If I remember the clauses in the Free Will Act, your being under age will not hamper your moving away from your father's house without his permission. You're of mobile age. On the other hand, according to law, you're not of nubile age. Biology, I know, contradicts that, but we also live in a social world, one of manmade laws. You may not get married without your father's consent. If you try to do so, he may legally restrain you. And will, no doubt."

"He can't do a thing," said Pete, fiercely. "We're not going to get married until Kate is of age."

He glared from under straw-coloured eyebrows. Kate's paleness disappeared under a flood of red, and she looked down at her slim legs, painted canary yellow with scarlet-tipped toenails. Her free hand plucked at her Kelly-green puffkilt.

Carmody's smile remained.

"Forgive a nosy priest who is interested because he doesn't want to see you hurt. Or to have you hurt anybody. But I know your father, Kate. I know he's quite capable of carrying out his threat against Pete. Would you want to see him kidnapped, brutally beaten up, perhaps killed?"

She raised her large eyes to him, her cheeks still flaming. She was very beautiful, very young, very intense.

"Daddy wouldn't dare!" she said in a low but passionate voice. "He knows that if anything happens to Pete, I'll kill myself. I said so in the note I left him, and he knows I'm just as stubborn as he. Daddy won't hurt Pete because he loves me too much."

"Just don't bother talking to him, honey," said Pete. "I'll handle this. Carmody, we don't want any interference, well meant or not. We just want to be left alone."

Father John sighed. "To be left alone is little enough to desire. Unfortunately, or perhaps fortunately, it's one of the rarest things in this universe, almost as rare as peace of mind or genuine love for mankind."

"Spare me your clichés," said Pete. "Save them for church."

"Ah, yes, I did see you once at St. Mary's, didn't I?" replied Father John, stroking the side of his nose. "Two years ago during that outbreak of hermit fever. Hmm."

Kate put her hand on the young man's wrist. "Please, darling. He means well, and what he says is true, anyway."

"Thank you, Kate."

Carmody hesitated, then, looking thoughtful and sad, he reached into the puffkilt's pocket and pulled out a slip of yellow paper. He held it out to Kate, who took it with a trembling hand.

"This was given to the steward just before our ship took off," he said. "It was too late then for anything to be done; unless it's a matter of supreme importance, the ship's schedule is adhered to."

Kate read the message and paled again. Pete, reading over her shoulder, became red, and his nostrils flared. Tearing the paper from her, he jumped up.

"If Old Man Lejeune thinks he can jail me by accusing me of stealing his money, he's crazy!" he snarled. "He can't prove it because I didn't do it! I'm innocent, and I'll prove it by volunteering for chalarocheil! Or any truth drug they want to give me! That'll show him up for the liar he is!"

Father John's eyes widened. "Meanwhile, you two will be held, and Kate's father will take steps to get her back or at least remove her to the other end of the Galaxy. Now, I'd like to suggest . . ."

"Never mind your needlenosing suggestions," barked Pete.

He crumpled the paper and dropped it on the floor. "Come on, Kate, let's go to our cabin."

Submissively, she rose, though she shot a look at Pete as if she'd like to express her opinion. He ignored it.

"Do you know," he continued, "I'm glad we're being forced to land on Abatos. From what I've read, the *Tokyo* determined that it's a habitable planet, perhaps another Eden. So Kate and I ought to be able to live fairly easy on it. I've got my Powerkit in my cabin; with it we can build a cabin and till the soil and hunt and fish and raise our children as we wish. And there'll be no interference from anyone—no one at all."

Father John cocked his head to one side and let his left eyelid droop. "Adam and Eve, heh? Won't you two become rather lonely? Besides, how do you know what dangers Abatos holds?"

"Pete and I need nobody else," replied Kate quietly. "And no interference from anyone—no one at all."

"Except your father."

But the two were walking away hand in hand; they might not have heard him.

He leaned over to pick up the paper, grunting as he did so. Straightening up with a sigh, he smoothed it out and read it.

Doctor Blake rose from the table and approached him. He smiled with a mixture of affability and reproach.

"Aren't you being a little bit too officious?"

Carmody smiled. "You've known me for a long time, Chandra. You know that this long sharp nose of mine is an excellent sign of my character, and that I would not put my hand in the flame to deny that I am a needlenosing busybody. However, my excuse is that I am a priest and that that is a professional attribute. No escaping it. Moreover, I happen to be interested in those kids; I want them to get out of this mess without being hurt."

"You're likely to get the shape of your nose changed. That Pete looks wild enough to swing on you."

Father John rubbed the end of his nose. "Won't be the first time it's been busted. But I doubt if Pete'd hit me. One good thing about popping off if you're a priest. Even the roughest hesitate about hitting you. Almost like striking a woman. Or God's representative. Or both. We cowards sometimes take advantage of that."

Blake snorted. "Coward?" Then, "Kate's not even of your religion, Father, and Pete might as well not be."

Carmody shrugged and spread his palms out as if to show that his hands were for anybody who needed them. A few minutes later, he was pressing the buzzer by the bishop's door. When he heard no answering voice, he turned as if to go, then stopped, frowning. Abruptly, as if obeying an inner warning, he pushed in on the door. Unlocked, it swung open. He gasped and ran into the room.

The bishop was lying face up on the middle of the floor, his arms and legs extended crucifix-wise, his back arched to form a bow, his eyes open and fixed in a stare at a point on the ceiling. His face was flushed and glistening with sweat; his breath hissed; bubbles of foam escaped from his lax mouth. Yet there was nothing of the classic seizure about him, for the upper part of his body seemed to be immobile, almost as if it were formed of wax just on the verge of melting from some internal heat. The lower part, on the contrary, was in violent movement. His legs thrashed and his pelvis stabbed upwards. He looked as if a sword had cut an invisible path through the region of his abdomen and severed the nerves and muscles that connected the two halves. The trunk had cast off the hips and legs and said, "What you do is no concern of mine."

Carmody closed the door and hastened to do that which needed doing for the bishop.

Chapter 3

The *Gull* chose to settle upon a spot in the centre of the only continent of Abatos, a globe-encircling mass large as Africa and Asia put together, all of it in the northern hemisphere.

"Best landing I ever made," said Tu to his first mate. "Almost as if I were a machine, I set her down so easy." Aside, he muttered, "Perhaps I've saved the best for the last."

Carmody did not come from the bishop's cabin until twenty-four hours later. After telling the doctor and the captain that André was resting quietly and did not wish to be disturbed, Carmody asked what they'd found out so far. Obviously, he'd been eaten up with curiosity while locked in the cabin, for he had a hundred questions ready and could not fire them out fast enough.

They could tell him little, though their explorations had covered much territory. The climate seemed to be about what you'd find in midwest America in May. The vegetation and animal life paralleled those of Earth, but of course there were many unfamiliar species.

"Here's something strange," said Doctor Blake. He picked up several thin disks, cross-sections of trees, and handed them to the priest. "Pete Masters cut these with his Powerkit. Apparently he's been looking for the best kind of wood with which to build a cabin—or maybe I should say a mansion; he has some rather grandiose ideas about what he's going to do here. Notice the grain and the distance between the rings. Perfect grain. And the rings are separated by exactly the same length. Also, no knots or worm-holes of any kind.

"Pete pointed out these interesting facts, so we cut down about forty trees of different types with the ship's Survival Kit saw. And all specimens showed the same perfection. Not only that, but the number of rings, plus the Mead method of photostatic dating, proved that every tree was exactly the same age. All had been planted ten thousand years ago!'

"The only comment I could make would be an understatement,"

said Carmody. "Hmmm. The even spacing of the growth rings would indicate that the seasons, if any, follow a regular pattern, that there have been no irregular stretches of wetness and dryness but a static allotment of rain and sunshine. But these woods are wild and untended. How account for the lack of damage from parasites? Perhaps there are none."

"Don't know. Not only that, the fruit of these trees is very large and tasty and abundant—all looking as if they'd come from stock carefully bred and protected. Yet we've seen no signs of intelligent life."

Blake's black eyes sparkled, and his hands seesawed with excitement.

"We took the liberty of shooting several animals so we could examine them. I did a fast dissection on a small zebra-like creature, a wolf with a long copper-coloured snout, a yellow red-crested corvine, and a kangarooish non-marsupial. Even my hasty study turned up several astonishing facts, though one of them could have been determined by any layman."

He paused, then burst out, "All were females! And the dating of their bones indicated that they, like the trees, were ten thousand years old!"

Father John's tufted eyebrows could rise no higher; they looked like untidy wings flapping heavily with a freight of amazement.

"Yes, we've detected no males at all among any of the millions of beasts that we've seen. Not a one. All, all females!"

He took Carmody's elbow and escorted him towards the wood.

"Ten thousand years old the skeletons were. But that wasn't all that was marvellous about them. Their bones were completely innocent of evolutionary vestiges, were perfectly functional. Carmody, you're an amateur paleontologist, you should know how unique that is. On every planet where we've studied fossil and contemporary skeletons, we've found that they display tag-ends of bones that have degenerated in structure because of loss of function. Consider the toes of a dog, the hoofs of a horse. The dog, you might say, walks on his fingers and has lost his big toe and reduced his thumb to a small size. The horse's splint bones were once two toes, the hoof representing the main toe that hardened and on which the fossil horse put his main weight. But this zebra had no splint bones, and the wolf showed no vestiges of toes that had lost their function. The same with the other creatures I studied. Functionally perfect."

"But, but," said Father John, "you know that evolution on other planets doesn't follow exactly the same pattern laid down on Earth. Moreover, the similarity between a terrestrial and a non-terrestrial type may be misleading. As a matter of fact, likenesses between Earth types may be deceiving. Look how the isolated Australian marsupials developed parallels to placentals. Though not at all related to the higher mammals of the other continents, they evolved dog-like, mouse-like, mole-like, and bear-like creatures."

"I'm quite aware of that," replied Blake, a little stiffly. "I'm no ignoramus, you know. There are other factors determining my opinion, but you talk so much you've given me no chance to tell you."

Carmody had to laugh. "I? Talk? I've hardly got in a word. Never mind. I apologize for my gabbiness. What else is there?"

"Well, I had some of the crewmen do some looking around. They brought in hundreds of specimens of insects, and of course I'd no time for anything except a hasty glance. But there were none with any correspondence to larval forms as we know them on Earth. All adult forms. When I thought of that, I realized something else we'd all seen but hadn't been impressed by, mostly, I suppose, because the deductions were too overwhelming or because we just weren't looking for such a thing. We saw no young among the animals."

"Puzzling, if not frightening," said Carmody. "You may release my elbow, if you wish. I'll go with you willingly. Which reminds me, where are you taking me?"

"Here!"

Blake stopped before a redwoodish tree towering perhaps two hundred feet. He indicated a very large hole in the trunk, about two feet from the ground. "This cavity is not the result of disease or damage by some animal. It obviously is part of the tree's structure."

He directed the beam of a flashlight into the dark interior. Carmody stuck his head into the hole and after a moment withdrew it, looking thoughtful.

"There must be about ten tons of that jelly-like substance inside," he said. "And there are bones embedded deep within it."

"Wherever you go, you find these jelly trees, as we now call them," said Blake. "About half of them hold animal skeletons."

"What are they? A sort of Venusian fly-trap?" asked the priest, involuntarily taking a backward step. "No, they couldn't be that, or you'd not have allowed me to stick my head in. Or does it, like many men, find theological subjects distasteful?"

Blake laughed, then sobered quickly.

"I've no idea *why* these bones are there nor what purpose the jelly serves," he said. "But I can tell you *how* they got there. You see, while we were flying around, mapping and observing, we witnessed several killings by the local carnivora. There are two types we were glad we didn't run into on the ground, though we've means to repel them if we see them soon enough. One's a cat about the size of a Bengal tiger, leopard-like except for big round ears and tufts of grey fur on the backs of its legs. The other's a ten-foot-high black-furred mammal built like a tyrannosaurus with a bear's head. Both prey on the zebras and the numerous deer and antelope. You'd think that their fleet-footed prey would keep the killers swift and trim, but they don't. The big cats and the struthiursines are the fattest and laziest meateaters you ever saw. When they attack, they don't sneak up through the grass and then make a swift but short run. They walk boldly into view, roar a few times, wait until the majority of the herd have dashed off, then select one from the several submissive animals that have refused to flee, and kill it. Those that have been spared then drift off. They're not frightened by the sight of the killer devouring one of their sisters. No, they just appear uneasy.

"As if that weren't extraordinary enough, the sequel positively astounds you. After the big killer has gorged himself and leaves, the small carrion-eaters then descend, yellowish crows and brown-and-white foxes. The bones are well cleaned. But they aren't left to bleach in the sun. Along comes a black ape with a long lugubrious face—the undertaker ape, we call him—and he picks the bones up and deposits them in the jelly inside the nearest jelly tree. Now, what do you think of that?"

"I think that, though it's a warm day, I have a sudden chill. I . . . oh, there's His Excellency. Excuse me."

The priest hurried across the daisy-starred meadow, a long black case in his hand. The bishop did not wait for him but stepped from the shadow of the ship into the light. Though the yellow sun had risen only an hour ago above the purplish mountains to the east, it was very bright. When it struck the bishop's figure, it seemed to burst into flame around him and magnify him, almost as if its touch were that of a golden god imparting some of his own magnificence to him. The illusion was made all the stronger by the fact that André showed no signs of his recent illness. His face glowed, and he strode swiftly towards the crowd at the forest's edge, his shoulders squared and his deep chest rising and falling as if he were trying to crowd all the planet's air into his lungs.

Carmody, who met him half-way, said, "You may well breathe this superb air, Your Excellency. It has a tang and freshness that is quite virginal. Air that has never been breathed by man before."

André looked about him with the slowness and sure majesty of a lion staking out a new hunting territory. Carmody smiled slightly. Though the bishop made a noble figure of a man, he gave at that moment just the hint of a poseur, so subtle that only one with Carmody's vast experience could have detected it. André, catching the fleeting indentations at the corners of the little priest's lips, frowned and raised his hands in protest

"I know what you are thinking."

Carmody bent his neck to gaze at the bright green grass at their feet. Whether he did so to acknowledge that the reprimand was just or to hide another emotion, he managed to veil his eyes. Then, as if realizing it was not good to conceal his thoughts, he raised his head to look his bishop in the eyes. His gesture was similar to André's and had dignity but none of the other man's beauty, for Carmody could never look beautiful, except with the more subtle beauty that springs from honesty.

"I hope you can forgive me, Your Excellency. But old habits die hard. Mockery was so long a part of me before I was converted—indeed, was a necessity if one was to survive on the planet where I lived, which was Dante's Joy, you know—that it dug deep into my nervous system. I believe that I am making a sincere effort to overcome the habit: but, being human, I am sometimes lax."

"We must strive to be more than human," replied André, making a gesture with his hand which the priest, who knew him well, interpreted as a sign to drop the subject. It was not peremptory, for he was always courteous and patient. His time was not his; the lowliest were his masters. Had Carmody persisted in dwelling on that line of thought, he would have allowed it. The priest, however, accepted his superior's decision.

He held out a slender black case six feet long.

"I thought that perhaps Your Excellency would like to try the fishing here. It may be true that Wildenwooly has a Galaxy-wide reputation for the best fishing anywhere, but there's something about the very looks of Abatos that tells me we'll find fish here to put a glow in our hearts—not to mention a whale of an appetite in our mouths. Would you care to try a few casts? It might benefit Your Excellency."

André's smile was slow and gentle, ending in a huge grin of delight. "I'd like that very much, John. You could have suggested nothing better."

He turned to Tu. "Captain?"

"I think it'll be safe. We've sent out survey copters. They reported some large carnivores but none close. However, some of the herbivores may be dangerous. Remember, even a domestic bull may be a killer. The copter crews did try to get some of the larger beasts to charge and failed. The animals either ignored them or ambled away. Yes, you may go fishing, though I wish the lake weren't so far off. What about a copter dropping you off there and picking you up later?"

André said, "No thank you. We can't get the feel of this planet by flying over it. "We'll walk."

The first mate held out two pistols of some sort.

"Here you are, Reverends. Something new. Sonos. Shoots a subsonic beam that panics man or beast, makes 'em want to get to hell and away as fast as they can, if you'll pardon the expression."

"Of course. But we can't accept them. Our order is never permitted to carry arms, for any reason."

"I wish you'd break the rule this time," said Tu. "Rules aren't made to be broken; no captain would subscribe to that proverb. But there are times when you have to consider their context."

"Absolutely not," replied the bishop, looking keenly at Carmody, who'd stretched out his hand as if to take a sono.

At the glance, the priest dropped his hand. "I merely wished to examine the weapon," said Carmody. "But I must admit I've never thought much of that rule. It's true that Jairus had his peculiar power over beasts of prey. However, that fact didn't necessarily endow his disciples with a similar gift. Think of what happened on Jimdandy because St. Victor refused a gun. Had he used one, he'd have saved a thousand lives."

The bishop closed his eyes and murmured so that only Carmody could hear. "*Even though I walk in the dark valley . . .*"

Carmody murmured back, "But the dark is sometimes cold, and the hairs on the back of the neck rise with fear, though I become hot with shame."

"Hmm. Speaking of shame, John, you always manage, somehow, while deprecating yourself, to leave me discomfited and belittled. It's a talent which, perhaps, should be possessed by the man who is most often with me, for it cuts down my inclination to grow proud. On the other hand . . ."

Carmody waved the long case in his hand. "On the other hand, the fish may not wait for us."

André nodded and began walking towards the woods. Tu said something to a crewman, who ran after the two priests and gave the little one a ship-finder, a compass that would always point in the *Gull*'s direction. Carmody flashed a grin of thanks and, shoulders set jauntily, bounced after the swiftly striding bishop, the case whipping behind him like a saucy antenna. He whistled an old old tune—"My Buddy." Though seemingly carefree, his eyes looked everywhere. He did not fail to see Pete Masters and Kate Lejeune slipping hand in hand into the woods in another direction. He stopped in time to keep from bumping into the bishop, who had turned and was frowning back towards the ship. At first Carmody thought he, too, had noticed the young couple, then saw he was gazing at Mrs. Recka and First Mate Givens. They were standing to one side and talking very intensely. Then they began walking slowly across the meadow towards the towering hemisphere of the *Gull*. André stood motionless until the couple went into the ship and, a moment later, came out. This time Mrs. Recka had her pocketbook, a rather large one whose size was not enough to conceal the outlines of a bottle within. Still talking, the two went around the curve of the vessel and presently came into sight of the priests again, though they could not be seen by Tu or the crew members.

Carmody murmured, "Must be something in the air of this planet . . ."

"What do you mean by that?" said the bishop, his features set very grim, his green eyes narrowed but blazing.

"If this is another Eden, where the lion lies down with the lamb, it is also a place where a man and woman . . ."

"If Abatos is fresh and clean and innocent," growled the bishop, "it will not remain so very long. Not while we have people like those, who would foul any nest."

"Well, you and I will have to content ourselves with fishing."

"Carmody, don't grin when you say that! You sound almost as if you were blessing them instead of condemning!"

The little priest lost his half-smile. "Hardly. I was neither condemning nor blessing. Nor judging them beforehand, for I don't actually know what they have in mind. But it is true that I have too wide a streak of the earth earthy, a dabble of Rabelais, perhaps. It's not that I commend. It's just that I understand too well, and . . ."

Without replying, the bishop turned away violently and resumed his longlegged pace. Carmody, somewhat subdued, followed at his heels, though there was often room enough for the two to walk side by side. Sensitive to André's moods, he knew that it was best to keep out of his sight for a while. Meanwhile, he'd interest himself in his surroundings.

The copter survey crews had reported that between the mountains to the east and the ocean to the west the country was much alike: a rolling, sometimes hilly land with large prairies interspersed with forests. The latter seemed more like parks than untamed woods. The grass was a succulent kind kept cropped by the herbivores; many of the trees had their counterparts among the temperate latitudes of Earth; only here and there were thick tangled stretches that might properly be called wild. The lake towards which the two were headed lay in the centre of just such a "jungle." The widely spaced oaks, pines, cypresses, beeches, sycamores, and cedars here gave way to an island of the jelly-containing redwoods. Actually, they did not grow close together but gave that impression because of the many vines and lianas that connected them and the tiny parasitic trees, like evergreens, that grew horizontally out of cracks in their trunks.

It was darker under these great vegetation-burdened limbs, though here and there shafts of sunlight slanted, seeming like solid and leaning trunks of gold themselves. The forest was alive with the colour and calls of bright birds and the dark bodies and chitterings of arboreal animals. Some of these looked like monkeys; when they leapt through the branches and came quite close, the resemblance was even more amazing. But they were evidently not sprung from a proto-simian base; they must have been descended from a cat that had decided to grow fingers instead of claws and to assume a semi-upright posture. Dark brown on the back, they had grey-furred bellies and chests and long prehensile tails tufted at the end with auburn. Their faces had lost the pointed beastish look and become flat as an ape's. Three long thick feline whiskers bristled from each side of their thin lips. Their teeth were sharp and long, but they picked and ate a large pear-shaped berry that grew on the vines. Their slitted pupils expanded in the shade and contracted in the sunlit spaces. They chattered among themselves and behaved in general like monkeys, except that they seemed to be cleaner.

"Perhaps they've cousins who evolved into humanoid beings," said Carmody aloud, partly because he'd the habit of talking to himself, partly to see if the bishop were out of his mood.

"Heh?" said André, stopping and also looking at the creatures, who returned his gaze just as curiously. "Oh, yes, Sokoloff's Theory of the Necessary Chance. Every branch of the animal kingdom as we know it on Earth seems to have had its opportunity to develop into a sentient being some place in the Galaxy. The vulpoids of Kubeia, the avians of Albireo IV, the cetaceoids of Oceanos, the molluscs of Baudelaire, the Houyhnhnms of Somewhere Else, the so-called lying bugs of Münchausen, the . . . well, I could go on and on. But on almost every Earth-type planet we find that this or that line of life seized the evolutionary chance given by God and developed intelligence. All, with some exceptions, going through an arboreal simian stage and then flowering into an upright creature resembling man."

"And all thinking of themselves as being in God's image, even the porpoise-men of Oceanos and the land-oysters of Baudelaire," added Carmody. "Well, enough of philosophy. At least, fish are fish, on any planet."

They had come out of the forest on to the lake shore. It was a body of water about a mile wide and two long, fed by a clear brook to the north. Grass grew to the very edge, where little frogs leaped into the water at their approach. Carmody uncased their two rods but disengaged the little jet mechanisms that would have propelled their bait-tipped lines far out over the lake.

"Really not sporting," he said. "We ought to give these foreign piscines a chance, eh?"

"Right," replied the bishop, smiling. "If I can't do anything with my own right arm, I'll go home with an empty basket."

"I forgot to bring along a basket, but we can use some of those broad leaves of the vines to wrap our catch in."

An hour later they were forced to stop because of the pile of finny life behind them, and these were only the biggest ones, The rest had been thrown back. André had hooked the largest, a magnificent trout of about thirty pounds, a fighter who took twenty minutes to land. After that, sweating and breathing hard but shining-eyed, he said, "I'm hot. What do you say to a swim, John?"

Carmody smiled at the use of his familiar name again and shouted, "Last one in is a Sirian!"

In a minute two naked bodies plunged into the cold clear waters at exactly the same time. When they came up, Carmody sputtered, "Guess we're both Sirians, but you win, for I'm the ugliest. Or does that mean that I win?"

André laughed for sheer joy, then sped across the lake in a fast crawl. The other did not even try to follow him but floated on his back, eyes closed. Once he raised his head to determine how the bishop was getting along but lay back when he saw that he was in no trouble. André had reached the other shore and was returning at a slower but easy pace. When he did come back and had rested for a while on the beach, he said, "John, would you mind climbing out and timing me in a dive? I'd like to see if I'm still in good form. It's about seven feet here, not too deep."

Carmody climbed on to the grassy shore, where he set his watch and gave the signal. André plunged under. When he emerged be swam back at once. "How'd I do?" he called as he waded out of the water, his magnificent body shining wet and golden brown in the late afternoon sun.

"Four minutes, three seconds," said Carmody. "About forty seconds off your record. But still better, I'll bet, than any other man in the Galaxy. You're still the champ, Your Excellency."

André nodded, smiling slightly. "Twenty years ago I set the record. I believe that if I went into rigorous training again, I could equal it again or even beat it. I've learned much since then about control of my body and mind. Even then I was not entirely at ease in the pressure and gloom of the underwater. I loved it, but my love was tinged just a little with terror. An attitude that is almost, you might say, one's attitude towards God. Perhaps too much so, as one of my parishioners was kind enough to point out to me. I think he meant that I was paying too much attention to what should have been only a diversion for my idle moments.

"He was correct, of course, though I rather resented his remarks at the time. He couldn't have known that it was an irresistible challenge to me to float beneath the bright surface, all alone, feel myself buoyed as if in the arms of a great mother, yet also feel her arms squeezing just a little too tight. I had to fight down the need to shoot to the surface and suck in life-giving air, yet I was proud because I could battle that panic, could defeat it. I felt always as if I was in danger but because of that very danger was on the verge of some vital discovery about myself—what, I never found out. But I always thought that if I stayed down long enough, could keep out the blackness and the threat of loss of consciousness, I would find the secret

"Strange thought, wasn't it? It led me to study the neo-Yoga disciplines which were supposed to enable one to go into suspended animation, death-in-life. There was a man on Gandhi who could stay buried alive for three weeks, but I could never determine if he was faking or not. He was some help to me, however. He taught me that if I would, as he put it, go dead here, first of all," and André touched his left breast, "then here," and he touched his loins, "the rest would follow. I could become as an embryo floating in the amniotic sac, living but requiring no breath, no oxygen except that which soaked through the cells, as he put it. An absurd theory, scientifically speaking, yet it worked to some extent. Would you believe it, I now have to force myself to rise because it seems so safe and nice and warm under there, even when the water is very cold, as in this lake?"

While he talked, he'd been wiping the water from his skin with his quilted dickie, his back turned to Carmody. The priest knew his bishop was embarrassed to expose himself. He himself, though he knew his body looked ugly and grotesque beside the other's perfect physique, was not at all ill-at-ease. In common with most of the people of his time, he'd been raised in a world where nudity on the beach and in the private home was socially accepted, almost demanded. André, born in the Church, had had a very strict upbringing by devout parents who had insisted that he follow the old pattern even in the midst of a world that mocked.

It was of that he spoke now, as if he'd guessed what Carmody was thinking.

"I disobeyed my father but once," he said. "That was when I was ten. We lived in a neighbourhood composed mainly of agnostics or members of the Temple of Universal Light. But I had some very good pals among the local gang of boys and tomboys, and just once they talked me into going swimming in the river, skin-style. Of course my father caught me; he seemed to have an instinct for detecting when sin was threatening any of his family. He gave me the beating of my life—may his soul rest in peace," he added without conscious irony.

"'Spare the rod and spoil the child' was ever his favourite maxim, yet he had to whip me just that one time in my life. Or rather, I should say twice, because I tore loose from him while he was strapping me in front of the gang, plunged into the river, and dived deep, where I stayed a long time in an effort to frighten my father into thinking I'd drowned myself. Eventually, of course, I had to come up. My father resumed the punishment. He was no more severe the second time, though. He couldn't have been without killing me. As a matter of fact, he almost did. If it weren't for modern science's ability to do away with scars, I'd still bear them on my back and legs. As it is, they're still here," and he pointed to indicate his heart.

He finished drying himself and picked up his puffkilt. "Well, that was thirty-five years ago and thousands of light-years away, and I dare say the beating did me a tremendous amount of good."

He looked at the clear sky and at the woods, arched his deep chest in a great breath, and said, "This is a wonderful and unspoiled planet, a testimony to God's love for the beauty of His creatures and His generosity in scattering them across the universe, almost as if He had had to do so! Here I feel as if God is in His heaven and all's right with the world. The symmetry and fruitfulness of those trees, the clean air and waters, the manifold songs of those birds and their bright colours . . ."

He stopped, for he suddenly realized what Carmody had just previously noticed. There were none of the noisy but melodious twitterings and chirpings and warblings nor the chattering of the monkeys. All was hush. Like a thick blanket of moss, a silence hung over the forest.

"Something's scared those animals," whispered Carmody. He shivered, though the westering sun was yet hot, and he looked around. Near them, on a long branch that extended over the lake's edge, sat a row of catmonkeys that had appeared as if from nowhere. They were grey-furred except for a broad white mark on their chests, roughly in the form of a cross. Their head-hair grew thick and forward and fell over their foreheads like a monk's cowl. Their hands were placed over their eyes in a monkey-see-no-evil attitude. But their eyes shone bright between their fingers, and Carmody, despite his sense of uneasiness, felt a prickling of laughter and murmured, "No fair peeking."

A deep cough sounded in the the forest; the monk-monks, as he'd tagged them, cowered and crowded even closer together.

What could that be?" said the bishop.

"Must be a big beast. I've heard lions cough: they sounded just like that."

Abruptly, the bishop reached out a large square hand and closed Carmody's little pudgy hand in it.

Alarmed at the look on André's face, Carmody said, "Is another seizure coming on?"

The bishop shook his head. His eyes were glazed. "No. Funny, I felt for a moment almost as I did when my father caught me."

He released the other's hand and took a deep breath. "I'll be all right."

He lifted his kilt to step into it. Carmody gasped. André jerked his head upright and gave a little cry. Something white was looming in the shadow of the trees, moving slowly but surely, the focus and cause of the silence that spread everywhere. Then it grew darker as it stepped into the sunshine and stopped for a moment, not to adjust its eyes to the dazzle but to allow the beholders to adjust their eyes to him. He was eight feet tall and looked much like a human being and moved with such dignity and such beauty that the earth seemed to give way respectfully at each footstep. He was long-bearded and naked and massively male, and the eyes were like those of a granite statue of a god that had become flesh, too terrible to look straight into.

He spoke. They knew then the origin of that cough that had come from the depth of lungs deep as an oracle's well. His voice was a lion's roar; it made the two pygmies clasp each other's hands again and unloosed their muscles so that they thought they'd come apart. Yet they did not think of how amazing it was that he should speak in their tongue.

"Hello, my sons!" he thundered.

They bowed their heads.

"Father."

Chapter 4

An hour before sunset, André and Carmody ran out of the woods. They were in a hurry because of the tremendous uproar that had aroused the forest for miles around. Men were yelling, and a woman was screaming, and something was growling loudly. They arrived just in time to see the end. Two enormous beasts, bipedal heavily-tailed creatures with bearish heads, were racing after Kate Lejeune and Pete Masters. Kate and Pete were running hand in hand, he pulling her so fast that she seemed to fly through the air with every step. In his other hand he carried his powersaw. Neither had a sono-gun with which to defend themselves, although Captain Tu had ordered that no one be without the weapon. A moment later it was seen that the gun would have made no difference, for several crewmen who had been standing by the ship had turned their sonos against the beasts. Undeterred by the panicking effects of the beams, the monsters sprang after the couple and caught them half-way across the meadow.

Though unarmed, André and Carmody ran at the things, their

fists clenched. Pete turned in his captor's grasp and struck it across the muzzle with the sharp edge of his saw. Kate screamed loudly then fainted. Suddenly, the two were lying in the grass, for the animals had dropped them and were walking almost leisurely towards the woods. That neither the sonos nor the priests had scared them off was evident. They brushed by the latter without noticing them, and if the former had affected their nervous systems at all, they gave no signs.

Carmody looked once at the young woman and yelled, "Doctor Blake! Get Blake at once!"

Like a genie summoned by the mention of his name, Blake was there with his little black kit. He at once called for a stretcher; Kate, moaning and rolling her head from side to side, was carried into the ship's hospital. Pete raged until Blake ordered him out of the room.

"I'll get a gun and kill those beasts. I'll track them down if it takes me a week. Or a year! I'll trap them and . . ."

Carmody pushed him out of the room and into the lounge, where he made the youth sit down. With a shaking hand, he lit two cigarettes.

"It would do you no good to kill them," he said. "They'd be up and around in a few days. Besides, they're just animals who were obeying their master's commands."

He puffed on his cigarette while with one hand he snapped his glow-wire lighter shut and put it back in his pocket.

"I'm just as shaken up as you. Recent events have been too fast and too inexplicable for my nervous system to take them in stride. But I wouldn't worry about Kate being hurt, if I were you. I know she looked pretty bad, but I'm sure she'll be all right and in a very short time, too."

"You blind optimistic ass!" shouted Pete. "You *saw* what happened to her!"

"She's suffering from hysterics, not from any physical effects of her miscarriage," replied Carmody calmly. "I'll bet that in a few minutes, when Blake has her calmed down with a sedative, she'll walk out of the hospital in as good a condition as she was in this morning. I know she will. You see, son, I've had a talk with a being who is not God but who convinces you that *he* is the nearest equivalent."

Pete became slack-jawed "What? What're you talking about?"

"I know I sound as if I were talking nonsense. But I've met the owner of Abatos. Or rather *he* has talked to me, and what *he* has shown the bishop and me is, to understate, staggering. There are a hundred things we'll have to let you and everybody else know in due time. Meanwhile, I can give you an idea of *his* powers. They range in terrible spectrum from such petty, but amazing, deeds as curing my toothache with a mere laying on of hands, to bringing dead bones back to life and reclothing them with flesh. I have seen the dead arise and go forth. Though, I must admit, probably to be eaten again."

Frowning, he added, "The bishop and I were permitted to perform—or should I say commit?—a resurrection ourselves. The sensation is not indescribable, but I prefer not to say anything about it at present."

Pete rose with clenched fits, his cigarette shredding under the pressure.

"You must be crazy."

"That would be nice if I were, for I'd be relieved of an awful responsibility. And if the choice were mine, I'd take incurable insanity. But I'm not to get off so easily."

Suddenly, Father John lost his calmness; he looked as if he were going to break into many pieces. He buried his face in his hands, while Pete stared, stunned. Then the priest as abruptly lowered his hands and presented once again the sharp-nosed, round and smiling features the world knew so well.

"Fortunately, the ultimate decision will not be mine but His Excellency's. And though it is cowardly to be glad because I may pass the buck on to him, I must confess that I will be glad. His is the power in this case, and though power has its glory, it also has its burdens and griefs. I wouldn't want to be in the bishop's shoes at this moment."

Pete didn't hear the priest's last words. He was gazing at the hospital door, just opening. Kate stepped out, a little pale but walking steadily. Pete ran to her; they folded each other in their arms; then she was crying.

"Are you all right, boney?" Pete kept saying over and over.

"Oh, I feel fine," she replied, still weeping. "I don't understand why, but I do. I'm suddenly healed. There's nothing wrong down there. It was as if a hand passed over me, and strength flowed out of it, and all was well with my body."

Blake, who had appeared behind her, nodded in agreement.

"Oh, Pete," sobbed Kate, "I'm all right, but I lost our baby! And I know it was because we stole that money from Daddy. It was our punishment. It was bad enough running away, though we had to do that because we loved each other. But we should never have taken that money!"

"Hush, honey, you're talking too much. Let's go to our cabin where you can rest."

Gently he directed her out of the lounge while he glared defiantly at Carmody.

"Oh, Pete," she wailed, "all that money, and now we're on a planet where it's absolutely no good at all. Only a burden."

"You talk too much, baby," said Pete, a roughness replacing the gentleness in his voice. They disappeared down the corridor. Carmody said nothing. Eyes downcast, he, too, walked to his cabin and shut the door behind him.

A half hour later, he came out and asked for Captain Tu. Told that Tu was outside, he left the *Gull* and found an attentive group at the edge of the meadow on the other side of the ship. Mrs. Recka and the first mate were the centre of attraction.

"We were sitting under one of those big jelly trees and passing the bottle back and forth and talking of this and that," said Givens. "Mostly about what we'd do if we found out we were stranded here for the rest of our lives."

Somebody snickered. Givens flushed but continued evenly.

"Suddenly, Mrs. Recka and I became very sick. We vomited violently and broke out into a cold sweat. By the time we'd emptied our stomachs, we were sure the whisky had been poisoned. We thought we'd die in the woods, perhaps never to be found, for we were quite a distance from the ship and in a rather secluded spot.

"But as suddenly as it had come, the illness went away. We felt completely happy and healthy. The only difference was, we both were absolutely certain that we'd never again want to touch a drop of whisky."

"Or any other alcoholic drink," added Mrs. Recka, shuddering.

Those who knew of her weakness gazed curiously and somewhat doubtfully at her. Carmody tapped the captain's elbow and drew him off to one side.

"Is the radio and other electronic equipment working by now?" he asked.

"They resumed operation about the time you two showed up. But the translator still refuses to budge. I was worried when you failed to report through your wrist radios. For all I knew, some beast of prey had killed you, or you'd fallen into the lake and drowned. I organized a search party, but we'd not gone half a mile before we noticed the needles on our ship-finders whirling like mad. So we returned. I didn't want to be lost in the woods, for my primary duty is to the ship, of course. And I couldn't send out a copter crew, for the copters simply refused to run. They're working all right now, though. What do you think of all this?"

"Oh, I know *who* is doing this. And *why*."

"For God's sake, man, *who*?"

"I don't know if it is for God's sake or not. . . ." Carmody glanced at his watch. "Come with me. There is someone you must meet."

"Where are we going?"

"Just follow me. *He* wants a few words with you because you are the captain, and your decision will have to be given also. Moreover, I want you to know just what we are up against."

"Who is *he*? A native of Abatos?"

"Not exactly, though *he* has lived here longer than any native creature of this planet."

Tu adjusted the angle of his cap and brushed dust flakes from his uniform. He strode through the corridors of the noisy jungle as if the trees were on parade and he were inspecting them.

"If *he* has been here longer than ten thousand years," said the captain, unconsciously stressing the personal pronoun as Carmody did, "then *he* must have arrived long before English and its descendant tongue, Lingo, were spoken, when the Aryan speech was still only the property of a savage tribe in Europe. How can we talk with him? Telepathy?"

"No. *He* learned Lingo from the survivor of the crash of the *Hoyle*, the only ship *he* ever permitted to get through."

"And where is this man?" asked Tu, annoyedly glancing at a choir of howling monkeys on an overhead branch.

"No man. A woman, a medical officer. After a year here, she committed suicide. Built a funeral pyre and burned herself to death. There was nothing left of her but ashes."

"Why?"

"I imagine because total cremation was the only way she could put herself beyond *his* reach. Because otherwise *he* might have placed her bones in a jelly tree and brought her back to life."

Tu halted. "My mind understands you, but my sense of belief is numb. Why did she kill herself when, if you are not mistaken, she had eternal life before her or at least a reasonable facsimile thereof?"

"*He*—*Father*—says that she could not endure the thought of living forever on Abatos with him as her only human, or humanoid, companion. I know how she felt. It would be like sharing the world with only God to talk to. Her sense of inferiority and her loneliness must have been overwhelming."

Carmody stopped suddenly and became lost in thought, his head cocked to one side, his left eyelid drooping.

"Hmm. That's strange. *He* said that we, too, could have *his* powers, become like *him*. Why didn't *he* teach her? Was it because *he* didn't want to share? Come to think of it, *he's* made no offer of dividing *his* dominions. Only wants substitution. Hmm. All or none. Either *he* or . . . or what?"

"What the hell are you talking about?" barked Captain Tu irritatedly.

"You may be right at that," said Carmody absently. "Look, there's a jelly tree. What do you say we do a little poking and prying, heh? It's true that *he* forbade any needlenosing on the part of us extra-Abatosians; it's true that this may be another garden of Eden and that I, a too true son of Adam, alas, may be re-enacting another fall from grace, may be driven out with flaming swords—though I wouldn't mind being expelled back to some familiar planet—may even be blasted with lightning for blaspheming against the local deity. Nevertheless, I think a little delving into the contents of that cavity may be as profitable as any dentist's work. What do you say, Captain? The consequences could be rather disastrous."

"If you mean am I afraid, all I can say is that you know better than that," growled Tu. "I'll let no priest get ahead of me in guts. Go ahead. I'll back you up all the way."

"Ah," said Carmody, walking briskly up to the foot of the enormous redwood, "ah, but you've not seen and talked to the Father of Abatos. It's not a matter of backing me up, for there's little you could do if we should be discovered. It's a matter of giving me moral courage, of shaming me with your presence so that I won't run like a rabbit if *he* should catch me red-handed."

With one hand he took a small vial out of his pocket and with the other a flashlight, whose beam he pointed into the dark O. Tu looked over his shoulder.

"It quivers, almost as if it were alive," said the captain in a low voice.

"It emits a faint humming, too. If you put your hand lightly on its surface, you can feel the vibration."

"What are those whitish things embedded in it? Bones?"

"Yes, the hollow goes rather deep, doesn't it? Must be below the surface of the ground. See that dark mass in one corner? An antelope of some sort, I'd say. Looks to me as if the flesh were being built up in layers from the inside out; the outer muscles and skin aren't re-created yet."

The priest scooped out a sample of the jelly, capped the vial, and put it back in his pocket. He did not rise but kept playing his beam over the hollow.

"This stuff really makes a Geiger counter dance. Not only that, it radiates electromagnetic waves. I think that radio waves from this jelly damped out our wrist speakers and sonos and played havoc with our ship-finders. Hey, wait a minute! Notice those very minute white threads that run through the whole mass. Nerve-like, aren't they?"

Before Carmody could protest, Tu stooped and dipped out a handful of the quivering gelatinous mass. "Do you know where I've seen something like this before? This stuff reminds me of the protein transistors we used in the translator."

Carmody frowned: "Aren't they the only living parts of the machine? Seems to me I read that the translator wont rotate the ship through perpendicular space unless these transistors are used."

"Mechanical transistors could be used," corrected Tu. "But they would occupy a space as large as the spaceship itself. Protein transistors take up very little area; you could carry the *Gull*'s on your back. Actually, that part of the translator is not only a series of transistors but a memory bank. Its function is to 'remember' normal space. It has to retain a simulacrum of real or 'horizontal' space as distinguished from perpendicular. While one end of the translator is 'flopping us over', as the phrase goes, the protein end is reconstructing an image of what the space at our destination looks like, down to the last electron. Sounds very much like sympathetic magic, doesn't it? Build an effigy, and shortly you establish an affinity between reality and counterfeit."

"What happened to the protein banks?"

"Nothing that we could tell. They functioned normally."

"Perhaps the currents aren't getting through. Did the engineer check the synapses or just take a reading on the biostatic charge of the whole? The charge could be normal, you know, yet any transmission could be locked."

"That's the engineer's province. I wouldn't dream of questioning his work, any more than he would mine."

Carmody rose. "I'd like to talk to the engineer. I've a layman's theory, but like most amateurs I may be overly enthusiastic because of my ignorance. If you don't care, I'd rather not discuss it now. Especially here, where the forest may have ears, and . . ."

Though the captain had not even opened his mouth, the priest had raised his finger for silence in a characteristic gesture. Suddenly, it was apparent that he *did* have his silence, for there was not a sound in the woods except the faint soughing of the wind through the leaves.

"*He* is around," whispered Carmody. "Throw that jelly back in, and we'll get away from this tree."

Tu raised his hand to do so. At that moment a rifle shot cracked nearby. Both men jumped. "My God, what fool's doing that?" cried Tu. He said something else, but his voice was lost in the bedlam that broke out through the woods, the shrieks of birds, the howling of monkeys, the trumpetings, neighings, and roarings of thousands of other animals. Then, as abruptly as it had begun, it stopped, almost as if by signal. Silence fell. Then, a single cry. A man's.

"It's Masters," groaned Carmody.

There was a rumble, as of some large beast growling deep in its chest. One of the leopard-like creatures with the round ears and grey tufts on its legs padded out from the brush. It held Pete Masters' dangling body between its jaws as easily as a cat holds a mouse. Paying no attention to the two men, it ran past them to the foot of an oak, where it stopped and laid the youth down before another intruder.

Father stood motionless as stone, one nailless hand resting upon his long red-gold beard, his deeply sunken eyes downcast, intent on the figure on the grass. He did not move until Pete, released from his paralysis, writhed in a passion of abjectness and called out for mercy. Then he stooped and touched the youth briefly on the back of his head. Pete leaped to his feet and, holding his head and screaming as if in pain, ran away through the trees. The leopardess remained couchant, blinking slowly like a fat and lazy housecat.

Father spoke to her. While he stalked off into the woods, she turned her green eyes upon the two men. Neither felt like testing her competence as a guard.

Father stopped under a tree overgrown with vines from which hung fat heavy pods like white hairless coconuts. Though the lowest was twelve feet high, he had no difficulty in reaching up and squeezing it in his hand. It cracked open with a loud report, and water shot from the crushed shell. Tu and Carmody paled; the captain muttered, "I'd rather tackle that big cat than him."

The giant wheeled, and, washing his hands with the water, strode towards them. "Would you like to crush coconuts in one hand too, Captain?" he thundered. "That is nothing. I can show you how you may also do that. I can tear that young beech tree out of the ground by the roots, I can speak a word to Zeda here, and she will heel like a dog. That is nothing. I can teach you the power. I can hear your whisper even at a distance of a hundred yards, as you realize by now. And I could catch you within ten seconds, even if you had a head start and I were sitting down. That is nothing. I can tell instantly where any of my daughters are on the face of Abatos, what state of health they are in, and when they've died. That is nothing. You can do the same, provided you become like that priest there. You could even raise my dead, if you had the will to be like Father John. I may take your hand and show you how you could bring life again to the dead body, though I do not care to touch you."

"For God's sake, say no," breathed Carmody. "It's enough that the bishop and I should have been exposed to that temptation."

Father laughed. Tu grabbed hold of Carmody's hand. He could not have answered the giant if he had wished, for his mouth opened and closed like a fish's out of water, and his eyeballs popped.

"There's something about his voice that turns the bowels to water and loosens the knees," said the priest, then fell silent. Father stood above them, wiping his hands on his beard. Aside from that magnificent growth and a towering roach on his head, he was absolutely bald. His pale red skin was unblemished, glowing with perfect blood beneath the thin surface. His high-bridged nose was septumless, but the one nostril was a flaring Gothic one. Red teeth glistened in his mouth; a blue-veined tongue shot out for a moment like a flame; then the black-red lips writhed and closed. All this was strange but not enough to make these star-travelled men uncomfortable. The voice and the eyes stunned them, the thunder that seemed to shake their bones so they rattled, and the black eyes starred with silver splinters. Stone come to flesh.

"Don't worry, Carmody. I will not show Tu how to raise the dead. Unlike you and André, he'd not be able to do it, anyhow. Neither would any of the others, for I've studied them, and I know. But I have need of you, Tu. I will tell you why, and when I have told you, you will see there is nothing else for you to do. I will convince you by reason, not by force, for I hate violence, and indeed am required by the nature of my being not to use it. Unless an emergency demands it."

Father talked. An hour later, he stopped. Without waiting for either of them to say a word, even if they'd been capable, he turned and strode away, the leopardess a respectable distance behind his heels. Presently, the normal calls of the wood animals began. The two men shook themselves and silently walked back to the ship. At the meadow's edge, Carmody said, "There's only one thing to do. Call a Council of the Question of Jairus. Fortunately, you fill the bill for the kind of layman required as moderator. I'll ask the bishop's permission, but I'm sure he'll agree it's the only thing to do. We can't contact our superiors and refer a decision to their judgment. The responsibility rests on us."

"It's a terrible burden," said the captain.

At the ship they asked about the bishop, to be told he had walked away into the forest only a short time before. The wrist radios were working, but no answer came from André. Alarmed, the two decided to go back into the forest to search for him. They followed the path to the lake, while Tu checked every now and then through his radio with a copter circling overhead. They'd reported the bishop was not by the lakeshore, but Carmody thought he might be on his way to it or perhaps was just sitting some place and meditating.

About a mile from the *Gull* they found him lying at the foot of an exceptionally tall jelly tree. Tu halted suddenly.

"He's having an attack, Father."

Carmody turned away and sat down on the grass, his back to the bishop. He lit a cigarette but dropped it and crushed it beneath his heel.

"I forgot *he* doesn't want us to smoke in the woods. Not for fear of fire. *He* doesn't like the odour of tobacco."

Tu stood by the priest, his gaze clinging to the writhing figure beneath the tree. "Aren't you going to help him? He'll chew off his tongue or dislocate a bone."

Carmody hunched his shoulders and shook his head. "You forget that *he* cured our ills to demonstrate *his* powers. My rotten tooth, Mrs. Recka's alcoholism. His Excellency's seizures."

"But, but . . . '

"His Excellency has entered into this so-called attack voluntarily and is in no danger of breaking bones or lacerating his tongue. I wish that were all there were to it. Then I'd know what to do. Meanwhile, I suggest you do the decent thing and turn your back, too. I didn't care for this the first time I witnessed it; I still don't."

"Maybe you won't help, but I sure as hell am going to," said Tu. He took a step, halted, sucking in his breath.

Carmody turned to look, then rose. "It's all right. Don't be alarmed."

The bishop had given a final violent spasm, a thrusting of the pelvis that raised his arched body completely off the ground. At the same time he gave a loud racking sob. When he fell back, he crumpled into silence and motionlessness.

But it was not towards him but towards the hollow in the tree that Tu stared. Out of it was crawling a great white snake with black triangular markings on its back. Its head was large as a watermelon; its eyes glittered glassy green; its scales dripped with white-threaded jelly.

"My God," said Tu, "isn't there any end to it? It keeps coming and coming. Must be forty or fifty feet long."

His hand went to the sono-gun in his pocket. Carmody restrained him with another shake of his head.

"That snake intends no harm. On the contrary, if I understand these animals, it knows dimly that it has been given life again and feels a sense of gratitude. Perhaps *he* made them aware that *he* resurrects them so that *he* may warm himself in their automatic worship. But, of course, *he* would never stand for what that beast is doing. *He,* if you've not noticed, can't endure to touch *his* secondhand progeny. Did you perceive that after *he* had touched Masters, *he* washed *his* hands with coconut water? Flowers and trees are the only things *he* handles."

The snake had thrust its head above the bishop's and was touching his face with its flickering tongue. André groaned and opened his eyes. Seeing the reptile, he shuddered with fear, then grew still and allowed it to caress him. After determining that it meant him no harm, he stroked it back.

"Well, if the bishop should take over from Father, he at least will give these animals what they have always wanted and have not got from *him*, a tenderness and affection. His Excellency does not hate these females. Not yet."

In a louder voice, he added, "I hope to God that such a thing does not come to pass."

Hissing with alarm, the snake slid off into the grass. André sat up, shook his head as if to clear it, rose to greet them. His face had lost the softness it had held while he was caressing the serpent. It was stern, and his voice was challenging.

"Do you think it is right to come spying upon me?"

"Your pardon, Your Excellency, we were not spying. We were looking for you because we have decided that the situation demands a Council of the Question of Jairus."

Tu added, "We were concerned because Your Excellency seemed to be having another attack."

"Was I? Was I? But I thought that *he* had done away . . . I mean . . ."

Sadly, Carmody nodded, "*He* has. I wonder if Your Excellency, would forgive me if I gave an opinion. I think that you were not having an epileptoid seizure coincidentally with sparking the snake with its new life. Your seeming attack was only a mock-up of your former illness.

"I see you don't understand. Let me put it this way. The doctor on Wildenwooly had thought that your sickness was psychosomatic in origin and had ordered you to Ygdrasil where a more competent man could treat it. Before you left, you told me that he thought that your symptoms were symbolic behaviour and pointed the way to the seat of your malady, a suppressed . . ."

"I think you should stop there," said the bishop coldly.

"I had intended to go no further."

They began walking back to the ship. The two priests dropped behind the captain, who strode along with his eyes fixed straight ahead of him.

The bishop said, hesitantly, "You too experienced the glory—perhaps perilous, but nevertheless a glory—of bringing the dead back to life. I watched you, as you did me. You were not unmoved. True, you did not fall to the ground and become semi-conscious. But you trembled and moaned in the grip of ecstasy."

He cast his eyes to the ground, then, as if ashamed of his hesitancy, raised them to glare unflinchingly.

"Before your conversion, you were very much a man of this world. Tell me, John, is not this fathering something like being with a woman?"

Carmody looked to one side.

"I want neither your pity nor your revulsion," said André. "Just the truth."

Carmody sighed deeply.

"Yes, the two experiences are very similar. But the fathering is even more intimate because, once entered upon, there is no control at all, absolutely no withdrawal from the intimacy; your whole being, mind and body, are fused and focused upon the event. The feeling of oneness—so much desired in the other and so often lacking—is inescapable here. You feel as if you were the recreator and the recreated. Afterwards, you have a part of the animal in you—as you well know—because there is a little spark in your brain that is a piece of its life, and when the spark moves you know that the animal you raised is moving. And when it dims you know it is sleeping, and when it flares you know it is in panic or some other intense emotion. And when the spark dies, you know the beast has died too.

"Father's brain is a constellation of such sparks, of billions of stars that image brightly their owner's vitality. *He* knows where every individual unit of life is on this planet, *he* knows when it is gone, and when *he* does, *he* waits until the bones have been refleshed, and then *he* fathers forth . . ."

"*He fathers-forth whose beauty is past change:*
Praise him!" André burst out.

Startled, Carmody raised his eyes. "Hopkins, I think, would be distressed to hear you quoting his lines in this context. I think perhaps he might retort with a passage from another of his poems.

"Man's spirit will be fleshbound when found at best,
But uncumbered: meadow-down is not distressed
For a rainbow footing it nor he for his bones risen."

"Your quote supports mine. *His bones risen.* What more do you need?"

"*But uncumbered.* What is the penalty for this ecstasy? This world is beautiful, yes, is it not sterile, dead-ended? Well, never mind that now. I wished to remind Your Excellency that this power and glory come from a sense of union and control over brutes. The world is *his* bed, but who would lie forever in it? And why does *he* now wish to leave it, if it is so desirable? For good? Or for evil?"

Chapter 5

An hour later, the three entered the bishop's cabin and sat down at the bare round table in its center. Carmody was carrying a little black bag, which he put under his chair without commenting on it. All were dressed in black robes, and as soon as André had given the opening ritual prayer, they put on the masks of the founder of the order. For a moment there was silence as they looked at each other from behind the assumed anonymous safety of identical features; brown skin, kinky hair, flat nose, thick lips. And with the intense West Africanness of the face, the maker of the masks had managed to impart to them the legendary gentleness and nobility of soul that had belonged to Jairus Cbwaka.

Captain Tu spoke through rigid lips.

"We are gathered here in the name of His love and of His love to formulate the temptation, if any, that confronts us, and take action, if any, against it. Let us speak as brothers, remembering each time we look across the table and see the face of the founder that he never lost his temper except upon one occasion nor forgot his love except on one occasion. Let us remember his agonies caused by that forgetfulness and what he has directed us, priest and layman, to do. Let us be worthy of his spirit in the presence of the seeming of his flesh."

"I would like it better if you didn't rattle through the words so fast," said the bishop. "Such a pace destroys the spirit of the thing."

"It doesn't remedy anything for you to criticize my conducting."

"Rebuke well taken. I ask you to forgive me."

"Of course," Tu said, somewhat uncomfortably. "Of course. Well to business."

"I speak for Father," said the bishop.

"I speak against Father," said Carmody.

"Speak for Father," said Tu.

"Thesis: Father represents the forces of good. *He* has offered the Church the monopoly of the secret of resurrection."

"Antithesis."

"Father represents the forces of evil, for *he* will unloose upon the Galaxy a force which will destroy the Church if she tries to monopolize it. Moreover, even if she should refuse to have anything to do with it, it will destroy mankind everywhere and consequently our Church."

"Development of thesis."

"All *his* actions have been for good. Point. *He* has cured our illnesses major and minor. Point. *He* stopped Masters and Lejeune from carnal intercourse and perhaps did the same to Recka and Givens. Point. *He* made the former confess they had stolen money from Lejeune's father, and since then Lejeune has come to me for spiritual advice. She seemed to consider very seriously my suggestion that she have nothing to do with Masters and to return to her father, if the chance came, in an attempt to solve their problems with his consent. Point.

She is studying a manual I gave her and may be led to the Church. That will be Father's doing and not Masters', who has neglected the Church though he is nominally a member of our body. Point. Father is forgiving, for *he* didn't allow the leopardess to harm Masters, even after the youth's attempt at killing *him*. And *he* has said that the captain may as well release Masters from the brig, for *he* fears nothing, and our criminal code is beneath his comprehension. *He* is sure that Masters won't try again. Therefore, why not forget about his stealing a gun from the ship's storeroom and let him loose? We are using force to get our goal of punishment, and that is not necessary, for according to the laws of psycho-dynamics which *he* has worked out during ten thousand years of solitude, a person who uses violence as a means to an end is self-punished, is robbed of a portion of his powers. Even *his* original act of getting the ship down here has hurt *him* so much that it will be some time before he recovers the full use of *his* psychic energies.

"I enter a plea that we accept *his* offer. There can be no harm because *he* wishes to go as a passenger. Though I, of course, possess no personal funds, I will write out an authorization on the Order for *his* ticket. And I will take *his* place upon Abatos while *he* is gone.

"Remember, too, that the decision of this particular Council will not commit the Church to accept *his* offer. We will merely put *him* under our patronage for a time."

"Antithesis."

"I have a blanket statement that will answer most of thesis's points. That is, that the worst evil is that which adopts the lineaments of good, so that one has to look hard to distinguish the true face beneath the mask. Father undoubtedly learned from the *Hoyle* survivor our code of ethics. He has avoided close contact with us so we may not get a chance to study his behaviour in detail.

"However, these are mostly speculations. What can't be denied is that this act of resurrection is a drug, the most powerful and insidious that mankind has ever been exposed to. Once one has known the ecstasies attendant upon it, one wishes for more. And as the number of such acts is limited to the number of dead available, one wishes to enlarge the ranks of the dead so that one may enjoy more acts. And Father's set-up here is one that 'combines the maximum of temptation with the maximum of opportunity.' Once a man has tasted the act, he will seriously consider turning his world into one like Abatos.

"Do we want that? I say no. I predict that if Father leaves here, *he* will open the way to such a possibility. Won't each man who has the power begin thinking of himself as a sort of god? Won't he become as Father, dissatisfied with the original unruly rude chaotic planet as he found it? Won't he find progress and imperfection unbearable and remodel the bones of his creatures to remove all evolutionary vestiges and form perfect skeletons? Won't he suppress mating among the animals—and perhaps among his fellow human beings—while allowing the males to die unresurrected until none but the more pliable and amenable females are left and there is no chance of young being born? Won't he make a garden out of his planet, a beautiful but sterile and unprogressive paradise? Look, for example, at the method of hunting that the fat and lazy beasts of prey use. Consider its disastrous results, evolutionarily speaking. In the beginning they picked out the slowest and stupidest herbivores to kill. Did this result in the survivors breeding swifter and more intelligent young? Not at all. For the dead were raised, and caught and killed again. And again. So that now when a leopardess or bitch wolf goes out to eat, the unconditioned run away and the conditioned stand trembling and paralysed and meekly submit to slaughter like tame animals in a stockyard. And the uneaten return to graze unconcernedly within leaping distance of the killer while she is devouring their sister. This is a polished planet, where the same event slides daily through the same smooth groove.

"Yet even the lover of perfection, Father, has become bored and wishes to find a pioneer world where *he* may labour until *he* has brought it to the same state as Abatos. Will this go on for ever until the Galaxy will no longer exhibit a multitude of worlds, each breathtakingly different from the other, but will show you everywhere a duplicate of Abatos, not one whit different? I warn you that this is one of the very real perils.

"Minor points. *He* is a murderer because *he* caused Kate Lejeune to miscarry, and . . ."

"Counterpoint. *He* maintains that it was an accident that Kate lost her foetus, that *he* had *his* two beasts chase her and Masters out of the woods because they were having carnal intercourse. And *he* could not tolerate that. Point. Such an attitude is in *his* favour and shows that *he* is good and on the side of the Church and of God."

"Point. It would not have mattered to *him* if Pete and Kate had been bound in holy matrimony. Carnal intercourse *per se* is objectionable to *him*. Why, I don't know. Perhaps the act offends his sense of property because *he* is the sole giver of life on this world. But I say *his* interference was evil because it resulted in the lost of a human life, and that *he* knew it would . . ."

"Point," said the bishop, somewhat heatedly. "This is, as far as we know, a planet without true death and true sin. We have brought those two monsters with us, and *he* cannot endure either one."

"Point. We did not ask to come but were forced."

"Order," said the moderator. "The Question first, then the formulation of the temptation, as laid down in the rules. If we say yes, and Father goes with us, one of us must remain to take *his* place. Otherwise, so *he* insists, this world will go to wrack and ruin in *his* absence."

The moderator paused, then said, "For some reason, *he* has limited the choice of *his* substitutes to you two."

"Point," said the bishop. "We are the only candidates because we have sworn total abstinence from carnal intercourse. Father seems to think that women are even greater vessels of evil than men. *He* says that bodily copulation involves a draining off of the psychic energy needed for the act of resurrection and implies also that there is something dirty—or perhaps I should say, just too physical and animal—about the act. I do not, of course, think *his* attitude entirely justified, nor do I agree at all that women are on the same plane with animals. But you must remember that *he* has not seen a woman for ten thousand years, that perhaps the female of *his* own species might justify *his* reaction. I gathered from *his* conversation that there is a wide gap between the sexes of *his* kind on *his* home planet. Even so, *he* is kind to our women passengers. *He* will not touch them, true, but *he* says that any physical contact with us is painful to *him*, because it robs *him* of *his*, what shall I say, sanctity? On the other hand, with flowers and trees . . ."

"Point. What you have told us indicates *his* aberrated nature."

"Point, point. You have confessed you dare not say such a thing to *his* face, that you are awed by the sense of the power that emanates from *him*. Point. *He* acts as one who has taken a vow of chastity; perhaps *his* nature is such that too close a contact does besmirch him, figuratively speaking. I take this religious attitude to be one more sign in *his* favour."

"Point. The devil himself may be chaste. But for what reason? Because he loves God or because he fears dirt?"

"Time," said Tu, "time for the chance of reversal. Has thesis or antithesis altered his mind on any or all points? Do not be backward in admitting it. Pride must fall before love of truth."

The bishop's voice was firm. "No change. And let me reaffirm that I do not think Father is God. But *he* has Godlike powers. And the Church should use them."

Carmody rose and gripped the table's edge. His head was thrust aggressively forward, his stance was strange in contrast to the tender melancholy of the mask.

"Antithesis reports no change, too. Very well. Thesis has stated that Father has Godlike powers. I say, so has man, within limits. Those limits are what he may do to material things through material means. I say that Father is limited to those means, that there is nothing at all supernatural about *his* so-called miracles. As a matter of fact, man can do what Father is doing, even if on a primitive scale.

"I have been arguing on a spiritual level, hoping to sway thesis with spiritual points before I revealed to you my discoveries. But I have failed. Very well. I will tell you what I have found out. Perhaps then thesis will change his mind."

He stooped and picked up the little black bag and laid it on the table before him. While he spoke, he kept one hand upon it, as if to enforce attention towards it.

"Father's powers, I thought, might be only extensions of what we humans may do. *His* were more subtle because *he* had the backing of a much older science than ours. After all, we are able to rejuvenate the old so that our life span is about a hundred and fifty. We build organs of artificial flesh. Within a limited period we may revive the dead, provided we can freeze them quickly enough and then work on them. We've even built a simple brain of flesh—one on the level of a toad's. And the sense of the numinous and of panic is nothing new. We have our own sonobeams for creating a like effect. Why could he not be using similar methods?

"Just because we saw *him* naked and without a machine in *his* hand didn't mean that *his* effects were produced by mental broadcast. We couldn't conceive of science without metal mechanisms. But what if *he* had other means? What about the jelly trees, which display electromagnetic phenomena? What about the faint humming we heard?

"So I borrowed a microphone and oscilloscope from the engineer, rigged up a sound detector, put it in the bag, and set out to nose around. And I observed that His Excellency was also making use of his time before the Question, that he was talking again to *him*. And while doing so, the jelly trees nearby were emitting subsonics at four and thirteen cycles. You know what those do. The first massages the bowels and causes peristalsis. The second stimulates a feeling of vague overpowering oppression. There were other sonics, too, some sub, some super.

"I left Father's neighbourhood to investigate elsewhere. Also, to do some thinking. It's significant, I believe, that we have had little chance or inclination to do any meditating since we've been here. Father has been pushing us, has kept us off balance. Obviously, *he* wants to keep our minds blurry with too rapid a pace of events.

"I did some fast thinking, and I concluded that the resurrection act itself was not touched off by *his* spark of genesis. Far from it. It is completely automatic, and it comes when the newly formed body is ready for a shock of bio-electricity from the protoplasm-jelly.

"But *he* knows when it is ready and taps the wavelengths of life blooming anew, feeds upon them. How? There must be a two-way linkage between *his* brainwaves and the jelly's. We know that we think in symbols, that a mental symbol is basically a complex combination of brainwaves issuing as series of single images. *He* triggers off certain pre-set mechanisms in the jelly with *his* thoughts, that is, with a mental projection of a symbol.

"Yet not anyone may do it, for we two priests, dedicated to abstention from carnal intercourse, were the only ones able to tap in on the waves. Evidently, a man has to have a peculiar psychosomatic disposition. Why? I don't know. Maybe there is something spiritual to the process. But don't forget that the devil is spiritual. However, the mind-body's actions are still a dark continent. I can't solve them, only speculate.

"As for *his* ability to cure illnesses at a distance, *he* must diagnose and prescribe through the medium of the tree-jelly. It receives and transmits, takes in the abnormal or unhealthy waves our sick cells broadcast and sends out the healthy waves to suppress or cancel the unhealthy. There's no miracle about the process. It works in accordance with materialistic science.

"I surmise that when Father first came here, *he* was fully aware that the trees originated the ecstasy, that *he* was merely tuning in. But after millennia of solitude and an almost continuous state of drugging ecstasy, *he* deluded *himself* into thinking that it was *he* who sparked the new life.

"There are a few other puzzling points. How did *he* catch our ship? I don't know. But *he* knew about the translator motor from the *Hoyle* survivor and was thus able to set up the required wavelengths to neutralize the workings of the protein 'normal space' memory banks. *He* could have had half the jelly trees of Abatos broadcasting all the time, a trap that would inevitably catch a passing ship."

Tu said, "What happened to *his* original spaceship?"

"If we left the *Gull* to sit out in the rain and sun for ten thousand years, what would happen to it?"

"It'd be a heap of rust. Not even that."

"Right. Now I suspect strongly that Father, when *he* first came here, had a well-equipped laboratory on *his* ship. *His* science was able to mutate genes at will, and *he* used *his* tools on the native trees to mutate them into these jelly trees. That also explains why *he* was able to change the animals' genetic pattern so that their bodies lost their evolutionary vestiges, became perfectly functional organisms."

The little man in the mask sat down. The bishop rose. His voice was choked.

"Admitting that your researches and surmises have indicated that Father's powers are unspiritual gimmickry—and in all fairness it must be admitted that you seem to be right—admitting this, then, I still speak for Father."

Carmody's mask cocked to the left. "What?"

"Yes. We owe it to the Church that she get this wonderful tool in her hands, this tool which, like anything in this universe, may be used for evil or for good. Indeed, it is mandatory that she gets control of it, so that she may prevent those who would misuse it from doing so, so that she may become stronger and attract more to her fold. Do you think that eternal life is no attraction?

"Now—you say that Father has lied to us. I say *he* has not. *He* never once told us that *his* powers were purely spiritual. Perhaps, being of an alien species, *he* misunderstands our strength of comprehension and took it for granted that we would see how *he* operates.

"However, that is not the essence of my thesis. The essence is that we must take Father along and give the Church a chance to decide whether or not to accept *him*. There is no danger in doing that, for *he* will be alone among billions. And if we should leave *him* here, then we will be open to rebuke, perhaps even a much stronger action from the Church, for having been cowards enough to turn down *his* gift.

"I will remain here, even though my motives are questioned by those who have no right to judge me. I am a tool of God as much as Father is; it is right that we both be used to the best of our abilities;

Father is doing no good for Church or man while isolated here; I will endure my loneliness while waiting for your return with the thought that I am doing this as a servant who takes joy in his duty."

"What a joy!" Carmody shouted. "No! I say that we reject Father once and for all. I doubt very much that *he* will allow us to go, for *he* will think that, faced with spending the rest of our lives here and then dying—for I don't think *he*'ll resurrect us unless we say yes—we will agree. And *he*'ll see to it that we are cooped up inside the ship, too. We won't dare step outside, for we'll be bombarded with panic-waves or attacked by *his* beasts. However, that remains to be seen. What I'd like to ask thesis is this: Why can't we just refuse *him* and leave the problem of getting *him* off Abatos to some other ship? *He* can easily trap another. Or perhaps, if we get to go home, we may send a government craft to investigate."

"Father has explained to me that we represent *his* only sure chance. *He* may have to wait another ten millennia before another ship is trapped. Or forever. It works this way. You know that translation of a vessel from one point in normal space to the other occurs simultaneously, as far as outside observers are affected. Theoretically, the ship rotates the two coordinates of its special axis, ignoring time, disappears from its launching point, reappearing at the same time at its destination. However, there is a discharging effect, a simulacrum of the ship, built of electromagnetic fields, which radiates at six points from the starting place, and speeds at an ever-accelerating rate at six right-angles from there. These are called 'ghosts.' They've never been seen, and we've no instrument that can detect them. Their existence is based on Guizot's equations, which have managed to explain how electromagnetic waves may exceed the speed of light, though we know from Auschweigh that Einstein was wrong when he said that the velocity of light was the absolute.

"Now, if you were to draw a straight line from Wildenwooly to Ygdrasil, you would find that Abatos does not lie between, that it is off to one side of the latter. But it is at right-angles to it, so that one of the 'ghosts' passes here. The electromagnetic net that the trees sent up stopped it cold. The result was that the *Gull* was literally sucked along the line of power, following this particular ghost to Abatos instead of to Ygdrasil. I imagine that we appeared for a flickering millisecond at our original destination, then were yanked back to here. Of course, we were unaware of that, just as the people on Ygdrasil never saw us.

"Now—the voyages between Ygdrasil and Wildenwooly are

infrequent, and the field has to mesh perfectly with the ghost, otherwise the ghost passes between the pulses. So that *his* chances of catching another are very few."

"Yes, and that is why *he* will never allow us to leave. If we go without him and send a warship back to investigate, it may be able to have defences built in to combat his trees' radiations. So we represent *his* sole ticket. And I say *no* even *if* we must remain marooned!"

So the talk raged for two hours until Tu asked for the final formulations.

"Very well. We have heard. Antithesis has stated the peril of the temptation as being one that will make man a sterile anarchistic pseudo-god.

"Thesis has stated that the peril is that we may reject a gift which would make our Church once again the universal, in numbers as well as in claim, because she would literally and physically hold the keys to life and death.

"Thesis, please vote."

"I say we accept Father's offer."

"Antithesis."

"No. Refuse."

Tu placed his large and bony hands on the table,

"As moderator and judge, I agree with antithesis."

He removed his mask. The others, as if reluctant to acknowledge both identity and responsibility, slowly took off their disguises. They sat glaring at each other, and ignored the captain when he cleared his throat loudly. Like the false faces they had discarded, they had dropped any pretence of brotherly love.

Tu said, "In all fairness, I must point out one thing. That is, that as a layman of the Church, I may concur in the agreement to reject Father as a passenger. But as a captain of the Saxwell Company's vessel, it is my duty when landing upon an unscheduled stop to take on any stranded non-active who wishes to leave, provided he has passage money and there is room for him. That is Commonwealth law."

"I don't think we need worry about anybody paying for *his* passage," said the padre. "Not now. However, if *he* should have the money, *he'd* present you with a nice little dilemma."

"Yes, wouldn't *he*? I'd have to report my refusal, of course. And I'd face trial and might lose my captaincy and would probably be earthbound the rest of my life. Such a thought is—well, unendurable."

André rose. "This has been rather trying. I think I'll go for a walk in the woods. If I meet Father, I will tell *him* our decision."

Tu also stood up. "The sooner the better. Ask *him* to reactivate our translator at once. We won't even bother leaving in orthodox style. We'll translate and get our fixings later. Just so we get away."

Carmody fumbled in his robe for a cigarette. "I think I'll talk to Pete Masters. Might be able to drive some sense into his head. Afterwards, I'll take a walk in the woods, too. There's much hereabouts to learn yet."

He watched the bishop walk out and grimly shook his head.

"It went hard to go against my superior," he said to Tu. "But His Excellency, though a great man, is lacking in the understanding that comes from having sinned much yourself."

He patted his round paunch and smiled as if all were right, though not very convincingly.

"It's not fat alone that is stuffed beneath my belt. There are years of experience of living in the depths packed solidly there. Remember that I survived Dante's Joy. I've had my belly full of evil. At its slightest taste, I regurgitate it. I tell you, Captain, Father is rotten meat, ten thousand years old."

"You sound as if you're not quite certain."

"In this world of shifting appearances and lack of true self-knowledge, who is?"

Chapter 6

Masters had been released after he had promised Tu that he would make no more trouble. Carmody, not finding the youth inside, walked out and called him over the wrist radio. No reply.

Still carrying his black bag, the padre hurried into the woods as fast as his short legs would go. He hummed as he passed beneath the mighty branches, called out to the birds overhead, stopped once to bow gravely to a tall heron-like bird with dark purple mask-markings over its eyes, then staggered off laughing and holding his sides when it replied with a call exactly like a plunger withdrawing from a stopped drain, finally sat down beneath a beech to wipe his streaming face with a handkerchief.

"Lord, Lord, there are more things in this universe . . . surely You must have a sense of humour," he said out loud. "But then, I mustn't identify a purely human viewpoint with You and make the anthropomorphic fallacy."

He paused, said in a lower tone as if not wanting Anyone to hear, "Well, why not? Aren't we, in one sense, the focus of creation, the Creator's image? Surely He too likes to feel a need for relief and finds it in laughter. Perhaps His laughter does not come out as mere meaningless noise but is manifested on a highly economical and informative level. Perhaps He tosses off a new galaxy, instead of having a belly-laugh. Or substitutes a chuckle with a prodding of a species up the Jacob's ladder of evolution towards a more human state.

"Or, old-fashioned as it sounds, indulges in the sheer joy of a miracle to show His children that His is *not* an absolutely orderly clockwork universe. Miracles are the laughter of God. Hmm, not bad. Now, where did I leave my notebook? I knew it. Back in my cabin. That would have made such a splendid line for an article. Well, no matter. I shall probably recall it, and posterity won't die if I don't. But they'll be the poorer, and . . ."

He fell silent as he heard Masters and Lejeune nearby. Rising, he walked towards them, calling out so they wouldn't think he was eavesdropping.

They were facing each other across a tremendous fringe-topped toadstool. Kate had quit talking, but Pete, his face red as his hair, continued angrily as if the priest did not exist. He gestured wildly with one fist, while the other hung by his side clenching a powersaw handle.

"That's final! We're not going back to Wildenwooly. And don't think I'm afraid of your father, 'cause I'm afraid of nobody. Sure, he won't press charges against us. He can afford to be noble-hearted. The Commonwealth will prosecute us for him. Are you so stupid you don't remember that it's the law that the Board of Health must take into custody anyone who's been put on notice as guilty of unhealthy practices? Your father must have sent word on to Ygdrasil by now. We'll be detained as soon as we put foot on it. And you and I will be sent to an institution. We won't even get to go together to the same place. They never send partners-in-misdoing to the same resort. And how do I know that I won't have lost you then? Those rehabilitation homes do things to people, change their outlooks. You might lose your love for me. Probably that would be fine with them. They'd say you were gaining a healthy attitude in getting rid of me."

Kate raised her large violet eyes to his. "Oh, Pete, that would never ever happen. Don't talk such stuff. Besides, Daddy wouldn't report us.

He knows I'd be taken away for a long time, and he couldn't stand that. He won't inform the government; he'll send his own men after us."

"Yeah? What about that telegram to the *Gull* just before we left?"

"Daddy didn't mention the money. We'd have been held for a juvenile misdemeanour only."

"Sure, and then his thugs would have beaten me up and dropped me off in the Twogee Woods. I suppose you'd like that?"

Tears filled Kate's eyes. "Please, Pete, don't. You know I love you more than anybody else in the world."

"Well, maybe you do, maybe you don't. Anyway, you forget that this priest knows about the money, and his duty is to report us."

"Perhaps I am a priest," said Carmody, "but that doesn't automatically classify me as nonhuman. I wouldn't dream of reporting you. Needlenose though I am, I am not a malicious trouble-maker. I'd like to help you out of your predicament, though just now I must confess to a slight inclination to punch you in the nose for the way you are talking to Kate. However, that is neither here nor there. What is important is that I'm under no compulsion to tell the authorities, even though your act was not told to me in confession.

"But I do believe you should follow Kate's advice and go back to her father and confess all and try to come to an agreement. Perhaps he would consent to your marriage if you were to promise him to wait until you had proved yourself capable of supporting Kate happily. And proved that your love for her is based on more than sexual passion. Consider his feelings. He's as much concerned in this as you. More, for he's known her far longer, loved her a greater time."

"Ah, to hell with him and the whole situation!" shouted Pete. He walked off and seated himself under a tree about twenty yards away. Kate wept softly. Carmody offered her a handkerchief, saying, "A trifle sweaty, perhaps, but sanitary with sanctity." He smiled at his own wit with such self-evident enjoyment, mingled with self-mockery, that she could not help smiling back at him. While she dried her tears, she gave him her free hand to hold.

"You are sweet and patient, Kate, and very much in love with a man who is, I'm afraid, afflicted with a hasty and violent temper. Now, tell me true, is not your father much the same? Wasn't that part of the reason you ran away with Pete, to get away from a too-demanding, jealous, hotheaded father? And haven't you found out since that Pete is so much like your father that you have traded one image for its duplicate?"

"You're very perceptive. But I love Pete."

"Nevertheless, you should go home. Pete, if he really loves you, will follow you and try to come to an honest and open contract with your father. After all, you must admit that your taking the money was not right."

"No," she said, beginning to weep again, "it wasn't. I don't want to be a weakling and put the blame on Pete, for I did agree to take the money, even if it was his suggestion. I did so in a weak moment. And ever since, it's been bothering me. Even when I was in the cabin with him and should have been deliriously happy, that money bothered me."

Masters jumped up and strode towards them, the power-saw swinging in his hand. It was a wicked-looking tool, with a wide thin adjustable blade spreading out like a fan from a narrow motorbox. He held the saw like a pistol, his hand around the butt and one finger on the trigger.

"Take your paws off her," he said.

Kate withdrew her hand from Carmody's grip, but she faced the youth defiantly. "He isn't hurting me. He's giving me real warmth and understanding, trying to help."

"I know these old priests. He's taking advantage of you so he can hug and pinch you and . . ."

"Old?" exploded the padre. "Listen, Masters, I'm only forty . . ."

He laughed. "Almost got me going, didn't you?" He turned to Kate. "If we do get off Abatos, go home to your father. I'll be stationed at Breakneck for a while; you may see me as often as you wish, and I'll do my best to help you. And though I foresee some years of martyrdom for you, placed between two fires like Pete and your father, I think you're made of strong stuff."

His eyes twinkling, he added, "Even if you do look fragile and exceedingly beautiful and very huggable and pinchable."

At the moment a deer trotted into the little glade. Rusty red, flecked with tiny white spots edged in black, her large liquid black eyes unafraid, she danced up to them and held out her nose inquiringly towards Kate. She seemed to know that Kate was the only female there.

"Evidently one of those unconditioned to being killed by the beasts of prey," said Carmody. "Come here, my beauty. I do believe that I brought along some sugar for just such an occasion. What shall I call you? Alice? Everybody is mad at this party, but we've no tea."

The girl gave a soft cry of delight and touched the doe's wet black nose. It licked her hand. Pete snorted with disgust.

"You'll be kissing it next."

"Why not?" She put her mouth on its snout.

His face became even redder. Grimacing, he thrust the blade-edge of the saw against the animal's neck, and pressed the trigger. The doe dropped, taking Kate with it, for she had no warning to remove her arms from around its neck. Blood spurted over the saw and Pete's chest and over her arm. The fan-edge of the tool, emitting supersonic waves capable of eating through granite, had sliced a thin plane through the beast's cells.

Masters stared, white-faced now. "I only touched it. I didn't really mean to pull the trigger. I must have nicked its jugular vein. The blood, the blood . . ."

Carmody's face was also pale, and his voice shook.

"Luckily, the doe won't remain dead. But I hope you keep the sight of this blood in your mind the next time you feel anger. It could just as easily be human, you know."

He quit talking to listen. The forest sounds had ceased, overcome by a rush of silence, like the shadow of a cloud. Then, the striding legs and stone eyes of Father.

His voice roared around them as if they were standing beneath a waterfall.

"Anger and death in the air! I feel them when the beasts of prey are hungry. I came quickly, for I knew that these killers were not mine. And I also came for another reason, Carmody, for I have heard from the bishop of your investigations and of your mistaken conclusions and the decision which you forced upon the captain and the bishop. I came to show you how you have deceived yourself about my powers, to teach you humility towards your superiors."

Masters gave a choked cry, grabbed Kate's hand with his bloodied hand, and began half-running, half-stumbling, dragging her after him. Carmody, though trembling, stood his ground.

"Shut off your sonics. I know how you create awe and panic in my breast."

"You have your device in that bag. Check it. See if there are any radiations from the trees."

Obediently, the man fumbled at the lock of his case, managed after two tries to get it open. He twisted a dial. His eyes grew wide when it had completed its circuit.

"Convinced? There are no sonics at that level, are there? Now—

keep one eye on the oscilloscope but the other on me."

Father scooped from the hole of the nearest tree a great handful of the jelly and plastered it over the bloodied area of the doe's neck. "This liquid meat will close up the wound, which is small to begin with, and will rebuild the devastated cells. The jelly sends out probing waves to the surrounding parts of the wound, identifies their structure and hence the structure of the missing or ruptured cells, and begins to fill in. But not unless I direct the procedure. And I can, if necessary, do without the jelly. I do not need it, for my power is good because it comes from God. You should spend ten thousand years with no one to talk to but God. Then you would see that it is impossible for me to do anything but good, that I see to the mystical heart of things, feel its pulse as nearer than that of my body."

He had placed his hand over the glazed eyes. When he withdrew it, the eyes were a liquid shining black again, and the doe's flanks rose and fell. Presently it got on its hoofs, thrust a nose towards Father, was repelled by a raised hand, wheeled, and bounded off.

"Perhaps you would like to call for another Question," roared Father. "I understand that new evidence permits it Had I known that you were filled with such a monkey-like curiosity—and had reasoning powers on a monkey's level—I should have shown you exactly what I am capable of."

The giant strode away. Carmody stared after him. Shaken, he said to himself, "Wrong? Wrong? Have I been lacking in humility, too contemptuous of His Excellency's perceptiveness because he lacked my experience . . . I thought. Have I read too much into his illness, mistaken its foundations?"

He took a deep breath. "Well, if I'm wrong, I will confess it. Publicly, too. But how small this makes me. A pygmy scurrying around the feet of giants, tripping them up in an effort to prove myself larger than they."

He began walking. Absently, he reached up to a branch from which hung large apple-like fruit.

"Hmm. Delicious. This world is an easy one to live in. One need not starve nor fear death. One may grow fat and lazy, be at ease in Zion, enjoy the ecstasy of re-creation. That is what you have wanted with one part of your soul, haven't you? God knows you are fat enough, and if you give others the impression of bursting with energy, you often do so with a great effort. You have to ignore your tiredness, appear bristling with eagerness for work. And your parishioners, yes, and your superiors, too, who should know better, take your labour for granted and never pause to wonder if you, too, are tired or discouraged or doubtful. Here there would be no such thing."

Half-eaten, the apple was discarded for red-brown berries from a bush. Frowning, muttering, he ate them, his eyes always on the retreating shoulders and golden-red roach of Father.

"Yet . . . ?"

After a while, he laughed softly. "It is indeed a paradox, John I. Carmody, that you should be considering again the temptation after having talked Tu and André out of it. And it would be an everlasting lesson—one that you are not, I hope, too unintelligent to profit from— if you talked yourself into changing your mind. Perhaps you have needed this because you have not considered how strong was the bishop's temptation, because you felt a measure—oh, only a tinge, but nevertheless a tinge—of contempt for him because he fell so easily and you resisted so easily.

"Hah, you thought you were so strong, you had so many years of experience packed beneath your belt! It was grease and wind that swelled you out, Carmody. You were pregnant with ignorance and pride. And now you must give birth to humiliation. No, humility, for there is a difference between the two, depending on one's attitude. God give you insight for the latter.

"And admit it, Carmody, admit it. Even in the midst of the shock at seeing the deer killed, you felt a joy because you had an excuse to resurrect the animal and to feel again that ecstasy which you know should be forbidden because it *is* a drug and *does* take your mind from the pressing business of your calling. And though you told yourself you weren't going to do it, your voice was feeble, lacking the authority of conviction.

"On the other hand, doesn't God feel ecstasy when He creates, being The Artist? Isn't that part of creating? Shouldn't we feel it, too? But if we do, doesn't that make us think of ourselves as godlike? Still, Father says that *he* knows from whence *he* derives *his* powers. And if *he* acts aloof, *noli me tangere,* he could be excused by reason of ten thousand years of solitude. God knows, some of the saints were eccentric enough to have been martyred by the very Church that later canonized them.

"But it's a drug, this resurrection business. If it is, you are correct, the bishop is wrong. Still, alcohol, food, the reading of books, and many other things may become drugs. The craving for them can be controlled, they may be used temperately. Why not the resurrection, once one has got over the first flush of intoxication? Why not, indeed?"

He threw away the berries and tore off a fruit that looked like a banana with a light brown shell instead of soft peelings.

"Hmm. *He* keeps an excellent cuisine. Tastes like roast beef with gravy and a soupçon of onions. Loaded with protein, I'll bet. No wonder Father may be so massively, even shockingly, male, so virile-looking, yet a strict vegetarian.

"Ah, you talk too much to yourself. A bad habit you picked up on Dante's Joy and never got rid of, even after *that* night when you were converted. That was a terrible time, Carmody, and only by the grace . . . Well, why don't you shut up, Carmody?"

Suddenly, he dropped behind a bush. Father had come to a large hill which rose from the forest and was bare of trees except for a single giant crowning it. The huge O at the base of its trunk showed its nature, but where the others of its kind were brown-trunked and light-green-leaved, this had a shiny white bark and foliage of so dark a green that it looked black. Around its monstrous white roots, which swelled above the ground, was a crowd of animals. Lionesses, leopardesses, bitch wolves, struthiursines, a huge black cow, a rhino, a scarlet-faced gorilla, a cow-elephant, a moa-like bird capable of gutting an elephant with its beak, a man-sized crested green lizard, and many others. All massed together, moving restlessly but ignoring each other, silent.

When they saw Father, they gave a concerted, muted roar, a belly-deep rumble. Moving aside for him, they formed an aisle through which he walked.

Carmody gasped. What he had mistaken for the exposed roots of the tree were piles of bones, a tumulus of skeletons.

Father halted before them, turned, addressed the beasts in a chanting rhythm in an unknown tongue, gestured, describing large and small wheels that interwove. Then he stooped and began picking up the skulls one by one, kissing them on their grinning teeth, replacing them tenderly. All this while the beasts crouched silently and motionless, as if they understood what he was saying and doing. Perhaps, in a way, they did, for through them, like wind rippling fur, ran a current of anticipation.

The padre, straining his eyes, muttered, "Humanoid skulls. *His* size too. Did *he* come here with them, and they died? Or did *he* murder them? If so, why the ceremony of loving, the caresses?"

Father put down the last grisly article, lifted his hands upwards and out in a sign that took in the skies, then brought them in so they touched his shoulders.

"*He's* come from the heavens? Or *he* means *he* identifies *himself* with the sky, the whole universe, perhaps? Pantheism? Or what?"

Father shouted so loudly that Carmody almost jumped up from behind the bush and revealed himself. The beasts growled an antiphony. The priest balled his fists and raised his head, glaring fiercely. He seemed to be gripped with anger. He looked like a beast of prey, so much did his snarling face resemble the assembled animals'. They, too, had been seized with fury. The big cats yowled. The pachyderms trumpeted. The cow and bears bellowed. The gorilla beat her chest. The lizard hissed like a steam engine.

Again Father shouted. The spell that held them in restraint was shattered. *En masse,* the pack hurled itself upon the giant. Without resistance, he went down beneath the heaving sea of hairy backs. Once, a hand was thrust above the screaming *melee*, making a circular motion as if it were still carrying out the prescribed movement of a ritual. Then it was engulfed in a lioness' mouth, and the spurting stump fell back.

Carmody had been grovelling in the dirt, his fingers hooked into the grass, obviously restraining himself from leaping up to join the slaughter. At the moment he saw Father's hand torn off, he did rise, but his facial expression was different. Fright showed on it, and horror. He ran off into the woods, doubled over so the bush would conceal him from the chance gaze of the animals. Once, he stopped behind a tree, vomited, then raced off again.

Behind him rose the thunder of the blood-crazed killers.

Chapter 7

The enormous melon-striped moon rose shortly after nightfall. Its bright rays glimmered on the hemisphere of the *Gull* and on the white faces gathered at the meadow's edge. Father John walked out of the forest's darkness. He stopped and called out, "What is the matter?"

Tu disengaged himself from the huddled group. He pointed at the open main port of the ship, from which light streamed.

Father John gasped. "*Him?* Already?"

The majestic figure stood motionless at the foot of the portable steps, waiting as if he could stand there patiently for another ten thousand years.

Tu's voice, though angry, was edged with doubt.

"The bishop has betrayed us! He's told *him* of the law that we must accept *him* and has given *him* passage money!"

"And what are you going to do about it?" said Carmody, his gravelly voice even rougher than usual.

"Do? What else can I do but take *him* on? Regulations require it. If I refuse—why, why, I'd lose my captaincy. You know that. The most I can do is put off leaving until dawn. The bishop may have changed his mind by then."

"Where is His Excellency?"

"Don't Excellency that traitor. He's gone off into the woods and become another Father."

"We must find him and save him from himself!" cried Carmody.

"I'll go with you," said Tu. "I'd let him go his own way to hell, except that the enemies of our Church would mock us. My God, a bishop, too!"

Within a few minutes, the two men, armed with flashlights, ship-finders and sonabeams, walked into the forest. Tu also wore a pistol. They went alone because the padre did not want to expose his bishop to the embarrassment that would be his if confronted by a crowd of angry men. Moreover, he thought they'd have a better chance of talking him back into his senses if just his old friends were there.

"Where in hell could we find him?" groaned the captain. "God, it's dark in here. And look at those eyes. There must be thousands."

"The beasts know something extraordinary is up. Listen, the whole forest's awake."

"Celebrating a change of reign. The King is dead; long live the King. Where could he be?"

"Probably the lake. That's the place he loved best."

"Why didn't you say so? We could have been there in two minutes in a copter."

"There'll be no using the copter tonight."

Father John flashed his light on the ship-finder. "Look how the needle's whirling. I'll bet our wrist radios are dead."

"Hello, *Gull, Gull,* come in, come in . . . You're right. It's out. Christ, those eyes glowing, the trees are crawling with them. Our sonos are kaput too. Why don't our flashes go out?"

"I imagine because *he* knows that they enable *his* beasts to locate us more quickly. Try your automatic. Its mechanism is electrically powered, isn't it?"

Tu groaned again. "Doesn't work. Oh, for the old type!"

"It's not too late for you to turn back," said Carmody. "We may not get out of the woods alive if we do locate the bishop."

"What's the matter with you? Do you think I'm a coward? I allow no man, priest or not, to call me that."

"Not at all. But your primary duty is to the ship, you know."

"And to my passengers. Let's go."

"I thought I was wrong. I almost changed my mind about Father," said the priest. "Perhaps *he* was using *his* powers, which didn't depend entirely on material sources, for good. But I wasn't sure. So I followed *him*, and then, when I witnessed death, I knew I'd been right, that evil would come from any attempted use of *him*."

"*His* death? But *he* was at the *Gull* a moment ago."

Carmody hurriedly told Tu what he'd seen.

"But, but . . . I don't understand. Father can't stand the touch of *his* own creatures, and *he* exercises perfect control over them. Why the mutiny? How could *he* have come back to life so quickly, especially if *he* were torn to pieces? Say, maybe there's more than one Father, twins, and *he's* playing tricks on us. Maybe *he* just has control over a few animals. He's a glorified lion tamer, and *he* uses his trained beasts when *he's* around us. And *he* ran into a group *he* couldn't handle."

"You are half-right. First, it was a mutiny, but one that *he* drove them into, a ritual mutiny. I felt *his* mental command; it almost made me jump in and tear *him* apart, too. Second, I imagine *he* came back to life so quickly because the white tree is an especially powerful and swiftly acting one. Third, *he* is playing tricks on us, but not the kind you suggest."

Carmody, slowing his pace, puffed and panted. "I'm paying for my sins now. God help me, I'm going on a diet. I'll exercise, too, when this affair is over. I loathe my fat carcass. But what about when I'm seated hungry at a table piled high with the too-good things of life, created in the beginning to be enjoyed? What then?"

"I could tell you what then, but we've no time for talk like that. Stick to the point," Tu growled. His contempt for self-indulgers was famous.

"Very well. As I said, it was obviously a ritual of self-sacrifice. It was that knowledge which sent me scurrying off in an unsuccessful search for the bishop. I meant to tell him that Father was only half-lying when *he* said *he* derived *his* powers from God and that *he* worshipped God.

"*He* does. But the god is *himself*! In his vast egoism *he* resembles the old pagan deities of Earth, who were supposed to have slain themselves and then, having made the supreme sacrifice, resurrected themselves. Odin, for instance, who hung himself from a tree."

"But *he* wouldn't have heard of them. Why would *he* imitate them?"

"*He* doesn't have to have heard of our Earth myths. After all, there are certain religious rites and symbols that are universal, that sprang up spontaneously on a hundred different planets. Sacrifice to a god, communion by eating the god, sowing and reaping ceremonies, the concept of being a chosen people, like symbols of the circle and the cross. So Father may have brought the idea from *his* home world. Or *he* may have thought it up as the highest possible act *he* was capable of. Man must have a religion, even if it consists of worshipping himself.

"Also, don't forget that *his* ritual, like most, combined religion with practicality. He's ten millennia old and has preserved *his* longevity by going from time to time into the jelly tree. *He* thought *he*'d be going with us, that it'd be some time before *he* could grow a tree on an alien world. A rejuvenation treatment is part of the re-creation, you know. The calcium deposit in your vascular system, the fatty deposits in your brain cells, the other degenerations that make you old, are left out of the process. You emerge fresh and young from the tree."

"The skulls?"

"The entire skeleton isn't necessary for the re-creation, though it's the custom to put it in. A sliver of bone is enough, for a single cell contains the genetic pattern. You see, I'd overlooked something. That was the problem of how certain animals may be conditioned into being killed by the carnivores. If their flesh is rebuilt around the bones according to the genetic record alone, then the animal should be without memory of its previous life. Hence, its nervous system would contain no conditioned reflexes. But it does. Therefore, the jelly must also reproduce the contents of the neural system. How? I surmise that at the very moment of dying the nearest jelly-deposit records the total wave output of the cells, including the complex of waves radiated by the 'knotted' molecules of the memory. Then it reproduces it.

"So, Father's skulls are left outside, and when *he* rises, *he* is greeted with their sight, a most refreshing vision to *him*. Remember, *he* kissed them during the sacrifice. *He* showed his love for *himself*. Life kissing death, knowing *he* had conquered death."

"Ugh!"

"Yes, and that is what will happen to the Galaxy if Father leaves here. Anarchy, a bloody battle until only one person is left to each planet, stagnation, the end of sentient life as we know it, no goal . . . Look, there's the lake ahead!"

Carmody halted behind a tree. André was standing by the shore, his back turned to them. His head was bent forward as if in prayer or meditation. Or perhaps grief.

"Your Excellency," said the padre softly, stepping out from behind the tree.

André started. His hands, which must have been placed together on his chest, flew out to either side. But he did not turn. He sucked in a deep breath, bent his knees, and dived into the lake.

Carmody yelled, "No!" and launched himself in a long flat dive. Tu was not long behind him but stopped short of the edge. He crouched there while the little waves caused by the disappearance of the two spread, then subsided into little rings, moonlight haloed on a dark flat mirror. He removed his coat and shoes but still did not leap in. At that moment a head broke the surface and a loud whoosh sounded as the man took in a deep breath.

Tu called, "Carmody? Bishop?"

The other sank again. Tu jumped in, disappeared. A minute passed. Then three heads emerged simultaneously. Presently, the captain and the little priest stood gasping above the limp form of André.

"Fought me," said Carmody hoarsely, his chest rising and falling quickly. "Tried to push me off. So . . . put my thumbs behind his ears . . . where jaw meets . . . squeezed . . . went limp but don't know if he'd breathed water . . . or I'd made him unconscious . . . or both . . . no time to talk now . . ."

The priest turned the bishop over so he was face downward, turned the head to one side, straddled the back on his knees. Palms placed outwards on the other's shoulders, he began the rhythmic pumping he hoped would push the water out and breath in.

"How could he do it?" said Tu. "How could he, born and raised in the faith, a consecrated and respected bishop, betray us? Who'd have thought it? Look what he did for the Church on Lazy Fair; he was a great man. And how could he, knowing all it meant, try to kill himself?"

"Shut your damn mouth," replied Carmody, harshly. "Were *you* exposed to *his* temptation? What do you know of his agonies? Quit judging him. Make yourself useful. Give me a count by your watch so I can adjust my pumpings. Here we go. One . . . two . . . three . . ."

Fifteen minutes later, the bishop was able to sit up and hold his head between his hands. Tu had walked off a little distance and stood there, back turned to them. Carmody knelt down and said, "Do you think you can walk now, Your Excellency? We ought to get out of this forest as quickly as possible. I feel danger in the air."

"There's more than just danger. There's damnation," said André feebly.

He rose, almost fell, was caught by the other's strong hand.

"Thank you. Let's go. Ah, old friend, why didn't you let me sink to the bottom and die where *he* would not have found my bones and no man would have known of my disgrace?'

"It's never too late, Your Excellency. The fact that you regretted your bargain and were driven by remorse . . ."

"Let's hurry back before it does become too late. Ah, I feel the spark of another life being born. You know how it is, John. It glows and grows and flares until it fills your whole body and you're about to burst with fire and light. This one is powerful. It must be in a nearby tree. Hold me. John. If I go into another seizure, drag me away, no matter how I fight.

"You have felt what I did, you seem to be strong enough to fight against it, but I have fought against something like it all my life and never revealed it to anyone, even denied it in my prayers—the worst thing I could do—until the too-long-punished body took over and expressed itself in my illness. Now I fear that—Hurry, hurry!"

Tu grabbed André's elbow and helped Carmody propel him onwards through the darkness, lit only by the priest's beam. Overhead was a solid roof of interlacing branches.

Something coughed. They stopped, frozen.

"Father?" whispered Tu.

"No. His representative, I fear."

Twenty yards away, barring their path, crouched a leopardess, spotted and tufted, five hundred pounds ready to spring. Its green eyes blinked, narrowing in the beam; its round ears were cocked forward. Abruptly, it rose and stalked slowly towards them. It moved with a comic mixture of feline grace and overstuffed waddle. At another time they might have chuckled at this creature, its fat sheathing its spring-steel

muscles and its sagging swollen belly. Not now, for it could—and probably would—tear them to bits.

Abruptly, the tail, which had been moving gently back and forth,
stiffened out. It roared once, then sprang at Father John, who had
stepped out in front of Tu and André.

Father John yelled. His flashlight sailed through the air and into
the brush. The big cat yowled and bounded off. There were two sounds:
a large body crashing through the bushes and Father John cursing
heartily, not with intended blasphemy but for the sake of an intense
relief.

"What happened?" said Tu. "And what are you doing down on
your knees?"

"I'm not praying. I'll save that for later. This perilous flashlight
went out, and I can't find it. Get down here and help me and be useful.
Get your hands dirty for once; we're not on your perilous vessel, you
know."

"What happened?"

"Like a cornered rat," groaned Carmody, "I fought. Out of sheer
desperation I struck with my fist and accidentally hit it on its nose. I
couldn't have done better if I'd planned it. These beasts of prey are fat
and lazy and cowardly after ten thousand years of easy living on conditioned victims. They have no real guts. Resistance scares them. This
one would not have attacked if it hadn't been urged by Father, I'm
sure. Isn't that so, Your Excellency?"

"Yes. *He* showed me how to control any animal on Abatos anywhere. I'm not advanced enough as yet to recognize the individual
when she's out of sight and transmit mental commands, but I can do
so at close range."

"Ah, I've found this doubly perilous flashlight."

Carmody turned the beam on and rose. "Then I was wrong in
thinking my puny fist had driven off that monster? You instilled panic
in it?"

"No. I cancelled out Father's wavelengths and left the cat on its
own. Too late, of course—once it had begun an attack, its instinct would
urge it on. We owe its flight to your courage."

"If my heart would stop hammering so hard, I'd believe more in
my courage. Well, let's go. Does Your Excellency feel stronger?"

"I'll keep up with any pace you set. And don't use the title. My
action in defying the Question Council's decision constituted an automatic resignation. You know that."

"I know only what Tu has told me Father told him."

They walked on. Occasionally, Carmody flashed his light behind him. While doing this he became aware that the leopardess or one of its sisters was following them by some forty yards. "We are not alone," he said. André said nothing, and Tu, misunderstanding him, began to pray in a very low voice. Carmody did not elucidate but urged them to walk faster.

Suddenly, the shadow of the forest fell away before the brightness of the moon. There was still a crowd on the meadow, but it was away from the edge, gathered beneath the curve of the ship. Father was not in sight.

"Where is *he*?" called Father John. An echo answered from the meadow's other side, followed at once by the giant's appearance in the main port. Stooping, Father walked through it and down the steps to the ground, there to resume his motionless vigilance.

André muttered, "Give me strength."

Carmody spoke to the captain. "You must make a choice. Do what your faith and intelligence tell you is best. Or obey the regulations of Saxwell and the Commonwealth. Which is it to be?"

Tu was rigid and silent, cast into thought like bronze. Without waiting for a reply, Carmody started to walk towards the ship. Halfway across the meadow, he stopped and raised clenched fists and cried, "No use trying that panic trick on us, Father! Knowing what *you* are doing, and how, we may fight against it, for we are men!"

His words were lost to the people around the ship. They were yelling at each other and scrambling for a place on the steps so they could get inside. Father must have evoked a battery of waves from the surrounding trees, more powerful than anything used before. It struck like a tidal wave, carrying all before it. All except Carmody and André. Even Tu broke and ran for the *Gull*.

"John," moaned the bishop. "I'm sorry. But I can't stand it. Not the subsonics. No. The betrayal. The recognition of what I've been fighting against since manhood. It's not true that when you first see the face of your unknown enemy you have the battle half-won. I can't stand it. The need I have for this damnable communion . . . I'm sorry, believe me. But I must . . ."

He whirled and ran back into the forest. Carmody chased after him, shouting, but his legs were quickly outdistanced. Ahead of him, out of the darkness, came a coughing roar. A scream. Silence.

Unhesitatingly, the priest plunged on, his light stabbing before him.

When he saw the cat crouching over the crumpled form, one grey-furred paw tearing at its victim's groin, he shouted again and charged. Snarling, the leopardess arched its back, seemed ready to rear on its hind legs and bat at the man with its bloodied claws, then roared, turned, and bounded away.

It was too late. There'd be no bringing back the bishop this time. Not unless . . .

Carmody shuddered and lifted the sagging weight in his arms and staggered back across the meadow. He was met by Father.

"Give me the body," thundered the voice.

"No! You'll not put him in your tree. I'm taking him back to the ship. After we get home we'll give him a decent burial. And you might as well quit broadcasting your panic. I'm angry, not scared. And we're leaving in spite of you, and we're not taking you. So do your damnedest!"

Father's voice became softer. It sounded sad and puzzled.

"You do not understand, man. I went aboard your vessel and into the bishop's cabin and tried to sit down in a chair that was too small for me. I had to sit on the cold hard floor, and while I waited I thought of going out into vast and empty space again and to all the many strange and uncomfortable and sickeningly undeveloped worlds. It seemed to me that the walls were getting too close and were collapsing in upon me. They would crush me. Suddenly, I knew I could not endure their nearness for any time at all, and that, though our trip would be short, I'd soon be in other too-small rooms. And there would be many of the pygmies swarming about me, crushing each other and possibly me in an effort to gape at me, to touch me. There would be millions of them, each trying to get his dirty little hairy paws on me. And I thought of the planets crawling with unclean females ready to drop their litters at a moment's notice and all the attendant uncleanliness. And the males mad with lust to get them with child. And the ugly cities stinking with refuse. And the deserts that scab those neglected worlds, the disorder, the chaos, the uncertainty. I had to step out for a moment to breathe again the clean and certain air of Abatos. It was then that the bishop appeared."

"You were terrified by the thought of change. I would pity you, except for what you have done to him," said Carmody, nodding down at the form in his arms.

"I do not want your pity. After all, I am Father. You are a man who will crumble into dust forever. But do not blame me. He is dead because of what he was, not because of me. Ask his real father why he did not give him love along with his blows and why he shamed him without justifying why he should be shamed and why he taught him to forgive others but not himself.

"Enough of this. Give me him. I liked him, could almost stand his touch. I will raise him to be my companion. Even I want someone to talk to who can understand me."

"Out of the way," demanded Carmody, "André made his choice. He trusted me to take care of him, I know. I loved the man, though I did not always approve of what he did or was. He was a great man, even with his weakness. None of us can say anything against him. Out of the way, before I commit the violence which you say you so dread but which does not keep you from sending wild beasts to bring about your will. Out of the way!"

"You do not understand," murmured the giant, one hand pulling hard upon his beard. The black, silver-splintered eyes stared hard, but he did not lift his hand against Carmody. Within a minute, the priest had carried his burden into the *Gull.* The port shut softly, but decisively, behind him.

Some time later, Captain Tu, having disposed of his major duties in translating the ship, entered the bishop's cabin. Carmody was there, kneeling by the side of the bed that held the corpse.

"I was late because I had to take Mrs. Recka's bottle away from her and lock her up for a while," he explained. He paused, then, "Please don't think I'm hateful. But right is right. The bishop killed himself and doesn't deserve burial in consecrated ground."

"How do you know?" replied Carmody, his head still bent, his lips scarcely moving.

"No disrespect to the dead, but the bishop had power to control the beasts, so he must have ordered the cat to kill him. It was suicide."

"You forget that the panic waves which Father caused in order to get you and me quickly into the ship also affected any animals in the area. The leopardess may have killed the bishop just because he got in the way of her flight. How are we to know any different?

"Also, Tu, don't forget this. The bishop may be a martyr. He knew that the one thing that would force Father to stay on Abatos would be for himself to die. Father would not be able to endure the idea of leaving *his* planet fatherless. André was the only one among us that could take over the position Father had vacated. He was ignorant at that time, of course, that Father had changed *his* mind because of *his* sudden claustrophobia.

"All the bishop could know was that his death would chain Father to Abatos and free us. And if he deliberately slew himself by means of the leopardess, does that make him any less a martyr? Women have chosen death rather than dishonour and been canonized.

"We shall never know the bishop's true motive. We'll leave knowledge of that to Another.

"As for the owner of Abatos, my feeling against *him* was right. Nothing *he* said was true, and *he* was as much a coward as any of *his* fat and lazy beasts. *He* was no god. *He* was the Father . . . of Lies."

. . . Son

The luxury liner blew up, and with it went Jones.

He had been leaning on the railing, his eyes on the moon's image dancing on the waves and his thoughts on his wife. He had left her in Hawaii; he would, he hoped, never see her again. He had also been thinking of his mother in California and wondering how it would be to live again with her. He wasn't unhappy or happy about either prospect. He had just been meditating.

Then the enemy, in one of the first moves of the undeclared war, had torpedoed the ship from beneath. And Jones, utterly unwarned, was thrown high into the air as if he had bounced off a tremendous springy diving board.

He plunged deep. The blackness crushed him. He became panicky, and lost that delicate sense of poise that he was able to maintain when he was swimming in the sunlit open waters. He wanted to scream and then to ascend on the scream, like a circus acrobat on a rope, to the uncloseted air and the bright moon.

Before the cry for help came, before the waters' poured their heavy blackness down his lungs, his head broke the surface, and he gulped in light and breath. Then he looked around and saw that the ship was gone and that he was alone. There was nothing for him to do but seize a floating piece of debris and hang on with the hope that the day would bring airplanes or another ship.

An hour later, the sea suddenly heaved and split, and a long dark back emerged. It looked like a whale, for it had the rounded head and the sloping-away body. Yet it did not move the tail up and down to propel itself forward, nor roll to one side nor do anything but lie there. Jones knew that it must be a new type of submarine, but he was not sure because it looked so alive. There was about it that indefinable air that distinguishes the animate from the inanimate.

His doubts were settled a moment later when the smooth, curved back was suddenly broken by a long rod pushing up from the centre. The shaft grew until it was twenty feet high, halted, and then flowered at its end into grids of various sizes and shapes. Retractable radar antennae.

So this was the enemy. It had come up from the depths where it had been hiding after its deadly blow. It wished to survey the destruction and, perhaps, pick up any survivors for questioning. Or to make sure that none lived.

Even with that thought he did not try to swim away. What could he do? Better to take a chance that they would treat him decently. He did not want to sink into the abyss below, into the darkness and the pressure.

He trod water while the sub turned its blind snout towards him. No men appeared from the hatches suddenly popping open upon the sleek deck. There was no sign of life except that men must be presumed to be below and turning the faceless, eyeless grids of the radar towards him.

Not until it was almost upon him did he see how it planned to take him prisoner. A large, round port in the whale-shaped head swung in. The sea rushed into it and carried Jones with it. He struggled, for he could not endure the idea of being scooped up in this monstrous parody of a cow catcher, gulped like a sardine chased by a mobile can. Moreover, the very thought of a door swinging open and showing him nothing but blackness beyond was enough to make him want to scream.

In the next moment, the port slid shut behind him, and he found himself hemmed in by water and walls and darkness. He struggled frantically against an enemy that he could not hold in his hands. He cried out from the bottom of his being for a breath of air and a spark of light and a door that would lead him out of this chamber of panic and death. Where was the door, the door, the door? Where . . . ?

There were moments when he almost awoke, when he was suspended in that twilight world between dark sleep and bright wakefulness. It was then that he heard a voice that was new to him. It sounded like a woman's, soft, caressing and sympathetic. Sometimes it was urgent with the hint that he'd better not try to hold anything back.

Hold back? Hold back what? What?

Once he felt rather than heard a series of tremendous impacts—thunder from somewhere, and a sense of being squeezed in a giant fist. That, too, passed.

The voice returned for a while. Then it faded off and sleep came.

He did not awaken swiftly. He had to struggle up through blanket after blanket of semiconsciousness, throwing each one off with desperation tempered with a frantic hope that the next would be the last. And just as he was about to give up, to sink again beneath the choking and heavy layers, to quit breathing and fighting, he awoke.

He was crying out loud and trying to wave his arms and he thought, just for a moment, that the closet door had opened and light and his mother had entered.

But it was not so. He was not back in the locked closet. He was not six years old, and it was not his mother who had rescued him. Certainly that was not her voice, nor was it the voice of his father, the man who had locked him in the closet.

It came from a speaker set into the wall. It did not talk in the tongue of the enemy, as he had expected, but in English. It droned on and on, oddly half-metallic, half-maternal, and it told him what had been taking place in the last twelve hours.

He was shocked to know he had been unconscious that long. While he assimilated that knowledge, he ran his eyes over his cell, taking stock. It was seven feet long, four wide, and six high. It was bare except for the cot on which he lay and certain indispensable plumbing. A bulb burned directly above him, hot and naked.

The discovery that he was hemmed within such a place, narrow as a tomb and with no exit that he could see, made him leap from the cot. Or try to, for he found that his arms and legs were bound inside broad plastic bands.

The voice filled the cell.

"Do not be alarmed, Jones. And do not try to make those hysterical and hopeless struggles that you made before I was forced to give you a sedative. If you suffer from severe claustrophobia, you must endure it."

Jones did not struggle. He was too numbed by the disclosure that he was the only human being upon the submarine. It was a robot speaking to him—perhaps the sub itself, directed electronically from a mother ship.

He took some time, turning the matter over in his mind . . . but he could bring himself to feel no lessening of the terror. It would have been bad enough to be imprisoned with the living enemy, but an enemy that was steel skin and plastic bones and electronic veins and radar eyes and germanium brains was an enemy that filled him with an overpowering dread. How could you fight against anybody—anything—like that?

He checked his fear with the thought that, after all, he was in no way worse off. How would this machine differ from the enemy itself, the creature from the creator? It was the enemy who had built this automatic fish, and he would model it exactly after his own thought processes, his own ideology. Whichever way the living enemy would have acted, just so would this monster.

Now that he was conscious, he remembered what the robot had said to him and what he had answered. He had awakened from his near-drowning and seen a long, plastic arm withdrawing into a hole in the wall. The hole had been covered with a small port, but not before he had caught a glimpse of the needles at the end of the arm. Later, he was to understand that the arm needles had shot adrenalin into him to stimulate his heart, and another chemical—unknown to the American—to cause his internal muscles to reject the water he had swallowed.

The sub wanted him alive. The question was, for what?

It was not long until he knew. The machine or mechanical "brain" or whatever you wanted to call it had also injected a drug that would put him in a light hypnotic state. And it had given him a key word which, uttered after the effect of the drug died off, would enable him to remember what had happened. Now that the voice had uttered that magical key to his unconscious—it was from the enemy's language so he did not understand it—everything came back in a rush.

He understood everything that the sub had thought fit to tell him. In the first place, she was one of the new experimental craft the enemy had built shortly before the war began. She was wholly automatic, not because the enemy had no men to spare, for God knew they had millions to throw away on the battlefield, but because a submarine that did not have to carry a great amount of supplies and air-making equipment for a crew and that did not have to consider living space, could be much smaller and efficient and stay at sea longer. The machinery required to run her occupied much less space than sailors.

The entire craft was designed for sleekness and speed and

deadliness. She carried forty torpedoes, and when these were expend-
ed she would return to her mother ship somewhere in the Pacific. If
need be, she did not have to rise to the surface at any time during her
entire cruise. But her makers had put in orders to the effect that she
should, if it was safe, take some prisoners and pry loose from them
valuable information.

"Then," said the voice with its hint of metal, "I would have shot
you back into the sea from which I picked you. But when, during the
questioning, I found that you were an electronics specialist I decided
to keep you and take you back to the base. I am required to bring back
any valuable prisoners. It is lucky for you that you turned out to be a
man we can use. Otherwise . . ."

The cold echoes hung in the room. Jones shivered. He could see
in his mind's eye, the port swinging inward, the sea rushing in, his
own struggles, and then the irresistible plastic arms shoving him out
into the black and silent depths.

He wondered briefly how much *Keet VI* had found out about him.
No sooner thought than answered. Memory flooded in, and he knew
all the rest that had happened.

To begin with, the sub was as human as it was possible for a
machine to be. It "thought" of itself as *Keet VI*—which meant *Whale
VI*—and spoke in terms that might have fooled a nonexpert into thinking it was conscious of itself. Jones knew better. No mechanical "brain"
had been built yet that was self-conscious. But it was set up so that it
gave that impression. And Jones, after a while, adopted the natural
fallacy of thinking of it as a living being. Or as a woman. For *Keet's*
makers had fallen into their own trap and, believing that ships are
female, had unconsciously built and endowed *Keet* with a feminine
psychology.

Otherwise, how could you explain that *Keet* seemed almost tenderly solicitous of him? Knowing that he was a valuable male, that the
men back upon the mother ship wanted a man like Jones who had
information and talents they could use, *Keet* was prepared to do all
she could to keep his body alive. That was why she had fed him intra-
venously and why she had stopped questioning him when she had
stumbled upon a particularly tender and painful area of his brain.

What was that sensitive part? Why, nothing other than that night
long ago in time, but so near in effect, when his father had locked him
in that dark closet because he, Jones, would not confess that he had
stolen a quarter from his mother's purse. And he had refused to confess,

for he knew he was innocent, until the darkness had become thick and heavy and hot, like a strangler's blanket thrown around him, and he, unable to endure any longer the terror, the blackness, and the walls that seemed to be moving in on him to crush him, had screamed and screamed until his mother, thrusting his father aside, had opened the door and given him light and space and a broad, deep bosom upon which to weep and sob.

And since then . . .

Keet's voice, somehow not so cold now, said, "I could not get much from you other than that you were an electronics specialist, that you had been on the luxury liner *Calvin Coolidge*, that you were leaving your wife for a trial separation and going to live with your mother who resides upon a university campus. There you were going to take up the old, safe, academic life, teaching, and there you were going to spend the rest of your days with your mother until she died. But when I struck that thought, you suddenly reverted to the closet incident, and I could do nothing more with you. Unfortunately, I am equipped with only the lightest of drugs and cannot put you under deep hypnosis. If I could, I could penetrate past that episode or set it to one side. But every time I begin the questioning, I touch that particular territory of the past."

Was it his imagination or did he detect a slightly querulous or plaintive note? It was possible. If the enemy had built in a modulator so it could imitate sympathy and kindness, he could also install circuits to mock other emotions. Or was it possible that the machine, which was, after all, a highly intelligent "brain," could manipulate voice mechanism to reproduce desired effects?

He would probably never know. Yet there was no doubt that the voice contained at least a hint of emotion.

He was glad that he was intrigued by the potentialities of *Keet*. Otherwise, he would have been struggling like a thing out of its mind to loose himself from these bonds strapping him down to the cot. The walls were too close, too close. And while he could endure them now, as long as the light was on, he knew he would go mad if that light were to go out.

Keet must have known that by now, too, yet she had made no threat, no attempt to utilize the knowledge. Why? Why hadn't she tried to scare his knowledge from him? Such would have been the methods of the men who had made her, and she was, after all, only a reflection of them. Why hadn't she tried to terrify him?

The answer was not long in coming.

"You must understand that I am in trouble. At the same time, that means that you, Jones, are also in trouble. If I sink, you do, too."

Jones tensed. Now would come the crux of it. He was surprised to hear the almost pleading tone in her voice. Then he remembered that her builders would have put the whole range of emotions in her voice for her to use whenever occasion required.

"While you were unconscious I was attacked by planes. They must have been carrying some device unknown to me, for I was a hundred fathoms deep, yet they spotted me," *Keet* said.

Jones was sure now. There *was* emotion in her voice, and it was half-way between sullenness and hurt feelings. When *Keet* had been sent to sea, the stage, thought Jones, had lost a great actress.

Despite his situation, he could not help chuckling. *Keet* overheard, for she said, "What is that noise, Jones?"

"Laughter."

"Laughter?"

There was a pause. Jones could imagine *Keet* waiting while she searched through the channels of her electronic memory-banks for the definition of the thing called laughter.

"You mean like this?" *Keet* said.

The speaker burst out with a blood-chilling cackle.

Jones smiled tightly. Evidently the creators of *Keet* had included the definition of laughter and ability to reproduce such in her make-up. But the laughter they had given her was just what you would expect from them. It was designed to frighten their victims. There was nothing of amusement or gaiety in this. He told her so. Another pause. Then the speaker chuckled. But this expressed contempt and scorn.

"That is not what I mean," he answered.

Keet's voice trembled. Jones wondered about that. Surely the enemy engineers had not meant for her to express her own emotions. Machines, he knew, could be frustrated, but they did not "feel" such disappointments as human beings did. But it was possible that in their desire to make her emulate a human as much as possible, they had included this device. It would be carrying construction to a fantastic limit, but it could be so.

It was then that he received another slight shock. *Keet* had started telling him why she needed help, but she had suddenly switched to this discussion and this vain attempt to reproduce his laughter.

Keet could be sidetracked.

He filed away that information. Perhaps he could use it against her later on if he ever got in a position where he could use it. At present, with the bands locking him down, there did not seem to be much hope.

"What were you saying?" he asked.

"I said that I was in trouble, and that, therefore, we both are. If you want to survive, you must aid me."

She paused as if searching her metal-celled brain for the psychologically right combination of words. He tensed, for he knew that this was his only chance, and listened carefully.

"While you were sleeping," she said, "these planes—which I suppose were bourgeois Yankee aircraft—somehow located me and dropped depth charges. They exploded quite close, but I am built rather strongly and compactly, and they did little external harm. But they did shake me up quite a bit.

"I dived at a slant and got away from them. But when I had come to the bottom, I stopped. My nose is in the abysmal ooze, and I cannot back away."

Good Lord, thought Jones, how deep are we? Thousands of feet?

The thought brought back his claustrophobia. Now the walls did indeed seem to crowd in on him. They bent beneath the mountain-heavy weight of the fathoms above him.

Black and crushing.

Keet had paused, as if to allow him time to dwell upon the terror that hovered beyond her thin skin. Now, as if she had gauged his reactions correctly, she continued.

"My walls are strong and they are flexible enough so they will not, even at this depth, collapse. But I have sprung a leak!

"It is a very small one, but it is filling a compartment between my outer wall and my inner. And, I must confess, a panel from my inner wall has been dislodged by the impact of the explosions. They were quite close."

She spoke as if she were a woman telling her doctor that she had a diseased kidney.

"My pumps are working well enough so that I can keep this water from eventually filling up my ulterior," she said. "Unfortunately, the wetness has affected part of the circuits that direct my steering gear. I can direct myself in but one direction because my diving rudders are now locked."

She paused dramatically and then said, "That direction is downwards."

Her words brought terror. There would be no opening of this door. It would only bring in the blackness and the crushing, not light and air and his . . .

He clenched his fists and summoned the strength to hurl back the panic. She would know what effect her words were having; she'd be counting on them. The chances were very strong that the bonds around his arms contained instruments to measure his blood pressure and heart beats. She could tell when he was lying to her and also when he was in a state of fear.

"I have means with which to repair myself," she continued, "but this leak has, unfortunately, also put out of commission those circuits that direct the repairing arms. Most unfortunate."

His voice was tight as his clenched fists. "So?"

"So I wish to release you from your cell and allow you to stop the leak and to repair the circuits. The material for stopping the leak and the box containing the blueprints are in my engine room. You can read the circuits from these."

"And if I do this?"

"I will take you back unharmed to the mother ship."

"And if I don't?"

"I will shut off your air. But first, I will turn off your light."

She might as well have struck him on the head and slammed the coffin lid shut in his face. He knew he couldn't stand against what she threatened. He didn't want to admit himself a coward; he wanted desperately to believe that he was strong. But he knew that there was something buried in him that would betray him.

When the darkness came and the air grew hot and stuffy, he would be as a child again, a child shut up inside a closet that seemed to him to be sinking down towards the earth's centre, never to rise again. And above him would be the weight of the earth itself, its seas and mountains and the people walking far, far overhead.

"Well?" Her voice was impatient.

He sighed. "I'll do it."

After all, as long as he lived, he had hopes of escaping. Perhaps of seizing this monstrosity . . .

He shook his head wryly. Why try to fool himself? He was a coward and no good. If he hadn't been, he'd never have been running away from fear all his life, running home to his mother. He'd not have given up that prominent teaching job at a big midwestern university and come out to the coast to teach because he could be close to his mother there.

She had refused to leave her home, so he had come to her.

And afterwards, when he met Jane and allowed her to talk him into working at that big electronics laboratory in Hawaii, he had thought several times that he'd like to have his mother come and visit them. And when, after many bitter quarrels, Jane had refused to allow it because she said his mother was smothering the manhood out of him, he had walked out on her.

And now, here he was back in the closet sinking ever deeper into the crushing abyss, back in the closet because he had run away again. If he had had the guts to stay with Jane, he wouldn't be in this predicament.

The terrible part about it was that he recognized that Jane was right. He'd known his mother had her hold over him because of this curious twist in his brain. Yet he'd not been able to do anything about it except struggle feebly, just as he had been swept into the open maw of this monster and was now obeying her every word. And all because of a fear that he could not face.

Her sharp voice drove into his reverie.

"There is only one thing holding me back from releasing you."

"What is that?"

"Can I trust you?"

"What can I do? I don't want to die, and only by staying with you can I live. Even if it is as a prisoner."

"Oh, we treat our co-operative technicians very well."

He did not miss the stress on co-operative. He shivered and wondered what was ahead for him and if, perhaps, it would not be as well to refuse her. He would at least go down with honour.

Honour was such a meaningless word, here so many solid fathoms under the seas, where nobody would ever know the sacrifice that he had made. He'd just be one of the missing, forgotten by all except his mother and Jane. And she—she was young and pretty and intelligent. She'd find somebody else, soon enough. The thought sent a wave of anger through him.

Keet said, "Your blood pressure went up. What were you thinking?"

He wanted to tell her it was none of her business, but he knew that she might suspect he was devising some ways of tricking her. He confessed.

Indifferently, she said, "You bourgeois Yankees should learn to control your emotions. Or, better yet, get rid of them. You will lose the war because of your stupidity and your sheep-like emotions."

Under other circumstances, Jones would have laughed at the idea of a machine spouting off such patriotisms, but now he was only slightly interested to know that *Keet*'s builders had not neglected even the ideological side of the well-brought-up, mechanical brain.

Besides—and this was a thought that made him wince—she might be right.

"Before I let you loose, Jones," she said, her voice taking on more of an edge, "I must warn you that I am taking precautions against any sabotage on your part. I will be very frank with you and confess that, while you are in the engine room, I cannot keep as close a check on you as I can while you are here. But I have all sorts of means for following your movements. If you should touch any unauthorized parts—or even get near them—I will be warned.

"Now, I will admit that I have only one aggressive weapon against you. If you do not behave, I will at once release an anaesthetic gas. I will leave the cell door open so the gas will eventually flood the rest of me. As the corridors are very narrow—being designed solely for maintenance men who work on me when I am in port—these quarters will quickly fill up. You will be overcome."

"And after that?" asked Jones.

"I will keep up the flow until you die. Then we both perish. But I will have the satisfaction of knowing that no capitalist boot-licker conquered me. And I am not afraid of death, as you are."

Jones doubted that last statement. It was true she would not be afraid in the sense he was. But her makers must have built into her a striving for survival that would be as strong as his. Otherwise, she would not be the fighting machine the enemy wanted, and they might as well construct the more conventional type of sub manned with beings who would fight for their lives.

The main difference was that, being a machine, she was not neurotic. He was a man, much more highly organized. Therefore, he was much more capable of having something go wrong with him. The higher the creature, the greater the downfall.

His plastic bonds snapped back. He rose, rubbing his tingling arms and legs. At the same time, the cell door slid back into a hollow in the wall. He walked towards it and then peered down the passageway. He drew back.

"Go ahead!" said *Keet*, impatiently.

"It's so dark," he said. "And so low and narrow. I'll have to crawl."

"I can't give you any light," she snapped. "There are flashlights for the maintenance men, but those are located in a locker in the engine-room. You'll have to go get them."

He could not. It was impossible to urge his legs into that solid blackness.

Keet swore an enemy oath. At least, he supposed it was an oath. It certainly sounded like one.

"Jones, you bourgeois coward! Get out of this room!"

He whimpered, "I can't."

"Ha! If all Yankee civilians are like you, you will surely lose the war."

He could not explain to her that everybody was not like him. His weakness was special; it excused him. There was just no fighting against it.

"Jones, if you do not get out of here, I will flood this cell with the gas."

"If you do, you will be lost, too," he reminded her. "You will stay here forever with your nose in the mud."

"I know that. But I have a stronger directive than survival. If I have to take a choice between being captured or perishing, I accept the latter. Without the qualms that distinguish you bourgeois."

She paused and then, with a contempt so strong he could almost see the curl of the speaker's lip, she said, "Now *get!*"

He had no doubt she meant what she said. Moreover, so burning had been the derision in her voice, he felt as if a flame had lashed out and burnt the back of his legs. He crouched down and plunged into the darkness and the narrowness.

Even then, he knew that she was not capable of any real contempt. It was just the makers had put into her electronic brain the directives that she treat the captured enemy in such and such a fashion. She was aware of his psychological states, and she automatically turned on contempt or whatever emotion was needed when the time came. Nevertheless, there had been a sting in her voice, and it had struck deep.

Bent over, knuckles almost touching the plastic floor, he walked like an ape in a strange forest. His eyes burned through the darkness as if they would furnish their own light. But he could see nothing. Several times he glanced nervously over his shoulder and was always comforted by the square of light that the cell globe threw out. As long as he had that in sight, he wouldn't be too lost.

The corridor took a little curve. When he looked behind him, there was only the faintest glow to show that all was not black, that he was not, after all, shut up in a closet. His heart beat fast, and something welled up from the lowest and deepest part of his being. It brought with it an oily, heavy, black scum of fear and reasonless panic. It filled his heart and crept up into his throat It tried to choke him.

He stopped and put both hands out against the walls on either side. They were solid and cold to the touch and they were not shifting in towards him to crush him. He knew that. Yet, for just the flicker of a feeling, he had felt them *move*. And he had felt the air thicken, as if it were a snake about to coil around his neck.

"My name is Chris Jones," he said aloud. His voice rang along the .corridors. "I am thirty years old. I am not a child of six. I am a specialist in electronics and capable of making my own living. I have a wife, whom I realize now, for the first time, dear God, I love more than anything else in the world. I am an American, and I am now at war with the enemy, and it is my duty and right and privilege, and should be my joy, if I were of the heroic mould, to do everything in my power to cripple or destroy that enemy. I have my own good hands and my knowledge. Yet God knows I am not doing what I should. I am creeping along a tunnel like a small child, shivering in my boots, ready to run crying for mother, back to the light and the safety. And I am aiding and abetting the enemy so that I may have that light and safety and my mother's voice once again."

His voice shook, but he firmed it. Its hardening was an indication of what was taking place within him. Now or never, he breathed to himself. Now or never. If he turned back, if his legs and heart failed him, it was all up with him. It would not matter at all that he might eventually reach safety as a prisoner of the enemy. Or even that he might be rescued and go home to his own people, free. If he did not break that fault in him, throw it down and march over it, he would always be a prisoner of the enemy. He had always been a captive of the enemy, he realized, and the enemy was himself. Now, deep under the sea, caught in this confined and lightless corridor, he must wrestle with that enemy whose face he couldn't see but knew well, and he must overthrow it. Or be thrown.

The question was, how?

The answer was, go ahead. Do not stop.

He moved slowly, feeling the wall with his right hand. *Keet* had given him directions; if he followed them he could locate the locker in the engine room. And he did. After what seemed hours of groping and fighting off the choking sensation around neck and breast, he felt an object whose dimensions answered *Keet*'s description. The key was hanging by a chain from a staple; he inserted it and unlocked the door. Another minute, and he had turned on the flashlight.

He played it like a hose about him. Beside him was the huge cube of the atomic reactor. Its exterior consisted of newly invented alloy that blocked radiation, yet did not weigh nearly as much as the now obsolete lead shielding. Nevertheless, knowing that there was some radiation leaking through and that the maintenance men would wear anti-radiation suits, he felt uncomfortable. If, however, he did not linger long, he would be safe.

He located, easily enough, the dislodged panel. It was in itself evidence that *Keet*, though she may have been well-planned, had been hastily built.

He changed that conclusion. Perhaps one of the men who had helped build her had been a member of the underground, a saboteur. This weak part of *Keet* was his handiwork.

He turned his flashlight into the opening. It showed a fine spray of water spurting at intervals of several seconds through an invisible hole. This might be further evidence that there were hands among the enemy working for the so-called bourgeois swine. The sub was formed of parts welded together for greater strength, instead of being riveted. *Keet*'s body should not leak unless a projectile had shattered a hole in the metal. That did not seem likely. So it was possible that this section had been deliberately flawed.

It did not matter, Jones thought. Whether on purpose or by accident, the deed had been done. It was up to him to take advantage of it.

He examined the compartment. The circuits inside were under water, but it was not because of their immersion that they were not working. Incased in plastic, they could operate inside a water-filled chamber. But due to a series of safety devices, this section of circuits had an automatic shut-off in case of emergencies such as the present. *Keet* could not turn them on until the leak was stopped up.

Jones returned to the locker and took out a spray gun. He squirted a semi-fluid over the spray which came through the wall rhythmically. The stuff congealed and dried. The spray was at once shut off.

Jones rose and turned to walk, stooped over, back to the locker. There he would look for a dipper with which to remove the water faster, inasmuch as the pumps were not working swiftly enough. But he stopped, one foot ahead of the other, as if he had been frozen in mid-stride.

What a fool he was! Why hadn't he noticed this before? He must have been in a hell of a blue funk not to have thought at once of this!

Keet had said that her nose was buried in the mud and that she could not withdraw until the circuits governing the steering mechanism were turned on again.

Yet there was no evidence at all that the craft was tilted. He could walk without having to lean one way or the other to compensate for the supposed incline.

Keet, then, was lying for reasons of her own.

He forgot about the fear that was still pressing around him, kept back only by an effort of strong will. This problem demanded all of his attention, and he gave every bit of it.

He had taken her word for the true state of their situation because it had not occurred to him that a robot could lie. But now that he thought about it, it was only natural that the machine should be cast in the mold of the makers. They boasted that lying was a good thing if it got them what they desired. And they would, of course, have built a lie-fabricator into *Keet*. If the occasion demanded it, she would make up something contrary to reality.

The big, million-dollar question was—why should she feel it necessary to do so?

Answer: She must feel weak, exposed.

Question: Where did she feel weak?

Answer: He, Jones, was her tender spot.

Why?

Because he was a man. He could walk around, and he could think. He might get nerve enough to take action against her. If he did, he might overcome her.

Keet was not nearly as bold and strong as she pretended. She had had to play upon his own weakness, his fear of the dark and the narrow, of the awful weight of water supposedly hanging over him. She had relied on that to make him meekly repair the damage and then, like the sheep he was, return to the pen. And, he thought, probably to the slaughter. He doubted now that she would take him back to the mother ship. She might be out to sea for a year or more until she found enough targets at which to shoot all of her forty torpedoes. In the meantime, she would have to be feeding him and giving him air.

She was not built large enough for that; she did not have much cargo space.

The cell in which he had lain must have been for the temporary keeping of prisoners who could be questioned. Also, it was probably meant for the cabins of spies and saboteurs, who would be let out, some dark night, on America's coast. *Keet* had been lying to him from the beginning.

The irony of it was that, in forcing him to repair her damage, she had had to use his particular fault of character to get him to do so. Yet, in so doing, she had forced him to overcome his weakness; she had made him strong.

For the first time since he had left his wife, he smiled with sincerity.

At the same instant, his flashlight picked out the spray gun where he had laid it. His eyes narrowed. *Keet* had been correct in her fears. In essence, she was a machine with a machine's limitations, and he was a man. He was mobile, and he had an imagination. Therein lay the enemy's defeat.

He could hear her voice echoing down the corridors, asking where he was and threatening to release the gas if he did not report at once to her.

"I'm coming, *Keet*," he called. His one hand held a screwdriver which he had taken from the locker, and the other held the spray gun.

***

Two days later, a navy patrol boat dived towards the sub, which lay helpless upon the surface. The alert observer spotted the man standing upon the sleek back and waving a white shirt. The plane did not release its bombs, but, after a judicious scouting, landed and picked up the man, who turned out to be an American with the good old American name of Jones.

He told his story over the radio on his way back to Hawaii. A destroyer close by immediately set out to take over *Keet*. When Jones landed, he had to make an official report and repeat in greater detail what had happened. In reply to a question a naval officer put to him, he answered, "Yes, I did take a chance, but I had to. I was sure that she—pardon me, the robot—was lying to me. If we'd had our nose stuck in the mud, I should have detected at once that the cell and the corridor were on a slant. Moreover, the water was not coming out steadily, as it would have if it had great pressure behind it. It spurted through the fissure, true, but only at intervals. It didn't take much deduction to see that we were on the surface, and that every time a wave hit that side, it forced some of its water through.

"*Keet* was depending on me not to notice this, to be so overwhelmed by our supposed situation that I would fix up the trouble and then creep back into the cell."

And I would have, too, he thought grimly, if it had not been for that unutterable scorn in her voice and the fact that then was the moment in which I had to prove myself forever a man or a coward.

I'm still afraid of the dark and the narrow, but it is a fear that I can conquer. *Keet* did not think I could. But to make sure, she told me that I was at the bottom of the sea. She did not want me to know that her steering gear was set so that she was on the surface, an easy prey to the first American ship that came by. She calculated that if I knew that, I might get nerve enough to revolt. Unfortunately for her, she did not give me any credit for brains. Or else she banked on my fear neutralizing my intelligence. And she was so near to being correct.

"Now, just what did you do with the spray gun?" asked the Lieutenant-Commander.

"First, I held my breath and ran into the cell where I had been prisoner. I located the vent from which the gas was coming and sprayed the stop-leak cement on it. That blocked it. Then I retreated to the locker, read the blueprints there, and located *Keet*'s 'brain.'

"It took me only a minute to disconnect her from her 'body.'"

He grinned. "That did not stop her voice, which gave me an unladylike cussing. But, inasmuch as it was in the enemy's tongue, I didn't understand a word of it. Funny, isn't it, that she, like a human being, should revert to her native tongue in a moment of fury and frustration?"

"Yes, and then?"

"I stimulated the circuits that opened the deck hatch and let in air from the outside."

"And you weren't sure whether or not air or water would come flooding in?"

He nodded. "That is right." He did not add that he had stood there, cold and shaking, while he waited.

"Very well," said the Lieutenant-Commander with an admiring glance that warmed Jones and for the first time made him realize that he had, after all, done something in the heroic mold. "You may go. We'll call you if we want to hear any more. Is there anything you wish before you go?"

"Yes," he said looking around. "Where's the telephone? I'd like to call my wife."

. . . My Sister's Brother

The sixth night on Mars, Lane wept.

He sobbed loudly while tears ran down his cheeks. He smacked his right fist into the palm of his left hand until the flesh burned. He howled with the anguish of loneliness. He swore the most obscene and blasphemous oaths he knew, and he knew quite a few after ten years in the U.N.'s Space Arm.

After a while, he quit weeping. He dried his eyes, downed a shot of Scotch, and felt much better.

He wasn't ashamed because he had bawled like a woman. After all, there had been a Man who had not been a man who had not been ashamed to weep. Moreover, one of the reasons he had been chosen to be in the first party to land on Mars was this very ability to cry. No one could call him coward or weakling. A man with little courage could never have passed the battery of tests on Earth's space school, let alone have made the many thrusts to the Moon. But though male and masculine, he had a woman's safety valve. He could dissolve in tears the grinding stones of tension within; he was the reed that bent before the wind, not the oak that toppled, roots and all.

Now, the weight and ache in his breast gone, feeling almost cheerful, he made his scheduled report over the transceiver to the circum-Martian vessel five hundred and eight miles overhead. Then he did what men must do any place in the universe. Afterwards, he lay down in the bunk and opened the one personal book he had been allowed to bring along, an anthology of the world's greatest poetry.

He read here and there, running, pausing for only a line or two, then completing in his head the thousand-times murmured lines. Here and there he read, like a bee tasting the best of the nectar . . .

> It is the voice of my beloved that knocketh, saying,
> Open to me, my sister, my love, my dove, my
> undenied . . .

> We have a little sister,
> And she hath no breasts;
> What shall we do for our sister
> In the day when she shall be spoken for?

> Yea, though I walk through the valley of the
> shadow of death,
> I will fear no evil: for Thou art with me . . .

> Come live with me and be my love
> And we shall all the pleasures prove . . .

> It lies not in our power to love or hate
> For will in us is over-ruled by fate . . .

> With thee conversing, I forget all time,
> All seasons, and their change, all please
> alike . . .

He read on about love and man and woman until he had almost forgotten his troubles. His lids drooped; the book fell from his hand. But he roused himself, climbed out of the bunk, got down on his knees, and prayed that he be forgiven and that his blasphemy and despair be understood. And he prayed that his four lost comrades be found safe and sound. Then he climbed back into the bunk and fell asleep.

At dawn he woke reluctantly to the alarm clock's ringing. Nevertheless, he did not fall back into sleep but rose, turned on the transceiver, filled a cup with water and instant, and dropped in a heat pill. Just as he finished the coffee, he heard Captain Stroyansky's voice from the 'ceiver. Stroyansky spoke with barely a trace of Slavic accent.

"Cardigan Lane? You awake?'

"More or less. How are you?"

"If we weren't worried about all of you down there, we'd be fine."

"I know. Well, what are the captain's orders?"

"There is only one thing to do, Lane. You must go look for the others. Otherwise, you cannot get back up to us. It takes at least two more men to pilot the rocket."

"Theoretically, one man can pilot the beast," replied Lane. "But it's uncertain. However, that doesn't matter. I'm leaving at once to look for the others. I'd do that even if you ordered otherwise."

Stroyansky chuckled. Then he barked like a seal. "The success of the expedition is more important than the fate of four men. Theoretically, anyway. But if I were in your shoes, and I'm glad I am not, I would do the same. So, good luck, Lane."

"Thanks," said Lane. "I'll need more than luck. I'll also need God's help. I suppose He's here, even if the place does look Godforsaken."

He looked through the transparent double plastic walls of the dome.

"The wind's blowing about twenty-five miles an hour. The dust is covering the tractor tracks. I have to get going before they're covered up entirely. My supplies are all packed; I've enough food, air, and water to last me six days. It makes a big package, the air tanks and the sleeping tent bulk large. It's over a hundred Earth pounds, but here only about forty. I'm also taking a rope, a knife, a pickaxe, a flare pistol, half a dozen flares. And a walkie-talkie.

"It should take me two days to walk the thirty miles to the spot where the tracs last reported. Two days to look around. Two days to get back."

"You be back in five days!" shouted Stroyansky. "That's an order! It shouldn't take you more than one day to scout around. Don't take chances. Five days! Otherwise, court-martial for you, Lane!"

And then, in a softer voice, "Good luck, and, if there is a God, may He help you!"

Lane tried to think of things to say, things that might perhaps go down with the *Doctor Livingstone, I presume,* category. But all he could say was, "So long."

Twenty minutes later, he closed behind him the door to the dome's pressure lock. He strapped on the towering pack and began to walk. But when he was about fifty yards from the base, he felt compelled to turn around for one long look at what he might never see again. There, on the yellow-red felsite plain, stood the pressurized bubble. That was to have been the home of the five men for a year. Nearby squatted the glider that had brought them down, its enormous wings spreading far, its skids covered with the forever-blowing dust.

Straight ahead of him was the rocket, standing on its fins, pointing towards the blue-black sky, glittering in the Martian sun, shining with promise of power, escape from Mars, and return to the orbital ship. It had come down to the surface of Mars on the back of the glider in a hundred-and-twenty-mile-an-hour landing. After it had dropped the two six-ton caterpillar tractors it carried, it had been pulled off the glider and tilted on end by winches pulled by those very tractors. Now it waited for him and for the other four men.

"I'll be back," he murmured to it. "And if I have to, I'll take you up by myself."

He began to walk, following the broad double tracks left by the tank. The tracks were faint, for they were two days old, and the blowing silicate dust had almost filled them. The tracks made by the first tank, which had left three days ago, were completely hidden.

The trail led north-west. It left the three-mile-wide plain between two hills of naked rock and entered the quarter-mile corridor between two rows of vegetation. The rows ran straight and parallel from horizon to horizon, for miles behind him and miles ahead. A person flying above them would have seen many such lines, marching side by side. To observers in the orbital ship the hundreds of rows looked like one solid line. That line was one of the so-called canals of Mars.

Lane, on the ground and close to one row, saw it for what it was. Its foundation was an endless three-foot high tube, most of whose bulk, like an iceberg's, lay buried in the ground. The curving sides were covered with blue-green lichenoids that grew on every rock or projection. From the spine of the tube, separated at regular intervals, grew the trunks of plants. The trunks were smooth shiny blue-green pillars two feet thick and six feet high. Out of their tops spread radially many pencil-thin branches, like bats' fingers. Between the fingers stretched a blue-green membrane, the single tremendous leaf of the umbrella tree.

When Lane had first seen them from the glider as it hurtled over them, he had thought they looked like an army of giant hands uplifted to catch the sun. Giant they were, for each rib-supported leaf measured fifty feet across. And hands they were, hands to beg for and catch the rare gold of the tiny sun. During the day, the ribs on the sides nearest the moving sun dipped towards the ground, and the furthest ribs tilted upwards. Obviously, the daylong maneuver was designed to expose the complete area of the membrane to the light, to allow not an inch to remain in shadow.

It was to be expected that strange forms of plant life would be found here. But structures built by animal life were not expected. Especially when they were so large and covered an eighth of the planet.

These structures were the tubes from which rose the trunks of the umbrella trees. Lane had tried to drill through the rocklike side of the tube. So hard was it, it had blunted one drill and had done a second no good before he had chipped off a small piece. Contented for the moment with that, he had taken it to the dome, there to examine it under a microscope. After an amazed look, he had whistled. Embedded in the cement-like mass were plant cells. Some were partially destroyed; some, whole.

Further tests had shown him that the substance was composed of cellulose, a lignin-like stuff, various nucleic acids, and unknown materials.

He had reported his discovery and also his conjecture to the orbital ship. Some form of animal life had, at some time, chewed up and partially digested wood and then had regurgitated it as a cement. From the cement the tubes had been fashioned.

The following day he intended to go back to the tube and blast a hole in it. But two of the men had set out in a tractor on a field exploration. Lane, as radio operator for that day, had stayed in the dome. He was to keep in contact with the two, who were to report to him every fifteen minutes.

The tank had been gone about two hours and must have been about thirty miles away, when it had failed to report. Two hours later, the other tank, carrying two men, had followed the prints of the first party. They had gone about thirty miles from base and were maintaining continuous radio contact with Lane.

"There's a slight obstacle ahead," Greenberg had said. "It's a tube coming out at right angles from the one we've been paralleling. It has no plants growing from it. Not much of a rise, not much of a drop on the other side, either. We'll make it easy."

Then he had yelled.

That was all.

Now, the day after, Lane was on foot, following the fading trail. Behind him lay the base camp, close to the junction of the two *canali* known as Avernus and Tartarus. He was between two of the rows of vegetation which formed Tartarus, and he was travelling northeastward, towards the Sirenum Mare, the so-called Siren Sea. The Mare, he supposed, would be a much broader group of tree-bearing tubes.

He walked steadily while the sun rose higher and the air grew warmer. He had long ago turned off his suit-heater. This was summer and close to the equator. At noon the temperature would be around 70 degrees Fahrenheit.

But at dusk, when the temperature had plunged through the dry air to zero, Lane was in his sleeping tent. It looked like a cocoon, being sausage-shaped and not much larger than his body. It was inflated so he could remove his helmet and breathe while he warmed himself from the battery-operated heater and ate and drank. The tent was also very flexible; it changed its cocoon shape to a triangle while Lane sat on a folding chair from which hung a plastic bag and did that which every man must do.

During the daytime he did not have to enter the sleeping tent for this. His suit was ingeniously contrived so he could unflap the rear section and expose the necessary area without losing air or pressure from the rest of his suit. Naturally, there was no thought of tempting the teeth of the Martian night. Sixty seconds at midnight were enough to get a severe frostbite where one sat down.

Lane slept until half an hour after dawn, ate, deflated the tent, folded it, stowed it, the battery, heater, food-box, and folding chair into his pack, threw away the plastic sack, shouldered the pack, and resumed his walk.

By noon the tracks faded out completely. It made little difference, for there was only one route the tanks could have taken. That was the corridor between the tubes and the trees.

Now he saw what the two tanks had reported. The trees on his right began to look dead. The trunks and leaves were brown, and the ribs drooped.

He began walking faster, his heart beating hard. An hour passed, and still the line of dead trees stretched as far as he could see.

"It must be about here," he said out loud to himself.

Then he stopped. Ahead was an obstacle.

It was the tube of which Greenberg had spoken, the one that ran at right angles to the other two and joined them.

Lane looked at it and thought that he could still hear Greenberg's despairing cry.

That thought seemed to turn a valve in him so that the immense pressure of loneliness, which he had succeeded in holding back until then, flooded in. The blue-black of the sky became the blackness and infinity of space itself, and he was a speck of flesh in an immensity as large as Earth's land area, a speck that knew no more of this world than a new-born baby knows of his.

Tiny and helpless, like a baby . . .

No, he murmured to himself, not a baby. Tiny, yes. Helpless, no. Baby, no. I am a man, a man, an Earthman . . .

Earthman: Cardigan Lane, Citizen of the U.S.A. Born in Hawaii, the fiftieth state. Of mingled German, Dutch, Chinese, Japanese, Negro, Cherokee, Polynesian, Portuguese, Russian-Jewish, Irish, Scotch, Norwegian, Finnish, Czech, English, and Welsh ancestry. Thirty-one years old. Five foot six. One hundred and forty pounds. Brown-haired. Blue-eyed. Hawk-featured. M.D. and Ph.D. Married. Childless. Methodist. Sociable mesomorphic mesovert. Radio ham. Dog breeder. Deer hunter. Skin diver. Writer of first-rate but far from great poetry. All contained in his skin and his pressure suit, plus a love of companionship and life, an intense curiosity, and a courage. And now very much afraid of losing everything except his loneliness.

For some time he stood like a statue before the three-foot-wall of the tube. Finally, he shook his head violently, shook off his fear like a dog shaking off water. Lightly, despite the towering pack on his back, he leaped up on to the top of the tube and looked on the other side, though there was nothing he had not seen before jumping.

The view before him differed from the one behind in only one respect. This was the number of small plants that covered the ground. Or rather, he thought, after taking a second look, he had never seen these plants this size before. They were foot-high replicas of the huge umbrella trees that sprouted from the tubes. And they were not scattered at random, as might have been expected if they had grown from seeds blown by the wind. Instead, they grew in regular rows, the edges of the plants in one row separated from the other by about two feet

His heart beat even faster. Such spacing must mean they were planted by intelligent life. Yet intelligent life seemed very improbable, given the Martian environment.

Possibly some natural condition might have caused the seeming artificiality of this garden. He would have to investigate.

Always with caution, though. So much depended on him: the lives of the four men, the success of the expedition. If this one failed, it might be the last. Many people on Earth were groaning loudly because of the cost of Space Arm and crying wildly for results that would mean money and power.

The field, or garden, extended for about three hundred yards. At its far end there was another tube at right angles to the two parallel ones. And at this point the giant umbrella plants regained their living and shining blue-green colour.

The whole set-up looked to Lane very much like a sunken garden. The square formation of the high tubes kept out the wind and most of the felsite flakes. The walls held the heat within the square.

Lane searched the top of the tube for bare spots where the metal plates of the caterpillar tractor's treads would have scraped off the lichenoids. He found none but was not surprised. The lichenoids grew phenomenally fast under the summertime sun.

He looked down at the ground on the garden side of the tube, where the tractors had presumably descended. Here there were no signs of the tractors' passage, for the little umbrellas grew up to within two feet of the edge of the tube, and they were uncrushed. Nor did he find any tracks at the ends of the tube where it joined the parallel rows.

He paused to think about his next step and was surprised to find himself breathing hard. A quick check of his air gauge showed him that the trouble wasn't an almost empty tank. No it was the apprehension, the feeling of eeriness, of something *wrong*, that was causing his heart to beat so fast, to demand more oxygen.

Where could two tractors and four men have gone? And what could have caused them to disappear?

Could they have been attacked by some form of intelligent life? if that had happened, the unknown creatures had either carried off the six-ton tanks, or driven them away, or else forced the men to drive them off.

Where? How? By whom?

The hairs on the back of his neck stood up.

"Here is where it must have happened," he muttered to himself. "The first tank reported seeing this tube barring its way and said it would report again in another ten minutes. That was the last I heard from it. The second was cut off just as it was on top of the tube. Now, what happened? There are no cities on the surface of Mars, and no indications of underground civilization. The orbital ship would have seen openings to such a place through its telescope . . ."

He yelled so loudly that he was deafened as his voice bounced off the confines of his helmet. Then he fell silent, watching the line of basketball-size blue globes rise from the soil at the far end of the garden and swiftly soar into the sky.

He threw back his head until the back of it was stopped by the helmet and watched the rising globes as they left the ground, swelling until they seemed to be hundreds of feet across. Suddenly, like a soap bubble, the topmost one disappeared. The second in line, having reached the height of the first, also popped. And the others followed.

They were transparent. He could see some white cirrus clouds through the blue of the bubbles.

Lane did not move but watched the steady string of globes spurt from the soil. Though startled, he did not forget his training. He noted that the globes, besides being semi-transparent, rose at a right-angle to the ground and did not drift with the wind. He counted them and got to forty-nine when they ceased appearing.

He waited for fifteen minutes. When it looked as if nothing more would happen, he decided that he must investigate the spot where the globes seemed to have popped out of the ground. Taking a deep breath, he bent his knees and jumped out into the garden. He landed lightly about twelve feet out from the edge of the tube and between two rows of plants.

For a second he did not know what was happening, though he realized that something was wrong. Then he whirled around. Or tried to do so. One foot came up, but the other sank deeper.

He took one step forward, and the forward foot also disappeared into the thin stuff beneath the red-yellow dust. By now the other foot was too deep in to be pulled out.

Then he was hip-deep and grabbing at the stems of the plants to both sides of him. They uprooted easily, coming out of the soil, one clenched in each hand.

He dropped them and threw himself backward in the hope he could free his legs and lie stretched out on the jelly-like stuff. Perhaps, if his body presented enough of an area, he could keep from sinking. And, after a while, he might be able to work his way to the ground near the tube. There, he hoped, it would be firm.

His violent effort succeeded. His legs came up out of the sticky semi-liquid. He lay spreadeagled on his back and looked up at the sky through the transparent dome of his helmet. The sun was to his left; when he turned his head inside the helmet he could see the sun sliding down the arc from the zenith. It was descending at a slightly slower pace than on Earth, for Mars' day was about forty minutes longer. He hoped that, if he couldn't regain solid ground, he could remain suspended until evening fell. By then this quagmire would be frozen enough for him to rise and walk up on it. Provided that he got up before he himself was frozen fast.

Meanwhile, he would follow the approved method of saving oneself when trapped in quicksand. He would roll over quickly, once, and then spreadeagle himself again. By repeating this manoeuvre, he might eventually reach that bare strip of soil at the tube.

The pack on his back prevented him from rolling. The straps around his shoulders would have to be loosened.

He did so, and at the same time felt his legs sinking. Their weight was pulling them under, whereas the air tanks in the packs, the air tanks strapped to his chest, and the bubble of his helmet gave buoyancy to the upper part of his body.

He turned over on his side, grabbed the pack, and pulled himself up on to it. The pack, of course went under. But his legs were free, though slimy with liquid and caked with dust. And he was standing on top of the narrow island of the pack.

The thick jelly rose up to his ankles while he considered two courses of action.

He could squat on the pack and hope that it would not sink too far before it was stopped by the permanently frozen layer that must exist . . .

How far? He had gone down hip-deep and felt nothing firm beneath his feet. And . . . He groaned. The tractors! Now he knew what had happened to them. They had gone over the tube and down into the garden, never suspecting that the solid-seeming surface covered this quagmire. And down they had plunged, and it had been Greenberg's horrified realization of what lay beneath that dust that had made him cry out, and then the stuff had closed over the tank and its antenna, and the transmitter, of course, had been cut off.

He must give up his second choice because it did not exist. To get to the bare strip of soil at the tube would be useless. It would be as unfirm as the rest of the garden. It was at that point that the tanks must have fallen in.

Another thought came to him: that the tanks must have disturbed the orderly arrangement of the little umbrellas close to the tube. Yet there was no sign of such a happening. Therefore, somebody must have rescued the plants and set them up again.

That meant that somebody might come along in time to rescue him.

Or to kill him, he thought.

In either event, his problem would be solved.

Meanwhile, he knew it was no use to make a jump from the pack to the strip at the tube. The only thing to do was to stay on top of the pack and hope it didn't sink too deeply.

However, the pack did sink. The jelly rose swiftly to his knee then his rate of descent began slowing. He prayed, not for a miracle but only that the buoyancy of the pack plus the tank on his chest would keep him from going completely under.

Before he had finished praying, he had stopped sinking. The sticky stuff had risen no higher than his breast and had left his arms free.

He gasped with relief but did not feel overwhelmed with joy. In less than four hours the air in his tank would be exhausted. Unless he could get another tank from the pack, he was done for.

He pushed down hard on the pack and threw his arms up in the air and back in the hope his legs would rise again and he could spread-eagle. If he could do that then the pack, relieved of his weight, might rise to the surface. And he could get another tank from it.

But his legs, impeded by the stickiness, did not rise far enough, and his body, shooting off in reaction to the kick, moved a little distance from the pack. It was just far enough so that when the legs inevitably sank again, they found no platform on which to be supported. Now he had to depend entirely on the lift of his air tank.

It did not give him enough to hold him at his former level; this time he sank until his arms and shoulders were nearly under, and only his helmet stuck out.

He was helpless.

Several years from now the second expedition, if any, would perhaps see the sun glinting off his helmet and would find his body stuck like a fly in glue.

If that does happen, he thought, I will at least have been of some use; my death will warn them of this trap. But I doubt if they'll find me. I think that Somebody or Something will have removed me and hidden me.

Then, feeling an inrush of despair, he closed his eyes and murmured some of the words he had read that last night in the base, though he knew them so well it did not matter whether he had read them recently or not.

Yea, though I walk through the valley of the shadow of death, I will fear no evil; for Thou art with me.

*   *   *

Repeating that didn't lift the burden of hopelessness. He felt absolutely alone, deserted by everybody, even by his Creator. Such was the desolation of Mars.

But when he opened his eyes, he knew he was not alone. He saw a Martian.

A hole had appeared in the wall of the tube to his left. It was a round section about four feet across, and it had sunk in as if it were a plug being pulled inwards, as indeed it was.

A moment later a head popped out of the hole. The size of a Georgia watermelon, it was shaped like a football and was as pink as a baby's bottom. Its two eyes were as large as coffee cups and each was equipped with two vertical lids. It opened its two parrot-like beaks, ran out a very long tubular tongue, withdrew the tongue, and snapped the beak shut. Then it scuttled out from the hole to reveal a body also shaped like a football and only three times as large as its head. The pinkish body was supported three feet from the ground on ten spindly spidery legs, five on each side. Its legs ended in broad round pads on which it ran across the jellymire surface, sinking only slightly. Behind it streamed at least fifty others.

These picked up the little plants that Lane had upset in his struggles and licked them clean with narrow round tongues that shot out at least two feet. They also seemed to communicate by touching their tongues, as insects do with antennae.

As he was in the space between two rows, he was not involved in the setting up of the dislodged plants. Several of them ran their tongues over his helmet, but these were the only ones that paid him any attention. It was then that he began to stop dreading that they might attack him with their powerful looking beaks. Now he broke into a sweat at the idea that they might ignore him completely.

That was just what they did. After gently embedding the thin roots of the plantlets in the sticky stuff, they raced off towards the hole in the blue.

Lane, overwhelmed with despair, shouted after them, though he knew they couldn't hear him through his helmet and the thin air even if they had hearing organs.

"Don't leave me here to die!"

Nevertheless, that was what they were doing. The last one leaped through the hole, and the entrance stared at him like the round black eye of Death itself.

He struggled furiously to lift himself from the mire, not caring that he was only exhausting himself.

Abruptly, he stopped fighting and stared at the hole.

A figure had crawled out of it, a figure in a pressure-suit.

Now he shouted with joy. Whether the figure was Martian or not, it was built like a member of homo sapiens. It could be presumed to be intelligent and therefore curious.

He was not disappointed. The suited being stood up on two hemispheres of shiny red metal and began walking towards him in a sliding fashion. Reaching him, it handed him the end of a plastic rope it was carrying under its arm.

He almost dropped it. His rescuer's suit was transparent. It was enough of a shock to see clearly the details of the creature's body, but the sight of the two heads within the helmet caused him to turn pale.

The Martian slidewalked to the tube from which Lane had leaped. It jumped lightly from the two bowls on which it had stood, landed on the three-foot-high top of the tube, and began hauling Lane out from the mess. He came out slowly but steadily and soon was scooting forward, gripping the rope. When he reached the foot of the tube, he was hauled on up until he could get his feet in the two bowls. It was easy to jump from them to a place beside the biped.

It unstrapped two more bowls from its back, gave them to Lane, then lowered itself on the two in the garden. Lane followed it across the mire.

Entering the hole, he found himself in a chamber so low he had to crouch. Evidently, it had been constructed by the dekapeds and not by his companion for it, too, had to bend its back and knees.

Lane was pushed to one side by some dekapeds. They picked up the thick plug, made of the same grey stuff as the tube walls, and sealed the entrance with it. Then they shot out of their mouths strand after strand of grey spiderwebby stuff to seal the plug.

The biped motioned Lane to follow, and it slid down a tunnel which plunged into the earth at a forty-five-degree angle. It illuminated the passage with a flashlight which it took from its belt. They came into a large chamber which contained all of the fifty dekapeds. These were waiting motionless. The biped, as if sensing Lane's curiosity, pulled off its glove and held it before several small vents in the wall. Lane removed his glove and felt warm air flowing from the holes.

Evidently this was a pressure chamber, built by the ten-legged things. But such evidence of intelligent engineering did not mean that these things had the individual intelligence of a man. It could mean group intelligence such as Terrestrial bisects possess.

After a while, the chamber was filled with air. Another plug was pulled; Lane followed the dekapeds and his rescuer up another forty-five-degree tunnel. He estimated that he would find himself inside the tube from which the biped had first come. He was right. He crawled through another hole into it.

And a pair of beaks clicked as they bit down on his helmet!

Automatically, he shoved at the thing, and under the force of his blow the dekaped lost its bite and went rolling on the floor, a bundle of thrashing legs.

Lane did not worry about having hurt it. It did not weigh much, but its body must be tough to be able to plunge without damage from the heavy air inside the tube into the almost-stratospheric conditions outside.

However, he did reach for the knife at his belt. But the biped put its hand on his arm and shook one of its heads.

Later, he was to find out that the seeming bite must have been an accident. Always—with one exception—the leggers were to ignore him.

He was also to find that he was lucky. The leggers had come out to inspect their garden because, through some unknown method of detection, they knew that the plantlets had been disturbed. The biped normally would not have accompanied them. However, today, its curiosity aroused because the leggers had gone out three times in three days, it had decided to investigate.

The biped turned out its flashlight and motioned to Lane to follow. Awkwardly, he obeyed. There was light, but it was dim, a twilight. Its source was the many creatures that hung from the ceiling of the tube. These were three feet long and six inches thick, cylindrical, pinkish-skinned, and eyeless. A dozen frond-like limbs waved continuously, and their motion kept air circulating in the tunnel.

Their cold firefly glow came from two globular pulsing organs which hung from both sides of the round loose-lipped mouth at the free end of the creature. Slime drooled from the mouth, and dripped on to the floor or into a narrow channel which ran along the lowest part of the sloping floor. Water ran in the six-inch-deep channel, the first native water he had seen. The water picked up the slime and carried it a little way before it was gulped up by an animal that lay on the bottom of the channel.

Lane's eyes adjusted to the dimness until he could make out the water-dweller. It was torpedo-shaped and without eyes or fins. It had two openings in its body; one obviously sucked in water, the other expelled it.

He saw at once what this meant. The water at the North Pole melted in the summertime and flowed into the far end of the tube system. Helped by gravity and by the pumping action of the line of animals in the channel, the water was passed from the edge of the Pole to the equator.

Leggers ran by him on mysterious errands. Several, however, halted beneath some of the downhanging organisms. They reared up on their hind five legs and their tongues shot out and into the open mouths of the glowing balls. At once the fireworm—as Lane termed it—its cilia waving wildly, stretched itself to twice its former length. Its mouth met the beak of the legger, and there was an exchange of stuff between their mouths.

Impatiently, the biped tugged at Lane's arm. He followed it down the tube. Soon they entered a section where pale roots came down out of holes in the ceiling and spread along the curving walls, gripping them, then becoming a network of many thread-thin rootlets that crept across the floor and into the water of the channel.

Here and there a dekaped chewed at a root and then hurried off to offer a piece to the mouths of the fireworms. After walking for several minutes, the biped stepped across the stream. It then began walking as closely as possible to the wall, meanwhile looking apprehensively at the other side of the tunnel, where they had been walking. Lane also looked but could see nothing at which to be alarmed. There was a large opening at the base of the wall which evidently led into a tunnel. This tunnel, he presumed, ran underground into a room, or rooms, for many leggers dashed in and out of it. And about a dozen, larger than average, paced back and forth like sentries before the hole.

When they had gone about fifty yards past the opening, the biped relaxed. After it had led Lane along for ten minutes, it stopped. It's naked hand touched the wall. He became aware that the hand was small and delicately shaped, like a woman's.

A section of the wall swung out. The biped turned and bent down to crawl into the hole, presenting buttocks and legs femininely rounded, well shaped. It was then that he began thinking of it as a female. Yet the hips, though padded with fatty tissue, were not broad. The bones were not widely separated to make room to carry a child. Despite their curving, the hips were relatively as narrow as a man's.

Behind them, the plug swung shut. The biped did not turn on her flashlight, for there was illumination at the end of the tunnel. The floor and walls were not of the hard grey stuff nor of packed earth. They seemed vitrified, as if glassed by heat.

She was waiting for him when he slid off a three-foot-high ledge into a large room. For a minute he was blinded by the strong light. After his eyes adjusted, he searched for the source of light but could not find it He did observe that there were no shadows in the room.

The biped took off her helmet and suit and hung them in a closet. The door slid open as she approached and closed when she walked away.

She signalled that he could remove his suit. He did not hesitate. Though the air might be poisonous, he had no choice. His tank would soon be empty. Moreover, it seemed likely that the atmosphere contained enough oxygen. Even then he had grasped the idea that the leaves of the umbrella plants, which grew out of the top of the tubes, absorbed sunlight and traces of carbon dioxide. Inside the tunnels, the roots drew up water from the channel and absorbed the great quantity of carbon dioxide released by the dekapeds. Energy of sunlight converted gas and liquid into glucose and oxygen, which were given off in the tunnels.

Even here, in this deep chamber which lay beneath and to one side of the tube, a thick root penetrated the ceiling and spread its thin white web over the walls. He stood directly beneath the flesh growth as he removed his helmet and took his first breath of Martian air. Immediately afterwards, he jumped. Something wet had dropped on his forehead. Looking up, he saw that the root was excreting liquid from a large pore. He wiped the drop off with his finger and tasted it. It was sticky and sweet.

Well, he thought, the tree must normally drop sugar in water. But it seemed to be doing so abnormally fast, because another drop was forming.

Then it came to him that perhaps this was so because it was getting dark outside and therefore cold. The umbrella trees might be pumping the water in their trunks into the warm tunnels. Thus, during the bitter subzero night, they'd avoid freezing and swelling up and cracking wide open.

It seemed a reasonable theory.

He looked around. The place was half living quarters, half biological laboratory. There were beds and tables and chairs and several unidentifiable articles. One was a large black metal box in a corner. From it, at regular intervals, issued a stream of tiny blue bubbles. They rose to the ceiling, growing larger as they did so. On reaching the ceiling they did not stop or burst but simply penetrated the vitrification as if it did not exist.

Lane now knew the origin of the blue globes he had seen appear from the surface of the garden. But their purpose was still obscure.

He wasn't given much time to watch the globes. The biped took a large green ceramic bowl from a cupboard and set it on a table. Lane eyed her curiously, wondering what she was going to do. By now he had seen that the second head belonged to an entirely separate creature. Its slim four-foot length of pinkish skin was coiled about her neck and torso; its tiny flat-faced head turned towards Lane; its snaky light blue eyes glittered. Suddenly, its mouth opened and revealed toothless gums, and its bright red tongue, mammalian, not at all reptilian, thrust out at him.

The biped, paying no attention to the worm's actions, lifted it from her. Gently, cooing a few words in a soft many-vowelled language, she placed it in the bowl. It settled inside and looped around the curve, like a snake in a pit.

The biped took a pitcher from the top of a box of red plastic. Though the box was not connected to any visible power source, it seemed to be a stove. The pitcher contained warm water which she poured into the bowl, half filling it. Under the shower, the worm closed its eyes as if it were purring soundless ecstasy.

Then the biped did something that alarmed Lane.

She leaned over the bowl and vomited into it.

He stepped towards her. Forgetting the fact that she couldn't understand him, he said, "Are you sick?"

She revealed human-looking teeth in a smile meant to reassure him, and she walked away from the bowl. He looked at the worm, which had its head dipped into the mess. Suddenly, he felt sick, for he was sure that it was feeding off the mixture. And he was equally certain that she fed the worm regularly with regurgitated food.

It didn't cancel his disgust to reflect that he shouldn't react to her as he would to a Terrestrial. He knew that she was totally alien and that it was inevitable that some of her ways would repel, perhaps even shock him. Rationally, he knew this. But if his brain told him to understand and forgive, his belly said to loathe and reject.

His aversion was not much lessened by a close scrutiny of her as she took a shower in a cubicle set in the wall. She was about five feet tall and slim as a woman should be slim, with delicate bones beneath rounded flesh. Her legs were human; in nylons and high heels they would have been exciting—other things being equal. However, if the shoes had been toeless, her feet would have caused much comment. They had four toes.

Her long beautiful hands had five fingers. These seemed nailless, like the toes, though a closer examination later showed him they did bear rudimentary nails.

She stepped from the cubicle and began towelling herself, though not before she motioned to him to remove his suit and also to shower. He stared intently back at her until she laughed a short embarrassed laugh. It was feminine, not at all deep. Then she spoke.

He closed his eyes and was hearing what he had thought he would not hear for years: a woman's voice. Hers was extraordinary: husky and honeyed at the same time.

But when he opened his eyes, he saw her for what she was. No woman. No man. What? It? No. The impulse to think *her, she,* was too strong.

This, despite her lack of mammaries. She had a chest, but no nipples, rudimentary or otherwise. Her chest was a man's, muscled under the layer of fat which subtly curved to give the impression that beneath it . . . budding breasts?

No, not this creature. She would never suckle her young. She did not even bear them alive, if she *did* bear. Her belly was smooth, undimpled with a navel.

Smooth also was the region between her legs, hairless, unbroken, as innocent of organ as if she were a nymph painted for some Victorian children's book.

It was that sexless joining of the legs that was so horrible. Like the white belly of a frog, thought Lane, shuddering.

At the same time, his curiosity became even stronger. How did this thing mate and reproduce?

Again she laughed and smiled with fleshy pale-red humanly everted lips and wrinkled a short, slightly uptilted nose and ran her hand through thick straight red-gold fur. It was fur, not hair, and it had a slightly oily sheen, like a water-dwelling animal's.

The face itself, though strange, could have passed for human, but only passed. Her cheekbones were very high and protruded upwards in an unhuman fashion. Her eyes were dark blue and quite human.

This meant nothing. So were an octopus's eyes.

She walked to another closet, and as she went away from him he saw again that though the hips were curved like a woman's they did not sway with the pelvic displacement of the human female.

The door swung momentarily open, revealed the carcasses of several dekapeds, minus their legs, hanging on hooks. She removed one, placed it on a metal table, and out of the cupboard took a saw and several knives and began cutting.

Because he was eager to see the anatomy of the dekaped, he approached the table. She waved him to the shower. Lane removed his suit. When he came to the knife and axe he hesitated, but, afraid she might think him distrustful, he hung up the belt containing his weapons beside the suit. However, he did not take off his clothes because he was determined to view the inner organs of the animal. Later, he would shower.

The legger was not an insect, despite its spidery appearance. Not in the terrestrial sense, certainly. Neither was it a vertebrate. Its smooth hairless skin was an animal's, as lightly pigmented as a blond Swede's. But, though it had an endoskeleton, it had no backbone. Instead, the body bones formed a round cage. Its thin ribs radiated from a cartilaginous collar which adjoined the back of the head. The ribs curved outwards, then in, almost meeting at the posterior. Inside the cage were ventral lung sacs, a relatively large heart, and liver-like and kidney-like organs. Three arteries, instead of the mammalian two, left the heart. He couldn't be sure with such a hurried examination, but it looked as if the dorsal aorta, like some terrestrial reptiles, carried both pure and impure blood.

There were other things to note. The most extraordinary was that, as far as he could discern, the legger had no digestive system. It seemed to lack both intestines and anus unless you would define as an intestine a sac which ran straight through from the throat half-way into the body. Further, there was nothing he could identify as reproductive organs, though this did not mean that it did not possess them. The creature's long tubular tongue, cut open by the biped, exposed a canal running down the length of tongue from its open tip to a bladder at its base; apparently these formed part of the excretory system.

Lane wondered what enabled the legger to stand the great pressure differences between the interior of the tube and the Martian surface. At the same time he realized that this ability was no more wonderful than the biological mechanism which gave whales and seals the power to endure without harm the enormous pressures a half mile below the sea's surface.

The biped looked at him with round and very pretty blue eyes, laughed, and then reached into the chopped open skull and brought out the tiny brain.

"*Hauaimi,*" she said slowly. She pointed to her head, repeated, "*Hauaimi,*" and then indicated his head. "*Hauaimi.*"

Echoing her, he pointed at his own head. "*Hauaimi.* Brain."

"Brain," she said, and she laughed again.

She proceeded to call out the organs of the legger which corresponded to hers. Thus, the preparations for the meal passed swiftly as he proceeded from the carcass to other objects in the room. By the time she had fried the meat and boiled strips of the membranous leaf of the umbrella plant, and also added from cans various exotic foods, she had exchanged at least forty words with him. An hour later, he could remember twenty.

There was one thing yet to learn. He pointed to himself and said, "Lane."

Then he pointed to her and gave her a questioning look.

"Mahrseeya," she said.

"Martia?" he repeated. She corrected him, but he was so struck by the resemblance that always afterwards he called her that. After a while, she would give up trying to teach him the exact pronunciation.

Martia washed her hands and poured him a bowlful of water. He used the soap and towel she handed him, then walked to the table where she stood waiting. On it was a bowl of thick soup, a plate of fried brains, salad of boiled leaves and some unidentifiable vegetables, a plate of ribs with thick dark legger meat, hard-boiled eggs and little loaves of bread.

Martia gestured for him to sit down. Evidently her code did not allow her to sit down before her guest did. He ignored his chair, went behind her, put his hand on her shoulder, pressed down, and with the other hand slid her chair under her. She turned her head to smile up at him. Her fur slid away to reveal one lobeless pointed ear. He scarcely noticed it, for he was too intent on the half-repulsive, half-heartquickening sensation he got when he touched her skin. It had not been the skin itself that caused that, for she was soft and warm as a young girl. It had been the *idea* of touching her.

Part of that, he thought as he seated himself, came from her nakedness. Not because it revealed her sex but because it revealed her lack of it. No breasts, no nipples, no navel, no pubic fold or projection. The absence of these seemed wrong, very wrong, unsettling. It was a shameful thing that she had nothing of which to be ashamed.

That's a queer thought, he said to himself. And for no reason, became warm in the face.

Martia, unnoticing, poured from a tall bottle a glassful of dark wine. He tasted it. It was exquisite, no better than the best Earth had to offer but as good.

Martia took one of the loaves, broke it into two pieces, and handed him one. Holding the glass of wine in one hand and the bread in the other, she bowed her head, closed her eyes, and began chanting.

He stared at her. This was a prayer, a grace-saying. Was it the prelude to a sort of communion, one so like Earth's it was startling?

Yet, if it were, he needn't be surprised. Flesh and blood, bread and wine: the symbolism was simple, logical, and might even be universal.

However it was possible that he was creating parallels that did not exist. She might be enacting a ritual whose origin and meaning were like nothing of which he had ever dreamed.

If so, what she did next was equally capable of misinterpretation. She nibbled at the bread, sipped the wine and then plainly invited him to do the same. He did so. Martia took a third and empty cup, spat a piece of wine-moistened bread into the cup, and indicated that he was to imitate her.

After he did, he felt his stomach draw in on itself. For she mixed the stuff from their mouths with her finger and then offered it to him. Evidently, he was to put the finger in his mouth and eat from it.

So the action was both physical and metaphysical. The bread and the wine were the flesh and blood of whatever divinity she worshipped. More, she, being imbued with the body and the spirit of the god, now wanted to mingle hers and that of the god's with his.

What I eat of the god's, I become. What you eat of me, you become. What I eat of you, I become. Now we three are become one.

Lane, far from being repelled by the concept, was excited. He knew that there were probably many Christians who would have refused to share in the communion because the ritual did not have the same origins or conform to theirs. They might even have thought that by sharing they were subscribing to an alien god. Such an idea Lane considered to be not only narrow-minded and inflexible, but illogical, uncharitable, and ridiculous. There could be but one Creator; what names the creature gave to the Creator did not matter.

Lane believed sincerely in a personal god, one who took note of him as an individual. He also believed that mankind needed redeeming and that a redeemer had been sent to Earth. And if other worlds needed redeeming, then they too would have got or would get a redeemer. He went perhaps further than most of his fellow religionists, for he actually made an attempt to practise love for mankind. This had given him somewhat of a reputation as a fanatic among his acquaintances and friends. However, he had been restrained enough not to make himself too much of a nuisance, and his genuine warmheartedness had made him welcome in spite of his eccentricity.

Six years before, he had been an agnostic. His first trip into space had converted him. The overwhelming experience had made him realize shatteringly what an insignificant being he was, how awe-inspiringly complicated and immense was the universe, and how much he needed a framework within which to be and to become.

The strangest feature about his conversion, he thought afterwards, was that one of his companions on that maiden trip had been a devout believer, who, on returning to Earth, had renounced his own sect and faith and become a complete atheist.

He thought of this as he took her proffered finger in his mouth and sucked the paste off it.

Then obeying her gestures, he dipped his own finger into the bowl and put it between.her lips.

She closed her eyes and gently mouthed the finger. When he began to withdraw it, he was stopped by her hand on his wrist. He did not insist on taking the finger out, for he wanted to avoid offending her. Perhaps a long time interval was part of the rite.

But her expression seemed so eager and at the same time so ecstatic, like a hungry baby just given the nipple, that he felt uneasy. After a minute, seeing no indication on her part that she meant to quit, he slowly but firmly pulled the finger loose. She opened her eyes and sighed, but she made no comment. Instead, she began serving his supper.

The hot thick soup was delicious and invigorating. Its texture was somewhat like the plankton soup that was becoming popular on hungry Earth, but it had no fishy flavour. The brown bread reminded him of rye. The legger meat was like wild rabbit, though it was sweeter and had an unidentifiable tang. He took only one bite of the leaf salad and then frantically poured wine down his throat to wash away the burn. Tears came to his eyes, and he coughed until she spoke to him in an alarmed tone. He smiled back at her but refused to touch the salad again. The wine not only cooled his mouth, it filled his veins with singing. He told himself he should take no more. Nevertheless, he finished his second cup before he remembered his resolve to be temperate.

By then it was too late. The strong liquor went straight to his head; he felt dizzy and wanted to laugh. The events of the day, his near-escape from death, the reaction to knowing his comrades were dead, his realization of his present situation, the tension caused by his encounters with the dekapeds, and his unsatisfied curiosity about Martia's origin and the location of others of her kind, all these combined to produce in him a half-stupor, half-exuberance.

He rose from the table and offered to help Martia with the dishes. She shook her head and put the dishes in a washer. In the meantime, he decided that he needed to wash off the sweat, stickiness, and body odour left by two days of travel. On opening the door to the shower cubicle, he found that there wasn't room enough to hang his clothes in it. So, uninhibited by fatigue and wine, also mindful that Martia, after all, was *not* a female, he removed his clothes.

Martia watched him, and her eyes became wider with each garment shed. Finally, she gasped and stepped back and turned pale.

"It's not that bad," he growled, wondering what had caused her reaction. "After all, some of the things I've seen around here aren't too easy to swallow."

She pointed with a trembling finger and asked him something in a shaky voice.

Perhaps it was his imagination, but he could swear she used the same inflection as would an English speaker.

"Are you sick? Are the growths malignant?"

He had no words with which to explain, nor did he intend to illustrate function through action. Instead, he closed the door of the cubicle after him and pressed the plate that turned on the water. The heat of the shower and the feel of the soap, of grime and sweat being washed away, soothed him somewhat, so that he could think about matters he had been too rushed to consider.

First, he would have to learn Martia's language or teach her his. Probably both would happen at the same time. Of one thing he was sure. That was that her intentions towards him were, at least at present, peaceful. When she had shared communion with him, she had been sincere. He did not get the impression that it was part of her cultural training to share bread and wine with a person she intended to kill.

Feeling better, though still tired and a little drunk, he left the cubicle. Reluctantly, he reached for his dirty shorts. Then he smiled. They had been cleaned while he was in the shower. Martia, however, paid no attention to his smile of pleased surprise, but, grim-faced, she motioned him to lie down on the bed and sleep. Instead of lying down herself, however, she picked up a bucket and began crawling up the tunnel. He decided to follow her, and, when she saw him, she only shrugged her shoulders.

On emerging into the tube, Martia turned on her flashlight. The tunnel was in absolute darkness. Her beam, playing on the ceiling, showed that the glow-worms had turned out their lights. There were no leggers in sight.

She pointed the light at the channel so he could see that the jetfish were still taking in and expelling water. Before she could turn the beam aside, he put his hand on her wrist and with his other hand lifted a fish from the channel. He had to pull it loose with an effort, which was explained when he turned the torpedo-shaped creature over and saw the column of flesh hanging from its belly. Now he knew why the reaction of the propelled water did not shoot them backwards. The ventral-foot acted as a suction pad to hold them to the floor of the channel.

Somewhat impatiently, Martia pulled away from him and began walking swiftly back up the tunnel. He followed her until she came to the opening in the wall which had earlier made her so apprehensive. Crouching, she entered the opening, but before she had gone far she had to move a tangled heap of leggers to one side. There were the large great-beaked ones he had seen guarding the entrance. Now they were asleep at the post.

If so, he reasoned, then the thing they guarded against must also be asleep.

What about Martia? How did she fit into their picture? Perhaps she didn't fit into their picture at all. She was absolutely alien, something for which their instinctual intelligence was not prepared and which, therefore, they ignored. That would explain why they had paid no attention to him when he was mired in the garden.

Yet there must be an exception to that rule. Certainly Martia had not wanted to attract the sentinels' notice the first time she had passed the entrance.

A moment later he found out why. They stepped into a huge

chamber which was at least two hundred feet square. It was as dark as the tube but during the waking period it must have been very bright because the ceiling was jammed with glow-worms.

Mania's flash raced around the chamber, showing him the piles of sleeping leggers. Then, suddenly it stopped. He took one look, and his heart raced, and the hairs on the back of his neck rose.

Before him was a worm three feet high and twenty feet long.

Without thinking, he grabbed hold of Martia to keep her from coming closer to it. But even as he touched her, he dropped his hand. She must know what she was doing.

Martia pointed the flash at her own face and smiled as if to tell him not to be alarmed. And she touched his arm with a shyly affectionate gesture.

For a moment, he didn't know why. Then it came to him that she was glad because he had been thinking of her welfare. Moreover, her reaction showed she had recovered from her shock at seeing him unclothed.

He turned from her to examine the monster. It lay on the floor, asleep, its great eyes closed behind vertical slits. It had a huge head, football-shaped like those of the little leggers around it. Its mouth was big, but the beaks were very small, horny warts, on its lips. The body, however, was that of a caterpillar worm's, minus the hair. Ten little useless legs stuck out of its side, too short even to reach the floor. Its sides bulged as if pumped full of gas.

Martia walked past the monster and paused by its posterior. Here she lifted up a fold of skin. Beneath it was a pile of a dozen leathery-skinned eggs, held together by a sticky secretion.

"Now I've got it," muttered Lane. "Of course. The egg-laying queen. She specializes in reproduction. That is why the others have no reproductive organs, or else they're so rudimentary I couldn't detect them. The leggers are animals, all right, but in some things they resemble terrestrial insects.

"Still that doesn't explain the absence also of a digestive system."

Martia put the eggs in her bucket and started to leave the room. He stopped her and indicated he wanted to look around some more. She shrugged and began to lead him around. Both had to be careful not to step on the dekapeds, which lay everywhere.

They came to an open bin made of the same grey stuff as the walls. Its ulterior held many shelves, on which lay hundreds of eggs. Strands of the spiderwebby stuff kept the eggs from rolling off.

Nearby was another bin that held water. At its bottom lay more eggs. Above them minnow-sized torpedo shapes flitted about in the water.

Lane's eyes widened at this. The fish were not members of another genus but were the larvae of the leggers. And they could be set in the channel not only to earn their keep by pumping water which came down from the North Pole but to grow until they were ready to metamorphose into the adult stage.

However, Martia showed him another bin which made him partially revise his first theory. This bin was dry, and the eggs were laid on the floor. Martia picked one up, cut its tough skin open with her knife, and emptied its contents into one hand.

Now his eyes did get wide. This creature had a tiny cylindrical body, a suction pad at one end, a round mouth at the other, and two globular organs hanging by the mouth. A young glow-worm.

Martia looked at him to see if he comprehended. Lane held out his hands and hunched his shoulders with an I-don't-get-it air. Beckoning, she walked to another bin to show him more eggs. Some had been ripped from within, and the little fellows whose hard beaks had done it were staggering around weakly on ten legs.

Energetically, Martia went through a series of charades. Watching her, he began to understand.

The embryos that remained in the eggs until they fully developed went through three main metamorphoses: the jetfish stage, the glow-worm stage, and finally the baby dekaped stage. If the eggs were torn open by the adult nurses in one of the first two stages, the embryo remained fixed in that form, though it did grow larger.

What about the queen? he asked her by pointing to the monstrously egg-swollen body.

For answer, Martia picked up one of the newly-hatched. It kicked its many legs but did not otherwise protest, being, like all its kind, mute. Martia turned it upside down and indicated a crease in its posterior. Then she showed him the same spot on one of the sleeping adults. The adult's rear was smooth, innocent of the crease.

Martia made eating gestures. He nodded. The creatures were born with rudimentary sexual organs, but these never developed. In fact, they atrophied completely unless the young were given a special diet, in which case they matured into egg-layers.

But the picture wasn't complete. If you had females, you had to have males. It was doubtful if such highly developed animals were self-fertilizing or reproduced parthenogenetically.

Then he remembered Martia and began doubting. She gave no evidence of reproductive organs. Could her kind be self-producing? Or was she a Martian, her natural fulfilment diverted by diet?

It didn't seem likely, but he couldn't be sure that such things were not possible in her scheme of Nature.

Lane wanted to satisfy his curiosity. Ignoring her desire to get out of the chamber, he examined each of the five baby dekapeds. All were potential females.

Suddenly Martia, who had been gravely watching him, smiled and took his hand, and led him to the rear of the room. Here, as they approached another structure, he smelled a strong odour which reminded him of clorox.

Closer to the structure, he saw that it was not a bin but a hemispherical cage. Its bars were of the hard grey stuff, and they curved up from the floor to meet at a central point. There was no door. Evidently the cage had been built around the thing in it, and its occupant must remain until he died.

Martia soon showed him why this thing was not allowed freedom. It—he—was sleeping, but Martia reached through the bars and struck it on the head with her fist. The thing did not respond until it had been hit five more times. Then, slowly, it opened its sidewise lids to reveal great staring eyes, bright as fresh arterial blood.

Martia threw one of the eggs at the thing's head. Its beak opened swiftly, the egg disappeared, the beak closed, and there was a noisy gulp.

Food brought it to life. It sprang up on its ten long legs, clacked its beak, and lunged against the bars again and again.

Though in no danger. Martia shrank back before the killer's lust in the scarlet eyes. Lane could understand her reaction. It was a giant, at least two feet higher than the sentinels. Its back was on a level with Martia's, its beaks could have taken her head in between them.

Lane walked around the cage to get a good look at its posterior. Puzzled, he made another circuit without seeing anything of maleness about it except its wild fury like that of a stallion locked in a barn during mating season. Except for its size, red eyes, and a cloaca, it looked like one of the guards.

He tried to communicate to Martia his puzzlement. By now, she seemed to anticipate his desires. She went through another series of pantomimes, some of which were so energetic and comical that he had to smile.

First, she showed him two eggs on a nearby ledge. These were larger than the others and were speckled with red spots. Supposedly, they held male embryos.

Then she showed him what would happen if the adult male got loose. Making a face which was designed to be ferocious but only amused him, clicking her teeth and clawing with her hands, she imitated the male running amok. He would kill everybody in sight. Everybody, the whole colony, queen, workers, guards, larvae, eggs, bite off their heads, mangle them, eat them all up, all, all. And out of the slaughterhouse he would charge into the tube and kill every legger he met, devour the jetfish, drag down the glow-worms from the ceiling, rip them apart, eat them, eat the roots of the trees. Kill, kill, kill, eat, eat, eat!

That was all very well, signed Lane. But how did . . . ? Martia indicated that, once a day, the workers rolled, literally rolled the queen across the room to the cage. There they arranged her so that she presented her posterior some few inches from the bars and the enraged male. And the male, though he wanted to do nothing but get his beak into her flesh and tear her apart, was not master of himself. Nature took over; his will was betrayed by his nervous system.

Lane nodded to show he understood. In his mind was a picture of the legger that had been butchered. It had had one sac at the internal end of the tongue. Probably the male had two, one to hold excretory matter, the other to hold seminal fluid.

Suddenly Martia froze, her hands held out before her. She had laid the flashlight on the floor so she could act freely; the beam splashed on her paling skin.

"What is it?" said Lane, stepping towards her.

Martia retreated, holding out her hands before her. She looked horrified.

"I'm not going to harm you," he said. However, he stopped so she could see he didn't mean to get any closer to her.

What was bothering her? Nothing was stirring in the chamber itself besides the male, and he was behind her.

Then she was pointing, first at him and then at the raging dekaped. Seeing this unmistakable signal of identification, he comprehended. She had perceived that he, like the thing in the cage, was male and now she perceived structure and function in him.

What he didn't understand was why that should make her so

frightened of him. Repelled, yes. Her body, its seeming lack of sex, had given him a feeling of distaste bordering nausea. It was only natural that she should react similarly to his body. However, she had seemed to have got over her first shock.

Why this unexpected change, this horror of him?

Behind him, the beak of the male clicked as it lunged against the bars.

The click echoed in his mind.

Of course, the monster's lust to kill!

Until she had met him, she had known only one male creature. That was the caged thing. Now, suddenly, she had equated him with the monster. A male was a killer.

Desperately, because he was afraid that she was about to run in a panic out of the room, he made signs that he was not like this monster; he shook his head, no, no, no. He wasn't, he wasn't, he wasn't!

Martia, watching him intently began to relax. Her skin regained its pinkish hue. Her eyes became their normal size. She even managed a strained smile.

To get her mind off the subject, he indicated that he would like to know why the queen and her consort had digestive systems, though the workers did not. For answer, she reached up into the downhanging mouth of the worm suspended from the ceiling. Her hand, withdrawn, was covered with secretion. After smelling her fist, she gave it to him to sniff also. He took it, ignoring her slight and probably involuntary flinching when she felt his touch.

The stuff had an odor such as you would expect from predigested food.

Martia then went to another worm. The two light organs of this one were not coloured red, like the other, but had a greenish tint. Martia tickled its tongue with her finger and held out cupped hands. Liquid trickled into the cup.

Lane smelled the stuff. No odor. When he drank the liquid, he discovered it to be a thick sugar water.

Martia pantomimed that the glow-worms acted as the digestive systems for the workers. They also stored food away for them. The workers derived part of their energy from the glucose excreted by the roots of the trees. The proteins and vegetable matter in their diet originated from the eggs and from the leaves of the umbrella plant. Strips of the tough membranous leaf were brought into the tubes by harvesting parties which ventured forth in the daytime. The worms partially digested the eggs, dead leggers, and leaves and gave it back in the form of a soup. The soup, like glucose, was swallowed by the workers and passed through the walls of their throats or into the long straight sac which connected the throat to the larger blood vessels. The waste products were excreted through the skin or emptied through the canal in the tongue.

Lane nodded and then walked out of the room. Seemingly relieved, Martia followed him. When they had crawled back into her quarters, she put the eggs in a refrigerator and poured two glasses of wine. She dipped her finger in both, then touched the finger to her lips and to his. Lightly, he touched the tip with his tongue. This, he gathered, was one more ritual, perhaps a bedtime one, which affirmed that they were at one and at peace. It might be that it had an even deeper meaning, but if so, it escaped him.

Martia checked on safety and comfort of the worm in the bowl. By now it had eaten all its food. She removed the worm, washed it, washed the bowl, half-filled it with warm sugar water, placed it on a table by the bed, and put the creature back in. Then she lay down on the bed and closed her eyes. She did not cover herself and apparently did not expect him to expect a cover.

Lane, tired though he was, could not rest. Like a tiger in its cage, he paced back and forth. He could not keep out of his mind the enigma of Martia nor the problem of getting back to base and eventually to the orbital ship. Earth must know what had happened.

After half an hour of this, Martia sat up. She looked steadily at him as if trying to discover the cause of his sleeplessness. Then apparently sensing what was wrong, she rose and opened a cabinet hanging down from the wall. Inside were a number of books.

Lane said, "Ah, maybe I'll get some information now!" and he leafed through them all. Wild with eagerness, he chose three and piled them on the bed before sitting down to peruse them.

Naturally, he could not read the texts, but the three had many illustrations and photographs. The first volume seemed to be a child's world history.

Lane looked at the first few pictures. Then he said, hoarsely, "My God, you're no more Martian than I am!"

Martia, startled by the wonder and urgency in his voice, came over to his bed and sat down by him. She watched while he turned the pages over until he reached a certain photo. Unexpectedly she buried her face in her hands, and her body shook with deep sobs.

Lane was surprised. He wasn't sure why she was in such grief. The photo was an aerial view of a city on her home planet—or some planet on which her people lived. Perhaps it was the city in which she had—somehow—been born.

It wasn't long, however, before her sorrow began to stir a response in him. Without any warning, he, too, was weeping.

Now he knew. It was loneliness, appalling loneliness, of the kind he had known when he had received no more word from the men in the tanks and he had believed himself the only human being on the face of this world.

After a while, the tears dried. He felt better and wished she would also be relieved. Apparently she perceived his sympathy, for she smiled at him through her tears. And in an irresistible gust of rapport and affection she kissed his hand and then stuck two of his fingers in her mouth. This, he thought, must be her way of expressing friendship. Or perhaps it was gratitude for his presence. Or just sheer joy. In any event, he thought, her society must have a high oral orientation.

"Poor Martia," he murmured. "It must be a terrible thing to have to turn to one as alien and weird as I must seem. Especially to one who, a little while ago, you weren't sure wasn't going to eat you up."

He removed his fingers but, seeing her rejected look, he impulsively took hers in his mouth.

Strangely, this caused another burst of weeping. However, he quickly saw that it was happy weeping. After it was over, she laughed softly, as if pleased.

Lane took a towel and wiped her eyes and held it over her nose while she blew.

Now, strengthened, she was able to point out certain illustrations and by signs give him clues to what they meant.

This child's book started with an account of the dawn of life on her planet. The planet revolved around a star that, according to a simplified map, was in the centre of the Galaxy.

Life had begun there much as it had on Earth. It had developed in its early stages on somewhat the same lines. But there were some rather disturbing pictures of primitive fish life. Lane wasn't sure of his interpretation, however, for these took much for granted.

They did show plainly that evolution there had picked out biological mechanisms with which to advance different from those on Earth.

Fascinated, he traced the passage from fish to amphibian to reptile to warm-blooded but non-mammalian creature to an upright ground-dwelling apelike creature to beings like Martia.

Then the pictures depicted various aspects of this being's prehistoric life. Later, the invention of agriculture, working of metals and so on.

The history of civilization was a series of picture whose meaning he could seldom grasp. One thing was unlike Earth's history. There was a relative absence of warfare. The Rameseses, Genghis Khans, Attilas, Caesars, Hitlers seemed to be missing.

But there was more, much more. Technology advanced much as it had on Earth, despite a lack of stimulation from war. Perhaps, he thought, it had started sooner than on his planet. He got the impression that Martia's people had evolved to their present state much earlier than homo sapiens.

Whether that was true or not, they now surpassed man. They could travel almost as fast as light, perhaps faster, and had mastered interstellar travel.

It was then that Martia pointed to a page which bore several photographs of Earth, obviously taken at various distances by a spaceship.

Behind them an artist had drawn a shadowy figure, half-ape, half-dragon.

"Earth means this to you?" Lane said. *Danger? Do not touch?*

He looked for other photos of Earth. There were many pages dealing with other planets but only one of his home. That was enough.

"Why are you keeping us under distant surveillance?" said Lane. "You're so far ahead of us that, technologically speaking, we're Australian aborigines. What're you afraid of?"

Martia stood up, facing him. Suddenly, viciously, she snarled and clicked her teeth and hooked her hands into claws.

He felt a chill. This was the same pantomime she had used when demonstrating the mindless kill-craziness of the caged male legger.

He bowed his head. "I can't really blame you. You're absolutely correct. If you contacted us, we'd steal your secrets. And then, look out! We'd infest all of space!"

He paused, bit his lip, and said, "Yet we're showing some signs of progress. There's not been a war or a revolution for fifteen years; the U.N. has been settling problems that would once have resulted in world war; Russia and the U.S. are still armed but are not nearly as close to conflict as they were when I was born. Perhaps . . . ?

"Do you know, I bet you've never seen an Earthman in the flesh before. Perhaps you've never seen a picture of one, or if you did, they were clothed. There are no photos of Earth people in these books. Maybe you knew we were male and female, but that didn't mean much until you saw me taking a shower. And the suddenly revealed parallel between the male dekaped and myself horrified you. And you realized that this was the only thing in the world that you had for companionship. Almost as if I'd been shipwrecked on an island and found the other inhabitant was a tiger.

"But that doesn't explain what you are doing here, alone, living in these tubes among the indigenous Martians. Oh, how I wish I could talk to you!

"*With thee conversing,*" he said, remembering those lines he had read the last night in the base.

She smiled at him, and he said, "Well, at least you're getting over your scare. I'm not such a bad fellow, after all, heh?"

She smiled again and went to a cabinet and from it took paper and pen. With them, she made one simple sketch after another. Watching her agile pen, he began to see what had happened.

Her people had had a base for a long time—a long long time—on the side of the Moon the Terrestrials could not see. But when rockets from Earth had first penetrated into space, her people had obliterated all evidence of the base. A new one had been set up on Mars.

Then, as it became apparent that a terrestrial expedition would be sent to Mars, that base had been destroyed and another one set up on Ganymede.

However, five scientists had remained behind in these simple quarters to complete their studies of the dekapeds. Though Martia's people had studied these creatures for some time, they still had not found out how their bodies could endure the differences between tube pressure and that in the open air. The four believed that they were breathing hot on the neck of this secret and had got permission to stay until just before the Earthmen landed.

Martia actually was a native, in the sense that she had been born and raised here. She had been seven years here, she indicated, showing a sketch of Mars in its orbit around the sun and then holding up seven fingers.

That made her about fourteen Earth years old, Lane estimated. Perhaps these people reached maturity a little faster than his. That is, if she were mature. It was difficult to tell.

Horror twisted her face and widened her eyes as she showed him what had happened the night before they were to leave for Ganymede.

The sleeping party had been attacked by an uncaged male legger.

It was rare that a male got loose. But he occasionally managed to escape. When he did, he destroyed the entire colony, all life in the tube wherever he went. He even ate the roots of the trees so that they died, and oxygen ceased to flow into that section of the tunnel.

There was only one way a forewarned colony could fight a rogue male—a dangerous method. That was to release their own male. They selected a few who could stay behind and sacrifice their lives to dissolve the bar with an acid secretion from their bodies while the others fled. The queen, unable to move, also died. But enough of her eggs were taken to produce another queen and another consort elsewhere.

Meanwhile, it was hoped that the males would kill each other or that the victor would be so crippled that he could be finished off by the soldiers.

Lane nodded. The only natural enemy of the dekapeds was an escaped male. Left unchecked, they would soon crowd the tubes and exhaust food and air. Unkind as it seemed, the escape of a male now and then was the only thing that saved the Martians from starvation and perhaps extinction.

However that might be, the rogue had been no blessing in disguise for Martia's people. Three had been killed in their sleep before the other two awoke. One had thrown herself at the beast and shouted to Martia to escape.

Almost insane with fear, Martia had nevertheless not allowed panic to send her running. Instead, she had dived for a cabinet to get a weapon.

A weapon, thought Lane. I'll have to find out about that

Martia acted out what had happened. She had got the cabinet door open and reached in for the weapon when she felt the beak of the rogue fastening on her legs. Despite the shock, for the beak cut deeply into the blood vessels and muscles, she had managed to press the end of the weapon against the male's body. The weapon did its work, for the male dropped on the floor. Unfortunately, the beaks did not relax but held their terrible grip on her thigh, just above the knee.

Here Lane tried to interrupt so he could get a description of what the weapon looked like and of the principle of its operation. Martia, however, ignored his request. Seemingly, she did not care to reply. He was not entirely trusted, which was understandable. How could he blame her? She would be a fool to be at ease with such an unknown quantity as himself. That is, if he were unknown. After all, though she did not know him well personally she knew the kind of people from whom he came and what could be expected from them. It was surprising that she had not left him to die in the garden and it was amazing that she had shared that communion of bread and wine with him.

Perhaps, he thought, it is because she was so lonely and any company was better than nothing. Or it might be that she acted on a higher ethical plane than most Earthmen and could not endure the idea of leaving a fellow sentient being to die, even if she thought him a bloodthirsty savage.

Or she might have other plans for him, such as taking him prisoner.

Martia continued her story. She had fainted and some time later had awakened. The male was beginning to stir, so she had killed him this time.

One more item of information, thought Lane. The weapon is capable of inflicting degrees of damage.

Then, though she kept passing out, she had dragged herself to the medicine chest and treated herself. Within two days she was up and hobbled around, and the scars were beginning to fade.

They must be far ahead of us in everything, he thought. According to her some of her muscles had been cut. Yet they grew together in a day.

Martia indicated that the repair of her body had required an enormous amount of food during the healing. Most of her time had been spent in eating and sleeping. Reconstruction, whether it took place at a normal or accelerated rate, still required the same amount of energy.

By then the bodies of the male and of her companions were stinking with decay. She had had to force herself to cut them up and dispose of them in the garbage burner.

Tears welled in her eyes as she recounted this, and she sobbed.

Lane wanted to ask her why she had not buried them, but he reconsidered. Though it might not be the custom among her kind to bury the dead, it was more probable that she wanted to destroy all evidence of their existence before Earthmen came to Mars.

Using signs, he asked her how the male had got into the room despite the gate across the tunnel. She indicated that the gate was ordinarily closed only when the dekapeds were awake or when her companions and she were sleeping. But it had been the turn of one of their number to collect eggs in the queen's chamber. As she reconstructed it, the rogue had appeared at that time and killed the scientist there. Then, after ravening among the still-sleeping colony, it had gone down the tube and there had seen the light shining from the open tunnel. The rest of the story he knew.

Why, he pantomimed, why didn't the escaped male sleep when all his fellows did? The one in the cage evidently slept at the same time as his companions. And the queen's guards also slept in the belief they were safe from attack.

Not so, replied Martia. A male who had got out of a cage knew no law but fatigue. When he had exhausted himself in his eating and killing he lay down to sleep. But it did not matter if it was the regular time for it or not. When he was rested he raged through the tubes and did not stop until he was again too tired to move.

So, then, thought Lane, that explains the area of dead umbrella plants on top of the tube by the garden. Another colony moved into the devastated area, built the garden on the outside, and planted the young umbrellas.

He wondered why neither he nor the others of his group had seen the dekapeds outside during their six days on Mars. There must be at least one pressure chamber and outlet for each colony. And there should be at least fifteen colonies in the tubes between this point and that near his base. Perhaps the answer was that the leaf-croppers only ventured out occasionally. Now that he remembered it, neither he nor anyone else had noticed any holes in the leaves. That meant that the trees must have been cropped some time ago and were now ready for another harvesting. If the expedition had only waited several days before sending out men in tracs, it might have seen the dekapeds and investigated. And the story would have been different.

There were other questions he had for her. What about the vessel that was to take them to Ganymede? Was there one hidden on the outside, or was one to be sent to pick them up? If one was to be sent how would the Ganymedian base be contacted? Radio? Or some—to him—inconceivable method?

The blue globes? he thought. Could they be a means of transmitting messages?

He did not know or think further about them because fatigue overwhelmed him and he fell asleep. His last memory was that of Martia leaning over him and smiling at him.

When he awoke reluctantly his muscles ached and his mouth was as dry as the Martian desert. He rose in time to see Martia drop out of the tunnel, a bucket of eggs in her hand. Seeing this, he groaned. That meant she had gone into the nursery again, and that he had slept the clock around.

He stumbled up and into the shower cubicle. Coming out much refreshed, he found breakfast hot on the table. Martia conducted the communion rite, and then they ate. He missed his coffee. The hot soup was good but did not make a satisfactory substitute. There was a bowl of mixed cereal and fruit, both of which came out of a can. It must have had a high energy content, for it brought him wide awake.

Afterwards, he did some setting-up exercises while she did the dishes. Though he kept his body busy he was thinking of things uncon- nected with what he was doing.

What was to be his next move?

His duty demanded that he return to the base and report. What news he would send to the orbital ship! The story would flash from the ship back to Earth. The whole planet would be in an uproar.

There was one objection to his plan to take Martia back with him.

She would not want to go.

Half-way in a deep knee-bend he stopped. What a fool he was! He had been too tired and confused to see it. But if she had revealed that the base of her people was on Ganymede she did not expect him to take the information back to his transmitter. It would be foolish on her part to tell him unless she were absolutely certain that he would be able to communicate with no one.

That must mean that a vessel was on its way and would arrive soon. And it would not only take her but him. If he was to be killed, he would be dead now.

Lane had not been chosen to be a member of the first Mars expe- dition because he lacked decision. Five minutes later he had made up his mind. His duty was clear. Therefore he would carry it out, even if it violated his personal feelings towards Martia and caused her injury.

First, he'd bind her. Then he would pack up their two pressure suits, the books, and any tools small enough to carry so they might later be examined on Earth. He would make her march ahead of him through the tube until they came to the point opposite his base. There they would don their suits and go out to the dome. And as soon as possible the two would rise on the rocket to the orbital ship. This step was the most hazardous, for it was extremely difficult for one man to pilot the rocket. Theoretically, it could be done. It had to be done.

Lane tightened his jaw and forced his muscles to quit quivering. The thought of violating Martia's hospitality upset him. Still, she had treated him so well for a purpose not altogether altruistic. For all he knew, she was plotting against him.

There was a rope in one of the cabinets, the same flexible rope with which she had pulled him from the mire. He opened the door of the cabinet and removed it. Martia stood in the middle of the room and watched him while she stroked the head of the blue-eyed worm coiled about her shoulders. He hoped she would stay there until he got close. Obviously, she carried no weapon on her nor indeed anything except the pet. Since she had removed her suit, she had worn nothing.

Seeing him approaching her, she spoke to him in an alarmed tone. It didn't take much sensitivity to know that she was asking him what he intended to do with the rope. He tried to smile reassuringly at her and failed. This was making him sick.

A moment later he was violently sick. Martia had spoken loudly one word, and it was as if it had struck him in the pit of his stomach. Nausea gripped him, his mouth began salivating, and it was only by dropping the rope and running into the shower that he avoided making a mess on the floor.

Ten minutes later, he felt thoroughly cleaned out. But when he tried to walk to the bed, his legs threatened to give way. Martia had to support him.

Inwardly, he cursed. To have a sudden reaction to the strange food at such a crucial moment! Luck was not on his side.

That is, if it was chance. There had been something so strange and forceful about the manner in which she pronounced that word. Was it possible that she had set up in him—hypnotically or otherwise—a reflex to that word? It would, under the conditions, be a weapon more powerful than a gun.

He wasn't sure, but it did seem strange that his body had accepted the alien food until that moment. Hypnotism did not really seem to be the answer. How could it be so easily used on him since he did not know more than twenty words of her language?

Language? Words? They weren't necessary. If she had given him a hypnotic drug in his food, and then had awakened him during his sleep, she could have dramatized how he was to react if she wanted him to do so. She could have given him the key word, then have allowed him to go to sleep again.

He knew enough hypnotism to know that that was possible. Whether his suspicions were true or not, it was a fact that he had been laid flat on his back. However, the day was not wasted. He learned twenty more words and she drew many more sketches for him. He found out that when he had jumped into the mire of the garden he had literally fallen into the soup. The substance in which the young umbrella trees had been planted was a zoogloea, a glutinous mass of one-celled vegetables and somewhat larger anaerobic animal life that fed on the vegetables. The heat from the jam-packed water-swollen bodies kept the garden soil warm and prevented the tender plants from freezing even during the forty degrees below zero Fahrenheit of the midsummer nights.

After the trees were transplanted into the roof of the tube to replace the dead adults, the zoogloea would be taken piecemeal back into the tube and dumped into the channel. Here the jetfish would strain out part and eat part as they pumped water from the polar end of the tube to the equatorial end.

Towards the end of the day, he tried some of the zoogloea soup and managed to keep it down. A little later, he ate some cereal.

Martia insisted on spooning the food for him. There was something so feminine and tender about her solicitude that he could not protest.

"Martia," he said, "I may be wrong. There can be good will and rapport between our two kinds. Look at us. Why, if you were a real woman I'd be in love with you.

"Of course, you may have made me sick in the first place. But if you did, it was a matter of expediency, not malice. And now you are taking care of me, your enemy. Love thy enemy. Not because you have been told you should but because you do."

She, of course, did not understand him. However, she replied in her own tongue, and it seemed to him that her voice had the same sense of simpatico.

As he fell asleep, he was thinking that perhaps Martia and he would be the two ambassadors to bring their people together in peace. After all, both of them were highly civilized, essentially pacifistic, and devoutly religious. There was such a thing as the brotherhood, not only of man, but of all sentient beings throughout the cosmos, and . . .

Pressure on his bladder woke him up. He opened his eyes. The ceiling and walls expanded and contracted. His wristwatch was distorted. Only by extreme effort could he focus his eyes enough to straighten the arms on his watch. The piece, designed to measure the slightly longer Martian day, indicated midnight

Groggily, he rose. He felt sure that he must have been drugged and that he would still be sleeping if the bladder pain hadn't been so sharp. If only he could take something to counteract the drug, he could carry out his plans now. But first he had to get to the toilet

To do so, he had to pass close to Martia's bed. She did not move but lay on her back, her arms flung out and hanging over the sides of the bed, her mouth open wide.

He looked away, for it seemed indecent to watch when she was in such a position.

But something caught his eye—a movement, a flash of light like a gleaming jewel in her mouth.

He bent over her, looked, and recoiled in horror.

A head rose from between her teeth.

He raised his hand to snatch at the thing but froze in the posture as he recognized the tiny pouting round mouth and little blue eyes. It was the worm.

At first, he thought Martia was dead. The thing was not coiled in her mouth. Its body disappeared into her throat.

Then he saw her chest was rising easily and that she seemed to be in no difficulty.

Forcing himself to come close to the worm, though his stomach muscles writhed and his neck muscles quivered, he put his hand close to its lips.

Warm air touched his fingers, and he heard a faint whistling.

Martia was breathing through it!

Hoarsely, he said, "God!" and he shook her shoulder. He did not want to touch the worm because he was afraid that it might do something to injure her. In that moment of shock he had forgotten that he had an advantage over her, which he should use.

Martia's lids opened; her large grey-blue eyes stared blankly.

"Take it easy," he said soothingly.

She shuddered. Her lids closed, her neck arched back, and her face contorted.

He could not tell if the grimace was caused by pain or something else.

"What is this—this monster?" he said. "Symbiote? Parasite?"

He thought of vampires, of worms creeping into one's sleeping body and there sucking blood.

Suddenly she sat up and held out her arms to him. He seized her hands, saying, "What is it?"

Martia pulled him towards her at the same time lifting her face to his.

Out of her open mouth shot the worm, its head pointed towards his face, its little lips formed into an O.

It was reflex, the reflex of fear that made Lane drop her hands and spring back. He had not wanted to do that, but he could not help himself.

Abruptly, Martia came wide awake. The worm flopped its full length from her mouth and fell into a heap between her legs. There it thrashed for a moment before coiling itself like a snake, its head resting on Martia's thigh, its eyes turned upwards to Lane.

There was no doubt about it, Martia looked disappointed, frustrated.

Lane's knees, already weak, gave way. However, he managed to continue to his destination. When he came out, he walked as far as Martia's bed, where he had to sit down. His heart was thudding against his ribs and he was panting hard.

He sat behind her, for he did not want to be where the worm could touch him.

Martia made motions for him to go back to his bed and they would all sleep. Evidently, he thought, she found nothing alarming in the incident.

But he knew he could not rest until he had some kind of explanation. He handed her paper and pen from the bedside table and then gestured fiercely. Martia shrugged and began sketching while Lane watched over her shoulder. By the time she had used up five sheets of paper, she had communicated her message.

His eyes were wide, and he was even paler.

So—Martia *was* a female. Female at least in the sense that she carried eggs—and, at times, young—within her.

And there was the so-called worm. So called? What could he call it? It could not be designated under one category. It was many things in one. It was a larva. It was a phallus. It was also her offspring, of her flesh and blood.

But not of her genes. It was not descended from her.

She had given birth to it, yet she was not its mother. She was neither one of its mothers.

The dizziness and confusion he felt was not caused altogether by his sickness. Things were coming too fast. He was thinking furiously, trying to get this new information clear, but his thoughts kept going back and forth, getting nowhere.

"There's no reason to get upset," he told himself. "After all, the splitting of animals into two sexes is only one of the ways of reproduction tried on Earth. On Martia's planet Nature—God—has fashioned another method for the higher animals. And only He knows how many other designs for reproduction He has fashioned on how many other worlds."

Nevertheless, he was upset.

This worm, no, this larva, this embryo outside its egg and its secondary mother . . . well, call it, once and for all, larva, because it did metamorphose later.

This particular larva was doomed to stay in its present form until it died of old age.

Unless Martia found another adult of the Eeltau.

And unless she and this other adult felt affection for each other.

Then, according to the sketch she'd drawn, Martia and her friend, or lover, would lie down or sit together. They would as lovers do on Earth speak to each other in endearing, flattering, and exciting terms. They would caress and kiss much as Terrestrial man and woman do, though on Earth it was not considered complimentary to call one's lover Big Mouth.

Then, unlike the Terran custom, a third would enter the union to form a highly desired and indeed indispensable and eternal triangle.

The larva, blindly, brainlessly obeying its instincts, aroused by mutual fondling by the two, would descend tail first into the throat of one of the two Eeltau. Inside the body of the lover a fleshy valve would open to admit the slim body of the larva. Its open tip would touch the ovary of the host. The larva, like an electric eel, would release a tiny current. The hostess would go into an ecstasy, its nerves stimulated electro-chemically. The ovary would release an egg no larger than a pencil dot. It would disappear into the open tip of the larva's tail, there to begin a journey up a canal towards the centre of its body, urged on by the contraction of muscle and whipping of cilia.

Then the larva slid out of the first hostess' mouth and went tail first into the other, there to repeat the process. Sometimes the larva garnered eggs, sometimes not, depending upon whether the ovary had a fully developed one to release.

When the process was successful, the two eggs moved towards each other but did not quite meet.

Not yet.

There must be other eggs collected in the dark incubator of the larva, collected by pairs, though not necessarily from the same couple of donors.

These would number anywhere from twenty to forty pairs.

Then, one day, the mysterious chemistry of the cells would tell the larva's body that it had gathered enough eggs.

A hormone was released, the metamorphosis begun. The larva swelled enormously, and the mother, seeing this, placed it tenderly in a warm place and fed it plenty of predigested food and sugar water.

Before the eyes of its mother, the larva then grew shorter and wider. Its tail contracted; its cartilaginous vertebrae, widely separated in its larval stage, shifted closer to each other and hardened. A skeleton formed, ribs, shoulders. Legs and arms budded and grew and took humanoid shape. Six months passed, and there lay in its crib something resembling a baby of homo sapiens.

From then until its fourteenth year, the Eeltau grew and developed much as its Terran counterpart.

Adulthood, however, initiated more strange changes. Hormone released hormone until the first pair of gametes, dormant these fourteen years, moved together.

The two fused, the chromatin of one uniting with the chromatin of the other. Out of the two—a single creature, wormlike, four inches long, released into the stomach of its hostess.

Then, nausea. Vomiting. And so, comparatively painlessly, the bringing forth of a genetically new being.

It was this worm that would be both foetus and phallus and would give ecstasy and draw into its own body the eggs of loving adults and would metamorphose and become infant, child, and adult.

And so on and so on.

He rose and shakily walked to his own bed. There he sat down, his head bowed, while he muttered to himself.

"Let's see now. Martia gave birth to, brought forth, or up, this larva. But the larva actually doesn't have any of Martia's genes. Martia was just the hostess for it

"However if Martia has a lover, she will, by means of this worm pass on her heritable qualities. This worm will become an adult and bring forth, or up, Martia's child."

He raised his hands in despair.

"How do the Eeltau reckon ancestry? How keep track of their relatives? Or do they care? Wouldn't it be easier to consider your foster mother, your hostess, your real mother? As, in the sense of having borne you, she is?

"And what kind of a sexual code do these people have? It can't, I would think, be much like ours. Nor is there any reason why it should be.

"But who is responsible for raising the larva and child? Its pseudo-mother? Or does the lover share in the duties? And what about property and inheritance laws? And, and . . ."

Helplessly, he looked at Martia.

Fondly stroking the head of the larva, she returned his stare.

Lane shook his head.

"I was wrong, Eeltau and Terran couldn't meet on a friendly basis. My people would react to yours as to disgusting vermin. Their deepest prejudices would be aroused, their strongest taboos would be violated. They could not learn to live with you or consider you even faintly human.

"And as far as that goes, could you live with us? Wasn't the sight of me naked a shock? Is that reaction a part of why you don't make contact with us?"

Martia put the larva down and stood up and walked over to him and kissed the tips of his fingers. Lane, though he had to fight against visibly flinching, took her fingers and kissed them. Softly he said to her, "Yet . . . individuals could learn to respect each other, to have affection for each other. And masses are made of individuals."

He lay back on the bed. The grogginess, pushed aside for a while by excitement, was coming back. He couldn't fight off sleep much longer.

"Fine noble talk," he murmured. "But it means nothing. The Eeltau don't think they should deal with us. And we are, unknowingly, pushing out towards them. What will happen when we are ready to make the interstellar jump? War? Or will they be afraid to let us advance even to that point and destroy us before then? After all, one cobalt bomb."

He looked again at Martia, at the not-quite-human yet beautiful face, the smooth skin of the chest, abdomen, and loins, innocent of nipple, naval, or labia. From far off she had come, from a possibly terrifying place across terrifying distances. About her, however, there was little that was terrifying and much that was warm, generous, companionable, attractive.

As if they had waited for some key to turn, and the key had been turned, the lines he had read before falling asleep that last night in the base came again to him.

It is the voice of my beloved that knocketh, saying,
Open to me, my sister, my love, my dove, my undenied.

We have a little sister,
And she hath no breasts:
What shall we do for our sister
In the day when she shall be spoken for?

With thee conversing, I forget all time,
All seasons, and their change, all please alike.

"*With thee conversing,*" he said aloud. He turned over so his back was to her, and he pounded his fist against the bed.

"Oh dear God why couldn't it be so?"

A long time he lay there, his face pressed into the mattress. Something had happened; the overpowering fatigue was gone; his body had drawn strength from some reservoir. Realizing this, he sat up and beckoned to Martia, smiling at the same time.

She rose slowly and started to walk to him, but he signalled that she should bring the larva with her. At first, she looked puzzled. Then her expression cleared, to be replaced by understanding. Smiling delightedly, she walked to him, and though he knew it must be a trick of his imagination, it seemed to him that she swayed her hips as a woman would.

She halted in front of him and then stooped to kiss him full on the lips. Her eyes were closed.

He hesitated for a fraction of a second. She—no, it, he told himself—looked so trusting, so loving, so womanly, that he could not do it

"For Earth!" he said fiercely and brought the edge of his palm hard against the side of her neck.

She crumpled forward against him, her face sliding into his chest. Lane caught her under the armpits and laid her face down on the, bed. The larva, which had fallen from her hand on to the floor, was writhing about as if hurt. Lane picked it up by its tail and, in a frenzy that owed its violence to the fear he might not be able to do it, snapped it like a whip. There was a crack as the head smashed into the floor, and blood spurted from its eyes and mouth. Lane placed his heel on the head and stepped down until there was a flat mess beneath his foot.

Then, quickly, before she could come to her senses and speak any words that would render him sick and weak, he ran to a cabinet. Snatching a narrow towel out of it, he ran back and gagged her. After that he tied her hands behind her back with the rope.

"Now you bitch!" he panted. "We'll see who comes out ahead! You would do that with me, would you! You deserve this; your monster deserves to die!"

Furiously he began packing. In fifteen minutes he had the suits, helmets, tanks, and food rolled into two bundles. He searched for the weapon she had talked about and found something that might conceivably be it. It had a butt that fitted to his hand, a dial that might be a rheostat for controlling degrees of intensity of whatever it shot, and a bulb at the end. The bulb, he hoped, expelled the stunning and killing energy. Of course, he might be wrong. It could be fashioned for an entirely different purpose.

Martia had regained consciousness. She sat on the edge of the bed, her shoulders hunched, her head drooping, tears running down her cheeks and into the towel around her mouth. Her wide eyes were focused on the smashed worm by her feet

Roughly, Lane seized her shoulder and pulled her upright. She gazed wildly at him, and he gave her a little shove. He felt sick within him, knowing that he had killed the larva when he did not have to do so and that he was handling her so violently because he was afraid, not of her, but of himself. If he had been disgusted because she had fallen into the trap he set for her, he was so because he, too, beneath his disgust, had wanted to commit that act of love. Commit, he thought, was the right word. It contained criminal implications.

Martia whirled around, almost losing her balance because of her tied hands. Her face worked, and sounds burst from the gag.

"Shut up!" he howled, pushing her again. She went sprawling and only saved herself from falling on her face by dropping on her knees. Once more, he pulled her to her feet, noting as he did so that her knees were skinned. The sight of the blood, instead of softening him, enraged him even more.

"Behave yourself, or you'll get worse!" he snarled.

She gave him one more questioning look, threw back her head and made a strange strangling sound. Immediately, her face took on a bluish tinge. A second later, she fell heavily on the floor.

Alarmed, he turned her over. She was choking to death.

He tore off the gag and reached into her mouth and grabbed the root of her tongue. It slipped away and he seized it again, only to have it slide away as if it were a live animal that defied him.

Then he had pulled her tongue out of her throat; she had swallowed it in an effort to kill herself.

Lane waited. When he was sure she was going to recover, he replaced the gag around her mouth. Just as he was about to tie the knot at the back of her neck, he stopped. What use would it be to continue this? If allowed to speak, she would say the word that would throw him into retching. If gagged, she would swallow her tongue again.

He could save her only so many times. Eventually, she would succeed in strangling herself.

The one way to solve his problem was the one way he could not take. If her tongue were cut off at the root, she could neither speak nor kill herself. Some men might do it; he could not.

The only other way to keep her silent was to kill her.

"I can't do it in cold blood," he said aloud. "So, if you want to die, Martia, then you must do it by committing suicide. That, I can't help. Up you go. I'll get your pack, and we'll leave."

Martia turned blue and sagged to the floor.

"I'll not help you this time!" he shouted, but he found himself frantically trying to undo the knot

At the same time, he told himself what a fool he was. Of course! The solution was to use her own gun on her. Turn the rheostat to a stunning degree of intensity and knock her out whenever she started to regain consciousness. Such a course would mean he'd have to carry her and her equipment, too, on the thirty mile walk down the tube to an exit near his base. But he could do it. He'd rig up some sort of travois. He'd do it! Nothing could stop him. And Earth . . .

At that moment, hearing an unfamiliar noise, he looked up. There were two Eeltau in pressure suits standing there, and another crawling out of the tunnel. Each had a bulb-tipped handgun in her hand.

Desperately, Lane snatched at the weapon he carried in his belt. With his left hand he twisted the rheostat on the side of the barrel, hoping that this would turn it on full force. Then he raised the bulb towards the group . . .

He woke flat on his back, clad in his suit, except for the helmet, and strapped to a stretcher. His body was helpless, but he could turn his head. He did so, and saw many Eeltau dismantling the room. The one who had stunned him with her gun before he could fire was standing by him.

She spoke in English that held only a trace of foreign accent "Settle down, Mr. Lane. You're in for a long ride. You'll be more comfortably situated once we're in our ship."

He opened his mouth to ask her how she knew his name but closed it when he realized she must have read the entries in the log at the base. And it was to be expected that some Eeltau would be trained in Earth languages. For over a century their sentinel spaceships had been tuning in to radio and T.V.

It was then that Martia spoke to the captain. Her face was wild and reddened with weeping and marks where she had fallen.

The interpreter said to Lane, "*Mahrseeya* asks you to tell her why you killed her . . . baby. She cannot understand why you thought you had to do so."

"I cannot answer," said Lane. His head felt very light, almost as if it were a balloon expanding. And the room began slowly to turn around.

"I will tell her why," answered the interpreter. "I will tell her that it is the nature of the beast."

"That is not so!" cried Lane. "I am no vicious beast. I did what I did because I had to! I could not accept her love and still remain a man! Not that kind of man . . ."

"*Mahrseeya*," said the interpreter, "will pray that you be forgiven the murder of her child and that you will someday, under our teaching, be unable to do such a thing. She herself, though she is stricken with grief for her dead baby, forgives you. She hopes the time will come when you will regard her as a—sister. She thinks there is some good in you."

Lane clenched his teeth together and bit the end of his tongue until it bled while they put his helmet on. He did not dare to try to talk, for that would have meant he would scream and scream. He felt as if something had been planted in him and had broken its shell and was growing into something like a worm. It was eating him, and what would happen before it devoured all of him he did not know.